VALERIOS

ROAD TO MASTERY

2

aethonbooks.com

ROAD TO MASTERY 2
©2023 Valerios

Aethon Books
www.aethonbooks.com

Print and eBook formatting by Josh Hayes.

Published by Aethon Books LLC.

Aethon Books is not responsible for websites (or their content) that are not owned by the publisher.

ALSO IN SERIES

Road to Mastery

Road to Mastery 2

Road to Mastery 3

Road to Mastery 4

PROLOGUE

"He was your grandson!" the lioness growled, pacing alone in an empty room at the very top of the Integration City white tower. She was Galicia Lonihor, Earth-387's assigned overseer. Though her voice was deafening, the strength of her Dao prevented the slightest whisper from exiting the room.

She was supreme, and sound was not.

"*He was your charge,*" a male voice calmly replied, seemingly out of nowhere and distorted, like a telephone transmission from across the planet. "*His death is your responsibility. So is losing the tournament rewards.*"

"The Barren High blocked me! What was I supposed to do, break their prophet's spiritual projection?"

"*You were supposed to handle things. The cost of the treasures is yours to bear. And know that the Grand Elder awaits your explanation the moment you return.*"

She gritted her teeth. The power to level the entire Integration City sparked in her eyes, then disappeared. "Fine. Let the Grand Elder know I will subdue this planet completely the moment the grace period is lifted. Then, I will rush back to report."

"*And the offender?*" the voice pushed. "*The boy who took your treasures,*" *killed the disciple you were supposed to raise with all your strength, and spat on our faction's face?"*

His emphasis was clear, but how could she retort? Both knew he was right. She was just fishing for any support she could garner.

"I have people tracking him down as we speak. He was heavily injured, and the teleporter had low range; only a hundred destinations. Moreover, he knows nothing of the galaxy. How far could he have gone?"

"He's only an untrained native. How could he defeat Rufus? And yet, he did. Do not underestimate our enemies like the low factions do. We will not suffer the fate of the Glacial Pole."

She gritted her teeth harder. This man was an elder with similar status to hers, yet his power was greater. She could bargain and argue, but in the end, his authority prevailed.

"I will not," she replied.

"Good. Announce a bounty on his head. Something that will entice even D-Grades to actively search for him."

Easy for him to say, considering it wasn't his money. The burden of paying the bounty would naturally fall on Galicia, who had let Jack reap all benefits and escape. Moreover, if someone got to Jack Rust before them, they would never return the Dao Soul, and its value would obviously be compensated from her credit card.

While she could afford that, she didn't want to.

"That would harm our reputation," she argued. "The other B-Grade factions will say we can't even take care of an E-Grade ourselves."

"Then let them nag. Little criminals like this boy can grow up before you know it, especially with all the resources you gifted him. The Glacial Pole faction took their chances, and you saw what happened."

"They were only C-Grade."

"And the Sword Emperor was E-Grade three years ago. They ignored him and paid the price. Do not make me repeat myself. Announce a heavy bounty."

"Can you at least foot part of the cost? This boy killed your grandson."

"Rufus's death saddens me, but such is life. He only died because he was weak... and for another reason, of course."

Because Galicia failed to protect him. He didn't say the words—she wouldn't suffer an insult like that from someone of the same rank—but his intentions were clear. Galicia wanted to break something.

"Very well. Be ever strong," she said, and abruptly cut the connection.

The three ceramic vases that decorated her new office exploded. They were nothing to a C-Grade, but it was the intention that counted.

It didn't make her feel better. Perhaps crushing Jack Rust's faction would; she only had to wait a bit. Besides, there was no way he would grow strong enough to match her in less than a year—the notion was moot. He would be captured within the day. As for his faction, she wouldn't let anyone swoop in and rescue them. They were cattle waiting for slaughter.

With a few thoughts, she navigated the System screens to contact a deacon in the nearby border fortress. "Post a bounty on the head of Jack Rust, a low E-Grade human from Earth-387 who leads the Bare Fist Brotherhood. He uses the Dao Seed of the Fist and the Dao Root of Indomitable Will." She also sent a mental picture of Jack Rust's appearance.

"*Understood, Elder,*" an obedient voice came from the other side. "*And the amount?*"

Galicia consoled herself with the thought that her hunters would catch him before the bounty even made it to whatever random planet he'd teleported to. "One billion credits alive, a hundred million dead."

The Immortality Serum was gone, but the Dao Soul could be salvaged from his corpse, and it was by far the most expensive reward of the tournament. She could at least cut her losses.

The professor looked at the System screen before her, showing her choices from the faction shop. In the short few weeks since Jack went to the tournament, she managed to gather a million credits, including the ones he sent her.

Now, most of that was going to vanish in a heartbeat. She took a deep breath to steady herself, then accepted. The ground shook under her feet. The trees swayed. She grabbed her armrest out of reflex, but of course, it was shaking too.

Thankfully, nobody in the Bare Fist Brotherhood were weak enough to be toppled by a mere earthquake.

The professor ran to the window—thanking the System for invigorating her old body. Energy walls rose around the forest: tall, shimmering blue energy fields like the ones the System used to enclose dungeons. However, these were transparent, and people could easily walk through.

As if on cue, someone crossed a wall, releasing small fireworks. Her heart hurt. Every time someone activated the wall, one more credit was removed from her credit card. She had already instructed everyone to stay away, but some confusion was expected at the start.

The walls left a gate for people to enter or leave the forest, of course, guarded by the second strongest being on planet Earth: Sparman, the D-Grade robot bodyguard. Too bad he could only be used to defend.

She directed her gaze lower, toward the base of her house, where a small starship had just materialized out of thin air. It was shaped as an elongated pyramid hovering sideways and looked like it could barely fit a few people, but it remained a vehicle faster than a plane. With the Sage and his starship gone, this one would serve them well.

It was yellow, too. She hadn't chosen that, but she liked the color.

The rest of the credits had gone to strengthening the faction. A pool of hot water now lay hidden in the ice pond's cave. That was the reason for the earthquake, actually.

It had taken half a million credits, but she managed to summon an additional E-Grade body strengthening resource. With that, the members of the Bare Fist Brotherhood would have a higher chance of survival against whatever the world threw at them.

That would never come to pass, hopefully. There was Sparman, and before the grace period was over, Jack would be back with salvation... *hopefully*.

Professor Margaret Rust was always ready for the worst.

———

Edgar and Vivi faced each other on the edge of Integration City. "Are you sure?" Edgar asked.

"Very," Vivi replied. "We cannot let them have all the firepower of

Earth. Many factions decided to join Flame River after the battle in the arena, and even more went neutral. Some governments joined too —especially those close to our main encampment in Burkina Faso. We have enough power to keep the Ice Peak from acting... at least openly."

Edgar gave her a sad smile. "This will be the Cold War all over again."

"But we have a nuke called Jack Rust. We *will* win, Edgar. And if we don't... we're dead anyway."

"Yeah."

They stood for a moment, considering each other's words and the situation. Then, side by side, they boarded the private jet that the Flame River managed to secure. It would drop Edgar off at Valville, then head for Burkina Faso.

After Jack and Rufus had left the arena, the Ice Peak was forced to face the Flame River, Dorman, the Sage, an injured Brother Tao, and Vanderdecken. Even though Vivi was injured, the Ice Peak couldn't possibly win that battle. Dorman alone could sear through them.

In the end, victory had gone to the Flame River alliance. Of the five Ice Peak members that had come to the tournament, only their leader, Alexander Petrovic, escaped, and only because Dorman couldn't fly. Coupled with Jack slaying Rufus, it had been an overwhelming victory... but not without sacrifices.

Li Xiang, the honorable elderly master, had fallen. Brother Tao lost an arm. Sadaka, the second-in-command of Flame River, had also fallen in battle.

Casualties had been expected. The important thing was that the battle had been broadcasted to the entire planet, and all knew they'd won overwhelmingly.

Fesh Wui and the elef scion had both survived and left the planet shortly after the tournament's conclusion. There was an inner division between their two families and the other three, giving them no reason to risk their lives for Earth. Plus, with Dorman here, there was no guarantee of victory.

Gan Salin's whereabouts remained a mystery.

However, Dorman and the Sage had also secretly left the planet. Nobody knew where they'd gone, only that they promised to return when Jack did. In fact, the only ones who knew they'd left were Edgar, Vivi, and the professor back at the Forest of the Strong.

In light of all that, there was no reason to go to war anymore. Jack and the scions were gone. Nobody would benefit from millions of dead. One way or the other, everything would be settled in eleven months—the Integration and the tournament had already taken one.

This didn't mean the planet would be unified. Many places remained neutral, allowing the Ice Peak and their allies, with the implicit support of the Animal Kingdom, to take control of around half the world. The Flame River and Bare Fist Brotherhood, along with their allies, controlled the other half.

These two large alliances had already begun scheming at one another, planning discreet strikes, assassinations, and all sorts of shadowy war. They competed at everything, from the level of their strongest cultivators to the number of starships they could buy. The hottest competition was the number of dungeons they could claim. After all, there were 1,111 dungeons on Earth—a thousand F-Grade, a hundred E-Grade, ten D-Grade, and one C-Grade—and only a few had been conquered. Wherever they met, the forces of the two alliances secretly tried to slaughter each other.

The System's arrival had altered the nature of war, both open and in the shadows, and everyone needed some time to adjust, but they would manage.

Maybe they had no nuclear weapons anymore—the Star Pact forbade them, and the System deactivated them upon arrival—but they would soon have cultivators with the strength to achieve similar destruction. In such a tense situation, any spark would be enough to set the planet aflame.

Nobody could contact Jack Rust. And while he was missing, a second Cold War settled over Earth.

CHAPTER ONE
MEET THE GALAXY

STARS FILLED THE SKY, THE GROUND, AND EVERYTHING IN BETWEEN. BROCK hurtled through space, feeling nothing and seeing everything. Meteors drifted past, followed by long tails—but only when they were close to stars. Some meteors didn't have their tails behind them, but rather in front, and Brock stared in wonder until they disappeared.

He saw a giant purple squid surrounded by small fish made of dust. He even saw a small iron-thing with a plate on its top, lazily drifting through an endless void.

All the while, Brock desperately gripped the arm of his big brother, afraid that if he let go for even a second, Jack would be lost forever.

The trip could have taken ages, or it could have taken the blink of an eye. Brock wasn't certain. All he knew was that, when the world flashed and all was still again, he was no longer home.

Brock found himself in a room painted black with yellow dots. The floor was white, and an open door poured daylight inside the room. Across him stood a woman dressed in gray armor without a helmet, revealing deep purple eyes and sapphire hair.

She looked at him with question, alternating her gaze between Brock and his big brother. Brock didn't know what the woman wanted, or who she was, but he didn't care. His big bro was injured; he had to get him to safety. Hide him somewhere.

Once again slinging Jack over his back—with his feet dragging across the floor due to the height difference—Brock walked to the door.

"Wait," the woman said. Brock froze. His instincts told him she was much stronger than he was—similar to his big bro. She stepped before him, blocking the way. "Name and affiliation, please."

Brock understood the words, but he had no means to reply. He only knew one word!

"Bro!" he replied, pointing at Jack with urgency. "Bro! Bro!"

"You cannot speak?" the guard asked, and her gaze swept over Jack. "Can you understand me?"

Brock nodded. He wanted to run away, but he learned from his mistakes. Impulsiveness did not suit a bro. Composure did.

"Are you his spiritual companion?"

Brock wasn't sure, but he nodded.

"Who injured him?"

Brock hesitated.

"It's okay. No need to tell me, then." The guard waved her hands from side to side.

Brock wondered why she even asked if she didn't want to know, but it was tough to judge someone who could break you like a ripe banana.

"I won't meddle in your affairs. If anybody is after you, I don't want to be involved. I will note down your faction, species, and level. However, please promise to return and give me your name when your friend heals. Okay?"

Brock nodded without hesitation. He had zero intention to return. Bros should keep their word, but there was a fine line between dishonor and deception.

The woman stepped aside. "Go."

Brock nodded excitedly to thank her and walked outside, dragging Jack behind him. He was blinded by the light, but he flexed his eye muscles and recovered. Then, his brain was blinded by information.

There were so many oddly-shaped Big Brothers and Big Sisters here. Their nests were colorless and ugly, the sky was green, and a big metal bird hovered in the sky.

Weird looks were directed at them, though Brock sensed no overt hostility. Therefore, he ignored everyone and turned to the side. Exactly fifteen steps later, he stood at the mouth of a dark alley. It smelled horrible, making him wrinkle his nose, but it seemed empty.

Brock was very clear about what he should do. When his little dog bros had been weak, they hid in dark alleys. Therefore, while his big bro was sleeping, Brock should do the same.

I hope my little bros are okay... he thought wistfully, then refocused.

Still ignoring the many eyes on them, Brock stepped into the alley, blending into the darkness. He found a large garbage bin and tucked Jack behind it. Then, he stood before his big bro, crossing his arms and glaring at the stream of people that moved outside the alley.

His big bro was sleeping, and Brock would die before letting anyone near.

———

Jack awoke with a groan. His consciousness drifted back from a hazy dream, and his eyes fluttered open.

The first thing he noticed was the unbelievable stench that flooded his nose. The second were the city noises that surrounded him. The third was that he was crammed, unable to move freely. Trapped.

What's happening! he barely managed to think, panic rising. His groggy consciousness recovered in a heartbeat, and he pushed harder. Something large and green to his side gave way, sliding over stone before tipping over with a large crash. Jack had no idea what was going on.

"Bro!"

A happy cry from the side reined in his growing panic. Brock fell on him, embracing him in a big hug.

"Brock," Jack said raspily, realizing how dry his throat was. "What the..."

Brock hurriedly let go, stepping back and looking at Jack with a big smile. He patted his chest and said proudly, "Bro!"

Jack allowed himself a smile before looking around. Tall stone walls stretched high on either side, enclosing them in an alley that was barely six feet wide. A strip of sky was visible, except it was green.

Why green? his scholar's mind wondered, but he had better things to ponder.

On either side of Jack were fast moving streams of people outside the alley. At first glance, they seemed human. At second, none of them were. Something was a little off about everyone. Purple eyes here, gray skin there...

He turned his gaze away before confusing himself any further. He focused on his immediate vicinity.

Nobody was there besides himself and Brock, which was good. The green thing he'd pushed away was a large, brick-shaped garbage bin that now lay on its side, garbage spilling from its mouth. There was rotting food in there—most certainly the cause for the stench—and Jack thought he saw a small dark shape dart away.

It could have been a rat. Or anything else, really, given the aliens outside.

Where are we? Jack wondered, thoroughly confused. This place reminded him of nothing. *What happened?* With a thought, he summoned what always grounded him: his status screen.

Name: Jack Rust
Species: Human, Earth-387
Faction: Bare Fist Brotherhood (E)
Grade: E
Class: Fiend of the Iron Fist (Elite)
Level: 50

Strength: 184
Dexterity: 184
Constitution: 184
Mental: 23
Will: 23

Skills: Iron Fiend Body (II), Ghost Step (I)
Dao Skills: Meteor Punch (II), Iron Fist Style (I)
Daos: Perfect Dao Seed of the Fist (early), Dao Root of Indomitable Will
Titles: Planetary Frontrunner (10), Planetary Torchbearer (1)

The assurance of those numbers allowed him to refocus on the present.

Memories came in a trickle. The Integration, as well as the dungeon that had spawned around him. His struggles to escape and the strength he'd obtained in the process. The friends he'd made: Harambe, the gym-obsessed brorillas, and the cheerful, poop-throwing gymonkeys. He remembered Valville, Henry's Fang, Gan Salin, Edgar, and his foster mother—the professor. The Bare Fist Brotherhood.

He recalled the tournament and the people he'd met there—Vivi, Sadaka, Dorman, the Sage, Li Xiang, Master Shol, Brother Tao, even Vanderdecken and his Dao of Metal. He also remembered the enemies he'd made: the Animal Kingdom, the C-Grade Planetary Overseer, as well as Rufus Emberheart, whom he'd pummeled to death after winning the tournament.

He patted the secret pocket behind his left thigh, where he'd stashed the two Trial Planet tokens—shaped as old gold coins—and the final tournament reward, the Dao Soul—a purple, mystical disc whose use was still unclear.

Right, he thought as the memories washed over him. *That's it. I killed Rufus Emberheart, then some dogs appeared, and then... we teleported.* He looked at Brock, then at the alley. This wasn't a teleporter. Brock had somehow gotten him out and hidden him here until he could recover. Now, he felt fully healthy, if completely exhausted. His regeneration came at a price—or maybe it was just the fight before. Still, he could move, though his entire body yearned for food.

He turned a gaze of fondness at the brorilla, who waited with his brown-furred chest puffed out. "Thank you, Brock. You took care of me. I'm very proud of you."

"Bro!" Brock replied, as if that explained everything. His toothy grin was so wide it almost split his face.

Jack smiled for a moment longer, then his previous wariness returned. At least controlled this time and not spiraling into blind panic. He took stock of the situation.

We are on a foreign planet. Alone. We know nothing about the world around us, and the Animal Kingdom is probably hunting us right now. There is no way they will let me be after all that—unless I'm being paranoid. Hmm. But they've shown how petty they can be. They are definitely after us. Better paranoid than dead.

Most importantly, we're now outside Earth, and there is no Star Pact or grace period protecting us. The moment an immortal shows up, we're dead.

The situation was grim. Jack was thrust into an unknown world with zero information, and he was hunted.

We must move, he realized with growing fear. Even if they don't know where exactly the teleporter took us, how many injured E-Grade cultivators with a small gorilla teleport every day? They will track us down soon. If they haven't already.

Jack jumped to his feet, eyeing the overturned garbage bin. It'd been loud when it fell. There could be people approaching, and the last thing he needed was an alien policeman detaining him.

"Come on, Brock," he said, pacing to the end of the alley. Further thinking could wait. For now, they needed to change hiding spots.

Brock followed obediently. As he only reached up to Jack's thigh, he had to take multiple steps for each of Jack's, lending him a silliness that didn't fit the grim situation. Jack walked out of the alley, momentarily blinded by light, and ran straight into someone. The collision pushed him back.

"Hey!" a rough voice came from above. "Watch it."

Jack was staring at a bare gray chest. Tilting his head back, he found the face as well. This was a hardened-looking man with red eyes, and his features were much too angular to be human. His chin was almost completely square, his skin taut over his bones, and even his arms lacked the smoothness they should have. He only wore a set of short brown pants and black boots.

This was like a human, except with barely enough flesh to cover his bones. If someone found a human skeleton and recreated it like humans did with dinosaurs, this is what the result would look like.

Except this guy was seven feet tall and gray.

Feshkur, Level 84
Faction: Gray Mercenaries

"What are you looking at?" the feshkur growled in Jack's face—or rather, above it—and Jack hurried to step back. He raised his open palms.

"Sorry," he said. "My bad."

The mercenary shot Jack another glare, then snorted and walked away. Jack noticed he was carrying a big-ass saber on his back.

Brock pulled his wrist, and Jack realized with satisfaction that the brorilla hadn't made a peep despite the other man's provocations. He was certainly angry, but he kept it in.

My little bro is growing, he thought with pride, and refocused on the task at hand: getting away from here.

He looked around. The street was dirty, browned in the corners and with the occasional trash on the ground. There were no vehicles that he could see. They were surrounded by tall, gray buildings that seemed empty of life. Some had broken windows. There was a similarity here to Earth, and Jack got the feeling that bad neighborhoods looked alike no matter the planet or culture.

Above the buildings, metal ships occasionally flickered by in utter silence, moving at great speeds. He couldn't make out their shape, but they must have been starships.

Jack pulled Brock through the crowd. He tried to come up with a plan, but he was overwhelmed by all the different alien species.

There were humanoids with sapphire hair and purple eyes called saphiras. Who knew what other differences they had with humans. The saphiras and the feshkurs—the gray giants—were by far the most populous, as far as Jack could tell. Maybe they were the natives of this planet.

But there were many more. He saw djinns—like Ar'Tazul or Ar'Karvahul—and ifrits, who looked like desert santa clauses. There was a group of snakemen—humans from the waist up and snakes from the waist down. There was a unicorn walking in the middle of the street—and its species was aptly named Unicorns.

That goes to say, Jack was the only human around. Moreover, it suddenly occurred to him that though his body had recovered, his attire had not. He was still covered in blood, reeked of sweat, his pants were torn in places, and he was shirtless and barefoot. Even the unicorn received fewer stares than him.

They didn't seem too surprised by the presence of a small gorilla in their midst, though nobody else had a companion. As far as Jack was aware, he could be out here with three heads and seven noses, and nobody would care. At least their clothing sense was similar to Earth's.

Jack reorganized his priorities. There is no way we can hide like this. I must find food, clean clothes, and a shower. And then, I must get the hell away from this planet. Or maybe I should teleport away first. How long do I have?

It was hard to make an estimation. The Animal Kingdom could already be here, tracking him down, or they might need a day to scout out all the teleporter's destinations. How many were there? He didn't know, and Brock only shrugged when asked.

Then again, even if he teleported again, he wouldn't become any harder to locate. A bloodstained human with a brown brorilla stood out anywhere.

I could return to Earth...

He let the sweet thought linger before squashing it. Returning to Earth would save him from the pursuit, as there was nobody strong enough to harm him there, but there was no telling what tricks the Animal Kingdom would employ. They'd already shown how much they cared about rules and laws. Maybe the Planetary Overseer would just find an excuse to end him herself.

Plus, he left Earth to gain the strength to protect it. He couldn't go back now.

I must reach the Belarian Outpost, then teleport to Trial Planet.

That was what Master Shol had instructed. Jack's first destination in the galaxy was Trial Planet, where the strongest E-Grade cultivators found their fortune. It was perilous, but Jack was confident in his abilities. All he needed to do was reach it, and according to Master Shol, the easiest way to do that was through the Belarian Outpost.

Can I just teleport to this Outpost? he considered. *I can try. Maybe the Animal Kingdom is watching the teleporter's exit there, or they've already located me and have people stationed at this teleporter... What choice do I have? How long was I unconscious?*

The sun was just setting, dying the green sky red, but that meant nothing.

"Hey, Brock, how high was the sun when you arrived?"

Brock thought for a moment, then pointed at a spot roughly in the middle of the sky.

"An entire afternoon, then..." Jack grumbled. "But there's no reason for this planet's day to be twenty-four hours long, like on Earth. Still, how different can it be?"

Unfortunately, Jack had no clue about the rotation speed of planets. Fortunately, he had an easy way of finding out.

"Excuse me," he said, stopping a random saphira passerby. Of all the species here, they looked the least intimidating, and this one was F-Grade. She shrunk back as Jack approached. "Don't be afraid. I would just like to know, how long is a day on this planet?"

She was hesitant, then replied, "Half a galactic day."

"And how many galactic hours is that?"

A galactic hour was thankfully the same as an Earth-387 hour—sixty-one minutes, to be exact.

"Around nine."

"Oh."

Nine hours. That was a short day. With quick calculations, it meant Jack had only been unconscious for a couple hours. *Not bad! Though, as I grow stronger, my regeneration will get less and less effective unless I upgrade it.*

"Thank you," he told the saphira, who mumbled a response and slipped away in relief.

Jack fell in thought, ignoring the few people around him. The crowd was getting sparser by the minute.

A few hours... Will the Animal Kingdom be prepared yet? Possibly. If I don't take the teleporter, what other choice do I have?

As if in response to his thoughts, a muffled boom shook the sky. Jack looked up. A large metallic shape tore through the clouds, disappearing in a single second as if space had swallowed it. His eyes widened. Such speed should be impossible.

A space-warping starship...

Master Shol had mentioned them a few times, but it was the first he'd seen one with his own eyes. They were used for space travel, though Jack couldn't imagine why anyone would choose that method over teleportation.

It's less controlled, he realized. Perfect for anyone hunted by the constellation's overlords. Wait. Could I have left the Animal Kingdom constellation?

It was unlikely. Why would the Animal Kingdom connect Earth to another constellation, given a teleporter's limited range?

So starships are an option, if I can board one, Jack thought. But that means all sorts of trouble. Maybe I should bet on teleportation. Hmm. Possible death on one hand, a long journey between the stars on the other—and possible death by a ton of different things.

If he successfully teleported from here to the Belarian Outpost, he would reach his target in moments. After all, Master Shol said that if he arrived at the Belarian Outpost teleporters, he could use his Trial Planet token to teleport directly to Trial Planet, where only E-Grade cultivators could enter.

What if the Animal Kingdom sent peak E-Grades after him? Strong as he was, Jack had no illusions of beating anyone at level 124. The E-Grade got five stat points per level.

Jack was unsure, but he had to choose fast. Every moment increased the chances of Animal Kingdom lookouts standing beside the teleporters.

"You look troubled," a voice came from behind him.

Jack turned to find a feshkur—one of those gray giants—towering over him.

Feshkur, Level 61
Faction: -

"I am," he replied, looking up to meet the other man's eyes. They were not kind. Suddenly, Jack realized the crowd had thinned so much that it wasn't a crowd anymore, just the occasional passerby, most of whom were feshkurs. And they were pointedly not staring in his direction any longer.

The gray giant smiled and drew a dagger. "You're about to become poor, too. Hand over your credit card."

CHAPTER TWO
NIGHT-TIME MUGGING

THE FESHKUR BRANDISHED HIS DAGGER, SEEMING EAGER TO USE IT. "DID YOU hear me, brightskin? Credit card. Now."

Half an hour into the galaxy and I'm getting robbed... Jack thought, frowning. *No, wait. Three hours, if we count the time I was unconscious.*

The feshkur took his silence as resistance. A hand rose to slap Jack. He leaned back, letting it sail before his face. The feshkur snarled. "You don't want to do this," he warned. His dagger tip rose as his grip tightened.

Jack got the distinct feeling that this man would use the dagger if he had to.

Level 61... he considered. Eleven over me. But I drank the Immortality Serum, which gave me fifty stat points, the equivalent of ten levels. And I have +25% efficacy to all my stats from my titles, which this grunt probably doesn't. Plus, a perfect Dao Seed.

Everyone was dodged Jack's gaze, assuming he was pleading for assistance. He wasn't. He was looking for the mugger's allies, of which he saw none. There was just this one desperate guy in a back alley.

And Jack was the champion of his entire planet. He was the Fiend of the Iron Fist. A hint of rage entered his psyche. He was exhausted, starving, and dehydrated, and he wanted to stay low-key, but he would be damned if he let himself be robbed by someone weaker.

Brock stepped back, sensing what was going to happen.

"Fine. I can—" Before the feshkur could finish his words, a hard fist smashed into his face. He couldn't react in time. His bony nose broke under Jack's iron knuckles, and his entire body was flung into a wall. The dagger dropped to the ground, useless, as the would-be robber slumped against the wall, looking at Jack in terror.

"Sorry!" he cried out. "I made a mistake! I made a mistake!"

Jack didn't reply. He only looked at his fist. A level 61 opponent had fallen just like that? The feshkur hadn't even had the chance to show off his Dao, whatever it was.

How strong am I? Jack wondered. The Dao Seed at the center of his soul seethed.

Plenty, it whispered. Jack raised his gaze to look at the quivering feshkur. His aggressive and arrogant stance was no more. Now, he could only lie there, weak and terrified. Worthless. Suddenly, a thirst for blood rose inside Jack, an urge to crush this bug and assert his dominance.

He quenched that urge. He was neither a beast nor a fiend. He was simply Jack.

And though he quenched his thirst for blood, a hint of it showed in his aura, making the robber shiver harder. Jack squatted beside him, keeping an eye out for surprise attacks.

"How about this?" he said sternly. "I have some questions. If you answer them, we can pretend this never happened."

"Yes, sir." The alien nodded intensely. The few spectators had already dispersed entirely, leaving them completely alone in this side street.

"Good. What's the fastest way to get to the Belarian Outpost?"

"Teleportation, sir," the robber replied. "From here, you can reach the Outpost in six leaps."

"Leaps?"

"Teleportation leaps," the robber replied, braving an odd look at Jack.

Jack nodded slowly. He had imagined this. Teleporters didn't have infinite range. Depending on how far away the Belarian Outpost was, he thought he might need to teleport several times to reach it.

He then took a moment to consider how much information he was willing to give this guy. "Can I perform these leaps in quick succession?"

The robber looked at him in confusion. Jack's eyes narrowed. "This is the first time outside my planet. I don't know how things work. Look at me like that again, and I'll break your chin."

"Yes, sir," the robber replied. Some light entered his eyes—Jack didn't like that. "To use a teleporter, you must register yourself to the presiding guard and pay a fee. It's easy here, but there is usually a line for larger teleporters, and not even peak E-Grades are allowed to cut in line."

Jack suspected that anyone could cut in line with a large enough bribe. "How much is the fee?" he asked. A moment of thought later, he added, "And where is here?"

"Pearl Bay," the feshkur explained. A thousand thoughts passed behind his eyes as he tried to piece together the information Jack revealed. "The fee is ten thousand credits, flat."

Jack grimaced. He reached inside the secret pocket behind his left thigh, not caring whether this guy saw him or not, and retrieved his credit card, habitually turning it so the robber couldn't see the amount. The number 3096 shone softly on its surface.

Not even enough for one teleportation... Fuck.

"How easy would it be to hijack the teleportation and keep leaping all the way to the Belarian Outpost?"

He was shooting blindly now, but there was a chance. Once inside the teleporter, maybe he could just teleport again before the guards stopped him. The robber dashed his hopes.

"You would have to neutralize the high E-Grade guards, sir. They have a device to interrupt outgoing teleportation, and more than enough time to use it."

"I see."

Teleporting to the Outpost seemed more and more impossible. At least he'd found this perfectly willing local to answer all his questions.

He remembered the starships hovering overhead. "Is that why they use these ships? To avoid paying for teleportation?"

"Yes, sir."

"And how long would it take to reach the Belarian Outpost by starship?"

"Three months, sir." Clearly, this was a number he knew by heart. Jack frowned.

"What about space-warping starships?"

"That number was for space-warping starships, sir."

Jack's frown deepened. "Is there no faster way?"

This time, the robber hesitated before he said, "That's the best I know of, sir."

Jack cursed inwardly. He had one year to reach the C-Grade and defeat the Planetary Overseer. That was already near impossible, but now he had to spend *three months* just traveling?

"Is there a faster way to reach the Trial Planet besides the Belarian Outpost?" he finally asked.

The robber's eyes widened imperceptibly. "There is one. The Animal Kingdom has a border station a month away from here—on space-warping starships. Their teleporter should be fully upgraded, letting you reach Trial Planet."

Jack wanted to drive his fist into the wall. He couldn't go there. The place would be teeming with hostile immortals. He also couldn't tele-port to the Outpost, and he didn't want to spend three months traveling.

Again, what choice do I have?

If he stayed here, he could probably find a way to earn the required money in less than three months. But he couldn't stick around saving money with the Animal Kingdom after him. They would track him down within days, at the latest. He had to keep moving.

Even if his travels took some time, he could use it to train, meditate, and stabilize his strength. He'd just broken through to the E-Grade, after all. Everything was new.

In the training cycle of expansion and stabilization, Trial Planet was sure to give him plenty of expansion—meaning battles and opportuni-ties. If he handled some stabilization beforehand, he could maybe save some time. He would also get to see how the world worked outside his home planet.

Trial Planet was chock-full of danger. Doing well there was extremely important. Perhaps taking some time to prepare himself beforehand was a better idea than rushing in blindly.

Of course, traveling by starship also meant high chances of getting captured by the Animal Kingdom, but... it was the best he could do. And it would be fun. Who knows what amazing sights he would see and adventures he would have on the way. It wouldn't take long, either. Trial Planet was already within sight.

Jack's mind was made, and he finally let himself relax, forgetting about the titanic weight on his shoulders for a moment.

His eyes swiveled upward, taking in the still forms of the hovering starships. As he looked closer, he noticed they weren't hovering randomly. They were mostly gathered around a metallic building that rose in the near distance.

It was a straight tower with a wide disk at its top. It reached at least three hundred feet into the sky, and was circled by large, open windows that led to nothing except a steep drop down.

Except they weren't windows. They were docks. Those starships hovered right next to the openings, connected to the building with wooden ramps while people moved crates back and forth.

"Is that the dock?" Jack asked—made sense for a place named Pearl Bay.

"Yes, sir," the robber replied. By now, he had relaxed slightly, but he still seemed on guard. "This planet's largest starship dock. With a bit of luck, you'll find a ship headed to the Outpost—it's the trade center of the constellation."

Jack looked at the guy, who suddenly seemed somewhat intelligent. Not only was his stance appropriately respectful and submissive, but he'd also adapted to what Jack had revealed. Now, his information was fine-tuned just for Jack.

Jack feared that. If this guy was smart, maybe telling him so much was a mistake. He could have split his questions between strangers.

A mistake I'm too late to correct.

"Will they take me?" he asked.

"Most ships carry merchandise, but a few are meant for travelers. They usually ask for five thousand credits a head."

That was ten thousand, if Brock counted as a head. Jack had three. The robber must have noticed his frown, because he added, "Sometimes they give discounts to people who promise to help with security or menial labor. Sir is only a low E-Grade, but with your strength, I am confident you could be of use."

This was good news, but it raised another important question.

"Why are E-Grades so weak?" he asked curiously. "I thought only one in a hundred people reached the E-Grade, so they ought to be important. But you're just a thug. Are low E-Grades really so useless that they can't even serve as crew on a starship?"

If the feshkur was insulted, he didn't show it.

"F-Grades cannot do much, sir," he replied. "They mostly deal with mundane professions. For space travel, low E-Grades are the weakest around. And as for me..." He chuckled helplessly. "This is Pearl Bay. It's crawling with E-Grades."

Jack nodded. When he had observed the crowd earlier, about one in four people was at the E-Grade, though very few were above level 75—the line between low E-Grade and middle E-Grade.

"I see. Thank you, random thug."

"No prob—"

Before the robber could reply, Jack's fist met his skull so hard that it bounced against the concrete below. He lost consciousness immediately.

Jack couldn't have this guy spewing his secrets left and right. Better let him sleep for a few hours. By the time he woke up, Jack would hopefully be off this planet. The concept managed to raise his mood a little. *I'm a space traveler*, he thought. *And a fist-wizard.*

Dragging the unconscious body to a nearby alley and throwing the knife away, Jack made to leave, followed by an excited Brock.

Two more feshkurs rounded the corner. They were levels 58 and 59 respectively, and they wore blue vests over brown pants. Their eyes did not hold the malevolence of the robber. Instead, they channeled their roughness and intimidating looks into what resembled authority.

"Hold still, human," the level 59 said, looking between the blood-covered Jack and the unconscious body that lay just behind him. "What happened here?"

Jack frowned in worry. The alien policemen he dreaded had arrived. "This man tried to rob me. I knocked him out in self-defense. I apologize for any disturbance I may have caused."

The policemen looked at him and the body, then exchanged a glance. "Did you beat him yourself, human?" one asked.

"Is that your blood?" the other added. They seemed in tune, like long-time partners.

"I did beat him, yes. But this blood is from another battle—not in

Pearl Bay." He smiled and raised his hands in a peaceful gesture. Beside him, Brock did the same.

The policemen exchanged a glance full of meaning. "You can go," the level 59 said. "But no more trouble. Okay?"

"Yes, sir," Jack replied. Dipping his head, he hurried to leave before they changed their mind. That could have gone much worse. If they insisted on detaining him, he might have been forced to fight.

In fact, he couldn't help but wonder why they'd let him go. Was it his intimidating visage? His apparent strength, since he'd easily beaten someone ten levels above him? Or had the Animal Kingdom publicized his appearance, and they recognized him but were afraid to engage?

I need to hurry, Jack told himself. He rushed toward the docks, thinking he saw eyes in every alley and dark corner.

CHAPTER THREE
PEARL BAY DOCKS

THE DOCKS REMINDED JACK OF A RISING WATERDROP, LIKE THE ONES THAT TRY to jump up when you throw a rock but don't manage to dislodge themselves from the neck of water that ties them to the sea.

Jack thought it was close-by. It wasn't. The building rose higher than he estimated, and its size practically dwarfed everything around. It was like the entire city was built as an afterthought to this behemoth.

On the bright side, he found a pleasant surprise on the way there. Someone had left a bucket of water on the street, under a leaking pipe. Jack had no idea why anyone would do that, but the water smelled okay, and he needed it.

Quickly raising the half-filled bucket over his head, he drenched himself. Despite the cold water and the night chill, it was barely an annoyance to his System-enhanced body. He shook his head to get the water out. Brock yelped as some drops landed on him.

Jack still wasn't clean, but at least the blood all over him was mostly gone. He would no longer seem like a mad murderer on the loose.

He placed the bucket back in its position, silently thanking and apologizing to whomever put it there in the first place. This was a disadvantage to using only credits as currency; he couldn't leave a coin as a token of his gratitude.

When Jack reached the base of the building, he was already covered in its great shadow. Craning his head back, all he saw was large, inter-locking plates of metal rising up and behind him. The waterdrop-shaped curve seemed smooth from a distance, but up close showed it was just a long series of tiny angles.

Idly, he wondered just how they built this thing. Could it stand on its own, or was it magic? That would surely take away from the wonder of architecture. He also wondered *why* they would do this. However, when he spoke, all he managed to say was, "Wow."

Brock nodded, panting with his tongue out—they'd ran to save time.

The tower that supported the docks—the neck of water tying the waterdrop to the sea—was a massive gray column erected in the middle of Pearl Bay. It was surrounded by people and riddled with entrances. A dozen different lines of people stretched out in different directions, stumping Jack.

He then noticed that, of those entrances, most were large, meant for cargo. Only one was the height of humans—slightly larger, actually, to accommodate the many species of the galaxy—and it also had the shortest line. Presumably, there was another entrance just like it on the other side of the tower, but Jack couldn't see.

He hurriedly made his way there. People gave him odd looks and a wide berth, but nobody spoke up about his smudged, bloodstained clothes and body. However, there were at least fifty people in line, all waiting patiently, and a rising urgency filled Jack. He had to board a starship and get out of here *fast*. He couldn't wait for this entire line to finish.

Just as he was considering asking people to let him pass, the door at the front of the line slid open. Behind it was a rectangular empty space, much wider and deeper than it was tall. A mirror covered the back wall, reminding Jack of an elevator.

No, scratch that; of course it was an elevator. They had to get up the tower somehow. He didn't know what he expected.

People streamed in, and the line advanced. When forty people entered, slightly cramped but not much, the last person held out a hand, and the line stopped. A woman inside pressed a button, the doors slid closed, and—presumably—the elevator went up without a sound.

Jack was satisfied. He was now twelfth in line, which meant he and Brock could easily get into the next elevator. He just had to wait a bit.

More doors slid open to the left and right, revealing large spaces filled with crates of all sizes. The task of carrying them appeared daunting until Jack saw two feshkurs grab a cube-shaped crate ten feet to a side and lift it easily, moving it through a wide empty corridor.

He shook his head. *Right. The System. Very helpful for menial labor.* Those two feshkurs weren't even at the E-Grade.

As they waited, Jack took a moment to admire the scenery, this time with peace of mind. Pearl Bay was a tapestry of species and a hub of buzzing activity. There were similarities to Earth, but also many differences, and Jack found this contrast aesthetically pleasing. He took a deep breath, enjoying the clean breeze—there were no factories or cars to pollute it, and the starships moved with the Dao, not fuel.

If the town wasn't entirely painted in shades of gray, it could have been beautiful.

A ruckus from farther behind grabbed Jack's attention. He turned to find three rough-looking feshkurs walking next to the line of people, approaching the front of the line like it was nothing. They didn't even give anyone a glance. Jack inspected them.

Feshkur, Level 102
Faction: Gray Mercenaries

They were levels 100, 102, and 105. High E-Grade. Each would have hundreds of stats on Jack. They could probably wipe the floor with him.

Seeing them cut in line, anger rose inside him, which he quenched at once. The Dao Seed of the Fist demanded war against this injustice, but he held it down with an iron will. That sort of mindset could work on Earth, but he was no longer the biggest fish in the pond. Now, he was just a random guy. He had to act with caution—at least for now.

Brock grumbled a bit but kept his voice down. Though he burned with anger, he trusted his big bro. Sometimes, the best way forward was peace.

Not everyone understood that. The ruckus Jack had heard came from a feshkur in a sleeveless shirt farther back the line. Without counting, Jack suspected the man was around the forty-people mark. If these feshkurs cut in line, he would have to wait for the next elevator.

As they passed by him, the sleeveless-shirt man grumbled something with restrained anger. The gray mercenaries ignored him. When his eyes sparked, two of his friends grabbed him, while another slapped his mouth shut. The angry man resisted for a second, then calmed down and angrily waved at them to let him go. He stayed in place with folded arms, glaring at the backs of the mercenaries. They simply walked to the very front of the line and waited, as if their strength was all the proof of their dignity they needed.

Jack didn't appreciate their cutting in line, but he acknowledged that they didn't start a fight against a weaker party.

"See that, Brock?" he said, nudging the little monkey. "That is how the strong should act. No need to brag or prove your strength."

"They just don't want to get in trouble," a voice came from behind him. Turning, Jack found a saphira smiling at him. Her eyes were purple, her hair sapphire, and her smile radiant. "If they get into a fight here, the guards will show up, and they will have to wait in line like everyone else. Otherwise, they would beat that guy to a pulp!"

Saphira, Level 67
Faction: -

"I see," he responded. "We're not from around here."

"Oh, I can tell."

"What gave it away? The blood on me, my species, or Brock here?"

"Blood is not uncommon around here. Pearl Bay is not the kindest neighborhood in the galaxy, and everyone is okay with that. Being drenched from hair to toe is more surprising—and you're dripping, by the way." She extended a hand. "My name is Vlossana."

"Jack." Her hand felt... human. What were the differences that made them a different species? Hair and eye color hardly qualified. "And this is Brock. He can't speak a lot yet, but he's a brave warrior."

Brock nodded, then shook her hand.

"Nice to meet you," she said. The doors to the elevator opened, and the three of them were squeezed inside along with everyone else. People gave the gray mercenaries a wide berth, but they also gave that to Jack, which made the thirty-four remaining people crowded. Brock counted as a person for this elevator, much to the dismay of the next person in line.

The doors slid closed, and with the sound of rolling gears, they began their ascent.

"What brings you to Pearl Bay, Jack?" Vlossana asked cheerfully. Her attempt to make conversation could have been annoying in such a crowded space, but to Jack, who was filled with enthusiasm at the alien city and fear of getting hunted down, it was a godsend.

"Coincidence," he replied. "In fact, I can't wait to get out of here."

"That's delightful!"

She didn't ask where he was headed. Jack noticed that and reminded himself not to ask either. He was neck-deep in multiple new cultures, and he had to absorb knowledge like a sponge, lest he accidentally find himself in trouble.

"What about you?" he asked. Since she'd asked him why he was here, he could ask the same.

"I'm just passing through," she replied. "My ship made a short stop, so I came down to see the sights. It was..." She looked around, at all the natives listening to her every word. Though they were almost whispering, nobody else was speaking. "...intriguing."

"Tell me about it." Jack now knew why this girl seemed so excited to chat. She had tourist syndrome. "And what made you approach a blood-stained stranger?"

She shrugged. "Curiosity. I enjoy meeting interesting people!"

"Ah, of course."

The rest of the ride went by in silence. The elevator stopped, the doors slid open, and Jack found himself in an eight-year-old's fondest dreams. Starships hovered everywhere, ranging from the size of a gondola to a large yacht. The largest ones remained outside, though they could fit through the large openings in the wall. The smallest ones hovered anywhere they wanted, crowding the empty wooden floor that stretched for hundreds of feet in every direction.

Aliens—mostly feshkurs—moved cargo, while others streamed in and out of ships on wooden ramps. There were a million different clothing styles. Hundreds of voices shouted at each other, struggling to be heard over the chaos. The passengers of Jack's elevator dissipated among the starships, leaving him and Brock gaping just outside the doors.

The starships were fascinating themselves. They were shaped as elongated pyramids and painted in various colors—mostly dark ones, though Jack did spot a small pink starship. They had round windows on their sides and one or two doors at the back where the base of the pyramid would be if they weren't hovering sideways. The first door of each ship was roughly human-sized, and through an open one, Jack caught sight of a sleek interior. The largest ships had a second entrance, which was large enough to accommodate the transportation of cargo.

If teleporting a person cost ten thousand credits, Jack could only imagine how much large crates would cost. The Animal Kingdom—who probably ran the teleporters—were fleecing people for all they were worth.

"Gape all you want, just move away from the door before the next elevator arrives," Vlossana said from the side, laughing merrily. She waved at them. "It was nice meeting you, Jack and Brock. I wish you the best of luck in any endeavor you pursue!"

Jack refocused. "Thank you, Vlossana. Best of luck to you, too."

She disappeared into the crowd.

Right. We must move, Jack thought, tearing his sight from the starships and aliens to inspect the docks themselves.

The floor was wooden, wide, and empty of furniture or buildings. The tower in the middle continued behind Jack, stretching another fifty feet up to support the ceiling, a dome-shaped construction of wood filled with little arcs. It spread from the highest point in the very center, where the tower met it, to end in wooden walls that reached the floor between the openings for the starships.

Everything appeared wooden, but Jack suspected that was only for decor. There had to be metal underneath—at the very least, the exterior was metallic.

Though it was currently night, the docks were filled with light. Squat chandeliers hung from the ceiling, emitting what felt like sunlight to Jack's skin. Outside the openings, dots of light shone from the city below.

Brock grabbed Jack's forearm and pulled him toward an opening. Unable to resist the temptation, Jack followed, quickly reaching the edge, just before a two-foot-tall protective fence. The opening was a half-circle rising from the floor, with a radius of around fifteen feet. There was no starship on this particular opening, which gave Jack and Brock an unobstructed view.

And it was beautiful.

They were hundreds of feet in the air. From this height, they could see Pearl Bay stretching before their eyes, illuminated by discreet lighting—less than an Earthen city would have. The buildings reached halfway to the horizon, whereupon they were replaced by rolling green hills filled with purple trees. Water glimmered at the very ends of their vision, somehow radiating faint light, while two moons—one whole and one-half—filled the night sky. At least night was the same color as it was on Earth. Without any pollution to hide them, stars shone in the thousands, and Jack could only recognize a few of the constellations he was familiar with.

He was captivated by wonder. A moment later, he shook himself awake.

"Come on, Brock. We must find a ship to get us out of here."

Looking around, one side of the dock area was occupied by what seemed like an open bar between two openings. People of all kinds sat on stools around tall tables, discussing animatedly or in hushed tones. Most drank what looked like beer. A counter was at the very back, and a metal sign above it spelled, "Morning Star."

"A bar at the docks..." Jack chuckled. "I guess some things never change, right, Brock?"

Brock gave an excited cry, and together, they headed for the bar.

CHAPTER FOUR
CAPTAIN DORDOK

THE MORNINGSTAR BAR WAS PRECARIOUSLY PLACED. SURROUNDED BY FIVE-hundred-foot falls on either side, it only had a flimsy fence protecting its patrons. Coupled with the cityscape stretching beneath, it gave the impression of a bar in the sky—which it was, in a way.

In fact, the bar had commandeered one of the openings along the wall, laying out tall tables for people to enjoy the view.

As Jack approached, he was assaulted by raucous laughter and strong winds. The patrons' clothes flapped furiously in the night wind. Their drinks threatened to spill outside their glasses. The patrons themselves remained steady; even the least of them was an E-Grade.

Most were dressed similarly to humans of Earth. Of course, their body's resistance to both heat and cold gave them more fashion options. Some wore shorts and t-shirts, showcasing tattoo-sleeved arms. Others donned cloaks that covered them top to bottom, and another few were garbed in long veils that flapped in the wind.

Most of the patrons were feshkurs, a few saphiras, as well as kovans, the spinning-top-like merchant species that had been present in the Integration Tournament. There were also lone representatives of other species—an orange-skinned ogre drank alone. Jack's mind was overwhelmed by new sights. If he paid attention to every peculiarity, he would never walk a step.

With Brock following closely, he approached the counter, where a level 110 feshkur woman chatted with a couple of saphiras.

"Excuse me," Jack said. The barwoman turned to him, while the saphiras kept speaking by themselves.

"Yes?" the barwoman asked, scanning him up and down. Her gaze was hard, but not aggressive. Her thin arms were covered by a white apron.

"I'm looking for a ride to the Belarian Outpost," Jack explained politely. "Do you know if any starships are heading that way?"

She smirked. "Take it easy, honey. First things first: Would you like to buy a beer?"

Jack wasn't sure whether this was bargaining or simple hospitality, but it rushed to the forefront how dehydrated and starving he was. The food could wait until he was done finding a ship, but the beer... "Yes, please."

"Comin' right up."

Nobody here seemed to mind Jack's appearance, which was a relief. The most he received was odd stares. Back on Earth, before the Integration, people would be running away screaming at the sight of him.

The bartender grabbed a thick glass from the wall behind her and placed it under a tap, filling it until the foam licked the edge. "There," she said, handing it to him along with a green credit card that showed no numbers—a merchant's staple. "That's five credits."

Similar to the dollar price... Does a credit in the galaxy equate to a dollar on Earth?

Jack reached for his card and touched it to hers, waiting until the -5 sign appeared on its surface. The cards could hide or show their balance at the owner's discretion, and Jack had naturally chosen to hide his. It wasn't much, but it wasn't nothing, either.

He took a sip. It was heavenly. "Wanna try, Brock?" he asked, letting the brorilla have a sip as well.

"Of ships heading to the Outpost," the barwoman said, returning to Jack's question, "we have plenty. There's a departure every three days, roughly. If you just wait a bit, you'll find a ride."

"When is the next one? I'm in somewhat of a hurry."

"In two days, I believe." Seeing Jack's deep frown, she added, "There's a starship leaving for the Outpost in an hour from now, but I believe they're full. You could ask, since you're in a hurry. Maybe they'll take you along."

"I'll do that," Jack said. "Could you direct me?"

She jabbed her head to the side. "See that big orange guy? That's the captain."

She was referring to the orange ogre Jack had spotted on his way in. "Good. Thank you."

"No problem. Safe travels."

The barwoman returned to her saphira friends, while Jack took his beer and walked toward the ogre. It wasn't difficult, the bar tables spread out in a sixty-foot wide semi-circle around the counter, so there was plenty of space despite the crowd. And, in any case, the orange man was sitting just down the long counter. Jack reached him in a heartbeat.

"Excuse me," he said politely. "I heard you're the captain of a starship heading to the Belarian Outpost. Is that true?"

The ogre turned to look at him.

It was suspicious how close Earth's mythology fell to the actual aliens. Not only were some galaxy names in latin, like Ursus Mountain and its bears, but djinns and efreetis were also real.

Now, as Jack looked at this person, he found another familiar creature.

The ogre was large, orange, and hairless, with a pot belly and only a dirty cloak, black pants, and black boots for clothes. Though he was seated, Jack thought he must have been tall. Certainly taller than himself. His face was rough-cut, with a wide nose and square teeth. There was also a metallic greatclub resting against the counter.

Most importantly, the ogre only had a single, blue eye.

Cyclops, Level ??? (D-Grade)
Faction: -
Title: Far Traveler

Jack's thoughts about aliens and mythological connections were abruptly cut off as he realized he was face-to-face with an immortal.

On second thought, he should have imagined it. Space-warping starships could only be operated by immortals. He'd just forgotten that little detail.

"I am," the cyclops replied in a gruff voice. His disinterest was obvious, but he still humored Jack. "Friends call me Dordok. You can call me Captain."

"I—Yes, Captain." Jack regained his bearings. He had to remember that he was in a civilized place. This immortal wouldn't just kill him for wasting his time... right? "My name is Jared, and this is Monk." Since they were on the run, they obviously needed fake names—though he'd accidentally given his real one to the girl in the elevator line. "We are also headed to the Outpost. If there's any space in your ship, could we—"

"We're full," Dordok cut him off.

"We don't even need a room, Captain! Any random corner will do. We are just in a real hurry."

The cyclops considered him for a moment. His eye narrowed as he scanned Jack and Brock from top to bottom. "Fine. If you complain even once about your living conditions, I will drop you off at the next stop. And I will charge you extra for all the trouble your "hurry" might bring to me and my ship."

He didn't seem bothered to ask just who was after them—who knows what he assumed—and Jack wasn't an idiot to give more information. He had even been prepared to lie about it. After all, if this person knew they were hunted by the Animal Kingdom, he would probably deny them boarding on the spot.

"Thank you, Captain," Jack replied, nodding deeply. Then, gritting his teeth, he continued. "I was also hoping to offset some of the cost by serving as a guard for the ship."

"Out of the question. A low E-Grade is only qualified to scrub the floors on my ship, and I already have a crew for that." His one brow fell lower. "You *can* pay, right?"

"If I may, Captain," Jack insisted, painfully aware that he was speaking with an immortal. "I may be only a low E-Grade in level, but my strength reaches the middle E-Grade." He wasn't sure about this, but he had to risk it.

At this, the cyclops showed a hint of interest. "Are you certain?"

"Yes," Jack replied. He wasn't, but only a fool would say no.

"Hmm. Earth-387... That's the newly-Integrated planet, isn't it? About a month ago?"

"Two months, Captain," Jack lied. The cyclops could see his species listed as Human (Earth-387), so he never expected to hide that. However, since he was given the opportunity, he increased the timespan to make him reaching the E-Grade less notable. The Integration had actually happened around a month and a week ago. "I ranked in the top sixteen of the Integration Tournament. Then I met a scion of the Animal Kingdom, and, well... Not much I could do."

A hint of rage burned in the captain's eye. Jack almost blurted everything out.

"They're still doing that, then. Dishonorable cretins," the captain said. "If you're lying to me, boy, you will regret it." Jack remained silent. After a moment, the captain continued. "My ship always has space for talented young cultivators. If you really possess the strength you claim, I will slot you in and even give you a bed to sleep in at half the normal price—two thousand five hundred credits a head. So five thousand for you and your monkey."

"We—" Jack bit back his rise of panic, looking down. "We only have three thousand, Captain. I know this is too much to ask, but could we pay you the remaining two thousand at a later date? We... We are in need."

The cyclops didn't reply immediately, but Jack didn't dare raise his gaze. Finally, the voice that replied was both surprised and annoyed. "Do you not have a shred of fear, boy?"

"I do, Captain. I'm shaking in my boots."

At this, the cyclops chuckled a bit, the sound of two rocks grinding. "Wait a moment," he said, turning back to the counter.

Jack obliged. However, Captain Dordok seemed to be ignoring him, lazily sipping on his beer as if waiting for something. Without a choice, and hoping it wasn't considered disrespectful, Jack did the same.

After an entire minute, someone approached them from behind. "You called, Captain?"

Jack turned to find a lean feshkur staring at him oddly. He was tall, at least two heads above Jack, with scars on his bare chest and a red bandana wrapped around his forehead. A mace hung from his belt.

Feshkur, Level 85
Faction: -

"This boy claims to have the power of a middle E-Grade," the cyclops said, motioning at Jack. "Interesting, isn't it?"

"Very," the feshkur replied, understanding his captain's meaning in a heartbeat. "My name is Vashter. What say you, boy? Wanna prove your words?"

"Always," Jack responded. "But how?"

"What's your Dao?" Vashter asked. Jack kept his mouth shut. One's Dao and skills were highly personal information.

"Answer him, boy," Captain Dordok chimed in. "If you want to join my crew, revealing your Dao is the very least you can do."

"The Dao of the Fist," Jack replied.

Vashter smiled. "That makes things simple." He drew his mace. "If you can last a few strikes against me, you pass."

"Wha—Here? Now?"

"Yes. And remember, the loser pays for the damages."

"I—"

Before Jack could finish his words, an orange hand grabbed his neck from behind and flung him out. Jack was drowned in overwhelming strength. Even if he was ten times as strong, he would still be like a baby faced with that hand.

He landed on the wooden floor with a roll and jumped upright. He'd flown over some tables to reach an empty area fifteen feet in diameter, surrounded by bar patrons on all sides. Seeing him, they looked confused, then erupted into cheers. Vashter appeared across him like a blur. The crowd cheered harder.

With only fifteen feet to move, the place was extremely cramped for a battle between E-Grades. It was only suitable for a brawl.

"Come on, boy," Vashter taunted, twirling his mace. "Show me the power of a genius."

Mid-twirl, his mace lashed out in a stab. It was faster than a whip or an arrow. Jack barely caught a glimpse before his fighting skill—the Iron Fist Style—activated, pulling his head to the side. The air exploded next to his ear.

"Not bad," Vashter said, already back in his previous position, twirling the mace with nonchalance. His eyes held a hint of intrigue now. "But let's see how you deal with a *real* attack."

Jack clenched his fist, desperately trying to enter his battle mode faster. That was a weakness of his. Most of his battles so far had been either him ambushing someone else or a tournament fight, so he always had time to prepare. Now, he was thrust into full-on combat out of nowhere.

The mace blurred. Jack barely had time to raise his forearm. The impact sounded like steel on steel, and Jack's arm barely held. If not for his regeneration, he would have a purple bruise spanning from wrist to elbow the next day.

Vashter didn't retreat. He flowed into more attacks, swinging his mace like a hurricane. Jack dodged one strike and redirected the next, no longer daring to block, defending was all he could do. There was no time to counterattack.

Ghost Step, he thought, flashing behind Vashter in a heartbeat and striking out.

"Oho! We're using Skills, then!" Vashter shouted, then disappeared. Jack jumped aside before the mace crushed down from above, halting its momentum just before it broke the floor. Jack punched again. Vashter blocked one strike, then swept his mace widely. Jack stepped back—

—and reached the edge of the tiny arena. A pair of firm hands pushed his back, making him stumble right into the attack. It was too late to defend. The mace struck his ribs at the same time that he used his forward momentum to unleash a Meteor Punch right at Vashter's face. There was no time for his punch to connect, so all he could do was shoot it out as a projectile and hope for the best. Blinding pain enveloped him.

The world tumbled as Jack flew away, crashing through two tables before a tall and wide feshkur caught him. The same feshkur screamed obscenities in his ear, but jokes on him—that ear had been deafened earlier.

Jack stumbled upright, struggling and regaining his balance. His entire body ached. Maybe he still wasn't fully healed from his battle with Rufus.

A path of broken wood and glass was strewn before him, leading all the way to the brawl circle. A dozen E-Grade eyes glared at him. In the brawl circle, Vashter was just standing up—Jack's meteor had taken him to the ground.

However, the feshkur's eyes weren't disappointed or triumphant. Instead, they gazed at Jack with what seemed like... surprise? Respect?

Jack lost sight of Vashter as a crowd of angry feshkurs gathered around him, but an orange giant blocked their path. The moment the feshkurs saw him, they all stepped back and shut up. Seeing the captain standing for the first time, Jack realized he was shorter than the feshkurs, only a head taller than Jack himself, but double as wide in all dimensions.

"Don't worry, everyone," Captain Dordok said, laughing. "The boy will buy your next two rounds of drinks."

"Will he also pay for my damages?" the barwoman said, having appeared just behind the captain. Her fingertips glowed with green light, and the wood splinters floated and recombined into whole tables and chairs. It was like nothing had happened.

"Of course," the captain responded. "This young man enjoys taking responsibility. He will repay you in full."

"Good. Thank you, Captain," she replied, turning to stare at Jack and extending her credit card. "That will be two thousand credits."

Jack failed to see why he needed to pay that much. The barwoman had clearly restored everything with a moment's effort. Her losses were zero. He also failed to see why *he* should be the one to pay, even though he'd been forced into this battle.

"Because the loser pays, always," Captain Dordok said as if reading his thoughts. "Consider it the fee for having us test you."

Jack couldn't retort to that. He touched his credit card to the barwoman's. "So..."

Dordok stepped forward and held out a large, orange hand that made Jack's seem tiny. "That was impressive, Jared. The crew of the *Trampling Ram* can use someone of your talents. Welcome aboard."

CHAPTER FIVE
THE TRAMPLING RAM

THE *TRAMPLING RAM* WAS THE LARGEST STARSHIP JUST OUTSIDE THE DOCKS. IT floated before one of the openings in the wall, five hundred feet over the city. Any random item dropped from this height could incapacitate the weaker people below.

The starship didn't bob with the wind as one would expect. Instead, it was completely still, as if anchored to space itself. Despite this stability, thick chains extended from the edge of the docks to the starship ten feet away, holding it in place should anything go wrong.

The *Trampling Ram* had a similar shape to the other starships: like an elongated pyramid hovering sideways, though it dwarfed most of them in size. It was about a hundred feet long and fifty wide at the back end.

It also had some differences compared to other starships. First, it was covered in windows, especially around the middle, making its exterior walls seem like they were made half of glass and half of metal. The other starships only had small, circular windows. Second, it did not end in a sharp tip, but rather in a large goat head made of solid steel. Hence its name.

"The *Trampling Ram*," Captain Dordok declared proudly, puffing his chest as he gestured at his ship. "Her top aerial speed is ten thousand miles an hour. Weighs only ten tons, made of void steel, and can warp twice a day."

"It looks... intimidating," Jack said.

"Sure does. Imagine her running into a planet at full speed; they won't live to tell the tale. We ran through a large pack of space monsters with her prow once. Tell me, do you think those boring tip-prowed ships can do the same?"

"No, Captain."

The captain looked genuinely happy to see his starship, and was very proud to show it off. Jack had the feeling that, if he let him be, he would go on and on about previous adventures without actually showing him anything. They were here so he could take a look at the ship before it was crowded with people.

"Does the inside look as good as the outside, Captain?"

"Good? Of course it looks good! But remember, kid, the important beauty is in the inside. The outside is only a bonus—the *Trampling Ram* just happens to have both."

"I will remember it, Captain. And after this introduction, I can't wait to see what the inside looks like."

"Well then, let me show you!"

Captain Dordok waved a hand, and a door on the back of the ship—the flat part that was the pyramid's bottom—slid open. "Place the ramp."

"The ramp?"

"Yes. Lesson one: open your eyes and look around before you ask stupid questions."

Jack did look around and found a wooden ramp about twenty feet in length and five in width lain strewn to the side. He grabbed one side, Brock grabbed the other—both were at the same end, just on opposite sides—and together, they placed it down to connect the starship to the docks.

"After you, Captain," Jack said. The captain nodded and went ahead, walking the narrow ramp like he'd been born on it. His wide feet found easy purchase on the wood. His tattered cloak fluttered behind him, held in place by the massive steel greatclub that hung diagonally across his back: the handle was at the side of his neck, and the fat end reached to his thighs.

The captain's short dark pants had clipped edges, only going to just above his knees, leaving his muscular legs as bare as his chest.

Jack walked the plank after him. His footing was steady, as was Brock's, but he still felt a moment of unease when he was suddenly five hundred feet above the ground, suspended only on a flimsy wooden ramp. A moment later, fear turned to awe as he saw the city stretching in all directions, illuminated by a myriad tiny lights. The wind rapped his face, making the whole sight even more real.

Brock shared the awe, skipping the fear part. He was a brorilla. High places didn't scare him.

A cube-shaped room nine feet at a side surrounded them a moment later. The walls were made of gray metal with lamps of yellow, natural light illuminating the room from the corners.

"That's the cargo hold," the captain said, pointing at a closed door to the right. "It's empty now. It will be your room."

The doors inside the ship weren't sliding, but were old-fashioned, made of metal, and had a handle you either pushed or pulled. The captain reached for a door straight ahead—the only other door in the room—and pulled it open, revealing a corridor.

It stretched both up—with a ladder—and to the right. The part heading right had one door to the right and two to the left, then ended in another ladder headed up.

"This is the main corridor," the captain explained. "We're at the third deck—the lowest floor, if you will. There are two identical corridors above us, connected by the ladders you see, each housing one floor of the ship. You can imagine these three corridors—which we collectively refer to as the main corridor—as parallel to the stern of the ship—stern is what we call the back part."

"I'm familiar with the word."

"Good. Now, I won't show you everything at once, but I will describe the general idea. Picture the stern in your mind. Imagine three floors just inside it, all connected by the corridor in front of you, the two above you, and the ladders. The lower deck—at the very bottom—houses storage and utility rooms, as well as the cargo hold and the people's exit. The upper deck—at the very top—is living quarters, both for the crew and for passengers. The main deck is in the middle, and it leads to the core parts of the ship: the bridge, the escape shuttles, the secondary exit, and the main room."

"Okay," Jack said, struggling to visualize all those. He pictured the pyramid-shaped ship hovering sideways, then two lines splitting it horizontally into three floors. The top and bottom ones couldn't stretch far due to the ship's shape. The middle was the only floor that continued deeper, occupying the entire ship.

"Working as a guard means you rarely work. You will only be needed if trouble presents itself. At other times, you will either be lazing about or cleaning," Captain Dordok explained. "But when there *is* trouble, you will need to get your ass to the main room immediately no matter what you're doing. Follow me."

They climbed the ladder to the next floor—the main deck—then walked to the only door within the corridor and opened it. A large room stretched before Jack—as large as it could be, in any case. Its ceiling, walls, and floor were all diagonal—probably the ship's outer walls— and its far side was occupied by three doors leading deeper.

The room itself was spacious. There were couches, tables, a kitchen, a walled-off bathroom, even a mostly empty library. Accessories of all kinds filled the bottom of that library, from dice to cards.

However, the room's most striking feature was its surroundings. The floor, the walls, the ceiling... All of them were made of glass, looking out into the city and the dark sky above.

"The view is amazing when we're in space," Captain Dordok said with a hint of longing. "You'll see. In any case, this is where we spend most of our time when not cultivating in our rooms. It's also where you will need to be if the alarm sounds."

"Who would attack us in space?"

"Space monsters and pirates, of course," the captain said as if it made perfect sense. "Now, from left to right, those three doors lead to the secondary exit—from where you can go fight space monsters, if need be—the bridge, where we power and navigate the ship, and the escape shuttles. Pray that we never have to open that last door."

Having said that, the third door seemed in perfect condition, as did the others. The captain clearly didn't skimp on maintenance.

"Any questions?" he asked.

"It is beautiful, Captain," Jack replied. "But aren't these glass panels dangerous? I mean, if people or... space monsters... attack us, wouldn't they break easily?"

"That's three feet of tempered glass you're talking about, boy," the captain replied proudly. "It isn't exactly as sturdy as steel, but it's close. And much, much more beautiful. The only issue is that they're expensive—cost almost as much as the rest of the ship combined—but I couldn't give her anything less than the best."

"They are indeed beautiful, Captain..." Jack said. Though the glass floor was disorienting, he had no doubt that it would be amazing when he got used to it. "If I may, how much does a good starship cost?"

The Sage had gotten one for a few hundred thousand credits. If a credit here was similar to a dollar back on Earth, Jack suspected the Sage had gotten himself quite the deal.

Captain Dordok turned to Jack and gave him a look full of meaning. "You cannot *buy* a good starship, boy. You can buy a starship. It only becomes good after you have sailed the galaxy together for centuries, when you know its every inch like the back of your hand, when you have seen its every screw and bolt replaced so that nothing remains of the original. Then, and only then, does a starship become *good*."

"I see," Jack said. Though Captain Dordok hadn't really answered his question, he didn't press.

"Don't view ships as objects, boy," the captain continued in an earnest tone. "They are more than just a collection of parts. They have a soul. They are one with the captain and the crew. Just another old friend. A ship will never abandon you in your time of need, and you should treat it the same way. That is all they ask of you: loyalty. And that is also the very essence of our crew."

Jack looked around with new eyes. "I see, Captain," he said, though he really didn't. Perhaps he would in time. Earthen sailors used to say similar things. "Indeed, the gift you gave your ship—the glass walls of the main room—look great. Much better than the tiny windows of other ships."

"They do, don't they?" Dordok puffed up, full of pride. "Well, it was also a gift to myself, if I'm being honest. I grew up as a sailor on my home planet. I've transitioned from the seas to space now, but I still couldn't handle being locked up in a box for months on end. What I love about traveling is the wind and sand on my face, the sea breeze and salt.

I want to keep my ship as close to that as possible, though most things are certainly... different."

"Why did you leave, then?" Jack asked. "If you preferred the sea, why become a starship captain?"

"There isn't much for an immortal to do at sea." Dordok shrugged. "Becoming an immortal is my greatest regret. I was forced to move to a larger ocean, that of space, which is lacking in many parts—though it does offer sights that I would never see on any planet."

"Like what?"

"You'll see. Surprise is part of the experience." Dordok smiled, revealing a set of square teeth. "Now then. This will be all for now. It's time to meet your shipmates. They should be here in a moment."

"How do you—"

The door behind them opened slowly, revealing three people. Two were feshkurs. The last was a hulking, brown-furred minotaur.

Vashter was one of the feshkurs; the weakest one.

Feshkur, Level 85
Faction: -

Feshkur, Level 99
Faction: -

Minotaur, Level 111
Faction: -

Before Jack could introduce himself, two more people entered the main room. One was a chubby, overdressed male saphira. The other was Vlossana.

"Oh!" she said, seeing him. "Hi!"

CHAPTER SIX

A SKY FULL OF STARS

GAN SALIN UNDERSTOOD THE CONCEPT.

Yes, he'd fucked up. Yes, he lost in single combat against Jack Rust, Vivi Eragorn, Li Xiang, and Edgar Allano. Yes, three of those fights had been broadcasted across Earth-387 and the Animal Kingdom home world. And yes, he'd even been assaulted by a pack of oddly muscular dogs.

But those things could happen to everyone, right? So why was he getting bullied now?

Not fun, man... he thought as space around him stabilized. They had reached their destination.

The three Hounds stepped off the teleporter. When Salin followed a moment later, they were already interrogating the guard, who claimed to know nothing. Salin looked above the door, where a sign declared their current location. *Pearl Bay...* he thought to himself, biting into a six-sided orange bar and tearing off a chunk. Earth-387 had some rather tasty snacks. *Another dud...*

They'd been on the search for several hours already. Earth-387's teleporter could reach a hundred and twelve destinations, and they had to check them all. Salin was dragged along because he knew Jack—and also as punishment for losing so many times in what was supposed to be an easy Integration Tournament.

But it wasn't my fault... He sighed. Okay, maybe it was. But how could I know those guys were all monsters?

He didn't even care about finding Jack Rust. In fact, if he was being honest with himself, he kinda liked the guy. Jack was fun and unpredictable, always finding a way to make things amusing.

Too bad he angered an elder.

Gan Salin bit off another chunk of the dog food bar. At least he didn't have to do much. The three Hounds would handle everything. The guard seemed to know nothing about Jack Rust, but they would also go out and ask the pedestrians, scout out for his Dao signature, speak to some important people, and generally make inquiries. They had to do this in every possible destination, lest they miss him and have to start over.

Not that Jack could escape. A bounty on his head was already beginning to circulate. Nobody could hide from the Animal Kingdom in their constellation. Not for long.

Suddenly, a pale feshkur—one of Pearl Bay's two native sapient species—arrived in front of the open door. He waited nervously. "Excuse me..." he muttered.

One of the Hounds turned to him, covering him in the aura that all D-Grades had. The feshkur shivered again.

"I heard you asking about someone with a pet monkey..." he muttered.

The rest of the Hounds turned to him as well. The aura pressing against his body tripled in intensity. The feshkur sweated.

"If you lie to us," one of the Hounds said, her face covered by a dark veil, "we will devour you."

"I wouldn't dare," the feshkur said. "I met that person. In fact, he even told me a few things, and I waited here in case someone was hunting him."

"Tell us everything," another Hound said, his voice raspy. Having caught sight of his prey, he was barely holding back his excitement. All Hounds were like that. Gan Salin rolled his eyes.

Unless Jack Rust grew wings, there was no way he could escape.

———

"Hey," Jack responded numbly as five people streamed into the main room. Even with seven of them present, it didn't feel crowded, just full.

"I didn't expect you to join the *Ram*'s crew!" Vlossana said, full of excitement.

"Neither did I."

"Or I, for that matter," the captain spoke up, laughing. "But here we are. Jared, these are Count Plomer and his daughter, Vlossana. They are our passengers for this trip."

"Oh, we've already met!" Vlossana spoke up, then narrowed her eyes at him. Jack wouldn't have noticed it if he wasn't paying attention.

When he met her in the elevator line, he'd given her his real name, Jack. Now, the captain had introduced him as Jared.

Ugh... This will be trouble, I can feel it. At least she isn't saying anything.

"A pleasure," Vlossana's father replied, not sounding very pleased. "But I thought, Captain, that we had booked the entire ship for ourselves..."

"You have. Jared here is a member of my crew, not a passenger."

Count Plomer nodded. He had sapphire hair and purple eyes, like the rest of the saphira, as well as an otherwise normal human body. There were slight wrinkles on his face, likely caused by years of stress, and his purple hair was fainter than his daughter's, inching toward white.

He donned a full suit, complete with a tie, but the air he radiated was unusual. He possessed the confidence that came with being an authority figure, but he was also steeped in exhaustion.

He reminded Jack of a professor he'd met briefly, once. A man with prestigious academic achievements but failure in every other part of his life.

More importantly...

Saphira, Level 49 (F-Grade)
Faction: -

...he was only F-Grade.

"That said," Captain Dordok continued, "this is the rest of the crew. Jared, you've already met Vashter. This is Achilles" —he pointed at the other feshkur, then the minotaur— "and this is Bomn. Everyone, this is Jared, our newest member. I believe you all saw his brawl against Vashter in the bar, so you understand his potential. In time, and with a bit of luck, he might even surpass me—something I expect from all of you. Also, this little guy is Monk, Jared's companion."

The three crew members greeted Jack, who responded politely. Brock shook their hands and nodded in a manly way.

Achilles looked like a slightly older version of Vashter. He had more scars and carried a heavy saber instead of a mace. Bomn was the silent, serious type, and he carried a large greataxe.

A greatclub, a mace, a saber, and a greataxe. Everyone in this crew were strength-based; just like him.

"Now," the captain said, clapping his large orange hands. "Introductions complete, our break is over. Let's get started. Bomn, handle our ascent. Achilles and Vashter, make sure nothing goes wrong. And Jared..." He winked—or blinked. It was tough to tell when he only had one eye, but it felt like a wink. "Watch the view."

"Yes, Captain!" Vashter and Achilles cried out, followed by Jack a moment later. Bomn simply nodded and went to the middle door at the far end of the main room. Before it closed, Jack caught a glimpse of sparkling machinery, a small goat head, and a glowing circle on a table.

Jack remained in the main room, along with Brock, the captain, Vlossana, and her father—Count Plomer.

"Have you ever been to space before?" Vlossana asked, already pouring excitement over his head. She seemed to have forgotten about his fake name—maybe she thought she'd heard wrong the first time. Jack prayed for that. "Oh, you're going to love it! The stars, the swirls, the galaxy... It's amazing!"

"Let the man rest, Vlossana," her father responded tiredly.

"Children are great," the captain said. His laughter was loud and booming, filling every nook and cranny of the room.

Jack felt space click around him. It was like he got detached and reattached from the world. He looked around wildly, but everyone seemed calm. Only Brock stared at him with wide eyes.

Before they could ask anything, the ship rumbled under their feet.

"Goodbye, Pearl Bay!" Vlossana shouted, waving backward. Then, they shot out.

Jack was disoriented, his senses unable to match up. They accelerated from nothing to top speed in an instant. He barely got a glimpse of the town under their feet before it disappeared, the entire planet shrinking at mind-numbing speed.

And yet, despite the massive acceleration, he felt nothing. No force pulling him back, no urge to puke. In fact, the entire ship was steady under his feet like they were still hovering next to the docks. He even thought they were joking, and the windows were just playing an illusion.

"What the...?" was all he managed to blurt out.

"Spatial independence," the captain explained with pride. "Space-warping starships exist in their own, independent spatial bubble. If space was a sheet, you can imagine us floating just an inch above it, unbothered by things such as gravity or inertia. Otherwise, only immortals could bear the pressure of acceleration—and certainly not any furniture."

Jack exhaled. He was trembling. Excitement was soaring through him. He looked beyond the windows, and he saw everything.

It was magnificent.

He was surrounded on all sides by the great nothingness. Empty darkness deeper than his mortal mind could comprehend. Multicolored dots of light spread out in the dark—white, blue, red, yellow—like Christmas lights. Where there were many, they formed rivers, floating on for unfathomable distances.

Everywhere was packed with stars, and cold darkness filled the void in between. In Jack's mind, their starship shrunk until it was invisible. Everything around them was so unimaginably large, even the void. His mind tried to comprehend the scale and was overwhelmed, both by it and by the beauty.

Soon after the Integration, Jack had seen the night sky for the first time—the true night sky, unblocked by pollution and artificial lights. It had been one of the prettiest sights of his life, and it had been burned into his mind. The difference between the sky he was used to seeing was tremendous.

He experienced that wonderous feeling again. This was on a completely different level than the sky from Earth. He was surrounded by the pure, untouched beauty of the universe, and it felt like looking at a canvas that God himself had filled with all the artistry and skill He could muster.

Jack lost himself in the sight. A hand landed on his shoulder and shook him awake.

"This is how we all felt on our first time," Captain Dordok said. "But don't worry. The stars aren't going anywhere. You will have the time to enjoy them all you want as we travel."

Tearing his sight away was a challenge, but Jack managed it. "Yes, Captain," he replied, whispering without intending to. The cyclops had a wide smile.

A voice came from somewhere on the ceiling. Jack recognized it as Bomn's. "Warping."

"About damn time," Captain Dordok said, still sporting his smile. He turned to Jack. "We don't usually come this far from the planet to warp. Bomn took things slow for you. He may not speak much, but his heart is made of gold."

Jack tried to respond, but his voice caught in his throat. The entire ship shook once. Then, his stomach lurched, space rippled around them, and they pierced into it like a stone falling in the sea.

Stars and comets flew around them, darting backward like trees at the side of the road. Jack vaguely remembered such a scene from when Brock and he had teleported, just before he fainted.

"Teleportation!" he cried out.

"Exactly," the captain replied.

"But... But how?"

"I asked a wizard once," Dordok explained, looking into the stars above them. "He said that space is a sheet, and black holes weigh it down so hard that the entire sheet creates folds, one for each black hole. Instead of traveling along the surface of space, we can simply drill through the folds, crossing impossible distances at the blink of an eye. Imagine trying to get past a giant wave at sea. Drilling through the base of the wave is much faster than swimming all the way up, then all the way down to the other side."

Jack simply stared at him.

"Of course, I'm not too clear on *how* this is done," Dordok continued, "but I know it works. Teleporters operate by the same principle, except they're much stronger than what can be mounted on a ship."

Brock whistled. Jack nodded absently. Vlossana laughed. Her father looked at the captain and nodded. Dordok himself gave Jack a wide smile just as space around them solidified again.

"I've said it before, boy, but welcome to the *Trampling Ram*. You are going to love this."

CHAPTER SEVEN
E-GRADE CULTIVATION

SPACE SOLIDIFIED AROUND JACK. ANOTHER SUCCESSFUL WARP HAD JUST ENDED. With a deep breath of relief, he looked inside himself.

It had already been a week since he boarded the *Trampling Ram*. In that time, they'd met no other starships, planets, or any sort of civilization. They were alone in an endless void, light-years away from anything else that could speak, with only each other as company.

Jack did not dislike it. He had used this time to finally relax and inspect everything new about him. There was plenty.

He had transformed a Dao Root into a Dao Seed. He'd broken through to the E-Grade. He received a new Dao Vision and finally achieved his fighting style Dao Skill. His body had been enhanced tremendously, and he had overall ascended to an entirely new level.

The Dao Seed was the most intimate change. Before, his Dao Roots —the Fist and Indomitable Will—had been two dots of power hovering inside his soul. He pictured them as small collections of mist floating through an otherwise empty jar.

Now, one of them had spread to encompass the entire jar. In evolving, the Dao of the Fist had seeped into every nook and cranny of Jack's soul, becoming a perfect whole with him. This greatly increased his aptitude with that particular Dao, and it also enhanced the power of the Dao Seed itself.

However, Jack remained himself, he and the Fist were one, but the Fist had no mind of its own, only power. Power that Jack could harness.

At least, it *usually* didn't have a mind. Jack felt like he'd struck a bargain with a devil. The power stayed inside him, perfectly dormant, but it started becoming upset the farther he strayed from its path. If he started acting as a weakling, not keeping the promise he made to the Fist during the breakthrough, his Dao would weaken.

On the other hand, while he remained loyal to the Dao of the Fist, its power was easy and malleable, and further breakthroughs were just outside his reach.

The Dao Root of Indomitable Will still hovered within his soul. Now that he fused with the Dao Root of the Fist, he could sense that the Indomitable Will was used ineffectively. He was just calling upon it when needed, but the connection between them could be far more intimate, far more efficient.

Jack was certain he could truly connect with the Dao Root of Indomitable Will, but only if he found the perfect way in which it fit with the Fist. Once that perfect fusion was achieved, the Dao Root of Indomitable Will would become a part of the Dao Seed of the Fist, and his power would rise yet again.

That was the way through the E-Grade. One had to forge as many Dao Roots as they desired, then connect them all to their Dao Seed. Only when the seed and roots were fully connected could a Dao Tree sprout.

Of course, the more Dao Roots one had, the stronger they would be. But power came with a price. Even if you reached the peak of the E-Grade—level 124—you couldn't advance to the D-Grade unless you connected all Dao Roots to your Dao Seed. And connecting them was difficult. Therefore, one had to choose the perfect number of Dao Roots.

One root was naturally the minimum.

Moreover, every Dao Root carried a tremendous risk. Not all Dao Roots could connect with all Dao Seeds. In fact, most couldn't. A cultivator had to be extremely careful in what Dao Roots they chose to cultivate, as very few could achieve a perfect fusion with the Dao Seed, and a single unfusable one would doom them to forever remain at the E-Grade.

For that reason, most D-Grades only had one Dao Root along with their Dao Seed. Those with two were considered elites even amongst immortals. Those with three were hailed as prodigies. And in the galaxy's million-year history, there had only been a handful of people who advanced to the D-Grade with four Dao Roots.

Nobody had ever achieved five.

The compatibility between a Dao Seed and the various Dao Roots was the most important reason why factions and masters were crucial. Every person's Dao was unique, but if you walked a well-documented path, you would have a measure of knowledge in what Dao Roots were and weren't suitable for you.

For example, Rufus Emberheart cultivated the same Dao of Supremacy that his entire family did. Their Dao Roots were recorded in secret archives. By perusing them, he could see what Dao Roots worked for other holders of the same Dao—they would have a good chance of working for him, too.

Jack didn't have that luxury. The Exploding Sun must have had records on previous holders of the Dao of the Fist, since that bald man from his first Dao Vision was Master Shol's ancestor, but he had no way to contact them. Apparently, neither did they.

Therefore, Jack was alone in uncharted waters, and he had to carve a perfect route on the first try. One mistake would be enough to completely sever his future. He had to be very careful.

Which was bad news, because he was also in a terrible hurry. He only had one year until he fought the C-Grade Planetary Overseer.

Of course, he could also find some other way to rescue his people, but there was no guarantee it would work. As nice as Captain Dordok seemed, Jack doubted he would risk himself, his ship, and his entire crew to oppose the Animal Kingdom just for Jack's sake.

Not to mention that Dordok visiting Earth would break the Star Pact, which would give the Planetary Overseer an excuse to act herself.

Therefore, Jack's best bet was to become as strong as possible while keeping an eye out for other opportunities. And, since he already had the Dao Root of Indomitable Will, he figured that he might as well start there.

The second thing he really itched to do was explore his new Dao Vision, but he figured that could wait a bit. It would teach him things, and he wanted to stabilize before expanding.

However, he had been working on connecting his Dao Root for the past week, to little effect. This time was no different. He had let his thoughts wander instead of concentrating.

If cultivating was easy, everyone would do it.

Jack opened his eyes, sighing. *Perhaps it's time...* he thought, touching the back of his left thigh. His secret pocket was there, where he kept the Dao Soul, among other things. He took it out and stared at it.

It was a purple, plate-shaped gem that could easily fit in Jack's hand. It seemed normal at first glance. On the second, it was anything but. Two thick lines swam inside it like eels, one black and the other white, cutting circles around each other. It reminded him of the yin-yang sign.

And it was damn frustrating.

The Dao Soul was one of Jack's rewards for winning the Integration Tournament. He was sure it was precious. Except he still hadn't found a way to use it. The head judge's description had been vague, and the System description wasn't helping either.

Dao Soul

The crystallized essence of the Dao. Dao Souls are formed in places where the presence of the Dao is so thick that it congeals. Over millions of years, it forms a rudimentary conscience that is extremely sensitive to the Dao.

They are very precious.

He sighed. That was nice, but it didn't tell him how to use it. For the millionth time, he recalled the head judge's description:

The Dao Soul is a mystical item said to split one's soul into two. It can help a cultivator practice their Dao against themselves, rising their cultivation speed tremendously. Ingesting it takes time.

That was all she'd said. Ingesting it takes time.

But how much? Jack asked himself, exasperated. *And how am I supposed to know!*

He had half a mind to smash it, hoping that would work, but what if it didn't? He didn't want to waste such a valuable resource. Plus, if smashing it was the answer, the head judge wouldn't say it needed time.

Then again, nothing changes the more I wait. Maybe I should smash the gem and be done with it.

He toyed with the idea, not actually intending to do it, but thinking about it was fun.

With a sigh, he slid the Dao Soul back into his pocket and closed his eyes to cultivate again. A blaring siren howled over his head and made him jump so fast that his head met the ceiling.

"Son of a—" he exclaimed. "What the hell?"

"Jared. Can you hear me? Come to the main room immediately," Captain Dordok's voice reached his ears.

Jack grumbled. He was alone in the cargo hold; a large, mostly empty room that served as his. He'd fashioned a hammock at the back with some rope Bomn had given him.

All thoughts of cultivation put aside, Jack opened his door to reach the exit room, then another to enter the main corridor. He climbed the stairs and opened a third door that led to the main room. He hurried through them all—he was a part of the crew now, and when the captain called, he should not tarry.

Captain Dordok was waiting for him alone in the middle of the main room, surrounded by stars in all directions. The scenery still awed Jack, but he snapped out of it. So did Brock, who had followed Jack.

"There's another monster approaching us," the captain said with a smile. "This time, it's a weak one. A baby, let's say; perfect for our weakest member."

"Which is me."

"Which is you."

Space monsters were fairly common. They were amalgamations of the Dao formed spontaneously in space. They came in various colors, and their forms weren't always steady. Most were barely conscious blobs of power. The best they could do was summon tentacle-like appendages and try to consume anything that came near them radiating the power of the Dao.

According to Captain Dordok, these monsters grew in stability and intelligence the stronger they got—either by time or by consuming Dao sources. D-Grade space monsters had a stable physical form. C-Grade ones were allegedly able to communicate.

Of course, higher Grade monsters were exceedingly rare in System space. All the ones they'd met were E-Grade, and naturally, they could never threaten the *Trampling Ram*. Captain Dordok alone could dispatch them easily.

But he didn't.

Every time, he would gauge the monster's strength and send out the most appropriate crewmember to face it. Claimed it was good practice.

Of the previous three monsters, Vashter had taken two. The third was pretty strong, forcing Bomn the minotaur to face it. It hadn't even been a battle. Bomn roared as he hefted his greataxe, its edge shining with a piercing red light, and then he slashed it down. The monster had been seared into two equal halves.

Now, the fourth monster showed up, and it was finally Jack's turn.

"It's coming fast from below. We have half a minute. Wear this and go through the exit," Captain Dordok said, tossing Jack a large helmet. It resembled a fishbowl, and wasn't airtight, but it had been enchanted to protect its wearer from space for a short period of time. According to the captain, it was standard equipment for all starships, space-warping or not.

Wizards could do amazing things.

Jack put it on, sensing a thin film spread to cover his whole body. Brock cheered. Captain Dordok laughed. Vlossana burst through the door, eager to watch the fight and flashing him a bright smile.

Jack opened the leftmost door at the end of the main room and came face-to-face with a window looking into space. There was no glass. All that protected the ship was a film stretching over the opening, similar to the one produced by Jack's helmet.

He took a deep breath and jumped out. It was his first time in bare space.

Before he could admire the sensation, a Dao-powered shriek, giving life to what would have otherwise been a silent war cry, crossed space to fill his ears. Three tentacles swept at him from below.

CHAPTER EIGHT
SPACE MONSTER

JACK WAS IN SPACE, FLOATING AND COVERED IN A THIN FILM THAT PROTECTED him from the lack of pressure and heat, as well as the radiation. The *Trampling Ram* awaited behind him, several faces watching through the main room's glass walls. The ship stood still—they'd stopped their flight to let the space monster approach.

Jack had never been outside the ship before. He didn't know what to expect besides the obvious.

The moment he stepped into space, even the obvious fled from his mind. He lost his balance and started rotating head over heels. He had nothing to grab onto, nothing to give him leverage. He was simply floating—and mid-rotation, he spotted flashes of a purple shrieking bubble approaching, waving three tentacle-like appendages.

Space Monster, Level 53
Experts speculate that, when large quantities of the Dao are left
undisturbed for a long time, they can spontaneously coalesce into a
Space Monster. While this is a very rare occasion, the vastness of the
void lends itself to the phenomenon. Space is filled with such monsters,
especially outside System space.
However, due to the phenomenon's relative rarity and the
requirement of a long-time undisturbed Dao, it has never been

observed in controlled environments. The exact procedure of a Space Monster's birth has never been documented in the Immortal Archives. Space Monsters are mostly mindless existences that seek only to feed on sources of the Dao, like natural treasures or cultivators. They grow larger and more intelligent in proportion to their strength.

Jack skimmed over the description, then grimaced as the monster's shriek somehow crossed the void to reach his ears. In the same way, the captain's voice rang in his mind.

"Fighting in space is different than anything else," he explained leisurely, *as if there wasn't a purple monstrosity hurling at Jack. "Even moving is difficult at first, until you get the trick."*

"What's the trick!" Jack shouted, but the sound was confined inside the thin, multicolored film covering his body.

The space monster towered over him, spherical in shape and the size of a small hill. Each of its appendages was many feet long and partially transparent.

When one tried to slap him, he didn't wait to find out what would happen. He smashed out a Meteor Punch, hurling a beautiful line of purple that exploded on the tentacle. The recoil of his punch sent him spinning backward into space.

"Ahhh!" Jack shouted.

"There's the trick!" the captain's voice reached him again. *"Good job. Now go beat it up."*

Jack thought he saw people laughing from the window. The space monster ignored the starship, perhaps sensing the immortal inside, and lunged for Jack. Its three tentacles flailed wildly.

Jack fired a weak Meteor Punch to steady himself but he miscalculated, and now he was spinning forward instead. "Son of a—" A tentacle smashed into him, hurtling him away. To his horror, Jack realized he wasn't decelerating. He sent a Meteor Punch backward to stop his flight, then another to shoot forward. He was spinning the whole time, but at least now he was doing it slowly enough to focus. His fighting style could help incorporate the rotation into his moves.

Jack eyed the purple monster and gritted his teeth. One tentacle was singed where he'd hit it before, but still swinging. Not for long.

With a roar, Jack smashed out a Meteor Punch, then a second, then a third. At the same time, he used his Dao to counterbalance the recoil. Having reached the E-Grade, he now had fine enough control over his Dao to send small bursts out of anywhere in his body. It was like using Meteor Punch to shoot meteors, but way too ineffective and unfocused to be used in battle.

Those bursts left his body like small clouds and dissipated almost immediately, but it was the act of leaving his body that mattered. If Meteor Punch could propel him backward, then using the Dao of the Fist through his butt, feet, or elbows was enough to propel him forward.

He also jumped in random directions, as this was too difficult to control at once, but at least he wasn't flying into the stars anymore.

Mid-battle, he realized he was farting Dao. He chuckled.

The three meteors crashed into the purple blob, making it shriek wildly. There were dents in its form now. Those three tentacles fell on Jack at the same time.

Two tried to slap him. He met them both with Meteor Punches, ricocheting them backward, but the third tentacle had time to coil around his waist. It grabbed him and tried to crush him like a constrictor snake.

Jack felt the pressure. His face paled, his ribs tightened... but they didn't break. The Iron Fiend Body held strong.

There were a few different ways to escape this grasp, but only one was suited to the Dao of the Fist, to the Field of the Iron Fist.

Jack reached for the tentacle with both his arms, grabbed it, and ripped it apart. It felt like jelly. He roared. The space monster shrieked, waving its stump of a tentacle and the two whole ones. Jack was slowly acclimating to battle in space, and he was far stronger than this monster.

Ghost Step.

He disappeared. His form darted sideways at tremendous speed, and of course, didn't stop decelerating. He flew off into space again.

Cursing, Jack used Ghost Step again in the opposite direction. He accelerated explosively. This time, when he arrived behind the confused space monster, he used a Meteor Punch to stop himself, then unleashed a barrage of attacks. Meteor Punches fell into the monster like rain. Its bubble-like form was covered in deep dents, parts of it dissipating into nothing.

It whipped its tentacles at Jack again. This time, he knew what to expect. The Iron Fist Style activated at full throttle. Jack leaned past a tentacle, then grabbed the second mid-swing and used it to swing the monster around. It shrieked.

As they were spinning, he roared and punched the tentacle twice in the same spot until his fist penetrated it completely, sending the tentacle monster careening in a random direction. He decided to call it "down."

A burst of Dao shot him downward, dodging the tentacle stump that tried to take his head off, and he shot up again to dodge another tentacle. Suddenly, he was above the creature. A hail of Meteor Punches fell again, a Meteor Shower, and how could this little space monster resist? Even Rufus Emberheart had been felled by this attack.

Its top bulged inward, about to pop like a bubble. Suddenly, a hole appeared under Jack, revealing a hollow interior. The monster shot up, swallowing him. The hole closed.

For a moment, the monster stayed still. Then, its body bulged outward from multiple spots. Jack was going berserk. It did its best to remain steady, even used its tentacles to keep the largest bulges down, but it was useless. Its form warped as Jack tried to break it from the inside, recklessly attacking in all directions.

In the end, there was only so much punishment the space monster could take. The force inside it became too great. With a loud *pop*, the monster broke apart. Its skin was rags dissipating in space, as were the remains of its tentacles.

Jack was left hovering where the space monster used to be, covered in a purple substance that resembled chewing gum—which was also dissipating, thankfully. He was panting, and the protective film covering his body flickered.

Level Up! You have reached Level 51.

Finally! he thought, grinning despite the disturbing bodily fluids coating him. The battle with Rufus had given him a lot of experience, and one weak space monster was apparently all he needed to advance.

Well, weak compared to him. They were around the same level.

Still grinning, Jack used bursts of Dao to reach the starship's secondary exit, then passed through. He immediately stumbled. Gravity had returned, and that took him a second to process.

At least the remains of the monster had completely evaporated. He was clean again.

He took off his helmet, placing it on one of the glowing pedestals that would recharge it, then opened the door to return to the main room.

Brock and Vlossana were clapping. "Bravo!" she shouted.

"That was a... showy fight," Captain Dordok said.

"Thank you, Captain."

"It wasn't a compliment. Getting swallowed by space monsters is not a good idea. If this one wasn't much weaker than you, you might have been in trouble. Their insides are highly corrosive."

Jack cringed. "Yeah, I felt that. I'll be careful."

"Good." The captain's expression melted into a smile. "Other than that, good job. It was like watching an experienced space wrestler. Not bad for a first time."

"You mean, when I wasn't flying around like a kite?" Jack replied, laughing.

"That happens to everyone, but not everyone wins. Achilles here, for example, needed me to rescue him on his first space battle."

"Captain!" Achilles, the second feshkur after Vashter, cried out. Dordok only laughed in return.

"So, at least you weren't the worst. But don't forget the feeling. This was just a weak opponent to get you used to the movements. Next time, you'll have to fight for real."

"Yes, Captain!" Jack said, sticking out his chest. "Can I practice on our downtime? Without space monsters, I mean."

The captain shook his head. "We cannot stop the ship for you to practice. Best save the time for when space monsters appear. It's more effective then."

"And more dangerous."

"So what? Are you afraid of danger?"

"No."

"Good. That's the least I expect from my crew." Captain Dordok turned around. "The show is over, everyone. Get back to work—or cultivating, or whatever it is you were doing."

Somehow, everyone had gathered to watch Jack fight, from Vlossana and her father, to the two feshkurs, to Bomn the minotaur. As everyone was dispersing, Bomn approached Jack and clapped a heavy hand on his shoulder. Jack had to look up—Bomn was as tall as the feshkurs. Truly, in this crew, he felt like a dwarf.

Despite the large greataxe on Bomn's shoulder, his horns, or his large physique, he didn't seem intimidating. There was a sense of calmness radiating off him that put Jack at peace.

Bomn looked into Jack's eyes and said only one word: "Good."

He kept walking, disappearing into the bridge. Jack still hadn't been to that room, but he tried to sneak peeks whenever anyone opened the door. This time, he spotted a glowing circle on the ground, as well as something radiating green light from outside his vision.

"Thanks!" he shouted behind the minotaur's back as the door closed.

Even the captain had left, perhaps going to cultivate in his cabin or read a book, leaving only Brock beside Jack.

"Whew," Jack said. "That was quite something, bro. When you reach the E-Grade, you'll be able to step into space yourself."

"Bro!" Brock shouted. Jack inspected him out of habit.

Brorilla, Level 37 (Elite)

A gorilla variant from planet Green. Brorillas usually live with Gymonkeys and train them in the ways of working out. It is due to the Brorillas' unmatched pecks that Gymonkeys use poop to fight—they consider themselves too weak for anything else.

Brorillas are usually calm, measured animals. However, if anyone harms their little cousins or invades their territory, they go bananas.

This particular brorilla is a variant that visually resembles a gymonkey. Though not weaker than other brorillas, the members of this variant are often shunned due to their lack of bulging muscles. That is not the case for this specimen. Through intense determination, it has achieved greater strength than its species' norm, as well as a Dao Root. Despite that, it remains an adolescent. Due to this specimen's potential, taming or slaying it are advised.

A new paragraph had, at some point, appeared at the end of Brock's description. Jack didn't enjoy it. Brock was his friend, but the System was treating him like... an object.

Besides that, Brock kept growing in size. He now reached up to Jack's waist. If he kept at it, he might soon resemble his dad, Harambe.

I wonder what everyone is doing on Earth... Jack thought, letting his mind wander. Are they still alive? Are they fighting, or is Sparman protecting them? Is the Flame River still standing? Is there a war?

He had no way to find out, at least for now. Master Shol had mentioned a telepathy System function for people of the same faction, and Jack could only hope the professor would find a way to buy it, because he sure couldn't. When he'd checked the faction shop, it cost ten million credits. A whopping number.

But the professor was smart, and she had Edgar, too. Perhaps they'd find a way.

In the meantime, all he could do was cultivate, train, and get stronger as fast as possible. If he wanted to save them, there was no time to waste.

Besides, if he delayed, even Brock might catch up to him. He was already a level 37 Elite, growing at a prodigious rate. Soon, he would be as strong as the black wolves that guarded the Forest of the Strong, and then...

Well, who knows how far Brock would reach.

With that thought in mind, Jack took Brock and headed back to his room. If he wanted to reach the C-Grade in less than a year, he only had a couple months to spend at the E-Grade at most. He should fuse the Dao Root of Indomitable Will into his Dao Seed as soon as possible, then decide how many and which Dao Roots he was going to pursue.

There was no time to waste.

However, the moment he stepped out of the main room and headed right to the ladder leading to the lower deck, a whisper came from behind him.

"Psst."

Jack paused.

"Pssst!" the whisper insisted. "Jared. Over here!"

He turned around to find Vlossana waiting at the other side of the door, sticking to the wall. "Psss—Oh, you saw me! Finally."

"Hey, Vlossana," Jack replied tiredly. "What is it?"

"Not much. I just wanna talk. What do you say, Ja..." She paused for a moment. "...red."

Jack sighed. *So, she* does *remember my real name. Crap.* He looked back at her—she wiggled her eyebrows in a sketchy manner.

"Okay," he said with resignation. "Mi casa, su casa."

"What?"

"Nevermind. Let's go to my room. I suspect what you have to say won't be fit for the main room."

She grinned. "Now you're talking!"

CHAPTER NINE

THE PLIGHT OF THE FAIR WAY

"WELL?" VLOSSANA ASKED, JUMPING ON A CRATE. JACK'S ROOM, THE CURRENTLY unused cargo hold, didn't have much in the way of furniture. A hammock he'd made in the back, a chair and table that Vashter had brought him on the second day, and some old crates by a side wall. It was on one of those crates that Vlossana had jumped, staring at him with bright eyes. Her shirt was the same color as her eyes—sapphire— and her long skirt the same as her hair—purple.

"Well, what?"

"Well, why did you give the captain a fake name?"

"Hey!"

As an immortal, Captain Dordok could stretch his senses farther than should be possible. He could spy on everyone in the ship if he wanted to. And, though he'd assured Jack that he wasn't going to do that... Well, if he did, how would anyone know?

Vlossana laughed. "Don't worry. I've been traveling on the *Ram* for a month now. Dordok isn't the sort of person who would eavesdrop on others. He may look tough, but he's actually a big softie!"

Jack wasn't sure if he would classify the hulking cyclops captain as a softie.

"Fine," he said, accepting that Vlossana wouldn't drop the subject. "How do you know I didn't give *you* a fake name?"

"Because I was a random girl in the elevator line."

"So? Do you never lie to strangers?"

"Oh, come on, Jack," she said, dropping to a seated position. "I could understand lying to the captain and me both. But only to me? That's so far-fetched. Any reason that would make you lie to me would apply tenfold to the crew of the *Trampling Ram*."

Jack sighed inwardly. Vlossana may be childishly excitable, but she wasn't an idiot. "Maybe I lie to strangers for fun," he tried weakly, but not even he believed it. Vlossana raised a brow.

"Really? Then I should let the captain know. I'm sure he'd love to know your hobbies."

"Please don't call me Jack, even in private," he said. "It might slip out in public."

"Oh, don't worry. I'm good with secrets." She leaned forward, her eyes full of expectation. "So? What are you hiding? Are there people after you? Are you a criminal? Are people hunting you out of jealousy? Dad told me you were integrated very recently, and you're already E-Grade. Oh, I know! Did you steal from someone important in Pearl Bay and are now trying to abscond with the treasure? Or did you... *kill someone*?"

Her eyes widened in fear, and she leaned away.

"Of course not. What are you thinking?" Jack replied out of reflex. "Hmm. Well, actually, I did kill someone, but it's not what it sounds like. I had no choice."

"That's what they always say."

"No, really! I... There was a person who was my enemy, and I had to kill him or he would do terrible things to the people I care about."

"I see. And then?"

"Well, his family wasn't too happy about it."

"Really? Who would have thought?"

"Hey, no sass here. I'm telling a story."

"I'll *try*!" she replied, laughing.

Jack shot her a glare before continuing. That also gave him time to think. He had to phrase things in a way that wouldn't sound too vague, but which also wouldn't give her enough clues to connect him with the Animal Kingdom's scions.

"So, I had to run away from them. Though I'm strong, there are some real monsters on my planet, and the guy I killed just happened to be their relative. An ally promised to keep my family safe for a while, but..." He shook his head for dramatic effect. "That protection won't last long. That is why I'm touring the galaxy now. I must get strong enough to face my enemies, and fast, or everyone I know will die."

"Oh, wow." Vlossana gasped, her eyes wide as saucers. "Wait. You aren't lying to me again, are you?"

"Everything I said was the truth." Not the complete truth, but the truth regardless.

"Hmm..." she hummed, inspecting him. She turned her gaze to Brock, who crossed his arms and stared back at her.

"Okay, I believe you," she said, bubbling with energy. "You have quite the weight on your shoulders. How are you holding up? Are you stressed? Afraid? Anxious?"

He laughed at her ill-timed excitement, then took a moment to think about it. His expression turned somber.

"I'm not sure, honestly," he said. "I suppose I should feel all those things, but I don't; not really. I'm already doing my best. I guess worrying about it will change nothing."

"I see. Were you always like that?"

"Hmm, no, not always."

"Then, what changed?"

The System did. My entire world. My perspective.

"My Dao, I guess." He looked at his hands and clenched them. "A fist does not worry. It only advances. It conquers."

"Sounds like quite a fist."

"It's mine." He shrugged. "And the farther I go, the stronger it becomes."

"Hmm. Cryptic. I like that." She jumped up, leaping to the next crate and balancing on its edge. "So, what's your plan? To get stronger fast, I mean."

"Travel the galaxy. Try to get a Trial Planet token, if possible." He shrugged. Of course, he already had two Trial Planet tokens. He just wasn't willing to share that information. "Otherwise, I can just throw myself in dangerous situations and hope I survive. Opportunity comes with danger."

"You know what else comes with danger? Death."

"I've been through worse... What about you? What are *you* doing?"

"That's a personal question, isn't it?"

He glared at her until she laughed.

"Okay, okay, I was just joking. I'm... Well, I guess I'm just being my father's daughter. Following him around on business."

"How come? You're already E-Grade. You can do whatever you like."

"I *can*, but this is a good opportunity to see the world outside my home planet," she replied, sitting back down and propping her chin in both palms. "Traveling off-planet is very dangerous. All sorts of things could happen. Now that my father has to report to the Animal Kingdom office in the Belarian Outpost, it's a good chance for me to follow and see what the galaxy looks like under his protection."

"His protection? He's only F-Grade."

"He's a count. Captain Dordok has sworn to protect us with his life."

"I see," Jack replied. "And you can't teleport because he's only F-Grade. That's why you have to ride a starship."

"Exactly," she replied sadly. "My father is the only F-Grade high noble on the continent, but the Animal Kingdom requested *him* personally. They did it to shame us. To make the Fair Way continent look weak."

"That's not very nice."

"It isn't, no." She shook her head. Suddenly, her eyes were filled with joy again. "On the bright side, it means I can travel with safety, comfort, and for free! The Viceroy's paying for our trip, obviously."

"A silver lining."

"Exactly!"

Jack stayed quiet for a moment. "What's your Dao?"

"Excuse me?"

"I told you my Dao. Isn't it fair that you do the same?"

"No you didn't."

"It's the fist. I thought that much was clear."

She mumbled something. "Yeah, okay, it was... Why do you want to know?"

"I'm simply curious. How did a girl full of joy and excitement like you manage to reach level 49, let alone form a Dao Seed?"

He really was curious. Back on Earth, reaching level 49 took the apex of skill and sacrifice. There was a difference between Earth and the galaxy, sure, but seeing such a seemingly immature girl reach such heights... It contrasted hard with what he knew.

Vlossana looked at him like he was an idiot. "I reached level 49 with experience balls, of course."

"Yeah, but do you mean to tell me you fought *nothing*? No monsters, no enemies, absolutely nothing?"

"I mean... I do have a Physical instructor," she muttered. "But my Dao isn't combat-oriented. Why would I fight anyone?"

"Of course," he replied. "We don't have many of those on my planet. Integration favors combat."

"Oh, I can imagine! Goblins jumping out of bushes, meteors raining from the sky, dragons roaring from volcanoes... It must have been really scary!"

"Well, it wasn't exactly like that, but yes. It was scary."

"Ohhh... Well, non-combat Classes advance differently. We just have to apply our Dao to its field. Someone with the Dao of Management, for example, just needs to manage people effectively and grow their skills, and then bam, they level up."

"That's handy. So, no danger of death everyday."

"No... but in return, progress is slower." Her eyes glimmered like she'd gotten a puppy and was *dying* to show it to someone. "Well, since you asked, I follow the Dao of Joy! You may see me as too excited right now, childish even, but that's only because I'm missing some Dao Roots. When my set is complete, I will be the greatest Countess ever!"

"A set of Dao Roots!" Jack's eyes widened. "How will you form a Dao Tree like that? I thought anything above one was risky."

"My Dao isn't intended to reach the D-Grade." She shook her head with a sad smile. "In our entire continent, only the Viceroy has reached that level. There's no way I could do it. Collecting a few Dao Roots and becoming a fine Countess would be more than enough for me. I will make all my people happy!"

"If you want to make people happy, why not the Dao of Happiness?"

Vlossana's face soured. Jack felt that he'd said something wrong. He hurried to change the subject.

"Anyway, um... Is that all you wanted?"

"Yeah!" She flashed him a bright smile, recovering instantly from the previous sourness. "Information and a chat. Cultivating alone can be so boring sometimes... We should chat more often, if you don't mind. Which you don't. Right?"

"Sure," Jack said, and he meant it. Though he had to be careful not to expose his connection with Earth, he had to admit that cultivating alone for a week had been... tiresome. Even the occasional chores he had to do were beginning to seem like fun breaks.

Plus, Vlossana was fun. Her joy was contagious—as was apt, given her Dao. Even Brock seemed happy, and his number of thrown poops so far was zero.

"I'll be going now," Vlossana said, hopping off the crate. "See you later, Jack."

"Can you please call me Jared?"

"No." She laughed and left. Purple hair drifting behind her was the last thing he saw before she closed the door, and Jack was once again alone with Brock, closed in a barely illuminated room with no windows —only a fool would expose their cargo hold to potential thieves, and crates had no need to see the view.

Hmm. Should I try meditating in the main room? he asked himself, only to leave thought for later. He had something more important to consider now.

His conversation with Vlossana reminded him that, outside this isolated starship, the world was still turning. The Animal Kingdom's machinations were reaching beyond Earth. Who knows what was happening on that planet.

He *needed* to get strong fast.

I've stabilized enough, he decided, face tightening in seriousness. It was time to explore his new Dao Vision.

———

Harambe watched the little humans training in front of his bananarm tree with disinterest. Their forms were perfect, their stances balanced. He had already shown them everything once. There was nothing more he could—

One human bent a bit, making the push-ups easier. Harambe growled, scaring the offender back in line. He snorted, crossing his large, burly arms, and throwing a bananarm at her head as punishment. It bounced off into the grass.

Why couldn't these humans follow instructions?

Times were... confusing for Harambe. He was the big bro around here, but even he didn't understand everything. Humans came occasionally to take bananarms. Others joined his forest gym, begging him to train them. There was a terrifying metal human wandering the woods, and a weak little human ordering others around. There was also a magic human occasionally coming to the forest to talk by himself.

Harambe didn't understand much of that and let them be. He could sense they meant good. And, most importantly, he trusted Jack Rust, the human big bro.

Enough to entrust his only son to him. Compared to that, letting these human little bros into his forest was nothing.

A void appeared in Harambe's heart, and his eyes became tinged with sadness. He had given away his own son to another man. He missed him so much. But it had to be done. Brorillas *must* be strong, and Jack Rust could make Harambe's son stronger than Harambe ever could.

So why did he feel so sad?

He was worried, too. There had been no news of Jack Rust or his son for a long time. The magic human and the frail human had come to Harambe some days ago, saying that Jack and Brock went on a trip and would return eventually... but what if something went wrong? What if he sent his son to die alone?

It had to be done, he reassured himself. Brorillas are strong. Son will surpass father, and father will be proud. Strength then is more important than sadness now... Even if Aya worries. Even if I, Harambe, worry.

No. Brock will return. He is strong. And Jack Rust is strong. We are bros. Bros must believe in bros.

There was something gradually developing inside Harambe. It felt like a thought that kept coming back, stronger every time. Stronger than any other. More complete.

A Big Thought.

But every time he tried to focus on it, it escaped again.

No matter, Harambe thought. I, Harambe, will Big Think it. Eventually.

CHAPTER TEN

ENTERING THE DAO VISION

JACK MADE HIMSELF COMFORTABLE. HE PATTED THE FLOOR BEFORE HE SAT, straightened his pants, shook his upper body once. There was great urgency, yes, but a few seconds of calmness before the storm could mean the world.

Brock gave him a supportive pat on the back. Jack nodded. He closed his eyes, and the world changed around him.

It was finally time to explore his new Dao Vision.

The spotless starship walls gave way to a desert. Jack found himself in an overcast world, hovering high over a field of broken bodies. Blood and weapons littered the barren dirt. Jack himself was only a ghost, lacking material form.

He'd seen this before, and knew where to look—who the main character was.

A big-bodied human stood alone in the field of battle. He was bare-chested, with wide shoulders and bulging muscles. His hands were clasped behind his back, and he stood straight like a ramrod. Three long, gray lines were tattooed on the right side of his chest, like a wound left by an animal's claws.

He did not look like a kind person. His long gray hair fluttered in a bloody breeze, while his gray eyes were harsh and narrowed into slits.

His skin was bronze. His face hard. In Jack's eyes, this man resembled a merciless, brutal master.

Gedritch, Level ??? (C-Grade)
Faction: Iron Fist Empire (C-Grade)
Title: Leviathan Slayer

Facing him was a fortress. Colossal dark walls stretched three hundred feet into the air and many miles on either side. Squinting at their top, Jack could make out a host of people preparing to defend. They sported all sorts of weapons, as well as magic. With a few random scans, he confirmed they were also gedritch, the same human-like species as the bare-chested man, and they were all in the E-Grade.

Dozens of figures assembled into battle formations, flying over the walls—immortals.

A single woman stood on the wall ledge, clad in golden plate armor from head to toe. She radiated bright power, and was also at the C-Grade—though the fact that she stood on the town walls indicated she was weaker than the bare-chested man.

In contrast, the man stood completely alone, facing down a fortress of immortals.

"We are willing to pledge our allegiance, Baron Longform," the woman shouted. Her voice echoed to the nearby mountains, easily reaching everyone's ears. "Promise the safety of our descendants and disciples, and we will swear a soul oath here and now. We will serve the empire without a word of protest."

The bare-chested man shook his head. "Once a traitor, always a traitor." His voice was deep and harsh, sharp enough to cut through stone, and that wasn't a metaphor. The walls and ground shook. The E-Grade defenders atop the walls screamed before a wide curtain of golden light spread over the entire length of the wall, shielding them. Jack was glad he had no body in this vision.

The woman's eyes were hard now.

"Very well," she responded commandingly. Her entire body erupted in a column of golden light that reached all the way to the sky, splitting the dense clouds, and ethereal wings spread from her back. "Then, let the emperor's dog die here."

Thundering shouts came from the immortals in the sky, joined by the still-reeling E-Grade defenders on the walls. Jack couldn't see behind them, though he thought he heard many more voices rising from inside the fortress—either civilians or backup forces.

He prepared himself. The main part was coming.

The bare-chested man smiled grimly. Though he hadn't moved a muscle, a wave rolled out of him.

It was invisible and formless. Jack only sensed it when it washed over him, and he was instantly flooded with unease. The man's form had changed, although not visibly. He'd become sharper, stronger, more intimidating. Like he was a bomb of violence ready to explode. Like a killer, a tyrant, a monster, a devil.

A fiend.

An aura of palpable violence spread in all directions, drowning the town in fear. Screams rose all over. The immortals in the air dropped like flies. Only a few were able to resist, but were unable to advance on the man.

Jack felt true terror grip his heart. This man would grab him and tear him limb from limb, bringing unimaginable pain. There was nothing he could do to resist, only despair.

He lost all power. His Dao was suppressed, his soul shivered, and he couldn't stop shaking. If not for the protection of the System letting him experience this vision, he was sure he would have crumbled on the spot.

Jack sensed people were dying in droves behind the wall, their souls and wills crushed beyond redemption, overwhelmed by terror.

And the more people that fell, the stronger the bare-chested man grew. He fed on their death until his body overflowed with power, and the black-and-red aura around him grew so thick that it seemed to form horns over his head and leathery black wings on his back.

This all happened in an instant. The woman's golden light did nothing to stop this aura. A second later, her face contorted in fury and despair. She charged, screaming, "Have you no honor! No shame?" at the top of her lungs, so hard it tore her throat and shook the heavens.

A lance of pure light materialized in her hand, filling the world with heat. The man clenched his fist and stepped forward. Then, abruptly, the vision cut off. It had shown what it wanted. The rest of the battle did not concern it.

Jack's eyes snapped open, his body drenched in sweat.

"Damn..." he muttered. "I'd forgotten how terrible it was."

This was the Dao Vision he'd acquired after upgrading his Class. There were a few key differences and one similarity compared to his first, the one with the bald, caped man.

Both visions showcased the same level of power. The bald man and the bare-chested man were at the C-Grade. Idly, Jack wondered who of the two was stronger. Logically, it should be the bare-chested man, since he appeared at a later Dao Vision—but even his terror failed to overshadow the bald man's sense of unfathomable power.

Jack shook his head and let the thought go. It was like seeing two mountains from below and wondering which was taller. Perhaps, when he was stronger, he would understand.

Besides the power level, the two visions were different in everything else.

The bald man taught Jack the Dao of the Fist, along with a hint of a skill that he transformed into Meteor Punch. The bare-chested man's vision seemed entirely dedicated to the aura he used. It was a Dao Skill of extremely high caliber, and one that Jack couldn't wait to get his hands on.

Feeding on the enemies' terror and death. How cool was that?

Another difference was that this more recent vision gave a lot of context. Jack now knew the Iron Fist Empire existed—or used to exist— and was a C-Grade faction at the time of the vision. He knew the bare-chested man's identity—Baron Longform—and the circumstances surrounding the battle.

Was there a reason for these differences, or were all Dao Visions random? Were there different kinds? And, if so, which was better? A vision focused on the Dao, or one focused on a skill? Or was the skill a mere stepping-stone to a Dao Root?

The third and final difference was the intimacy involved. When the bald man punched, Jack was only a watcher. When the bare-chested man unleashed his aura, Jack was affected. He felt it deep in his soul. He experienced the terror of violence that aura brought. Perhaps the nature of the Dao Vision had shielded him from the aura's full effects—even immortals had fallen like flies—but he had still experienced it.

Presumably, that would make understanding it easier. But it would also make watching the vision harder. The aura was a deeply unpleasant feeling, like sinking into a nightmare you had no control over.

Jack wouldn't be stopped by mere fear. Yet he wouldn't rush into the vision more than necessary, either. Not unless he had to.

Let's see, he considered, closing his eyes to concentrate. *He tried to remember the sensation of the aura. Terror. Violence. Like being held down by a butcher you cannot overpower, or trapped between a hungry lion's jaws. Being at the mercy of someone else. Running from a nightmare, but no matter how hard you try, you remain at the same spot, and the monster approaches from behind.*

And then what?

He came up short.

Man, I wish I had a coffee.

The Dao held a hint of magic. It transformed feelings, thoughts, and emotions into reality. Jack's Dao of the Fist was the physical incarnation of his resolve to fight, his belief in his power, his determination to survive and triumph, his love for violence. By simply channeling those thoughts, Jack gained access to the power of the Dao of the Fist, which he utilized by staying true to its path.

In a way, pursuing the Dao was a long process of understanding the world, understanding yourself, then angling yourself to look at the world through a specific perspective.

Dao Skills, in turn, were an application of one's Dao, a particular train of thoughts and emotions that resonated with the Dao. They were akin to miniature Dao Roots.

Jack's Meteor Punch was an explosion of power and violence, his determination to break the enemy. The Iron Fist Style was a Dao Skill that encompassed all physical components of his Dao.

Therefore, to comprehend what the Dao Vision was trying to teach him, he needed more than just a superficial understanding. It was extreme terror in the enemy leading to increased power for the wielder, yes. But how, exactly, did that work? What triggers were pulled in their minds?

Jack decided to break it into two parts. Part one was projecting his intention to unleash violence and causing terror so extreme that the weaker enemies died outright. Part two was harnessing that terror for himself.

It feels... evil, Jack thought. *Fiendlike.* There was a love for violence hidden deep in his soul. It was part of his Dao. Now, this new skill struck a chord close to that, which Jack usually kept hidden. He was apprehensive.

But why? I am neither ashamed or afraid. I am simply myself.

There was no space for doubts in the path of the fist.

Jack dived into the first part of the vision. It actually felt like the easy part, because he could already do something similar.

More than once during the tournament, he'd released an air of brutality around him. It was when he really wanted to beat up someone, like when he fought Shard Presht after realizing how fucked up things were, or when he decided to murder Rufus Emberheart.

Shard Presht had flinched, and the spectators appeared terrified both times. Even Rufus Emberheart's final mistake could be attributed to his fear, which was partly a result of Jack's unwavering determination to kill him or die trying.

In other words, this skill would be great for eliminating a large number of weaker opponents or weakening strong ones. Being able to activate it at will would certainly come in handy.

In fact, people didn't need the Dao to achieve this. When someone was enraged, the minds of everyone in the vicinity rang with alarm bells. It was a survival instinct developed through evolution.

Is the skill building on top of that? Jack wondered. Hmm. How, exactly, do people broadcast their rage? Tense bodies? Wide eyes? Gnashed teeth? Shouting?

No. Those are mundane things. They can maybe lead me to a skill, but not a Dao Skill. I need something deeper.

Is it the feeling? Do I need to embrace my intent to maul the enemy?

Okay. Let's take another look at the vision.

Jack's world faded away—

"Jared," a voice came from the ceiling. "Jared. Are you there?"

Jack opened his eyes, letting the vision dissipate before it could begin. He sighed. "Yes, Captain?"

Dordok couldn't hear him—though he could if he wanted to. He also didn't need a speaker to reach Jack. He just didn't spread his senses to this room to respect Jack's personal space.

"Well, I hope you can hear me. Come to my cabin. We have to talk."

CHAPTER ELEVEN

HORDE

"Captain?" Jack said, knocking on the door. As the captain had only called him, he'd left Brock behind. "It's Jared."

"I know. Come in."

Jack pulled the handle, opening the door. The captain's cabin was a tidy mess of color. The walls were built to resemble polished wood, as were the floor and ceiling. A small window was at the side, circular and made to look like a fenster.

The floor was covered by a sideways, oblong carpet of concentric rings, all illuminated by an old lamp hanging from the ceiling, flickering with yellow light.

Trophies mounted the walls, most of them parts of monsters the captain had personally slain. There was also a cupboard with souvenirs whose significance eluded Jack—a snowball, a rusty gear, a miniature of a ship, a little doll, among many others.

At the back of the office stood a solid, heavy-looking, wooden desk, and behind it sat Captain Dordok, lounging on a wide chair and scribbling on a parchment with a feathered quill. He raised his gaze as Jack walked in.

Jack took this in all at once. "You asked to see me, Captain?"

"Yes. Take a seat."

The captain seemed to be in an excellent mood. His square teeth flashed a smile, his orange skin was shiny, and his one eye glimmered with joy.

Oh no. Did Vlossana get to him, too?

Jack made himself comfortable in one of the two chairs before the desk.

"Are you enjoying the trip, Jared?" the captain asked.

"As much as I can," Jack replied cautiously. "The view still awes me, the company is pleasant, and cultivation is a good way to pass the time."

"I'm surprised to hear that. Not many enjoy cultivation. They find it a tedious, boring, exhausting experience that sucks them dry for little to no benefit."

"Is the strength to crush mountains a little to no benefit?"

The captain smirked. "It can seem so. Most people have to spend decades on a single insight, going over the same thoughts again and again to find one tiny mistake. It drives them crazy."

Jack pictured that. It was not pretty.

"You see, Jared," the captain continued, "not everybody advances at breakneck speed. Bless your lucky stars. And don't waste your talents." He blink-winked.

"Yes, Captain," Jack replied, puffing out his chest. He made a mental note to show off less. He didn't want to attract any more attention than necessary.

"Good. But I did not call you here for that. I am happy that you're enjoying your time on the *Trampling Ram*. I also find you satisfactory as a crew member, at least for now. Therefore, it is time to discuss your payment."

"Payment? I thought taking me to the Belarian Outpost was payment enough. That's what we'd discussed, no?"

The captain laughed. It was a deep, rumbling sound, like rocks rolling down a hill that filled the little room and Jack's heart all the same.

"I only said that to send you away, boy," Dordok said, wiping away a large tear. "I did find it strange that you weren't put off. Then again, you're newly-Integrated; how could you know how things work?"

"I do lack experience, Captain."

"For a middle E-Grade guard, the normal fee is five thousand credits a month," the captain explained. His eye shone with a glimmer of fierce intelligence, the one that was usually hidden under carefree, simple-minded conduct. "I could give you more. However, given the circumstances of your arrival and the secrecy you carry, I believe sticking to the five thousand is the fair choice."

Jack considered denying the secrecy part, but there was no point. Plus, he really didn't want to. His responsibility to his people might be stronger than his guilt, but the nicer the captain became, the harder it was for Jack.

"Absolutely, Captain. In fact, we could even go lower. Truth is, I'm in such a rush to reach the Belarian Outpost that I wouldn't mind traveling for free."

The captain shook his head. "We can't have that. I take pride in being generous, and I can't let a rut who's still wet behind the ears spoil that. Five thousand it is."

"Then, thank you, Captain," Jack said, lowering his head in gratitude. A new pang of guilt seared his heart. The captain and everyone onboard the ship were being so good to him, and he was putting them all in danger to save himself.

That familiar thought hit him: what choice did he have?

"No big deal," Dordok replied, reclining in his chair. "Besides, you're going to need that money soon."

"I will?"

"You will. It's been almost two weeks now, and we're approaching our next stop: the Amethyst Mountain. Ever heard of it?"

Jack's eyes shone. "No."

"It's a dock built at the top of a lush mountain. Pretty practical if you ask me, since starships come from the sky. It's on Earth-321. And the town can be quite novel for young people such as yourself, so I'd recommend taking Vashter and Achilles and going for a stride. Maybe Vlossana, too—the girl could use some company."

"Has she been pestering you too, Captain?"

"Like you cannot imagine." They exchanged a pain-filled gaze. "Thank the System you came along. At least I get some moments of peace now." Jack's gaze turned to one stunned by utter betrayal.

The captain laughed again. "As I was saying, you could use some fresh air after being cooped up in here for weeks. We'll only stay for three hours, so I expect you to make the most of it."

"Yes, Captain."

Dordok must have seen his disappointment. "I would normally dock for a couple days, but we're booked for a fast trip. There's no time to waste. I believe that coincides with your interests, as well?"

"It does," Jack said. "I can handle some isolation. Reaching the Outpost quickly is more important. I can just cultivate to pass the time. Besides, traveling in space isn't that bad."

"Of course it isn't. In any case, our stop will hopefully prove uneventful. If nothing goes wrong, we'll be there in two hours."

"Don't say that, Captain," Jack replied, laughing. "What could possibly go wrong?"

"When you tour the galaxy for as long as I have, you know that something always does." With a smile, the captain reached into a drawer under his desk and pulled out a cigar, as well as an ash tray. Without offering Jack one, he said, "Now, if there's nothing else..."

"I actually have a question to ask you, Captain. Nothing important, just a small curiosity that's been bugging me."

Dordok snapped his fingers at the end of his cigar, lighting it up through sheer physicality. He drew a deep breath, then exhaled smoke toward the roof, where the magical ventilation would recycle it into breathable air. "Go ahead."

"I was just wondering..." Jack said, leaning forward. "I've heard of cyclopses before. Minotaurs, too. They're part of my planet's mythology."

"They are?"

"Yeah. The ancient Greeks had an entire pantheon built around creatures like you, even with the same names. There were also satyrs, mermaids, nymphs... Do any of those ring a bell?"

The captain snorted with amusement. "A few of them. What are you getting at?"

"Well, I understand that the galaxy is large, and all sorts of creatures exist. That can be a coincidence... but how come the names are shared?" Jack asked. "Is it part of the System's universal translation? Does it translate the actual name of your species into cyclops, the one I'm familiar with? Or is it something else?"

Dordok puffed from his cigar. "Your suspicions are correct. The System can translate the names of common animals, like ants or lions, but it wouldn't translate the name of my species. No, we really are named cyclopses. If your planet was familiar with the name, that's probably because some of us had visited that ancient civilization of yours."

"How? I thought that's impossible. We weren't Integrated yet."

"Nothing is impossible." The captain drew another big puff of smoke, then blew it out. "Sometimes, people get fed up with the world we live in. There are too many rules, too many conflicts, too much oppression by the strong... In those cases, it's not uncommon for people to board a ship and travel outside System-integrated space, looking for a quiet, inhabited planet to live out the rest of their lives."

Jack's eyes widened. "Are you saying the ancient Greek gods were cultivators from your planet?"

"They could be. Your Earth was just Integrated, so it must have been close to System space anyway. It wouldn't be too strange for a rogue starship to find their way there. If you are familiar with cyclopses, minotaurs, and satyrs, that was most likely the case."

Jack considered Zeus. Technically, he could have been a D-Grade cultivator with the Dao of Lightning—or the Dao of Loose Morals. Maybe even an E-Grade, though there would have to be *someone* at the D-Grade to pilot a space-warping starship. It would also explain why they lived atop a mountain—at those Grades, a cultivator could easily destroy their surroundings if they lost their temper or decided to fight each other.

But was it truly possible that the entire Greek mythology was the result of a rogue starship landing on their planet? Then, after they died off, what happened to that starship? And what about other pantheons? The Egyptians, the Norse, the Aztecs... How many of those were imaginary, and how many were alien cultivators?

"What about their descendants?" he asked. "Wouldn't we still be filled with satyrs and gods?"

"Gods, certainly not. It doesn't matter if your parents are D-Grades; if you're born on an unintegrated planet, maybe you can cultivate a little bit, but it's unlikely you'll ever find your way to true power. As for satyrs and the rest... Well, how many people could a starship carry? After a period of interbreeding, they're bound to die off."

Jack shook his head. "Why did you have to challenge my worldview like that, Captain?"

"Hah! You're the one who asked."

"Yeah... Well, no matter. I'll be a God soon, too."

"Of course you will. It's easy, right?"

"I'll manage. I have people to protect."

"Everyone does. And yet, the vast majority fails." Dordok pressed his cigar into the ash tray, extinguishing it. "Motivation does not run the world, Jack. Power does, and talent. Pray that you have both or you'll end up like those old gods of yours, leaving the real world to spend your final years bullying mortals. It is sad, you know. The weight of—"

A knock on the door interrupted whatever the captain was going to say next. "Bomn," a voice came from outside.

Dordok sighed, putting away his cigar. "Come in."

Bomn entered, looking even larger here. His horns scraped the ceiling, almost carving trenches in the captain's woody paint, and his width almost matched the door's. However, despite his size, the aura he exuded was one of calmness, like a still pond. Jack felt at peace.

It was the exact opposite of the bloodthirsty beast he became during battle.

Bomn nodded at Jack and the captain both, then took a seat opposite Jack. Unarmed, of course.

"Welcome, Bomn," the captain said. "Jared here was just telling me he wants to see the mines under the dock on Amethyst Mountain. If you're interested, you could take him, Achilles, Vashter, and Vlossana for a tour. The mines are too dangerous for just them."

Bomn thought about it. "Okay."

Not a man of many words, Bomn. But he was strong and kind-hearted. Jack still remembered on their departure from Pearl Bay how Bomn traveled farther than necessary before warping. Simply to give Jack a chance to enjoy the scenery.

After traveling on the *Trampling Ram*, Jack had realized there were two groups of people. The seniors, which included the captain, Bomn, and—more reluctantly—Count Plomer, and then were the rest of them.

In theory, Bomn should be hanging out with the captain when they landed, not with the "kids."

However, Jack had once been a PhD student—still was, technically —so he understood why the captain was putting Bomn in this position. He was training him to be the next captain—the first mate. If anything happened to Captain Dordok, Bomn would take over, and he ought to have the crew's trust and loyalty by then.

Since he didn't talk much, protecting and leading them through dangerous areas ought to do the trick. It was a bonding exercise.

"Very well," Dordok said joyfully, clapping his hands. "If there is nothing else, you are dismissed."

"Actually," Jack cut in, drawing both their gazes. "There is something I've been planning to ask you, Bomn. If you don't mind."

The minotaur inclined his head, giving Jack the go-ahead.

"Well, I've been struggling with a new skill recently, and I thought you could maybe weigh in a bit. It's about inciting terror in your enemies, and well... I've seen you fight."

The captain beamed at the suggestion. Since he was looking for ways to assert Bomn over the crew, this fit like a good shoe.

Bomn himself nodded. "Come."

He stood and headed for the door. Jack threw the captain a hasty glance and a nod before following. Surprisingly, Dordok himself followed behind. Perhaps he was curious. Or bored.

They went to the main room, seeing stars all around. Vashter was reclining on a chair, dozing off, but he jumped to his feet the moment everyone entered.

"Easy, Vashter," the captain said. "Bomn has some things to show Jared."

Vashter hesitated.

"I don't mind you staying," Jack said. Bomn also acknowledged this, and Vashter relaxed a bit, though he remained upright in his seat.

"What is this about?" he asked curiously.

Surprisingly, Bomn was the first to respond. "Bloodlust."

Gone was the calm Bomn. A beast stood before Jack, a minotaur drenched in the blood of his enemies and desperately thirsting for more. He was a monster of muscle and violence, a relentless slayer of men, a gigantic, bipedal, red-eyed bull. From the side, Vashter gasped, and the sound of a tumbling chair soon followed.

Jack didn't expect the change to come so abruptly. Bomn's pressure washed over him, a Dao far stronger than Jack's, and he backpedaled two steps before steadying himself.

His fists balled on reflex. Power coursed through his veins, pumping him up. Though his heart shook like a leaf, he stood defiantly against Bomn's presence like a tree to a storm.

A moment later, he caught himself. Bomn reverted to his normal self. "This?" he asked.

Jack had to blink a few times. His body was filled with tension like he was about to enter a battle. Bomn's aura had been similar to the bare-chested man's, but only to a degree and infinitely weaker. Jack could stand against it—though his heart was flooded by primitive fear, he hadn't collapsed like the people did in the vision.

And there was also another difference, one Jack couldn't quite put his finger on, but he knew was important.

"Yes, kind of like this," he replied. "But I was hoping to ask you some questions about the specifics. You see, I have a Dao Vision about this skill, and—"

Something changed in the air. Jack's skin stung with pinpricks. He turned around to find that Captain Dordok's smile had been wiped off, and his eyes were dangerously narrow. The power of a D-Grade immortal rolled out of his body, most of it contained, though the barest hints were enough to make Jack sweat.

For a moment, Jack thought the captain was participating in their demonstration. Then, he realized that his single eye was lost in the distant stars.

"Every hand on deck. Grab your weapons," the captain said. His voice was projected over the entire starship. "We face a horde."

CHAPTER TWELVE

FACING THE HORDE

"Horde?" Jack asked, growing worried. "What's that?"

The captain didn't reply. His eye increasingly widened and he rushed to the bridge, slamming the door open and not bothering to close it. Jack got a good look for the first time.

A ram-headed rod occupied the middle of the room, rising from the floor in the center of a circle of glowing runes. A large screen in front of it showed a three-dimensional compass, a map folded in on itself multiple times, and several buttons and switches with no indication of their purpose. The only thing Jack recognized was a large sonar that took up an entire wall—two sonars, in fact, which showed slightly different things. The details weren't important.

What *was* important were the dozen red dots heading their way. Fast.

Jack got a glimpse of everything before the captain fell on the ram-head, pushing it forward all the way. Its eyes flared blue. The ship's space stabilization flickered. Jack felt the floor shaking under his feet. They accelerated hard.

"All hands on deck!" the captain called again, his strained voice echoing throughout the ship.

Achilles flashed in the main room, holding the handle of his saber. "Captain!" he shouted.

"We have a horde!" Dordok roared back. "Heed my commands. Bomn, take the helm and get us the hell out of here. Achilles, Vashter, take the helmets and be ready to defend the ship. Jared, you're the backup. Be ready to replace whoever gets injured."

"Yes, Captain!" Achilles, Vashter, and Jack roared at the same time, while Bomn raised his head and released a mighty bellow. Brock arrived then, rushing to stand beside Jack and waiting to help however he could. Vlossana and her father came last, entering the main room just as Vashter and Achilles charged into the secondary exit room. They could put on their helmets and rush out at a moment's notice.

"What's happening?" Count Plomer asked in a tired yet commanding voice.

"A horde, sir," Jack replied, looking out the windows, though he couldn't help but wonder: A horde of *what*?

The stars answered. Purple dots appeared in the star-lit darkness, growing larger by the second. A green dot was in their middle. Jack gasped.

But they had the captain. An immortal. No matter how many space monsters appeared, he could handle them, right?

Captain Dordok stepped into the main room just as Bomn reached the bridge, still keeping the door open. He kept the ram-head at its farthest position, the equivalent of stepping on the gas, and glanced between the screens and indications with utmost focus. Occasionally, he flicked a switch or pressed a button.

"No need to panic," the captain's authoritative voice reached every-one. He spoke to Count Plomer. "Bomn is an outstanding pilot. If anyone can outrun the monsters, it's him."

"And what if he can't?" the count asked.

"Then, we fight."

The flurry of activity had died down, at least temporarily—the purple dots were still growing in his vision. "What's a horde?" he braved the question.

"Space monsters are solitary," the captain replied. "But when a D-Grade monster appears, it tends to form a horde and rove space in search of food."

"A D-Grade monster!"

"Exactly." The captain nodded somberly. "I should be able to handle it, but D-Grade battles are not simple. I will need some time to beat it. Until then, the four of you are responsible for protecting us against the thirteen E-Grade monsters. Who knew your practice would pay off so soon."

"But—"

"Pray that you don't need to fight. None of us should, actually. There is only half an hour until we're ready to warp. They shouldn't catch up by then..."

"But?"

"But they might." His one eye darkened. "So prepare yourself for combat."

Jack wasn't unfamiliar with the concept. However, for the first time, he wasn't the strongest of the group, but the weakest. The backup. He chuckled darkly.

The captain glanced at him, visibly surprised by his composure, though he said nothing.

Brock crossed his arms and waited. Vlossana hopped from foot to foot. Count Plomer looked exhausted. "By the Immortals..." he muttered. "Are the gods determined to destroy me?"

Tense silence fell throughout the ship. Everyone waited with bated breath, watching the purple dots steadily growing. Jack could now make out flailing tentacles, but not on the middle-most dot—the green one. That one looked to be of similar size to the others, but an extra flicker of green occasionally flashed at its sides, something Jack couldn't quite make out.

Ten minutes passed. Fifteen minutes.

The dots were close enough to make out clearly. They were faster than the ship, and their leader was especially so. It seemed much larger than the others, not because it actually was larger, but because it was closer.

Captain Dordok's gaze became increasingly grim.

Twenty minutes.

The leading space monster had approached enough that Jack could make out its shape. It wasn't a blob, more resembling a green crocodile. The extra flicker of green that Jack had noticed was its tail, moving from side to side as the crocodile swam through space at a speed that would put Earth's spacecrafts to shame.

It opened its mouth to roar, and the entire ship shook, though no sound reached them.

"In position!" the captain roared.

Jack gulped. This crocodile pressured him by merely *approaching*. He understood that, the moment it reached them, the captain would have to go out and do combat. The ship would have to stop or decelerate significantly—they couldn't abandon him—and the rest of the space monsters would have their opportunity to catch up.

They hadn't been able to outrun the monsters. They would have to fight.

Twenty-five minutes.

The crocodile was almost upon them now. Jack could make out the gaps between its teeth, the depths of its throat as it opened wide to bite on them, the glimmer of hunger in its reptilian eyes.

"*CULTIVATORS!*" a voice that shouldn't exist rang in their heads. Count Plomer screamed and cupped his ears. He was only F-Grade. Vlossana was at his side, but there was nothing she could do. "*GIVE ME YOUR DAO!*"

Captain Dordok drew his steel greatclub. The air sparked around him. A sense of oppression filled the ship, like being in the presence of a God. An immortal. Jack held his breath.

The moment the captain drew his weapon, he was out for blood. "We only need to last five minutes," he said calmly, his voice permeating the space, alleviating Count Plomer's pain. "I believe in you, everyone. Make me proud."

His form blurred. Jack's eyes barely caught him rushing through the film of the secondary exit—without a helmet. He was facing space with his bare body.

The crocodile's jaws clamped shut, and a steel greatclub met them head-on. The entire ship shook and tumbled by the force of the collision, sending the chairs and books of the library to the ground.

Jack felt invincible power wash over him, followed by an urge to kneel. "Immortals..." he whispered, breathless. "This is what a battle between immortals looks like..."

Next to him, Brock had eyes as wide as saucers, fully captivated by the power in display.

"*GIVE ME YOUR DAO!*" the crocodile screamed in their minds, but it was muted this time. There was no pain. The captain was keeping them safe.

"*The only thing you'll get,*" his voice filled everyone's head like a large wave about to crash, "*is death.*"

The crocodile roared and darted forward, its tail propelling it through the void. The captain stood tall, his body bursting with incredible power. Compared to the massive crocodile, he was an ant. He swung. Greatclub met teeth. Space dipped and rippled between them, straining to handle the aftermath of the collision. The explosion of Dao made Jack feel like a shaky boat in a storm.

The captain represented Strength. His every swing was unstoppable, his every attack irrefutable. His tattered cloak fluttered behind him. As he stood there, he commanded space itself.

The crocodile was an amalgamation of different Daos without any rhyme or reason. Jack thought he sensed speed in there, along with a sharp sense of hunger. It was difficult to distinguish. But whatever its Dao was, the crocodile held its own. It bit down again and again, shrugging off hits that could have leveled mountains. Its tail swung faster than Jack could follow, and it surrounded the captain as a shark would circle a bloodied swimmer at sea.

Their every collision carried incredible force, like hundreds of Meteor Punches exploding at once. Jack was glad they were thousands of feet away. Even the aftermath of their attacks made the ship feel unsteady.

"Wow!" Vlossana cried out, her face stuck to the window. Jack wondered if she had any sense of self-preservation at all. "No wonder that crocodile caught up to us! It's a high D-Grade!"

"High D-Grade?" Jack raised both brows. "How do you know?"

"Easy, silly. Dordok is high D-Grade as well!"

Jack turned back to the battle. They weren't just immortals; they were *strong* immortals. No wonder they felt so... godly.

Wow... The captain was a high D-Grade all along...

Jack believed her, though he couldn't help but wonder. Immortals were highly revered across the galaxy. Every step signified a tremendous change. The captain should have exponentially higher status than most immortals, who were already sky-high... So why was he riding a starship in the middle of nowhere, hanging out in dock bars and ferrying passengers across the constellation?

Does he love sailing that much?

"Wait!" he yelled, realization slamming into him. "If the crocodile is that strong... How strong must its horde be?"

Vlossana's eyes widened in terror. As the ship had slowed to a crawl, the other space monsters had almost reached them. Jack inspected the largest ones.

Space Monster, Level 121

Space Monster, Level 113

Space Monster, Level 107

Space Monster, Level 91

Space Monster, Level 78

There were three high E-Grade monsters, two middle E-Grade, and eight low E-Grade. Thirteen in total. The *Trampling Ram* had one high E-Grade and two middle E-Grade, along with Jack as a backup.

The comparison didn't look good.

Everyone else must have come to the same conclusion. The ship came to a stop as Bomn barreled out of the room. "Jared!" he bellowed. "When the red light turns green, press the big green button!"

It was the most words Jack had ever heard him speak, but the situation had no room for delays. "Understood!" he shouted back.

Bomn rushed to the secondary exit room. Jack looked outside the window, seeing Achilles and Vashter floating side by side. They faced the incoming horde with bravery, just a hundred feet away from the ship.

"Wait. There's no third helmet!" he shouted at Bomn, but the minotaur ignored him and jumped through the protective film anyway. He reached space, enduring it with his bare body. It was clearly a struggle. His eyes widened and he pushed through, appearing just in front of the two feshkurs.

"He can do that!" Jack asked in shock.

"Wow!" Vlossana cried out.

"He can't," Count Plomer's grim voice reached them. They turned to look at his resigned face. "Bomn is only at the high E-Grade. Even if he's stronger than most of his level, it's not enough to survive in space. Every second out there is harming him... But we are out of options, aren't we?"

Jack's heart reached his throat. Bomn had been nice to him on multiple occasions, and to put himself at such risk... He swiveled to look outside, admitting that the count was right. Even with those three protecting the ship, it was a herculean task. With only two... it would be downright impossible.

Jack clenched his fists so hard that his nails dug into his palms. He hadn't been with these people for a long time, but he desperately wanted to be out there fighting. They were protecting him, risking their lives for him without a moment's hesitation.

And he'd lied to them. Dragged them into danger without their knowledge. If the Animal Kingdom discovered he was on board, which they might, who knows what they would do to the *Trampling Ram* and its crew.

Jack had never felt shittier. If they made it out alive, he swore to tell them everything, and damned be the consequences. They deserved to know. And if Earth wanted his protection, then he would make the decision on Earth's behalf. They would not survive like this.

A life built on corpses was not worth living.

However, as he saw it, they wouldn't even get there. Just how were Bomn, Achilles, and Vashter supposed to face thirteen space monsters by themselves?

Bomn bellowed. His entire body burned blood-red, and the edge of his greataxe seemed so sharp and brutal that Jack instinctively wanted to look away. Achilles drew his saber, ready to fight to the death. Vashter gripped his mace, whose head glowed with silver light.

The space monsters arrived, a screeching mass of writhing tentacles. The two sides collided. Combat ensued.

CHAPTER THIRTEEN
TRAMPLING RAM VS. SPACE MONSTERS

THE *TRAMPLING RAM* FLEW FORWARD AS THE THREE DEFENDERS STOOD ON TOP of it. Bomn, Achilles, and Vashter stared down a horde of space monsters. To the side, Captain Dordok was desperately fighting to prevent the D-Grade monster from nearing the ship.

As they needed to stay close to the fighting captain, the ship's speed had decreased significantly, letting the other monsters reach them. They were purple blobs of power, and each was surrounded by an arbitrary number of tentacle-like appendages.

Bomn bellowed. Blood-red light swam over his body, and the edge of his greataxe radiated an impossible sharp brutality. Achilles drew his saber, ready to fight to the death. Vashter gripped his mace, its silver light intensifying.

The space monsters fell on them. The defenders jumped off. They clashed and the impact shook the ship, making Brock grab a wall to steady himself.

Jack watched the battle from the bridge.

Bomn was a menace. He swung his greataxe in wide swings, using unstoppable force to cleave through space monsters like butter. Two were pushed away, and another—a low E-Grade one—was cleanly slashed in half. Bomn roared harder, the Dao carrying his voice where space could not. As he stood there, a tall, steady form above a writhing mass of tentacles, he filled Jack's sight.

Three monsters—the high E-Grade ones—split off from the horde to face him. They had sensed his power. They hungered for it. Each had at least six tentacles, and they shot out at Bomn like hail.

He did not falter. His dodges were few. The brunt of his defense came in the form of his greataxe, which he swung at the forest of tentacles with a massive bellow. Blood-red, sharp light shone around its edge, making Jack's eyes sting.

Technically, each of these monsters should be able to fight Bomn one-on-one. When all three attacked at once, he held them back. His greataxe cleaved through their tentacles, sending the tips flying. He slashed down, hacking off five tentacles, then changed his grip and slashed upward, slicing another three. The monsters screamed and screeched as they dove for him, but he flew backward, keeping them at bay with sheer strength.

Clearly, Bomn was not a normal high E-Grade. But even he could not face three opponents at the same time. The monsters roared. Their tentacles regenerated. Their onslaught intensified.

A third bellow left Bomn's mouth, and this time, his entire body shone red. Jack was beholding a butcher. An executioner. Rage and violence oozed out of him so abundantly they were almost physical, and even the mindless space monsters didn't dare stray too close. They kept their distance and pummeled him with tentacles, slowly but surely whittling him down.

After all, not only was Bomn fighting the three of them by himself, he also didn't have a helmet. He had to use part of his Dao to keep the void at bay.

Achilles was facing the two middle E-Grade monsters. His saber carried deadly sharpness and great strength. His swings were violent. He dodged some tentacles and slashed at others, cutting them clean from the root. However, no matter how many he severed, more appeared, and he did not possess the strength to dive in and inflict meaningful damage.

Regardless, he persisted. He couldn't beat the two monsters, but he wouldn't lose, either. All they had to do was protect the ship for five minutes. Then, the warp would be ready, and they would be out of here.

With three monsters occupied by Bomn, two by Achilles, and one killed at the start by Bomn, that left seven of them, all low E-Grade.

And they were all stopped by Vashter.

Individually, he was stronger than each of his opponents. But he was one, and they were seven. Their tentacles blotted the stars, and their gaping maws sought to devour him.

Vashter danced among the tentacles, using his mace to break through any openings he could find. Unfortunately, the tentacles were simply too many. He was surrounded. Attacks rained on him, each small in power, but they added up. More importantly, every hit sent him off-balance, leading to even more attacks landing.

The seven monsters resembled a pack of wolves that managed to isolate a particularly durable bison. Vashter did his best, and he remained whole for now, but even defending was a tall task against such predators.

His mace danced regardless. Silver light flared on every hit. Tentacles were smacked aside, his weapon blurring. He was playing whack-a-mole, except on all sides at once, and the moles were too many.

He managed to break off a few tentacles—the low E-Grade monsters couldn't regenerate—but for every tentacle he broke, five slapped his body, tossing him around like a ragdoll.

Getting overwhelmed was a matter of time. The question was, was that time longer than five minutes?

Inside the ship, Jack's teeth-gritting intensified. He had half a mind to jump out and shield his body like Bomn was doing, but that was impossible. He simply didn't have the power. The vacuum would boil his blood in a heartbeat, leaving him a dead, twisted, frozen straw man.

But he wanted to help so fucking much. These guys were putting their lives on the line to protect him, and he could only watch from the sidelines like some weakling.

"Hey." A soft hand touched his shoulder. Turning, he met Vlossana's earnest, sapphire eyes. "It's okay."

Jack wrestled down the urge to shake her off. "I'm fine," he responded, turning back to the battle. She didn't reply, though her hand didn't leave his shoulder. Jack felt his weight lessening, acceptance coming faster than it should.

He turned back to Vlossana. "Is that a skill?"

She smiled. "Emotional Daos have many uses."

"I appreciate it, but please stop. I can control myself. I won't disrespect their battle by turning my eyes away."

She seemed hurt at this. "I know you can control yourself. I'm simply reducing the pain."

Jack shook his head. "Don't. Thank you, but this is enough."

She hesitated, then lifted her hand. Jack's mental turmoil returned in full, his helplessness, but he stood tall through it. Emotions were the crucible on which the mind grew, and weakness was the way to strength.

Master Shol had taught him that.

Jack simply remained still, keeping one eye on the battle, another on the red warp light, and his hands on the ram-head, tilting it slightly forward so the ship never stopped advancing.

It was a good thing the E-Grade space monsters were mindless. Otherwise, they could have split up and destroyed the ship as well. All of them would die.

Vashter was struggling. One of his legs was bent oddly, and his entire body must have been covered in bruises under his clothes. Who knew how many bones were broken or fractured.

But he continued to fight. At least, he'd protected his helmet. His mace drew silver lines around himself, exploding on any tentacle that came close. More tentacles pushed through, but he persisted, his eyes filled with a wild, unyielding look.

Holy shit, Jack thought. He just might die.

The plan was for anyone too injured to retreat so Jack could take over. He was a backup... but that was a lie. If he had to fill in for either of the feshkurs, let alone Bomn, he would die in seconds. He was the weakest member of the crew. If they couldn't handle it, neither could he, and his helplessness was enraging.

He yearned to fight. Purple light flared on his fists as his fighting spirit rose, and he noticed that Vlossana had taken several steps back as if afraid.

He looked back outside. Besides Vashter, Bomn was also struggling. The three high-level monsters were gaining on him, forcing him to fight while in retreat. His sleeves were torn, he was panting, and blood oozed from every orifice on his face—the result of staying in space too long without a helmet.

His greataxe swings came slower, each remaining equally dominating, keeping the monsters back at all costs. He was losing, but he did not let them advance. Perhaps he could last until the warp.

Only Achilles was in a better situation. He could fight the monsters equally, but he could not push them back, though he unleashed large attacks at every opportunity. His grip was white—Jack had to help Vashter, but he couldn't.

Two minutes remained until the warp.

Captain Dordok still fought the crocodile in the distance. He only had one opponent, but it was no joke. The crocodile was similar to him in strength. They exchanged titanic strikes that made Bomn's greataxe seem like a toy. Space rippled in waves around them, the stars behind them lost their luster.

Captain Dordok was only lightly injured, smashing his steel greatclub into the crocodile as many times as he could. Every strike was strong enough to make Jack flinch. The crocodile itself was in a worse state, green Dao leaking from several wounds on its body, but its eyes hadn't lost their hunger.

It could speak, but it remained a mostly mindless beast. It would not retreat, choosing to feast or die.

The captain was infuriated. His face was warped into an expression of pure rage, and he leaned his entire body into each attack. His crew needed him, but if he drew the crocodile to them, everyone would die. He had to kill it first, and he wasn't fast enough.

But maybe they could last.

One minute remained until the warp.

Jack watched the battles with rapt attention. He always kept one eye on the warp light, too, and his hand was ready to smack the button at a moment's notice. The warping wouldn't be instantaneous. Bomn and the captain would have time to return, though barely, and the two feshkurs were connected to the ship through their helmets. The warp would drag them along.

Suddenly, silver light flared in the middle of the melee. Vashter shot out like a cannonball, flying for the ship at full speed. He was bleeding from several places, and his face was twisted by pain.

His eyes scanned the windows to find Jack.

"Brock!" Jack shouted. "You heard the instructions. Take over!"

He dashed away and Brock grabbed the ram-shaped helm and stared at the persistent red light.

Jack reached the secondary exit room just as Vashter flew in, crashing against the far wall. There was no time to lose. Jack ripped the helmet from the feshkur's head, slapped it on his, and jumped out. The protective film barely had time to manifest. The familiar disorientation of space hit him in an instant, but his adrenaline-filled mind pulled through.

Seven space monsters were hot on Vashter's heels. Seeing them screaming and charging, endless tentacles flailing, Jack understood why the feshkur had been in such a bad shape. There was no way he could keep track of so many attacks.

Jack grimaced, but he was ready. He only had to last for a few moments. He could do this.

He roared and dived into the beasts. "Meteor Shower!" he screamed. The sound remained in his helmet, ringing in his ears. His fists flared purple as they smashed into the void, again and again, over and over, sending a rain of meteors at the monsters.

They were barely slowed. No matter how fast Jack punched, the monsters had over twenty tentacles in total. His meteors were slapped aside or endured. Some missed. One was dodged.

Fear gripped his heart, but survival instinct prevailed.

The monsters fanned around Jack, trying to surround him. If that happened, he was dead. He flew to the side, using Meteor Punches to propel himself faster. He tried—and succeeded—to draw the monsters away from the ship. If it got damaged, they were all dead.

As he ran, his Meteor Punches still flew at the monsters, slowing them down a little—enough, hopefully. But they were gaining ground. They were far more proficient at moving through space, and much faster, even though Jack was individually stronger than any of them.

He lost track of time. His entire being focused on survival. Everything else faded away. The seconds stretched into eons.

His existence became a constant check around him for tentacles, punching, and retreating. He didn't have the stamina to shoot out endless Meteor Punches. He was already getting tired, and it had only been a few seconds. His arms had slowed imperceptibly, and that allowed the monsters to close the distance at twice the speed.

I won't make it, he thought. Perhaps it had only been ten seconds. Perhaps it had been thirty. He had no idea, and not knowing brought a greater fear than the space monsters themselves. They towered over him, their tentacles swinging and their bulbous bodies ripping open to swallow him whole.

In the corner of his eye, Jack saw one of the monsters break off. It flew to the side, screeching and waving its tentacles through space. Relief flooded him before a thought occurred.

Where is it going?

He braved a glance. Achilles, absorbed in his fight against the two middle E-Grade monsters, hadn't noticed the low E-Grade that now creeped toward him. The purple bastard had slowed down and wasn't screeching any longer—it instinctively understood the concept of stealth.

Jack felt so angry at this.

"ACHILLES!" he screamed, but all he achieved was to bleed his own ears. He couldn't transmit his voice through space. He didn't know how.

In that momentary pause, the space monsters had caught up. Their tentacles reached for him, slimy appendages of pure power. The ship still wasn't warping. There was no guarantee he would survive this, even if he focused completely on the battle.

Fuck me.

Jack's entire body flared with the power of his Dao. This was his fault. He would save Achilles or die trying. And if the space monsters got in his way, he would destroy them.

A formless ripple emanated from him, giving the monsters pause. It was momentary, barely a blink's worth. But it was enough.

Jack shot through their tentacles, dashing to the side. They followed, slapping the space around him, passing inches by his skin. He swerved to the left and right, dodging desperately. Two attacks landed. They were heavy, like punches to the gut, but he grunted through the pain.

He was looking back, shooting out Meteor Punches to propel himself faster. Since he was in space, his speed kept mounting. He was accelerating, and no force worked against him. There was no wind to indicate his speed, but he could see the ship flying sideways like an arrow. If this was Earth, he would have broken the sound barrier.

He was so fast that he momentarily felt terrified, but he kept punching. He couldn't be too fast, only too slow. He risked a glance behind him, where he was headed. The tentacle monster was right there, tentacle raised to ambush Achilles.

Jack shot out a final Meteor Punch, then turned his body around, directly at the space monster. He no longer cared about his pursuers—he couldn't afford it. A tentacle clipped his ankle, jolting him downward and bending his foot the wrong way. Another fell past his ear, missing him by sheer luck.

Achilles sensed something and turned around to a tentacle descending on his face at full force. He had no time to dodge. His eyes widened with terror.

Jack screamed. The distance between him and the space monster evaporated. He was too fast.

He slammed into it with his fists extended, channeling his Dao to make a meteor out of himself. The poor space monster couldn't even respond. He tore through it, breaking it like a bubble and disintegrating its tentacles, then rammed into one of the middle E-Grade monsters, destroying that one as well.

Jack wasn't unhurt from the collision. His entire body was in pain, multiple bones were fractured or dislocated, and his mind was in disarray. It was like slamming into water at five hundred miles per hour. Even his fists, which were augmented by several skills, had been twisted beyond recognition, the bones showing.

The low E-Grade space monsters that hunted him fell on Achilles, caught in between. He shouted something—Jack could only see his lips moving—and turned to face them.

The second middle E-Grade monster towered over Jack. It would be a hard opponent if he had his full power. As he was, even F-Grades could defeat him. He was no match.

The space monster screeched and brought a tentacle down on him. Jack moved his maimed hand, throwing out whatever little power he had left as a desperate means of escape, but he wasn't nearly fast enough.

Space rippled around him. It tore. The tentacle fell on him—then a colossal power swept by, picking up Jack and carrying him toward the ship. He barely caught a glimpse of Captain Dordok, whose chest sported a long, bleeding wound.

A second colossal power appeared immediately afterward. Large jaws snapped shut around Jack, each tooth the size of a hill.

Space rippled, and Jack was no longer there. Neither was Captain Dordok. They had warped.

CHAPTER FOURTEEN
REVELATION

Space cracked as the *Trampling Ram* pierced through it, sinking between its folds. Jack's helmet pulled him along. The crocodile's teeth snapped at nothing, and the tentacles of lower-level space monsters flailed ineffectively.

A frustrated roar was the last thing Jack heard before the darkness around them warped into a kaleidoscope, and they were hurtling through space from the outside.

Level up! You have reached Level 52.
Level up! You have reached Level 53.
Level up! You have reached Level 54.

He'd killed both a low E-Grade and a middle E-Grade monster, netting him three levels. It was a welcome benefit, though it didn't pacify Jack's worries. He invested the points in Physical and took in his status screen, which always gave him a sense of anchoring.

Name: Jack Rust
Species: Human, Earth-387
Faction: Bare Fist Brotherhood (E)
Grade: E

Class: Fiend of the Iron Fist (Elite)
Level: 54

Strength: 204
Dexterity: 204
Constitution: 204
Mental: 23
Will: 23

Skills: Iron Fiend Body (II), Ghost Step (I)
Dao Skills: Meteor Punch (II), Iron Fist Style (I)
Daos: Perfect Dao Seed of the Fist (early), Dao Root of Indomitable Will
Titles: Planetary Frontrunner (10), Planetary Torchbearer (1)

Jack took a trembling breath.

He was heavily injured, but he maintained enough clarity to feel terrified. He was warping while *outside* the starship. That couldn't be good.

Thankfully, Captain Dordok was right next to him. He grabbed Jack under his arm and flew to the *Trampling Ram*'s secondary exit, pushing him through first before entering himself.

Jack fell to the floor, suppressing a scream. His foot was broken, his fists were maimed, and he sported various cracked or dislocated bones. Truly, he was quite shit. At least his enhanced body kept him from losing consciousness.

Captain Dordok appeared next to Jack in a flash and used the power of the Dao to levitate him. They moved into the main room, which was filled with groans, moans, and the smell of blood. Brock rushed to Jack, making concerned monkey sounds.

A cupboard on the side had been opened to reveal three soft mattresses, which were now unrolled on the floor. Vashter lay on one, groaning intermittently. He was worse than Jack thought. One of his arms hung limp at the side, and the shoulder blade jutted out of his back, wetting his shirt with blood. One of his legs was blue and bloated at the knee—despite the feshkur's gaunt body—and his breaths came in short rasps. With every inhale, a low moan escaped his lips, and his chest trembled—something was broken there.

That he had fought with such injuries was beyond commendable.

Bomn was sprawled on the next bed. His face was covered in frozen blood that stretched out of his nose and mouth. Even his eyes were marred by bloody tears. He was pale and shivering, and looked so weak, Jack wondered how he'd even made it back.

It was thanks to these two that they managed to survive, if barely. Had the warp been ten seconds late, there was a good chance all of them would be dead.

"I'm proud of you," Captain Dordok said. "All of you." Though he was clearly strained, his injuries were light, same as Achilles. They didn't take a bed and stayed standing, attending to the injured. Vlossana and Count Plomer were also helping.

"These injuries won't heal themselves, but don't worry. We escaped the horde. When the warp ends, we'll be less than an hour away from Earth-321 and Amethyst Mountain. We will find you medical assistance promptly on arrival."

Vashter made pained noises of gratitude, only for Vlossana to push him back down. "No talking!" she said cheerfully, slapping his good shoulder. "Only resting! I'll get you some chocolate later."

Jack had no idea where she would find that, but it was good to know that chocolate was a thing outside Earth. Anything to keep his mind away from the pain.

His broken foot was a pain he could handle. His minor injuries were just blips on the radar. But his hands... Oh, that was agony. They felt frozen and electrocuted at the same time. Continuously. He was pretty sure that enhancing his body had given him some pain resistance, because he could *sense* his nerves close to fraying from the constant, high-volume output.

Not screaming was a struggle. But if Vashter could handle it, so could he.

Achilles approached from the side. "Jared," he said, looking Jack in the eye. They hadn't spoken much, but the honesty in his gaze was soothing. "Thank you. You saved me back there."

"It... was... my... fault," Jack managed to grit out. Achilles shook his head.

"It was a battlefield. There was no guarantee the enemies would stick to their targets. I should have been more careful." He glanced at the captain, who nodded in approval. "A feshkur never forgets his favors. I owe you my life. One day, I will repay you."

Jack tried to speak, but Captain Dordok beat him to the punch.

"Don't deny your bravery," he said. "You couldn't even guarantee your own life, but you took a risk to save another, a friend. In my eye, this is loyalty—the most important quality of a crewmember."

Without warning, Achilles stabbed a needle in Jack's thigh. Jack grunted in surprise. Next thing he knew, the pain was receding. It didn't disappear, but at least he could speak now. Captain Dordok's powers levitated Jack to the third mattress and let him down gently, sending a muted jolt of pain through his body.

"I had my doubts about you, Jared," the captain continued. "Our crew is tight-knit because we don't accept others easily. We are strong, and we would all die for each other without a second thought. The *Trampling Ram* is our home and cradle. I only took you in because you showed promise, and you, my boy, proved me right at the very first opportunity you got. You saved Achilles; that means a lot."

His face split into a large grin, uncaring about the grim situation they were in.

"From today onward, Jared, you really are a member of the crew. Wherever you go in your life, whatever happens, know that the *Trampling Ram* will always be a home for you. For anything you need, we'll be there. And we hope you feel the same way."

"I don't deserve such kind words..." Jack muttered.

"Of course you do!" The captain roared in laughter. "Take pride in yourself, Jared. You did the right thing!"

Every word of the captain was a jab at Jack's heart. These people had been nothing but kind to him. They'd accepted him with open arms, respected him, been polite and friendly. They risked their lives to protect him, and he had done the same.

But it was built on lies the whole way. The guillotine over his head was too massive. Anyone near him was at risk of getting cut, and he'd thrown the *Trampling Ram* and its crew into danger to save himself and his planet.

Perhaps it was the sedative, but the pain in Jack's heart eclipsed that of his hands.

"Captain..." he said in a trembling voice, deciding to open his heart. They deserved to know. "I'm sorry, Captain... I've been lying to you."

Captain Dordok stopped in confusion. His celebratory smile faltered. "What?"

"I... My name is not Jared. It's Jack. Jack Rust. I'm hunted by some people, as you have suspected, but they aren't weak. They are... I don't know who they are, exactly, but they're strong—It's the Animal Kingdom. I'm being hunted down by the Animal Kingdom... or at least, there is a good chance I am."

Everyone had fallen silent. Captain Dordok didn't respond immediately. His one eye narrowed, filled with a glint of fierce intelligence that usually remained hidden.

"Tell me everything," he said.

Jack glanced at Brock, who nodded, and he started speaking. He told them everything from the dungeon he spawned in, to Gan Salin in Valville, to the faction he created, to the Integration Tournament. He spoke about the scions and how they treated the natives. How his conflict with them started, and how it had escalated. The times he insulted them.

The conclusion of the tournament, where he defied the C-Grade Planetary Overseer and took what the Animal Kingdom had prepared for Rufus. How they dropped all pretense to kill him, but he killed them back. He murdered Rufus in front of the entire world, dragging the Animal Kingdom's face through the mud. That even the Planetary Overseer had acted against him at the very end but had been blocked.

How he was his planet's greatest hope.

His story took some time to tell. Space had stabilized around them, revealing new constellations in the distance, and Achilles had wordlessly gone to direct the ship toward Earth-321.

Nobody interrupted Jack. Brock stayed by his side throughout, listening calmly. The captain kept a sharp stare on him, occasionally nodding or tightening his jaw.

By the end, the captain's expression was grim.

"That's all," Jack finished his story, filled with shame. He looked away, not daring to meet the captain's eye.

A few moments of silence went by as the captain considered his response. Nobody else spoke up. Eventually, Dordok said, "So you plunged us all into danger."

"Yes," Jack admitted, not attempting to defend himself.

"Do you regret it?"

"I knew... I was tricking you. I will not make excuses. I came here intending to sacrifice strangers to save my people. That was my choice, and I still believe it was reasonable at the time. But if I could go back now, with what I know about you... I would tell you everything before we set off. I would let you make the call."

"And I would decline without a second thought," the captain replied.

"As you should. But that's fine. Everything is my fault to begin with. I'm the one who exposed my people to danger. I'm the reason why they need saving. But despite that, if I am to save them, I simply cannot do it like this. I cannot backstab good people like you. I will walk my path, and I will either succeed or die trying. The people I protect will fall or rise with me." He chuckled darkly, lost in regrets. "I put them in danger, but I am ready to sacrifice them a second time in the name of morality. How fucked up is that?"

"It is not," the captain replied. "In deciding to accept you as their leader, those people agreed to follow you wherever you go and embrace your decisions, even if those decisions led to their death. They tied themselves to your carriage, accepting that the carriage moves wherever it wants. If you want to antagonize the Animal Kingdom, they are in it with you. If you want to sacrifice some of them, they have already agreed to it."

"But I can't do that!" Jack protested. "I have a responsibility to them!"

"You have many responsibilities," Dordok retorted, his voice steely. "You cannot do everything at the same time. Sometimes, you have to let things go. You respect them and try to help them, but accepting someone as your leader has consequences. These are the consequences. Followers are there to help you and be helped, not to shackle you. You have the responsibility to protect and help them rise, but they have the responsibility to accept your decisions and follow you wherever you go, even into death. If your path is honor or death, they will follow it without a word of protest. And if they didn't know what they were signing up for, or if they weren't strong enough to make decisions for themselves, that is their fault."

"That's..." Jack gritted his teeth. This was just too harsh. "How can you think like that, Captain?"

"Because I am a leader," the cyclops said. "And when you have been traveling the galaxy for as long as I have, you will see the same truth. The world isn't soft or easy. Hard decisions need to be made all the time. And these hard decisions must often be shouldered by the people who believe in you."

It was like a massive weight had appeared on the captain's shoulders. His one eye was hazy, looking off into the distance, and his posture was slightly hunched. For a moment, he did not resemble a strong immortal, but a weary old man.

The feeling disappeared as quickly as it had come, and Dordok was bursting with the steely authority of a captain. "Watch me, Jack," he said, then turned around.

"Crew of the *Trampling Ram*, heed my words," he declared in a tone that brooked no disobedience. "Jack lied to us, used us, and shoved us into danger. That will not go unpunished. However, he also fought with us, risked his life for us as we did for him, and saved one of us. We accepted him as a member of this crew. We will remember his mistake, and we will punish him for it, but we will not abandon him to the tyrants of the constellation. He never had malice—he simply had no choice. And when he became one of us, he told us everything, putting himself at risk. He betrayed strangers, but he stayed loyal to the crew of the *Trampling Ram*. We will not be disloyal in return. As the captain, and as the eldest here by far, I say we let him stay."

He swept the crew with his eyes. Bomn's trembling voice was the first to answer. He pushed himself to sit up, then said, "I trust you, Captain."

Achilles threw Jack a complex glance, then said, "I trust you, Captain."

Vashter hesitated, and the captain's gaze lingered. Finally, he said, "I trust you, Captain."

Jack couldn't believe what was happening. He expected to be berated, beaten up, and abandoned at the nearest planet. Maybe even surrendered to the Animal Kingdom. He had accepted that his journey might end here.

He never expected such a good conclusion. He almost couldn't believe this—and the guilt in his heart burned even hotter. Did he deserve this kindness?

"Good," Dordok replied, turning to Jack. This time, his eye was angry. "You are a member of the crew. We will not abandon you or turn you in to save ourselves. However, know that our protection will be limited. Loyalty is important, but you have brought this upon yourself. If a C-Grade comes here and asks for you, we will not commit suicide. Is that understood?"

Jack almost choked. The galaxy was full of dictators, scions, and arrogant, power-driven overlords... but it also had people like Captain Dordok and Master Shol. People whose hearts were filled with genuine kindness.

The world hadn't been nice to Jack since the Integration. Sometimes, it seemed like everyone was out to get him, and impossible obstacles filled his path. But when it came to people like these, he was so grateful to have met them. They were his benefactors. He owed them everything.

The *Trampling Ram* was a beautiful oasis in a harsh world.

"Thank you," he said from the bottom of his heart. Through his pain, he bowed his head. "I will not drag you down. Even if they torture me, I swear that I will tell them nothing about you."

"Good." The captain nodded. "Remember the kindness we have shown you. We will discuss this more after we provide medical care to Bomn and Vashter—you don't seem to need any."

Jack blinked in surprise, then looked down. His foot had at some point righted itself, and the twisted bones in his hands were setting themselves right. His chest wasn't in as much pain anymore. He wasn't in fighting condition, but he could walk. His regeneration was no joke.

"Wow," he said breathlessly.

"That's an impressive skill," the captain commented. "If you want to progress fast, it will be invaluable... but enough talk. Earth-321 is right there."

Jack looked to the side, still combing through his emotions. A blue planet shone in the distance, quickly increasing in size. The green strips on its surface unraveled into continents. It looked just like Earth—his Earth—but with even more water. It rotated slowly, lending a new sense of majesty to the sight.

Jack had seen a planet disappearing in the distance, but it was the first time he saw one approaching.

"Slow us down," Captain Dordok told Achilles, who was at the helm. "One tenth of relative speed. Amethyst Mountain is at the northern hemisphere, right where those two conti—"

Whatever he said next was lost. A new voice flooded the starship, echoing in everyone's ears with almost the same intensity as the crocodile's roar.

"Pilot of the *Trampling Ram!*"

It was a harsh, commanding voice. Jack couldn't tell its gender.

"Stop the ship!" the captain shouted, and the *Trampling Ram* stilled. Jack looked out of the window. Three figures appeared, closing the distance from the planet. Each were garbed in black, with a cape stretching behind them. Their faces were covered by green, opaque veils that fell from their foreheads.

And all three of them were floating in space.

They came to a stop a hundred feet away from the prow of the *Trampling Ram*. "In the name of the Animal Kingdom," one of them said, "surrender Jack Rust."

CHAPTER FIFTEEN

PILOTING IS DIFFICULT

"In the name of the Animal Kingdom, surrender Jack Rust!"

The voice echoed through the starship, commanding authority and arrogance. Who could blame them? There were three immortals hovering before the *Trampling Ram*. Three!

Inside the starship, everyone swiveled to look at Jack, then at the captain.

"Sons of bitches," Dordok cursed. "They sent out Hounds to hunt a mere child!"

"Hounds?" Vlossana asked, her eyes forming into wide circles. "Woooow."

"Hounds, Captain?" Jack risked asking.

"The hunters of the Kingdom. The terror of the constellation." Captain Dordok gritted his teeth. "But they only wear green veils. They have to show me respect."

"Captain," Bomn said in a warning voice, but Dordok raised an orange palm.

"Don't worry," he said. "My strength matches theirs, and we have done nothing wrong yet. They will not attack."

Jack watched their exchange with wide eyes. Just a moment ago, he'd revealed the truth to everyone, and he was so glad about it. If he hadn't, there was no way he could survive this.

However, also a moment ago, the captain had said they wouldn't commit suicide for him. And contradicting the Animal Kingdom sounded a little too much like suicide.

Thankfully, it seemed the captain had a way out of this.

"We have no idea who that is," the captain spoke in normal volume, yet his voice crossed the void to reach the Hounds, carrying the full force of a high D-Grade immortal.

"Come out immediately!" the voice responded.

"One moment."

The captain turned to everyone inside. "The glass windows have obscuring properties when in space. They cannot see us. Listen closely. I will go out there and delay them for as long as I can. I will pretend to be angry and stubborn, as people often accuse cyclops of being, and I will also block their spiritual perception. Jack, you grab Brock, take one of the escape shuttles, and run to the planet."

"But they'll see me."

"No. You will drive the shuttle away from the planet first, in such a direction that the *Ram* is always between you and them, so they cannot see you. Once far enough, circle around and approach from a distance. The Amethyst Mountain is where the two continents cross. You can't miss it."

Unprompted, Achilles stabbed another syringe into Jack's thigh. Jack's pain receded even further. He was still injured, and he sure as hell couldn't fight, but he could make a run for it.

His heart was filled with warmth. After everything he'd done, they were still willing to help him. His gratitude was so suffocating that he felt the need to hug them all one by one.

That feeling was immediately overshadowed by guilt. Even if he escaped...

"Focus, boy," Captain Dordok said with increasing urgency. "We'll be fine. Even if they catch you, we'll say we knew nothing. You were Jared and Monk to us. They cannot prove anything if you don't speak, and galactic law protects us until we're proven guilty. Even if—"

Glass moaned. The entire starship jolted to the side. Everyone looked toward the Hounds, and they saw that the massive, thick glass walls had been dented by a powerful strike, almost breaking. The entire wall was so fractured they could barely see outside.

The Hounds had attacked the *Trampling Ram*.

Dordok was stunned silent. As he stared at the fractured glass in disbelief, Jack felt something give way inside the captain. He'd fought a battle and almost lost a crew member. Two more had been injured. One had been injured *and* confessed to lying to them all along.

Throughout all that, the captain had been calm and reasonable. He was the strong person. Even under increasing strain, he kept a level head and made good decisions one after the other.

But every man's patience had a limit. And Captain Dordok's had just been reached.

"They touched my ship," he muttered, still unable to believe his eyes. "The *Trampling Ram*... They..."

His wide eye narrowed slowly. His large fists balled. His entire body arched and tensed, his mouth forming into a vicious snarl. He reached out, and the steel greatclub flew to his hand, shaking the air where it passed. He held it in a death grip.

"HOW DARE YOU!" he roared and disappeared. In the next moment, he was outside, facing the three Hounds from thirty feet away—barely an inch to an immortal. "What the hell do you think you're doing?" he screamed in their faces.

"Show respect to the Hounds," the middle Hound commanded. These three didn't have an apparent leader.

"Show respect to *my ship*!" Dordok retorted. He was furious, and his anger was clearly barely kept at bay.

Jack didn't know how much of that was fake, nor did he have time to ponder. "Thank you for everything," he said, swiping his gaze around the room. Bomn and Achilles met it, nodding. Vashter looked the other way. Vlossana smiled and waved. Count Plomer glared at him.

Grabbing Brock, Jack ran to the far right door and smashed it open. He'd never been here before. He never expected to come alone.

Two small, oblong shapes waited for him; the escape shuttles, each were in front of a sliding door that led directly to space. He opened the door to one and barged in. They were also pretty tiny. He could barely fit in them without ducking, and they were made to host two people.

And there came the real problem. He had no idea how to drive this thing. He looked around in haste, cataloging everything. The shuttle was only a few square feet in size, its walls reinforced and with one small window on each side. The front was occupied by a control panel, where Jack rushed.

A small helm—similar to the starship's but without the ram-shaped head—dominated the panel. There was a lever, a big green button, a big red button, as well as an inactive sonar. There were also a dozen other buttons, flicks, switches, displays, and light bulbs, all inactive.

"Fuck my life," Jack muttered, slapping the green button. "Green means go."

The shuttle came to life and the control panel lit up like a Christmas tree. The light bulbs switched on in random colors, the displays showed graphs and statistics Jack couldn't understand, and a low hum came from under his feet.

The top of the helm glowed green. There was an item embedded there; a transparent, veined stone. Jack had no idea what it was. A power source? Was there a similar one in the bridge of the *Trampling Ram*, just hidden under the helm's ram-shaped head?

He had no time to care.

Mechanical sounds came from all around as the doors in front of the shuttle opened, revealing a dark, empty nothing. "Okay," Jack said, "but how do I activate this thing? If you have any ideas, Brock, now is the time."

He had only been to the bridge for a few moments, and it was mid-battle. He didn't remember much besides the helm. Thinking up to there, he grabbed the helm and inched it forward. The shuttle tilted downward an inch, but it didn't budge.

"Goddammit!" he cursed.

Brock made monkey noises, grabbed the lever next to the helm, and gave it a good push. The shuttle bounded forward like a wild horse. Jack flew backward, still holding onto the helm, and the shuttle's nose turned upward so hard that they began spinning over themselves. Thankfully, Brock had been drawn back too, releasing the lever and stopping the ship.

"SHIT!" Jack shouted. They'd only traveled a few feet, still hidden behind the *Trampling Ram*, and they were spinning in place. There was no inertia in space to stop them.

He pushed through the centrifugal force, reaching the helm and tilting it forward. The shuttle's rotation decelerated, leaving them facing away from the *Trampling Ram*. Meanwhile, a terrifying, Dao-infused clash reached their ears and shook their shuttle. He knew this feeling. Captain Dordok was fighting. That wasn't part of the plan.

The captain had said the Hounds would not attack. Something had gone wrong. But no matter what, the greatest help Jack could offer was not getting captured.

"Brock!" he shouted. "Grab the lever. You control speed, I control direction. Ready? Go!"

Brock bounded forth, grabbing the lever and tilting it gently. The shuttle barely moved. He tilted it harder, and they shot forward so hard that they almost revealed themselves from behind the *Trampling Ram*. Thankfully, the starship covered a lot of space.

Jack struggled with the helm. It wasn't as simple as pointing it where they wanted to go. The helm controlled the shuttle's rotation speed, so if he tilted to the right and then let it rest dead-center, they would keep spinning right for eternity. He had to control it very carefully, struggling to cancel out their rotation so they wouldn't overextend. Moreover, the helm was insanely delicate. Every tiny movement had great effect.

It was like playing a badly-designed video game, and having a second person control the speed wasn't helping, but it was the best they could do. Jack couldn't spare the concentration to control both things at once. Thank God he had his monkey bro.

Brock was struggling in his own right. The ship had been designed to achieve great speeds, so keeping it slow enough for Jack to maintain control was nearly impossible. He had to minimally nudge the lever every time, and just the slightest overextension would send them bounding forth like rockets.

"FUCK WHOEVER MADE THIS SHIP!" Jack shouted, glad for once that sound couldn't travel in space—not his sound, in any case.

They were darting left and right like a drunk fly. Their speed was increasing and decreasing randomly, and they were turning in all directions at once. They barely managed to remain in the shadow of the *Trampling Ram*. They must have looked ridiculous.

Moreover, Jack's hands were still seriously injured. The only reason he could operate the helm at all were the two shots of anesthetic Achilles had jutted in his thigh. The regeneration brought by Iron Fiend

Body was superb, if the captain's surprise was anything to go by, but E-Grade bodies were difficult to repair. Even after almost an hour of rest, he was only barely functional.

Very slowly, even moving as haphazardly as they were, they managed to make some distance. The shuttle didn't have outside lights —Jack had checked before boarding—and the interior was dimly lit, so from this distance, they would seem like a star unless someone paid attention for long enough to notice them moving.

Hopefully, even immortals couldn't stargaze mid-battle.

"Let's circle around, Brock!" Jack shouted. "I'm turning right!"

"Bro!" Brock responded. He did his best to maintain a constant speed, but it was a struggle. Jack suspected the lever was as unwieldy as the helm.

"Why in the world would they make such terrible ships?" he wondered aloud. He turned bit by bit, not daring to make any large movements lest they find themselves spinning again. Space turned in his eyes until the corner of a blue planet appeared in his vision.

"That's it!" he shouted in joy.

He couldn't see the battle from the front window—it was fairly limited in width—but he could still feel the shockwaves. *Captain Dordok will be fine, right?*

The captain had said he'd play it stubborn. Perhaps a few warning shots, a demonstration of his power, was all part of the show. Besides, he'd said it himself. Unless Jack gave them away, nobody could prove that the crew of the *Trampling Ram* knew anything.

Jack shook the thoughts away. He couldn't afford distractions with this blasted helm. They had to reach the planet as fast as possible while circling far around the battle. Then, they could—

A knock on the glass drew him out of his thoughts. Jack turned to the side in mounting horror.

Gan Salin was floating right outside the window, wearing a protective helmet. He was holding onto the shuttle and drifting along. He waved cheerfully.

CHAPTER SIXTEEN
THE RETURN OF GAN SALIN

CAPTAIN DORDOK FACED THE THREE HOUNDS IN SPACE. A BLUE AND GREEN planet hovered behind them, humongous beyond imagination. Dordok himself was only framed by stars and the *Trampling Ram*.

"We have no Jack on board," he said furiously. He really was angry, but he was playing it up even more. Nobody became an immortal by losing their temper. "All we have is people in need of immediate medical assistance. We were just attacked by a horde of space monsters. Let us through at once!"

"Not happening." The middle Hound shook his head. "You will not move an inch until we inspect your ship."

"My crew is *dying!*" the captain roared and jabbed a finger at them. "You are overstepping your authority. I demand passage. You can inspect the ship after we land."

"No."

Dordok frowned. His aura flared, covering his body in a sun of strength. Conveniently, it also blocked the Hounds' spiritual perception, shielding the starship behind him.

"I am a high immortal," he growled, his voice steadily growing in volume. "You damaged my starship. You are harming my crew. Get out of my way."

"No," the rightmost Hound replied, laughing. Her voice was raspy and harsh. "High or low immortal, we don't care. The Animal Kingdom rules this constellation. You will do what we say."

Captain Dordok's anger rose—for real this time. His chest was hot and stuffed with rage. They were disrespecting him.

"This is preposterous," he said with barely contained rage. "I demand fair treatment. I *will* report you."

At the same time, his mind turned quickly. Why are they so stubborn? he insisted. Will they really break decorum with a high immortal over an E-Grade brat?

Canine, Level 175
Faction: Animal Kingdom (B-Grade)
Title: Third Ring Conqueror

Canine, Level 178
Canine, Level 171

They were all affiliated with the Animal Kingdom and showed the same Title: Third Ring Conqueror, which should increase the efficacy of their attributes by 15%, enough to shoot their strength into the middle D-Grade.

On the other hand, Dordok was injured and exhausted. These three may be low D-Grades, but they had all the titles, enhancements, and Dao skills that a B-Grade faction could give them. If things really came down to combat, he struggled to predict the victor.

At times like this, Dordok regretted not visiting Trial Planet when he was younger.

"Report us?" the leftmost Hound laughed. "To whom? Kneel to your superiors, slave!" His voice was tinged with frenzied bloodlust. Dordok finally understood why these three were so heavy-handed. They didn't care about laws or fairness. They were just itching for a fight. They were maniacs, and he was only an unaffiliated D-Grade. Even if they killed him here, the Animal Kingdom wouldn't care.

Dordok paled. Fear and rage warred inside him as he gripped his greatclub tighter. It had been long enough. Jack might have reached the planet by now. He had to protect his crew and the *Trampling Ram*.

But that didn't mean he would let himself be pushed around by low D-Grades. He was the captain.

"If you think I will let you touch my crew, you're sorely mistaken," he said. His one brow fell low. "I will let you come close and inspect the ship with your spiritual perception. You will not board."

"We will do whatever we want," the leftmost Hound, the most battle-crazed one, spoke again. "And you better step aside, slave, or we will touch you as well. I don't see you kneeling."

Dordok's grip tightened. His pride raised its head. He followed the Dao of Strength, not the Dao of Weakness.

It wasn't even about Jack anymore. This became personal.

"And I never will," he growled. Things had gotten out of hand, but it didn't matter. This was a battle. He just had to win.

All three Hounds laughed. Their Daos emanated from their bodies, casting a blanket of insanity on him. His reason crumbled bit by bit. He tried to fight back, but Strength was not a good match against them. His blood went cold.

With a battle cry, Captain Dordok raised his greatclub overhead and swung. The three Hounds dodged, fanning out to surround them, their laughter rising to hysteria.

———

Jack looked through the escape shuttle's window. He looked away, wiped his eyes, then looked again. Gan Salin was still there, waving, a big smile on his face.

"Brock," he said, "are you seeing what I'm seeing?"

He turned around, only to find Brock looking at the same window like he'd seen a ghost. Reality finally settled in. Gan Salin, a scion of the Animal Kingdom, was here. He was wearing a protective helmet. All he had to do was strike the shuttle, or somehow alert the Hounds, and Jack would be dead beyond the shadow of a doubt.

So why wasn't he doing that?

Canine, Level 51
Faction: Animal Kingdom (B-Grade)

Jack's control of the shuttle faltered a bit as he directed most of his attention to Gan Salin. The canine gave Jack a thumbs-up, then pointed at the back of the ship. Jack turned to look.

The door?

He looked back at the window, but Gan Salin had disappeared. The knocking came again, this time from the door. Jack and Brock exchanged an incredulous gaze.

"He can't be serious," Jack said.

"Bro..." Brock replied hesitantly. The ship wobbled a bit, but they quickly put it back on track. The knocking sound came again.

"We... We have no choice," Jack muttered in disbelief. "We have to open the door."

Brock gave him a slow, determined nod. Jack took a deep breath and pressed the button at the doors side. It slid open, revealing nothing but space and an excited canine. A terrible whooshing power drew Jack and Brock toward the outside. They lost control of the helm and lever, letting the shuttle spin endlessly in the void.

"Let me iiiiin!" Gan Salin shouted, shooting inside as fast as he could. Jack almost punched him. Instead, he jabbed the button again, closing the door as fast as he could. The sucking power had almost gotten the best of them. The shuttle was still spinning, and they hurried to rebalance it.

At least there was no gravity.

"What the fuck is going on?" Jack asked, staring at Salin from an inch away. The escape shuttle wasn't designed for three people. They could barely fit.

"We haven't met in so long, and that's the first thing you say? *What's going on?*" Gan Salin complained. "How are you doing, Salin? Are you alright, Salin? I missed you, Salin. But did you say any of that? No. Some friends you are."

"I..." Jack wondered if he was having a stroke. "We aren't friends."

"But we can be!" Salin replied excitedly.

Jack blinked a few times, then shook his head. It occurred to him that if he killed Gan Salin, he couldn't alert the Hounds. If he wasn't so heavily injured, he might have tried.

"What's happening?" Jack asked again. "Why are you here?"

"Oh, that. Well, you made a lot of people angry. The overseer, especially, and she can be a bitch sometimes—but don't tell her I said that. Anyway, the Hounds were tasked with hunting you down, and they dragged *me* along because I know your face—supposedly. The real reason is that I'm punished for sucking in the tournament. Also, I suspect they don't like me."

"What?"

"I know. How is that possible? So yeah, they dragged me along, but I don't like that, man. They're reaaaally treating me like shit, and I thought, you know what? If we find Jacko, I could join him instead. Travel the galaxy while outsmarting our pursuers. Have wacky adventures. Go to Trial Planet with the two tokens he *hopefully* still has. Those kinds of things."

"What?"

"I said, let's travel together. I'll use my status to get us through the teleporter, and you use your extra token to let me into Trial Planet. I was supposed to get one after the tournament, but uh, that's not really happening anymore. Good thing you have a spare one, right?"

"What?"

"What this, what that. Did the suction from before steal your brain? Am I not speaking clearly? I can repeat everything slower if you want. Weeee haaaveeen't meeeeet in soooo looo—"

Jack, again, thought he was having a stroke. This was too much to process.

"Wait," he said, cutting off Salin's rapid-fire bullshit. "Wait, wait, wait. You want to join me and go to Trial Planet?"

Salin reverted to normal speaking. "My phrasing was better, but yeah."

"And you can get us through the teleporters?"

"Yep."

"And you will betray the Animal Kingdom."

"Oh, we canines betray the Kingdom all the time, don't worry about it. Comes with the territory. We're their crazy frontliners, so some extra initiative here or there is nothing odd."

Jack was struggling to comprehend. By his side, Brock had completely quit this conversation and was focused on the distance. They were approaching the planet now, and they could see the immortals fight in the side window, exchanging herculean attacks like it was nothing. Despite being injured and exhausted, the captain was holding his own, though he was clearly defending more than attacking.

"This is all... too sudden," Jack said. "You're an enemy. You tried to kill me and my friends, and you set a terrorist loose in my hometown. I kicked your ass."

"Hey, no need to brag," Salin replied, pouting. His long canines stuck out a bit. "You weren't even the only one to kick my ass."

"But— I mean—How did you even catch up to us?"

He raised a brow. "With that driving? Are you kidding me?"

"I—"

"So, um, not to pressure you or anything, but we're kind of in a hurry here. The Hounds will notice us eventually if we keep moving like turtles. Do you mind?" He gestured at the helm and speed lever.

"You can drive this?" Jack asked. Brock gave Gan Salin a suspicious look.

"Of course! What kind of scion would I be if I couldn't even drive a little escape shuttle?"

He moved to the front, gently pushing Brock to the side. The brorilla struck him with the most insulted glare Jack had ever seen.

Gan Salin grabbed the lever and pushed it forward, keeping his other hand on the helm. Their flight accelerated somewhat. He then flicked a switch, making their ship jump. Jack and Brock both crashed into the ceiling. Brock's tail slapped Gan Salin. It was certainly accidental.

"Whoops," Salin said. "Wrong switch."

"Are you sure you can drive this?" Jack shouted.

"Yes, don't worry about it! My middle name is pilot." He flicked a different switch. The shuttle calmed down, its flight stabilizing. "There you go. You sillies forgot to turn off the race setting."

"The what?"

Everyone was thrown backward as Salin accelerated massively. This time, the shuttle wasn't jumping in random directions every time someone touched the helm. It almost resembled smooth sailing. The planet was quickly growing in their sight.

"All set!" Gan Salin said. "And it only took me two tries!"

Jack and Brock exchanged a look. "For the record," Jack said, "I still hate your guts."

"No problem! I'm sure you'll come around in no time at all."

Salin rockily turned the tip toward a point where two green strips—two continents—crossed. Evidently, he also knew about Amethyst Mountain.

"Can you land this thing?" Jack asked.

"Jacko, Jacko, Jacko," Gan Salin replied, shaking his head.

"Don't call me that."

"Of course I can land this thing! I mean, I've never *done* it before, but how tough can it be?" He gave them a bright smile and accelerated.

Jack and Brock braced themselves.

CHAPTER SEVENTEEN
THE CAPTAIN'S BURDEN

The people of Amethyst Mountain were stony, composed individuals. When immortals started fighting near their planet, leading to an explosion of fireworks, they only looked up to admire the view.

However, when a space shuttle barreled through the planet's atmosphere, heading directly for the town, even they had to frown. The shuttle was burning red like a comet, its surface ignited by friction with the atmosphere. The course was jagged, rigidly shifting to one side or the other. The two metallic surfaces that were supposed to slow its descent were facing the wrong way.

It was out of control.

People screamed and ran away, using F and E-Grade powers to jump from the skyscraper docks, leap over food carts and slower people, or jump to the rooftops where they kept running.

Jack saw all that from a tiny window. They were falling from outer space like a rock, without parachutes or anything of the sort. The one slowing device they had, Gan Salin managed to fumble it so hard that it spun the wrong way and wouldn't come around.

"You said you knew how to drive!" Jack screamed to be heard over the wind pounding against the ship walls.

"I do! I just never practiced!" Gan shouted back, wrestling with the helm.

The metal walls of the shuttle were made to diffuse the heat, so they weren't boiling, but the temperature still resembled a mid-summer heat wave, and the cramped, stuffy space didn't help. Due to his fur, Brock was especially hot. He was sweating buckets.

"Do something!" Jack shouted with rising panic. The ground was fast approaching, and they weren't slowing down.

"I'm trying!" With a great heave, the helm ripped from its base. Gan Salin stared at it, then at the ground, then back at it. "Whoops."

"I'LL FUCKING KILL YOU!"

"Ha, joke's on you. Looks like *I'll* kill us first."

A hard poop splatted into Salin's face, making him retch. Brock waved his fist through the air, screaming obscenities in monkey.

I refuse to go down like this, Jack thought. I refuse!

He had survived the Forest of the Strong. He triumphed in the Integration Tournament. He escaped the pursuit of a constellation-spanning space kingdom. He'd overcome insurmountable odds again and again. If he died because of an amateurish crash-landing, that would be the world's stupidest joke.

He wrung his brain dry, but nothing came to mind. If he went out right now, he would burn to death in seconds. The shuttle's helm had broken. They had already tried all the buttons, but nothing happened.

"I hate you, Gan Salin!" Jack screamed in the canine's ears.

The town was now so close they could easily make out the running people. Suddenly, green clouds rose from below. They formed into shiny green platforms in front of the shuttle—they looked like glass.

The shuttle rammed into a platform and shattered it, only to find another behind. It shattered that one as well. A long series of platforms stretched between the shuttle and the town below, with every collision slowing it down, cushioning the fall, but throwing the ship into a spin. Jack, Brock, and Gan Salin were smacked up and down with every crush like ragdolls.

In the middle of all this movement, Jack caught a glimpse of a furious-looking, half-dressed, green woman floating in the middle of the sky.

When he looked ahead again, he saw the ground. "Brock!" he screamed, grabbing the brorilla and hugging him tight, protecting his little bro with his body. He pulled in his limbs. Then, they crashed.

Everything in the shuttle shattered. Buttons and broken glass flew everywhere. Jack, Brock, and Gan Salin were plastered to the front as the shuttle dug a trench through the soil and two buildings—empty ones, thankfully.

When everything came to a stop, Jack was alive. His chest felt like he'd been hit by a cannonball, his head swam, and he felt like puking, but Brock looked fine. Jack heaved a huge sigh of relief. He was so glad.

"All things considered," Gan Salin said, standing and dusting himself off, "I'd say this went pretty well!"

"I'll fucking murder you."

"WHAT DO YOU THINK YOU'RE DOING!" a furious voice washed over them, shaking Jack to his core. He thought back to the floating woman. An immortal.

"Oh, crap. Quick!" Gan Salin said. "Put these on!"

He fished a pair of steel manacles from his jacket—a neat, dark blue leather—and tossed them to Jack. Jack looked between the manacles and the canine.

"You must think I'm stupid."

"Come on! We'll pretend I captured you, okay? That's our only chance."

"We're enemies. You'll just turn me in."

"If I wanted to turn you in, I would have pointed the Hounds in your direction," Salin pleaded. "If you don't put them on, I'll have to surrender you to the Amethyst Mountain, who will deliver you to the Kingdom in a heartbeat. There's a bounty on your head—a large one."

Jack felt like exploding—he had no other choice.

"Hurry! She could scan us anytime!" Salin urged him.

Jack punched him in the face. "That's for before!" he shouted, snapping the manacles shut around his wrists. If this was all part of the canine's plan, Jack had been outsmarted. Then again, if Gan Salin was lying, Jack had already lost the moment his shuttle was spotted.

"Ow!" Gan said, holding his nose. "Why did you do that?"

"Because you almost killed us!"

"Hey, you're the one that flew a space shuttle without knowing how to drive! They should revoke your license!"

"I DON'T HAVE A LICENSE!"

"And whose fault is that?"

Jack bit back a response. Gan Salin made so little sense that arguing with him was like speaking to a toddler. He was insane—hopefully in a good way.

This guy is a headache, Jack thought, deeply irritated. What did I get myself into... At least it's better than dying.

"Let's go! We gotta hurry!" Gan Salin said, pressing the button next to the door. When nothing happened, he scratched his head. The door was ripped off its hinges and tossed aside. A green-skinned woman hovered before them, her brown eyes glinting furiously. She looked to be in her thirties, though she was certainly older.

She wore a blue skirt that didn't sit well on her waist, a white shirt with only one sleeve down, and her hair—also green, just paler—was disheveled. Whatever she was doing before, she had come to stop them in a terrible hurry.

Dryad, Level ??? (D-Grade)
Faction: Amethyst Mountain (D-Grade)
Title: Fifth Ring Conqueror

"What is the meaning of this?" she demanded in a voice that could have been pleasant if it wasn't angry.

"Apologies, Mountain Lord," Gan Salin said, bowing deeply. "This criminal brought allies and tried to escape, but we apprehended him. The Hounds are still fighting. I must get him through the teleporter as soon as possible."

Jack stared at her with the hatred a captured criminal should have. She only threw him a cold glance.

"You damaged my town," she said.

"The Animal Kingdom will pay you back. But please, Mountain Lord, help us reach the teleporter as soon as possible. And, if possible, you should help the Hounds. They're fighting a high immortal! I'm afraid for their lives!"

Gan Salin's voice was filled with urgency and honesty. If Jack didn't know he was lying, he would have spotted nothing out of place. The dryad glared, brows furrowed. However, in the end, she didn't dare risk the Kingdom's rage.

For once, Jack was happy that the Animal Kingdom was a heavy-handed dictator.

"Fine," she said. "Run to the teleporter. I'll assist the Hounds."

She turned into a flash of green that took to the sky. The captain was about to be in even bigger trouble. His worry redoubled. There were still fireworks in the sky.

Captain Dordok had said things would be fine, and had seemed pretty confident... Was he wrong?

Regardless, Jack couldn't help. All he could do was not get captured. He just had to believe in the captain.

Gan Salin turned to him, his face a cold mask of wrathful arrogance. "Come, you worthless scum," he ordered, grabbing the chain that hung from Jack's manacles and pulling. Brock followed from the side, shooting Gan Salin a glare of hatred.

Jack let the chain drag him forward, wearing a look of impotent anger. They hopped off the space shuttle. A crowd had formed around them, full of angry faces, but nobody dared speak to Gan Salin.

The canine may have failed the landing, but at least he'd set them on the right course. They were only two blocks away from the teleporter.

Gan Salin started running, dragging Jack along. He pretended to resist for a bit. Two bulky humans—both at the high E-Grade—stepped out of the crowd and picked him up, running after Gan Salin. One punched Jack in the face. A third man joined, grabbing Brock in a headlock.

Jack saw houses made of gems and rainbow windows, but he wasn't in the mood to sightsee.

They crossed the street in a flash, reaching the teleporter. It was an oven-like building similar to Earth's, except constructed entirely out of transparent, green glass. They stepped in, and the three men dropped Jack and Brock on an empty, circular platform that served as the actual teleporter.

Two comets hurtled down from the atmosphere at breakneck speed, one green and the other brown. It was the dryad and a Hound. They were onto them.

The three men glanced up at the approaching immortals, then at the teleporter's guard. They exchanged a look full of meaning. The guard turned to Gan Salin. "Wai—"

He didn't have time to finish his words. Gan Salin attacked out of nowhere and slashed the guard's throat open. In the same moment, he activated the teleporter. Green motes of light rose around them, forming swirling ribbons.

The three E-Grade humans stood frozen. A cry of utter rage flooded the town from above as the Hound swiped a claw, sending a gray column of power directly at the teleporter. It had the width of an entire building and the speed of a bullet. It crossed the sky like lightning. A second cry followed as the dryad tried to stop the attack, but she wasn't fast enough.

The Hound's attack struck the teleporter, evaporating the building and demolishing an entire neighborhood, killing hundreds. Unfortunately, it was too late. Jack, Brock, and Gan Salin were no longer there.

Stars swirled around a tunnel of warping space. Gan Salin tossed a key to Jack. "Untie yourself, quick! This teleport will be fast!" he said.

Jack didn't dare tarry. The manacles fell to his feet, and before he could rub his wrists, space stabilized around them. The air was filled with voices.

They were in a large hub, with a dozen teleporters arrayed around them. Guards were everywhere, supervised by a chubby D-Grade woman, and a long line of E-Grades of all species waited for their turn to teleport.

The moment the three of them materialized, Salin pocketed the manacles and the key, then decisively stepped out of the teleporter.

They were in a large building that resembled a buzzing, cathedral-shaped train station. Besides the teleporters, there were small starships where people boarded or disembarked. Beyond the station's open door, he could make out throngs of people.

Gan Salin didn't look around. He headed for the only teleporter that had no line. It was the largest of them all, with its platform encrusted by diamonds and a D-Grade feshkur guard stationed before it. Jack scanned him; he belonged to the Hand of God.

Before they could reach, a level 124 human guard stopped Gan Salin. "Apologies, sir, but the man behind you matches the description of a wanted criminal," he said, hand at his weapon's hilt. Said weapon looked like a revolver.

"You're the tenth person to tell me so," Gan Salin replied with annoyance. "There are more E-Grades with pet monkeys out there. He's my assistant, and I am a canine of the Animal Kingdom. Let me pass."

"But his faction—"

"Your head is full of shit. Let me pass, or I'll make sure you rot in Hell."

The guard hesitated for a single second before stepping aside. He stared at Jack the whole way.

They reached the large teleporter, where the D-Grade stretched a hand to stop them. He didn't say anything, just looked. Salin turned to Jack. "The tokens," he said.

Jack reached into his secret pocket—now inconveniently located behind his left thigh—and fished the two golden coins. One had been with him since he beat the black wolves in the Forest of the Strong, which seemed like so long ago. The other was one of the tournament rewards.

The guard received the coins, stared at them for a moment, then nodded. "Brace yourselves," he said, "and good luck. The Hand of God awaits your success."

Jack, Brock, and Gan Salin stepped into the teleporter. Purple ribbons formed around them, far thicker than the ones in the previous teleporter. Jack felt a lurching sensation, like he was falling. And then, the world erupted in flash so blinding that he yelled.

The galaxy warped around them. Space parted where they passed. Stars only appeared as blinks before disappearing again.

Next to him, hovering in the empty void, Gan Salin took a deep breath and sat down on nothing. "Can't believe that worked," he said, smiling. "Feel free to relax. This will take a while."

————

Bomn's heart was filled with helplessness as he looked through the *Trampling Ram*'s cracked window.

Captain Dordok was floating in the void, unconscious. All three of the Hounds had been injured, but only lightly. The captain had tried his best, but with his exhaustion and injuries of the previous battle against the crocodile, he simply couldn't best them.

One of the Hounds held his steel greatclub, admiring the workmanship. The other two approached the ship, still shivering from the tension of battle. Bomn could see their wide grins.

There should have been no reason to fight. The Hounds had no proof, and the captain was a reasonable man. He wouldn't instigate anything.

They only came to blows because the Hounds were itching for a fight. Because they were insane and completely unfit for any job. But the Animal Kingdom let them be. It wanted the terror they caused.

Bomn's hatred burned hotter and bitterer.

The Hounds paused. Their faces went from excitement to rage. They must have scanned the starship with their immortal perceptions and noticed the missing escape shuttle.

Of the two, one shot off in a burst of speed, heading for the planet behind them. Bomn could only hope that Jack managed to escape in time, but there were more pressing matters at hand.

"You colluded with criminals!" the other Hound declared. Her voice was filled with rage and excitement, like she couldn't wait to punish them, though she should have no right to. Bomn knew the law. They were innocent until proven guilty. As long as they denied everything, they should be fine.

If not for the insanity of the Hounds.

"As punishment, your captain will be dragged to Hell, and the Fair Way continent will pay. As for you... You are all guilty. You will be executed on the spot!" the Hound declared. She stretched a claw-like palm, her fingertips glistening like five diamonds of death.

Achilles rushed before her, already wearing his protective helmet. His saber was sheathed, his palms stretched and open. Bomn could see his lips moving without sound. Achilles couldn't project his voice through space, but the Hound could use her Dao to hear him. He was asking for mercy, declaring their surrender, saying they had injured on board, and that they knew nothing. That the law clearly protected them.

His head left his body. Bomn watched it fly away, saw the Hound's body rock with laughter as Achilles froze and shattered in space, leaving nothing behind. A brave man had died, just like that.

"The only law in this constellation," the Hound declared, "is the Animal Kingdom!"

Bomn's mind was buried in grief. He had never felt so useless before. This was unfair. He bellowed deeply with despair, a mere scrap of his mind remaining. "Vlossana!" he yelled. "Grab the helm. Take us away!"

He couldn't see her through his tears, but the ship jerked away, accelerating in the spasmodic way that only newbies achieved. The Hound sent a column of gray force at them, tipped with five diamond-like points. The entire ship shook from the impact, but it remained whole.

They couldn't charge a warp without an immortal on board, but the *Trampling Ram* was fast. It could outrun most D-Grades.

Bomn looked outside the window again. The captain's body was wrapped in red ribbons. He would be taken to Hell.

Leaving him behind drove a stake of pain through Bomn's heart, but this was the right call. The captain had explained this long ago. Suicide wasn't loyalty. Against an impossible fight, it was better to retreat, regroup, and return. Where there was life, there was a way. They would rescue the captain or die trying, but not now. Now, they had to escape.

But it hurt so much.

Bomn bellowed again, shaking everyone in the ship. They were two heavily injured sailors, a non-combat E-Grade, and a non-combat F-Grade. The situation was grim, but they would pull through. He would make sure of that. It was *his* responsibility now.

From the side, Vashter's eyes were full of pain. He said, "I believe in you... Captain."

Bomn hesitated. He nodded, his heart full of grief. That word had never been heavier.

CHAPTER EIGHTEEN
TRIAL PLANET

STARS FLEW BY JACK. THERE WERE HUNDREDS OF THEM, THOUSANDS. GALAXIES swirled in the distance, their spires barely discernible even with his new senses. Something flashed periodically from a distant point, and he saw a column of light stretching up and down from the center of a far-off galaxy.

They traveled through the Milky Way galaxy. There were blue, yellow, and red stars. Some large, and some so titanic that his mind couldn't comprehend their scale. They crossed a dust cloud so immense that it made even those astral giants seem like fish to an ocean.

Their speed was unnatural. They floated through space not at the speed of light, but the speed of thought, untouched by anything. The fabric of space itself was their vehicle.

Jack lost track of time, but it couldn't have been more than a few hours.

When the world stabilized, Jack found himself on a moon. He stood on a large teleportation platform, like the one he'd departed from, except his surroundings were mostly empty.

Before anything else, he fell to his knees and violently emptied his stomach. Next to him, Gan Salin did the same. Brock seemed unaffected. The vomit disintegrated when it touched the platform. Only after a good minute did Jack look up.

A dome of glass surrounded them like an Inuit's igloo, about a hundred feet in height and another hundred in diameter. Outside its walls, he could see gray dirt lined with craters. There was no sky. Space was directly observable from here, like the pictures Jack had seen of Earth's moon.

Perhaps I could go to the moon now, he thought, before realizing he was much farther than any Earth-387 human had ever been in the entire history of their planet. He was a pioneer.

In the horizon, a large sphere rose over the moon. It did not look like Earth. Jack didn't know what he expected, but it was certainly not this. This planet looked... dead.

"Step off the teleporter," a commanding voice reached their ears, cutting off Jack's train of thought. He looked around, then followed the command to step away. The person who called out to them was a human of Earth-199, dressed in a silver uniform with the Hand of God's emblem at the front—an open palm facing the observer, with an open eye in the center.

He was at the D-Grade, as were the other two guards flanking him: one ant-like humanoid—an antfolk—and one that resembled a djinn but was even smaller in size, barely reaching Jack's waist. This last one was also floating on a tiny cloud. Its species was called vonanan.

"Are you expecting more people?" the human guard asked. Gan Salin shook his head.

"Nope. Just us."

"Good." He took out two pieces of paper. "Name, affiliation, and Dao, please."

"Gan Salin, Animal Kingdom, Dao of Insanity," Gan Salin replied. "And my friend here is Jack Rust, Bare Fist Brotherhood of the Animal Kingdom constellation, Dao of the Fist."

Jack glared at him. Salin leaned in, whispering, "Don't worry. The Hand of God doesn't care about the B-Grade faction grudges."

"You told them my Dao." That was personal information.

"We *have* to tell them," Salin said, shrugging. "Everybody does it. And lying to the Hand of God is a terrible idea."

Jack grumbled. "Speak for me like this again, and we go separate ways. Understood?"

Gan Salin smiled. "Perfectly so."

"And the brorilla?" the guard asked. Gan Salin didn't reply, shooting Jack a glance.

"He's my spiritual companion," Jack replied.

"Okay." The guard scribbled down some things. "Does he have a name and Dao?"

Jack glanced at Brock, who frowned but nodded. "Brock," Jack replied honestly. "Dao of Muscles."

The guard nodded, still writing. Unless he was describing their physical appearance in text, Jack had no idea how an immortal could be this slow at transcribing.

"All done," the guard said. "You may proceed."

Another guard stepped forth—the antfolk. "Follow me, please," it said in an odd voice, like it came through a series of long pipes. Jack, Brock, and Gan Salin followed it to the side, where three sleek, dark starships awaited. They were shaped as elongated needles, giving Jack an impression of great speed.

Seeing the starships reminded him of Captain Dordok and the crew of the *Trampling Ram*. He hoped they were okay. They had saved his life.

He wouldn't forget that.

The antfolk reached the first starship, and its door slid open by itself. "After you," it said. Jack, Brock, and Gan Salin entered a cramped space with two lines of seats facing each other. It could fit ten people in total, which gave them some space to move. The antfolk walked to the front, placed its ant-like hand on a glowing blue helm, and the starship slowly rose off the ground. It passed through the entrance of the building—a tunnel-like space covered by a transparent, protective film on both ends—and sped toward the dead planet.

"Is that Trial Planet?" Jack asked. "It looks..."

"Destroyed?" Gan Salin said.

"Yeah."

"It is. Well, its surface. I hear that the inside is pretty colorful." The canine shuffled in his seat. Everybody got only one chance to visit Trial Planet, and unlike Jack, Gan Salin had been waiting for it his whole life. He was beyond excited. His explanation poured out. "Trial Planet is made up of nine rings—hence its other name, the Hollow Planet. Imagine nine hollow planets of increasing size that encapsulate each other."

Jack raised both brows. "Are you telling me that planet has more planets inside it? Like a matryoshka?"

"I don't know what that is, but yes. And they're all hollow. It's like nine worlds nested in each other. The nine rings. As you descend into deeper rings, the danger rises exponentially, but so do the rewards. Trial Planet is filled with all sorts of opportunities, from natural treasures to Dao inheritances."

Jack drew a sharp breath. From a physics standpoint, this nested planet thing shouldn't be possible. Then again, after everything he'd experienced, he was beginning to suspect that the physics he understood was somewhat incomplete. At least, it seemed pretty small for a planet—maybe even smaller than Earth's moon, though size was hard to gauge at this scale.

Brock leaned in, listening to the description with rapt attention. The antfolk didn't seem to care about their discussion.

"What you see now," Gan Salin continued, pointing at the approaching planet's surface, "is actually the first ring. But not really. Research shows that there used to be cities and civilizations there, but now it's just an empty, ravaged hellscape."

"Are you saying someone destroyed that ring? Who would do such a thing? And why?"

"Nobody knows!" Salin shrugged. "Trial Planet actually precedes our galaxy. When the System arrived a million years ago, this planet came with it, and it already looked like this. There has been much research, of course. The most prevalent theory is that this planet used to belong to the Ancients, the fabled race that created the System, but that its surface was ravaged during the crusade against the Old Ones.

"But that doesn't matter, at least not to us," Salin concluded. "Nobody is allowed on the surface anymore. We'll start our delve in specific entrance points that lead directly to the second ring. The first is out of order."

"But the rest of the rings are still okay? They aren't destroyed like this surface world?"

"Exactly. Trial Planet is protected by the System itself. Anyone above the E-Grade cannot descend below the surface. Perhaps this is why the lower rings were spared."

"Hmm. What can you tell me about those rings? What do they look like?"

"They're all unique! The second ring, for example, is the Giant Ring —though I won't spoil any surprises by telling you why. The point of that ring—like most of them—is to find an exit heading to the next. They're hidden under large, monster-infested landmarks and oddities, so if you see one, head directly there and get to searching. There are very few rewards on the upper rings, so just try to get through them as fast as possible. That's what everyone does.

"The third ring—the Barbarian Ring—is similar, though its environment is more hostile, and the monsters stronger. At the fourth ring, the Village Ring, just try to find the village. Things get more complicated deeper down... but you don't need to worry about that for now. Besides, we'll meet again in the village of the fourth ring, so we can talk about it then."

"Meet again?"

"Oh. I didn't mention we would be separated, did I?"

"No. No, you didn't."

"Well, people obviously come here in teams, but the Hand of God doesn't want weaklings to delve far just because of their connections. Everyone is scattered before they enter the second ring. The fourth ring is small enough and open enough that teams can reconvene, though. With your strength, you should be able to make it there. Me too, I hope. Unless I'm unlucky. Then, I'll just die." He laughed.

Jack looked at Brock with worry.

"Oh, don't worry. Spiritual companions aren't separated," Gan Salin hurried to add. "You and little Brock will be just fine."

Brock punched his shoulder.

"Big Brock, I meant big Brock," Salin corrected himself, laughing.

"So Trial Planet is only for combat Classes?" Jack asked.

"Well... Partly. Non-combat Classes can also delve, and they often do, but they have to go through the trouble of reconvening with their teammates at the second ring—which can take months—or surviving alone for some time. For us, it's better to just go solo until the fourth ring."

"I see..."

Jack looked outside the window. They had reached the planet and were sailing over its surface. The ground was ravaged with razor-sharp ravines kilometers in length, like they'd been slashed open by swords. There were craters the size of cities, one of which was shaped exactly like a palm print.

Jack even saw areas covered in multicolored mist, as well as ruins where the shadows seemed to flicker wrong.

Who could have done all this? he couldn't help but wonder.

"So, that's the plan," Gan Salin repeated, drawing Jack's attention. "We meet at the fourth ring's village. If one of us hasn't made it there in a month... the other just keeps going. Okay?"

"Okay."

"And by the way, if you see anything resembling a trial, go for it!"

"What? What do Trials look like?"

"You'll know it when you see it."

Jack rolled his eyes. "By the way, how difficult is it to conquer the entire Trial Planet?"

"Oh, it isn't difficult. It's *impossible*. Nobody has done it before, and nobody ever will—probably."

"Really?" Jack raised a brow. "Why?"

"You'll see if you make it to the eighth ring—which is already highly unlikely, by the way. So, uh, I think this is our stop. Do you see a stop button anywhere?"

The starship slowed. Jack noticed a massive hole dug into the earth under them. It was circular, with a diameter of a few hundred feet, and seemed to stretch down endlessly. It was like a deep dark maw carved into the earth—or just a really large and deep well.

The starship touched down on the land right next to the hole. "Jack Rust and Brock, please descend," the antfolk said. Jack and Brock stood up.

"Gan Salin," Jack said, throwing the canine a complex gaze. "I have no idea what you're thinking, but you saved me. I appreciate that and can confidently say we are no longer enemies."

"Of course not. We're friends!"

"I don't know about that yet, but not enemies. Probably." Jack smiled. "Be careful down there."

"Same to you!" Gan Salin flashed his own smile.

Jack caught the antfolk's gaze and decided not to delay any longer.

He and Brock walked away. The moment they stepped onto the ground, the door behind them slid closed, and the starship took off. Gan Salin kept waving from the little window until he disappeared in the distance.

Jack looked at the sky for a moment. It was red and hazy. The air was stingy, like he was breathing through a lemon. His eyes were watering. "So, this is Trial Planet. What do you think, bro?"

Brock gave him a thumbs-up and a monkey grin. Jack grinned back. "That's what I thought. Let's go! For Earth! For us!"

The hole behind them resembled a gate to hell. They found stairs swirling its edge and climbed down, one man and one brorilla.

They didn't even have a backpack.

CHAPTER NINETEEN

GIANT RING

"Oof," Jack said, panting. He and Brock had just climbed down a staircase that could have reached from the heavens to the earth. He didn't even know how many miles down they'd traveled. Maybe a hundred.

Even for an E-Grade cultivator with almost two hundred Physical, it hadn't been easy. To save time, they'd been jumping from one side of the massive, stair-ridden hole to the other. As if that wasn't enough, his anesthetic had run out halfway, and his self-healing still wasn't done repairing the damage. His hands burned with every jump. He'd had to grit his teeth through the final two hours of their descent.

At least those two hours had given his regeneration time to work. He was mostly fine now, though starving.

"Well, Brock," Jack said, looking around, "I guess we're here."

Now he knew why the first ring was called the Giant Ring. They were surrounded by a forest of gigantic proportions. The trees stretched hundreds and thousands of feet into the sky, with barks the width of apartment buildings. The grass blades reached up to Jack's thigh and Brock's neck, making the brorilla look funny.

Jack felt tiny. It was like he had been shrunk to the size of a large bug and shoved into a forest. At least his gray pants and dark blue t-shirt didn't stick out too much, and his black boots were sturdy enough to protect him from anything sharp on the ground. Brock's only garment, a red pair of shorts, weren't nearly as protective, but forests and jungles were his natural environment. He'd manage.

A deep roar washed over them, shaking every molecule in their bodies. Jack couldn't tell what animal might be making that sound, but he sure as hell wouldn't like to find out.

Brock looked around with wide eyes. They were currently at the base of a long column that stretched from the ground all the way to the sky—or, at least, what passed as the sky here. This ring was a massive cave, with its roof being the underside of the planet's surface, a rock layer of unknown width. It was so high up that it really did resemble the sky—there were even a few clouds drifting about.

Based on how long they'd been descending, the cave ceiling could be a hundred miles tall. The sheer enormity of this space was enough to blow his mind. For a few moments, he was consumed by awe.

What god could have made this... he thought, his gaze lost above.

Enormous mushrooms hung from the ceiling. Each was clearly titanic in size, and they shone like miniature suns. With one of them every few miles, the forest below was illuminated as bright as day. The cave ceiling between the mushrooms was a bright gray, covered in still shadows. Jack wondered if there was night here.

Finally, the air itself was odd. Jack didn't notice it at first, panting as he was, but he eventually caught on. Every breath seemed to fill him with life and energy. His heart beat faster, his thoughts rolled quicker—almost too quick.

Am I hyperventilating? he realized, consciously slowing himself down. I see! The oxygen here is thick. That's why everything is so large.

He'd once read a novel by Jules Verne, *Journey to the Center of the Earth*, which described a giant forest in a deeper layer of the planet. Many subsequent storytellers had been inspired by that, and the deep-earth gigantic forest caught on. Funny how that ended up having a hint of truth.

Only the dinosaurs were missing—for now.

Wait. Jack's eyes widened. Will there be dinosaurs!

He reined in his inner child and biologist. He wasn't here for fun. He was here to punch stuff, meditate on punching stuff, and get stronger.

A second roar echoed through the thick trees. "Was that closer?"

Jack asked. Brock shrugged. "Okay, bro. You know what they say: the first step to getting stronger is not dying. Let's move."

Brock cheered—together, they left the column behind and delved deeper into the forest.

It was nostalgic, in a way. Being lost in a forest teeming with dangerous, unknown creatures. It reminded him of the first days after the apocalypse. Back then, the Forest of the Strong had been a hive of danger. Before he'd conquered it.

Funny how the world moved in circles sometimes. Jack had grown stronger, but so had his environment. Suddenly, he was back to the start. He didn't dislike the feeling. Here, there were no scions with strong daddies, no planetary overseers, no complex diplomacy and rules.

He was just a man in a forest. A predator amongst many. He felt life spread through his limbs. The satisfaction of the hunt. He buzzed with anticipation. His soul, his Dao Seed of the Fist, was shivering. His fists itched. He couldn't help grinning.

He'd conquered the Forest of the Strong and triumphed. It had been his first step onto the path of the strong—the tournament his second.

This oversized forest would be the third.

However, he wasn't alone this time. Jack smiled at Brock, who grinned back. There was excitement in that grin. Brock mirrored Jack's thoughts. For the thousandth time, Jack felt glad to have him. He was the best little bro ever.

But this wasn't the time to ruminate. Jack turned back to the front, on the lookout for the danger that was sure to appear.

He didn't know what to expect. Gan Salin had said this ring wouldn't be too dangerous for someone of his strength. That gave Jack courage, but he still kept his eyes peeled for danger. He crouched through the tall undergrowth, parting grass blades with his hands to pass. His gaze scanned the large branches above, the inconspicuous tree barks, the towering, thick bushes.

He almost didn't see the enemy.

As he pushed a grass blade aside, a hint of black was the only indication he got. He froze, ready to fight or flee. Brock froze beside him.

The ants before him turned to look. They were the size of small dogs, each reaching his knee in height. They were black with hints of brown, along with six thin legs and fierce mandibles that clicked and clacked as they inspected him. Antennae rose from where their eyes should be.

Jack saw three ants at a glance, one behind the other. Looking closer, there were more; far more. They'd stumbled upon a long ant line.

Conqueror Ant, Level 28 (F-Grade)
Conqueror Ants are invasive species that can survive in most environments. Their colonies typically contain hundreds of workers, with larger colonies rising up to tens of thousands, along with multiple queens. If left alone, they will expand at great speed, annihilating anything in their path despite their relatively low individual levels.
A Conqueror Ant colony is considered a peak E-Grade threat. Immediate extermination is advised.

Jack's first reaction was to back up a bit. He was a biologist focusing on evolution, with insects being one of the most fascinating sub-topics. He knew a lot of things about them, and everything came back to him at once. Ants were terrifying.

He did *not* want to mess with dog-sized variants.

The ants' antennae waved, probably spreading pheromones—their preferred way of communication. Jack held his breath.

Eventually, the ants seemed to reach a consensus. One broke off the line to watch Jack and Brock, while the rest carried on, heading to wherever.

Jack took slow steps back, followed by a confused Brock, until they were out of sight. Then, he kept going for a bit.

Brock made questioning sounds.

"Because they're *ants*, Brock," Jack replied. "Trust me. I don't care what their level is, they'll mark us, hunt us down, and overwhelm us by sheer numbers. Plus, ants have incredible strength for their size. If they bite us, goodbye." He shook his head. "No. Better to avoid them at all costs and just find the way down. Gan Salin said so, too: up here, there are few benefits to get. The lower rings are our targets."

But where could the entrance to the next tunnel be? Gan Salin had also mentioned that there were many of them, each usually indicated by some landmark.

"Knowing the System, I'd bet my right arm these ants have built their nest right on top of a tunnel," Jack said. "But it doesn't matter. My biologist sense is tingling; attacking them is too dangerous."

Brock nodded. Whether because he agreed or because he trusted Jack, that was hard to say.

"Let's find a way across the ant line," Jack suggested. "Perhaps we could go over it?"

He looked up. Their ears were suddenly filled with buzzing. A dragonfly zoomed high over their heads, as long as Jack was tall. It was painted in bright colors, almost like a rainbow.

Agathan Dragonfly, Level 56
Contrary to what their name suggests, dragonflies have no relation to dragons. Agathans range in length from 3 to 15 feet. Despite their beautiful appearance, they are deadly hunters. They are carnivorous, fast flyers, highly perceptive, and require a large amount of sustenance to survive. Caution is advised.

This particular dragonfly didn't seem to have noticed them. It darted down from between tree branches and flew into a bush, hiding itself from sight. Jack heaved a sigh of relief.

Suddenly, he was torn. The biologist inside him screamed that every single creature here was a walking dissertation. However, his more prudent parts yelled that insects were fucking dangerous. He'd take dinosaurs over them any day of the week.

Trial Planet was no joke.

"Let's go, Brock," he said quietly. "We should climb a tree and see what's around us. According to Gan Salin, the tunnels are in obvious locations. Perhaps we'll find a few."

"Bro!" Brock said. Then, he frowned. Jack raised a brow.

"What is it?"

Brock's frown intensified. He opened his mouth and closed it again. A moment later, he said, "...Yes."

Jack's eyes widened. "Brock!" he yelled in joy. "You said another word! Yes! That's amaz—"

Buzzing filled their ears. The dragonfly shot out of the bushes next to them like a bullet, mandibles wide open and ready to rip.

Edgar sat in the safety of his study. His desk was filled with orderly stacks of paper, each covered in detailed notes. The window was open, letting in a light breeze and the sight of the far-off mountains—the view from the top floor of the Bare Fist Brotherhood's new headquarters.

However, Edgar's eyes were on the brown ceiling. He was slumped in his chair, neck resting on its back.

He was sad.

Magic was beautiful. It was everything he'd ever dreamed about. When the opportunity appeared, he grasped it with both hands, forcing the world to make him a powerful wizard. He succeeded.

So why were things not as he expected?

Where was the joy of discovery and exploration that accompanied magic? Where were his faithful wizard companions, with whom he would forge a new life? Where were the grizzled professors that would teach him their ways, and where was the childlike wonder of bending the world with the power of will and imagination?

Edgar chased his dream and caught up, but all he found was ugliness. Selfishness. Competition. Hatred, death, and war.

He did not want that. His notes were of theories on how to best weaponize his abilities, but his heart wasn't there. He wanted to make butterflies. To host light shows and recreate the nice little spells of his favorite books. He wanted to be a wizard, not a warrior that happened to use magic.

He'd tried his best since the Integration, all the way from Valville to the tournament, and he succeeded in getting stronger, but that didn't mean he *enjoyed* it.

His notes and research were guided by duty, but his mind simply traveled other paths. There wasn't much he could do about it. Every minute he forced himself to focus was pain. The little moments of peace like right now, when he allowed himself to simply relax, were his final haven.

I hate this world, he realized in a moment of clarity, but I love magic.

How could dreams and reality be reconciled? That was supposed to be precisely a wizard's job. He didn't want to fight. He wanted to research magic and explore its applications, lose himself in the bright world of possibilities. He wanted to master magic and spread the gift to everyone, so that gifted little children would no longer have to suffer in a mundane world that didn't fit them.

Was war the only path to peace? Did he have to live through hell *again* to protect others? When would that end? When would he finally be free?

Edgar did not know, and that scared him. *Help me*, he thought, but no God answered his prayer.

He sighed as he sat up. He would weaponize magic as he was told, but here, where it was calm and safe.

The Forest of the Strong would be safe with or without him, thanks to Sparman, the D-Grade robot guard that Jack got for them. In truth, Edgar should have been in Burkina Faso with Vivi and the rest of Flame River. He could bolster their defenses.

But the Flame River headquarters were at war. Nobody had time for research. He would be reduced to a weapon, called to the front lines all the time, having to risk his life to kill his fellow men and waste his time in under-leveled dungeons instead of progressing his research. He would have to live in an environment he hated.

For once, he had a choice, and he would stay in the Forest of the Strong until he was needed. He was working on his magic every waking second to become as strong as possible and help everyone. He deserved some calmness.

And more than that, safety. Because there was only one thing that truly scared Edgar.

He could live through the current crucible. He could flatten and exhaust himself on the altar of war. He could do the right thing. He could endure years of being at the wrong place because he was powered by the anticipation of the good years to come. When everything was over, he would become a strong wizard and build a wizarding school. It was the dream of his life.

Which was why he feared death. If he endured years of despair only to die before he was rewarded, all would have been for naught. He would have wasted everything.

So he would remain in the Forest of the Strong for as long as possible. While the Flame River and their allies exhausted themselves to conquer as many dungeons as possible, fighting the Ice Peak's forces at every turn, he would study, achieving strength in his room's peace, so he could fight well at the time of need.

Because he deserved it. And if his decision brought casualties, so be it.

CHAPTER TWENTY

THE LAY OF THE LAND

THE DRAGONFLY SHOT AT JACK LIKE AN ARROW THE SIZE OF AN ADULT HUMAN. He turned around as fast as he could, but not fast enough. A set of sharp mandibles snapped at his arm, ripping off a good chunk of skin on the way.

"Holy shit!" Jack shouted, both in pain and surprise. He tried to grab its tail, but it was long gone. It flew behind a tree and disappeared. His ears were still buzzing, and he didn't know if it was due to actual buzzing or because its wings had passed right next to his head.

Brock pointed at Jack's arm, making worried noises. Jack took a glance. "I'm fine. 'Tis just a scratch."

It really was. A long red line crossed his forearm, but it was shallow. His regeneration would handle it. Though that wouldn't cure Jack's anger.

"The fucker!" he shouted, inspecting the surroundings. "It was such a happy moment, Brock. You said a second word! That's worthy of celebr—"

The buzzing intensified. The dragonfly shot at them from above, this time aiming at Brock. Perhaps it realized Jack was tough prey. But Jack was ready. He pivoted and smashed his knuckles into its face, hitting it so hard that the insect burst into a shower of gore around his arm. Only half its body remained, a broken, bleeding husk that fell to the ground.

"That's what you get," he told it, glaring. "Nobody touches my little bro."

Thankfully, the dragonfly had been pretty light, so his hand remained whole. It just bruised a bit. Compared to the maiming from his fists crashing into the space monsters a few hours ago, this was nothing.

"Yes!" Brock cried out, raising his arms in celebration. He pointed at Jack's biceps and made faces of admiration.

"Of course I am," Jack replied smugly.

Hints of movement interrupted them. The grass blades were swaying without wind. Jack and Brock backpedaled.

Brown-black shapes came into view. It was the conqueror ants from before—five of them. They'd probably noticed something and came to check.

The moment they found the dragonfly's corpse, the leading ant's antennae waved frantically. A light, stinging smell, like the remains of lemon juice, assaulted the noses of Jack and Brock, who watched from the distance. It was slightly unpleasant.

The other ants apparently thought otherwise because they crowded the first like there was no tomorrow. One of them grabbed what remained of the dragonfly between its mandibles, easily carrying it despite the size difference, and started walking back—probably heading to its nest.

The rest of the ants fanned out and started searching the area. One of them stared at Brock. He and Jack didn't wait to see what would happen. They bolted away.

The ants searched around for a bit more. Then, after not finding anything else, returned to their lines. Jack watched them from behind a leaf the size of his torso. Even the waterdrops were larger here. He saw one the size of his closed fist.

"Are there only insects around here?" he asked. "No, it can't be. We heard a deep roar before. That wasn't an insect."

Brock nodded in acceptance, then pointed upward. Jack followed Brock's finger with his eyes.

"The treetops," he said. "Good idea. We can survey our surroundings from there. Let's go."

Defeating the dragonfly so easily had curbed his fear a bit. The ants were only F-Grade. He could take them by the dozens if needed. He'd avoided them just for the sake of caution.

No other insects or animals appeared as Jack and Brock made their way to the nearest tree. It was a monumental column of wood and bark reaching higher than trees had any right to. Jack had to tilt his head all the way back, and he still couldn't see its top.

The prospect of climbing this tree reminded him of the endless stairs just before.

"Well," he said, lifting his sleeves, "no time like the present."

And so began the climb.

Jack wasn't a climber before the Integration. He still wasn't. However, his physical strength was greater than his body weight would indicate, letting him move easily on the almost vertical trunk.

There was also no shortage of outcroppings or handholds. The bark was rough, reminding Jack less of a tree and more of a climbing wall.

It still wasn't easy. His first goal was the tree's lowest branch, a highway of wood stretching overhead, but even that was far away. He kept his body close to the trunk to defend from errant wind gusts. Halfway up the climb, he saw a termite—an F-Grade insect that ignored them.

Brock, on the other hand, was right at home. He dangled from outcroppings with one hand, jumped from one handhold to the other, and generally ran circles around Jack. He seemed glad to be the better party for once. Jack had the strength to do those things, too, just not the skill. He re-appreciated just how useful his Fistfighting skill—and the subsequent Iron Fist Style—was, for giving him the skill to go with his ever-increasing stats.

When he took a glance behind him, he saw an endless forest stretching far and wide. The trees were enormous, and they were many. He also saw multiple insects going about their business, including ants, beetles, and bees.

If this place has wasps, he thought, I'm fucked.

Regardless, he kept climbing. When he finally reached the first branch, he was panting. It must have been a thousand feet in height.

Not bad for an amateur climber, he thought with pride. Perhaps I should get a skill about this. Then again, immortals can fly.

"Are you okay, Brock?" he asked, wiping the sweat off his brow.

Brock looked back and raised a brow. "Bro," he said, as if he meant, *you can't be serious.*

"Yeah, yeah. I know." Jack looked up. He wasn't slow in climbing, but Brock was at least twice as fast. The problem was, Brock wasn't nearly as strong as Jack. A random dragonfly here could be a mortal opponent. They had to stick together. "Two minutes of rest?" he asked.

"Yes," Brock replied, eager to use his shiny new word. Jack noticed his accent was a bit hard, like he was saying every word with a frown.

Nothing attacked them on the branch, which was a welcome change of pace. Two minutes later, they set back out.

The branches were more densely arrayed. Jack took his second break on what he estimated was two-thirds of the way up—already so high that there might have been clouds if this was Earth. But there weren't any clouds here, only moisture.

Where does it come from? he wondered. If not above... Could it be from below?

The higher they went, their view broadened, but they remained under the forest's canopy. Then, they entered it, and were enclosed in the tree's foliage. All they could see was leaves.

The climb went on. After the first half an hour, Jack had fallen into a rhythm: reach, grab, pull, repeat. He didn't need to think as much now, besides keeping an ear out for any suspicious buzzing.

He used the time to consider this forest. This ring, really.

Everything was enlarged here. By a lot. His inner scientist yearned to explore the forests workings. Jack recalled the knowledge stored in his brain after years of study.

Higher oxygen ratio leads to larger species, he remembered. Most animals can't handle this, but insects can. Arachnids, scorpions, and all their relatives too. But not larger animals. A magnified elephant would just collapse under its own weight. So would a dog, probably.

That explained why he had seen only insects so far, though the roar from before remained a mystery. Insects had highly durable bodies and could handle an upscale. Most larger animals, not so much.

Am I in the insect kingdom? he wondered. I bet I could outline ten publications in a day if I wanted to.

He wouldn't do that, of course. Becoming a superhuman immortal sounded more important than getting a slightly higher h-index.

However, one thing kept bugging him—pun intended. Earth, by itself, had endless diversity when it came to insects. Ants alone had ten thousand recorded species, including many exotic variants. So why did all four insect kinds he'd observed so far—ants, dragonflies, bees, and termites—resemble their Earth versions so closely?

Had they managed to converge? Were insects the hallmarks of evolution, just moving in circles? Were they adapting too much, but only the most resilient variations would survive the eons?

Or were they moved here from somewhere else?

The galaxy's history went back a million years, and Trial Planet preceded it. A million was a lot by human standards, but it was nothing compared to the endless eons that Earth had weathered. The dinosaurs were eradicated sixty-five million years ago, and life had existed on the planet for billions of years. If Trial Planet had been established a few million years back, at what evolutionary stage had its original inhabitants been?

Or, a less scientific theory entered Jack's mind, *is there magic at play?*

This nested planet was absolutely not natural. It was artificial, and there had to be some sort of magic holding it steady, otherwise it would just collapse in on itself. What if there was also magic that kept the rings relatively unchanged over the eons?

If Trial Planet was an ancient testing ground, as Jack assumed, this would make sense.

His ruminations were cut short when he entered a new, thicker layer of leaves. Climbing became more difficult. Brock let out an exclamation from somewhere above. Jack accelerated, eager to see what made Brock so excited...

...and broke through the leaves. He was in the sky. And he lost his breath.

The tree they'd chosen to climb had been one of the tallest ones. He could see the forest stretching around him, a canvas of fluttering green. Leaves swayed in the moist wind, while winged creatures he couldn't identify—either birds or insects—swirled in the distance.

The ceiling stretched over his head, still impossibly high. It was the underside of the planet's surface layer, stretching endlessly in all directions. He *knew* there was a curve, but he couldn't see it. From where he looked, it was perfectly straight, its ends lost in mist.

The shiny mushrooms hanging from the cave ceiling were like a host of miniature suns, and brown stone columns rose intermittently from earth to heaven, like toothpicks supporting a mountain. Jack could see dozens of them. Across the planet, there must have been tens of thousands, if not more.

"Just... Just who could create such a thing?" he asked aloud. The wind grabbed his hair and pulled it back, exposing his full face to the view. Jack took a deep breath. His lungs filled to the point of almost bursting. He felt so energized.

Then he paced himself, remembering that too much oxygen wasn't good.

Brock was by his side, and he pointed in one direction. Jack turned his gaze over.

A few miles away, a massive mound of upturned dirt rose between the trees. It was shorter than them, of course, but it still resembled a large hill in size. It was an anthill. Its surface was teeming with workers, rushing everywhere in semi-orderly lines. There must have been hundreds of them, possibly thousands, and even more inside the nest.

It seemed extremely dangerous.

According to Gan Salin, large landmarks—like this ant hill—indicated the position of tunnels heading down to the next ring. But Jack didn't want to infiltrate an oversized ant colony. He'd just have to find another landmark.

He looked around. He found none. He looked back at the ant hill.

"Oh, fuck me."

CHAPTER TWENTY-ONE
SPOTTING OPPORTUNITIES

THE MASSIVE ANT HILL DOMINATED THE SCENERY. IT ROSE BETWEEN THE TITANIC trees, shorter but thicker than all of them. It was built on a bed of dirt, and its slanted sides were teeming with conqueror ants. There were hundreds of them, possibly thousands.

Jack had no illusions of being able to rush the place. So what if the ants were only level 30 or so? There were so many, they could simply body-pile him and bury him under their corpses. Moreover, he understood that the world didn't play nice. There were bound to be stronger variants inside the ant hill, conveniently waiting out of sight until he attacked.

Unfortunately, it didn't seem like he had a choice. Gan Salin had mentioned that the tunnels to the next ring hid under special landmarks, and the ant hill was the only such thing he saw.

Should I wander the forest until I find another? he wondered. It was certainly a possibility. The issue was, there was no guarantee the next tunnel would be easier to access. And testing would take time.

"What do you think, Brock?" Jack asked, leaning on one of the tree's higher branches. "Do we stay, or do we go?"

Brock hung from a nearby leaf. One of his hands held onto the leaf's stem, bending it to support his weight, while the other scratched his armpit. Then, he let go of the leaf, landing on the wide branch under-neath. He smashed his fists together.

"We fight?" Jack asked.

"Yes!" Brock replied. His throat still wasn't used to speaking human, but he was getting more proficient as time passed. Jack was optimistic. If Brock could say two words, he could say all of them. Eventually.

"Alright. We can scout the ants a bit. Outside the nest, I don't think they can do much to us, even if they attack."

It was funny. Once upon a time, he had to risk his life to take down the level 15 earth bears, facing each of them in drawn-out combat where the tiniest misstep could lead to death. Now, the prospect of facing a swarm of level 30 monsters didn't even bother him.

Heck. Even his little monkey bro could easily beat up any earth bear, or even their leader, the rock bear. After all, Brock was now a level 37 Elite. He was even stronger than his own father.

Going down the tree was harder than going up. When they made it, Jack's entire body was sore, while Brock seemed fresh as a daisy.

"Bro!" he said, jumping up and down in excitement.

"Bro," Jack replied, laughing. The light of the mushrooms hadn't dimmed at all during the few hours they'd spent climbing. Was there no night here? Or was the day just longer than Earth's?

He hoped for the former, as he couldn't see in the dark. The faster they got out of here, the fewer chances they would sink into a long night. Just one more reason to hurry.

Jack and Brock crouched into the underbrush. They moved around leaves the size of cars, hid themselves in waist-high grass. The ground was wet, even muddy in places, and the air smelled of moisture. It was also filled with extra oxygen, but Jack and Brock kept their breaths slow.

Intermittent buzzing reached their ears. They couldn't tell where it came from, or what sort of bug produced it. They were trapped in an ocean of green. Predators could hide anywhere—hundred-foot centipedes crawling along the grass, praying mantises hiding between leaves, wasps descending from above. All sorts of creatures, known and unknown, could be lying in wait.

The only thought keeping them inside the greenery was that, as soon as they were out of it, they would be visible to all would-be preda-tors. But was one enemy in the dark really better than ten in the light?

"Let's go in the open," Jack whispered. "I can fight off these things, but only if I see them coming."

Brock agreed, and they slipped out of the bushes into a more open part of the forest. Besides the grass around their legs, they had good visibility of their surroundings.

Jack instantly felt much better. "Now we're talking. Keep your eyes peeled for surprises, Brock."

The brorilla saluted like a soldier. *Where did he learn that?* Jack wondered.

Fortunately, no threats appeared on the way, though they did see three bees fly overhead, all around level 60.

They made it back to where they'd first seen the ants. They weren't there, but after a bit of searching, they found them. As they approached the root of a tree, the grass stopped, revealing the ants in full display. Their mandibles were just as fierce as before, and from this position he noticed spaced-out short hairs covering their body, which were lean and wiry, with a thin torso and a thick behind.

They truly resembled Earth ants, just magnified a thousand times.

Their target was a hole in the base of the large tree. The ants streamed in endlessly, antennae raised and mandibles poised to strike. There were dozens of them, all disappearing into the hole like stones dropped into the sea.

Jack narrowed his eyes and focused on his hearing. Thuds and low hissing screams came from inside the tree. The ants were attacking something, but what?

The answer became apparent soon. A conqueror ant emerged from the hole, carrying the corpse of a different ant. This one had heavier mandibles and was many times larger than the conqueror ants. Jack couldn't inspect it, as it was dead, but it sure as hell seemed to be a different species.

They're attacking other ants! Jack realized. Then, could it be...

He turned his gaze to the back of the conqueror ant line. A massive form lumbered in the distance, slowly approaching. It was twice as large than most of the other conqueror ants and had a pair of wings at its back.

A queen!

Conqueror Ant Queen, Level 39 (F-Grade)
Queens are the core of a colony, with each laying hundreds of eggs per mating season.

Jack had focused on the part of the description unique from the last, though he really didn't need the System's confirmation. Once upon a time, he had been a PhD candidate in biology. He was also focused on evolution. As a result, insects were his area of expertise. He'd studied them for years.

That goes to say, he knew what was happening. Some ant species were hostile against their fellow ants, especially if they were a different species. If they located another colony in their territory, they would attack and destroy it.

However, some species were even crueler. They didn't just destroy an enemy colony. They invaded it, culled its numbers, and stole their eggs. They would take the eggs back to their own colony, and when they hatched, they would use pheromones to brainwash the captured hatchlings into slaves.

Additionally, if they conquered a colony, they would send one of their own queens into the enemy colony mid-battle. The queen would take advantage of the chaos to reach the chamber of the enemy queen and murder it in heated combat. If it succeeded, it would then coat itself in the pheromones of the dead enemy queen, essentially taking her place as the ruler.

The enemy ants would tend to her and her brood, unaware that their real queen was long dead, until she and her children killed them all.

The animal kingdom was brutal—or, as some would say, nature was metal. No wonder the Animal Kingdom faction was so tyrannical.

Jack and Brock watched the invasion from behind some leaves, unable to tear their eyes away. Soon after the conqueror queen entered the enemy nest, a few conqueror ants emerged, carrying green, pulsating sacks—the enemy brood. They skittered back toward their own nest.

The attack died down soon after. The conqueror ants stopped coming, and a few emerged from the nest to retreat. Some of the opposing ants chased them for a while, giving Jack a chance to inspect them.

Carpenter Ant, Level 37 (F-Grade)

Carpenter Ants usually make their colonies inside trees. Their heavy-set mandibles can be used to dig through wood, hence their name. They aren't particularly aggressive, but their bite can easily cut off limbs.

He barely suppressed an exclamation. He knew carpenter ants! They were one of the most widespread variants on Earth. Did the System translate their true name to something he would recognize, or did many sapient species individually settle on the same name for these ants?

The latter made sense. Carpenter ant wasn't the most difficult of names to come up with.

But in that case, Jack wondered, could conqueror ants exist on Earth as well, just with a different name?

He thought back to everything he had seen. He inspected the ants' behavior and appearance with a biologist's eye. There were many details he noticed but didn't care about before—their multi-segmented antennae, their uneven thorax... Coupled with their highly invasive behavior and other patterns, he quickly narrowed it down to one species.

Argentine ants! he exclaimed mentally.

They were one of Earth's most invasive ant species. In fact, human traveling had accidentally spread them around the world, and they were currently at war against pretty much all other ants. The various argentine ant colonies didn't fight each other. They used superior, cruel tactics and stratagems to kill any other ants they came across, slowly but steadily conquering the insect world.

They were assholes.

Assholes Jack had studied. New excitement bubbled in his heart—the equivalent of *finally* using the Pythagorean theorem outside school. He could put his theoretical knowledge to good use!

Take that, society! Who's a nerd now? he thought with a smug smile.

Ants were scary, but less so if he knew their ins and outs. In fact,

Jack was half-certain they could sneak through without much trouble. He knew some tricks.

However, even with a plan, infiltrating an ant colony was a terrifying prospect. Things would be much easier if they took the time to pick off the ants, hunting and killing them by the dozens outside the colony. That would make infiltrating much easier.

But did they have time? Gan Salin had said they should hurry, that these higher rings had no opportunities, only danger.

"Hmm," Jack muttered, cupping his chin. "What do you think, Brock? Should we risk hurrying, as Gan Salin advised, or take our time whittling them down so it's safer?"

Brock considered it for a moment. He then gave Jack a doubtful look.

"What? You disagree with something?"

Brock nodded.

"Why?"

This was trickier to respond. Brock pretended to run in place, then trip on something and fall on his face. He then wagged a finger from side to side.

"Hurrying is no good? But Gan Salin said—" Jack's eyes flashed. "Wait. Brock! You're a genius!"

Brock stuck out his chest—though he seemed a bit confused, too. Jack continued.

"Why should we hurry? Gan Salin said what he said, but there has to be a reason for this ring's existence. If I was the creator of Trial Planet, I wouldn't go through all this trouble just to test the survival skills of people. I could easily do that *before* sending them to Trial Planet. No, this ring can't be useless. Even if there aren't any treasures here, there has to be *something*. And I think I see it. Look around you, Brock."

Brock looked around, seeing nothing. He scratched his head.

"Exactly!" Jack said excitedly. "Mindless enemies ranging from the middle of the F-Grade to the low E-Grade. Doesn't this remind you of something? It's goblins!"

Brock reached out to touch the human's shoulder. He twisted a finger around his temple, then gave a gentle smile. He seemed to say, "You're crazy, but that's okay."

"No, Brock." Jack laughed. "What were goblins? Weak enemies, stupid, and lacking humanity. *Level up material.* That's why they were so common during the Integration, and *that's* why this ring exists. It's a sharpening stone! It's so weaker E-Grades can gather levels and battle experience, using their superior minds to outsmart and overpower the insects. That way, they level up fast, and they practice real combat at the same time. The creators of Trial Planet tried to mimic the Integration's mechanisms!"

Finally, Brock's eyes lit up a little. Jack grinned.

"Why should we hurry? This ring may have no treasures, but it's a treasure trove by itself. Master Shol warned us against using experience balls in the E-Grade, and the deeper rings of Trial Planet will no doubt require us to have extraordinary strength. Where else will we find such a perfect hunting ground? Moreover, a hunting ground where *I know all enemies by heart.*"

He smashed his fists together, eyeing the far-off conqueror ants. "Let's go, Brock. It's time to fight to our heart's content." He grinned savagely. "It's time to level up."

CHAPTER TWENTY-TWO
BROCK THE WARRIOR

IT HAD BEEN A WHILE SINCE JACK STALKED PREY FROM A BRANCH. SOME THINGS remained the same. The thrill of the hunt, the adrenaline rush of watching without being watched, the tension that came from the possibility of battle erupting at any moment.

But, of course, most things were completely different than last time.

Jack wasn't stalking goblins or earth bears, but giant conqueror ants the size of large dogs. He wasn't hiding on an actual branch, but on the stem of some gigantic plant. A torso-sized leaf hung in front of him.

He was also much, much stronger than he used to be. His prey... not so much.

And he had a friend this time. Brock was next to him, keeping his body close to the branch and his breathing deep and slow. Soundless.

Brock's body, now reaching up to Jack's waist, was already toned with muscles that his Dao of Muscles made all the more apparent. Brorillas were made for strength, not stealth.

Still, he tried. He watched Jack's movements and copied them, learning the basics of stealth from his big brother.

A line of conqueror ants marched thirty feet under them. The ants were five in total, all between level 25 and 30, and the reason why Jack and Brock were stalking them was to make sure they were completely detached from the rest of the colony. That way, they could fight without worrying about enemy reinforcements.

Five ants weren't many, but this was just a first experiment. Jack would attack and fight for a bit, scout out their patterns and tactics—see what surprises they hid.

"Go," Jack whispered. They crawled off the stem and onto the plant's main body, then slid down like firefighters on a pole. The only sound was the gentle rubbing of their fingers against the stalk. Their fingers were sticky, but that was only a minor inconvenience.

They followed the ants in stealth, then circled around them. Jack looked to the left and right, making sure they weren't watched. He made to step in the open.

A hand grabbed his arm. He turned to find Brock, standing there with a hard gaze. He pointed at himself, then the ants.

"You want to fight?"

Brock nodded.

In truth, the brorilla was more than strong enough. He was a level 37 Elite. He should be able to handle at least two or three of them.

Jack still hedged. Brock had never seen real combat. He was strong, yes, but not enough to steamroll the opposition. And if something went wrong, he didn't have the regeneration Jack had.

Jack couldn't help but worry.

"Are you sure?" he asked. "This could get dangerous. We don't know what they can do. Why not let me fight first, and you can participate next time?"

Brock shook his head. "Nu," he said—probably trying to say no. He pointed to his heart, then his head, then down.

"You must fight now?" Jack translated. "You are tired of watching?"

Brock nodded. He flexed his biceps, then shook his head sadly.

"I see," Jack said. "You are strong, but you want to be more than that. A warrior. You want to take risks because a coward could never rise?"

Brock nodded again.

"Okay," Jack said. "I understand how you feel. If I scout them out first, that's not real battle, it's target practice. You aren't wrong... However, you must learn to walk before you can run. Your attitude is commendable, but five ants is too much for your first real battle. I'll take out three of them. How does that sound?"

Brock shook his head, then raised two fingers.

"...Fine. But your dad will kill me if anything happens to you, so be careful, okay? Do you promise?"

Brock's face split into a monkey grin. "Yes."

"Okay..." Jack threw him a final look, then took a deep breath. Suddenly, this easy battle was full of tension. He was worried sick. But if he didn't let Brock face real danger, he would never mature. Jack couldn't protect him forever. "Be careful," he repeated, then stepped into the open.

———

Brock was flooded with excitement. His body shivered. His fur was rising.

He stepped after his big brother, feeling every muscle in his body flex in anticipation. His first real battle. It was finally time for him to become an adult.

The only other opponents he'd fought were his little dog bros in Integration City, but they were too weak to count. Only now could he feel it. The thrill of battle. The fear that made him grin. The sharpening of the world, the total clarity and thirst for battle that came with risking his life.

What his big bro always felt.

Now, it was Brock's turn.

Big Bro released a mighty cry. The ants stopped and turned. Brock sensed the power that flooded Big Bro's body, so great that it filled Brock's mind with terror. It was strength. *Power.*

Big Bro shot out, falling on the ants like a rock from the sky. A set of mandibles wrapped around his arm, but they could barely pierce the skin. Two punches shot out in an instant. Two ants fell to the ground, their heads cracked open.

The three remaining ants shuffled around, then opened their mouths and released a shrill sound that made Brock frown. The smell of ash filled the forest—the smell of the ants' fear.

They turned and tried to run. Big Bro didn't pursue them. It was time for Brock to act.

He stood in the ants' way, facing down their barreling bodies and mandibles snapping at the air. His heart shook—but his mind muscles were too strong, and they overpowered the fear. They turned it into power. His limbs burst with strength, and his mouth released a cry that contained his resolve to fight to the death.

Brock would no longer be weak. He would no longer be abandoned by his family—even if Father claimed it was for his own good. Brock knew better. They had discarded him because of his weakness, because Father was ashamed of him.

But no more.

The ants arrived, reaching up to his chest. Brock's world changed. Everything slowed down, becoming less detailed. He became faster.

He stretched out both arms and jumped in.

They bit at him. Mandibles snapped, barely missing his face or fingers. They weren't fast enough. Brock slapped one ant so hard it spun around, then caught the second in a headlock. It struggled, but he was stronger. He swung it around from its neck and crashed it into the third ant, sending them both tumbling.

The first ant returned to the fight, but the other two were gone for the moment. Brock let it snap once, then grabbed its mandibles in one hand and held them shut. He bent under it, grabbing the ant's underbelly with his other arm. He placed his shoulder under it, and he *pushed*.

The ant wrestled. Its face moved from side to side, desperately trying to dislodge his hand, but he kept it tightly wrapped over the ant's mandibles. It tried to squirm out of his grasp, tried to bend its legs to stay on the ground, but Brock was stronger. His core and leg muscles flexed with power, straining, and he pushed harder. He yelled. The ant gave way.

Brock rose to his full height, flipping the ant on its back. He also let go of its mandibles. The ant squirmed on the ground, snapping left and right as it struggled to right itself.

Brock brought his hands together, then raised them over his head. His entire body pulsed with power. His muscles tensed, clearly visible under his short brown fur. With a mighty cry, he brought his hands down with all his power, smashing them into the ant's thin abdomen.

It exploded.

With a sickening crunch, the ant broke in two, snapping like a twig. Yellow blood erupted from the point of impact. The ant only made a low sound before dying, and immediately, it smelled like dirt.

Brock didn't have time to celebrate. He jumped forward, sensing the burst of air as a set of mandibles snapped behind his back, then whirled around. The other two ants had recovered and were pursuing him, desperately trying to catch him in their mandibles.

Brock wasn't a fool to let them. His mind spun, coming up with a plan.

As they came at him from the left and right, he unexpectedly stepped forward. They both missed, snapping on either side of him, and he wrapped his arms around them. Now, he held the mandibles of both ants shut under his armpits. The ants struggled and failed to escape in time.

Brock fell back. The ants rose. Their mandibles dug into the soft soil, getting lodged there, while Brock rolled upright. He began smashing his fists into one ant's underbelly, cracking its spine with every hit. The ant snapped. It fell to the ground, lifeless.

The final ant managed to extricate itself from the soil and turned to face Brock. However, it was now alone, and Brock was a menace. It tried regardless.

The mandibles shot forward. Brock sidestepped, letting them pass him harmlessly. He grabbed the ant by the spine and raised it into the air. It squirmed helplessly. With Brock holding it from the middle of its back, it couldn't reach him at all.

Brock bared his fangs. He brought a second hand to the ant's spine, holding it steady. Then, he gritted his teeth. His muscles flexed. His entire body tensed. His grip was iron. Hundreds of pounds of force pulled the ant's spine toward either side until, with a massive *rip*, the entire ant was pulled apart.

Brock let the two pieces fall to the ground. He stood on the remains of his enemies, uninjured. He had achieved victory. Honor. He was a warrior. A true brorilla.

He raised his face to the sky and unleashed a loud holler of triumph, shaking the nearby leaves as he beat on his chest. The excitement was more than he'd ever felt. He'd triumphed! He felt alive!

Brock looked aside, searching for Big Bro, who was staring with a mix of satisfaction and wonder.

"That was pretty brutal," he said. Then, before Brock's heart had time to drop, he continued, "But you won. I'm so proud of you, Brock. I knew you could do it. You are a true warrior!"

Brock cheered harder. Big Bro cheered with him, and for a moment, the forest echoed with their joy.

Then, it echoed with the sounds of marching. They both looked in the same direction: toward the anthill. An army of ants were streaming their way, and they were... more than Brock could count on his hands and feet.

"Good," Big Bro said, stepping forth. He cracked his knuckles. "My turn. Stand back, Brock!"

Brock obliged, ready to admire his big bro's strength, and he wasn't disappointed.

Big Bro yelled, then ran into the ant army. His strength and speed were overwhelming. The few mandibles that managed to bite him could only inflict superficial wounds. He was a maelstrom of violence, destroying ants left and right. They tried to pile on him, but they weren't enough.

He ripped through them. For a short while, the forest rained yellow blood. It was carnage.

CHAPTER TWENTY-THREE

THE BEAST THAT ROARS

Jack stood over a field of broken corpses. Ant corpses. He raised his gaze, going from their drying yellow blood to the dirt mound that dominated the distance. He tightened his fist.

After the pent-up frustrations of getting cheated and chased by the Animal Kingdom, letting loose was nice. This wasn't even his first ant swarm. Or the second.

System, he thought, show me my progress.

Name: Jack Rust
Species: Human, Earth-387
Faction: Bare Fist Brotherhood (E)
Grade: E
Class: Fiend of the Iron Fist (Elite)
Level: 60

Strength: 204 (+)
Dexterity: 204 (+)
Constitution: 204 (+)
Mental: 23 (+)
Will: 23 (+)
Free points: 30

Skills: Iron Fiend Body (II), Ghost Step (I)
Dao Skills: Meteor Punch (II), Iron Fist Style (I)
Daos: Perfect Dao Seed of the Fist (early), Dao Root of Indomitable Will
Titles: Planetary Frontrunner (10), Planetary Torchbearer (1)

For most people, leveling through the E-Grade took years. Decades. They had to find monsters at the right level and at large quantities, which was made more difficult by the fact that everyone else was searching too. As a result, most E-Grade cultivators took high-paying jobs, hunting the odd monster wherever they found it, slowly trudging through the levels. Eventually, most got the money to buy E-Grade experience balls, but by that point, they were so used to the peaceful life that giving up everything to advance was difficult.

Jack, on the other hand, was surrounded by abundant prey at all the right levels. He had hordes of middle and high F-Grade enemies, as well as E-Grade ones under every second stone. Moreover, his power helped him slay them effortlessly.

He had risen by six levels in one day. He'd also made slight progress in his fear aura skill, though he was currently prioritizing levels.

"Not bad for a day's work." He smiled. "Right, Brock?"

The brorilla yelled a cheer in monkey. After defeating those ants at the start, Brock had been beside himself with joy. He kept flexing his muscles and pointing at himself with pride. Jack shared in the joy.

Harambe would be proud... he thought with a gentle smile.

Brock couldn't level up like Jack could, as the System still considered him a monster, but he could gain battle experience and Dao insights. Fighting allowed him to use his muscles in new ways, sharpening his Dao of Muscles. Jack could see him pondering at times, taking breaks to sit on rocks with his fist under his chin.

He couldn't stop wondering how Brock's Dao would progress in the future.

They had also discovered a large stream with clear water, as well as a tree with apples the size of living rooms. Sustenance wouldn't be a problem no matter how long they stayed here.

After that, they'd spent most of the day fighting conqueror ants and scouting out their patterns. Small parties of five to nine ants would leave the colony at random intervals, spreading out in all directions to find food. If they succeeded, they would bring it back to the colony. If the food was too much to be carried by a few ants, they would summon a host of a dozen workers to help them.

If they didn't find food, they would keep searching until they died.

When one of those raiding parties ran into strong predators—Jack and Brock, for example—they would scream as loudly as possible. They would also release a flood of pheromones. The sound alerted other ants to come in the general direction of the battle, while the pheromones had shorter range, guiding the reinforcements to the exact point of combat.

These reinforcements usually contained around two dozen ants— there was no soldier caste in argentine/conqueror ants, so they were all the same. It was a number large enough to overpower most low E-Grade insects, but not enough to defeat Jack. To him, they were just walking bags of levels.

Fifteen such hunting groups later, he'd slain hundreds of ants, and managed to reach level 60. Unfortunately, his leveling speed had begun to stagnate. F-Grade opponents could only take him so far.

Brock had also practiced and was now able to face five ants at the same time, but he, too, had reached his limit. He'd even gotten injured in the last fight, and he now sported a gash on his right upper arm. Jack had tied it with a strip of his dark blue shirt, which was now so dirty he chose to take it off, returning to the bare-chested look he'd donned in the Forest of the Strong.

It brought back memories.

"Thirty stat points..." Jack muttered. "That's a lot. What do you think, Brock? Time to allocate them?"

The brorilla cheered. Jack smiled.

"Okay. Now, let's see. Master Shol said I should keep my Physical balanced until I have a reason not to, so all Physical points are split evenly between the three sub-stats. He also said I should keep an 8-1-1 distribution between my main stat—Physical—and the auxiliary ones —Mental and Will. To maintain that distribution, I should allocate... Hmm..." He frowned. "Oh boy, this is calculus all over again. You don't happen to have pen and paper, do you, Brock?"

The brorilla didn't respond, too busy playing with a flat stone he'd found. Jack didn't blame him.

"Okay then. Let's approximate. Physical should be eight times more than the others. If I raise Mental and Will to 30 points each, then Physical should be around 240. Hmm. I don't have enough points for that, but it's close, and putting them at 28 or 29 points is just... Ugh. Okay. Let's do that. I'll just put the next few levels into Physical as well."

Before he could change his mind, he allocated the points.

Strength: 220
Dexterity: 220
Constitution: 220
Mental: 30
Will: 30

"Ohh! Brock, check this out! Round numbers everywhere!"

Brock cheered in the flattest way Jack had ever heard.

"Hmph, spoilsport. If you ever become a cultivator, we'll see who's excited about numbers then."

Brock snorted as if to say, "That is never happening, bro."

Two striped, yellow shapes shot down from the sky. Buzzing filled the air. Jack looked up only to find a stinger right above his face.

He stepped back. The stinger almost scratched his nose as it descended at the speed of a bullet and buried itself in the soil. Jack came face-to-face with a terrifying, black-and-yellow creature.

He ignored it for now.

The second wasp came at him from the side. His hand grabbed the thin stinger midair and yanked, turning the entire creature mid-flight and slamming it into the first one. They rolled on the ground. He didn't let them stand.

The forest sounds disappeared. The lush greenery lost its vibrancy. Purple swirls gathered around Jack's fist, and it smashed down on them both.

Meteor Punch, he thought.

The world exploded on impact. The wasps screeched as they were torn apart, sending pieces of flesh and yellow blood flying everywhere. One stinger clinked on a nearby stone.

Where the wasps used to be, only a blackened crater was left.

"Fuckers," Jack said with irritation, shaking his hand. "You just don't learn, do you?"

Ants weren't his only opponents in the forest. Throughout the day, they'd been ambushed by dragonflies, wasps, beetles, even a horse-sized praying mantis. Thankfully, they were low level, which let Jack handle them easily as long as he kept his guard up at all times. Only the praying mantis had been a slight challenge, being level 70 with wicked scythe arms, but even those arms couldn't resist a Meteor Punch at point-blank. After it was disarmed, the rest was history. At least, they all attacked Jack first, as he represented a larger target than Brock.

Those ambushes had contributed significantly to Jack's leveling speed. In fact, he was actively looking for more of those praying mantises—he hadn't managed to find any.

As for the wasps, he just hated them on principle.

"What do you say, Brock? Wanna travel a bit farther away? The ants are no longer leveling me."

"Yes."

"Excellent. Let's go!"

They left the pile of dead ants and two wasps where they lay.

The forest was gigantic, but they were fast. Even with Jack matching Brock's pace, they were zooming through the titanic trees, jumping from root to root or running on the leaf-covered soil.

Jack ran at the front, keeping an eye out for danger. He was actively resisting the level-up arrogance that gnawed at his caution. Despite his strength, he was not the apex predator here. Not even close.

For example, there was a large beehive hanging from a tree branch near the anthill. A massive, yellow hub of death and honey. If those bees wanted to, they could skewer him easily. And, of course, there was still the—

A deep roar echoed throughout the forest. Leaves shook, the ground shook. *Speak of the devil.* Jack clicked his tongue. *The big guy.*

These roars came in random intervals. He still had no idea what beast produced them, but he also didn't *want* to find out. Even insects were E-Grade here. A beast that could make the ground shake... It was probably beyond Jack's abilities.

Unfortunately, the forest made it difficult to discern the direction of the roar. For all Jack knew, they could be heading right into it. And was it louder than normal?

Thinking to that point, he signaled Brock to slow down. They came to a stop. "I think this is the wrong direction. The roar got louder."

"Yes," Brock agreed.

"We should head the other way."

"Yes."

They were in agreement, yet before they could move, the roar came again. It was different this time. Less a declaration of supremacy and more a cry of war. Jack jumped and looked around, but he saw nothing.

"What the—"

A third roar came, followed by stomps that shook the ground, along with crashing sounds. A pained growl came shortly afterward.

"The beast is fighting. What could stand against it?"

The roars and crashing sounds kept coming. Brock perked his ears, then looked to the right. "It's that way?" Jack asked. "Okay. Let's go."

Brock nodded.

Going to witness the battle of a massive beast sounded dangerous—and it was. But they weren't here to take the easy way out. Opportunities and danger came hand in hand. If they didn't dare to take risks, they would never defeat the Planetary Overseer.

Jack and Brock darted through bushes the size of buildings. The ground was soft, with the occasional leaf under their feet, but they were too light to make them crunch. Green parted before them as they made haste.

Two minutes later, the roars intensified. The very air shook, and many insects were running the opposite way. A trio of wasps even ignored them to escape faster.

Jack and Brock were inside a bush, but they'd slowed down. They shouldn't be spotted. Carefully, he parted a leaf to witness the battle beyond.

His breath caught in his throat.

That's... That's not a beast!

A green-skinned giant stood between the trees. It held a large club and must have been at least fifty feet tall, if not more. It was hairless, only wearing a loincloth around its waist, and its eyes held no glimmer of intelligence. It resembled a wild animal. When it opened its mouth, yellow teeth were revealed, and buckets of saliva flew out. The roar that escaped was the same one they'd been hearing all the while.

Forest Giant, Level 118
Forest Giants are bestial humanoids that inhabit forest biomes. Their main habitat is the Giant Ring of Trial Planet. They can reach up to a hundred feet in height, are fast, resilient, and extremely strong. Moreover, their sense of smell is heightened, able to pick out prey from a mile away.
Many aspiring cultivators have found their end under the clubs of Forest Giants. They find you before you find them.

Jack's blood went cold. If they had tried to approach this creature when it wasn't fighting, it would have smelled them coming, and they would have had to outrun it. There was no way he could match a level 118 creature in combat.

Fortunately, it was currently too preoccupied to notice them. Red blood streamed from where its left ear used to be, its bare chest was covered in shallow cuts, and it was limping. Oddly, hints of frost surrounded its chest wounds.

Three cultivators stood against it, fully focused on the giant. They didn't seem to have noticed Jack.

One was a man with long, dark hair, wielding an extremely long, sharp sword. The second was a young-looking woman in a white robe, whose silver hair fluttered in a non-existent breeze. Her outstretched arms were covered in frost to the elbow, while snowflakes danced around her open palms. The third and final cultivator was a towering minotaur in full plate armor, who was currently standing in front of the forest giant, seeming tiny, and roared back.

Jack inspected them.

Human (Earth-74), Level 104
Faction: Wide Swirls (B-Grade)
Title: Gifted

Human (Earth-74), Level 121
Faction: Wide Swirls (B-Grade)
Title: Wide Swirls Prodigy

Minotaur, Level 109

Faction: Animal Kingdom (B-Grade)
Title: Resilient

CHAPTER TWENTY-FOUR
TRUE CULTIVATORS

"HOLY SHIT!" JACK WHISPERED. "BROCK!"

A second face emerged from the leaves, right next to his. Nobody would notice them in such a heated battle, anyway.

The giant roared again, shaking the entire forest. It raised its club high, then brought it down on the minotaur, who raised a tower shield.

The clash was cataclysmic. The earth moaned. The wind stirred. Even the titanic trunks around groaned a bit against the force of the giant. Jack was horrified. Even at this distance, over a hundred feet away, the ground shook under his feet, and his ears rang from the sound.

Holy shit.

The minotaur's allies were unbothered. As soon as the giant committed to the attack, the swordsman burst into motion. He was a human with long, dark hair and a narrow blade longer than he was tall. He wore a dark cloak with jagged edges, as if battle-tattered.

His feet pounded the ground. Instantly, he was next to the giant, and he slashed out. His blade slid over green skin like a razor whip. Blood spurt out. A long red line was carved into the giant's exposed ribs, and the creature screamed in pain, a sound even harsher than its previous roars.

The moment it opened its mouth, the witch acted. Ice extended from her fingertips, forming thin, smooth lines that materialized through the air like snakes. They reached the giant's open mouth in a heartbeat and dove inside. Its eyes widened in pain and terror. It tried to scream again, but only blood rose from its throat. Jack didn't even want to imagine what was happening in there.

At the same time, the giant's club rose from the ground. The minotaur was revealed under it; crouched, panting, and clearly battered, but still in good shape. His shield remained steady, ready to defend against any attacks.

Jack couldn't believe his eyes. That giant had attacked with the power of *at least* a peak E-Grade. It had struck hard enough to break a hill—and this minotaur defender just... took the blow.

Despite the hits it had received, the giant wasn't dead yet. It snapped its mouth shut, breaking the lines of ice, and whirled its club around to hit the swordsman, but he easily jumped past the blow. The three cultivators returned to their original positions, facing the giant with no injuries.

The giant tried to growl, but it winced. Whatever those ice lines had done to its throat, it wasn't good. It looked ready to keep fighting, but the result was already clear. They would just keep torturing this humanoid beast until it dropped dead. This wasn't a battle. It was a cold-blooded execution.

In fact, Jack suspected that any one of these three could fight the giant by themselves. They were high E-Grades, and additionally, they came from B-Grade factions and had earned the right to enter Trial Planet. They were undoubtedly stronger than normal high E-Grades. Way stronger than Jack himself.

And they were cold-blooded hunters. Merciless and efficient. They showed zero emotion or hesitation as they whittled this poor giant to death.

Jack felt growing terror. He only just realized he'd been frozen, watching this battle like he wasn't in danger. But he was. He needed to get the hell out of here before these people noticed him. Not only were they strong and ruthless, but one of them came from Animal Kingdom, Jack's enemy.

The giant swung its club overhead. Jack didn't stay to watch. He silently slid the leaves back to their original positions, then grabbed Brock under his armpit and made a mad—silent—dash toward the anthill. Brock didn't complain. If Jack had to guess, his blood was also frozen solid.

Even as the ground shook under his feet and the giant's desperate whimpering was cut short, Jack didn't look back. He kept running.

High E-Grade beasts that could smell him from a mile away. Ruthless, mighty cultivators. And who knows what else.

This forest was dangerous. He had to get the hell out of here.

And go where? he asked himself. The next rings will be even more dangerous. The monsters will be stronger, and so will the cultivators...

Even if he grew strong enough to fight strong people like them, he couldn't handle three at once.

I need to find allies, he realized. *Gan Salin and whoever else... I won't last long by myself. By ourselves*, he corrected himself, looking at Brock. Brock, still held under Jack's armpit, gave a thumbs-up.

They had already crossed several miles, approaching the anthill. The sounds of combat had disappeared, but Jack still didn't feel safe. Those people hadn't come from the direction of the anthill, that was for sure. So could they be headed there?

I need to hide and wait, Jack concluded. He looked around, then up. His eyes shone. "Brock. We're climbing!"

They were close to the anthill, next to a tree shorter than most—but still a thousand feet tall. Jack rushed there, threw Brock on the hard bark, then started climbing. He even went at the opposite side of the tree, so if those three were approaching, they wouldn't see him.

This time, he was trying to be fast. The bark flew under his feet, one handhold giving way to another in an endless cycle of reach, grab, pull, and repeat. Soon, Jack made it to the first branch, only to find Brock waiting there. Both were panting hard. It couldn't have been more than two minutes. Last time, it had taken thirty.

They were safe now. Up here, they could hide until the three cultivators went away. Even if they passed right underneath, it was virtually impossible to find Jack and Brock.

Unless the cultivators had some sort of detection magic, but in that case, what could Jack do? He'd just die.

He raised his head and came face-to-face with a bee. He almost shouted. Its low buzzing was clearly present now that he paid attention —he'd only missed it due to the volume of his thoughts.

Brock must have missed it too, because he jumped and yelled the moment he turned around. "Quiet!" Jack hissed. "Don't worry. It's just a bee."

The bee stared at them from a few feet away. Jack inspected it.

Silent Bee, Level 59
Silent Bees live in tree hives, usually in forest biomes. They are neither aggressive nor territorial. Their only battle instinct is self-defense, which makes them ideal for raising in captivity. Their honey is considered a delicacy in many cultures.
The buzzing of their wings is much more discreet than other bees, hence their name.

Jack had seen this description before. There were many such bees in the forest. He just hadn't fought them before for two reasons. One, they were pretty friendly, according to their descriptions, and biologists loved bees anyway.

Two, he'd spotted a big-ass nest on a tree close to the anthill. Who knows how many bees lived here. If he harmed one, maybe a hundred would come to kick his ass, and he wasn't about to risk it.

However, the bees never approached him either. This was the first he saw from up close. So why was it here?

Jack looked at the bee suspiciously. It looked back at him with exactly the impassiveness one expects from an insect. It didn't attack. It only landed on the branch near them, presumably deciding to rest.

When the bee landed, the buzzing sound didn't stop. Jack did a double take. Its wings had stopped moving. So where was the buzzing coming from?

He thought back to the giant hive hanging from a tree near the anthill. And he was *on* a tree near the anthill. He had only been looking at the bark while climbing.

"Oh, hell no..." he muttered. He reached the edge of the branch in three steps, then looked down. And there was the beehive. Right below him. Dozens of bees flew around it, all around level 60. There were so many that the usually low humming of their wings was audible as a droning buzz.

Jack really wanted to break something. "Un-fucking-believable," he cursed. "I... Fuck. What sort of terrible luck is this?"

He'd almost ran into a predator, then escaped three others, and now he suddenly found himself basically sitting on a giant beehive that could fill him with more holes than Swiss cheese. The only thing keeping him alive was their friendliness, but who knows what kind of misfortune would break that?

Sitting on a bomb was highly stressful.

Brock was scared too, but Jack watched his eyes slowly calm down. He seemed to have found inner peace—perhaps his bravery muscles were hard at work.

Jack took a deep breath, too. *I'm panicking*, he realized. *Calm down, Jack.*

He took another deep breath. Then a second. A third.

When he opened his eyes, the bee was still there, not attacking them. The giant was dead. Even if the cultivators came in this direction, he was well-hidden. They couldn't spot him up here.

And the bees weren't hostile.

He took a final deep breath, then relaxed. The situation was tense, but he was safe. And, if things went south, he would just have to find a way out.

His mind was calm now. Surprisingly, when the fear of the other cultivators was stripped away, another emotion was revealed: excitement.

Jack could not deny that he loved strength. It was his beacon in the darkness. Now that he had seen these people and witnessed how strong they were, his heart was jumping around with elation like a child window shopping.

He, too, wanted to become strong like that. To shrug off the giant's attack like it was nothing.

A fire had been lit inside him, and it reminded him of his impossible time limit.

"What are we even doing, Brock?" he asked. "We have to get stronger as fast as possible, and yet, here we are, hunting ants." He shook his head. By now, it took a lot of ants to give him a single level.

Soon, he would have to uproot entire colonies. It was no longer efficient —and, most importantly, it gave him very little experience Dao-wise.

However, if he could find a place like this, except with slightly stronger monsters... A place like the next ring...

"Here's the plan, Brock," he told the brorilla, more to gather his own thoughts. "We wait here for an hour. If the cultivators don't show up, we climb down and sneak through the anthill to reach the second ring. We've already stayed here for too long. Is that fine with you?"

Brock considered it. "Yes, bro."

"Okay. Then we—Oh! You connected two words to form a sentence! Nice going, Brock!"

The brorilla smiled widely and Jack found his worries swiftly evaporating.

"Okay then. Let's just wait a bit."

And so they did. Jack sat down, keeping one eye on the bee and the other on the tree trunk, just in case something tried to sneak up on them. He also kept his ears open.

Brock sat next to Jack and sank into meditation. Jack wished he could do the same.

There they waited, not daring to look below. The minutes ticked by. Half an hour passed. Jack had calmed down completely by now, embracing the fist's resolve that things would either work out or they wouldn't. Brock must have found a similar truth, because he was calm, too.

"Do you think it's safe?" Jack asked.

A deep, loud roar answered. Jack seized, but this wasn't the cultivators. It was the giant. *But I thought it died!* he wondered, then chided himself. *Idiot. Of course there's more than one. Maybe the cultivators are fighting it, too.*

A few minutes went by. No more roars came, indicating that there wasn't a battle going on.

The giant's roar came again, then descended into an oddly intense growl before going silent. *Poor guy,* Jack thought. *The cultivators must have found you. That sucks. Best of luck.*

As another minute passed and no more roars came, Jack began to wonder if the giant's odd growl was because it *smelled* the cultivators. *Poor guy's walking to his death,* he thought, shaking his head with pity.

Another roar came, though unlike the rest, this one was pretty fucking loud, like the giant was screaming in his ear. And it hid a sense of triumph.

Jack got goosebumps. "Oh..." These giants could smell prey from a mile away, and he wasn't that high. "Come on. You have got to be kidding me."

He walked to the edge of the branch and looked down. And there, staring at him triumphantly, was a green, club-wielding giant.

CHAPTER TWENTY-FIVE
THREADING THE NEEDLE

"You have got to be kidding me," Jack said in disbelief.

A hundred feet below him, the giant grinned, revealing a set of sharp, yellow teeth. Its eyes stared into Jack's, and there was no emotion there, only malice.

Forest Giant, Level 122

"Great. And it's even stronger than the last one!" Jack cursed out loud, still unable to believe what was happening.

Brock, on the other hand, was very much up to speed. He shot to his feet and looked at Jack for instructions. He seemed ready to go down fighting.

Jack bit his inner lip. He couldn't defeat it. Its level was simply too high. One hit from that club would flatten him like a fist pancake.

"Bro," Brock said, his gaze serious. He mimicked running. Jack shook his head.

"Its description says it's fast," he replied. "I think staying up here is our best shot. Maybe it can't climb."

But that's not safe either, he thought. Even if it can't climb, what are we supposed to do? Wait here until it grows tired? Will it ever? And what if the cultivators come here to investigate, then wonder what the giant was hunting? They'll tear us apart. That Animal Kingdom minotaur will eat me alive.

Does the giant want to eat me alive?

He looked back down. The giant's teeth were sharp like a carnivores. It was even salivating. Jack gulped. *It wants to eat me alive. Fuck whoever decided to put giants in an insect forest.*

Oh. That's why it's called the Giant Ring.

Unfortunately, trivia about Trial Planet wasn't very helpful right now.

We must escape, he thought. But how? We can try to run, but it will catch us as we climb down. Maybe I can fall on it like a meteor? Or will it baseball-club me into the cave ceiling?

At least it can't climb, so we have time.

Come on, Jack, think. What do we have? A guy who fists a lot, a buff brorilla who can say two words, the height advantage... What else?

The bee stared back at him. Jack felt like a lightbulb just shone over his head.

The bee's wings shook a bit like it'd read his thoughts. But that was impossible. Right?

"Brock," Jack said quietly, trying to act nonchalant. "I have an idea. Prepare to run, okay? I will count to—"

The tree shook a bit. Jack looked down. The giant had abandoned its club and was hugging the tree trunk with both arms, slowly but surely making its way up. In scale, it was like a human baby climbing a normal-sized tree, except they were both a hundred times larger.

"If you can climb, why wait until now!"

The giant growled, its face stuck to the tree as it struggled to climb. It wasn't good at it, but it was trying.

"Wow, fuck that guy," Jack said in anger. "And fuck this forest. We go at three. Ready? Three."

He turned and smashed a Meteor Punch into the unsuspecting bee, tossing it down from the branch. He mentally apologized—at least he'd taken care not to kill it. The droning buzz from the beehive at the end of the branch intensified. Jack didn't have a moment to waste.

Both his fists shone purple. "Meteor Shower!" he shouted, feeling stupid for calling his move out loud, but tension called for tension.

Meteors rained horizontally. The giant stopped, looking at Jack with incomprehension. The few bees hovering around their hive darted for him, but his meteors were already on the way.

The beehive was only attached to the branch by a thick column of wax. Jack's Meteor Punches exploded into it, cutting deep into the material. It broke on the second meteor. The beehive fell.

Jack held his breath. Brock's eyes widened. The giant followed the falling beehive with its eyes, then watched as it crashed and shattered against the ground. Tons of wax and honey fell into a pile. An army of a hundred bees buzzed out of it, ready to give their lives to annihilate the offenders.

Some noticed the bees attacking Jack on top of the branch, but that scene was far away. The giant was closer and larger. Their many eyes fell on him. The giant stared back and its skin tightened.

They lunged at the same moment the giant let go of the tree, falling back to the ground and picking up its club. It roared and swung. Just like its description said, it was fast. Its club whistled through the air despite its size, carving a line through the cloud of bees and injuring dozens, but they were too many.

They fell on him like a new coat. They covered him from legs to neck, each stinging him and injecting their venom, along with their life. Bees died after stinging. The giant roared in pain, smashing the club into his own body in a vain attempt to escape.

Meanwhile, Jack was fighting eight bees by himself. They were almost too many. Each was the size of a desk and zoomed around like it weighed nothing. He could keep up with their speed, but not if they came from every direction at once.

These bees were all at the same level he was. He couldn't afford to hold back. For the first time since arriving at Trial Planet, he was going all out. Meteor Punches exploded everywhere. His fists shot out even faster than the bees, and they struck like ogre-wielded sledgehammers. The Iron Fiend Body helped him twist and bend his body to difficult angles, and his perfect Dao Seed imposed his will onto the world, skewing reality in his favor a tiny bit.

The Iron Fist Style guided his movements, flawlessly transitioning from parries, to punches, to dodges. He danced amidst the stingers.

He grabbed one and turned it into another, forcing a bee to impale one of its own. Both bees went down. He ducked under a stinger and turned to avoid a second, shooting an uppercut into the abdomen of a bee and making its innards explode from the other side—Drill had been absorbed into Iron Fist Style, but its principle remained.

Level Up! You have reached Level 61.

As he drew back his hand, a bee flashed to his right and another to his left. He elbowed one. The other impaled his leg at the thigh. He screamed out in pain. It wasn't just the injury. A hint of venom flowed into his blood, causing searing pain all over his leg. At least the stinger had run clean through, causing most of the poison to drip from its tip to the bark below.

The bee dislodged itself with a sickening sound, but the stinger remained, sticking out of both ends of his leg like a sword.

Jack's eyes went bloodshot. Iron Fiend Body was already working to restore the wound, but it would take time. He left the stinger in his leg to contain the bleeding and kept fighting.

His fist smashed into a bee mid-flight, exploding into it like a meteor and clipping its wings. It tumbled down to the forest floor. Meanwhile, in the corner of his eye, Jack saw Brock dancing with a bee. He'd somehow managed to dodge its initial sting and grab onto the stinger with all his strength. He held on to it, flailing wildly as the bee flew around to shake him off, easily carrying his weight.

It flew away from the branch. The only thing separating Brock from the ground was a hundred feet. He let out a monkey cry and held on even tighter, straining his muscles to not fall off. His fingers were slipping off the stinger. It was only a matter of time.

Seeing that, Jack's mind was filled with urgency. He Ghost Stepped to the front, slipping behind the remaining bees. He struck one in the same movement, penetrating it with his fist, then back-fisted another. A weaker version of Meteor Punch appeared around his hand, blowing the bees head off.

Level Up! You have reached Level 62.

He panted. That was the last bee other than the one Brock was fighting. A stinger was still in his leg, limiting his movements, but Brock was struggling. He was only level 37, fighting off a level 60 monster. And he was dangling over a deadly fall.

Jack ran to the edge of the branch and jumped. The air screamed in his ears. Suddenly, he was a long way from the ground, and the only thing holding him aloft was his rapidly dwindling momentum.

He kept his eyes focused on Brock and the last bee. He was on the right course. Brock saw him, and his gaze was equal parts glee and terror.

The bee saw him too and its flight shifted. It jerked to the right to avoid him. Jack could no longer reach. Even if he struck it with a Meteor Punch, Brock might not survive the fall, and Jack couldn't fly.

Or could he?

"GHOST STEP!" he shouted. The world obeyed. His body moved contrary to physics, changing directions midair and dashing to the right. Unlike when he used the skill on land, the strain this time was immense. He immediately felt out of breath. He couldn't do this again.

But he didn't need to.

He fell on the bee, grabbing its wings and fighting to stay there. It tried to shake him off, but his fist smashed into its face, obliterating it. Its wings stilled as it fell from the sky.

"Brock!" Jack shouted, reaching out. Brock reached out, too, and managed to grab his arm. Jack pulled him in a hug. "Hang on!" he shouted.

They smashed against the forest floor like a cannon ball. Leaves went flying, and a dull thud echoed in their ears. Jack's Iron Fist Style told him to roll, but he couldn't do that while holding Brock. He landed on his feet. His knees creaked but thankfully held. Brock was ripped off his arms, tumbling on the soft soil with a pained grunt, but he looked fine.

"Oh, thank God," Jack said. He grabbed Brock under his armpit and bolted off. Behind him, the floor was littered with dead bees, some flattened and some simply crawling without their stingers, but the giant wasn't in better condition. Its skin was bloated and red. Bees covered it still, walking all over it without stingers and trying to bite, determined to do everything they could to save the hive.

The giant opened its mouth and screamed. It couldn't walk

anymore. Its club was on the ground, covered in the blood of its cracked palm. Its eyes met Jack, and they were full of hatred. Then, the giant collapsed.

Jack didn't look back anymore, either. He ran into the trees, determined to open as much distance as possible. Not only was he afraid of the bees seeking him for revenge, but the battle had been extremely loud. The cultivators would certainly come to check, and more giants might arrive, too—they were probably attracted to sound, which would explain why this giant had arrived in Jack's territory so soon after its predecessor died.

Jack's leg throbbed. The stinger was still there, burning him on every step, but he powered through the pain.

They had to get the hell away.

He ran until the sounds disappeared beside him. On the way, he met a bunch of conqueror ants but ignored them. He was injured and exhausted and needed a moment to rest and recover.

Suddenly, more notifications appeared.

Level Up! You have reached Level 63.
Level Up! You have reached Level 64.

Was it due to the giant's death? That was interesting. Jack willed all twenty points he'd gained in that bout into Physical. A little bit of extra energy entered his body, giving him the power to reach his destination.

There was a spot relatively near the anthill that he'd marked for future rest, back when he thought they'd stay here for days. It was a little cave carved in the base of a large tree trunk. It seemed natural. And, most importantly, empty.

The moment he made it there, he let Brock down and sat on the ground, leaning his head back and panting hard.

"Fuck," he said. He fished in his pockets for the strips that remained of his old shirt. When he grabbed a handful, he pulled the stinger out, gnashing his teeth to avoid screaming. He tossed it aside.

Idly, he wondered how he'd managed to run this far with a wrist-thick hole through his leg. Had the stinger missed all vital spots, or was it somehow due to Iron Fiend Body and his Dao Seed?

The sight of his streaming blood drew him back to the present. He wrapped the cloth strips around both ends of the wound and tightened them to slow the bleeding. The Iron Fiend Body's regeneration would do the rest. He'd be fine in a few hours as long as no cultivators, giants, or mega-insects attacked them in the meantime.

"I hate this place," he muttered. "Listen up, Brock. The moment I recover, we trick the fucking ants, and then we're out of here."

CHAPTER TWENTY-SIX
WALKING ONE'S PATH

THE HOURS TICKED BY. JACK AND BROCK REMAINED IN THEIR LITTLE CAVE between the tree roots, waiting out the consequences of their battle. They'd blocked the entrance with a big rock, casting them in near-total darkness.

This time, Brock was the one on guard duty. He sat on the soil with his ears perked up, ready to act at the first hint of danger. They had to be ready for anything. There could be colossal worms digging under them, or the tree roots could come alive, or another giant could smell them and come running.

Fortunately, it seemed that the two dead giants were the only ones in the vicinity. No other roars had come in hours. Nothing moved.

The reason Brock was on guard duty wasn't because Jack was injured. It was because he wanted to meditate.

There was something about killing monsters. Pushing yourself to the absolute edge to survive, facing an enemy knowing that one of you has to die, tasting the dread of death when all seems lost, and the triumph when you come up with a way to turn things around.

Even the simple act of butchering the conqueror ants gave Jack insights. They bubbled into his soul, pulled to the surface by the here and now, the total clarification of battle, and inflicting death.

Exterminating ants in direct combat, even if easy, was a world of difference from using experience balls. Jack was even beginning to suspect that these insights weren't all natural. Perhaps he absorbed more than levels when he killed things. Or maybe it was psychological.

Whatever the case, the fact remained that the day's fights had given him things to consider. There were thoughts flitting in the back of his mind, just waiting for him to give them proper attention so they could unravel.

Currently, he had nothing else to do while healing. Now was the time.

He recalled his battles against the ant armies. Well, not really armies. More like batches. Each was made up of around thirty ants, including the scouting parties he attacked until they called for reinforcements.

He had taken down fifteen of those batches. Almost five hundred ants, each stronger than anything in the Forest of the Strong besides the black wolves. Back then, every battle had been an uphill struggle. He'd only briefly experienced superiority at times. Most battles involved him outsmarting stronger opponents. The goblin tribe, the earth and rock bears, the wolves... Even if things ended up in heated combat most of the time, Jack was always the underdog.

Not this time, though. He was the hunter now. The conqueror ants were prey, and he was picking them off by the dozens. The battles against them were trivial matters. He was simply on a whole different level.

And there was something about those battles. His soul, the Dao Seed of the Fist, called out to him. Something was off, a tickling sensation at the back of his mind, but what?

He sank into the feeling.

What was the fist? The fist represented a path. Power. War. The carrier of his will. The unyielding resolve to grab the world and bend it to his wishes. To not accept things as they are, but rather change them. To not step back. To choose a path and fight for it until his knuckles bleed. To stand in the center of the world, bare and vulnerable, and demand that his voice be heard. To struggle.

And yet, what struggle was there in stomping ants?

Jack was stumped. The dichotomy was clear. The fist, or at least his fist, didn't include bullying weaker opponents. Had he miss-stepped?

No. He hadn't. The conqueror ants were simply on his path, and he had no reason to show them kindness. They were unfeeling, cruel, murderous machines. Stepping on them to advance further wasn't the most gracious thing to do, but it was part of his path. The Dao of the Fist agreed. He could feel that.

So, why was there a contrast? Why was this hunt clearly part of his path, but it somehow didn't fit into its current definition?

Jack became excited. By solving this riddle, he would be one step closer to mastering his Dao.

He acknowledged the excitement, then suppressed it to keep going. Meditation required a focused mind.

He thought back to what his fist signified. In one word, it was struggle, and there was no struggle in defeating the ants.

But there was overwhelming power.

He was on to something. Jack's mind spun in a whole new direction. He'd had similar thoughts in the past, and he always felt he was close to something but never reached the end of that thought process.

Power was at the core of his Dao. How did it relate to the ants?

He'd destroyed them because he was powerful. Against him, it didn't matter if they were tiny or dog-sized, they remained ants. It was their weakness that defined them. Their lack of power.

They had no mind of their own. They acted cruelly, but that was just their instinct. They were neither good nor bad—they were furniture. However, even if they did have a mind, so what? They were too weak. They would have no choice but to bow to Jack's will, hope and beg for his mercy.

When those cultivators butchered the forest giant, did it not want to live? Of course it did. But its opinion didn't matter, because the weight of opinion is power, and it didn't have any.

Power makes the world go round. Morality, desire, decision, emotions... Everything is supported by power. Only when one has power do they really exist. A powerless person can be a saint or a devil at heart, but it doesn't matter, because they are completely unable to affect the world, because they are powerless. Anyone with superior power can easily overwrite them.

Only when two creatures are on the same level of power does anything else matter.

Power is the foundation of everything.

The moment Jack that thought, his soul pulsed. His eyes snapped open and he was ejected from his own thoughts, and his realizations swirled and combined inside his soul, coalescing into the shape of a dark fist that moved in tandem with the other one, the dark blue Dao Root of Indomitable Will.

"Oh, man," he said, suddenly fully aware. "I messed up."

He looked to his status screen, noting that the stat points of his last four levels were there, invested in Physical and bringing it up to 240, but the most important change was in the Daos line: Dao Root of Power.

Another screen popped up by itself.

Congratulations! You have developed the Dao Root of Power.
To see through the veils of the world. To reach its deepest secrets. To understand that power is the foundation of all, the only truth of the universe. That is the one true path.

"Nooo!" Jack groaned. "I didn't want another Dao Root."

Brock walked up beside him and made monkey sounds. Though the darkness was deep, their eyes had adjusted somewhat.

"Because it's dangerous!" Jack replied. "I wanted to connect my previous Dao Root to my Dao Seed. Then, I would carefully plan on which extra Dao Roots to get—and how many."

Brock cupped his chin in question. He raised one brow and half a thumb.

"Yes, it is nice, and it feels suitable to my Dao, but I have two now! Don't you remember? Very few people manage to break through with two Dao Roots. Three is an incredible achievement. Four is the stuff of legends." He sighed. "I now have two... I was planning on either this or three, to be honest, but I wanted to research them first. Maybe find someone with an adjacent Dao to mine, or even a B-Grade faction with records on the Dao of Fist—like the Exploding Sun, which surely has people in Trial Planet. Now, I have to be reaaally careful not to acciden-tally develop a third Dao Root."

Brock shrugged.

"First world problem, I know." Jack smiled weakly. "But it's a problem nonetheless. I don't want to be careful. Too bad success takes temperance."

At this, Brock finally agreed. He nodded, then pointed to his flexed biceps and Jack's head.

"Practice my brain muscles? Yeah, I can do that. They're pretty strong, you know! I almost have a Ph—" Brock threw him a handful of dirt. Jack was startled, then laughed. "I've been saying that a lot, haven't I? Okay, okay. In any case, I suppose you aren't that wrong." He scratched the back of his head. "More power—heh—is always a good thing. I have a feeling this Dao Root will fit nicely with my Dao of the Fist, so it's as good a bet as any. Plus, I can probably use it offensively, somehow. I just have to be a little careful not to get a third one by accident."

Brock smiled. This time, he gave a double thumbs-up.

"Thanks, bro!" Jack smiled back. "You sure have your way with words. How did you turn me around so fast?"

Brock shrugged smugly. They exchanged a fist-bump.

"Okay," Jack said, putting the new Dao Root aside for the moment. He noticed he was almost fully healed. They would be ready to move soon. "Let's go over the plan again to make sure it's fool-proof—though we are no fools, right bro?"

Brock gave a big thumbs-up.

"Good. Now, remember all those ants we killed? Nobody came to pick up the corpses, at least until a few hours ago, so there will probably be many of them still around. All we have to do is..."

———

Professor Margaret Rust opened her eyes. She stayed in bed for exactly one minute, finding peace in counting down the seconds before getting up. These days, even her dreams were full of tension.

She got dressed and went to her bathroom. Three minutes later, with her face still dripping cold water, she descended to the living room. A hot cup of coffee waited on the table, poured by an assistant exactly two minutes ago—she didn't have time to brew it herself.

She took a sip, then sat on the couch. The clock on the wall indicated it was five minutes after six o'clock. Right on schedule.

"Good morning. Progress report," were her first words of the day.

"Morning, professor," the woman sitting across her—Emily—replied. "We got one dungeon during the night. The Ice Peak alliance also got one. However, they annihilated our team in that dungeon—the Stinky Marsh in China."

"I see. Survivors?"

"None."

"Was there anyone important?"

"No, professor. It was a dungeon of lesser significance. Our team was a group of ex-special forces from Egypt."

"I see. Send my condolences to Emir, and promise that Egypt will undertake more favorable assignments from now on."

"Understood, professor."

The professor sipped her coffee. Its warmth did little to alleviate the pain in her heart. She was talking about dead people like they were nothing more than assets... But the survival of many hinged on her efficiency. Between failing her alliance and numbing her heart, she would always choose the latter.

"Any news from the other major factions?" she asked.

Emily hesitated. The professor raised a brow.

"Yes," the brown-haired assistant finally replied. "Our two contacts in Ice Peak reported the presence of high-ranking lycan merchants in their headquarters. Both reports were made independently; we believe they are accurate."

"Lycan merchants means the Animal Kingdom."

"Yes. We believe they arrived to negotiate a further alliance with Petrovic."

"Bad news."

They were already losing the cold war. If the Animal Kingdom chose to assist the Ice Peak, they might as well pack up and retreat their entire alliance to the Forest of the Strong, where Sparman held the fort.

The Animal Kingdom couldn't interfere formally, but they had already shown how much they cared about the Star Pact. They could pressure the Merchant Alliance to raise prices for the Flame River and decrease them for the Ice Peak. They could send Fesh Wui and the elef scion back to Earth—since there were no E-Grades on the planet presently, just those two would steamroll anything Vivi and the professor threw at them.

"However, there are no further indications yet," Emily hurried to add. "We believe their negotiations are lagging."

"All the better for us. We must develop at least two combat E-Grades before the Animal Kingdom steps in, preferably three. I don't suppose Edgar broke through last night?"

"He did not. He says he's almost there, but... he's been saying that for a week now."

"Okay. Not much can be done. If push comes to shove, perhaps the pressure will tip him over the line." Another sip. "Inform Vivi to send her elites into the fray. Since Petrovic is willing to sellout our planet, we cannot afford to delay."

"She will complain."

"We will also send out the Rattlesnakes."

Emily looked up from her notes. "We're pulling them out of training so soon? After investing so much in them?"

"We knew our deadline. It has arrived. Now, we must increase the pressure and hope our cultivators bloom rather than die. But make sure they keep up their combat training until deployment."

"Very well." She scribbled down a few lines.

"Instruct everyone that we must overtake the Ice Peak in dungeons within two days," the professor continued. "Activate half our sleeper agents to disrupt their forces in dungeon boss battles. No doubt they will do the same. That's why the Stinky Marsh squad got eliminated, right?"

"We are unable to confirm that. But we suspect so, yes."

"We can only fight fire with fire—well, ice with fire." The professor allowed herself a chuckle. "If there's nothing else, let's move to resource allocation. With the Rattlesnakes entering the fray, we have some open slots. Allocate one high-end dungeon to Emir. He will ask for more, but we cannot risk that if his forces had spies. Spread half the remaining allocations to our most loyal allies and the rest to those who hesitate. Ask our allies if anyone has soldiers ready for battle—more resources must have run out in the night, anyway."

Dungeon resources, like the High Speed Bush or the Ice Pond, weren't endless. They eventually ran out and needed time to restore themselves. This was why the Forest of the Strong had been closed off to outsiders. It was also why they raced so hard to conquer more dungeons than their enemies. Not only was each dungeon a victory, it also offered useful resources that could tip the scales of battle.

Very few dungeons had E-Grade resources, though, and it wasn't easy to know beforehand. Whenever they discovered one, entire armies moved to battle. In this cold war situation, dungeons were the only places where open warfare took place.

Of the E-Grade resources discovered after the Integration Tournament, the Ice Peak had gotten two out of three. Things were looking grim.

"And advise Vivi to tighten her defenses," the professor added in a moment of inspiration. "The alliance between the Ice Peak and the Animal Kingdom is almost certainly happening... but there's always a chance those lycans are a feint to make us allocate forces from defense to attack. Petrovic is a selfish sellout, but a devious one."

"Yes, professor."

"Good. Now, walk me through last night's dungeons—in detail."

CHAPTER TWENTY-SEVEN
SNEAKING INTO AN ANTHILL

Jack and Brock peeked from behind a boulder. The anthill lay right before their eyes, a hundred-foot-tall mound of dirt smelling vaguely of metal. There were black ants running along the sides, but far fewer than before. Jack's hunting had seriously lowered their numbers.

Besides the ants carrying food to the colony, leaving to go search, or adding more dirt to the mound, there were also guards. These were shaped exactly like the other ants—argentine ants had no soldier caste —but waited around the colony, antennae extended outward to detect any invaders.

"Ready?" Jack asked, gulping. Brock nodded. "Let's go."

He dropped to all fours and started walking toward the colony. Brock followed right behind.

The moment they appeared, the nearest guard noticed them and stared intently. Its antennae flickered in hesitation. Jack and Brock kept walking on all fours like nothing was wrong.

The guard approached them to take a sniff. It tilted its head. Eventually... it let them pass, watching as they went ahead.

Jack grinned widely. *Success!*

They were dressed as ants.

Ants communicated mainly through a system of pheromones. They trusted those smells even more than their eyes, which is how a conqueror queen could infiltrate and take over the anthill of another species, pretending to be their queen. Even though she was obviously different in appearance, she was covered in the right pheromones, which was enough to trick the other ants.

Jack thought they could use the same trick.

For the past half hour, they'd traveled between groups of dead ants to find the right ones. When Jack had been hunting them before, he'd made sure to ambush one or two in each group, killing them before they could know what was happening. That way, they didn't release the danger pheromones that would alert nearby ants.

He and Brock had rummaged through the corpses to scavenge the most intact parts—be they legs, carapaces, or antennae. Then, they used the last strips of cloth remaining of Jack's shirt to tie those ant parts on them, basically dressing themselves as conqueror ants.

Each of them had two antennae sticking out of their head. Their back and ribs were covered in pieces of ant carapace, their limbs had ant legs attached to their outer side, and they had an extra pair of ant legs dangling between their arms and legs.

It was heavily ridiculous, to a degree that both couldn't stop laughing for five minutes. But Jack had bet on it working.

They resembled ants just enough for the guards to not attack immediately. Moreover, their disguise still carried the right ant pheromones.

If it didn't, they would just have to retreat and come up with a new plan. At worst, they could try fighting their way through.

The current idea was to infiltrate the anthill, then head directly down, where the tunnel to the next floor should be. Gan Salin had been very clear that anything large, striking, and monster-infested hid an exit. This anthill hit the mark perfectly. If there was no exit, Jack would be severely pissed.

If this plan worked, they could come and go from the colony as they wished.

And it was working so far! If even the guards didn't stop them, there was no reason for the workers to do it.

Jack and Brock slowly climbed the dirt mound toward the very top, where the hole leading downward lay. There weren't many ants around. After all, they had already killed around five hundred of them, and there were also many scouts outside the colony.

When they brushed against the occasional ant, it ignored them, too focused on its own tasks.

They eventually made it to the top of the hill, and just as Jack suspected, the tunnel leading into the nest was slanted. It would have been vertical in a real anthill, but the dirt here couldn't support the gigantic ants.

Without a word—Jack wasn't clear on the auditory senses of ants—they walked in. Darkness swallowed them.

There was little light in ant tunnels. The ants navigated using the senses of smell and touch. Jack and Brock weren't as skilled in those, and they could only barely detect the pheromones—they smelled like metal, lemon juice, ash, or dirt. Thankfully, though it was dark, the soil here was thin and porous, letting some light through. Coupled with their System-enhanced senses, they could see a bit after their eyes adjusted to the dark.

Jack considered lighting a torch. Ants were animals; they might be scared away and let them pass. However, he had a sneaky suspicion that whoever made Trial Planet wouldn't make things so easy. No one played fair in the System world. If he lit a fire, he suspected the entire forest would suddenly want to murder him, including ants.

He did carry an unlit torch, though. Just in case.

The tunnel they were in was long and rough, extending deep at a steep angle. It was also wide enough for Jack to stand, if needed, letting ants walk on the walls without colliding with the ones on the floor.

They followed the tunnel, with Brock ahead this time. He had the superior senses.

Chittering sounds came from all around. The darkness smelled vaguely of metal. Jack could see ants walk past them occasionally, sticking to the walls, and he could hear the little tapping sounds of their feet on dirt. He kept looking behind him, seeing the light grow smaller and smaller before they rounded a corner and it disappeared.

It was horrifying. If he died in here...

He didn't even want to think about it.

Brock was brave, too. If he was afraid, he didn't show it. His eyes remained glued ahead, squinting to pierce the darkness as he led them through turns and twists, heading ever downward. When crossroads appeared, he chose the steepest path down. The exit would be at the bottom of the anthill.

I wonder how many people fail here, Jack thought. Come to think of it, everyone I saw with Trial Planet titles had made it past the third ring. Is this second ring really so easy?

Or is it just so deadly that people don't have time to escape?

It was a sobering realization. Gan Salin had mentioned that Trial Planet hid dangers... but he'd never mentioned a survival rate, had he?

Jack gulped.

The darkness grew heavier and the ants more numerous. Jack spotted smaller tunnels branching off from the main ones, but Brock wisely chose not to follow any of those.

It occurred to Jack that his life was in Brock's hands. He felt proud.

They briefly stepped into a large room. Jack felt the air open up around them, but he couldn't see well enough to distinguish where exactly they were. Brock paused for a moment, then turned left and entered another tunnel heading even lower. As Jack followed, he caught a glimpse of dark, oblong shapes stuck to the walls, with ants tending to them.

The brood.

By now, the ants were so numerous that Brock couldn't give them a wide margin. One came too close and stopped and stared at Brock, wiggling its antennae. This was how ants recognized each other. They "smelled" each other's antennae to detect the colony's specific pheromone.

Brock's antennae had it, since he'd taken them from ants of this colony, but it was weakened. They also had the death pheromone that was released when an ant died. However, Brock was clearly alive. The ant would hopefully be more confused than wary.

Brock lowered his head, touching his antennae to the ant's. They stayed there for a second. Jack held his breath.

Then, the ant went on its way. So did they.

Soon after, the tunnel opened up into another chamber. Jack still couldn't make out the far walls. Brock paused for longer this time. He paced to a corner. Jack followed.

It was tough to make out Brock in the darkness, but he mimed some things. "The exit is here?" he whispered as low as he could. He barely heard himself, but it was enough.

"Yes."

"And let me guess. So is the queen."

"Yes."

Jack nodded. This was within expectations. At least, they confirmed that the exit to the next ring really was here—though Jack couldn't help but wonder how Brock knew.

Now that they stood still, Jack could tell there were many ants in this room. He could see patches of slightly deeper darkness move in the distance. The soft tapping of feet against dirt came from all around, echoing on the walls. Mandibles chittered calmly.

And the sound of ripping was dominant.

Something was tearing into something else. Jack assumed it was the queen feasting.

There were also oblong shapes stuck to the walls. A couple were close to their current corner, so Jack could make out that they really were ant brood. Transparent, pulsing sacks containing killers. They sent a chill down his spine.

"Okay," Jack whispered again. "Let's head to the exit?"

Brock wasn't done miming. There was something else he wanted to say, but Jack couldn't understand it.

"Bro!" Brock whispered in exasperation. He then mimed for Jack to follow.

They stuck to the walls, passing right by the brood sacks. Jack felt the urge to break them but held himself still. As they advanced through the chamber—which was larger than he expected—he began to make out a large shape lumbering in the darkness. He'd seen a queen outside the colony, when the conqueror ants attacked some other ants, but this one was larger still. It was far bigger than the other ants, reaching at about Jack's height, and its mouth moved a lot. That must have been the source of the ripping sounds.

He was glad he couldn't see the details.

They circled far around the queen, coming to a stop near an oddly flat section of the walls. Jack touched it. It was stone, and though its surface was slightly uneven, it was too flat to be natural.

It was a door.

Jack felt excitement flood him. They'd made it! Nothing had detected them! The plan had worked!

So why was Brock still hesitating? What was he trying to say?

The brorilla touched Jack's shoulder and pulled lightly. They kept walking past the door. They circled around the walls until they began approaching the queen. Brock didn't stop. They were close now. Her shape was clear in Jack's eyes through the darkness. She was stuck against a wall, leaning her behind against it. They came very close.

Jack wondered if Brock was *too* brave.

When they stopped, they were so close to the queen that Jack could touch her if he took another two steps. Thankfully, she was too preoccupied eating to notice them.

He didn't dare ask Brock what was happening. However, the brorilla pointed down. Jack followed his finger.

Something stuck out in the darkness, obscured by the deep, low light. Brock held Jack's hand and pushed it against the thing, letting him feel cloth. The shape suddenly registered in Jack's eyes.

A corpse! he realized. The head was missing, but the rest was still there. The ants got someone... But why did Brock come here? Does he want to loot it? I guess it has a credit card, probably, but—

Before he could think further, Brock took another short step toward the queen and pointed somewhere under her. Jack cursed—inwardly— before even looking.

Something was on the ground next to the queen, partially buried under her foot. It was long enough that Jack could feel its tip without approaching within three feet of the queen.

The item was surprisingly warm to the touch. It also felt hard, like stone, and it must have been engraved with something because Jack felt slight grooves under his fingers. He felt tempted to touch down its sides, but he didn't dare go further. If he moved it even a bit, the queen might notice. It was under her leg, after all.

Is that a staff? Jack wondered. Its shape—long, straight, and somewhat thin—matched. Come on, Brock... If you want a weapon, we'll find you one. We don't have to take the one that is right under an ant queen.

Brock didn't move. His intention was clear now. He waited for his big bro to decide.

Jack mulled it over. He couldn't understand Brock's obsession with this particular staff, but there had to be a reason. He trusted his little bro. Maybe there was something Jack couldn't see yet.

We could take it and run to the door, he thought. Get past it and shut it in their face or use it as a choke point to hold them back. Or just run. We're faster than F-Grade ants.

Getting surrounded inside the colony was dangerous, but they had an easy way out right behind them. How badly could it go?

Jack looked at Brock. He nodded. The brorilla gave a slow nod back.

Jack grabbed his unlit torch and passed it to Brock. He then raised three fingers. He lowered them down one by one, grabbed the edge of the staff, and yanked it out.

CHAPTER TWENTY-EIGHT
BREAKING THROUGH THE GATES

Jack yanked at the staff. Hard.

The chamber erupted into chaos. The queen screeched—a harsh, grating sound, the likes of which he'd never heard before. Chittering came from all around, feet stomping on dirt as the ants frantically darted for the entrance of the chamber, assuming there was an enemy coming. The stale air suddenly smelled of ash.

However, the staff in Jack's hands only budged a little before remaining still.

Fuck.

He couldn't see the queen well in the darkness, but he felt it stirring. He ducked. A set of mandibles snapped hard over his head. Much harder than the low-level ants he was used to. Much harder than it should be.

"Brock!" he shouted, abandoning stealth. The rest of the ants would realize what was happening, anyway.

A sharp sound came from behind him as Brock rubbed his hands around the torch head, creating friction. The tattered cloth caught on fire.

Jack was momentarily blinded. He Ghost Stepped away, feeling the familiar pull through space as a large body collapsed where he used to stand. His eyes recovered a moment later. Now, a tremendous ant stood before him.

A chitinous body the size of a horse. A thick, sturdy torso and a bulging behind. Two long antennae, each scraping the nine-foot-high chamber ceiling, and two membrane wings that shivered in anticipation. A hellish face with heavy-set mandibles dripped yellow saliva and exuded the worst smell Jack had ever experienced. It was like bug-infested meat left in the sun for far too long.

He almost puked on the spot. Only the battle tension saved him, but he still wrinkled his nose and felt his eyes watering. He had seen a queen outside the nest, when the conqueror ants attacked another colony. This was far bigger.

Conqueror Broodmother, Level 69
The leader of a conqueror ant mega-colony. Broodmothers hide in the heart of massive nests containing thousands of conqueror ants. Each mega-colony can span many square miles of land, with the broodmother being the leader of all nests in its territory.
They are breeding machines that can output hundreds of eggs a day.
They have the strength of a hundred ants. If one is spotted outside its nest, exterminate it immediately.

Jack had found the queen of queens. The mother of all ants. And she was *hideous.*

The broodmother vibrated her wings, the low ceiling ensuring she couldn't take flight. She hissed in Jack's direction, unleashing another wave of stench.

Level 69... he thought, paling. *Shit.*

He couldn't fight seriously down here, or the entire nest might collapse on their heads. He couldn't even use Meteor Punch. Thankfully, they wouldn't need to fight. The plan was to run.

Meanwhile, the rest of the ants had realized what was happening. They were charging back from the chamber's entrance, and the dirt shook under the marching stomps of every ant in the colony rushing here at top speed. The broodmother's description mentioned thousands of ants. What they had explored was likely only a fraction of the nest. They would be overwhelmed.

There was no time to go treasure hunting.

"Brock!" Jack shouted, keeping his eyes on the broodmother. "The door!"

The light and shadows moved as Brock dashed for the door, dropping the torch beside it. Jack wasn't looking that way, but he heard Brock's fists pounding on stone, then a cry of frustration. He risked a glance.

The passage leading to the next ring was hidden behind a double stone door. Carvings of insects and giants covered it, as well as other creatures that Jack didn't recognize. And no matter how Brock pushed, it remained stubbornly shut.

Jack felt his world sharpen to a point. They were trapped here. He forced himself to look ahead, where the broodmother was already rushing him. Her mandibles snapped next to his head, strong enough to cut through trees. Her massive body kept going, striking him in the chest and threatening to tip him over. He turned under her legs and found himself at her side.

He unleashed three punches in quick succession. One struck her where a leg met her torso, and the leg snapped off with a crunch. The other two struck her thick torso and rebounded.

Jack looked around, taking stock of everything in slow motion. The ants had almost reached him. Brock was pushing at the door, but it wasn't even budging. There was no lock, either. He'd have to break through, but it would take time.

"Change of plan," he said, dodging another bite from the broodmother. "Hold back the ants! I'll slay the queen and demolish the tunnel!"

Demolishing anything down here was dangerous, but not as dangerous as an army of ants a thousand strong in an enclosed space. They had to take risks or die. If this succeeded, he would Meteor Punch the door until it broke—hopefully before the ants dug a new tunnel in.

Brock yelled back in monkey and jumped at the ants. Jack only caught a glimpse of his arms and legs carving the ants apart before the broodmother blocked his sight. She was a hulking behemoth.

Jack met her head-to-head. His adrenaline and terror had long eclipsed any stench in his nostrils. She bit and tried to bulldoze him. Jack struck her in the face and mouth, flowing around her attacks with Iron Fist Style and Ghost Step.

He flashed left and right, jumping from one end of the chamber to the other before she could react. Egg sacks were crushed under his boots, further enraging the broodmother. Her wings vibrated so furiously that their razor tips were cutting lines into the dirt above.

His fist met her chin, shooting her face up. He capitalized, smashing four more into her throat, then sneaking under her and striking the thorax from below. She tried to fall on him, but he Ghost Stepped out of the way. He yanked on a leg, trying to rip it away. He failed, but at least he ruined her balance enough to make her fall completely, giving him time to punch another leg off. Breaking the contact point between the legs and the thorax was easier than breaking the actual leg.

The broodmother screeched, summoning her children for assistance. Two had already entered the chamber to assist their brethren in taking down Brock, who was struggling to hold seven of them at bay. It was more than he could handle. Jack had to hurry.

But the broodmother wasn't dying fast enough. Even with two legs missing, she unleashed a flurry of blows, trying to kick Jack. Since her bite wouldn't work, she switched tactics. She was intelligent.

Which changed nothing.

Jack tore into her, flowing between her legs and striking the contact points. She was twisting and protecting them, delaying his work. She knew she couldn't beat him. She was simply stalling, and it was working. Brock would fall before she did, and Jack wouldn't last long afterward.

He gritted his teeth. What could he do? If he went all out and used Meteor Punch, there was a high chance the chamber would collapse. After all, Meteor Punch created explosions. If he tried to help Brock, the broodmother would catch up, and Brock wouldn't survive the sandwich. If he rushed for the door, the broodmother would have a chance to turn to Brock. If he kept fighting as he was, Brock would lose before Jack won.

I have to use Mete—

His leg bumped against something. It was the corpse he'd seen before—a naked human missing a leg—and next to it lay the staff Brock wanted, what started this whole thing. He'd forgotten about it.

Now that there was light, he could see that the staff was gray. It was made of ancient, moss-covered stone, with the forms of various animals carved into its entire length, along with glyphs whose meaning escaped him.

Staff of Stone, Life Weapon (D-Grade)
An Ancient weapon that utilizes the Dao of Density to—

Jack didn't expect a screen to appear. It blocked his vision for a second, letting the broodmother land a heavy kick into his ribs that sent him flying into a wall. She tried to bite him, but he rolled out of the way and punched her eyes. She retreated, screeching.

A weapon with stats! Jack thought, reeling. He hadn't seen anything like it before. The galaxy was full of surprises. *Ghost Step.*

He arrived next to the weapon instantly. "Brock!" He tossed it to the brorilla, who took a step back, momentarily disengaging to glance over and catch it.

Jack didn't know what the staff did—there was no time for reading—but it was a weapon. It could help Brock survive.

That was the idea at least. In the short moment when he grabbed it, Jack realized that the staff was very handy to wield, neither too light nor too heavy. But he was much stronger than Brock. To the brorilla, it might as well weigh a ton.

Brock grabbed the staff, twirled it, and smashed it into an ant's face in one fluid motion. It was like he'd used a staff his entire life. The extra weight didn't seem to bother him one bit.

Jack didn't have time to ponder that. He was just glad Brock wouldn't die instantly. Now, he just had to hurry. The mysterious staff wouldn't help against the approaching army. Time was running out.

Jack roared, laying into the broodmother with all his strength. He let a kick land, taking it with Iron Fiend Body, and drove his fists into her body, breaking off leg after leg. She snapped at him, but he Ghost Stepped to the other side and kept pummeling. She was squirming and thrashing, making his job more difficult, but he simply attacked faster. If one punch missed, he would hit ten times. If ten missed, he would hit a hundred.

Yellow blood spurted out and flowed over the dirt, seeping into the soil. Jack's roars filled his ears. One leg broke after the other. Suddenly, the broodmother fell to the ground. She only had one leg remaining on the far side of her body. She couldn't move. She couldn't even stand.

She snapped with those terrible mandibles and he Ghost Stepped backward. He'd won, but there was no time to celebrate. He had to collapse the tunnel *now*. Maybe he was already too late.

As he turned around, he froze. He didn't want to believe his eyes. He *was* too late.

Ants streamed out of the opening, painting the walls and floor black. Dozens of them, with no end in sight. They were a flood.

It was the most terrifying sight he'd ever seen. It was death between the mandibles of ants, deep beneath the earth at some far-off corner of the galaxy. His limbs lost strength. He felt despair.

In the face of death, only two people came to mind. The professor... and Brock.

I'm sorry, he thought.

Brock was fighting bravely just in front, twirling his staff without much mastery, simply with the power of a strong brorilla using a stick to keep weaker enemies at bay. He was holding on, but he couldn't stop a flood. Even Jack couldn't. He could reach the door before them, but he couldn't open it. If he unleashed a Meteor Shower, he wouldn't get all the ants, and the chamber would collapse on his head.

But perhaps that was a better fate than death by a thousand mandibles.

Serenity filled Jack. He would die. But he would kill as many as he could. His rage dissipated, leaving only cold, dark resolve. A mixture of bitter hatred and pure, untainted will to kill. All questions disappeared from his mind. The ants would die.

His head lowered a bit. His veins swam in dark fire. His eyes were shining dots in the darkness, and his soul burned with all the power it could unleash.

His body was wreathed in violence. Strength and brutality flew out of him in waves, submerging the chamber. He felt like a dark god at the end of his life, facing a crowd of mortals.

He would kill the ants, but at this last moment, he felt no hatred toward them, only to his own weakness. He understood. They were just insects. He would kill them regardless because he could.

At that moment, Jack felt his vision rise above his body, like he was staring every single ant in the eyes simultaneously. The full brunt of his overwhelming strength and irrefutable decision to kill fell on them.

And the ants shuddered. They slowed a bit, as if pushing against an invisible force. Jack's mind was already set, but he was also fully present. He watched their reaction coldly.

They were scared. It was understandable. After all, they were facing an overwhelmingly strong enemy who would kill them with cold indifference. Even if he lacked bloodlust, that made it all the more terrifying because the only thing left behind was death.

So what if they would win in the end? So what if they would willingly lay down their lives for the colony? Even ants were afraid of death. Everyone was.

The image of the three cultivators from before popped into his mind. Why had he been so afraid of them that his blood ran cold? It wasn't because they threatened him. They hadn't even seen him. No, it was because he, too, was afraid of death. And, when all else disappeared, when there was no heat of the moment or any sort of stubbornness to counterbalance the fear, the coldness of death gripped one's soul and squeezed it so hard they might die.

Another image popped into his mind. The bare-chested man in the vision, facing an army by himself. His cold indifference promised them death, and it wasn't one they could refute with courage or self-sacrifice. It was simply the end.

This was true, heart-gripping terror.

Oh.

Everything came together.

Congratulations! Class Skill unlocked: Brutalizing Aura I.
Brutalizing Aura I: The fear of death is one of the most primal
instincts of all living creatures. You have learned to project your
Dao and intent in a way that targets this fear, amplifying it and
paralyzing all weaker targets in a wide range around you.

Now I see.

Jack used the skill. His chest was filled with dark ice. The finality of death, stripped of everything that might sweeten it, spread outside his body. It was an invisible aura that pulled at the souls of his enemies. A bare terror that froze them.

Brock screamed and jumped back. He almost dropped his weapon in surprise, but no attacks came at him.

The ants stopped. From the first to the last, all the way down the tunnels, they froze. The army came to a shivering halt. They lived for the colony, but even they had a hint of identity in their core, and that hint was currently paralyzed by the fear of death.

They were too weak compared to him.

Jack turned around. Even the queen whimpered, not daring to look at him. She was stronger than her children and should have been able to resist the aura, but perhaps the fact that he'd broken off her legs helped.

"Brock," Jack said slowly, "go to the fucking door."

The brorilla looked around, at the still flood of ants waiting to swallow him, and rushed for the door. He fell on it with all his weight, even screamed as his shoulder was smashed against it, but the door refused to budge.

The ants followed him with their eyes and antennae. Jack was sweating. This aura was a burst, not a constant effect. It weakened with time. They only had a few seconds at most before the ants were free again. There was no time to lose.

"Step aside," he ordered. He walked up to the door and charged a massive Meteor Punch, infusing it with all his desire to get through that door—and, thanks to their fast-approaching deaths, that desire was massive.

The chamber fell back into darkness. Even the torchlight was drawn into his fist, a shining purple aura, and all sound disappeared as only Jack, his fist, and the double door remained in the world. The door came into focus, its every detail pristinely clear.

"OPEN!" he screamed. He smashed out with all his strength. The world was swallowed by an explosion that blew both halves of the door off their hinges, sending them crashing against some far wall. The entire chamber shook. Dirt fell from the ceiling, slowly at first but quickly growing faster.

Jack and Brock dashed through the door as the chamber ceiling collapsed behind them, burying the army of ants under a forest's worth of dirt. Thankfully, the gate led to a stone passage, which saved them from the collapse.

Jack looked behind him, where only a dirt-blocked gate waited. "Turns out we couldn't avoid battle. I believe our approach was a bit unorthodox... but hey, it worked. Shouldn't we get levels from all those ants, System?"

No response came—or levels. Perhaps the System considered the collapse of the anthill too easy to reward with levels?

In any case, Jack didn't mind. Levels would come. For now, survival was good enough.

He looked around. The remains of the gate lay on the wall in front of them, while a smooth corridor carved into the rock spiraled down into the darkness. There was a lit torch on a wall, illuminating the space and just waiting to be picked up. A bunch of unlit torches waited in a basket underneath. There was no oil, though, and Jack would bet that the torches were enchanted to burn forever.

"Well, the path is clear," he said, picking up the torch. "But I have to say, that was an oddly designed exit. Why have multiple torches if the gates can only be opened once?"

Brock shrugged. In a flash of intelligence, he reached for two of the torches, broke off their tips, and stashed them in his pockets for a time of need. Jack nodded in acknowledgement.

He then looked at the broken double doors again. This time, when there was no death breathing down his neck, he could take a closer look, and he noticed two small openings. They were near the spot where the two doors connected, mirroring each other, and just the right size for a human to grab them.

Hoarse laughter escaped Jack's throat. "We just had to *pull*, not push!"

Brock looked confused for a second, then became extremely embarrassed. Jack, still laughing, patted his head.

"Don't fret, little bro. Look at how the openings are hidden between the engravings. I think it was meant to be a riddle, but we took the fist way out." He grinned, turning to the corridor heading down. "Come on, Brock. The next ring awaits."

CHAPTER TWENTY-NINE
BARBARIAN RING

THE PASSAGE LEADING TO THE NEXT RING WAS A ROUGH TUNNEL CARVED INTO the earth. It was bereft of sound. A single torch illuminated the darkness, creating a small bubble of light that spiraled ever downward with no end in sight.

Jack swung the torch left and right, looking for dangers or hidden passages. After the first few minutes, he got bored.

"Show me the staff again, Brock." His voice echoed oddly in the seemingly infinite tunnel. Brock handed it over. The moment Jack grabbed the staff, he once again appreciated how handy it felt. It had the perfect weight and form to swing—the perfect toy to any child, or the perfect weapon to any staff-wielding warrior. Brother Tao back on Earth would love it.

That it felt perfectly acclimated to Jack's current strength was impressive, given he was fifty times stronger than the average pre-System human. However, after reading the item's description, it wasn't as simple as it seemed.

Staff of Stone, Life Weapon (D-Grade)
An Ancient weapon that utilizes the Dao of Density to adjust its weight, matching the wielder's strength perfectly. Its max density is suitable for anyone with up to 1000 attribute points in Strength.

Carved and enchanted by Bozdom the Crafty.

Jack didn't know what a life weapon was, but it sounded awfully convenient. With how quickly people's strength rose in the System, a cultivator would need to change weapons every few levels to maintain their peak fighting strength, which sounded like a massive pain in the ass. Only a weapon that could adjust to its user, like this Staff of Stone, could accompany someone for a long time—maybe even their entire lives. Perhaps this was why it was called a life weapon.

Thankfully, Jack didn't use weapons, so he never had to consider this. But it did make him wonder. Were life weapons common? If so, why had he never heard about them before?

Brock made a small sound. Jack snapped out of his thoughts, handing him back the staff. The brorilla cheered and spun it in a circle.

My little bro got a weapon... Jack thought. How time flies. It feels like yesterday that he was sitting on my shoulder and trying to lift dumbbells.

It was a good weapon. Hopefully, it would help Brock get stronger quickly. Though Jack did worry. His own strength would rise tremendously in the near future, but Brock wasn't in the System. His current strength came simply from training and growing up, but he was bound to hit a ceiling soon.

Then what would happen? Could Brock still follow him, weak as he would be? Or would it be too dangerous?

Jack chased those thoughts away. They weren't pleasant, so he would consider them when the time came. Why burden himself for no reason?

Instead, he sent his thoughts in a different direction. They had just finished crossing the second ring—the first ring was the ruined surface —and his gains had been nothing short of tremendous.

Name: Jack Rust
Species: Human, Earth-387
Faction: Bare Fist Brotherhood (E)
Grade: E
Class: Fiend of the Iron Fist (Elite)
Level: 64

Strength: 240
Dexterity: 240
Constitution: 240
Mental: 30
Will: 30

Skills: Iron Fiend Body (II), Ghost Step (I)
Dao Skills: Meteor Punch (II), Iron Fist Style (I), Brutalizing Aura (I)
Daos: Perfect Dao Seed of the Fist (early), Dao Root of Indomitable Will, Dao Root of Power
Titles: Planetary Frontrunner (10), Planetary Torchbearer (1)

He'd gained many levels, had forged a new Dao Root, the Dao Root of Power. He developed Brutalizing Aura, a new Dao Skill. And Brock found a life weapon for himself.

That progress was vastly greater than everything Jack had achieved since breaking through to the E-Grade two weeks ago. And he had only spent one day in the second ring. There were seven of them remaining.

Just how strong will Trial Planet make me? he wondered.

As more time passed, his thoughts lost discipline. He let them roam free, jumping from one subject to the next to restore his mental energy. He remembered incidents from before and after the Integration. He wondered how his friends on Earth were doing—he'd never found time to visit them. He hoped the professor, at least, was okay, and that Sparman was holding the fort in Forest of the Strong.

The minutes bled into each other. Jack and Brock were running at superhuman speeds by now, eager to reach the next ring, but the tunnel seemed never-ending. They also didn't have a clock—he'd left his mobile phone in his house in Integration City.

After what felt like hours, they began to sense a change. The stuffy air of the tunnel warmed. It was imperceptible at first, but the feeling grew.

"We must be close!" Jack said, speeding up. Brock cheered and followed.

And the tunnel kept going. The air was warm, and it was also humid, making Jack's hair stick to his head. "What is this? Is the next level a sauna?"

It wasn't a sauna. Just as he thought the heat and humidity were getting seriously annoying, light appeared at the end of the tunnel.

They burst into a lush jungle. Light blinded them. "Wha—" Jack said, squinting and looking around. He'd never been to a tropical rainforest, but they probably looked like this.

Trees rose sparsely around them, tall and sleek. Bushes were everywhere. Branches, sticks, and wide leaves blocked visibility. The vegetation wasn't gigantic like in the previous ring. It felt normal-sized.

Animal cries filled his ears, coming from everywhere. There were chirps, roars, squeaks, and many other sounds he couldn't quite name. The ceiling was closer than in the previous ring, and the sunlight mushrooms were much more densely planted. Perhaps this explained the heat.

However, Jack couldn't shake the feeling that something was wrong. Everything felt *slightly* off. The roars did not come from something like a jaguar; they were harsher. The chirps were not by birds he knew. He saw a few flying far overhead. They sported bright colors, with long tails and bony wings. They reminded him of colorful, show-offish bats.

The vegetation was also wrong. He recognized some of it, but not all. There was a slim, tall tree with thin, yellow leaves that drooped downward. They glistened with moisture. He also spotted a bush that seemed ancient, like something he'd see in animated documentaries. Come to think of it, many things felt ancient here.

It can't be, he thought, eyes gradually widening.

He looked behind him, where a wide brown column stretched all the way to the cave ceiling—as impossibly high as in the previous ring. A new sky. He looked in front, where vegetation blocked his way. It didn't appear too dense, easily letting them pass. Even large animals could walk around without a problem.

Suddenly, a screen popped in his face.

Congratulations! For descending past the second ring of Trial Planet, you are awarded the Title: Second Ring Conqueror. Trial Planet Quest Interface unlocked.
Second Ring Conqueror: A title awarded to those who made it past Trial Planet's second ring. Efficacy of all stats +10%.

"Woah!" Jack said. "So these titles come as soon as I complete each ring, not at the end... Interesting. 10% is a lot, though. It's as much as my Planetary Frontrunner (10) title. I can see why Trial Planet tokens are so valuable."

He could already feel his body tightening, his muscles growing stronger, his eyes sharper, his reflexes faster. Ten percent was no small deal. Coupled with his previous titles, he now had an extra 35% efficacy in all stats. That was pretty massive.

Hmm. But what's that interface thing... System?

The Trial Planet Quest Interface details the achievements needed to acquire each ring's title.

Okay. So, just going through isn't enough?
No response.
What is this ring's quest?
Yes, a response!

Barbarian Ring Quest:
• **Defeat an opponent of Level 115 or above in a team of at most three individuals.**
• **Make your way to the Village Ring.**

Ohh... An actual quest. Not too complicated, but it might be hard. Can I even take down a Level 115 enemy? Probably not. And does Brock count as an individual?

He looked at the brorilla, who was still toying with his new staff. He tried to spin it behind his back, dropped it, and gave a sad monkey cry.

Probably yes.

Well, there's no time limit. I can fight whatever is on this ring, level up, and somehow defeat a level 115 enemy... But I should still hurry. There could be more strong cultivators here, or peak E-Grade monsters out for me.

He looked around, finding nothing. This changed his plan a bit—he couldn't simply rush to the Village Ring to find Gan Salin—but he could adapt. He simply had to increase his leveling speed.

Hmm. I wonder if there will be more complicated quests in the next rings.

He filed the information away for now and focused on the present.

Brock, who had watched Jack's interaction with great confusion, tapped him on the shoulder with his new staff. Jack turned around, remembering where he was and what he might discover here—his gaze filled with excitement.

"Let's go!" he said.

"Yes," Brock agreed.

They stepped deeper into the jungle. The heat wasn't as terrible as Jack originally imagined, it was simply the moisture worsening the feeling. The animal sounds intensified, coupled with the occasional shifting of leaves and rustling inside bushes. Brock was on full alert. He was walking at the front so Jack could keep an eye out and protect him if need be. There was no guarantee the enemies here would prioritize Jack as the insects had done.

However, no animal showed itself. The bushes slowly opened up, revealing a more expansive path that led into a clearing. A large creature was there, spotting them as they spotted it.

It stood on two claw-tipped legs, using its long, thick tail as a counterweight. It reached around nine feet in height and twelve in length, with short arms that ended in sharp talons. Most importantly, it had a large mouth bursting with needle-like teeth, exposed when it roared at them.

Jack's mouth opened wide in childlike wonder.

Allosaurus, Level 84
A carnivorous dinosaur boasting great speed and ferocity.
Allosauruses infest the subtropical biomes of many planets, hunting large prey. While not particularly social, different allosauruses often feed on the same corpse that one of them, or some larger predator, killed.
This particular specimen is juvenile.

"A dinosaur!" Jack exclaimed, unable to help himself.

The dinosaur wasn't as happy to see him. It opened its mouth terribly wide, like a snake unhinging its jaw, and charged at them. The jungle parted in its wake—the sparse vegetation wasn't much of an obstacle.

The danger snapped Jack out of his wonder. Suddenly it hit him that they were being charged by a level 84 predator. The thought of fighting a dinosaur lit him on fire. He clenched his fist.

"Stand back, Brock," he said, stepping forward to meet the allosaurus. It roared. He roared back.

A shape darted out of the jungle. An arrowhead glinted in the mushroom light before impaling the allosaurus, piercing into its large throat from the side. Its eyes bulged. With the thick, wooden arrow still stuck inside it, the dinosaur slowed, then toppled to the side, convulsing on the ground as it bled out.

Jack was caught off-guard. He eyed the new arrival.

A woman stood there, gazing back at him. A longbow was in her hands, while two quivers hung from her back. Her skin was pale, standing out in the bright jungle, and she only wore fur strips around her private areas and chest, revealing a highly toned body. Her features were slim, her hair was blonde and done in a ponytail, and her eyes were blue pools of suspicion.

Human (Trial Planet), Level 99
Faction: -
Title: Direct Descendant

He gaped at her, who had just killed a large dinosaur in one blow.

She frowned. "What are you looking at, delver?"

CHAPTER THIRTY

NAUJA

Jack was doubly stunned.

One, he had just seen and *been attacked* by a fucking dinosaur. In the flesh. If he ever made it back to Earth with one of these, he could publish half a library of research papers and win a bucketload of Nobel Prizes. It had no feathers!

Two, said dinosaur had been skewered by a woman dressed like a barbarian in the middle of a Jurassic jungle. Everything else aside, dinosaurs and humans shouldn't coexist!

She glared at him. "What are you looking at, delver?"

"You're in the wrong age," was all he could muster in reply. Her frown deepened over her inquisitive stare. Jack examined her back.

First of all, she was ripped. A six-pack dominated her abdomen, and her limbs were clearly lined with muscles, though not overly so. Under her blonde hair, her eyes were deep blue, and she even had a few freckles. If one got past her barbaric exterior, she could be pretty—although, Jack being here with his chest bare for all to see and roaring at dinosaurs seemed pretty barbaric himself.

She looked young, too. Couldn't be more than twenty-five. Perhaps twenty.

The main thing about this woman was how out of place she was in a dinosaur jungle. Again, dinosaurs and humans never coexisted in the same age. Her skin was also paper white, but she lived in a tropical rain-forest. Her people should have developed large quantities of melanin, though perhaps that was explained by the artificial nature of the light here. The mushroom light resembled sunlight, but they probably didn't exude the same radiation a star did, which would explain why the inhabitants of this ring didn't develop melanin.

Which brought Jack to the main question. This woman was a native here. Even the System called her race Human (Trial Planet).

He didn't know there were natives!

In hindsight, this ring is called Barbarian Ring. I should have seen it coming.

The woman grew wary of Jack as he stared, wondering how to approach her. How should he follow up to "you're in the wrong age?"

Before Jack could decide, Brock acted first. He approached her, undeterred by her cautionary gaze, and reached out for a handshake.

The woman looked at Brock like he was an alien—which he was, to her—and ignored his outstretched hand. Brock persisted, waiting. She alternated her gaze between him and Jack.

Jack finally decided to be honest. "Sorry for staring. I just didn't expect to find people here. Please don't take offense."

She seemed slightly taken aback by his comment.

"My bro's hand is still hanging, by the way," Jack advised. "It's rude to keep him waiting."

The woman snorted. She grabbed Brock's hand in a quick shake—but firm enough to make his face twitch—then took a few steps back. "Keep your wily words to yourself, delver," she said with clear distaste. "I know how your kind treats us. I will not fall for your schemes."

"I have no schemes," Jack tried to pacify her. He showed his palms in a peace gesture. "I truly didn't even know you existed until just now. Thank you for saving us, by the way."

He could probably take that allosaurus, but no use in revealing his strength now.

"Hmph." She snorted. "A barbarian saved your life. Next time your kin bad-mouths us, remember that. Remember how people should act and compare that against your heartless malice."

"Okay. I can sense some misguided hatred here. Perhaps you're mistaking me for someone else?"

"Mistaking you?" She snorted again, intensifying her glare. Despite being a young woman, there was nothing even remotely cute about her anger. Her eyes were hard, the kind that had seen life and death, and the sharp arrow waiting on her half-drawn bow could pierce his skin as easily as it had the allosaurus's. "I don't know what you are trying to achieve, but you're either stupid or a fool. I have the System's eyes. I know who you are."

"And who am I?"

"A delver."

"Is that the name for people who descend through this planet?"

"Of course."

"And these delvers are mean to you?"

"Mean?" Her eyes narrowed dangerously. He'd touched a sensitive subject. "You exploit us like monsters. You suck our land dry, burn it to the ground, kill our cattle, ruin the jungle's balance, and laugh about it. Your heart holds no respect, only greed."

Jack didn't mind her aggression—which was misguided, at any rate. In fact, unexpectedly, her words struck a chord inside him. He could sympathize.

The way she spoke and the things she said reminded him of other people. The native Americans. The age of colonialism on Earth. The way the Animal Kingdom stomped on their planet, treating them like garbage by the side of the road.

All of a sudden, her plight was familiar.

"That sounds awful," he said honestly. "I don't know what others do, but I have nothing to do with those people. I come from a newly-Integrated planet—if you know what that is—and I'm just trying to get stronger so I can protect my home from the same tyrants who are after yours."

His words did not have the desired effect. Her anger flared, and she pulled on her bowstring, holding it taut and aimed at the ground. "Of course I know what the Integration is," she spat back. "Spare me your mockery, delver. We barbarians are people, not animals. We aren't stupid."

"I... I apologize. I did not intend to mock you. I simply know *nothing* about this world, or any world. I'm lost. A month ago, I thought we were alone in the universe. I didn't even know the System existed. Then, the Integration happened, and my world was broken under the heel of some tyrannic galactic overlords, and everything I knew was turned upside down, and I suddenly had to fight for my life, and then everyone started relying on me. I have been thrust into a world I don't understand, my enemies are overwhelmingly stronger than me, everyone is after me, and yet I must somehow succeed or everyone else will die! Trust me, I couldn't give a second shit about mocking you."

He'd started venting at some point during that small speech, giving voice to the complaints about his fate. But he didn't care.

This girl had it bad, but so did he! His people and land were also disrespected and ruined!

The barbarian seemed surprised at his outburst. She bit her lip in thought—probably unconsciously. When she finally spoke, her voice was lower, but also calmer.

"Those were words of the heart," she said. "I can tell. I apologize for my assumptions. I thought... I thought you were someone else."

Jack didn't expect such a quick change of mind. Not that he was going to complain, of course, but he now understood better why these barbarians were preyed upon by the cultivators of the galaxy. They were naive. And the cultivators, if everyone thought like the Animal Kingdom, were cutthroat opportunists.

"Listen," Jack said, taking a careful step forward. "I understand we got off on the wrong foot here. How about we start over? I'm Jack, and this is Brock. We are simply passing through, and we have no intention of harming anyone who doesn't mean us harm."

Or who isn't a killer ant, he added mentally, but no need to complicate things.

"My given name is... Nauja, of the Tri Lake tribe."

"Okay, Nauja," Jack said, "thank you. Now, can you please tell me about this ring? We're on our way down, but it looks like I must kill something strong first, which means I have to level up. I will be respectful in doing so and direct my fists where you tell me to, and maybe I can even help your tribe in the process. Especially if there's anyone from the Animal Kingdom bothering you."

"There are, sometimes," she said, squinting at him. "I've never heard of anyone from the... Bare Fist Brotherhood? That's a good thing. Perhaps you are not lying."

"Of course not. I said words of the heart before, right?"

That wasn't the right time to joke. He could practically see her guard coming back up.

"Wait, wait," he added quickly. "Bad time to be funny. My bad. Now, if you can help us by explaining what's going on, we would be very grateful. If not, that's fine too. Just point us away from your tribe and we'll be on our way."

She examined him for another long moment.

"Barbarians are kind to strangers," she finally replied, still hesitant. "Kind delvers are rare. If you really are one of them, we would be happy to offer you our hospitality. But if you aren't... My father will run his spear through your heart. Trust me. We have people who can detect lies. If you don't mean your words, you will not survive."

"That's fine," Jack replied with relief. If they could just confirm he was telling the truth, things would go a lot smoother. "Being your guest would be my honor."

He was in a rush. Taking down a level 115 beast would take time, but the quest had mentioned a party of three, right? Maybe these people could help him.

"Very well," Nauja replied, turning around and presenting a clear target. If he was lying, she would be dead. Probably. "Follow me. I will take you to the Tri Lake tribe. Oh, and beware of dinosaurs. They bite."

———

Vivi was buried under endless decisions and the weight of her position.

"Send out our elites?" she said, frowning at her advisor. "That's risky."

"The professor advised it pretty strongly, Commander," the advisor, a middle-aged, hard-faced man, replied. "She said we must increase the pressure and hope our soldiers rise to the occasion. A harsh but appropriate decision, if you ask me."

Vivi wasn't going to ask him, but she let the comment slide.

"Fine. Deploy the Fire Snakes. Do we have a high-tier dungeon for them to conquer?"

"Negative, Commander. Our seers sensed one in India, but the three we've checked so far were duds."

"Yeah, well, India is huge. It doesn't take a seer to know there's a high-tier dungeon." She sighed, slumping in her chair. The advisor frowned slightly, but she had no energy to care about him, too. "We should reallocate the resources of the Fire Snakes. Do we have any elites waiting, allies to secure, or other suggestions by the professor?"

"She gave one entire dungeon to Emir of Egypt, since his squad got annihilated in the Stinky Marsh, but no instructions to us."

"Okay..." She massaged her brows. "Give him another half. He's a valuable ally, and Egypt has performed splendidly, besides the recent hiccup in Stinky Marsh. As for the rest... one fire- or water-related dungeon to our most promising recruits, and one to Babua. He's reliable."

"Yes, Commander."

Vivi took a moment to breathe. Unlike the professor, she had a combat Class. Keeping all variables in mind and making complex split-second decisions was taxing. When those decisions affected the course of war and millions of lives in the long run... she became overwhelmed.

She pushed through and didn't show it. But every once in a while she needed a breather.

The only reason she was still in charge was because of her strength and because people trusted her. But deep down, she felt inferior to the professor and Alexander Petrovic... Perhaps she was why they were losing.

On the plus side, she had strength. She was a warrior queen. And, in some cases, this more than made up for her other, slightly lacking qualities.

She looked up, remembering that the advisor was still here. "Dismissed—Actually, no. Prepare a small squad. I'll go conquer a dungeon myself."

Being a warrior queen had its perks.

"One more thing, Commander, the professor advised us to tighten our defenses," the man said. "It would be more prudent for you to stay here."

Vivi looked him in the eye. She didn't disregard his advice. The man was an experienced army general. However, there was little she could do. Her strength was the only thing that made up for her lack in experience. If she stayed cooped up in her palace, she would just be a clearly inferior leader compared to the other major factions.

"The odds are against us. We will never win by playing safe," she decided. "I'm going. Prepare a squad."

The man hesitated for a split-second. "As you wish, Commander."

CHAPTER THIRTY-ONE
THE TRI LAKE TRIBE

Nauja led Jack and Brock through the jungle, ducking under long leaves and parting bushes. The path was easy to follow. At some point, Brock abandoned the ground for swinging across branches, making excited monkey cries all the while.

"He's cute," Nauja said, a smile playing at the ends of her lips.

"Yes, but don't let him hear that or he'll be grumpy forever," Jack replied, laughing. "He's a big, strong warrior!"

Nauja laughed at that. Perhaps it was a trait of all barbarians, or just her, but her mood could change in a heartbeat. Her original distrust had already faded. Now, she laughed and joked with him like they were old friends. Once again, Jack wondered if this was why her people were exploited by cultivators. Were they too pure-hearted?

"Allosauruses are handy prey," she explained as they walked. "They are loners, easy to ambush. We usually send our lower-leveled hunters to train against them."

"And what if they die?" Jack wondered.

"They don't. Not often, in any case. The inexperienced ones have someone looking out for them, and the experienced ones... Well, they're just good."

"So you're one of the experienced ones?" Jack asked, looking around for a grisly barbarian veteran.

"Hah! Of course!" She flashed him a bright smile, revealing perfect white teeth. "I am the chief's daughter. Of course I'm good!"

"Really? That sounds awesome."

"I know, right? I once hunted an adult allosaurus all by myself! They're much bigger than the one you saw, and almost level 100. We usually send peak Hill Breakers to handle them."

"Hill Breakers?"

"Yes." She gave him an odd look. "You know. Between levels 50 and 125."

"Oh. The E-Grade."

"That's what the System says, but we just call them Hill Breakers. Because they can break hills. Well, the strongest ones, in any case. E-Grade is just words. It means nothing."

"I suppose." Jack scratched his head. This was an interesting naming scheme. Could he break hills?

If I Meteor Showered them, probably, he concluded.

"What do you call the other Grades?" he asked, intrigued. He'd never had a good frame of reference for the strength of immortals.

Nauja seemed all too happy to explain. "Well, there's Tree Snapper and Hill Breaker," she said, lowering her fingers one by one. "Then come Mountain Cutters. They are extremely strong, so much that they can even destroy entire mountains!"

"Entire mountains?" Mountains were large, dominating landscapes, and weighed millions or billions of tons. D-Grades could *break* those?

"Of course." She puffed out her chest in pride. "My dad is a Mountain Cutter. I once saw him topple a small mountain peak with one swing of his spear."

So, there is a D-Grade in her tribe. I should be careful.

"And *then*, there's Continent Crushers," Nauja continued, losing some of her enthusiasm. "Though we've never had one of those."

"So how do you know they can crush entire continents?"

"It's a legend. Supposedly, long, long ago, there were Continent Crushers and Mountain Cutters all over the place. Even Planet Crackers. The sky used to be blue, not gray, and our people lived in harmony with nature, creating new life everywhere they went..." She shook her head. "But that's just legends. I know the sky is blue outside this planet, but I believe the rest is just made-up. I mean, continents and planets are enormous things, right? It could take months to walk across them. There's no way anyone can crack such a thing."

"I guess." Jack certainly hoped that was the case. If the Planetary Overseer could just vanquish North America, he would be in for a treat. "Say, if you don't mind me asking, what is life like here? In the Barbarian Ring?"

"It's nice. Beautiful. We have our tribe, our family, our friends, our animals... We give to the land, and the land gives back. It is a blessed life, barring the occasional delver," she said. Then, she hesitated, as if she wanted to add something, but in the end, she stayed silent.

"But?" Jack helped her out.

"But, if I wanted to say something more, I would say it myself."

She flashed him a glare, taking him aback. She looked ready to go. Jack had to remind himself that this girl was level 99, a full thirty-five levels above him. That was almost two hundred stat points.

"Woah, sorry," he said. "I was just making conversation."

"Yes, not a problem. I just made sure you knew my limit."

She returned to her jovial mood. She named a couple of trees, then started talking about triceratopses. Jack hated himself for not listening intently, but his thoughts were talking amongst themselves.

Not exactly naive, he corrected his previous assessment of Nauja. *Just wearing her heart on her sleeve. Erratic. Like she only has one layer of thoughts. What an odd way to live.*

And yet, he found himself nodding along. This way of thinking fit his Dao of the Fist. He suspected he would like these barbarians.

Just as he got himself to focus on the undoubtedly priceless information she was dumping on him, the trees began to open up. "Ah!" Nauja shouted. "We've arrived! Look!"

She rushed forward, followed by Jack and a confused Brock swinging from vines overhead. Soon after, they crossed some bushes, and a small valley presented itself.

Palm trees—their ancestors, to be precise—dotted a shallow, bowl-shaped dent in the jungle ground. Lush grass reached down from the edges of the jungle, making it all the way to the shores of a crystal clear, blue lake. The mushroom light shimmered on its surface, making its waters glitter. The heat of this ring made the lake seem all the more appealing.

A small village rested by the waters. They had rough huts of wood and mud, a few dozen of them, each decorated with an abundance of colored feathers.

Pale-skinned people wearing only the barest garments of fur lounged on the grass or bathed in the lake. Some were practicing with weapons at the side of the village. Jack spotted a small group on the opposite side of the lake, tending to a pen containing roughly eleven triceratopses. A kid had climbed on the horns of one, laughing as the dinosaur's head under his butt dived into a basket of herbs. Everyone else seemed unconcerned.

The valley itself must have been only a few thousand feet long, roughly circular, while the lake was the size of an Olympic pool back on Earth, except wider. Colorful birds—dinosaurs, Jack corrected himself —flew overhead, shining in all colors of the rainbow.

It was like seeing a patch of heaven dropped in the middle of Jurassic nothingness.

"It's beautiful," Jack said, losing his breath. Next to him, Brock gaped too.

Nauja laughed. "Of course it is. I told you. It's a blessed life. Follow me!"

The jungle ended where the valley started. They walked out of the trees and into the grass, the heat and humidity immediately lessening. The valley's shape protected them somehow.

As soon as they started walking down—the descent wasn't too steep—the tribespeople noticed them. A few waved, but most stared warily. Jack felt unwanted.

"I'm back, everyone!" Nauja shouted as she reached the base of the valley, near the start of the village. "And I brought a friend!"

"That's a delver, Nauja," a man replied, stepping out of the small crowd. He was tall, broad, and completely bald.

"I'm not blind," she retorted with a smile. "Don't worry. His heart is louder than his thoughts."

At this, most of the tribespeople eased up, as if she'd said something profoundly calming.

"Hello," Jack said, approaching them. "My name is Jack Rust, and this is Brock. We have no ill intent toward anyone. In fact, your tribe looks beautiful."

"Welcome, Jack and Brock," the same man replied. "If Nauja vouches for you, we have nothing else to say. My name is Muka, a veteran hunter of the tribe. I look forward to hunting alongside you, my new friends."

Jack smiled. "The pleasure is all ours."

At the same time, he scanned most people present. None belonged to a faction, and they all shared Nauja's Direct Descendant title. He was very curious about it, but titles were personal information, so he hadn't asked.

Most of the people he scanned were at the low E-Grade. A few were at the high F-Grade or middle E-Grade. Only Muka and an older woman were at the high E-Grade—at levels 124 and 119 respectively. The children were all in the F-Grade.

Half the people here could steamroll anyone on planet Earth.

"Take your friend for a stroll, Nauja," Muka said. "Show him around the tribe. Your father will meet him at night."

"Yes, Muka," she replied, turning to Jack. "Come. You will meet everyone else later."

"There's a night here? I thought the mushrooms never went off."

"Of course they do. It just takes a while."

Jack was very happy he'd left the giant insect forest. Who knows what horrors would infest it in the darkness.

Nauja led him and Brock around the lake, pointing things out all the while. "Our tribe is called Tri Lake because of two things: this lake, and the triceratopses we raise. They are wonderful animals."

"I can imagine," Jack said, staring at the swiftly approaching pen. "I'm so glad they don't have feathers."

"Why would they? They aren't birds."

"I have some colleagues who'd tear their hair out at this."

"Okay... Well, triceratopses are our friends. If you meet a stray one in the jungle, *never* attack it. And I mean never. We'll have to kill you if you do."

Jack glanced at her, expecting to find her smiling, but she wasn't. She was dead serious. The contrast between her enthusiasm and deeply nested violence was impressive. If Master Shol and Vlossana made a baby, this is what it would feel like.

Like a happy maniac... he thought, realizing he was of similar make.

"And this is the pen," the happy maniac explained as they reached it. A sturdy-looking wooden fence surrounded a large area that included part of the lake. Eleven triceratopses of various sizes were currently gathered next to the fence—rhino-like creatures with stocky bodies, three horns, and a hard crest around their heads—where two tribes-people had emptied five large buckets of herbs. They nodded as Jack approached, and he returned the gesture.

"They eat a lot," Nauja said, gesturing at the triceratops. "Thankfully, the jungle has plenty of food. We offer them food, water, and protection, and they offer us their milk and meat."

"Protection from what?" Jack asked. "And what do you mean milk? They're reptiles."

"Yes?" She looked at him weird.

"Reptiles don't make milk."

"Sure they do. Look." She pointed at a nearby bucket filled to the brim with a white liquid.

"That's—" Jack wanted to retort but found himself unable to. With a sigh of resignation, he waved the issue away. "Nevermind... I guess Professor Else was right. Ugh. You mentioned that you offer them protection?"

"They need it," she explained. "Triceratopses are strong, but there are many larger predators in the jungle. Tyrannosauruses, gorillodinosaurs, pteranodons... The strongest dinosaurs are at the very peak of Hill Breakers, and there are even some Mountain Crushers deeper in the jungle... Not that I've ever seen one. They would flatten me with a single breath."

"Really? I didn't expect D-Grade monsters in Trial Planet," Jack replied, still observing the triceratopses and committing everything about them to memory. Earth's biologists had gotten them right, impressively. "Though I guess we aren't expected to fight them."

"Well..."

He glanced over in surprise. "Well?"

"There are rumors of delvers fighting the strongest dinosaurs," Nauja said hesitantly. "I don't know how that could be true, since all delvers are Hill Breakers, but we can sometimes sense the ground shudder and hear the echo of faraway battles. Father says it's delvers.

Such fights are very rare, but there are many delvers around these days, so..."

Jack remained glued to the first part of her words. Even though every cultivator that reached Trial Planet was highly talented, the gap between Grades was enormous. However, if they attacked in large numbers, maybe taking down a D-Grade was doable?

After all, Jack had once asked Captain Dordok if it was possible to fight someone of a higher Grade, and the answer had been a definitive no.

All at once, Jack noticed the colors of the world changing. He looked up. The mushrooms were slightly dimmer now, and their light was steadily fading.

"Night is approaching," he said.

"Yes," Nauja agreed. "But don't worry about it. With Father here, you are safe. Everyone is. Come on! It's time to meet him. I hope he doesn't kill you."

"You hope he what?" Jack asked, but Nauja was already walking toward the tribe.

She looked over her shoulder at him. "Well? Are you coming?"

CHAPTER THIRTY-TWO
THE NIGHT FLAMES DANCE

JACK FOLLOWED NAUJA BACK AS THE CEILING MUSHROOMS DIMMED. THEIR LIGHT lessened slowly at first, then faster, until night arrived in a matter of minutes. By the time they made it back to the tribe, darkness had fallen everywhere.

But not completely. Though the mushrooms had gone dark, their roots still pulsed with soft blue light. It wasn't enough to illuminate the entire ring, not even close, but it still shed a hint of light on the jungle beneath, like a moonless night on Earth.

As soon as darkness fell, the ambient sounds changed. The animals of day went to sleep, letting their nocturnal counterparts take over. Their cries were sparser, chillier. If he were in the jungle—or the insect forest—he would be terrified.

And yet, the valley of the Tri Lake felt safe. Peaceful, even. The leaves rustled in the night breeze like calming music to his ears, not a sign of danger. Fireflies danced around the lip of the valley.

It was almost mystical.

Brock's excited yells drew Jack's attention back to the front. A large bonfire had been lit in the middle of the tribe, right next to the lake. Bare-chested men had dragged over entire logs and stacked them into a pyramid, then set the dry grass beneath it ablaze.

Now, the crimson fingers of a pyre reached for the stony sky. The tribespeople were gathered around it, forming a circle at a moderate distance, their pale faces shining red from the flames. They waved at Nauja as she approached.

"This is our night," she whispered to Jack, pulling him forward. "We work hard during the day. At night, we dance, drink, celebrate, and sleep."

"What do you celebrate?" he asked, breathless.

"Everything."

His gaze opened up, taking in the new faces. Two dozen people sat around the fire, all staring at him. The previous crowd he met were amongst them.

Jack wanted to say something but held himself back. Nauja hadn't spoken yet. Nobody had, like they were all waiting for something.

The door of a hut creaked open and a man walked out, so tall he needed to duck through the door. His chest was bare, and a proud mane of red hair covered his head. His face was hard, with low cheekbones, and he wore only a skirt-like garment made of thin wood strips, like all other men of the tribe.

Human (Trial Planet), Level ??? (D-Grade)
Faction: -
Title: Direct Descendant

"Father," Nauja said respectfully, inclining her head, and everyone else followed suit. They weren't bowing, just expressing their respect.

"Hmm," the man replied, caressing his long red beard. Jack felt deep exhaustion in that voice. He wasn't old, he looked to be in his forties, though he exuded the air of a man who had experienced the vicissitudes of life.

Jack recalled that immortals lived for centuries. While this man looked forty, he could easily be seven hundred years old.

So much time in the same corner of the world... he thought, shaking his head. *No wonder he looks so tired.*

"Father, this is Jack and Brock," Nauja introduced them. "Friends who seek our hospitality."

"Delvers," her father replied, letting the word hang. A bit of tension seeped into the air. Jack had no doubt that, if this man gave the word, the tribesmen would chase them into the jungle instantly.

"Yes," Nauja replied, "but they know respect. This man speaks from his heart, Father. I could sense the bitterness in his words, the fire in his chest. He faces the same threat we do. He may have come from above, but he is more barbarian than delver."

Jack couldn't resist throwing her a surprised glance. They barely even knew each other. Not even an hour ago, she was cursing at him, and now she was vouching for him. Just how confident was she in her evaluation?

"Mm." The chief's hum rang heavy in Jack's ears, rocking his entire body, but he remained still. "My daughter praises you. Are her words true?"

"They are," Jack replied as respectfully as he could, not sure how to address the man. Chief? Sir? "Nauja told me you have ways to detect lies. I'm perfectly willing to accept such examination, if it helps alleviate your suspicions."

A hint of amusement entered the chief's eyes. "We have no such thing, but neither do we need it. The heart cannot lie."

Before Jack could respond, a heavy gaze bore deep inside him, as though the chief were staring directly into his chest. He shook, almost stumbling. He felt naked.

A moment later, the chief withdrew his skill—because it had to be one—and turned to Brock. "Can this young brorilla speak yet?" he asked.

"He—"

"Yes," Brock cut off Jack.

"Good. Are you pure-hearted?"

"Yes."

"Should we accept you among us?"

"Yes."

"Do you possess any sort of ill will?"

"No."

Brock had used two-thirds of his vocabulary, but his answers seemed to satisfy the chief, for whatever reason. A tired smile crept on his face, one that he probably forced himself to wear. "In that case, welcome to the Tri Lake tribe. You can be our guests for tonight, but we expect you to depart tomorrow."

Jack resisted the urge to raise his brows. He hadn't realized the invitation would be so short-lived, but it didn't really matter. It aligned with their purposes, anyway. They weren't here for tourism. They had come to level, rise in power, and descend through the rings. This Barbarian Ring was only one stop on their way.

"Thank you," Jack replied, inclining his head, and Brock did the same.

"Mm," the chief hummed again. His smile turned a tad more genuine as he said, "Now, let's drink."

The tribespeople cheered. Someone brought over a sturdy barrel, pulled open its cork, and started filling stone goblets. The people sat around the fire, chatting the night away, as the chief sat alone on a log and relaxed, letting his thick legs rest so close to the fire they were almost inside it.

"Here!" Nauja said, passing two goblets to Jack and Brock. They were filled with an amber liquid that smelled vaguely of milk.

"You lied to me," Jack said with a smirk. "You have no lie detectors."

"Telling you that *was* the lie detector." She winked.

"Ha! By the way, should Brock be drinking this?"

"Why wouldn't he?"

"I don't know. He's a child brorilla. Where I come from, dogs don't eat chocolate, so I don't know what a brorilla eats."

Brock gave him an insulted stare, while Nauja scowled. "Don't be a wuss, Jack. Let the man drink."

If they were the same species, Brock would have instantly fallen in love. As it was, he simply laughed, gave her a high-five—after Jack explained how she should respond to his raised hand—and then downed his goblet. Jack, letting some of his worries ease, did the same.

It wasn't strong alcohol. It felt like beer, only thicker and less bubbly.

They made their way to the barrel and refilled, learning that the person who'd brought it over was called Mayon. He made this drink with wheat they'd bought from another tribe, a particular fruit Jack didn't recognize—a juiceberry—and triceratops milk, which apparently wasn't really milk, but a milk-like substance they secreted from their mouths.

The surrounding people were laughing, chatting, and drinking in small groups. Nauja had gone off to speak with a friend of hers, a young man with blond hair.

Jack thought it was a good time to socialize, except most people looked busy in their tight-knit groups. He assumed they'd open up as the night advanced. Therefore, he approached the one person who sat alone.

"Excuse me," he said. "Can I sit?"

The chief raised his head, stared at Jack for a second, then motioned at the open spot next to him on the log. Despite not speaking, his gaze seemed inviting, even approving.

Jack took a seat. This close to the fire, the heat was scalding, but his enhanced body only perceived it as moderate warmth. Brock didn't agree, so he took off to hang out with other people. Jack caught him miming at people and replying with "yes," "no," or "bro." He quickly became the center of attention.

"It must be tough being immortal," said Jack, sipping from his goblet. Next to him, the chief hadn't touched his.

"When the tree stops growing, it sags," he replied in a slow, deliberate voice. This was an odd mixture of a man. He sat slouched, uncaring, not even trying. But Jack could feel the fire burning within him, an enormous reservoir of power simply waiting to be unleashed on the world. His voice was tired, but it remained rich and powerful, used to commanding and being heard. There was no weakness in this man. He was merely tired.

"Why would it stop growing?" Jack asked. He tried to detect if the chief was bored of conversing, but it didn't seem so. His short answers were preference, not rejection. A tiny smile played on the chief's lips, so small that Jack would easily miss it if he wasn't paying attention.

"Everything does," the chief replied. "The apple tree stops quickly. The pine takes long, and the eucalyptus longer, but nothing is born without a limit. Even people. Even you and me."

"I intend to rise far," Jack said. "There is someone I must beat. If I don't reach the C-Grade in ten months, the Continent Cracker level, my enemies will strike down my people and my planet."

It was a pretty blunt thing to say to someone who'd remained a D-Grade for centuries, but Jack suspected the chief was in no mood for anything but direct truth. Indeed, the chief frowned but showed no sign of anger. He scanned Jack with his gaze, seeing through his plight in an instant.

"The world is unfair," he said. "The strong oppress the weak. They will never let them rise. It is all a ruse, a false hope to keep the slaves obedient so they can rule by words and not by force."

Jack considered those words. He took his time. A few moments later, he asked, "Do you mean that I'm doomed?"

"Nothing is absolute... But the balance is enforced. Change is forbidden. The faster you rise, the harder they will strike, and their power is insurmountable. To survive ascension, you must either yield and become one of them, bearing the cloak of the oppressor, or rise faster and stronger than anyone ever has, suppressing the entire world with your power alone."

The chief's words sounded like a retelling of thoughts buried deep inside him, ones that existed at the very core of his soul. They were weary, like the chief himself, yet powerful. Jack wondered what his Dao was.

The truth of these words vibrated in his own heart. Defeating the Planetary Overseer was an almost impossible task, but then what? The Animal Kingdom wouldn't let him get away with it. They would throw B-Grades at him, and if the Galactic Alliance was corrupt, the entire galaxy might come down on his head for upsetting the balance and inspiring others to do the same.

Could he really triumph over everyone?

Strangely, the thought only raised his mood. It sounded despairingly difficult, but also simple. Straightforward. The perfect path for a fist to follow.

"You are wise, Chief," Jack said with a sigh.

For the first time, the chief chuckled, a deep sound that made many heads turn in surprise. "Not wise. I am simply old."

"How old?"

"Five hundred galactic years. Roughly."

"Wow... I'm twenty-eight. Roughly."

The chief smirked, sipped from his goblet, and Jack did the same.

Just as it emptied and he was about to refill it, excusing himself in the process, the chief spoke again.

"You are far from home."

Jack paused. "I am."

"You are brave. To fulfill your goals, the only way is to *conquer* Trial Planet. All of it—a feat that nobody has achieved in this galaxy. You will need power. Tomorrow, you and Nauja will hunt a beast near the Forbidden Cave, close to the delver camp. Fate will take its course. That is all the help I can offer."

That caught Jack off guard, stamping down his brief confusion lest he come across ungrateful to this titanic man.. "Thank you, Chief."

"May the will of our ancestors be with you."

Jack nodded, more thoughtful than he was a moment ago, and moved to refill his goblet.

"Jack," the chief's voice came again before he could take two steps.

"Yes, Chief?"

A strange light played in the chief's eyes. It was almost threatening. "Do not trust the System."

———

Alcohol flowed freely, and conversation gave way to bare excitement. A man and a woman drew out small bongos, beating them to a rhythm that danced with the flames. Jack found his body moving to the tune. Beside him, Brock did the same.

One by one, the tribespeople gathered around the crackling bonfire, dancing in a way Jack hadn't seen before. They shook their limbs wildly, rocking their bodies from side to side. In any club on Earth, they would be mocked. But here, Jack felt their movements strangely fitting. He grinned along, mustering the courage to dance himself, yet he stayed on the sidelines.

"What are you waiting for?" Nauja's voice came from behind him. Her hand grabbed his wrist. "Come on!"

She dragged him into the dance, where two dozen people shook their bodies, having fun. Not many were young. Besides Nauja, another girl, and a blond man, everyone else was either over forty or under twelve.

Their bodies moved before the flames, casting long, shifting shadows. The music seeped into every pore of Jack's body. He moved to the tune, without thinking, only dancing. It was liberating. He hadn't cut loose in so long—he'd never been good at dancing.

Nauja danced with him, helping him feel less awkward. It was unnecessary. After everything he'd been through, a little dance felt so insignificant. He couldn't be better.

A mass of rapidly writhing bodies surrounded him, shielding him in their midst. He'd lost Nauja at some point. A nearby woman danced with him for a bit, then a man whose moves reminded Jack of standing break dancing. Nauja reappeared by his side, and he grabbed her by the hand to spin her around. She laughed, holding his hand and spinning more. The mass of bodies packed tighter. Everyone came closer, a feeling of unity. The heat of fire became one with the warmth of people.

Jack found himself laughing. He realized he was drunk and he didn't care. This was nice.

And the night went on.

CHAPTER THIRTY-THREE
THE DAY OF THE HUNT

Jack awoke to a pair of strong hands shaking him.

"Orgh," he said groggily, rolling over.

"Bro," a commanding voice reached his ears.

"Ugh... Five more minutes?"

"No."

"Damn, man." A yawn. "Is it really time to go?"

"Yes."

Jack yawned again, then rose to a sitting position and rubbed his eyes. He was in the guest hut of the Tri Lake tribe—little more than a walled-off circle on the soil. There was a fur bed on the floor, made from the same material as the clothes of the tribespeople, and one window that was covered by a piece of wood. Jack could remove it to look outside or keep it there for privacy. He'd kept it on during the night.

Now, thin rays of sunlight slipped in through the cracks of the door and shut window, yellow and syrupy. Dust particles danced in the light, disappearing the moment they crossed its edge.

"How long was I asleep?" Jack asked.

Brock shrugged. They had no clock. How was he supposed to tell time?

Last night's events returned to Jack. They'd danced and drunk, and he had a cryptic but important-sounding conversation with Nauja's dad. Near the end of it, the tribe chief had mentioned Jack would be hunting a beast with Nauja tomorrow. Today.

Jack bolted up.

He was already dressed—black boots, white pants, and nothing else —so there wasn't much to do. He opened the door and strode out. Brock followed a step behind, still wearing his red shorts and holding the ancient-looking Staff of Stone in his right hand.

The tribe was already active. Jack had no way of knowing how long ago the day began, but he saw people tending to the triceratopses like yesterday, children fetching water from the lake, and a few groups of men and women heading into the jungle with big, woven baskets.

"Jack!"

Turning, he found Nauja walking his way. "Morning, Nauja."

"It is. Took you a while. It's already one hour after dawn!"

"What can I say? Multiple deadly combats in a row made me sleepy. Sorry."

"Oh, don't be cranky." Her smile widened as she squatted. "And good morning to you too, Brock. Did you sleep well?"

"Yes," the brorilla replied, nodding somberly.

"That's great!"

"Were you waiting for us?" Jack asked.

"Father called for you." Nauja raised her gaze from Brock. She was petting his fur—something Brock only allowed women to do, for whatever reason. "Said I should bring you to him the moment you woke up."

"I don't suppose there's breakfast on the way?"

"No. You'll have to bear with it. Come on!"

Under Nauja's lead, they crossed the small tribe to arrive at the largest and center-most hut. She knocked on the door.

"Who is it?" a tired, imposing voice came from inside.

"It's Nauja! I brought Jack and Brock."

"Come in."

There was no doorknob or lock. Nauja simply pushed the door open, revealing a dimly lit, sparsely furnished interior. A pile of fur on the floor served as the bed, while there was also a small table, a chair, and a knee-high bookcase containing five leather-bound tomes.

The chief sat in a wooden chair, somehow fitting his large body into it, and sipped from a clay mug. Muka, the veteran hunter Jack had met on his arrival to the tribe, was also there, standing by the chief's table with an odd expression. It looked like they'd just interrupted a conversation.

"Good morning, Father," Nauja said, and Jack hurried to say the same.

"Good morning, Chief."

"Hmm," he replied, while the three of them—Jack, Nauja, and Brock —also exchanged respectful nods with Muka.

Nauja cleared her throat. "Since I brought them over, Father, I will take my—"

He cut her off with a gentle shake of his head. "Stay. This involves you too."

"Me?" she asked in surprise.

"As you know, Jack must defeat an enemy of level 115," the chief said. "By himself, that will be a dangerous and time-consuming task. I fear the nearby delver camp will not let him be. Therefore, he should expedite."

He took a deep sip before continuing. His voice remained solid as a stone. "You, my daughter, must also defeat an enemy of that level to become a true hunter of the tribe. You will team up today. There is a tyrannosaurus picking off our animal friends near the Forbidden Cave. You shall head there, slay it, and return victorious."

As he spoke, Nauja's face showed increasing horror. "Father!" she cried out. "I—I apologize for my weakness, but I cannot defeat a tyrannosaurus! Much less while protecting a lesser Hill Breaker."

"I suspect he does not need your protection," the chief replied calmly. "My instructions are final."

"Then, what about the third member of our team?" She glanced at the nearby Muka. "It should be someone strong enough to protect us."

The chief only shook his head. "The third member of your team will be Brock, the brave brorilla."

"*Father!*" Nauja cried again, her voice rising higher. "What are you saying? This is suicide! I cannot fight a tyrannosaurus! It will kill us all. Muka, say something!" Muka gave her a helpless smile, then shook his head. That helplessness only fueled her frustration. "Father, I implo—"

The chief raised a hand. Despite her agitation, Nauja paused mid-word. His authority was absolute. "Do not doubt me," he said, and

Jack's heart sped up—for no apparent reason. "You will go, and you will return victorious or not at all. This is my command."

Nauja's mouth moved without sound. She seemed to be struggling with herself. Jack watched her silently, as did everyone. He knew his own strength. Even if he was weaker than her, it wasn't by much... but how could she know?

Regardless, he did not speak. This was not his place. Brock remained composed at Jack's side as well, face as stony as his staff.

"I do not understand, Father," Nauja finally said, her voice weak. "I will obey your will, but... can you at least help me understand? I... I do not see it. This is all too sudden."

"When fate knocks, there is no time to prepare." The chief revealed a small, sad, tender smile. "You must fight today, my daughter. Prove that you have the power to ride the wave of fate, should it manifest. I know you do not understand. Perhaps, one day, you will."

He hesitated for a moment—and, from Muka's raised brow, Jack got the impression that this wasn't common. "There will be no one guarding you this time," the chief continued. "All the veterans will remain in the tribe... Very well. I remedy my word. You may return alive. But you must fight first and give it your all. If defeat is certain, you may retreat, and the will of our ancestors will judge your life or death."

Nauja looked like she'd seen a ghost. Her eyes contained betrayal, pain, and fear, as well as massive incomprehension.

"I do not understand, Father..." she muttered, lost.

"It's okay, my child. This pains me as it pains you, but I have consulted with our ancestors, and I have thought about it deeply. This is the way. Go. And, if you die, remember that I love you. My heart will break with yours."

"Father..." She took a half-step forward, then caught herself, taking a deep, trembling breath. Jack imagined her heart fluttering, then settling. She still did not understand, but she would obey. "Very well. I shall do as you ask. Look forward to my victory, Father. When I return, even Muka will have to treat me as an equal."

Muka's expression changed into pained amusement. "May the ancestors be with you, child," he said.

"Farewell, Daughter," the chief said, and this time, his determined voice hid more than just tiredness. "May the ancestors be with you. You too, Jack Rust. You too, Brock the brorilla."

"We will not disappoint you, Chief," Jack said, inclining his head. Brock did the same, then they followed Nauja out of the hut. She walked silently for a few steps, her stormy expression scaring away an approaching child.

"I don't understand. What is happening?" she erupted, whirling around to glare at Jack. "What did you tell him yesterday?"

"Not much," Jack replied calmly. "Just some things about myself, but nothing related to this tyrannosaurus hunt."

"You will tell me everything," she said in a tone that brooked no disobedience, her blue gaze boring into his. "Give me some time to say my goodbyes. Wait behind the triceratops pen."

Her eyes indicated she had a slew of things to say to him, a storm of emotions to vent, but she chose to think things through by herself first. That was... more reasonable than Jack had expected.

"I'm stronger than I look," he couldn't resist saying.

"I sure hope so," she replied darkly. "Because the beast we're hunting is a killer."

And then, she took off, leaving them alone. Out of respect, Jack didn't follow her with his gaze.

"Is there anything you want to do, Brock?" he asked. The brorilla shook his head. "Me neither. Let's go wait."

He could quench his thirst by the lake. He was hungry, too, but he felt such guilt that he couldn't bear to take the tribe's food.

He was unsure what was going on. What did the chief's words mean? Why did he suddenly send his daughter on a near-suicide mission with a total stranger? Had Jack said anything yesterday that might have triggered this reaction?

As they made their way around the lake to the triceratops pen, his mind swam in doubts.

I didn't say anything. I just told the chief who I am... What did he see in my words? In me? Could he be insane? But he didn't look the part. He was odd, yes, but in a wise way. Like Master Shol.

When this connection was made, he drew a few more lines of similarity. This chief handled things in a way that reminded Jack of Master Shol. Cryptic and concise. He didn't explain his reasoning, as if Jack wouldn't understand, but there was something behind his words that made Jack trust that the chief knew better.

He hated this feeling. Once again, he was swept into the plans of another, unable to set his own course.

He could always run away. Nobody was holding him, and he doubted that the chief would come out and chase him personally. But Jack wouldn't run away. He believed he could trust this mystical man, so he would go and hunt the tyrannosaurus with Nauja. This was ultimately his plan, anyway. Make it through this ring quickly to find Gan Salin—and other allies, if possible—in Village Ring.

I wish I was stronger... Jack wished with every fiber of his heart. Only strength would allow him to choose his own path. If he were an immortal, the chief would have discussed things with him instead of simply spout instructions.

Only strength mattered. Jack's resolve reaffirmed itself.

He bent down by the lake, cupping some water into his hands and sipping greedily. It was perfectly clear. Tasty, even. He could see the bottom of the lake as if the water was glass. There wasn't the tiniest wave obstructing his sight. The only indication that the lake even existed were the gentle ripples caused by his cupping hands, along with the glint of mushroom light deeper in.

He raised his eyes, taking in the lush grass that filled the bowl-shaped valley, the smiling people who lay on it or tended to the dinosaur cattle, the jungle beyond.

It occurred to him, for the first time, that this valley was shaped as a crater. He liked that mental image. Life and peace in a former spot of intense violence.

He reached the back of the pen and waited, looking into the jungle ahead, not wanting to spoil Nauja's goodbyes with his stare. Brock lay on the soft grass, relaxing with his hands behind his head.

Eventually, soft footsteps approached. Nauja stood behind them, wearing the same, simple clothes as yesterday—fur strips around her privates and chest. A bow was slung on her back, along with two quivers: one containing normal-sized arrows, and the other large ones, the size of small spears.

Her gaze carried an intensity that Jack recognized. It was the same gaze everyone had adopted toward the end of the Integration Tournament. A warrior ready to battle.

"I am ready," she said. "On the way, you owe me an explanation."

"Sure. But you also need to explain all the things your father mentioned. What is the Forbidden Cave? How dangerous is that delver camp? And, most importantly, what's the deal with your title and ancestors?"

Her face cramped. "You ask a lot for a weakling."

"I risk my life alongside yours. I deserve to know."

Her face-cramping intensified before easing into a wary glance. "Fine. But only if we survive."

CHAPTER THIRTY-FOUR
THE BALANCE OF THE JUNGLE

JACK AND NAUJA PACED THROUGH THE JUNGLE. THE VEGETATION WAS DENSE enough to limit their sight but sparse enough to allow easy passage, while the cave ceiling a hundred miles in the air remained filled with enormous, glowing, yellow mushrooms.

The soil was soft and porous, caving easily under Jack's feet, and the incessant sounds all around them—from chirps, to buzzing, to rustling, to faraway roaring—indicated that the jungle didn't care much about their presence.

Brock jumped from branch to branch overhead. This place reminded him of home, the Forest of the Strong. Jack felt the same.

"So, that's all from me. More or less," Jack said.

As promised, he'd spent the last half an hour telling her his story, all the way from the first goblin to Trial Planet.

"Sounds infuriating," Nauja replied, shaking her head. "All those Animal Kingdom people on your planet... They're very similar to the ones I know. Birds of a feather flock together."

"How do you know that expression? Shouldn't it be, pterodactyls of a feather flock together?"

"Pterodactyls don't have feathers." She gave him a curious look. "You're an odd man, Jack Rust. Sometimes I wonder if you're actually stupid."

"Wow. Where's the enthusiasm you had when heading to the tribe?"

"That was before you messed with my life. Now, you're suspicious again. I don't believe that's everything you told my father. There is no reason for..." She gestured around. "...all this."

"I know." He shrugged. "But hey, I don't make the rules. He does. Go be angry at him if you dare." She glared at him. Jack smiled back. "Now, I told you everything. What about you?"

"What about me?"

"You promised to give me all the information you knew. About this place, the delvers, your Forbidden Cave, triceratops milk, your title..."

"I said I'd tell you *after* we survive."

"*Come on.* I gave you a lot of information. Reciprocate a bit."

She held her glare on him. Jack endured it calmly.

"Ungratefulness breaks the heart," she relented. "Fine. But nothing sensitive."

"Sure."

"What do you want to know first?"

"Let's start from the other delvers," he decided. "How strong are they? How many? What do they do here?"

"Plenty strong," Nauja replied. She bent down to inspect an animal track, then continued. Truthfully, following the tyrannosaurus wasn't difficult. It left footprints the size of a dining table. "Trial Planet isn't exactly packed with delvers, but there are usually hundreds of them in our ring. Even worse, most are stronger than us at the same level. They come from the B-Grade factions in the outside galaxy, who stuff their students full of resources and send them here like velociraptors on steroids."

"How the hell do you know about steroids?"

"We have contact with the outside world. We hear stories. Anyway, the point is that many delvers stop here to rest, recuperate, train, or gather allies. The terrain is much more hospitable than the ring above— or so I hear."

"It is." Jack agreed without a second thought. "Insects are terrifying."

"I don't understand that, but okay. However, our ring also has a quest: slay a level 115 enemy."

"Which wasn't the exact phrasing. It said, 'defeat.'"

"Same thing. That is not an easy task. Most delvers enter Trial Planet around the middle of the Hill Breaker range, around level 80 or 90. It is the level their factions judge as optimal. They also enter alone. As a result, even if they're a few levels stronger than they seem, hunting a level 115 dinosaur is risky. They have no reason to do it alone. To facilitate this, the factions have formed camps all around the ring, where delvers can find other people to team up with."

"Wait a moment," Jack said. "In the previous ring, I saw three delvers. They weren't alone, obviously, and all of them were high E-Grades."

Nauja paused at that, raising a brow. "That's unusual."

"So it seems. What do you think about them?"

She kept walking. They approached another tyrannosaurus track and angled their path to follow it. "It's not unheard of. Remember what I said about the optimal level being around 80 or 90? That's because their factions don't want to invest more yet. Trial Planet has a high death rate, so they're basically sending them in at the minimum level of preparedness, and only seriously invest in those who make it back with decent achievements."

"A high death rate? How high?"

"Seven out of ten delvers never return. Or so I heard."

"Spooky."

"It's because of arrogance. Starting at the Village Ring, everyone can choose to leave through teleporters. Even here, they can choose to backtrack to the surface if things get too difficult. But they're greedy and arrogant. They press on until they either die or almost die, at which point they finally retreat."

"But if they return early, they won't be deemed worthy, and their faction will sideline them."

"Exactly," Nauja replied with a hard smile. "It's what they deserve. They oppress us, but their factions oppress them. The world is merciless out there."

"And in here."

"It doesn't have to be that way here. They are the ones making everyone's life difficult."

Jack nodded thoughtfully. "So the ones I saw were precious members of their faction."

"Exactly. They raised them to a higher level before sending them in, which means their faction already invested in them. They don't do that for everyone. It's very rare, actually. And coming in as a team is even rarer. They would have to bribe someone at the outside to make that happen."

"Why am I not surprised that the Hand of God accepts bribes?" Jack replied cuttingly, thinking back to how Vocrich had just stood by and watched the Animal Kingdom gang up on him in the tournament. "Fucking fuckers."

"Everyone does." Nauja shrugged. "There are no good people out there, only less bad ones."

"There's me."

"Give it time." Her crooked smile turned more twisted. "So, you ran into big-shots. That is not good... but it is somewhat expected."

"Why?"

"There is an important event happening this time every year in the deeper rings. This is always when the big-shots come. That's also why we're hunting this tyrannosaurus now. The beasts of the jungle know not to touch our pens, but delvers grow more numerous this time of the year, so they kill a lot more prey. The large predators get hungry, and they either go after the delvers—which ends badly for them—or after our pens—which also ends badly for them. It is a shame. The delvers commit the same atrocities every year, ruining the balance we have to spend an entire cycle restoring. Why not respect nature just a bit?"

"Because they're assholes."

"Are you saying that because you mean it, or to flatter me?"

"Both." He gave her his best smile. She rolled her eyes, then inspected another tyrannosaurus footprint. "Why are you looking at these so intently, anyway? They're so large you could probably see them from the sky."

"Yes, but their size and depth hide information about the beast," she replied. "And more than that... We aren't the only ones who can track a tyrannosaurus. With footprints this large, everyone can, so I'm searching for humanoid footprints near it. If there are delvers already hunting it, we shouldn't approach."

"Oh," Jack said. "That's actually pretty smart."

"Of course it is. Why? Did you think I was stupid?"

She wasn't looking at him, but Jack still felt a chill. "Not at all. I just admired your knowledge. So, is there anyone else hunting it?"

"Not that I can see," she said. "Let's keep going. We're getting close."

"Mhm." They walked on. "So... About that Forbidden Cave of yours..."

"What about it?"

"Well, what is it?"

"Forbidden."

"I gathered that."

Silence fell again. Jack considered his next words before speaking. "Is there a particular reason why it's forbidden?"

"Why? So you can go ransack it?"

"I would never even consider that." He *had* considered it. "Besides, if there was anything to find there, I'm sure some delver would have gotten it already."

She stopped and glared at him, harder this time. Jack met her eyes calmly. He didn't glare back, but he also didn't look away, weathering her stare like a stone wall. Eventually, Nauja diverted her gaze and kept walking.

"It's nothing too important," she explained. "We have stories passed down by our ancestors. They mention that the cave should remain hidden and serene... but, as humiliating as this is to say, the delvers got wind of it long ago. They captured and tortured a few of us until someone spoke, more to protect the rest of the tribe than herself. There wasn't much to say. We know nothing else.

"The delvers have investigated it many times, but there's nothing. It's just a deep, empty cave complex. Some of them disappear some-times, but they're delvers. They're probably killing each other to steal their belongings, then blaming it on the cave."

"Sounds like something they would do."

"The point is, it's just an old story. We don't go into the cave for the sake of tradition. That's all there is to it."

"Mhm."

"You want to go inside and search for your luck." It wasn't a question, but a statement.

And, in truth, that was exactly what was going through Jack's mind. An empty, forbidden cave where people occasionally disappeared... This sounded too fishy. At worst, it would be empty. At best, he might discover something that everyone else had overlooked. It was a long shot, but it was a cave. How long could it take to explore?

"Of course not," he lied. Then, after hesitating, he added honestly, "It does sound intriguing, but your tribe took care of me yesterday. I will respect your wishes."

"Really?" This time, her gaze was earnest, like she believed him. Jack cursed. The girl *was* a truth detector.

"Really," he assured her. Not being a dick was more important than betting on the one-in-a-million chance he'd find something.

A wide smile blossomed on her face. "Thank you, Jack! This is basic propriety, but I know that even this much is challenging for delvers. I appreciate your sacrifice."

He wasn't sure if she was mocking him or not. Perhaps it was better not to know.

"How do you do that?" he asked instead. "How do you always know when I'm speaking the truth?"

"I told you. Words of the heart."

That made little sense. Either she was lying and had a relevant skill, or she'd simply gotten lucky so far. To be fair, Jack hadn't really lied about anything, so getting him right wasn't hard.

"Sure," he said. "Then, final question before we get to reptile milk. What's the deal with your title, the Direc—"

"Shh!" She put a finger on her lips. Jack froze. Above, Brock remained glued to his branch, frozen mid-movement. Nothing happened for a while.

Then, Jack heard it. A faint, deep, rhythmic sound. The subtle shaking of the earth under his feet.

"We're close," Nauja whispered, falling into a crouch and nocking an arrow on her bowstring. "Follow me."

Jack obliged. He did his best to remain stealthy, though he had no relevant skill. Nauja obviously did. Her movements left the environment completely undisturbed and made no noise, making Jack wonder whether she'd turned into an illusion. In comparison, his slow footsteps echoed in his ears like war drums.

There are more animals in the jungle, he consoled himself. There's no way it can hear me. It stomps like an elephant.

Following Nauja's lead, they crept closer. The small animals that used to flash on the canopy had disappeared, and the bird cries lessened, giving way to relative silence.

In it, the tyrannosaurus's heavy steps were even more audible.

Five minutes later, they entered a sparser part of the jungle. The trees weren't as thick, and the bushes clung to their roots, not spreading to block visibility. Jack could easily make out the lumbering beast that prowled through the woods, head scratching the canopy.

It was enormous. Long like an intercity bus and easily ten feet tall, with a thick tail, an oversized head, and a maw full of wicked teeth. Its two legs were thick and muscular, pressing heavily against the earth with every step, while its front limbs were short and stubby, ending in sharp talons that probably didn't find much practicality.

It was just like *Jurassic Park*, but far less comical. And also magically enhanced, probably. No normal beast had the power to smash hills.

Tyrannosaurus Rex, Level 121
The Tyrannosaurus Rex is one of the strongest dinosaur species. They are bipedal carnivores reaching up to forty feet in length and twelve high at the hips, with tails strong enough to act as weapons. Though solitary animals, they are not to be underestimated. Elite specimens have been observed using passive Physical Daos.

Perfect. Daos. Just what a t-rex needed, because it wasn't deadly enough.

At least this one wasn't an elite specimen.

The massive beast was currently walking away from them, probably seeking prey in some deeper section of the jungle. A small, rocky hill was visible in the distance, standing out of the jungle like a bald head, and a dark cave mouth hung open on its side.

"Is that your cave?" Jack asked, but Nauja brought a finger to her lips again, signaling silence.

He had detailed his strength on the way. Now, she saw him as an equal hunter—though she pridefully refused to treat him as such—which made this battle not as suicidal as it could have been.

Watching the tyrannosaurus, Nauja gulped. Jack saw her eyes harden. She was ready.

And he... He'd been born ready.

CHAPTER THIRTY-FIVE
FIGHTING REX

With a few hand signals from Nauja, Jack crept closer to a fern. Brock hid in the faraway canopy, ready to assist when and if he could. The barbarian herself climbed to a tree branch. She would start shooting the t-rex from afar to weaken it, and then Jack would ambush it as it approached. That was the extent of their plan. After that, they would improvise and hope to survive.

Jack crouched between the ferns, letting the ancient plant caress his skin. Wind slipped through the trees, calm and peaceful, unaware or uncaring of the violence about to ensue. The soil crunched softly under his boots, framing the intermittent animal cries that reached his ears.

The t-rex was a majestic creature. It awoke in Jack a childish wonder that only magic had matched so far. He'd seen so much about this beast, read so much, studied and theorized on it.

He expected a hint of hesitation at the thought of hunting one. Some unwillingness, a subtle feeling of desecration, like a child about to fight their hero. But he felt none of that. His wonder and fond memories manifested as an intense desire to fight. He yearned to test his might against this majestic beast and face it in combat. It was a sort of self-realization, along with an implicit understanding that combat was a mutually respectful experience, not manic slaughter.

Despite himself, he grinned.

An arrow was loosed between the trees. Its shaft was three fingers thick and as long as Jack's arm, especially devised for use against large creatures. It flew through the branches, heading for the tyrannosaurus's head so straight and unerringly that it simply couldn't miss.

It slipped into one of the dinosaur's eyes.

The bowstring's twang reached Jack right then. A crisp, deep sound, like an iron whip striking a mountain. It spoke of tremendous strength.

The jungle went quiet. The t-rex only then realized what happened, filling the silence with a deep, pained, furious roar. It turned in their direction and charged.

It was an apex predator. When a surprise attack occurred, it didn't think to run, only to fight back.

The dinosaur crashed through the trees as it made for him, taking long leaps and shaking the earth with each stomp. Its mouth was large enough to eat him whole, filled with long, sharp teeth. Its hulking body grew larger and larger as it approached, heading almost straight for Jack, though he was hidden.

Jack's world sharpened. All unnecessary thoughts and considerations fell away, leaving only the charging dinosaur, his allies, and the terrain. The entirety of his mind focused on combat. His body shivered in anticipation, mouth drew into a grinning snarl, fingers dug into his palm.

His being was fully aligned on the hunt.

The t-rex closed the distance in the blink of an eye. It wasn't just a large dinosaur. It was a peak E-Grade beast, enhanced by System, magic, or the Dao. Its physical capabilities were miles beyond its Earth equivalent.

But so was Jack.

A large foot stomped on the earth before his fern, imprinting it with a deep claw print. Jack jumped out. He flew into the air, right into the t-rex's path, right in front of its chest. He was like a fly.

But he stung.

Still midair, as the large chest threatened to flatten him, he reared back a fist, stretching his entire body. Purple light glowed. The world lost a hint of color, the dinosaur's roars lessened subtly. Jack's fist became the focal point, drawing the world's essence inside it until it shone brilliantly like a meteor about to fall.

He shot it forth.

The t-rex hadn't noticed him before and had no time to stop or turn. It fell into Jack, who used its momentum to drive his fist deep into its innards.

The explosion rocked the jungle. Jack's fist broke through smooth skin and scales, meeting a bone and snapping it. The t-rex roared in response to the blinding light and booming sound. Its body couldn't stop, and it crashed into Jack, sending him flying away like a ragdoll. His back smashed into a tree. All air was pushed out of his chest. He gasped silently, seeing stars as he slid down the bark.

A moment later, he recovered. His torso was in pain. His right fist sported cracked knuckles, having unleashed its strongest Meteor Punch yet. But he remained combative.

His eyes flicked to the t-rex. Besides the arrow stuck in its eye, it now sported a deep wound at the center of its chest. Blood flowed, and Jack could even spot the edge of a bone digging into the flesh underneath. Its gait was unsteady now, every step clearly bringing it pain.

Unfortunately, the t-rex was a large, System-enhanced beast. There was still plenty of fight left.

It was already charging again. When his eyes cleared, it was almost before him.

He rolled to the side, hearing a massive maw uproot the tree he'd been leaning against. It barely missed him. He pivoted, not sparing the time to even look back. A massive foot smashed the ground where he used to lie.

The tail got him. It whipped from the side and crashed into his chest, sending him flying again. Thankfully, he'd been close to the t-rex, so he only got hit by the part near its base, which couldn't gather too much momentum.

The impact was still like a massive sledgehammer. His ribcage groaned, and his entire body was bent backward like a bow. When he slammed into a tree back-first, and he bounced off to fall on the soil. By a herculean effort of will, he landed on his feet, stumbling but standing. He couldn't afford to fall prone again.

The t-rex was upon him instantly, a massive maelstrom of incredible strength. Even the weakest of hits threatened to maim him, and Jack's greatest attack had only managed to injure the beast, not kill it. It was at the peak of the E-Grade, and he was only at the early stage. No matter how overpowered he was, there was a limit to his strength.

Now, even surviving was a tall task.

An arrow drilled into the t-rex's head from behind, but its thick skull stopped it short. The beast ignored the arrow and lunged for Jack. He crouched, ready to defend.

The jaws came first. Despite its size, the t-rex was fast, its movements a blur. He barely managed to dodge the snapping teeth. Then, expecting another attack, he Ghost Stepped another few feet to the side. The massive tail whipped through the air where he used to stand—a debilitating strike, if it hit.

He kept moving. If he stayed still, he was dead. The sky darkened as a foot fell on him. He Ghost Stepped again, using the System's power to ignore the limitations of space, then turned and rolled. His boots dug into the soil, gravel slid against his shoulder and ribs. The world was dirt before he saw trees again.

He more felt than saw the next attack coming. He Ghost Stepped for the third time, sensing the air shudder where the jaws snapped shut around his previous position. He heard the twang of a bowstring and an arrow meeting flesh, but he couldn't see it. He was too slow. The t-rex was rotating through attacks faster than he could react.

His only saving grace was that the tyrannosaurus was a beast, and its attack pattern somewhat predictable.

A shadow on the ground was all the indication he had. He jumped aside, unable to breathe. The ground shook next to his head. He fell flat against it, letting the tail sail inches over him, then pushed against the dirt with all of his strength to fly out of the way. When no attack came to his previous position, he Ghost Stepped blindly. Again, no attack had come.

It came the moment his skill ended. The t-rex kicked at him. Its clawed foot met Jack's ribs, digging under him and shooting him upward with tremendous force. He barely even realized what happened before he smashed into the canopy, breaking through three branches, then starting to fall back down.

Pain was all-encompassing, but he was too deep into battle to really feel it. He managed to orient himself, catching a glimpse of a massive maw rushing up to get him. He Ghost Stepped away. Activating the skill midair took a lot out of him. He felt stitches in his ribs, his breath coming short.

He stumbled onto the ground, white stars swimming in his vision. He caught another glimpse of the dinosaur's massive body. Its hide was peppered with arrows, three of them sticking out of its head. A few were lodged deeper than others. Not only was the t-rex attacking him frantically, it was moving its body to make Nauja's aiming harder.

Those multiple wounds had to have an influence. An arrow was embedded in its eye. Its chest showed broken bones. And yet it still had the power to hunt Jack at such speed.

This can't go on, Jack thought. I'll die first.

The tail swiped at him. He jumped over it, sailing toward the t-rex's chest. Its head whipped around to bite at him. He Ghost Stepped midair, sensing the energy leave his body. He felt wrung out, empty, utterly exhausted.

Thankfully, survival was one hell of a motive.

He appeared on the dinosaur's back and fell against it, hugging the huge neck just as an arrow pierced the skin a few inches over his head. The t-rex growled and shook like a bull. Jack sensed the muscles below him tighten like steel cords, felt the power hidden in the dinosaur's body. Challenging it was a fool's errand.

Jack held on for dear life, his fingers digging into its skin. He was almost dislodged several times, but he grasped the dinosaur with all his strength. His jaw was clenched tightly to avoid biting his tongue. The t-rex's skin was hard and rough, scratching his chest as he held on tight. Its movements were erratic, unreadable, full of rage and desperation.

Arrows rained. They pierced all around him, but Nauja wasn't aiming too close to him to avoid accidents. Unfortunately, he was clinging on to a vital area, but he couldn't move now. She would just have to find a way. Jack placed all his faith in her, praying she would succeed.

How many arrows does she have? The thought passed through his head, filling him with terror. Her quiver wasn't that large.

Regardless, she kept shooting. Three seconds felt like a lifetime. The t-rex resembled a pincushion by now. Its life was bleeding out from all the wounds, especially the one in its eye. Jack felt it slow. His grasp was getting numb and weaker. He couldn't hold on too long.

The t-rex finally accepted that the archer was the priority. It stopped shaking and charged in the direction from where the arrows came, carrying Jack along as an unwilling passenger.

He was riding a dinosaur. If he wasn't dying, he would be elated.

The t-rex smashed headfirst into a tree, breaking it down. Jack couldn't see, but he felt the arrows stop coming. The dinosaur kept going, smashing into trees in quick succession, leveling this part of the forest, but Nauja must have been dodging, because he didn't hear her pained cries, nor did the t-rex's efforts abate.

It slowed further. There was a delay in its muscles now, Jack could sense it under him. They moved laboriously, as if pulling heavy weights instead of the limitless strength they used to exude. It was probably dying—but would it fall in time?

A great boom came. The t-rex smashed into a tree thicker than most, still cracking it but not with ease. Its entire body shook from the impact. Jack was dislodged, sent flying back-first into the falling canopy. Nauja's scream came from somewhere under him.

His gaze scanned the ground below, spotting Nauja dancing under the t-rex's body. Its jaws couldn't reach her there, but its legs could. She was faster than Jack, yes, but not as fast as the dinosaur. She could barely dodge. Her death was only a matter of time.

Pain came from all around Jack's body, but it was numb, distant. Riding the t-rex had allowed him to catch his breath, summon the last dregs of his energy. He had to act. Even as the canopy tumbled away from the fight, Jack pressed his feet against a branch's side and kicked against it so hard that it snapped.

He flew straight as if untethered by gravity. He came at the dinosaur from the side and above. His fist gathered energy, shining purple, sucking in the world. Just as the t-rex noticed him, Jack roared in its face, then fell on it like a meteor, fist-first.

His middle knuckle met the back of the arrow embedded in the t-rex's eye. The explosion splintered the wood, pushing the arrow tip even deeper. The t-rex's face erupted in a shower of blood and brain matter, and a chilling sound that was neither a roar nor a cry escaped its maw.

The explosion also arrested Jack's momentum, letting him fall straight down. He landed on his feet, almost dropping to his knees. Nauja was right behind him, face pale, eyes grim, and half-kneeling on the ground. The t-rex, somehow still alive, raised its head and released a final death rattle.

Then, it collapsed. Right on them.

Its body was large. Nauja inched away, but Jack's feet weren't working properly. He remained there, rooted. The t-rex wouldn't kill him if it fell on him, but it wouldn't be pleasant, either.

You have the power, a force inside him uttered—the Dao Root of Power. *Use it. Achieve dominance.*

Jack snarled. His fist shone purple again, glowing as he crouched and shot it upward, enhanced by his new Dao Root, and made unstoppable and dominating. A fierce uppercut connected with the falling t-rex's chest. The explosion threw Jack on his butt, and his knuckle bones cracked, but the massive body was flung back and swung to the other side like a pendulum. Without the t-rex consciously controlling its strength, its weight wasn't too great.

It landed on its back with a crash, then tumbled to the side and remained still, unmoving. A pool of gore formed under its head, and smaller ones around its body.

The tyrannosaurus rex was dead.

Level up! You have reached Level 65.
Level up! You have reached Level 66.
Level up! You have reached Level 67.
Level up! You have reached Level 68.
Level up! You have reached Level 69.

Through his exhaustion, one thought occurred to Jack. *Huh. Nice.*

He invested everything in Physical, some strength returning to his body. He could have waited a bit, but he didn't want to be vulnerable in the jungle.

Next to him, Nauja sat on the ground, panting, but her face was covered in a ruddy glow. Jack lay on his back.

"In hindsight," he said, panting himself, "this was stupid."

"Told you," she said. "Father went crazy."

"But we won. It wasn't even my toughest battle."

"That's stupid. If you keep going like that, you'll die." She glanced at him, a small smile playing on her lips. "Don't die."

He chuckled. "I'll try. You fought well."

"You too. I didn't expect you to survive."

"But you still sent me out to fight it. Thanks."

"No problem."

Brock came then, falling from a branch right next to Jack, making concerned monkey sounds, with some guilt mixed in. "I'm fine," Jack reassured him. "And don't worry about it. If push really came to shove, I know you'd save me."

That was more consolation than truth, but Brock seemed happy to hear it. Jack smiled, then willed the quest interface open.

Barbarian Ring Quest:
- **Defeat an opponent of Level 115 or above in a team of at most three individuals. (Completed)**
- **Make your way to the Village Ring.**

"So, what now?" he asked, eyeing the stony sky above. Since part of the canopy had collapsed, he had a view.

"Now, we get the hell out of here," Nauja said. "The battle was heard for miles around. Any delvers will be rushing here, and the scavengers of the forest as well. We aren't fit to face either of them."

"I could handle a scavenger."

"Allosauruses are scavengers, Jack. Think you could take one of them now?"

He thought back to the beast she'd slain the first time they met. Even as a juvenile, it was nine feet tall. "Let's get out of here."

"That's what I thought. Half a minute of rest and we're going."

"Got it."

CHAPTER THIRTY-SIX
THE DAO SOUL AWAKENS

THE NEXT FEW MINUTES PASSED QUIETLY. JACK AND NAUJA WERE RESTING NEXT to the dead t-rex, chests rising and falling with laborious breaths, while Brock kept watch from a high branch.

Nothing disturbed their rest, and all too soon, Nauja stood up. "Let's go. Can you walk?"

Jack groaned. "Letting our bodies go cold was a terrible idea."

He struggled to stand. When he succeeded, everything hurt. His ribs were cracked from the impacts. His back bled from a few lacerations where he'd smashed into trees, his legs wobbled, and he still felt like he'd run a marathon from the consecutive uses of Ghost Step.

"But can you walk?" Nauja insisted. She was in better shape, though also not fine. Whatever skill she used to dodge the dinosaur's attacks had taken its toll.

"Slowly."

"Good enough. We must get away from here."

"What about our trail?"

"Nobody will bother following. The scavengers will be more than happy with the tyrannosaurus itself, and delvers have no reason to come after us."

Jack nodded. Brock fell from the tree, and they headed out, leaving the corpse behind. He hadn't realized how pungent the smell was until they were a good twenty feet away. Then, he turned and gazed at the beast one last time. Sprawled on the ground like that, it resembled an overturned truck, just slightly larger. That they'd defeated such a beast was incredible.

To just leave its corpse untouched was more upsetting. They didn't need its meat, bones, or anything like that. It never harbored malice toward them—probably because it hadn't seen them. Jack pacified himself with the thought that it was eating the cattle of the Tri Lake tribe. They didn't kill it out of malice or arrogance; it had initiated a conflict, and it died because it was the weaker party.

Sometimes, there was no kind solution.

"Don't we need to take proof back?" he asked. "How will your tribe believe us?"

"They will believe me," Nauja replied confidently. "Only delvers lie. Barbarians, never."

"Hmm. Big words."

She did not reply.

They crossed the jungle, slower this time. Jack winced with every step, but he kept his mouth shut. The Iron Fiend Body was already working to patch him up, but it would take time. An hour at the least.

Nauja led them toward the Forbidden Cave. It was a cavernous opening in the side of a hill stretching down into the darkness, wide enough to fit a bus. Rocky outcroppings surrounded its entrance, and the grass stopped growing a few feet away from it.

According to Nauja, its inside was large and complex, akin to a maze. Going in without a map was a fool's errand. It was also completely empty.

They didn't enter. There was a cabin built next to the entrance, empty and dusty, but enough to shield them from any eyes. It shielded the tribe's guards, once upon a time. Inside was simple: a rectangular space with one bed—a pile of furs—on either end, and no windows. There was also a table with two chairs, a stool, and two thick paravans that could be drawn to isolate either bed.

Seeing those paravans, Jack barely resisted the urge to sigh in relief. He was in need of secrecy, and not because he was modest. In the half-minute of rest after the fight, something had happened. Something big. A pleasant warmth came from the secret pocket behind his left thigh, seeping into his skin. It felt familiar, somehow. Though Jack had never experienced such a thing before, he knew what it was.

The Dao Soul. It was finally awake.

"Do you mind?" he asked, motioning with his head to the paravan. If Nauja was surprised, she didn't show it.

"Of course not," she replied, moving to one of the beds. "How long do you think you need?"

"...An hour. Even if I'm not fully healed, I'll be ready to walk back to the tribe."

Now she was surprised. She raised both brows. "Are you serious?"

"Yeah."

"Those wounds would take me two days to heal, and I have a regeneration skill."

"Well, we can't all be awesome."

She glared at him. "Fine, awesome one. One hour. Then, we'll be on our way."

"You got it."

She walked to her bed and pulled the paravan on the far wall. Jack noticed with satisfaction that he couldn't see anything past it. It was so heavy that it even muffled sound. He did the same, isolating himself on the small bedding of fur that decorated the other side of the building, and sat cross-legged.

Brock was with him. Unlike Nauja, he understood that something was up. He threw Jack a questioning glance, but Jack said nothing. He simply reached into his hidden pocket and pulled out the Dao Soul.

The purple gem glowed. Jack had no idea why. He'd kept it for two weeks already, and nothing had ever changed.

But the why didn't matter. Somehow, the Dao Soul had awoken. Jack was giddy.

Not only was the gem glowing purple, but the black and white lines inside had changed their rotating pattern. Before, they were simply turning in circles. Now, they had stabilized into a particular shape.

"What the—" Jack said, cutting himself short.

The shape was a fist. Half of it was white and the other black, split roughly between the middle and ring fingers. As Jack stared at it mutedly, and as Brock watched with wide eyes from behind his shoulder, he realized that not only was this a fist, it was *his* fist.

Not his physical one, but his Dao. This fist looked exactly like the vision he'd seen when breaking through to the E-Grade. The only difference was the colors. It resonated deeply with him, pulsing to the beat of his heart and soul.

"What the fuck..." Jack said again, holding the gem with both hands. It was warm to the touch. "Do you see what I see, Brock?"

The brorilla nodded.

One part of Jack wanted to consume this immediately. He didn't know how, but he was certain there was a way. It looked like his soul; he *had* to have it.

However, another part of him was suspicious. He'd already been tricked and lied to many times. The world was not on his side. Was this gem really a reward, or was it maybe a hidden device planted by the Animal Kingdom to control him? It couldn't activate by itself, right? Someone had to give the signal.

I'm being paranoid, he scolded himself. That's too much. If the Dao Soul was fake, Master Shol would have noticed it. Perhaps it was just attuning to my Dao all this time, and now it's finally ready—thank God I kept it on me.

In any case, he had to take every advantage he could. He couldn't afford to waste opportunities on vague suspicions. If the Animal Kingdom had somehow snuck in a fake Dao Soul, so be it.

With that final thought, he let himself truly desire this object. It felt vital to him, like a long lost part of his soul. He touched it to his chest—on instinct. The Dao Soul melted, entering his body like a stream of pure power that ignored his skin.

A prick of panic followed. The Dao Soul reached his soul, and wrapped around it, tightening its grip. The pain was excruciating.

His entire body convulsed. He lost control. He tried to scream, but Brock's hand clamped his mouth shut and held his head still so he wouldn't injure it from all the thrashing.

The Dao Soul was a secret. Brock understood that. If Jack screamed, Nauja would come running, and they would have no choice but to reveal some of their secrets. As honest and peaceful as she seemed, there was no guarantee she wouldn't be tempted at the knowledge of the Dao Soul.

No, she couldn't find out. Better safe than sorry.

Therefore, Brock held Jack's mouth shut, muffling his screams despite his own panic. Their souls were connected. He could sense that Jack's pain was necessary, that the Dao Soul wasn't harming him, but he was still filled with worry.

It only lasted for a few moments.

Half a minute later, Jack was sprawled on the floor, panting and sweaty. His eyes were exhausted but clear. "Fuck that hurt." Brock nodded, giving Jack a double thumbs-up. "Heh. Yeah, I guess so. Thanks, brother."

Still on the ground, Jack shut his eyes and looked inward. Where his soul hovered, a fist-shaped container in the middle of a large void, there was now a second soul hovering just beside it. The two souls were identical, except for their size—the new soul was only a fraction of the original.

"Would you look at that..." Jack muttered tiredly, opening his eyes. "I have two souls."

Brock cheered, then looked at Jack questioningly.

"I don't know either," Jack responded. "But I suspect..."

He sat up, forcing himself into a sitting position despite the lingering phantom pain. He closed his eyes, settling into meditation.

What is the fist? he asked himself.

The moment he began pondering on the Dao, he became aware that his mindscape was different. His thoughts flowed oddly. The Dao Soul hadn't changed him, but it had enhanced him. As he considered the meaning of his fist, it felt like he had a second brain analyzing the thoughts of the first. He saw his own thoughts from outside, which easily revealed flaws he might have otherwise needed hours to uncover.

It was like discussing an idea with someone who knew exactly what you were talking about. Naturally, the results of this method would be vastly superior to thinking alone. His cultivation speed had just multiplied.

Jack's excitement threatened to overwhelm him, but he held it at bay. He could sense that there were still things to discover. He homed in on the feeling of that second brain, diving deep inside himself.

The next moment, he stood in the void of his soul, the same space he'd visited during his last breakthrough.

This time, the experience was much more disorienting. He could simultaneously sense himself standing here and sitting still in the jungle cabin. He moved his arms and legs. The him that was sitting remained still, but the him in the soul space moved as he indicated. And yet, he remained a single person.

It was like using one brain to control two bodies. Complicated.

What is this? Jack thought, focusing on the version of himself inside his soul. Now that he wasn't mid-breakthrough, he could investigate this place with his full mental awareness.

It felt just like space. He was hovering in seemingly endless nothingness, with only the Dao Root of Indomitable Will and the Dao Root of Power randomly floating around. Jack struggled to make them out, two colored fists lazily crossing the void.

He couldn't see the Dao Seed of the Fist because it had already become one with his soul. He was inside it. He could sense the fist in every inch of the surrounding space. Any rainbow-colored hints of the Rainbow Dao Pill had long dissipated.

Okay, he thought, looking around. *And now what?*

Suddenly, someone knocked on the door of his soul. It was a very peculiar feeling. Jack was baffled. "Come in?"

A head poked out of nothing, looking around the infinite blackness until it spotted him. It was his head. Except it wasn't. It moved on its own.

The head smiled. A hand appeared next to it, waving at him, and then the entire body appeared.

Jack was looking at a copy of himself, down to his white pants and black boots. He tilted his head. His copy smiled cheerfully and waved again. Jack, cautiously, waved back.

The copy looked around. There was only darkness as far as the eye could see. It turned its gaze back at Jack, and he could see a hint of questioning inside it.

"What? I didn't choose to make my soul black."

The copy shook its head, indicating around it.

"Can you not speak?" Jack asked. The copy kept pointing circles around it. "Do you mean I can... change the background?" he asked. The copy nodded. "But how?"

The copy shrugged. Jack frowned, picturing a grassland...

...and suddenly, they were in a grassland. The sky was bright blue over their heads, illuminated by a shining sun. A breeze caressed his skin, making his pants flap. His hair moved as well, dancing to the tune, as did the grass blades under his feet. Jack wished he was barefoot to feel them, and next thing he knew, he was! The grass now tickled his toes.

Around him, the grass stretched on endlessly, and there was absolutely nothing else in the world except for himself, the copy, the sun, and two colored moons floating lazily through the sky—his Dao Roots, one metallic silver and the other dark blue.

"What the heck?"

The copy smiled—a smile so bright and wide it reminded Jack of Vlossana. It was full of pure bliss.

"Wow," he said. "I know! Are you a child?"

The copy looked at him in confusion, then tilted its head and shrugged. Jack took that as, "I guess?"

"Wow. No wonder you seem so happy. Hey, look." Eager to test out his new powers, he willed a large toy box into existence. It was filled with all sorts of goods. The copy gave it one look, then glanced back at Jack. It balled its fists.

Jack frowned. "What? You wanna fight?"

The copy laughed without sound—a creepy sight—and shook its head. It pointed at its heart, then the floating lights in the sky.

"Oh!" Jack said. "You're the Dao Soul. You want to play with the Dao!"

The copy nodded excitedly. This time, Jack laughed, too. "Very well. Have at it!"

His fist flared with purple light. He charged, and the copy, full of joy, did the same. Their fists clashed.

CHAPTER THIRTY-SEVEN
CONSECUTIVE BREAKTHROUGHS

THE TWO FISTS CLASHED IN A TERRIFYING EXPLOSION. BOTH BORE THE DAO OF the Fist. They were strong, unrelenting, indomitable. None backed down. Jack's knuckles ground against the copy's, and all the amassed power erupted in a ring-shaped shockwave that blasted into the ground.

The grass disintegrated under their feet, leaving a blackened crater the size of a bathtub.

Jack turned and smashed a hook into the copy, which stepped into his guard and shot a straight right into his face. Jack took it head-on, flying backward, rolling midair, and skidding on his feet. He rubbed his lip—a hint of blood was left on his fingers.

"Heh. You can fight."

The copy smiled brightly. Of course it could fight. It was him.

Jack noticed that he couldn't use skills in here. What he just shot wasn't a Meteor Punch, just a punch infused with his Dao.

What he *could* use was the Dao, and its power was far greater than in the real world. Here, the Dao was part of everything. It existed in the air, the ground, the grass, the sky. He was simply utilizing the power that was freely available.

In the real world, trying to push his Dao outside his body was like wedging it into something that was already full. The world was flooded with its own Dao, one that included everything, and imposing his will on that was hard. So hard, in fact, that Jack couldn't do it. His Dao could only affect his own body, or at best influence the world in tiny manners. Every skill he used came from him or the System's assistance.

Even Brutalizing Aura, his newest skill, only interfered with the minds of other people, not the Dao or the world itself. That was the domain of D-Grade cultivators.

Here, however, Jack's Dao was one with the world's. They were in his soul, after all.

He took another moment to consider the implications of this. The copy gave him time.

What did it mean that he couldn't use his skills? Why? Because the System can't reach me here, he realized. The soul is inviolable. Even the System cannot access it.

He tried to bring up his status screen as an experiment. Nothing happened. His theory was right. Was this a good or a bad thing? Jack didn't know, but the tribe chief had warned him not to trust the System. Did Jack trust that guy? Probably. Did he know what this meant? No. But a System-free space inside his soul couldn't be a bad thing, right? At worst, he just wouldn't use it.

He returned his gaze to the copy, standing across a blackened crater on the grass. A thought later, the crater disappeared, leaving the ground pristine. Jack's torn lip recovered instantly.

I cannot practice skills, Jack considered, but I can use the Dao and amplify its effects.

He tested that theory. The Dao of the Fist flooded his body and seeped out, forming a purple halo around him. He could sense the world changing. There was no tangible difference, but the fabric of reality was now under the influence of the Fist. It was like coloring the air purple. Everyone would be able to see it, but it wouldn't really change anything. There was no conduit.

Dao Skills were that conduit. And, though the System wasn't here... How much did it help with those skills, really?

Jack clenched his fist, imagining a meteor around it. The Dao of the Fist rushed to it, cladding his fist in bright purple, and the world shuddered lightly around it, but nothing else happened. The sounds and colors weren't drawn in, and the power Jack had gathered felt like a pale imitation of the real thing.

Why? he considered. Is the System amplifying my power when I use skills?

But his Dao itself wasn't weakened. The power he poured into his fist was the same. It was just the effect that was severely lessened.

It's because I can't guide it, he thought, eyes shining. That's where the System helps. It doesn't empower. It facilitates.

On closer inspection, he could sense the Dao straining under his control. The skill he was using wasn't less powerful than the outside world's Meteor Punch, it was just far cruder. Power leaked out. As though a bunch of tiny people were pulling in different directions instead of the disciplined army that the System helped him form.

Can I get better? Jack wondered. A crazy thought entered his mind. What happens if I perfect the skill by myself? What will the System do, then?

He focused on the fist. Maintaining the skill was draining, but he clamped on with Indomitable Will. He focused every scrap of his mind into it. In the sky, the metallic silver light that was the Dao Root of Indomitable Will shone brighter, though Jack couldn't see it.

Controlling his Dao manually was a pain in the ass. It rebelled constantly. The fist was more than just a weapon, it was a concept, a will to go forward. It contained hints of defiance. Every time Jack willed it into his fist, a part of the Dao refused to follow his orders.

He could force it if he pushed harder, but it took a lot of power, and it wasn't as effective. A rebellious army was far less useful than one which believed in your cause.

Could I convince it?

This was a bit like his breakthrough into the E-Grade. The Dao was mindless, yet it spoke in feelings and ideas. It told him why it refused to follow his orders. It was like a stubborn child. Jack could debate it, constantly adjusting his outlook to perfectly match the Dao's. He explained why flowing into his fists and striking out was perfectly in line with the nature of the Dao of the Fist, why he deserved to wield it, why they were a perfect match.

It didn't work, of course. His control and understanding of his own Dao was too shallow to debate the Dao itself. His control slipped, letting most of the gathered power escape... but some remained. A small part of the power yielded to his control. His fist strengthened, forming a barely usable form of Meteor Punch. It was a far cry from the System-assisted one in the outside world, but it proved an important point.

Jack could get better at it. Here, with no distractions, where the power of his Dao was amplified enough to let him sense the tiniest changes, he could practice. And the skills were simply sharpening stones. The real target was the Dao. In the process of mastering his Meteor Punch skill, his flaws were made apparent. He was sharpening his own understanding, which brought him closer and closer to the Dao of the Fist itself.

Jack couldn't help grinning. Dao skills had five tiers, like normal skills, but were very hard to upgrade. None of his were at the third tier. Now, though... Now, he had a way forward.

This Dao Soul was an incredible treasure. It stabilized and enhanced his soul, letting him open up this space, and that was only half of the benefits.

Jack looked up. Not only did he have the perfect place to practice his Dao, but he also had a training buddy.

The copy grinned and clenched his fist. Jack did the same. This was like Sparman all over again, except less mocking—at least for now.

He shot forward. The Dao roared over his fist, mustering a bit more power than his previous attack. When he met the copy's fist, he overpowered it. Copy Jack flew away, back-flipping and landing on its feet. Its eyes narrowed. Jack felt the Dao flicker around the copy, changing subtly. He laughed.

The copy was also working on its Dao.

But that was good. It gave him yet another sharpening stone.

The copy's Dao gathered around its fist, imitating Jack's understanding but not exactly. There were subtle changes. Tiny insights that were more polished than Jack's, and others that were less.

That was interesting. The copy followed his path, but it had its own mind. It could show him things he couldn't see himself. Maybe point out his flaws.

"Come on!" Jack shouted.

The copy charged him. Their fists collided. Their auras ground against each other, both pulsing with the power of the fist. They exchanged a flurry of strikes, meeting each other punch for punch before moving to more advanced combat.

This time, Jack didn't underestimate the copy. It had his Fistfighting skills, too—though they were far cruder without the System's assistance. Still, he had experience fighting now, and the copy inherited it.

Jack ducked under a hook, stepping in with a straight. The copy saw that coming and slapped the strike away, retreating. Jack unleashed two jabs in a row, which the copy barely dodged. The three-jab was a feint. Right as the copy dodged, a heavy uppercut met its jaw, shooting it upward to crash hard into the ground where it stayed, its head bent at an odd angle.

Jack grimaced, panicked, and willed the copy to reform. Thankfully, it did, and it seemed just as gleeful as before.

That was a good point to remember. In this soul space, their bodies had the strength of a pre-System Jack. They also lacked his defensive skills, but they had his offensive Dao, so any attack that landed would be devastating. That was a pretty unbalanced way to fight.

However...

Jack's eyes narrowed. The Dao of Indomitable Will above shone bright. Once upon a time, he'd used it to augment his defense. As his will was indomitable, so was his body.

Perhaps he could do the same now.

When the copy attacked again, Jack crossed his arms and took the blow, channeling the Dao Root. He was indomitable. The attack shook him, but he'd defended against a weak Meteor Punch. The copy raised its brows. Jack grinned behind his guard, then smashed a fist into the copy's teeth.

The copy fell back, then quickly stood again. It squinted at Jack, considered his defenses, then copied it. The Dao Root above shone even brighter. Jack and the copy each had fists shining purple and bodies shining metallic silver—the color of Indomitable Will. They charged each other.

Jack's soul became a battlefield.

Fists carved the ground and shook the air. Small explosions landed on bare chests, shooting the recipient away. Though Jack was progressing in both attack and defense, one was fueled by a Dao Seed and the other by a Dao Root. There was a clear difference there.

However, this also meant the flaws of his defense were exposed faster. Jack's Dao of the Fist was qualitatively stronger than his Dao of Indomitable Will. As he and the copy fought, pitting themselves against each other, not only did they practice their Fistfighting skills without the System's assistance, but every attack that landed pitted the two Daos against each other.

The attacker always won, but their defense was gradually getting sturdier. They weren't pushed back as far anymore.

Jack lost himself in the fighting. Like the dance he'd experienced in the Tri Lake tribe, it was liberating. He loved combat. This time, he didn't have to worry about killing someone, dying himself, or holding back his power. He could completely let loose. The pain still existed, and every time he lost was agony, but it only fueled his resolve to get stronger.

Battle was an art. Punches whistled past heads. Jack and the copy targeted each other's weakness, learning the patterns of the enemy and changing their own. Every time they clashed, someone was sent flying. As time passed, their bouts became longer. They could attack and dodge better. They knew how the other moved. Though they shared the same experiences, they were two different entities, so they each acted slightly differently.

Time flowed freely as Jack was engrossed in the fighting, like a particularly intense video game. He got slightly sharper with every clash. It was the first time he'd trained like this, so his improvement was fast, and so was the copy's.

The annoying thing was that they still couldn't block. They were forced to always dodge. Every time an attack connected, the defender was blown back, and the defense of Indomitable Will only weakened the blow, not negated it. That greatly limited their options.

And, worst of all, there was nothing Jack could do about it. The world around them was his soul, which was one with the Dao Seed of the Fist. The Dao surrounding them was that of the Fist. Even though Indomitable Will was compatible, and even though Jack felt he had a pretty good understanding of it, that Dao simply had far less of a pool to draw from.

Unless I can use the fist to defend, Jack thought. But the Dao of the Fist is offensive. Hmm...

When they clashed again, Jack didn't use the Dao of Indomitable

Will to defend. He used the Dao of the Fist, drawing it around him like a mantle.

It failed. He was thrown backward. The copy scoffed at him.

"I'll show you when I get it," Jack thought, narrowing his eyes. "Again!"

They clashed. Jack tried different things. He made the Dao of the Fist into a shield, armor, or even a series of tiny fists that protected him. Every time, it failed.

Dammit! he thought, panting on the grass. *The fist is attacking!*

No matter how he used his understanding to rouse the Dao's power, its nature by itself was offensive. He could convince it to fight with him, but he couldn't talk it into changing its nature. It had to be the Dao of Indomitable Will.

Oh!

What if he convinced the power of the Dao of the Fist surrounding him to transform into the Dao of Indomitable Will? If one was part of the other, it should be possible.

He stood back up. He and the copy clashed another dozen times. Jack kept failing, but he sensed he was on to something here. The Dao resisted, but every time, he found new ways to counter it. When it claimed that the fist was meant to crush through anything, he showed how indomitability was a part of that. When it claimed the fist was power, he proved that indomitability was included. When it asked why indomitability was present in every aspect of the fist, he simply explained that indomitability was a part of the fist. The two Daos were interlinked, doubly nested.

He kept pushing. The Dao challenged every part of his understanding. It demanded that he fuse every aspect of the fist with indomitability. It was difficult, but his understanding of both was sharp enough. Eventually, he succeeded.

And the Dao complied. When he used the Dao of Indomitable Will to defend himself, it was powered by the same Dao of the Fist that fueled his Meteor Punch. Metallic, silver armor appeared on him. The copy's punch exploded on it, and Jack had to take a step back... but he remained standing.

The entire soul space shook. Jack looked up. The silver star that was the Dao Root of Indomitable Will stirred. Its color washed out, no longer stopping at its boundaries, and spilled into the air. In return, the air flowed in. The Dao Root shone purple, then turned colorless, becoming one with the soul world. Root-like lines stretched out of the Dao Root and into the air, fading the farther they went until they disappeared and stilled. Now, the Dao Root was colorless and anchored to the soul world, fused into it.

Suddenly, everything turned more solid. More real. Jack felt like the entire world had gotten denser, containing more power in every molecule. The grass was greener.

The copy looked at him in astonishment, and even he was surprised. He hadn't expected such a change. However, he understood what he'd done, and he smiled. He also realized he was exhausted.

How long was I in here?

"That's enough for today, Copy Jack," he told the copy. "Thank you. See you soon."

The copy waved at him.

Jack opened his eyes to find himself still cross-legged in the real world. He had no idea how long it had been, but since nobody had disturbed him, probably less than the agreed-upon hour. Brock was nowhere to be seen—probably standing guard outside.

Whatever the case, Jack couldn't stop a wide grin from spreading on his face. He perused the screens waiting for him.

**Congratulations! The Dao Root of Indomitable Will had been successfully fused with your Dao Seed.
Constitution +30
Will +30**

**Congratulations! Skill Iron Fiend Body (II) upgraded into Dao Skill, Indomitable Body (II).
Indomitable Body (II): You possess more than mere physicality. The Dao of the Fist reinforces your entire body, making it indomitable. You have significant durability, quick regenerative powers, and heightened control over your body, including its natural limiters. Additionally, your mind is fast enough to keep up.**

Trial Planet was a gift that kept on giving. Though, the Dao Soul came from earlier. This was his delayed reward for winning the Integration Tournament, and Jack could now understand why the Animal Kingdom would put such a huge bounty on his head. This thing was extremely precious. They probably hoped to recover it before he used it, but now...

Now, the tiger had been given wings. Even the days benefits were incredible. He wouldn't have such explosive gains all the time, but it was as the head judge had said. This Dao Soul would increase his cultivation speed by a lot.

He grinned. Trial Planet, here I come!

CHAPTER THIRTY-EIGHT
DIRECT DESCENDANTS

"Done!" Jack shouted, pulling open the curtain. The same little cabin waited for him, but he was not the same.

He'd fused a Dao Root. Had advanced a skill into a Dao Skill. He'd gotten sixty stat points—the equivalent of twelve levels, though only half of those went into his main stats.

Still, the doubled increase in Will was significant, and Jack felt so unfettered. It was like he had complete control over his mind, like the lamp light that illuminated his island of conscious in the sea of subconscious had expanded. All errant thoughts had seized. The noise that always filled his mind went silent, and only now did he realize just how strong its impact was. He'd just learned to ignore it so far in his life, but doing so was surprisingly tiring. Suddenly, many mental resources were just... available.

He felt like he could do anything.

Name: Jack Rust
Species: Human, Earth-387
Faction: Bare Fist Brotherhood (E)
Grade: E
Class: Fiend of the Iron Fist (Elite)
Level: 69

. . .

Strength: 265
Dexterity: 265
Constitution: 295
Mental: 30
Will: 60

Skills: Ghost Step I
Dao Skills: Meteor Punch II, Indomitable Body II, Iron Fist Style I,
Brutalizing Aura I
Daos: Perfect Dao Seed of the Fist (middle), Dao Root of Indomitable
Will (fused), Dao Root of Power
Titles: Planetary Frontrunner (10), Planetary Torchbearer (1), Second
Ring Conqueror

Perhaps I should invest in Mental, too, he considered. This feels so nice.

Jack didn't know what his Dao Seed advancing to the middle stage
meant. Was it because he'd fused a Dao Root?

"Do you need to shout?" Nauja's irritated voice came as her curtain
slid open. The barbarian girl revealed herself sitting on the bed with her
back against the wall, resting.

Jack smiled at her. His excitement was hard to contain. "I don't need
to be quiet either."

"How are you done already?" she asked, narrowing her eyes. "I
thought you needed an hour."

"My wounds were lighter than I thought."

Jack had no idea how long he'd spent training in his soul. It had felt
like hours, but perhaps the time inside and outside wasn't the same? In
any case, his upgraded body skill and the extra thirty points in Constitution worked wonders for healing. Besides some soreness in his muscles
and a lingering sense of exhaustion, he felt fine.

Nauja shrugged. "Well, whatever. I'm glad you're okay. In that case,
we can head back."

"Right," Jack said. Now that he wasn't in pain, he could think clearly again. In fact, he could think clearer than ever. Out of momentary curiosity, he scanned her to see how much she'd leveled up from the tyrannosaurus.

Human (Trial Planet), Level 101
Faction: -
Title: Direct Descendant

Two levels... Seems about right.

"Don't get me wrong, but I'm in a hurry," Jack said. "Since I completed the requirement of the Ring Quest, there's no need to come back and impose on your tribe further."

A hint of something went through her eyes. Jack saw it but failed to decipher it. It wasn't ill-intentioned, nor was it polite hesitation. She hadn't fallen for him, either. It was concern, in a way. Worry. But it wasn't for him.

Before he could consider it further, Nauja replied, "You aren't imposing at all. We are glad to have guests."

"I must still hurry. I have a friend—kind of—waiting for me at the Village Ring, and I must find allies to descend the tower. Plus, you know my deadline now. A year is very short. I have no time to waste."

Nauja bit her lip. "You are leaving too quickly."

"Too quickly for what?"

"I—Nevermind. Staying longer would give me more time to deal with a personal decision, but I cannot hold you back for my own weakness."

"What weakness?"

"I said, nevermind." She glared at him. He could see the flickering light in her eyes. She wasn't really looking at him. Her mind was busy, whirling around...

But about what? he considered, letting her glare slide over him. She doesn't seem to have fallen for me. Could it be she needs me as an excuse to stay away from her tribe? That can't be right, she just said we needed to go back. Then, what could it possibly be?

...Oh.

"Say," he asked leisurely, "can barbarians descend through the planet?"

Her gaze hardened, betraying nothing. "We can. But we have to fulfill the same requirements as you."

"Which you just fulfilled."

"What are you implying?"

"I'm just wondering... Are you considering coming with me?"

"Absolutely not." Hard rejection, emphasized. "It is something I could consider in the future, but it's still too early for me."

"Oh? How come?" Jack asked, not fully convinced. He remembered how she described her tribe. *It is a blessed life, but...* That but was never completed. She wasn't fulfilled here. She was missing something— which could only be adventure. He knew because he'd felt the same way, back before the System arrived on Earth.

Then again, barbarians never lied, according to her.

"Because you're a delver," she said, "and a stranger. I don't know you. I admit that I am intrigued by the deeper rings and the universe outside, and I struggle to wait now that I am a veteran hunter, but I cannot just tie my life with yours. I just met you yesterday. That isn't how we do things." She took a deep breath, calming down. "When we choose to delve, we form a carefully designed team of our own. Barbarians only. Only *we* are trustworthy. Everyone else is treacherous, greedy, prone to temptation, and unreliable. Just because you seem like a better person than everyone else doesn't mean you're one of us. My father would never trust you with my life."

"Hmm." Jack nodded somberly. "That's very reasonable. Sorry for pushing you."

"It's okay. If I didn't want to speak my thoughts, I wouldn't speak them. I can wait a couple years. I just toyed with the idea a bit, tasting the temptation, but that is weakness."

"Well, for what it matters, fighting the tyrannosaurus with you was a fun experience," Jack said. "I haven't fought alongside others in a long time."

"Same there!" A weight seemed to have been lifted off her shoulders. Now that she'd shared the thoughts she kept hidden, hints of her enthusiasm started resurfacing. "We make a good team!"

"Hardly. We're both muscleheads." He roared in laughter. She pouted. "I'm kidding! We fought well. Thank you for not skewering me on the back of the tyrannosaurus."

"I was aiming at you, I just kept missing." Her smile widened. Jack once again noticed how her pale face made a stark contrast against the jungle environment and the hut's dark walls, giving an out-of-place impression. "So. Since you're leaving, I suppose you need instructions to the nearest exit down."

"Yes please."

"Listen closely. There is one exit right under the nearby delver camp, but you want to avoid that one. If you show up alone, you will probably get in trouble."

Jack nodded.

"The second nearest is in the bowels of a close-by mountain. It's five days away—maybe more for you, since you're unused to the jungle. Just walk straight east until you spot the mountain. There is a ravine by its base, mostly empty save for the occasional delver. The exit is at the far end. There are pteranodons inhabiting the ravine, though, so be careful."

"I will. But how do I tell east here? There's no sun."

"I've heard of that." Her eyes took on a dreamy look. "A giant ball of light that travels through the sky... How incredible is that?"

"To each their own. I find the light mushrooms here equally amazing."

"I guess. Well, we may not have a sun, but we do have compasses. They work just fine. I don't have one with me, but" —she pointed— "east is that way."

"Wow. Did you swallow a compass when you were a kid?"

"I'm a hunter. Comes with the territory." She gave him a toothy grin. "You are always welcome to rest in our tribe before going. We can give you a proper compass, too."

"Thank you, but it's fine. Yesterday's rest was plenty."

"Very well. In that case, I suggest you leave quickly. You are healed, as I understand, so the faster you get going, the better. This place is not completely safe."

"Neither is the jungle."

"More than here. Delvers sometimes come to the Forbidden Cave, and if they find you here—"

"Trouble, I know. Are you *trying* to get rid of me? I thought you enjoyed my company."

"Hesitation is unbefitting of a barbarian. We know to let go."

"A great quality. Took me many years to learn."

"It does make life simpler."

Nauja paced toward the door, and Jack followed suit. There was nothing in the hut besides dust. His mind was already filled with thoughts about his next trip.

Five days in the jungle... he considered. Provisions won't be a problem, but what about predators? I would see a tyrannosaurus coming from a mile away, but... Hmm.

"Are there strong, stealthy predators in the jungle?" he asked.

"There are. They range between levels 60 and 100, so you should be careful."

"I might be able to take them, actually."

"A level 100 predator while you're still level 69?" She looked back and raised a brow. "You were pretty good at not dying against the tyrannosaurus, but don't get overconfident. Needless risks lead to death."

"Yeah, you're right," Jack lied. He still believed he could fight a level 100 creature. His titles gave him a cumulative +35% efficacy on all his stats, plus the Immortality Serum that was the equivalent of ten levels, plus his perfect Dao Seed, the fused Dao Root, the unfused one...

He had his chances. He just had to not get ambushed—which he had zero skills for.

Whoops.

"Can I ask you a final thing, Nauja?"

"Sure!" she said, hand on the doorknob. "What is it?"

"Why's your title Direct Descendant? I'm just curious. You said you'd explain to me after the tyrannosaurus fight."

"Oh, that?" She smiled awkwardly. "Everyone knows by now, so I guess it's no harm telling you. It's because we are direct descendants of the Ancients, the species that created the System."

"What!" He gaped. "Really?"

"Or so the title says." She shrugged. "We don't know anything about it, really. We've been in here for countless generations."

"Wow... What does it give you?"

She stuck out her tongue. "I'm not telling you that."

"Hah, fair enough."

"Is your curiosity sated?"

"It's reignited."

She chuckled. "Delvers." She pushed the door open, revealing a green clearing with the Forbidden Cave to their back. Jack had considered circling around and coming back to explore it, but the barbarians had been nice to him, and he didn't want to disrespect their wishes. Maybe another time.

Brock was right in front of the door. He seemed frantic. In fact, they opened the door just as he was about to dash into it, making him crash into Nauja before he could stop himself.

"Oof," she said, grabbing him. Her gaze was already scanning the perimeter, her bow drawn. "What is it?"

"What's going on, Brock?" Jack asked, feeling the brorilla's tension. Brock tried to mime something. He was indicating that four cultivators were approaching, led by the Animal Kingdom minotaur Jack had witnessed fighting a giant in the Giant Ring. Said minotaur had also leveled up rapidly, rising from level 109 to 115.

Of course, Brock's miming wasn't *that* good. Jack understood everything because the four cultivators had just stepped through the ferns and into the clearing. They were an odd assortment. One was a walking tree and another a walking... ferret? There was also a human with a shaved head and a purple robe covering her body.

Leading them was the plate-armored, hulking minotaur that Jack remembered clearly. The other two from before were missing, thankfully, and the three that had replaced them were of a lower level, each hovering in the mid-nineties.

"Can we help you?" Nauja asked.

Maybe he doesn't know me, Jack thought, trying to pace his thoughts. Perhaps this minotaur had never seen Jack's bounty, never received his information. Those hopes were dashed as the minotaur instantly locked eyes with him.

"You can't, but he will," the minotaur replied leisurely, seeming in complete control, mouth forming into a triumphant grin. His voice was deep and sure. Commanding. "You caused a lot of waves, Jack Rust."

CHAPTER THIRTY-NINE
CORNERED

FOUR CULTIVATORS LED BY THE ANIMAL KINGDOM MINOTAUR BLOCKED JACK'S way. The jungle went quiet as if the animals understood what was about to go down. A breeze came from behind the cultivators, making their long robes flutter, and pulling Jack and Nauja's hair back.

"Shit," Jack said, and inspected the group.

Minotaur, Level 115
Faction: Animal Kingdom
Title: Resilient

Treant, Level 96
Faction: Star Garden
Title: Second Ring Conqueror

Human (Earth-302), Level 93
Faction: -
Title: Second Ring Conqueror

Ferretfolk, Level 93
Faction: Animal Kingdom
Title: Second Ring Conqueror

Of the three cultivators surrounding the minotaur, only one was human—a tall, lanky woman with shaved hair.

The second cultivator, a treant, was an actual walking tree. Its skin was made of twisting bark, its arms were branches that split into thin, finger-like sticks at the end, and it walked on two sturdy roots. It stood a head shorter than Jack, but the crown of branches above it put them at the same height. However, all its branches were dry, and its bark was gray, gnarly, giving the impression of an old, withering tree. Its face had features that were little more than slits in the bark, with only the eyes exuding a menacing red light.

The final cultivator was a ferretfolk. It was short and lithe, with a black eyepatch covering its left eye and dark fur all over its body. It held two daggers, and its mouth was drawn into a predatory snarl.

They were very interesting, academically. Unfortunately, they were also enemies, which kind of extinguished Jack's interest.

"What is the meaning of this?" Nauja asked again. She knew Jack was hunted by the Animal Kingdom and was just trying to earn time.

"The man beside you is wanted by my faction," the minotaur explained with confidence. He reminded Jack of Bomn, but less like a berserker and more like an army officer. His entire being exuded authority and unshakable confidence. "Surrender him or perish together. Your choice."

"He is a guest of my tribe," Nauja tried, but the minotaur only laughed.

"I couldn't care less about your tribe. I gave you a choice. Make it."

"How did you find me?" Jack asked, stepping forward. He could see no way out besides running, but they had the cabin to their back. There had to be a way.

"You never tried to hide. Someone killed a forest giant and upset the conqueror ant colony a few hours before we went through. Yet, when we arrived at the nearest camp, there was no new arrival. Instead, our scouts reported a cultivator staying with the barbarian tribe—a bare-chested man with an ape companion." He grinned sharply. "It wasn't hard to connect the dots. Getting Lord Longsword to let me come was more difficult, but... a billion-credit bounty is worth wasting a few hours."

Jack was getting severely irritated. There were scouts around the Tri

Lake. The Animal Kingdom was everywhere, and everyone knew of his bounty. They were hunting him at every step.

Is the entire universe against me? Jack thought, anger mounting. Will I not get a moment of peace? One opportunity to rest? Is it too much to ask for!

"Surrender," the minotaur commanded. "I have to bring you back alive, but I can either do it peacefully or break all your limbs in the process. Your choice. And you, barbarian girl—your time is running out. I swear on my name, Bocor Aximar, that I will kill you if you help him." He grinned, like he'd just cornered her. "So, what will it be? Surrender or death?"

Jack had seen how the Animal Kingdom acted. Even if he surrendered quietly, they would break all his limbs anyway so he couldn't escape. No. He had to get out of here. His eyes scanned the surroundings as Brock clutched his Staff of Stone tightly.

An extra pang of worry pierced Jack's heart. If he surrendered, would they let Brock go?

The three cultivators had fanned out, surrounding them, while the minotaur waited in front, only thirty feet away. To an E-Grade, that distance was nothing.

Jack could probably take any of the three weaker cultivators, but only by themselves. Even if Nauja helped him—she was still gritting her teeth and considering her options—they could at most take on the three cultivators, but definitely not the minotaur.

Jack's mind raced. Bocor was level 115, but he could definitely fight above his level. He had to be as strong as the tyrannosaurus. However, Jack had seen him in combat. He focused on defense. Given his heavy armor, he might not be able to catch up to them if they started running.

But to do that, he'd have to get past one of the three weaker cultivators. The minotaur was too close. Just a moment's delay would end up with Jack captured and bound before he could say, "Whoops."

Nauja would help him, probably. She struck him as that kind. If they worked together, could they ensure the escape of all three of them? If she was captured... could Jack run away, knowing she'd sacrificed herself for him?

He gritted his teeth, wrestling with that possibility. *Probably not*, he concluded.

"Fine," Nauja's voice snapped him out of his thoughts. He looked over in shock. She was packed with tightly-controlled fury and frustration, but also resignation. "I know where barbarians stand. He is a stranger. You can have him, just let me go."

Jack chuckled bitterly. "Of course," he said. "The entire universe is against me. I was a fool to believe in you."

He didn't blame her, but his bitterness had to be vented.

Nauja glanced at him, her gaze pained, but he didn't care if his words hurt her. He was stuck in his own hell. The weight of his obstacles had never been so vivid. He had opposed a B-Grade faction. Its influence and power were beyond his wildest dreams. They would always find him, everywhere. And they would stomp on him until he died.

The world was dark and hostile, and he was alone.

A tug at his wrist shook him awake. Brock was there, clenching his jaw and staff. "Bro," he said, his voice rich with emotion.

Jack felt a hint of sweetness in the sea of bitterness. *Right,* he realized. *I'm not alone. The world, the universe, might oppose me... but I have Brock.*

"Bro," Jack replied softly. His eyes whirled around. He didn't even look at Nauja—not because he blamed her, but because he couldn't spare the attention. His mind set to work, his resolve renewed. He would make it out. He would not yield.

And, one day, he would destroy the Animal Kingdom.

For now, however, he had to run. The path of the fist was about fighting, not about breaking your head against a wall—especially since he had no reason to stay. Retreating wasn't always a weakness.

So... how do I survive this?

Four enemies. The minotaur, excelling in defense but hopefully slow. The ferretfolk with the daggers; a fast, sharp attacker. The treant had no visible weapons, but it didn't look particularly mobile, what with being a tree. And the human... Jack couldn't read her. She also didn't hold a weapon, and she gave no indication of her powers.

The ferretfolk must go, he decided. It could definitely catch up to him if he ran. He had to assassinate or cripple it, *then* escape. With any luck, he could outrun the rest of them and get lost in the jungle. He would have to carry Brock, too, as the brorilla couldn't run fast enough by himself.

"Personally, I prefer you run," Bocor said, reading his thoughts. "It's more fun that way."

As the minotaur approached, Bocor's form seemed to enlarge in Jack's eyes. He knew it was his fear acting up, but he couldn't stop it. The minotaur became a force of nature, a brutal torturer. Jack envisioned his limbs snapping, his Dao breaking, the world abandoning him, his body left to rot with nobody caring.

His despair was magnified, filling him completely, leaving him no room to think of anything else. His Dao rose instinctively to meet it, to calm it down, but this fear was solid, stubborn. It refused to die down, striking back at Jack's Dao with increasing intensity that threatened to swallow him.

His Dao roared in frustration.

This isn't right. It's too strong, Jack thought, barely holding the terror at bay. I... I just reaffirmed my resolve. I beat my despair. Why is it back? What is happening to me?

With a tremendous effort of will, his perfect Dao Seed erupted with power. The Dao Root of Indomitable Will, only recently fused, enhanced the Seed's effects, grabbing Jack's heart and asserting its control. He felt some resistance, but a moment later, it was ripped apart, receding like a torn veil.

Jack blinked, recovering from the terror, and found the bald woman's eyes locked with his. A hint of surprise crossed his gaze.

When did I look that way? he wondered. What is—

Panic welled up inside him. That woman had controlled his emotions, magnified his fear, and blinded him to reality. The minotaur was looking on with sadistic mirth. He wasn't approaching anymore, content to watch Jack's struggles.

A furred hand grabbed Jack's wrist and pulled it behind his back.

"Wait! He's awake!" the woman's shout crossed the air, her voice crisp, but it was too late. Jack roared, turned, and punched. The ferretfolk was behind him, ready to chain his wrists together. His reaction surprised it, but it still managed to react in time, leaning back to dodge.

As it did, an arrow tip emerged from the front of its throat. Nauja had stabbed it from behind, her hand manifesting an arrow out of thin air. She met Jack's eyes. "Run!" she shouted.

The world exploded into motion. A green torrent appeared around

Jack, filled with leaves that blocked his visibility and stuck on his body as if glued. They itched him terribly, and they were heavy, each limiting his movements.

A bellow was all the warning Jack got. A silver form flashed before him, a hulking minotaur clad in plate armor and smashing down a huge tower shield. Jack had no time to think. He roared and smashed out a Meteor Punch.

The world exploded before him. His fist met the shield, pain shooting all the way to his shoulder. He stumbled backward, stifling a cry. His hand was cracked again, bleeding from the knuckles. Bocor, on the other hand, hadn't moved a step. He'd tanked the Meteor Punch like it was nothing, smiling at Jack from above the shield. But he'd stopped his attack to defend, earning Jack a precious second. Like he'd assumed, the minotaur was slow.

Jack sensed more than saw the human and treant close in from both sides. He shot a blind Meteor Punch. The cabin behind him exploded. Wood flew everywhere, a splinter barely missing his eye. Brock screamed, covering his head with his arms. The cultivators ignored the shrapnel of the demolished cabin passing between them. Jack grabbed Brock and pulled him along as he dashed through the debris, frantically trying to escape the encirclement. Nauja was by his side, her feet stomping the ground and her face twisted by tension.

"Stop him!" came the minotaur's cry. Leaves flew at Jack, magical in nature, blocking his sight and forming a wall before him. He shouted and Ghost Stepped through it, carrying Brock along. The strain was tremendous, unlike anything before. Jack's breath cut short, but he'd escaped the treant's attack. The leaves closed behind him, wrapping around empty air.

Armored boots thundered on soil as Bocor joined the chase, howling like a red-eyed bull. Brock's eyes widened under Jack's arm. Risking a glance, he saw that the minotaur was running on all fours. Thankfully, he wasn't too fast—the distance between them remained the same.

Another bellow came, rocking Jack's ears. Fury rose inside him. He wanted to attack that minotaur, kill him even if it meant—

His Dao Seed roared to life, neutralizing the taunt. A second influence in his heart appeared right after. He sensed the taunt flare back to life, stronger than ever, but he knew the sensation now. His Dao Seed shone with the metallic silver sheen of Indomitable Will, nipping the influence at its root.

"Argh! He has a heart Dao!" the bald woman's voice echoed through the woods, followed by another bellow. Jack looked to the front. It had only been a second since he started running. The cave's mouth opened before him, and he had to avoid it, because he would be trapped in there.

The jungle waited on either side. Nauja ran beside him. Just as he was about to turn, more shapes surfaced through the trees. One cultivator on either side, a staff-wielding woman and a fire-haired man flanking him. The fire-haired one was especially livid with anger. "You took Fermek!" he roared, stretching out his hands and unleashing a torrent of flames at Jack.

The staff-wielding woman rushed him, trying to cut off his path, and the air shook by her side, like there was another, invisible enemy there.

The jungle was no longer an option. They were surrounded. "Cave!" Jack shouted, receiving a hard confirmation from Nauja, and they angled for the opening—they wouldn't make it.

A torrent of fire at the front, a staff-wielder at the side, and an unknown, invisible combatant—three more people seeking an opening to attack. A roaring minotaur, a walking tree, and a mental specialist closed in behind him. Jack didn't have many options. If he stopped or turned, he would be captured. If he kept running, the staff-wielder and invisible enemy would catch up before he could run past them.

Only one choice left.

Jack's features warped into a scowl. The full brunt of his hatred came to bear, along with bitterness and resolve. His Brutalizing Aura flared to life. It spread out like an invisible wave around him, and where it passed, the world turned grim, like death's scythe was arriving.

He'd imbued the aura with a simple thought, one that the skill amplified and clarified beyond any doubt: "If you stop me, I will kill you first." He meant it.

There was no rage, no emotion. He was simply stating a fact, which the aura injected deep into the hearts of his pursuers.

Jack had seen hard times. He survived the Forest of the Strong. Antagonized an impossible enemy. He was chased, cheated, and burdened, and he was constantly putting his life on the line since the Integration. Every step he took was painted by his blood.

In that regard, these scions were far too lacking. Whoever was afraid of death had no power against Jack Rust.

All the enemies reacted differently. The bald woman resisted the skill completely, as did the minotaur, but they were too far back to stop him. The flame-man gasped but pulled through, his desire for revenge overpowering the terror. The treant stumbled, then pressed the assault.

But the staff-wielding woman and the invisible enemy were the closest. As Jack's aura roared out, they slowed, eyes going wide. The staff woman almost ran away in fear. She recovered a moment later, too strong for the aura to hold her, but she'd lost a precious second.

In that second, Jack and Nauja burst through, heading for the cave opening.

The flame wizard's attack had persisted. The torrent of fire came from the front, cutting off their advance. Jack jumped right through it.

The pain was hellish, like diving into a burning oven. Jack resisted the urge to scream, keeping his mouth and eyes closed as he ran as fast as he could. It reminded him of the time he'd charged the goblin shaman, back in the Forest of the Strong, and pushed through a wall of flames.

The pain lasted but a second. Jack emerged from the flames with his skin red and ready to blister. His hair was on fire, but the wind of his dash quickly put it out. Even the insides of his nose were burning with pain. When he drew in a breath, the hot air reached his lungs, making him miss a step.

Thankfully, Brock was fine. Jack had held him in a tight embrace, trying to protect him as much as possible. Some of his fur was singed off, but it had served as protection. Nauja was still by his side, having jumped over the flames without losing any momentum. She screamed as she landed in a run. The air above the flames was also hot.

The flames winked out in the next second. The minotaur barreled forth, barely twenty feet behind Jack. The staff woman came at them diagonally from behind, the shuddering air just a step in front of her, and the flame-man readied another strike. A green aura surrounded the cave mouth, leaves spawning around it and forming a swiftly closing barricade, while Jack still felt errant thoughts attempt to invade his mind—the bald woman's influence.

There was no time to think. They reached the cave mouth and dove in, barely making it before the leaf barrier blocked their path. The minotaur tore through the leaves, hot on their heels, and the rest of the cultivators flooded in right after, joining the hunt.

Firebolts flew at Jack and Nauja, some hitting them and causing first-degree burns, and some missing and illuminating the dark, winding path ahead.

Nauja had said this cave complex was large and labyrinthic. Jack dearly hoped she was right.

CHAPTER FORTY
THE CAVE MARATHON

JACK'S FEET THUNDERED ON SOLID ROCK. THE LIGHT HAD DISAPPEARED, LETTING only his weak dark-vision steer him away from walls and outcroppings. Nauja was a step in front, running with large strides and leading him deeper. Jack really hoped she knew the way—and that she could see.

The minotaur, Bocor, was at the front of their pursuers, charging on all fours like a bull. Smoke rose from his nostrils, the ground shook and moaned under his hooves and arms, and he boasted enough strength to run at the same speed as Jack and Nauja while wearing full plate armor and carrying a big-ass tower shield on his back.

Level 115 wasn't for show.

The rest of his team followed: a treant, three humans, and what looked like shimmering air but was actually an invisible person.

The cave angled downward. Jack felt the slope under his feet, sensed his momentum threatening to tip him forward. With his limited vision, all he could do was follow Nauja's swaying back, her pale skin standing out just a bit in the darkness.

Sounds came occasionally from the left and right as if the wind was stopped by something. Jack imagined peculiar rock formations, but they could be dinosaurs plastered against the wall for all he knew.

Excluding Jack and Brock—who was carried by Jack—everyone else was over level 90. Their feet swallowed the distance at tremendous speed. It was like they were all racing motorcycles through the cave, which appeared endless.

They had already crossed miles. More than once, forks appeared in the path, Jack barely distinguishing the hints of lighter darkness that signified openings. Nauja always picked the one heading farther down, and he didn't dare disagree.

By now, it was clear they were in an enormous, underground cave complex. Its sheer scale was stunning. Endless miles of caves stretched in all directions, twisting and bending around each other, crossing at a thousand different intersections. Cold fear gripped Jack's heart.

Even if we escape them, will we find the way out?

With his sight impaired, other senses flared up. He could hear the rasping of Nauja's breath, the subtle change in his footsteps as they ran over different kinds of stone. His nose caught the moisture that suffused the caves, detected the slight hints of moss and rot in the air.

His breath was catching in his throat. His ribcage felt cramped. There was a limit to how far he could run.

"Do you know the way?" he finally asked, trying to keep his voice a whisper, but that was hard to do while running.

"Down!" she said, giving no further explanation.

"I thought you'd give me up!"

She snorted. "I am no coward!"

"But you said barbarians never lie!"

"Deception is not lying. There's a difference!"

"How is—" Nauja took a sharp right, and Jack almost slid ahead before barely managing to turn. "How is there a difference?"

"Is this really the time!" she growled.

"Why not? We have nothing else to do!"

They did have something else to do: run. However, a chase was a battle of minds as much as it was of bodies. Their pursuers didn't know how tired Jack was. If he made them believe they'd exhaust themselves first, they might be demoralized, even stop chasing altogether.

Nauja growled again, not indicating whether she understood or not, while Bocor's voice came from behind, washing over them in the narrow tunnels.

"I am a minotaur!" he roared. "You will never outrun me!"

If he was using the same trick as Jack, it was working. Those thunderous hooves were closing in faster, the entire party accelerating. They had fallen a bit behind since the start of the hunt five minutes ago, but they had remained within eyesight.

"Brock!" Jack yelled, keeping his eyes on Nauja's back. "Are they all there?"

Having climbed on Jack's back, Brock snuck a peek, then raised three barely visible fingers in front of Jack's face. "Three are left? Good. Which ones?"

Incoherent monkey noises by his ear.

"The minotaur?" he tried. "The staff? The invisible?"

"Yes. Yes. Yes."

"Good!"

The other three focused on Mental or Will. They couldn't follow everyone else in this mad rush. That left only the minotaur, the staff-wielder, and the invisible one.

Which was more than enough to destroy Jack and Nauja if they caught up.

Their only choice was to keep running. Unfortunately, the main reason Jack could match higher-level cultivators in combat was his perfect Dao Seed. Stat-wise, he was weaker, which hurt him in an all-out marathon. The only reason he could keep up in this never-ending chase was his Indomitable Body and Dao Root of Indomitable Will, which ensured he would die before giving up.

They kept heading down. The temperature steadily dropped, reaching the freezing point, and the moisture dampened. Jack's every breath was laborious now. He drew the cold in every time he inhaled, like icicles stabbing his lungs. His throat was parched. He was sweating all over, his vision was bleary, and his legs were made of lead.

But he couldn't stop.

Nauja's exhaustion was growing apparent, too. Her strides had shortened. Her breath came in shallow rasps, her form wobbled in his eyes.

He had no way of telling whether their pursuers were as tired. The footsteps remained on their heels, gnawing at the distance every time Nauja tried to slow down. It was incredible that the minotaur had persisted so far while carrying such massive weights. He wasn't fast for his level, but he was extremely durable.

Will we get captured? Jack wondered. Should we split up?

It could take him days to find the way back without Nauja. Weeks, even, and that's assuming he wasn't captured. But if they didn't have a choice...

The tunnel opened around them. Jack sensed himself entering a cavern, felt the open space surrounding them. For a moment, hope surged in his heart. This cavern signified change. Opportunity. Salvation.

Nauja kept running straight, not slowing down in the slightest. A few moments later, they were back in a tunnel, always running.

Jack wanted to ask what that cavern was about, but he no longer had the energy to spare. His focus sharpened to a point. The world fell apart, becoming a series of ragged breaths. Only keeping track of Nauja and placing one foot before the other mattered. His heart was drumming in his temples, his ribs stitching, his every breath simultaneously burning and freezing his throat.

He kept hoping for something to happen, anything. Their pursuers to let up. Some monster to appear.

But nothing. All this place had was empty stone tunnels. It really was empty.

The minutes slogged on with every step a new torture. Many times, Jack considered turning around and just fighting, even if it meant death, but his heart was made of fist, and it pushed him ever onward. Every time they turned, he thought he would fall over, barely staying on track.

His mind swam. Running was his entire existence, his purpose. The reason had stopped mattering, all directions were fused into one. He no longer felt pain. He simply moved his legs and kept going.

Suddenly, his exhaustion disappeared. It felt like he was flying on clouds. His heart surged with joy. His steps grew sturdier and stronger, his stride widened, and before long, he was flying through the tunnels, relaxed and free like a bird, euphoric. He was a gust of wind flowing through, a fist in trajectory to meet the next face.

Nauja must have felt the same, because she accelerated. They darted through the tunnels, making sharp turns, opening the distance. The encroaching footsteps were softer now, farther away. They were escaping.

The minotaur's bellows went from a voice next to their ears to a faraway, forgotten sound. The tunnels echoed it, but it was nothing but a memory. Their pursuers footsteps were disappearing. Jack laughed, a carefree, exalted peal. Nauja laughed with him. They were the Dao itself.

And then, as suddenly as it had come, their energy disappeared. They returned to reality so hard that Jack almost lost his steps. Everything became pain. His chest was shaven from the inside, his throat was filled with razors. His legs were numb. His muscles were no longer responding. He had the will to bear through the pain, but his body simply had nothing else to give.

He could no longer run. He slowed to a walking pace, his legs moving shakily by themselves, like they were no longer his. Nauja saw him and slowed down as well, only to groan with pain. She paused for a moment before forcing herself to keep going, but it was a slog.

Every step, they almost collapsed. Jack's eyes bulged out. He yearned for release, to stop, but kept himself going. When Nauja faltered and tripped, he grabbed her waist, put her on his shoulder, and kept trudging, for he could no longer run. They had to escape.

The footsteps that had almost disappeared were returning now. Slowly, steadily, they were getting louder. They went from whispers, to thumps, to stomps. Jack felt despair creep in. He couldn't fight in this condition. Escape was the only means.

His mind released all unnecessary functions. All that mattered was to keep walking.

The footsteps drew closer. The stomps became crashes, then peals of thunder. Jack maintained a smile of hope, a tiny prayer that, even at the last moment, the pursuers would collapse. He kept going.

The thunderous footsteps paused. He heard a faint gasp. A flicker of hope welled up inside him. It'd happened. They experienced the same euphoria he had, then crashed hard. Maybe this would make them stop. He just had to walk a little bit more. A little bit more.

He took another step and ran into a dead-end.

Brock started screaming, dropping down and dragging Jack backward. He barely stopped as a draft reached him from below. He forced his bleary eyes to focus. A lighter darkness was in front of his feet, a hole going down. He wanted to jump, but Brock was pulling at the back of his pants.

"Deep?" he managed to croak out.

"Yes!" Brock shouted. "Yes!"

At this state, a fall would leave them completely mangled. Easy pickings.

Jack wanted to laugh. This was it. He had tried so hard, pushed himself to the limit, endured this torture only to come within reach of escape... and be cursed with bad luck.

Now, even if the hole disappeared, his legs wouldn't carry him anymore.

"This world hates me," he muttered, throat scratched with every word. "It hates me!"

A bestial, guttural scream tore through what remained of his throat, crashing into the stones only to disappear. Jack collapsed into a heap. His arms had some power still, but he couldn't stand. Nauja fell with him, and she tried to draw her bow, tried to nock an arrow. It manifested halfway, out of thin air, then winked out of existence. Her arms fell to the ground, defeated.

Footsteps neared. A shape rounded the corner. A bull. No—a minotaur. A hulking beast on all fours that slowly stood up as it saw him on the ground, releasing a triumphant roar.

A final hint of hope blossomed inside Jack. The minotaur was alone and exhausted, like them. Maybe they could take him.

Yet even that bit of hope was dashed as he saw the darkness flickering. The invisible one was here, too. And, a moment later, the shadow of a staff peeked through the opening.

"I told you—" the minotaur's rough voice filled the tunnel, exhausted but satisfied. "You cannot... escape."

Stubbornness welled up inside Jack. He wasn't going to just wait for death. There was a hole behind him. What was the worst that could happen? Smash his head on a rock?

If the minotaur wanted to take him, he had to jump exhausted into a hole.

"Fuck you," Jack said, tilting back. He let his body topple, falling over the edge. Time slowed. The shimmering darkness flickered. A dagger crossed the air, its familiar whistle echoing in Jack's ears like the calling of death.

Gravity was pulling him, but at their level, everything was happening too fast. Gravity was slow. He could see the darkness deepening as the dagger approached his face, and he struggled to raise a hand to defend.

A staff smacked it out of the air. Brock stood before him, screaming in defiance and bitterness. He'd been carried all the way—he was fresh, but also too weak to help. These people were so far above him that he could do absolutely nothing.

Still, he tried.

The dagger veered off its path, only grazing Jack's ear instead of stabbing his eye. The minotaur roared. Somehow, he found the strength to lunge forward, raising his tower shield from its edge to bring it down like a club. However, Jack could see that the strike wouldn't be on time. He would fall before the shield did.

Brock, turned the other way, couldn't see that. He tried to smack the minotaur's side. The Staff of Stone whirled through the air, but in the end, he was far too weak. Bocor let it land, not even bothering to defend, then took a hand off his falling shield and slapped Brock across the face. The strike wasn't strong, but it was fast, faster than the shield could fall. Simply an insult.

Brock was thrown aside by the strike, his cheek red, gaze frozen in surprise and rage. In that moment, the shield crashed down.

The little brorilla recovered, but he still didn't retreat. He thought Jack was behind him, defenseless. He roared in anger and threw himself forward, ready to give his life to defend his big bro. Jack grabbed his tail just in time. He dragged Brock along, pulling him just an inch away from the falling wall of metal that almost broke his head. The shield slapped against the rock floor, barely missing Jack and Brock as they tumbled down the hole.

Brock hollered, throwing a poop at the minotaur, and his cry of rage followed them into the deeper darkness.

And they fell.

CHAPTER FORTY-ONE
ROCK BOTTOM

JACK REMEMBERED FALLING. HE TUMBLED THROUGH THE AIR, STRUGGLING TO control his descent through waves of crippling exhaustion, but it was difficult. His body was malfunctioning. His Dao, in disarray.

He accelerated for several seconds. By the end, he thought he was a goner.

Then, he crashed into icy water, and all went black.

———

Jack awoke with a groan, his eyes fluttering open. The darkness was all-consuming, impenetrable. As he'd already opened his eyes, a hint of panic threatened to consume him, thinking he was blind.

Then, someone leaned over him. Jack almost exploded with power before a calming voice said, "Bro."

Everything came back at once. The hunt, the chase, the fall... Jack let his body sag against cold stone, indifferent about the gravel massaging his waist. He realized now that he was exhausted. Every breath took effort, and just leaning against the ground was heaven.

He also realized he was wet. His pants stuck to his skin, and his hair was one with his scalp.

"What happened?" he croaked out. His voice was coarse, like sandpaper.

"We fell into a pond," a woman's voice came from the side. Nauja. "That was lucky. I think I broke my arm."

"What?" Jack asked. "Are you sure?"

"It's numb and unresponsive. I think it's bent wrong."

"Shit."

Nauja sounded calm, like it wasn't her arm she was talking about. *We need light*, Jack realized. He didn't know how long he'd been unconscious for, but it had to be several minutes. His regeneration had worked a bit. He was still utterly spent, but not crippled.

And, most importantly, the minotaur hadn't chased them.

"Brock," he said. "Is that torch tip still in your pocket?"

When they crossed the gate below the ant hill, there was a pile of torches waiting for them. They hadn't taken just one. Brock had broken off the tips of two torches and stashed them in his pockets.

Now, that decision was proven wise.

Brock stayed silent for a moment, making sure he had them. "Yes," he replied.

"Okay. Can you try to light one up?"

"Yes."

Sounds filled the room. Fur rubbing furiously against fur and fabric. A few moments later, the sounds ceased, but there was still no light.

Jack tsked. Not only had they plunged into a pond, wetting the torch tip, but the air down here was cold and damp. Setting it on fire was going to be difficult. "Can I try?" he asked, forcing himself to a seated position. It felt like pushing away his blankets on a cold winter morning.

Brock handed him something—a short piece of wood whose tip was wrapped in slippery cloth. Jack shook his hands once, then grabbed the cloth by both sides and started rubbing it between his hands. He was careful, going as fast as he could without ripping it.

It was hard without sight. He started off slowly, then gradually picked up the pace. His hands applied pressure and friction, creating heat. The cloth gradually dried up. The hotter it was, the faster Jack could go without tearing it.

It took the better part of five minutes. Eventually, Jack felt serious heat building up under his hands.

"Careful," Nauja said. "It might be steeped in oil."

"I know."

When he felt it was close, he pulled his hands away and dragged them against the stone to clear them of oil. It occurred to him that there was a pond nearby. After feeling around a bit, he found it just behind his feet, and cleaned the oil off as well as he could.

He then held his fingers to the torch tip and snapped them, hard. Once, twice, a small spark flew off, blinding in the darkness, illuminating hints of ragged skin and dark stone.

The sparks landed on the torch tip to no effect. He kept going for a while. Eventually, one took hold. The entire torch tip lit up, shedding bright light in a short radius. Jack closed his eyes—they were so adjusted to the darkness that the light hurt.

"Your fingers!" Nauja warned him.

Cranking up an eyelid, he saw that his palm was on fire. It was the leftover oil he hadn't managed to clean up. He shook his hand until the fire went out, and then was left with a brilliantly lit, short torch. There was only an inch of wood under the burning cloth, just enough to grab it from below.

"Let's see," he muttered, carefully swinging the fire around. His light illuminated Brock's awed face, excited to finally see properly again and full of admiration for his crafty big bro. He kept going, revealing a small expanse of dark gray stone. Blue glimmers came occasionally, hints of an unknown ore. A pond was behind him, about ten feet across, and a tunnel extended vertically over it. The wall ended just behind the pond.

He paused there, the light shining at the very end of the vertical hole. He remembered them falling for several seconds. That meant the hole was very deep, and since they hadn't crashed into its sides, it had to be straight, too.

Why would there be a perfectly vertical, five-hundred-foot-long hole right above a small pond in the bowels of an expansive cave complex?

Could it be man-made? he wondered. The edges of the hole were surprisingly smooth. *But who would make this? And why?*

At least the minotaur and his friends hadn't followed them. They probably feared injuries after knowing the hole's depth—maybe the splashes hadn't even reached them, and if it did, it must have taken a long time.

Whichever the case, Jack was glad. He didn't know how long he was out for, or which of his comrades had dragged him out of the pond, but if the minotaur had come down, they sure as hell would all be dead.

Speaking of...

Jack's face darkened. Right before they fell, the minotaur had dared to slap Brock. That would not go unanswered. Jack was filled with righteous fury.

For now, he focused on his immediate surroundings. Revenge would come later.

Since the pond was directly adjacent to the back wall, he directed the torch at the front. Nauja lay there, her moist skin reflecting the torchlight and her hair forming wet lines on the stone floor. Her face was calm, steady, and pointedly not looking at her twisted arm.

Jack shivered when he saw it. It was bent the wrong way at the elbow.

"Is it bad?" she asked, still not looking.

"Could be worse," he replied. "Keep your eyes on me. You said you had a regenerative skill, right?"

"It's weak. Just part of my body-enhancing skill. I doubt it can fix a broken arm within a week."

Jack nodded. Inwardly, he was shocked. His own regeneration could patch up his wounds within a few hours. What was that about?

Because I'm meant to fight body-to-body and get injured a lot? he theorized. *Because I have a perfect Dao Seed? Because I have an Elite Class, so better skills? Then again, maybe she's an elite, too.*

Maybe all those combined.

"Okay," he replied after a moment of thought. Thankfully, he knew some things about how bones work. "Focus on me. Look into my eyes."

She kept her gaze locked with his as he handed the torch to Brock and stepped around and reached for her arm. He admired her bravery. He grabbed her elbow and forearm, and with a sharp movement, twisted it to the right direction. Bone snapped. Nauja lost her breath, then gritted her teeth so as not to scream.

"It's okay, it's alright," he said softly. "We're done. That was the hard part."

She was shivering, wanting to scream but her pride not letting her. Her eyes remained glued to his, and he could see them widening until the vessels burst. With swift, confident movements, Jack reached for his pants and tore off parts below his thigh, being careful not to destroy his secret pocket. There was no other fabric left. His shirt was long used up.

Tearing the cloth into strips, he used them to tie Nauja's arm at the right position. Though he wasn't a paramedic, he was confident that it would last.

He tried his best to be gentle, but Nauja still had to hold back screams every time he touched her. Her arm quivered under his touch, surprisingly soft and silken. Thankfully, he felt no bones sticking out under her skin, besides the one at the elbow.

When he was finished, he took a deep breath and said, "Done. You were very brave. Not one scream."

"Of course I was," she replied, her voice weak. "Can I look now?"

"Yes."

She threw her arm a glance. Her elbow stuck out sideways. She groaned and turned her head the other way.

"I set the bone right," Jack said. "Now, we just have to wait for your regeneration to run its course."

"My tribe's healer could fix this in moments," she replied weakly.

"Well, I'm not a healer. This is the best I can do."

"That's not—" She bit her lip. "I was just talking to myself. Thank you. I appreciate what you did."

He cracked a smile. "You're welcome. Now, let's go see what's down here, okay?"

The tunnel extended farther than the torch could illuminate. After resting for a bit, he could move again, though his legs were sore to the point of numbness. And he was starving.

Unfortunately, no restaurant delivered to Trial Planet. He had to go find food.

Helping Nauja to her feet—she wobbled but stood—and making sure Brock was ready, he held the torch out front began walking into the tunnel.

They only got ten feet in.

The tunnel came to an abrupt dead-end. However, it didn't end in stone. A door was embedded in the far wall, taking up the entirety of the tunnel. It was eight feet high and wide enough for two people to fit side by side, and it looked positively ancient. Dust had accumulated on its surface, almost hiding it from sight.

"What is this?" Jack asked, wiping away some of the dust. Light gray metal was revealed underneath. He didn't recognize the material, but it felt hard, smooth, and cold. Steel?

"What's a door doing down here?" he asked again, filled with disbelief. When he looked back, Nauja seemed equally confused.

"I have no idea," she said. "I have never heard of anything man-made in the Forbidden Cave."

"I thought these tunnels were fully explored."

"They are... Father said so."

"Do you think they missed this?"

"I... don't think so. The delvers are blasted people, but pretty thorough when it comes to treasures. Someone must have discovered this before."

"Hmm. Are you saying they kept it secret?"

"Either that, or whoever found the door never made it back." She stared at its surface. Faint engravings were just barely distinguishable under the alighted dust.

Jack swiped his torch around, looking more carefully at the cavern. "There." He pointed at a corner. "People."

The barest hints were left. Food wrappings, a broken arrow without its tip, a credit card. They didn't look nearly as ancient as the door. "Someone has been here before us," Jack concluded. "But they kept it secret—or, at least, didn't tell many people."

"Why would they leave their credit card behind?" Nauja asked. "If they returned to their camp to report the door's existence, they would take it along."

Jack's eyes widened in realization. "Something happened to them. They never made it back."

"Exactly."

They remained very still. Jack held up his own credit card and touched it to the dropped one. Numbers shone on the surface. "Nine hundred thousand!" he exclaimed, drawing in a sharp breath. "This guy was rich."

Nauja raised a brow. "It isn't much. Most delvers carry that kind of money, if not more."

"Hah. Correction: I'm poor. But not anymore." The credits moved to his card. "There we go."

"Congratulations. I'm sure the tunnels will be full of merchants."

That reminded Jack of a grim reality. "Can you find the way back? We ran for a long time, made so many turns."

Nauja hesitated. "Maybe. I mostly kept heading deeper hoping they would let us go, but... they were really persistent. One of them must have a navigation skill."

"Which you don't have."

"No. I just know some tricks to find my way around caves."

"Great. So we're trapped here."

"I wouldn't say *trapped*. More like... temporarily stranded."

Jack grimaced. "Without food and water."

"There is water," she said, pointing back to the pond. "Our bodies can take it unless it's extremely poisonous."

"Then the sooner we start, the faster we'll be out of here," Jack said. However, his eyes stayed glued to the door. So did Nauja's.

"What do you think is behind it?" she asked in a low voice.

"Something dangerous. It took out whoever left that credit card."

"But there was only one card. One person."

"Perhaps we could take it," he finished her thought.

It didn't get any more intriguing than this. An ancient door at the bottom of a supposedly empty, enormous cave complex. "Maybe your tribe knows about this. That's why they call it the Forbidden Cave. Because they don't want anyone to find out."

"But why?" Nauja asked. Jack had no answer.

Brock pointed at the door, then mimed pulling it open.

"It might be dangerous," Jack said.

"For sure it is," Nauja replied.

"But we're here already. And this is Trial Planet, the land of opportunities. We might as well take a look, right? And if it's too dangerous, we retreat."

Brock said, "Yes."

"We really shouldn't," Nauja said, biting her lip. Her pale skin, blue eyes, and blonde hair all shone in the torchlight. "But we could."

"There's a saying on my planet: curiosity killed the cat."

"We have a similar one: the curious velociraptor springs the trap."

"But satisfaction brought it back."

"What?"

"That's the full saying. Curiosity killed the cat, but satisfaction brought it back. Though people don't say that second bit. The first sounds better."

Nauja narrowed her eyes. "Are you saying we should open it?"

"I know we will. I'm just demonstrating my knowledge."

Unable to hold back, she chuckled, cradling her broken arm. "You're right. We're already here. We might as well open it. Retreating now would be cowardly."

"Or cautious."

"Cowardly," she insisted. "Fear is the worst guide to follow."

Jack considered that, then chuckled. "Fine. Enough bantering. Let's go."

He reached the door in two steps and pushed. Nothing happened. Then, learning from past mistakes, he tried to find a handle to pull, but there was nothing. He groaned.

"Just once, I want something to be simple. Is that too much to ask?"

CHAPTER FORTY-TWO
THE ANCIENTS

THE ANCIENT DOOR REMAINED STUBBORNLY SHUT, ITS EXPOSED METAL glittering in the dwindling torchlight. Jack tried pushing, pulling, even sliding the door. Nothing worked.

"Guess I have to break it," he concluded.

"Oh, give me a rest," Nauja intervened. Raising her good hand, she wiped off some of the dust that had alighted on the door, revealing a line on the metal underneath it. "See? It's engraved."

She drove her open palm into the middle of the door. A gust of wind spread from it—a skill—clearing the door completely. A dust cloud enveloped them, sending all three into a coughing fit. When it finally settled, Jack took another look.

"Huh," he said.

Engraved in the hard metal, as smoothly as sculptors engraved clay, was an illustrated battle. Humans, along with smatterings of other species, filled one side of the door. They rode crab-shaped starships, were surrounded by colorless auras and were drawn in a way that indicated both Dao and technology. There were hundreds of them, each the size of Jack's palm, filling up half of the space.

The other half was occupied by larger creatures. Twelve of them in total, each completely different from the others. There was a smiling human at the very top, his body shackled by dark chains. A creature of pure darkness was in the middle, slightly larger than the rest. The other ten were all presented as featureless humanoid shapes, but their forms weren't as solid as the topmost, shackled man's. They were fainter, expertly carved as to appear translucent, and boasted differences compared to normal humans.

One was made of fire. Another, of stars. A third was comprised of many small spheres tightly assembled into a humanoid shape, and a fourth seemed normal, but everything around it was warped, as if it were drawing them in. The fifth creature was made of lightning, the sixth of blue and red sparks, the seventh and eight of explosions, though the latter depicted fewer yet larger ones. Finally, there were two creatures that only appeared as bodies of water, one resembling a rippling pond and the other a steady current.

Twelve large creatures. An army of humans and other species using the Dao, and technology to fight against them. Galaxies as the background.

"Wait," Jack said, taking a step back. Incredulousness creeped into his voice. "This rings a bell."

"Twelve gods..." Nauja said, voice shaking with awe. "The Old Ones..."

"Then, these ones..." Jack gently touched the army, "are the Immortals?"

Master Shol had talked about this once. The Immortals, the makers of the System, had waged the Immortal Crusade against the Old Ones.

"I..." Nauja narrowed her eyes. "I am not sure. The Immortals led the crusade, yes, but they are supposed to be machines, not humans. These are probably the Ancients." She took a trembling breath. "My ancestors."

Jack thought he'd heard something about the Ancients before, but he wasn't sure. "So the Ancients were soldiers of the Immortals?"

"No!" Nauja jerked away as if Jack had blasphemed, then caught herself, continuing in a lower voice. "No... The Ancients were the first people to ever exist in the universe. They flourished across the universe, spreading life to other galaxies. Every species you know came from the Ancients."

Jack was pretty sure everything on Earth evolved from amoebas, but he let her go on. It took only one sentence for his attention to be rewarded.

"Until they discovered the Old Ones," Nauja said.

Jack instantly homed in on her words.

"The Old Ones feared the Ancients' growing power. Using their divine powers, they eradicated them." She took a breath. "But it didn't end there. The Old Ones turned their gaze away, but though the Ancients were gone, they had left a heritage. Descendant species across the universe. And, most importantly, the Immortals.

"The Immortals were machines dedicated to the Ancients. Their first children, before they discovered how to create true life. When the Old Ones destroyed the Ancients, the Immortals swore revenge. They forged the System, an existence based on the Dao, meant to facilitate the development of sapient species. The System quantifies and streamlines the Dao, serving as a guide for everyone who wishes to attain true strength. It makes the path far more accessible, creating a host of warriors to fill the Immortals' armies against the Old Ones. That was the primary directive.

"When enough soldiers were ready, the ninety-nine Immortals went to righteous war, each wielding godlike powers. They were flanked by the strongest cultivators of all the galaxies, and that gave them the power to challenge the Old Ones. The war raged on for a millennium, destroying the Primordial Galaxy in the process. In the end, the Immortals pushed back the Old Ones, but couldn't kill them. Not a single God had fallen. But they had the System. The Old Ones were forced outside System space, and the Immortal Crusade remained inside, where their powers were greatest, and where the Old Ones didn't dare touch them. After that..." She bit her lip, frowning as if trying to remember. "Balance returned, but the promise of eternal revenge still stands. In time, the Second Immortal Crusade will come, and the Old Ones will be shorn off the face of the universe."

"Wow..." Jack said. "I had no idea."

"Maybe it's not accurate," Nauja said, suddenly bashful. "The legend has been in our tribe for countless generations."

"Does everyone know this?" Jack asked. "The version I heard from my master mentioned nothing about the Ancients."

"Probably. We don't freely share our culture with delvers, but they have gotten more valuable things out of us. Surely some people know."

"I see..."

More secrets. More lies. More hidden knowledge.

He returned his gaze to the engraving. He had context now. He saw the Ancients and their children-species—though that part was debatable—standing against the twelve Old Ones.

To be precise, it wasn't a battle. There were no attacks flying. This was the stand-off before the battle, where each side showed off their power—their godlike power. A concept that made him and his struggles, even the entire Animal Kingdom, feel insignificant.

What level had the soldiers and generals of the Immortal Crusade reached, to be qualified to stand against gods? C-Grade? B-Grade? Perhaps... even stronger?

Jack turned his gaze to the twelve Old Ones. He'd never been a religious man, but the System and magic existed. Gods belonged to the same domain. Suddenly, the awe and wonder that flooded him were strong enough to bring him to his knees, a sense of purpose flashing in his chest as some ancestral instinct urged him to devote his entire life to worship.

And yet, they were enemies. Jack wasn't a follower of the gods. He was their opponent, walking the path of divinity himself, because how else could man stand up to a God?

"So these are the gods..." he muttered, taking in their every detail and memorizing their individual shapes. He began drawing connections to things he knew. "I recognize some of their powers. This one is electricity, this is fire, obviously, this is... magnetism?" He stared at the creature made of pairs of blue and red sparks.

"The Old Ones represent the foundational forces of the universe," Nauja explained, still lost in disbelief. "Everything else is a combination of these twelve powers. I know some of them, but not all... See that one?" She pointed to the topmost man, the one that had a clear humanoid shape but was shackled by darkness. "That is Enas. He used to be the King of the Old Ones, but the others teamed up and cast him into a bottomless pit of darkness at the end of the world, where he will remain trapped for eternity. Nobody knows why. That one"—she pointed at the creature wrought of darkness—"is Axelor, the new King of the Old Ones after Enas. I'm afraid I do not know the rest."

"There is always something greater..." Jack said. These unfathomable heights of power should bring him a sense of fear, of futility, like all his struggles were for naught.

Instead, they gave him hope.

For the first time, he saw the Animal Kingdom not as an unsurpassable mountain, but as one force amongst many. The Kingdom and all their allies, the entire Galactic Alliance, only had B-Grades as their peak. If A-Grades existed, even gods, that meant there was a way out. Jack just had to reach that level of power. Then, nobody would bother him.

Just becoming a God... he thought, chuckling in amusement.

It was an impossible goal, but even that was better than total despair. The moment Jack realized there was a way out, his entire being realigned. Even if he never reached those heights, he had a clear target now, a destination at which to orient himself. He would just head there, try his best, and if he died or failed in the process, so be it.

His heart instantly felt lighter.

"Well, history is great and all," he said, "but we still need to get through this door. I could try breaki—"

Nauja's glare was sharp enough to cut through stone.

"I was *kidding*," he added quickly. "This is clearly a precious artifact. There has to be another way in."

"...Right. But what?"

Brock made monkey noises, pointing at something. Jack squinted to see it.

In the bottom left corner, behind the army of the Ancients, were more people. They were angular humanoids, their faces and bodies square. *Robots*, he thought with surprise. They were rushing at the army of Ancients from behind, probably to assist them in battle.

"Those must be the Immortals," he said.

"Yes," Nauja agreed. "But how does that help us open the door?"

Nobody knew, but Brock was happy to have spotted something they didn't. He raised a hand and high-fived Jack, while Nauja watched on with mild amusement. "Men..." she said.

Having discovered the Immortals, stuffed as they were in a corner, they thought there could be more hidden details. They scanned the engraving, searching for something, anything, but they came up short.

Nauja shook her head, taking a step back. "I think there's nothing. The engravings are just that—engravings. The answer must be hidden somewhere else."

"Hmm. Maybe there's a hidden button?" Jack tried.

He drew his hand across the door, gently pushing it all the while. He felt every line, steady and straight as he kept going down to up, side to side, slowly exploring the door's surface.

When he was a fifth of the way up, he felt something. The metal hadn't given way. But there was *something.*

"Hmm?"

His gaze sharpened, moving his hand back to where he'd had the feeling. It was the bottom-most Old One, the one that resembled a rippling pond. When Jack touched it, he felt a strange sense of emptiness, though the metal was clearly there. It took him a moment to place the sensation.

It was like a mental emptiness. Like some core aspect of the metal was just... not there.

In fact, it felt oddly similar to his fists when he was about to imbue them with his Dao.

"Hey, check this out," he said, pointing at the Old Ones. "I think I can push my Dao into this one."

"What?" Nauja approached, placing her good palm over the engraving and closing her eyes. A moment later, they snapped open. "You're right! I feel the same."

"Should we do it?"

"Hold on a second." Her fingers rose to the next Old One—the one that looked like a steady water current. "This one is empty too." She proceeded to the one, made of many small explosions. "And so is this."

After a quick inspection, all twelve of the Old Ones felt empty of Dao.

The world was filled with the Dao, every nook and cranny of it, making it impossible for an E-Grade to push their Dao into reality. But these spots were vacuums.

Jack and Nauja also confirmed that there were no other such vacuums.

"Are we supposed to fill them all up?" Nauja asked. "Doesn't feel too difficult."

"Hmm. That's almost too easy." Jack narrowed his eyes. Suddenly, they flashed with understanding. "Wait! Notice how each Old One is completely different from the others? You said they each represent the foundational forces of the universe. That everything else is just a combination of these twelve forces."

"Yes?"

"What if we have to fill up just the one that is most compatible with our Dao?" he explained excitedly. "Like, this one is fire, and that's electricity. I don't know what most of them are, to be honest, but maybe I just have to find the one most adjacent to the fist."

"Hmm. I don't know. I still think we have to fill them all up."

"Then let me go first. If I fill one up and nothing happens, we just fill the rest as well. We don't lose anything."

She considered it for a moment. "Okay. Let's do that."

Jack grinned and turned to the door. *The fist*, he thought, tuning out everything else to focus. With his recent increase in Will, it wasn't difficult. *Let's see...*

There were twelve Old Ones. A shackled man—though the shackles didn't seem like part of his power—a creature of death, then fire, electricity, magnetism, two creatures of explosions, stars, small spheres—mass, maybe?—one that warped everything around it, and the two water-like ones.

Channeling his Dao of the Fist, a few of those were immediately discarded.

The watery ones were a no-go. They felt completely unrelated to the fist. Electricity, fire, and magnetism were also out. That left seven.

What about the warping one? That could be gravity, or something similar, which didn't have much in common with the fist. Discarded.

The stars? He failed to see the connection. The small spheres? He didn't know what that was, but it felt unrelated, so also a no-go.

Eight down, four to go: the man, death, and the two explosions.

The explosions were the first he considered. His Meteor Punch was the closest skill he had to the Dao of the Fist, and it was an explosion. However, why were there two of them? One was made up of many small explosions, and the other of fewer but larger ones.

Jack didn't know what fundamental forces of the universe those represented, or why they were so similar. Did the explosion match with the Fist?

To a degree, he admitted. But it wasn't the core. There was more to the fist—or rather, his fist—than just exploding stuff. It wasn't just a weapon. It was a declaration of will, a way of life. It was the nature of his soul, and, as contradicting as it sounded, it involved way more than breaking things.

Reluctantly, he placed the two explosion Old Ones as a "maybe."

Which left just death and the man.

Death... he considered it. Death is a result of combat, but I don't think I aim at that. It's even farther than the explosions.

A "no," then.

Which left only the human. If he could discard that as well, he would know that one of the explosions was the answer.

But the human... Jack frowned. What exactly did it signify?

There was no discernible characteristic. Nothing supernatural about him. Just a human, a man, standing in space. His details weren't clear, though he seemed to have a calm, steady smile, like he saw through everything and simply enjoyed reality.

Could he signify people? he thought. Simplicity? Life? Intelligence?

All those could be true. However, this concept was more complicated than the others. For everything else, he could imagine fitting Daos. But what Daos would fit the image of a human?

It felt like the door was cheating, throwing in a wildcard. Jack ignored it and focused inwardly, sinking into his Dao and all the insights he'd gathered so far.

What was the fist? It was a path. It was freedom. It was battle. How could it connect to... whatever this human signified?

Well, my path is the natural one, he thought, though everyone probably feels the same about theirs. I embrace my instincts without losing track of myself. I stand, laugh, and fight when I have to, and die when I lose. That's how life should be. I feel complete in this path, happy.

It's how everyone should live, in my humble opinion.

But what did that have to do with being human?

Maybe this is all there is to it, he considered. I am simply who I am. This is what it means to be a human.

However, even he felt that this was slightly off the mark. A bit naive and overstated, even.

Hmm. What else? What is my fist?

It's all the things I mentioned before. However, if I abstract it, is it closer to explosions, or closer to being human?

When he thought of it like that, the answer came easy. Violence and battle were part of his Dao, but just that, a part, a manifestation. The true core of his Dao was the nature of the fist. He strived to make himself behave and think like a fist; steadfast, reliable, strong, honest.

In the end, the Dao was far more than just a weapon. It was a state of being, a way of life. The man he yearned to be.

Jack opened his eyes, gazing at the shackled human at the top of the door, and reached out to touch him. His Dao flowed in, barely a trickle before the vacuum was filled.

Nothing happened.

"Told you," Nauja bragged. "Now, let's—"

The cavern shook. The door shone, all twelve Old Ones glowed—starting from the human Jack had chosen—until the glow illuminated the entire engraving from behind. Colors appeared. Suddenly, it was a work of art, one of mesmerizing beauty that lasted a mere moment.

And then, soundlessly amidst the shaking tunnel, it swung open inward, revealing a patch of impenetrable darkness.

Nauja was left staring. So were Brock and Jack, but Jack was the first to recover.

"Jack one, Nauja zero," he said, full of pride. "Now come on. Let's go see what's behind it!"

CHAPTER FORTY-THREE
PROVING YOUR ANCESTRY

THE SPACE BEHIND THE DOOR WAS A DEEP, THICK DARKNESS. AT FIRST, JACK'S enhanced senses didn't pick up the slightest hint of light.

Thankfully, they had a torch. Jack waved it before the door, revealing a new corridor, but it was nothing like the tunnels they'd been traversing so far. This one was smooth. Sharp. Carved by tools. There was a slight slope downward but no steps.

Jack gulped. "Are you coming?"

"We can't just turn back now... Right?" Nauja asked. Her voice and rising chest betrayed a mix of exhilaration and fear. A hidden passage connected to her ancestors under the Forbidden Cave... It didn't get much more adventurous than that.

Brock was unbothered. He raised a fist and cheered, then impatiently motioned for Jack to get going.

He laughed and obliged.

The tunnel was deeper than his torchlight could reach. As he took three steps in, nothing happened. He kept walking, at any point expecting a monster to leap from the shadows. He couldn't shake the feeling that he was walking into the innards of some leviathan.

Brock followed, making "ooh" and "ahh" sounds, and Nauja brought up the rear. The moment she stepped through, the door behind them smashed shut with a terrible boom that made them all jump.

"What the fuck?" Jack exclaimed.

"That—The door closed," Nauja said in shock.

"I can see that. You didn't close it?"

"No, it just... *closed*."

They exchanged a look, fear in each other's faces. When Nauja tried to push, nothing happened, and there was no engraving or Dao vacuum on this side.

"What a good omen," Jack said bitterly.

"Do you think this is what happened to the delvers who found this place?" Nauja asked, looking around warily. "They were trapped here forever?"

Jack looked around again. Now, he understood why the walls were made of metal. He could have punched his way through rock, given time. But through this... He knocked on a wall, feeling sturdiness beneath. The door was equally impregnable.

"I think we're stuck," he said.

However, Brock shook his head. "No," he replied. He pointed down into the darkness.

"Oh, how could I forget about that," Jack replied sarcastically, slapping his forehead, while Brock nodded sagely.

"Not much choice," Nauja said. "We were heading down, anyway."

"I guess. Well, no point standing around. Let's go."

With that, they walked farther in, Jack at the front, Nauja at the back, and Brock in the middle. The door disappeared behind them, leaving them flanked by darkness. There were no side passages, only one straight line heading downward at an angle.

"Where do you think this leads?" Jack asked, his voice low by instinct.

"Honestly? No idea," Nauja replied in the same near-whisper.

A few minutes later, the tunnel opened. They couldn't see where it led, only that their torchlight reached no walls. It could be a chamber stretching for miles in every direction, or just ten feet.

The world flared with light all at once. They had to cover their eyes, used as they were to the darkness. Jack grabbed Brock and jumped to the side, dodging whatever attack might be coming. Nauja jumped the other way, stifling a cry as she landed on her broken arm.

There was no attack, however. When their eyes adjusted, all they met was a wide, empty room.

It looked like a fancy Earth basement. Flat, electrical lights were plastered in equal rows on the ceiling, illuminating the room, while the gray marble floor was strikingly clean. The walls were made of some dark metal that looked light to the touch, almost like plastic, and they were curved, shaping the room as a rectangle someone had pushed air into until it almost burst.

It looked so much like something he may find on Earth, that Jack was momentarily stunned. Going from the primordial environment of Trial Planet to this was a leap that took him some time to process.

Next to him, Nauja was also stunned, but for different reasons.

"What is this magic?" she said, gawking at the ceiling lights. "The torches... They do not dance. And they have the wrong color."

"It's called electricity," Jack explained. "What you see is glass with a thin iron cord behind it, through which courses power with enough intensity to make it glow without burning."

"Wow," she said, observing the lights for a moment longer before turning to the floor and walls.

Jack's attention was arrested by something else entirely. The room was empty, roughly a hundred feet long, fifty wide, and twenty tall. However, there was writing on the back wall, though it wasn't carved into the metal. It resembled projected computer text—he could find no projector in sight.

All it said was, *Scan nothing.*

"What's that supposed to mean?" he asked.

A new row of text appeared under the first one, as if the letters were surfacing from behind the wall.

Prove yourselves or die.

"How nice," he said. "More things trying to kill us."

"What?" Only now did Nauja notice the writing. "What does that say?"

"What?"

"I can't read. What does that say?"

She didn't seem bashful about it, so Jack didn't react. It made sense. Why would she need to read in the jungle?

"It says to scan nothing, and to prove ourselves or die."

Her eyes narrowed. "What does that mean?"

"It's when you stop living."

She threw him a cold stare. Jack laughed.

"I have no idea either," he said. "The 'scan nothing' part could only mean the System scan we can do at things. That's all I can think of. Either that, or it expects us to carry around scanners, which we don't."

"Why not scan things?"

"How am I supposed to know?"

"And what about that second part? To prove ourselves?"

"Well, I also don't know..." He looked around, licking his lips. "But I suppose we're about to find out."

He expected something to happen at the cue of his words. Disappointingly, nothing did. No enemies jumped at them, no traps sprung, no suspicious sounds. Nothing.

Belatedly, he noticed there were no other doors in the room.

"Do we have to find a way out or die of thirst? Or asphyxiation?" he wondered incredulously. "Okay, I take it back. Send in the things that want to kill us. Just underestimate us, so we kill them instead."

"What are you talking about?"

"Nothing. I'm just bantering against a wall."

At least there were no corpses, so if delvers had made it past the door, they'd made it past this room as well.

"Maybe the way out has something to do with that thing?" Nauja said.

"What thing?" He followed her pointing finger. "Oh!" Right under the letters was a device, of sorts, embedded in the wall.

"Let's take a look," Nauja said.

"Just be careful."

They inched their way across the room, keeping an eye out for traps or ambush. Tripwires, pressure plates, poisoned darts, illusions... They looked for anything but found nothing. The room was as empty as it appeared.

Once at the back, right under the letters, Jack noted how each of them was the length of his arm.

And the device in the wall under them was a... Well, a disappointingly primitive contraption. A short metal protrusion extended from the wall, with a small groove at its end, facing up. Directly above it was another protrusion, this one ending in a sharp needlepoint.

"What's that?" Jack asked. "Perhaps I should break it."

Nauja glared.

"I'll keep making the same joke until you stop glaring," he warned her.

"It's like we have to put something in that groove," she said. "But what? And why the needle?"

Jack reached out to touch the groove, but there was no Dao vacuum. He shook his head.

"You know..." Nauja said. "This reminds me of something that exists deeper inside Trial Planet: Trials."

"Trials?"

"Yes... The delvers talk about them a lot. They start appearing from the fifth ring down: testing grounds that reward those who complete them. Supposedly, they are the main allure of Trial Planet, besides the conqueror titles."

"Really? Now that's interesting."

"It is. Trial rewards are supposed to range from impressive to world-shattering. If this is a trial, that would be great for us. But as I said, Trials aren't supposed to exist before the fifth ring." She threw him a quick glance. "And they have nothing to do with the Ancients."

"Hmm. Are you saying we discovered a hidden trial?"

Hesitation clouded her face. "The door, this riddle, the instructions on the wall... It all seems to match, but the ring and Ancients don't. It should be impossible. If this is a trial, there could be something extremely valuable at the end. But maybe it's something completely different."

"Extremely valuable," Jack repeated. His chest burst with hope. His goal—defeating the Planetary Overseer within a year—was almost impossible. Extremely valuable treasures were exactly what he needed. "Well, only one way to find out. But how do we solve this... needle-groove thingy?"

He gazed at the two protrusions in thought, as did Nauja.

Brock tapped Jack's waist. When he turned to look, the brorilla pointed at the needle and mimed pricking his finger.

"Oh!" Jack said, eyes flashing with understanding. "Brock's right. It does look like a finger-pricking device. A drop of blood comes out, then falls into the groove. I've seen that before."

"Really? Where?" Nauja asked curiously.

"TV."

She looked on blankly.

"Delver stuff," he corrected, to which she nodded.

"But why would this machine want our blood?"

"Good question. It said we have to prove ourselves... Hmm."

"Maybe that we are humans?" Nauja tried. "Not robots?"

"Why would it care about that?"

"I don't know. What else could it want?"

"Maybe it will test our blood for something." He thought back to his lab, where they liked to put liquids in testing tubes and thoroughly examine them. This groove didn't look like a tube, but they also used small bowls to collect liquids. Then, they just had to use a dropper or needle to move it wherever. "Maybe it really does want to see if we're humans?"

That was strangely speciesist, and it also didn't make much sense.

"I know!" Nauja exclaimed, raising a finger. "It wants to see if we are Ancient!"

"What?"

"Think about it. The door depicted the Ancients. Trial Planet was constructed and used by the Ancients for millions of years before somehow appearing in your galaxy. If this place was a secret, it makes sense that they'd only want their people accessing it. Right?"

"Hmm. Right. That makes sense. And you're a direct descendant!"

She smiled ear to ear. She seemed very excited to contribute something other than hunting and killing dinosaurs.

"Wait," Jack said. "Does this mean that, if I wasn't here with a barbarian, I couldn't get past? That can't be right."

"It would explain why no delver ever made it back."

"I guess." A shiver went down his spine. "Then you should prick your finger there." He pointed at the needle. "Go for it."

"Okay," she said, placing her finger by the needle. "But what if that's not it?"

"I don't see what else it could be. That thing is out for blood, and there is nothing in mine that's better than yours."

"You're right, I guess."

Brock gave her a big thumbs-up, encouraging her. Taking a deep breath, Nauja pushed her finger against the needle.

Despite her enhanced skin, it broke through without any resistance whatsoever. A thick, red droplet tumbled down as Nauja retracted her finger.

The blood landed on the groove with a soft plop. Nothing happened for a moment. Then, it drained down, absorbed into the metal until it all disappeared.

"Wow," Jack said. "I have no idea if this is technology or magic. Maybe both."

The letters above them flickered and changed. They were sucked back into the wall, and when they returned, the second line was different. A third one had appeared, too:

Scan nothing.

Ancient blood confirmed.

Initiating test.

"Initiating? But we just finished it."

"What does it say, what does it say?" Nauja asked excitedly. Jack translated while looking around.

Then, blue light gathered, and a creature appeared in the middle of the room. It was a goblin.

"Kekekeke," it laughed, licking its long, clawed fingers. "Humans. I bity! I eaty!"

CHAPTER FORTY-FOUR
THE ANCIENT RUINS

A GOBLIN STOOD IN THE MIDDLE OF THE HIGH-TECH ROOM. THE CONTRAST WAS almost jarring.

Its bare green feet were planted on the immaculate marble floor. It was child-sized and covered in brown rags. Its teeth were sharp, like a dog's, its eyes were dark beads of hatred, and it rubbed its short claws together, enjoying the prospect of devouring them without the slightest idea of how massive the gap between them was.

"Kekekeke," it laughed again.

Jack did a double take. "Why would a goblin—"

He almost scanned it. *Almost.* The move was an ingrained reflex, but his surprise was such that he waited an extra moment, and that saved him. The words on the wall came to mind: "Scan nothing."

His thoughts were firecrackers. All connections were made instantly, and he dived in front of Nauja, shouting, "NO! Don't scan it!" He landed in a somersault, rising to his feet at once.

"What are you doing?" she asked, raising a brow. She ignored the goblin completely.

"Don't scan it!" he said again. "The wall said not to scan anything. This is what it meant. Don't scan the goblin. That's the only reason it would appear; it's too weak to test us in combat."

Nauja raised the other brow, too. "Okay." She looked to the little creature, which was now approaching them with an astonishing unawareness of danger. "What should we do with it?"

"Let me handle it."

Jack stood before her, facing the goblin. It broke into a sprint, covering the room as quickly as its little legs could take it. It was... painfully slow.

"Kekekekeke!"

"I don't think it's a threat," Nauja said from behind him.

"Let's not risk it," Jack retorted. "Since we can't scan it, it could be hiding its power."

Even Brock looked disinterested, but Jack had experienced the System's shenanigans before, and he was determined to play it safe. He shot a Meteor Punch when the goblin came within ten feet.

"Keke—" It exploded without even seeing the strike. In fact, the explosion was so strong that the goblin was torn into a million tiny pieces, covering the floor behind it in a red paste that spread across half the room.

"I think it's dead," Nauja said. "But you can hit it again if you want. Just to be sure."

"Caution is important," he retorted, rubbing the back of his head. "But man... I remember how one of them almost killed me once. Tough times to be a goblin."

"Eh. They're goblins." She shrugged. "Little sacks of hatred and sadism. They're better off dead."

"I thought you loved nature."

"I do. But not goblins."

"Well, it's dead now, anyway. I wonder if we succeeded this trial thingy already."

"Maybe there will be a kobold next. You should hit it even harder."

"You're welcome for my figuring out the trick, by the way."

"Just so you know, I figured it out myself, too."

"I didn't hear you shouting, 'Don't scan it!'"

"I trusted you."

"I call bullshit."

"*In any case,*" Nauja said, "what now?"

This time, the room took her cue. Just as her words finished ringing, a sliding sound made them turn toward a wall. A door had opened there —a door that had been indistinguishable before.

At the same time, the goblin's remains were absorbed into the floor, walls, and ceiling, leaving the room as spotless as when they entered.

Jack raised a brow. "Maybe that's what happened to the previous delvers," he said. "They died of dehydration, then were sucked into the floor."

"What a way to go, huh?"

"Yeah."

There was light beyond the door, so they didn't bother keeping their torch. It had almost burned out, anyway. Jack let it fall, and the floor absorbed it after a moment. "Think it can absorb us too?"

"Not so far. Let's hurry before it changes its mind."

They reached the door with quick steps and peered through.

"The fuck?" Jack said.

"This is..." Nauja's eyes went wide. "This is impossible!"

A civilization stretched before them.

The cave ceiling rose a mile above, but not as high as the sky. Mushrooms hung from it, illuminating rolling fields of wheat and vegetables. These stretched on for miles, all the way to the far wall, a rising cliff of stone that connected the ground with the ceiling.

There were cattle, too. Cows and pigs, sheep and goats, all grazing on a hill to the right. To the left stood a small lake, its edges bordering the wall.

People dotted the landscape. Some tended to animals, others to the fields. There were many of them, easily dozens, maybe hundreds, and they appeared human.

The entire thing looked like Earth, actually. The cattle and crops were the same. There was even a temple at the back, resembling a Buddhist shrine. The only differences were the houses, little picturesque huts with no roofs, and subtle hints of advanced technology. Everywhere Jack looked, he saw high-tech contraptions integrated into the seemingly simplistic lifestyle.

Here, a farmer tilled the field with a hoe that had a vibrating head. There, the cows were tied to a wooden stake that slowly moved around the fields on tiny legs, regulating their feeding. Farther back, a watermill scooped up the lake water, pouring it into an ingenious irrigation system that spanned the fields.

And everyone wore a smile. Nobody seemed tired. These were happy people. Simple. At peace.

"What?" he asked.

"That's..." Nauja could barely hold back her excitement. She stepped through the door, into the large cave beyond—

—and everything faded.

It was like a veil was pulled from their eyes. The vibrant farms were replaced by weeds and flat, barren soil. The cattle disappeared, their pens fading away. The houses stood the test of time, changing from homes to ruins. The smiling people were the final thing to go, turning to look at Jack and Nauja as they did. Their bodies became dust, from their legs to their heads, leaving their smiles for last.

Everything was gone. Thousands of years had passed in the blink of an eye. The flourishing civilization had turned into a wasteland, with only the ruins of a few houses standing out here and there like memories of a time long past.

"No!" Nauja said. "I... I thought..."

"An illusion," Jack said, stepping up beside her. "The past, maybe? But... how? And why?"

"I think these were my ancestors," Nauja muttered, tears welling up in her eyes. "I think... the Ancients used to live here."

"Really?" Jack thought back to their human forms, their Earth-like environment. Were Ancients really like that?

"I really do." She turned to look at him. "But now, they're all gone."

"Yeah, I guess they are."

There was one thing that remained unchanged. The temple at the back, the Buddhist shrine, was exactly as the illusion had shown. As if time held no grip there. It stood guard over the barren fields, exuding the same holiness it always did.

"What is this place?" Jack asked. "What's the point of it? All the tests, the door, the blood, the goblin... Why scan nothing? Why such secrecy? Why would Ancients—if they really were that—be living in Trial Planet, and why would they not want to be found?"

"They *were* Ancients, I know it," Nauja said. "We have stories about them. How they lived as one with nature, how they reached the apex of technology, saw its futility, then returned to the roots. It's exactly what we saw in the illusion."

"It is," Jack admitted. "But still, why?"

"I... don't know. Maybe... Maybe they disliked the delvers. They wanted to hide from them, escape the incessant conflict, the greed."

"Hmm... Wait! The Ancients were exterminated by the Old Ones, right? In your story. Maybe these ones got away somehow and hid here to escape the wrath of gods."

"You think? But why would they still hide? The Old Ones can't come here."

"Maybe they just... never knew." Jack took in the ever-sealed stone. "Maybe they were here for a looong time."

Her face soured. "They aren't stupid. They would know."

"How?"

"I don't know. But they would have a way."

"Maybe that place has answers," Jack suggested, pointing at the temple. "What do you say? Wanna take a look?"

"I absolutely do!" Despite her broken and bandaged arm, Nauja was brimming with energy. Her eyes sparked, her face glowing. "Let's go."

"Brock?"

The brorilla was nearby, watching over the ruins with them. He idly twirled the Staff of Stone around himself, lost in thought. When Jack called, he snapped out of it and pointed at the ruins. "Strong," he said.

Jack raised a brow. "A new word? Congrats, bro!"

Brock gave him a toothy grin.

"But strong..." Jack repeated, looking over the ruins. "What do you mean by that, my friend?"

The brorilla shrugged. He didn't even bother miming. "Strong," he said again, pointing to his heart.

"Hmm. Yeah. I understand."

Nauja puffed up in pride. "Of course, my ancestors were awesome!"

They paced into the ruins, not taking a straight line to the temple—they explored a bit. From up close, the contrast between past and present was even more striking. They passed by the watermill's remains, only finding rotten, wooden foundations where it used to stand. The irrigation system, all those wooden pipes, had been absorbed into the ground. The fields were overgrown with weeds, rugged patches of ground flowing over one another. The ruined houses still stood, and Jack realized that the wood which constructed them didn't look quite right. It shimmered. Perhaps that was why it lasted so long—from what he knew, Trial Planet had been in their galaxy for a million years.

In fact, the wood didn't just shimmer. There was a hint of something to it, an itch at the back of his mind, urging him to focus his will and scan it. Jack refused. Though curiosity burned him, he remembered the instruction to not scan anything. It didn't make any sense—but his heart chose to follow the will of these people.

The System-induced urge to scan grew the more he resisted. It went from an itch to an uncomfortable whisper at the back of his mind, like an addiction acting up. He was practically being offered a cup of coffee after not having any in three days. In fact, it was even worse, because all it would take to activate the scan was a moment of weakness, one misstep of intention.

Together, the three of them walked through the ruins like time had lost all meaning. When they reached the temple, they gawked at it.

It was smaller than it looked from afar. A small wooden fence, barely enough to stop livestock from walking over, enclosed a courtyard the size of the goblin room from before. At its back, attached to the stone wall of the cave, was a small shrine, its gates open.

They approached. Jack, feeling wary, took to the front. A small stone tablet was half-buried in the soil before the shrine's open entrance. Warily, he wiped its dusty surface, revealing ancient words carved into the stone.

May they who think themselves worthy enter. May they save us from the evil we have inflicted on the world.

That was promising.

The inside of the shrine was as simple as its exterior. A room of twenty by twenty feet, with a human-sized stone statue in the middle depicting a smiling man, thin and dressed in light robes, with long silken hair tumbling down his back. His smile... It was one filled with calmness and peace, but hiding under was all the vicissitudes of life, like he'd already seen through everything.

Unlike the Buddhist-like shrine, this man didn't resemble Earth's depictions of Buddha. He still reminded Jack of something, and it took him a moment to place the feeling. Last time he'd seen this man, there was no hair, no robes, and his features were indiscernible. But that smile was exactly the same. Jack's eyes widened the same time Nauja's did.

"That's Enas!" they exclaimed at the same time.

"Why is a shrine of an Old One here?" Jack said. "I thought they eradicated the Ancients. They were enemies."

"This doesn't make any sense," Nauja muttered. "The Old Ones supposedly destroyed the Ancients shortly after making contact. There shouldn't be any time for worship to occur."

"It is odd," Jack agreed. His attention was drawn to something else.

First, the statue created in him the same urge to scan it as the wood outside—like the Staff of Stone, the Dao Soul, and other scannable items.

Second, the statue wasn't the only thing in the room. As he took a step inside, a glimmer of white in a corner caught his eye. It wasn't visible from outside, as it was stuck to the entrance wall—there was a skeleton there. It was humanoid and in a cross-legged position, back pressed to the wall. Despite the ages it had been since this person died, their skeleton remained whole and pristine, and not just that. The bones exuded a sense of awe and wonder, like they radiated the power of the Dao even centuries or millennia after death. They were also scannable, as Jack's gut feeling hurried to inform him.

"What's the meaning of all this?" he asked. "A shrine to an Old One, a hidden pocket of Ancients, a corpse brimming with power after all this time, a testing room that still operates perfectly, the command to not scan anything... What the hell's wrong with this place?"

Nauja ignored his words. She touched her forehead to the ground before the corpse, struggling to bow with one hand tied up. "Ancestor..." she said reverently. "Nauja is here. May you rest in peace."

Seeing her, Jack inclined his head as well. "You have my respect, ancestor. Apologies for disturbing your rest."

Brock nodded, too. "Strong," he said, using his shiny new word.

A moment of somberness went by. Then, Jack asked, "Should we bury it?"

"Can you not feel its power, Jack?" Nauja asked from the ground. "If such a powerful person wanted to be buried, they would be. No. This ancestor chose to die here, to keep an eye on this shrine even after death. Let's leave it be."

"Alright," he whispered.

Then, while Nauja remained bowed, muttering a prayer to her ancestors, Jack looked about the room again. He felt small in this place. Insignificant. He couldn't shake the feeling that they'd intruded on a secret larger than they could handle, something they should never have found. A sense of power and awe entangled everything in this place—from the engraved door to the corpse—speaking of forces far stronger than Jack could comprehend.

This was a place meant for people far, far stronger than Jack and Nauja.

And there was a hint of wonder in that. Of achievement. That, by some stroke of blind luck, Jack was here, taking in the sights that his meager strength could never afford. Who knows what tremendous powers lay in wait, what secrets to uncover?

Even ruined as this place was, he refused to believe it was empty. There had to be something. Nauja had mentioned Trials with life-changing rewards. This could be such a place. And, secret as it was, the rewards would be ever greater. Something related to the Ancients and the Old Ones could only be unimaginable in importance.

His treasure hunting sense was going off. An opportunity that could make his impossible goal slightly more doable. But where?

If only he could scan things...

His gaze returned to the statue. It stood in the middle of the room, unbothered by their presence, stony gaze directed at the front, one hand extended with its palm facing forward.

Jack approached it, circled it, observed it. The craftsmanship was uncanny, as expected from people who could carve steel. It made him curious. What secrets could it hide?

He snuck a glance at Nauja. She was still bowed in reverence. Brock was looking, but he was a bro. He wouldn't speak.

Unable to resist, Jack raised a hand and touched the statue, meaning to feel its surface, to experience its age and meaning.

The moment he touched it, an ancient voice rang out, booming from every direction at the same time. "Let the trial begin."

And he teleported.

CHAPTER FORTY-FIVE
TRIALS OF THE DIVINE

THE MOMENT THE VOICE BOOMED OUT, ANCIENT AND RESOUNDING, JACK'S world changed. The familiar lurch of teleportation overcame him for an instant before everything stabilized.

He wasn't in a shrine anymore. He stood alone in the middle of a large, dome-shaped room, like an upturned bowl. Stone surrounded him on all sides, with a single sun mushroom hanging from the top of the ceiling, some fifty feet above his head, showering the room in yellow light.

Jack looked around with wide eyes, realization dawning. "Shit..." He couldn't stop a chuckle. "Curiosity killed the cat, I guess."

He didn't lose heart at the sudden teleportation. The voice had mentioned a trial—and Nauja said that Trials were tests, hiding danger and opportunity. There would be a way through—he just had to find it.

However, the more he observed the room, the more his frown deepened. There was no door. No wall with letters, no windows, no enemy, no nothing. Cold stone entombed him.

If I die here, will anyone ever find me? he wondered, but even he didn't know where he was, let alone Nauja and Brock.

Thankfully, the trial didn't leave him waiting long. The same voice as before boomed throughout the room, so loud that Jack felt an urge to clap his ears.

"A divine gift lies in wait, seeking its successor. Five trials stand between you and great power. Prove yourself worthy of wielding and protecting it—or die. The trials will be adjusted to your level."

Simple and succinct. Strangely, Jack wasn't pacified.

"Excuse me," he shouted back. "Can you tell me where this is?"

The voice did not reply. Jack was left alone with his thoughts, running the previous words over and over in his mind. Wait. It said "level." This place is aware of the System, the eradication, the Immortals. It wasn't simply forgotten. They chose to remain hidden even after the Old Ones were forced away... but why?

He had no more time to ponder, as a mist filled the room, manifesting out of thin air. Jack braced himself for battle, looking around warily, but no enemy came. The silence was as crisp as ever, broken only by his breath, the beating of his heart, the blood drumming on his temples.

A song cut through the mist. It was ephemeral and light, the voice carried on clouds, each note sung with unparalleled beauty and depth. So relaxing it was, Jack's entire body loosened, the knots in his back untied, his muscles turned to jelly, and euphoria coursed through his heart. If there was a heaven, this was how angels would sing.

He lay down, so engrossed in the music he couldn't think. The mists receded around him, revealing a palace of pleasure. Heavenly delicacies sat on golden plates, fruit soft enough it would surely melt in his mouth, meat that could lace his entire body with energy, youth, and virility.

He wasn't alone. People surrounded him on all sides. Their names eluded him, as did their past, but he remembered they were bosom friends, people he'd been through thick and thin together. He loved them almost more than himself.

Jack lay on cushions, stretched out and leaning to the side, where a platter of apples awaited him. He grabbed one and bit into it. The taste was heavenly. After this, how could he bear to consume anything else? Even the water he tried, from a blue bottle made of clouds, was made of liquid crystal, so pure that he felt all negative feelings wash out of his heart.

The song was still there, sung by a striking woman on a different set of cushions. She was one of his bosom friends, but she was also more.

She was beauty itself. Her hair fell down her shoulders to reach her waist. Her expression moved with the song, fully absorbed as she was, and her voice lit a fire inside him that made even the heavenly apples seem inconsequential.

This was love. Deep, true love. Yet something inside him resisted, denying the feeling, but he couldn't refuse his heart.

The woman poured her soul into the song. Jack couldn't quite catch the lyrics, but they spoke directly to his heart, recounting beauty, passion, breezy days, and hot nights. Each part struck a chord in Jack's heart and explored it, caressed it, massaged and kissed it. The most wonderful feelings in life were presented, expanded, and fulfilled. Every verse a story, so true that no other story could ever reach their height. All sung in a voice and way that could never be surpassed.

It was perfect.

Jack's eyes welled with tears, such was the beauty of every note, and his heart reveled in the music, expanding until it could fit the entire world.

He lost track of time. Or, rather, time lost its meaning. Before this song, nothing else mattered. The world was born and developed only to reach this moment in time, for this song to flow out of this woman's lips.

When the music came to an end, Jack was melted into a puddle of emotions. He felt every emotion there could be, overwhelmed by the sheer beauty of life, its ups and downs, struggles and rewards, the gems which hid on rainy nights and gave them meaning.

His friends felt the same, and their happiness bounced off each other until it could increase no more.

The woman turned to Jack, regarding him alone. "Did you like it?" she asked, sliding a strand of hair behind her ear.

"I loved it." The words left his lips of their own, true beyond the shadow of a doubt.

She smiled beautifully. He didn't know his heart could melt any more, but it did. "I have something for you," she said, removing a small, golden sphere from her dress. A triangle with a dot in its center was painted on its surface. "I made it especially for you. A gift as precious as my song."

"What is it?" he asked, receiving the sphere with tender care.

"Why don't you scan it and find out?" she replied, smiling.

Jack regarded the sphere. Indeed, why wouldn't he scan it? The song was still inside him, that love all-encompassing. Nothing could be wrong in the world. Everything ugly was simply another facet of beauty undiscovered. In this palace, surrounded by the warmest emotions known to man, he had nothing to fear.

So why didn't he scan it?

There was an awareness that he wasn't supposed to. It seeped out from inside him, making him hesitate until he was certain it was wrong. He shouldn't do it.

But how much did it matter? Her song had filled his heart. She'd given him the greatest gift there was, and here was another. Even if it was wrong, could he really refuse her this little favor?

But it *was* wrong.

"What is the matter, my love?" she said, inching closer. Her perfume reached Jack's nostrils. His brain turned pink. His every cell shivered with joy.

"I—"

"Shh, don't talk," she said again, laughing. "Just scan it. I made it with so much effort. Please?"

To refuse would be to break her heart. However, to refuse himself would be the same. "Can't I just open it?" he asked weakly, his voice coming out a low whisper.

"No, you silly!" She laughed again. "How can you open it without scanning it first?"

She's right, he thought. I should scan it.

But it's... wrong.

The insistence of wrongness was so deeply planted inside him that it persisted, rearing its head again and again, refusing to be side-tracked.

On one hand, he knew with absolute certainty that scanning this sphere was wrong. On the other... how bad could it be? Didn't she deserve for her gift to be appreciated?

Should he betray what he knew was right, or should he betray her feelings?

"Come on, Jack!" his friends shouted from the side, more voices joining in. Some were jesting, others laughing, all filled with joy. "Let us see! Scan it and open it up!"

"It looks so pretty!"

"Don't keep her waiting or she'll go away!"

They all burst out laughing at this last, well-intended comment, while the woman by his side blushed.

Jack felt so much momentum around him directed at scanning the sphere. To refuse would be to break the flow, to shatter such a wonderous moment, to endure his friends' and lover's disapproving stare.

But to scan it would be wrong.

He... He couldn't possibly ruin this moment for everyone.

Except, he had a path. A way. His friends would be fine. Betraying his path would be to break both it and himself. To lose everything.

"I'm sorry, everyone," Jack said, raising his head and laughing. "You know I can't do this." He returned the gift to the woman, whose gaze was deeply hurt. "I'm sorry if I'm ruining some surprise. If you can open it for me, I will love it all the same."

He smiled widely. And, before anyone could reply, the forms around him turned to mist, the apples, the water, the friends, the lover. The golden sphere with the dotted triangle remained last, and as it disintegrated, Jack caught a glimpse of a live scorpion inside before it, too, disappeared.

He was left alone in the mist, mind struggling to comprehend what occurred. That had been an illusion. He had remained himself, but reality had been bent to present him with a dilemma.

He suppressed a growl that threatened to rise from his chest.

But the song was real. It echoed inside him still. He couldn't remember the lyrics, nor the voice, or the music, but the soul of the song was etched into his heart. The perfect stories, the full emotions he was capable of experiencing.

Nothing would ever top it. Everything else he ever felt would be inferior to that one song, to the absolute peak of life. But that was okay. A bittersweetness enveloped him then, an appreciation of what he experienced, nostalgia for what had irreversibly passed.

Without Jack knowing it, at that moment, his smile resembled the one of the statue in the shrine.

"Will trial, passed," the voice boomed, drawing Jack back to the present. Then, it took a more educating tone. "Good intentions and the will to uphold them are the foundation of a full heart. But choosing the right path is meaningless if you cannot see it."

The mists changed. They swam and coiled around him, flashing through a thousand shapes before settling on one.

An expansive maze stretched out before him. He viewed it from above, like he was hovering on the ceiling, but he could also see himself standing at the entrance. Twisting paths led outward, merging and branching, ending at dead-ends or circling around themselves. A light glistened in the very center of the maze—the exit. Jack was nowhere near it. The sheer complexity of the shape before him was more than he could handle.

I have to solve this maze, he realized, still looking at it from above. He set to following the paths with his eyes, mentally crossing out the ones that didn't work, but they were simply too many, their branching endless. His brain wasn't capable of tracking them all.

An hourglass appeared by the maze, blue and made of crystal. It turned, as if by an invisible hand, and the sand tumbled down, siphoning through the tiny gap. Slowly but surely, it was diminishing.

Jack fervently set to work. He sent the mini version of himself exploring, hoping to stumble onto a good path by luck. He tried extending outward from the exit or inward from the entrance. He followed paths that were going in the right direction and ones that went directly opposite. Many times, he came close. Once, only one wall separated the path he'd chosen from one that led to the exit, but that *one* wall had no openings, no way to cross.

The sand tumbled, and Jack had found no solution. A large part of the maze remained unexplored. His brain was feverish with activity, devoting the entirety of his being to the puzzle, but no matter how he searched, he couldn't find the solution.

The hourglass was almost empty, the last grains of sand tumbling slower.

Jack accepted his failure. He had not found the path.

"There is no solution!" he shouted as the last grain tumbled down, a final gamble that he had no choice but to make.

The maze and hourglass disappeared. The mists returned, as enigmatic as ever, and Jack was gripped by the suffocating awareness of his failure.

"Mental trial, barely passed. Combat trial difficulty will be adjusted accordingly," the voice came. Jack heaved a huge sigh of relief before processing the last words.

Adjusted? Will that combat trial get harder because I almost failed this one? Hmm. At least, I passed. Was there really no solution?

He had no way to know, nor was there time.

"Recognizing the right path and choosing to follow it are the prerequisites to a full heart. However, one weakness is enough for doom. The mind means nothing if the body is weak."

Jack braced himself. The mists remained empty. A few moments later, the voice came again.

"Physical trial, passed by virtue of specialization."

Oh, Jack thought. Well, not that I'll complain. I wonder if someone with balanced stats could easily pass all three trials—the ones I've seen, anyway.

The voice came again.

"The absence of weakness is the first step. However, the road to mastery is fraught with conflict. Without power, one's impact on life is insignificant. All is for naught."

CHAPTER FORTY-SIX
TRIAL BY COMBAT

As the voice finished ringing, the mists receded completely, vanishing back into the nothingness they came from. The cavern was left empty, stone the shape of an upturned bowl.

Without power, one's impact on life is insignificant. All is for naught. The last words of the mysterious voice still rang in Jack's mind. He mulled them over and over, considering them.

Without power... That's actually similar to my Dao of Power, isn't it? he pondered, analyzing the trial's structure. He'd passed the Will, Mental, and Physical trials, proving he had no glaring weakness. Now, he had to prove he had power, too. It made sense.

What's the purpose of all this? he wondered. *This Ancient space—if it really was one—was so out of the ordinary. The voice mentioned a divine gift... The statue of an Old One... Could I be fighting for the direct blessing of a God?*

The thought sent shivers down his spine, an excitement that rattled his bones and opened his pores. *No way,* he concluded. *It wouldn't be this easy... right?*

A blue light in the center of the cavern interrupted his thoughts. A creature now stood there, facing him. It was humanoid, except with green skin, sharp ears, and beady eyes. Similar to a goblin, but with a few key differences: this creature was the same size as him, and its gaze lacked the telltale malevolence of goblins. In its place was neutrality, an absence of feeling, like this creature was more machine than person.

The urge to scan it became overwhelming, coupled with his own curiosity, but he held it at bay. Perhaps he'd know later what this thing was.

Most importantly, he didn't know its level. It stood there, clad in leather armor, holding a curved sword, scanning him up and down. Jack assumed his battle stance, raising both fists in front of his face and turning to show it a three-quarters profile. This creature was the combat trial. It couldn't be weak.

It charged him without warning. Bare feet kicked against the ground, the curved sword drawing a wicked arc as it aimed for his midsection.

It wasn't particularly fast.

Jack could see its movements clearly. Read them, even. Still watching out for any surprises, he smoothly stepped aside, letting the blade sail over his shoulder, and smashed out a straight punch into the creature's face, catching it in a textbook counter.

With a flash of purple, its head exploded.

Its body flopped to the ground, dropping the sword. As Jack watched warily, the body and dropped sword dispersed into motes of blue light.

"Huh. That was easy."

More light shone in the center of the cavern. This time, two creatures appeared, each identical to the previous one except for their weapon. One held a crossbow, and the other a short rod with a bejeweled top.

Jack blanched, then leaped aside. A bolt whistled through the air where he used to stand, impaling itself on the stone behind him with a *swish*, then an icicle shot at him from the outstretched rod, materializing out of nowhere.

Jack ducked under it, already dashing for the two creatures in a zigzagging pattern. More projectiles flew at him. Crossbow bolts screamed past at the speed of bullets, while icicles rushed past his exposed skin.

Mid-run, Jack shot out two Meteor Punches, both aimed at the crossbow creature. One met a bolt mid-flight and exploded, hiding Jack from their eyes. The second shot past the projectiles, arcing through the air like a purple, fist-shaped meteor, faint starlight trailing behind it, to crash into the creature's sternum.

It flew back, the crossbow thrown aside as the explosion took half its chest away. The creature disintegrated before it even landed.

The icicle one looked at its dying partner and displayed no emotion. It kept shooting at the explosion caused by the previous Meteor Punch, and when it cleared, Jack was no longer there. A fist met its neck from behind and destroyed it.

Jack was left alone again, panting slightly. These creatures weren't too strong—they were low E-Grades. Maybe level 60? He could take them easily. However, he suspected the trial wasn't over yet.

More light flashed in the center of the cavern. Jack was already there, since he'd approached to kill the ice wizard, so he simply watched the light manifest around him. When it settled into four more of those creatures, he shot out two punches, decimating them. A flail wielder and an unarmed creature disintegrated, leaving only two. One swung twin daggers, and the other tried to aim a longbow at his chest.

Jack sidestepped so the dagger wielder was between him and the longbow. He dodged one dagger, slapped away the wrist holding the other, and closed in on the creature to plant a fierce uppercut in its gut. He didn't use Meteor Punch, as it wasn't necessary, and if this turned into a battle of attrition, better to conserve his power.

His fist carried his Dao, along with almost three hundred points of Strength. It dug into the creature's gut like a mallet, lifting it off its feet and sending it flying over its comrade, blue blood leaking from its lips, both daggers dropping.

The longbow wielder was revealed as the dagger creature flew away. An arrow flew at Jack, its speed such that, had he not already moved aside the moment the dagger wielder's feet left the ground, he wouldn't have been able to dodge in time. He stepped in and threw two punches. The creature dodged the first, but the second caved its face in, and it collapsed in a heap.

Jack frowned. "Well, this is getting—"

The light came faster this time, and more blinding than ever. Eight opponents now surrounded him, wielding all sorts of weapons. Jack twisted and attacked wildly. The good thing about being surrounded was that he didn't need to aim. Three creatures fell before they could gather their bearings, but the other five pounced on him.

Fire covered him in a cone, a mace and longsword aimed for his chest and legs, while a great tower shield rose before him, blocking his line of sight.

Jack could no longer hold back.

Before coming to Trial Planet, this attack would have been overwhelming. However, he'd progressed tremendously since then. He had leveled up a lot, gotten new skills and Daos.

The problem with such rapid increases in power was that acclimating took time. He had barely even used his Dao of Power and Brutalizing Aura. The Indomitable Body's limitations were a mystery. He was becoming stronger fast, but stabilization was a core part of the process, and he hadn't had the time to do that yet. He felt lost, his reflexes biased, his body offbeat, his skills underutilized.

On the bright side, real combat was the best practice.

As four attacks flew at him—along with one he couldn't see—Jack let the Brutalizing Aura erupt from his body. The upcoming deaths of these creatures spread out of him with finality, irrefutable. They could not resist, plead, or beg. They would die by power overwhelming.

They stumbled. Whether by accident or design, the aura got to them despite their apparent lack of emotions. The mace missed, drawn back at the last second, and the longsword lost its power, easily slapped away. The fire guttered then went out, while the tower shield shook, the creature behind it momentarily losing the will to fight. An attack inside his mind, one that had been in the process of forming, collapsed by itself.

Brutalizing Aura was perfect for large groups of weaker enemies.

The moment his opponents faltered, Jack became a force of nature. His fists tore through their bodies, pulverizing heads and smashing torsos. Their weapons flew away, useless, and they all disintegrated in quick succession. Their lack of pain was unnerving, but their death was timely.

Jack cast a wary eye. The trial gave him no time to catch his breath.

Sixteen opponents flashed into existence, each holding a different weapon or not at all, and this time, he truly felt fear.

Brutalizing Aura erupted again, stunning them just as they spawned. His fists tore into their ranks with prejudice, exploding in their midst and sending them flying, disorganizing them. His eyes flicked from side to side, taking in everything, but he wasn't omnipotent, and neither was Brutalizing Aura.

When he'd gotten half of them, the rest recovered. Weapons and magic flooded him. He did his best. A mace clipped the back of his thigh, making him stumble. A sword grazed his forehead, a mallet met his forearm head-on, fire creeped up his back, and frost glued his feet to the ground.

With a massive bellow, Jack shook his feet free and Ghost Stepped away, narrowly dodging another onslaught. He appeared outside the encirclement. The moment he did, intense fear clouded his mind, making him forget what he planned to do next. His Dao roared, grabbing that fear and crushing it. Two empty-handed creatures at the back groaned.

The melee fighters were almost upon him, but Jack was awake. With a roar, he punched the air before him in quick succession, sending a dozen punches flying at them.

Meteor Shower!

The creatures exploded like balloons of blood, skin, and flesh, revealing a fire mage and the two Will-oriented attackers. Jack dodged the fire, dove in, and destroyed them.

Amidst heavy panting, he clutched his forearm, where a mallet had struck him hard. It was bruising already, every movement of his fingers painful.

Thirty-two creatures flickered into existence next, eliciting a cold spear that struck his heart. They would never stop coming. They would keep multiplying until he died.

He thought himself strong, much stronger than most, almost unmatched at his level. When the trial said it was adjusted based on that, he thought it would be easy. How wrong he was.

Just who is this trial intended for! Was all he managed to think before a small army fell on him. He Ghost Stepped away, enveloping them all in Brutalizing Aura, then rained meteors. Bodies exploded, weapons went flying, creatures were tossed to the far walls. Again, not a single cry of pain.

But he couldn't defeat thirty-two opponents like that.

They recovered and came for him. Most had fallen, tightly clustered as they spawned, but they remained more than he could handle. He fell back, shooting out more meteors, then was forced to dodge when the enemy backline fired back. Arrows, magic of all kinds, disorienting mind attacks, even illusory opponents sprung up out of nowhere.

This was an onslaught.

Jack roared, charging at the melee so the backliners couldn't easily get him. He ducked into them and punched furiously, each fist carrying the power to break a body. He swatted a warhammer, took a shortsword to the back, a spear butt to the ribs.

His fists tore through the assailants, destroying them inside and out. When the bodies thinned, he was left panting and injured, bleeding from several cuts. But the trial had no mercy. As the frontliners dispersed into blue motes, they revealed a back row of mages and ranged fighters that showered him with attacks. Jack Ghost Stepped, dodging most, but an arrow had embedded itself in his thigh, the bloody tip sticking out on the other side.

He sent out Meteor Punches, aiming at each enemy. Some attacks missed, others were dodged, and a few were shot midair and exploded, but some hit home. The backline erupted into gore and violence, and Jack Ghost Stepped within their midst, taking care of what his meteors missed. His fists dispersed quick deaths, stabbing through guts, rupturing chests, caving in ribcages, cracking skulls.

The Will attacks constantly gnawed at his attention, distracting him. He took care of those creatures first.

When all was said and done, Jack stood alone in a sea of blue motes, like a flock of fireflies. He was breathing heavily and sported several more wounds, the most serious of which was the arrow sticking through his thigh. He grabbed its back and snapped it, then pulled it from the tip and tossed it to the ground. Blood flowed from both sides of the wound, but Jack felt the iron grip his will had on his body, felt the influence he could exert.

He refused to let this wound stand. The blood slowed, gradually coming to a stop, and the skin began to slowly knit itself back together.

He didn't know he could do that.

I survived... he thought. *There's no way more enemies are coming. Still, this trial was more difficult than I expe—*

Blue light flashed.

Jack's whole body shuddered with terror as sixty-four assailants appeared around him, all staring with cold, murderous eyes. *Are you fucking kidding me? This is too much!*

CHAPTER FORTY-SEVEN
PUSHING ONESELF

HE BURST WITH POWER. HIS FRUSTRATION BECAME A DEEP ROAR, ECHOING through the stone walls of the cavern. Suddenly, the previously spacious battlefield was cramped, not leaving him much room to dodge. There were *sixty-four* enemies. Even if all of them were weaker than him, how was he supposed to handle them?

Even as the doubts formed in his mind, Jack lashed out with attacks. A lattice of explosions surrounded him, borne of his own Meteor Punches, filling the air with torn limbs. He was going all out now, striking with little concern for conserving power. Brutalizing Aura wreaked havoc through their numbers.

He didn't stay there long, Ghost Stepping away right as ranged attacks burst through, piercing the air where he once stood. Missing him, the attacks flew to the other side of the encirclement, claiming the lives of their allies.

Jack Ghost Stepped once more, appearing outside the mass of enemies, who were so spread out they almost reached the walls. Luckily, he appeared behind a group of mages. Brutalizing Aura erupted from his body, stunning all the creatures as he set to work on the mages, brutalizing them himself.

Nine mages fell. He Ghost Stepped twice in rapid succession to reach the other side, where archers lay in wait, and tore into them like a wild beast. His every punch claimed a life. He was covered in blood and gore, some his own, but most blue and rapidly disintegrating.

The creatures snapped out of the aura's effects, but Jack had dealt with most of the ranged attackers. Without Brutalizing Aura, he would have been a goner. Only the melee fighters were left now, a whole crowd of them, with a few Will wielders barraging his mind.

Those couldn't hurt him, only disturb him, and his fused Dao Root of Indomitable Will allowed him to brute force his way through. He ducked low and oriented himself on the crowd of melee fighters who were coming at him like a tide in a flood of metal.

His fists clenched tighter, his eyes narrowed dangerously. Brutalizing Aura swept out again, but its effects were greatly reduced the second time. He met the melee head-on.

His fists shot out rapidly, not bothering with aiming, just dodging and striking as fast as possible. He weaved through the hail of metal on instinct, letting his experience guide him through the net. Weapons raked weakly against his skin, leaving shallow gashes. His fists struck out with such intensity that the creatures had no time to charge up strong attacks, blown apart the moment they approached.

His arms were heavy now, the Meteor Punches coming with strain. He was running out of stamina. Gritting his teeth, Jack changed tactics. He stopped Meteor Punching. The Dao of Power filled him, fueling his attacks with the domination of superior power.

His knuckles met torsos, sending the creatures flying into their own. He kept his back to a wall and worked to disrupt their formation, so that only a few could attack him at a time. The drawback was that his punches were weaker now. Not all of them maimed the enemy. Some creatures returned, weak and battered, but alive still.

Jack didn't feel it mattered. They were a never-ending stream of enemies. For every creature he destroyed, another was there to take its place. His injuries were light, but they piled up. Scratches and bruises covered his body. A few, like the hole through his thigh or a persistent pain in his left shoulder, were more serious.

He sank into a red battle haze, equal parts ferocity, exhaustion, and pain.

The enemies remained unending, until they weren't. The final creature fell, revealing an empty room filled with blue motes of light, all struggling to disappear. Only the five Will wielders were left, and Jack quickly took care of them, breaking them apart more brutally than strictly necessary.

He was alone again. Some part of him expected more enemies to appear, a hundred and twenty-eight in total. If that happened, he would die. He couldn't handle them.

But there was a limit to the trial's cruelty.

How was this adjusted to my level? he wondered, gulping to steady his breathing. Even with Brutalizing Aura and Indomitable Will, which were both perfectly suited for this battle, I only barely made it. Just how high are the standards of this trial? Just how precious the reward?

And then, to Jack's utter horror, the blue light flashed. He froze. The light was more condensed now. It took more time to manifest the creatures, and it only covered the center of the cavern.

When it faded, four enemies appeared. They weren't the creatures from before. These ones had skin of metal and smooth, almost mesmerizing curves. Their faces were featureless ovals, their limbs long and lithe, their bodies bare, revealing them to be made of a single piece of metal, like humans of steel.

They held curved swords, so long they looked more like spears. Jack was relieved there were only four instead of over a hundred, but that relief was soon overshadowed by worry. These were far stronger than the previous creatures. Their stance was solid, their movements drawing perfect lines through the air, their bodies exuding a sense of strength.

They weren't stronger than him, but they weren't too far off, either.

He instinctively erupted with Brutalizing Aura, but he felt it slide off the robots with minimal effect. It only influenced them for a fraction of a second. If he wanted to use the aura against them, he'd have to time it just right.

The robots kicked against the ground and reached him in a heartbeat, moving in perfect silence and sync, their weapons reflecting the mushroom light as they slashed at his throat. They were arrayed in two rows of two.

Jack couldn't retreat. If he stepped back, they would beat him through longer reach. Instead, he dove under the crisscrossing attacks and into their guard, where they couldn't reach him easily.

However, as he'd stepped closer to the first line of robots, he was at the perfect distance for the ones at the back. The front robots stepped aside. Two more swords came at him, each blinding in speed, their blades glinting with sharpness. There would be no tanking these blows, as he'd done for the previous creatures. Every attack that hit would be a grievous wound.

Jack jumped and turned sideways. One blade passed above and the other below him, while the two front robots took a step back and raised their blades to crash them down on him. Jumping had been a bad idea, because at the speed they were fighting, gravity would be too slow to bring him back down. He was a sitting duck.

As the two swords rose, he went into overdrive. Only the Iron Fist Style, that had been supporting him throughout the battle, let him survive. He sank into it, becoming a fist-ended force of nature.

He grabbed one blade and held it still. It cut into his palm, the pain stinging, but there was no momentum behind it, its movement thrust backward. He pulled the blade down to lift himself higher, his weight negligible compared to his strength, and pushed against it to turn his body midair, letting the other blade scream past.

He spun around, still airborne, using the momentum to sweep a fist into a robotic head. The metal was hard under his knuckles, shaking his entire arm, but his fist was stronger. The purple glow on its surface pulsed, sucking in the colors and sounds of the world before exploding in a rupture of light.

Jack flew back, landing on his feet and reorienting on the robots as one of them tumbled to the ground, its head a dented mass of darkened metal. It dispersed into blue motes shortly after.

Three robots were left. Without any regard for their fallen comrade, they charged Jack again.

Jack gritted his teeth. He estimated each of them to be close to a middle E-Grade cultivator—perhaps level 70? He was lower than that. Moreover, these robots possessed excellent coordination. How exactly was this "adjusting to his level?" Just what did the trial creators take him to be?

One pale blade glinted in the mushroom light, a razor-sharp edge that could bisect him if it hit head-on.

But there was only one. After he killed a robot, their formation weakened. The two at the back remained as strong as they used to be, but the front one...

Jack ducked and sidestepped, letting the blade sail over his shoulder, then stepped in to deliver a straight Meteor Punch into the robot's head. Unfortunately, its reach was long, giving it time to respond, and it was fast. It managed to duck in time, turning the curved sword to smash its butt into Jack's ribs from below.

He gasped, taking a step back and fighting the urge to double over, as the other two robots swung at him. He took another step back, dodging the attacks, wondering how he should approach.

Brutalizing Aura erupted again, but it was the second time they faced it, so it had no effect. The robots created distance, and the front one swiped its blade at him. Jack charged in to meet it with his chest—

—and Ghost Stepped behind them, shooting a Meteor Punch into one of the back robots. It swung to meet him faster than he thought possible. It blocked his fist with the flat of its blade, the explosion lifting it off its feet and into the front robot.

For a precious second, the two robots were flying, unable to control themselves in the air. Jack was alone with one robot, which faced him squarely and backpedaled to approach the safety of its teammates. Their tactical awareness was annoying. These robots were no fodder.

Neither was Jack. He chased after the robot, closing in with Ghost Step. He appeared in front of its chest. Expecting it, the robot raised a leg to meet him, but Jack endured the attack. A spike of pain burned though his calf, which took the blow.

The other two robots were still midair, but they didn't just wait for gravity to do its job. As one, they stuck their swords into the stone, piercing it like cheese, then pushed against the side of the ground with the flat parts of their blades, reversing their momentum and shooting back toward Jack.

It was a maneuver he never even thought possible. He was momentarily awed by the level he'd reached, where he fought multiple enemies with such capabilities, but also irritated that these robots were so adept in battle.

Unfortunately, even with midair maneuvers, they just weren't fast enough. Jack had stepped into the guard of the retreating robot and took its hit.

He smashed out a Meteor Punch, imbuing it with the Dao of Power. It exploded as an uppercut into the robot's waist, storming into it with such power that its entire body flew off in a straight line, crashing into the cavern ceiling and getting embedded in the stone. Its midsection was broken. Its sword flew away, spinning through the air, to slide into the stone like it was nothing. Both sword and robot burst into blue light.

The other two robots reached him. In an act of unspoken communication, they broke their previous formation and faced him as two individuals instead of a team. They rushed to flank him—Jack wouldn't let them. He used Meteor Shower, enduring the increasing weight of his arms, forcing one enemy to stop and defend.

The other screeched to a halt, but Jack was already upon it. He rained blows. The robot's blade flashed, blocking everything, but Jack persisted, keeping it on the back foot. Even as the second robot joined in, he refused to relent, understanding that he couldn't afford to waste this opportunity.

CHAPTER FORTY-EIGHT
REACHING THE LIMIT

His arms were leaden, his body coal. Weakness suffused him, but his Indomitable Body pressed on, guided like a precise blade. He was only fighting two robots now—one attacking, one buried under his onslaught of strikes.

He feinted an attack to the right. The defending robot didn't fall for it, but the attacking one did, swinging where he pretended to go. He moved the other way and kept laying on the defender.

His fists erupted with the power of falling meteors, every hit shaking the cavern. The robot resisted, its metal feet digging trenches into the stone, but it was struggling to defend. Its grip faltered with every block, and Jack's strikes roared forth with overwhelming intensity.

The other robot's curved sword was imbued with rising panic. It swung widely, rushing to save its comrade and exploit Jack's insistence on attacking—

—and Jack Ghost Stepped behind it. The bending of space was exhausting, his temples drumming with blood, his own heartbeat thundering like the hooves of a horse, but he was in a good position. The robot had already committed to an attack, and its sword was too long, too slow to retreat.

It twisted blindly to the side, again dodging one of Jack's strikes, but he simply threw another, his fist clashing against hard metal and denting it, venting the power from inside, rummaging its interior, and cracking the robot sideways down the middle.

It disintegrated.

The final robot fell on him, exploiting his exhaustion to push on with a fierce offensive. Strikes rained faster than Jack could counterattack, the robot pushed into a frenzy by the loss of its comrades. Jack struggled to fight back, his body and mind heavy.

For all the robot's tactical understanding and brilliant maneuvering, its actual skill with the blade was lacking. Finally, one strike went wide. Jack spotted it in a haze of gray, stepped into the missed attack and slapped the blade near the handle, sending it completely off-position.

His slapping arm then formed a fist and back-fisted the robot in the side, making it bend, and Jack followed his momentum to smash his other fist into the side of the robot's head. A Meteor Punch erupted. The head flew back, the metal neck groaning under the strain, and Jack planted another fist straight into its chest, just to be sure.

The robot exploded mid-flight and burst into blue light before it even reached the wall.

Jack put his hands on his knees, gasping. His previous wounds had reopened. He was losing blood quickly, he was exhausted, his eyes were wavering, and his head was ringing.

But he'd succeeded. Fierce joy flooded his heart, overshadowing the pain, filling him with the satisfaction of a hard-earned victory.

He would have cheered if he wasn't trying to catch his breath, still afraid that more enemies would come, that an even harder battle would rear its head, that the trial would be cruel to the point of disgust.

A few moments passed, enough to make him think it was over.

Then, the voice said, "Adjusting difficulty due to barely passing the mental trial," and light flashed again, revealing eight robots holding wicked curved swords.

Despair washed through him. This battle was beyond his skills.

At the same time, intense resolve accompanied the upcoming death. His world sharpened to a point. Time slowed. All thoughts disappeared, leaving only the bitter desire to take as many enemies as he could with him. He didn't even care that the robots were clearly not living beings. He just wanted to destroy them.

As the blue light receded, Jack flowed into the spawned robots. They raised their swords and Brutalizing Aura swept out, fueled by Jack's awareness of his own death. The robots froze for a precious second.

In that time, Jack smashed one in the midsection, and another in the head. Both dispersed, leaving him with six. More than enough to destroy him.

His only thought was to optimize the battle, to survive for as long as possible, and deal as much damage as he could. The robots fell on him, one formation of four and one of two. He whirled, placing one formation before the other so they couldn't all attack him at the same time.

In his mind, damp exhaustion and intense resolve went hand in hand.

I have to disrupt the formations. He registered the thought like it wasn't his own. *I have to save my power, use my skills sparingly.*

No longer did Jack feel the pain or numbness from his wounds. He pressed on. The swords turned into blurs. He moved more on instinct than decision, surrendering himself to his Iron Fist Style and fighting experience. He ducked, sidestepped, bobbed, and weaved. He let the wicked blades sunder the air around him, carve and toil it like a fertile field, while he remained unhurt in the very center.

The Dao of the Fist roared inside him, lending him all its power alongside his two Dao Roots.

There was no sudden power-up, no miraculous breakthrough at the last moment. He could only depend on himself. His strength was what it was. So were his skills. In this sealed-off cavern, nobody would arrive to save him. There was no way out.

All Jack discovered was a profound sense of going all out. There was nothing to conserve anymore, no thoughts to make. Regrets would come at his final moment. Now, all he could do, all he wanted to do, was devote his entire being to battle, punch with every iota of his soul.

His brain was filled with calculations. He could see the swings before they came, move around them, punch in the gaps. His entire brain was laid bare, revealing depths that the conscious mind could never touch, and it was all devoted to battle. He even thought his heart would forget to beat. Perhaps it did.

Metal crumpled under his knuckles. The distant sound of an explosion reached his ears, and its glaring heat seared his eyes. He slapped a strike away, the movement almost impossibly precise, and let another flow before his eyes as he stepped in to punch a robot with all his strength. The impact was distant, dull, as it traveled up his arm and down his torso. The robot still exploded.

Yet there were more. There were always more.

He danced with the blades, no longer clear on his position, riding the swings as a leaf would ride the wind. Pain was a constant. The burn, cold, and air touched places in his body that it shouldn't be able to. He wasn't clear what happened, but he understood those injuries were deadly.

So what?

In one fluid motion, he ducked under a blade, leaned past another, and drove his fist into a robot's jaw. He Ghost Stepped blindly—and luckily—dodged two attacks, then buried his knuckles in a metal armpit, tearing an arm free.

He turned around, swinging his other fist in a wide arc, only to realize there was no fist there. No hand. No arm.

Huh.

He followed the momentum, spinning low and then high, jumping and somersaulting to crash his one remaining fist into a robot, smashing its head into the ground. Something caressed his chest like a light, stinging veil coated in blood. His vision was bleary, unfocused.

The attacks came slower now, but he was already dead. Even as he landed, he pressed on, ignoring the rapidly growing weakness in his limbs, the soreness of breath in his punctured lungs.

He fought and fought, dodged, and attacked. The battle was a stream of indecipherable colors, his moves nothing but instinct. If not for his Indomitable Body, he would already be unable to move. He could no longer use skills, nor did his mind work enough to remember he had them.

Only the Dao remained, a burning, roaring lump in his chest, a core of power that fueled him to keep going, like a clenched fist, like a punch shot out and the force of life carving through the world.

Everything became one, until he realized he'd stopped punching. He could no longer move his body. He was alive in dead flesh, only his will persisting, a guttering flame whose candle had expired.

He used the last of his tenacity to admire the devastation he wreaked, his parting tribute to the world. Blue motes of light swirled along the ground, robotic parts twitched, disintegrating swords glinted in the light, a human arm lay in a puddle of red blood.

No robots stood.

At some point, he'd won. Too bad he died in the process.

Pressure reached his ears. A faraway voice, like someone was speaking to him. He couldn't remember who it was. It didn't matter.

At least, he'd fought well.

CHAPTER FORTY-NINE
AND PUSHING PAST

As the last of Jack's flame whisked away with a final spark of infinite sadness, gentle warmth filled his entire being, suffocating him, completing and burying him under power the likes of which he couldn't even begin to imagine.

His world turned green, a plain of infinite vitality, a pond of life from which he was allowed to drink. Jack's ruined body sucked in the life like a cracked desert absorbs the rain, drinking greedily, desperately. His numbness became infinite pain, filling his every fiber. His stump of a shoulder sprouted new flesh, coiling around itself and tightening into an arm. His wounds closed, the skin regrowing and knitting itself shut.

And Jack Rust was made anew.

Suddenly, he snapped back into total lucidity. As the healing powers faded away, he was left flabbergasted.

His body, broken and mangled beyond recognition, had been completely restored. New, rosy skin had appeared over his wounds. His veins and arteries were filled with blood again. His heart beat strong as an ox, and his lungs were blissfully empty of liquids.

Even his cut-off arm had regrown. He flexed its fingers. They felt good as new, like they had always been there. Like the battle had been a dream. However, the sight of his previous arm in a puddle of blood served as a grim reminder of just how close to death he'd come.

But he had pushed through.

He survived. Succeeded.

"Combat trial, passed," the voice said, and this time, Jack imagined he heard a hint of approval in its tone. "Withheld rewards presented."

A slew of notifications clustered Jack's vision.

Level up! You have reached Level 70.
Level up! You have reached Level 71.
Level up! You have reached Level 72.

...

Level up! You have reached Level 80.

He lost his breath. He'd never seen so many level-ups at the same time.

No wonder! he thought. No wonder I didn't get any level-ups during the battle... The trial was holding them back. I didn't even know that was possible.

Despite his surprise and near-death experience, Jack didn't lose any time. He remembered that the voice had mentioned five trials—he'd only been through four so far.

In the few seconds of peace, he quickly checked his status screen.

Name: Jack Rust
Species: Human, Earth-387
Faction: Bare Fist Brotherhood (E)
Grade: E
Class: Fiend of the Iron Fist (Elite)
Level: 80

Strength: 265 (+)
Dexterity: 265 (+)
Constitution: 295 (+)
Mental: 30 (+)
Will: 60 (+)
Free points: 55

Skills: Ghost Step (I)

Dao Skills: Meteor Punch (II), Indomitable Body (II), Iron Fist Style (I),
Brutalizing Aura (I)
Daos: Perfect Dao Seed of the Fist (middle), Dao Root of Indomitable
Will (fused), Dao Root of Power
Titles: Planetary Frontrunner (10), Planetary Torchbearer (1), Second
Ring Conqueror

This time, allocating them wasn't so simple.

First, he decided to pour twenty points into Mental. This trial emphasized that having no weaknesses was important, as had his previous run-ins with Mental and Will cultivators. He would have liked to raise it to 60, like Will, but this was about survival. Twenty points was already plenty.

Following Master Shol's 8-1-1 distribution, he wouldn't need to reinvest in Mental until he reached four hundred points in the Physical attributes.

The remaining thirty-five points would go into Physical. Although would he allocate them uniformly, or would he emphasize Strength and Dexterity to balance Constitution?

He decided to balance.

These three were the Physical sub-stats, which meant each attribute point counted as three sub-points when split between them. The math was slightly complex, but it was nothing to the current Jack.

He invested twenty of his remaining points into Physical. They became sixty sub-points, which he split evenly to raise Strength and Dexterity to 295, just like Constitution. Then, with a satisfied grin, he split the remaining fifteen points evenly.

Strength: 310
Dexterity: 310
Constitution: 310
Mental: 50
Will: 60

Over three hundred Physical. The average pre-System human had *five*. Jack felt as strong as an elephant, dexterous like a snake, and durable like a steel wall—but without the intelligence of one.

The familiar surge of power coursed through his limbs, making the near-death experience fall away, replacing the dread with anticipation. He couldn't wait to test his new power—preferably against that minotaur who'd dared slap Brock.

The voice chose this moment to ring again, drawing Jack back to the present.

"You have proven the absence of weakness. You have proven strength. You have proven tenacity, intelligence, and a strong heart. You are worthy."

Space fissured. Verdant green floated before him, shaped as a droplet, but its small size failed to hide its majesty. Jack was looking at an ocean of life, a well of inexhaustible energy, a Dao at a level far beyond anything he'd ever seen. Even the Dao of the C-Grade Planetary Overseer, as he'd experienced it when she suppressed him in the arena, was tiny compared to this drop.

At the start of the trial, the voice had mentioned a divine gift. Jack didn't know what this was, but if someone told him it was the power of gods, he would believe them.

Before he could think further, the drop flew inside him with tremendous speed. It crossed his skin like it was non-existent, diving into his body, his spirit. For the first time, he felt something approach his soul.

"However," the voice boomed out again, its tone grim, "all those are nothing without an undying ambition, a will eternal, unbroken, unsatisfiable. You have succeeded in four of the trials, but the divine gift itself is the final crucible. If you cannot endure it, the powers of this place will heal your soul. You may exit and keep the benefits you have already received, but know that they are nothing compared to the true reward. Best of luck."

It was the first time the impassive voice gave him encouragement. Somehow, this scared Jack more than cold impassiveness.

The moment the voice ceased, he was plunged into hell.

The drop, whatever it was, finished seeping into his body. It spread across him from head to toe. It even invaded his mind. And then, it started pushing.

His entire body was covered in riveting pain. The drop pushed into him from every direction, not compressing him, but sinking into his body like an iron anvil might sink into particularly thick quicksand. It made him feel elastic, impossibly bent. His every cell refused this invasion, but the drop persisted, slowly but surely demolishing his resistance.

Jack felt like his body was disintegrating from the outside inward.

His first reaction was to fight back. He gathered his focus and pushed against the drop, finding with surprise that he could easily resist it. He could even expel it. The pain abated as he pushed out, and Jack wanted nothing more than to keep pushing.

But with the absence of pain came lucidity. He remembered the voice's words. If he accepted this gift, he would gain extreme power.

Was that worth the pain?

Jack closed his mouth, only now realizing he'd been screaming. Everything outside his body had long fallen away. He gnashed his teeth, wrestling against himself. The Dao Root of Indomitable Will came to his assistance, reinforcing his efforts, helping him control his impulses.

He stopped resisting. The drop sank again, as slowly as ever, its sweep though his body absolute. Not a single cell escaped. The hellish pain returned, consuming him, rupturing him.

His mouth flew open into a torturous scream, alone in a sealed stone cavern deep beneath the earth.

Despair blanketed Jack. The pain was so great—he had to escape it, to do something *right now*. And the worst part was, he could. He could push the drop away. Escape the pain.

But doing so meant he would fail. He would not have the power. Power he needed.

It felt like he had split into two people. One screamed and thrashed. The other held the first Jack captive, pinning him to the ground and forcing him to endure the pain, keeping his entire body glued to an oven's burning iron no matter how the first Jack screamed.

Jack was his own torturer. His sense of self ruptured. Inflicting such misery on oneself made no sense. Why not release it? Why not escape?

And yet, he persisted. Blind stubbornness, indomitable will, an unquenchable thirst for the power this pain would bring.

Why do you persist? he asked himself. Why do you do this to me?

The answer was not clear. It was inside him, however, and Jack pushed.

You are insane! We do not deserve this! Let me go!

NO!

Why?

Jack screamed again, the sound not even registering. Every nerve in his body was firing off like firecrackers. Every synapse in his brain was flaring.

The drop was like a bubble closing around him, with his heart as the center. But even after all this time, it was nowhere near done.

Why? One Jack demanded to know, while the other held his hands in a death grip around the neck of the first.

His thoughts were loose. His body jelly. His sense of self became torn, and he struggled to make even the slightest of thoughts. All he knew was that he had to push through, to endure, a desire which stemmed from somewhere deep inside him, from the very core of what made him Jack Rust. It came without thought, without consideration.

Why! Jack screamed again, the voice echoing inside his mind. *Why!*

He did not know. He could not see that far inside him. Why did he fight? Why did he progress? Why did he force himself forward when all that lay between him and triumph was pain?

Why had he fought in the dungeon instead of lying down to die? Why had he joined the Tournament? Why had he stood up for what was right, refusing to be enslaved? Why had he cornered himself, running out to a hostile galaxy to fight against insurmountable odds?

Why could he not just yield and be happy?

That's not happiness! the torturer Jack screamed back. *That's fake! Lies! Weakness! It is not my path!*

That was the core, wasn't it? The path he'd chosen, what he'd forged himself into, the filter through which he saw the world. His desires were set. His soul was settled. He wanted to be this Jack Rust, not any other. The Jack who fought.

Why! the tortured Jack insisted, desperate to understand the meaning for enduring such pain.

Jack felt like it had been a century already, yet the drop was only halfway through his body. His nerves were frayed, existing in an eternal state of pain. Could he persist all the way? He didn't know. But he would try. His outer self was shed away, revealing his deepest core underneath.

He had almost run out of power. He wanted to resist, but he simply couldn't any longer. The drop was approaching completion, but could he last? He needed something to fuel him, to support him. He dug deep inside himself, striving to find the core-most reason of why he fought and grab on to it like a drowning man on a floating log.

His thoughts screamed his fear, despair, and weakness.

At the end of his rope, he found the reason.

Because compared to the pain of being weak, this is nothing.

When all else was shed away, that was all that remained. That was Jack Rust. A man who would never yield, never give up, never stop striving for greatness. A man who had seen through the lies he told himself. And he knew.

Without strength, without freedom, life was meaningless.

He remembered the times before the Integration. He led a dull life, simply floating along without power, initiative, nor even control over his life. He always smiled and nodded, playing by the rules, seeking society's approval, burying himself deeper into the hurtful facade. The Integration had hurt, but it'd shown him a way out—a way that always existed, even before the Integration, but he was too weak of heart to pursue it.

Now that he saw the truth, he could never go back. He didn't want to return to those days. He feared them, and the person he used to be.

He wanted power. Freedom. Without those, he might as well die.

And the world had listened to his wishes. It provided him the opportunity. If he gave up now, if he betrayed himself at this critical juncture, he would never recover. His will would be shattered and he'd forever remain weak.

He anchored himself to this truth, holding on with tooth and nail, using his despair as fuel to grab on harder.

The pain did not abate, but the tortured Jack stopped resisting, accepting his fate and why it had to be so. Torturer and tortured became the same. He was one again, a unity of will and pain centered around one axis: Strength. Freedom. True life.

The pain came in crashing waves. Jack felt it all, but he no longer suffered as much. He knew he would not relent and would persist until he died. That resolve took a weight off his chest, turning him into a rock at sea, always battered by waves but never budging. His screams became a natural part of the world as his mind receded in a shell of acceptance, watching his own pain as if from afar.

It could have been a second or a year. Jack had no way to tell.

Until everything came to an end.

The pain disappeared. Jack was no longer in a stone cavern. In fact, he no longer had a body. He was in a vision similar to those he got from his Classes, but the scenery was on a whole other level.

He wasn't on a planet anymore. He was in space, surrounded by broken stars and swirling vortexes.

And right in front of him, the entire world was dark, like someone had stuck a black sticker in the center of his vision.

CHAPTER FIFTY
GROWING STRONGER

A HUGE CIRCLE OF DARKNESS SUPERIMPOSED ON JACK'S VISION. IT WAS CLOSE and far away at the same time. He could sense it just before his eyes, a threat of cosmic scale, but he could also see stars orbiting it in the distance, their shapes twisting and warping, elongated.

In this moment, Jack didn't have a mind to observe the universe around him. His gaze and soul were captivated by the darkness. Something waited in there, calling to him. It was gargantuan beyond belief.

Yet, the darkness showed nothing. It was a void so impenetrable that not even light could escape, a place where even time and space seemed to lose their meaning.

A place that could trap even Old Ones.

Despite the absence of any clues, Jack could feel it beyond the shadow of a doubt. Something hid in the darkness. A deity shielded by an impenetrable veil. An existence on such a high level that it felt as sacred as the Dao itself, as the large fist he'd glimpsed when he first touched upon his Dao of the Fist. It radiated life with such intensity that it overwhelmed everything else. It made death seem childish.

Jack was humbled. The incalculable physical distance between himself and that force of life was a fitting metaphor for the immeasurable difference between them.

His mind ground to a halt, frozen in incomprehension, paralyzed by being in the presence of something so superior. It was a self-defense mechanism. If not, he would go insane.

The God in that black hole spoke, though Jack couldn't understand the words. Each buffeted him like a tsunami, and blocking off reality was all he could do to shield his sanity.

Eventually, a tired sigh resounded through the stars, and the vision faded, returning Jack to reality. He instantly remembered the cruel, unending pain, a now inseparable part of his existence. He braced himself... but it never came.

From one moment to the next, the pain was simply not there. The sensation was jarring. It took him some time to adapt. The environment began to creep into his mind again, hesitantly.

Jack was in the stone cavern, lying on the floor. His entire body was sore. Wounds brushed against the crude stone, and that pain was almost funny.

He simply lay there. Not thinking, just waiting for reality to settle over him, for his brain to forget about hell and start operating again.

Many minutes later, Jack forced himself to stand. Tentatively, he rose to his feet. Nothing bad happened. Finally able to think again, he wondered, *What the hell happened?*

He first thought about the vision, but the mere memory filled him with horror. The vision's intensity was such that even considering it stretched his soul. However, Jack wouldn't be stopped by mere horror.

A God in bottomless darkness... he thought, suppressing a shiver. *Enas. The Old One trapped in a black hole by his peers, for reasons unknown. It was his statue I touched to come here. The voice spoke about a divine gift.*

Does this trial really have a direct connection to an Old One?

The thought was enough to fill him with anticipation. Just what would such an entity consider valuable enough to call a gift?

Jack admitted that this trial was no joke either. He was extremely strong for his level, and also well-suited to fighting crowds of weaker enemies, but the combat trial had still almost doomed him. And the pain of that drop entering his body...

Only his steel resolve, cultivated through many life-or-death situations, had pulled him through. How many people could boast the same decisiveness?

Who was this trial designed to find?

The rewards could only be suitable. Jack turned his gaze inward, afraid of what he might find.

There, inside his soul, was a new entity. A drop of liquid, vibrant green and floating around in his Dao Seed—his soul—alongside his two Dao Roots. No—it wasn't just floating. It was connected to him, fused. Little roots spread from its core to dive into the nearby space, resembling the Dao Root of Indomitable Will he'd only recently fused.

Besides that, the drop looked nothing like a Dao Root. Apparently, the System disagreed.

Congratulations! The Dao Root of Life had been successfully fused with your Dao Seed.
Strength +20
Constitution +20
Will +20

Congratulations! Indomitable Body II → Indomitable Body III.
Indomitable Body III: You possess more than mere physicality. The Dao of the Fist reinforces your entire body, making it indomitable. You have significant durability, *extreme* regenerative powers, and heightened control over your body, including its natural limiters. Additionally, your mind is fast enough to keep up.

Conveniently, the System italicized the differences from the previous tier of the skill. This time, it was only one word: his regenerative powers had become "extreme."

What? Jack opened his status screen, confirming what the screens told him—he indeed had a new Dao Root fused with his Dao Seed, which had increased from middle to late.

What? he asked again. This didn't make any sense. The drop was the Dao Root of Life? And it *fused* with him? *When?* What did he know about life? He'd never even pondered the issue.

It didn't even look like a Dao Root at all.

Something was wrong here.

Either there are many things I don't understand, or the System misinterpreted something, Jack thought. Still, I thought the Dao could only be understood, not transferred. Is this the power of a God? What happened? And how?

...And how do I get out of here?

The sun mushroom above still covered the cavern in still light, and the absolute silence was like heaven after all the trial's intensity. Since the voice didn't seem eager to speak up, Jack focused inward again, taking a better look at his new Dao Root.

No matter how he looked at it, it still didn't resemble one. The System could say whatever it wanted, but Jack knew this wasn't a Dao Root. Or maybe it was, except it was also much more.

It was a reservoir of unlimited energy, a well of infinite vitality, like an ocean of life compressed to the size of a droplet. It made sense that his regeneration would be ramped up so hard that his Indomitable Body rose an entire tier.

Still, there was more. He gazed into the drop, focusing more and more on it. As he did, its details sharpened, its ocean of life growing ever deeper. His current spiritual perception wasn't even enough to reach the bottom.

Just what is this thing? he wondered for the hundredth time in a single minute. His thoughts whirled in a new direction. *And what else can I do with it?*

He sensed the endless vitality, the power. There were roots connecting this drop to the rest of his soul, but they seemed tiny. The amount of power they could transmit to him was nothing in comparison to the drop's reserves, a tiny fraction of a fraction.

What happens if I draw more?

He tried. The drop was in his soul, after all, so he had good control over it. He sensed the thin barrier keeping the power of life contained, and he very gently parted it, letting a tiny portion of the drop's energy seep out, infiltrating his soul through osmosis and quickly reaching a point of balance. Something clicked.

The change was instantaneous. He was filled with such power that his body was about to burst. He let the barrier drop again, releasing a cry of surprise, but the energy that had already been released coursed aggressively to his every nook and cranny. It pushed at him from the inside like a flood, demanding that his body expand or explode.

He really was afraid that he would burst when somehow, he expanded.

Jack's eyes snapped open, observing the changes in his body. He couldn't believe it.

He grew taller and wider. His body was magnified—even his pants. He instantly grew a whole foot in height, all his proportions remaining constant. He sensed power course through him like when he leveled up. His overall power had just increased by a significant margin, though no System notification accompanied the change.

Before he could digest what happened, staring at his own hands with wonder, he realized that the life energy wasn't done yet. It circled around him, frustrated that he'd stopped growing, and focused under his armpits.

There was a momentary spike of pain as his skin ruptured. Then, to Jack's absolute shock, two more arms grew under his regular ones, flesh and muscles entwining to form elbows, forearms, hands, and fingers. It resembled the way his cut-off arm had regrown after the combat trial.

Jack had four arms.

Only now was the life energy satisfied, content to course around his body and continuously support its changes.

Jack was left as a four-armed giant. He was stupefied. He flexed his fingers in disbelief—all twenty of them—overawed by how he had complete and easy control over his two new arms like they'd always been there. Instinctively, he clenched one into a fist and punched out. A purple meteor unfurled, its starry line crossing the room to land on the floor ten feet away with an explosion.

"What the fuck?" he couldn't resist saying. He couldn't stop looking over himself, conflicted between shock and glee.

He'd suddenly grown massively stronger. The Life Drop was a tremendous boon to his combat abilities, and also gave him extra arms. He could punch much faster. But he had four arms.

He checked his status screen, but nothing had changed. His stats remained as they were, as did his titles and Dao Roots. There was no indication that his body had just changed completely.

Will I stay like this forever? he thought with a spike of horror. It wouldn't be too bad. He would be strong. Everyone would look at him weird, but did he really care?

He soon realized that wasn't the case. He hadn't noticed it before due to the shock, but the life energy coursing through his body was under his control. With an effort of will, he pushed it back inside the drop, where it remained.

The changes reverted. His new arms shrank, the skin closing without a trace of what used to be there, and he shrunk until he regained his normal size.

It was like nothing had changed.

Jack wasn't sure he could process this.

"Congratulations," the booming voice came again, fanning Jack's hopes of an explanation. This time, the voice carried emotion—deep, trembling joy. "You have succeeded in inheriting the divine gift, the Life Drop, a drop of blood from the Old God of Life himself. This is an unfathomable honor, as well as a great duty.

"You will notice that the Life Drop has joined your body as an already fused Dao Root. The System will say so, if it still exists, but that is false. It simply cannot comprehend the powers of an Old God. That is also a gift. If the System recognized the Life Drop for what it was, a sign of the Old Gods, its forces would descend on you and this place, demanding to take it away or destroy it.

"Fear not. The soul is inviolable. Neither the System nor anyone else can discover the Life Drop inside you without special means. However, there is yet more power in this divine gift. Look deep into it, let its power seep out to fill you, and you will assume a form that vastly increases your powers."

"I did that already," Jack replied. The voice either couldn't hear him or ignored him—probably the former, given how talkative it now was. Success really did change everyone's attitude.

It waited a few moments, expecting Jack to realize and experiment with the Life Drop's powers.

"That form is a great weapon which requires utmost secrecy," the voice continued. "If word of it gets around to the ones in power, they will know what it means. That will be your end. Therefore, that form should only be used as a final resort, when you are certain there is nobody watching, or when you are certain that those watching will not report your powers."

"I see," Jack replied, nodding. "An ace in my sleeve."

"Giving you access to that power is a gamble," the voice admitted, sounding hesitant. "But, if you are to achieve the feats we require of you, trusting your judgment is essential. You have attained great power today, young mortal. Use it wisely. Your path is endless, your potential limitless. Make us proud. Right our wrongs. Undo the evil we have created."

"I, uh... Thank you. I'll do my best," Jack replied. "Could you perhaps tell me more about this evil? I, uh, have no idea what you're talking about."

"You will exit this hall shortly. We ask that you use your power rightly, with the Dao as your guide, and with utmost secrecy. Tell no one about it, not even your closest allies, for it is always them who tempt betrayal. If you stand out sufficiently, as you doubtlessly will, the great forces of the universe will stop at nothing to get your secrets."

"Okay, that sounds dangerous. I noticed you keep talking about important things, like great forces and such, but not saying names. Could you maybe—"

"Goodbye, chosen one. May you scale the peak we failed to master."

"I—"

And just like that, Jack teleported away.

CHAPTER FIFTY-ONE
PULLING THE TRIGGER

JACK APPEARED IN THE MIDDLE OF THE SHRINE WITH A STUMBLE. THE MOMENT reality finished playing around, he scanned his surroundings.

Destruction. The skeleton by the corner was the only thing left untouched. The rest of the shrine was carnage, like someone took a sledgehammer and went to town on it. The thin walls were torn and battered. The floor was upturned. The ceiling had collapsed in places, showering the room with debris.

Not even the statue of Enas had escaped unscathed. It lay on the ground with tiny dents on its face, surrounded by chips of stone. Someone had tried and failed to break it.

Jack was seized by anxiety. He'd just received a divine gift by Enas. Now, someone had tried to break his statue? Was that considered blasphemy? Was Jack supposed to do something about it? Not that he'd ever agreed to such a thing, but still, it felt right to help those who helped you.

If the statue was destroyed, would I be stuck in that cavern? he wondered with rising brows.

"Jack!" a cry reached him, filled with elation. He looked outside the shrine, finding Nauja there.

Outside the little room, the wave of destruction continued

unabated. The flimsy fence was tattered, the soil carved, the nearby ruins of a house collapsed.

"Thank the System you're here!" Nauja said, rushing over. "Brock was worried sick. He tore the place up to find you."

"Brock did all that?" Jack asked, looking around again.

"He went berserk! I managed to stop him from destroying my ancestor's skeleton, but the rest of it..." She gestured widely at the disaster. "Well, let's just say it's a good thing the Ancients here are long, long gone."

"My little bro..."

Jack's heart fluttered. Brock had been so worried that he started searching... He wasn't even gone that long. The brorilla must have been frantic.

As if on cue, Brock spilled out from behind a hut at full tilt. The moment he saw Jack, his little eyes widened, and Jack could see the tension leaving the little brorilla's shoulders.

His fur was matted, covered in chips of wood and stone. His staff was dusty, his pants torn at the hems, his gaze filled with elation. He rushed to Jack like a cannonball of fur and slammed on him, sending them both to the ground.

"Oof!" Jack said, falling on his back. "I missed you too, bro."

"Yes! Bro! Yes!" Brock stood on Jack's chest, drumming on his chest and cheering to the heavens before realizing what he was doing. He quickly stepped back and helped Jack stand, then dutifully dusted off his big bro's pants.

Jack laughed. "It's alright, Brock. I'm glad to see you were worried about me."

"Bro!" Brock exclaimed, almost insulted. He pointed at Jack, then himself. "Bros."

"Oh, you even know the plural now? How long was I gone?"

"A few hours," Nauja replied. She gave him a pointed look. "Enough for Brock to wreck the ruins of my ancestors."

Jack paused. Should he scold Brock?

Then again, Brock had seen his big bro touch a statue and disappear. He didn't know how the world worked. In fairness, Jack might have acted the same way. He really couldn't blame his little bro.

But he had destroyed the ruins of Nauja's ancestors. Why didn't she stop him? Could she be worried, too?

"I understand your reaction, bro. It came from the heart," he declared, raising his hands in a peace gesture. "Still, we apologize for disrespecting your ancestors, Nauja. At least it all worked out."

"Yeah," she accepted the half-apology after a brief hesitation. "Where were you, anyway?"

So, Jack told them. Not everything—just most things. He detailed the simple stone cavern, the voice's instructions, and the trials he went through. In the end, he even told them about his reward. The only things he withheld were the vision, the battle form offered by the Life Drop, and its true identity as a drop of blood from Enas himself. He said it was simply the Dao Root of Life.

It pained him to lie, especially to Brock, but he remembered the voice's instructions. Closest friends were the ones whose betrayal stang the bitterest.

A moment later, he was ashamed by his own thoughts.

"No, you know what? I said some inaccuracies. Let me fix that."

And he told them the rest as well. In the end, he hid nothing. Such was the path of the fist. Perhaps there were mind-readers somewhere in the universe, but Nauja had journeyed here with him and risked her life to help him when the minotaur came knocking.

As for Brock... Well, Brock's importance and loyalty went without saying. They were brothers.

"Wow," Nauja said breathlessly. "An Old One? Really?"

"The voice called him an Old God, but yes. Basically, I'm super strong, but nobody can find out."

Brock gave him a thumbs-up.

"You should test out that form," Nauja said. "I look forward to seeing four-armed, big Jack."

"What, here?"

"Why not? This could be the most secretive place in Trial Planet."

Jack hesitated. He didn't fear discovery if he used his new power here, but the truth was, he felt a bit uncomfortable. He had already ignored the voice's instructions by sharing the secret—fairly, in his opinion. If he now demonstrated his powers for no reason, even if it was safe... Wouldn't he be a little too carefree? Almost disrespectful of the power he'd received?

"Maybe later," he finally said. "When the time comes, you will see it."

Nauja pouted but said nothing. Brock nodded calmly. He was obviously consumed by curiosity but acted like nothing was wrong.

"So, how do we get out of here?" Jack asked.

"There's an exit tunnel leading to the next ring. We discovered it while searching before."

He raised a brow. "We?"

"Obviously, I was searching too." Nauja crossed her arms. "What did you expect, that I'd just sit back and let Brock wreck this place alone?"

"Good point. But what about you? You don't want to come to the next ring. Is the way back open?"

She bit her lip. "I took a look, but the door remains sealed. I think... I think there is no way back. Or, if there is, I don't know where."

"I could try breaking the door."

"I don't think that's wise."

"Then, what are you going to do?" Jack asked.

"Come along, obviously. At least for a bit. I can backtrack when we reach the next ring and climb up through another tunnel."

"Hmm." Jack took a close look at her, not believing her hard attitude. "If you're there already, you could come to the village with us. Meet Gan Salin. See the world a bit. And you backtrack later."

Her gaze remained somber, but Jack saw the redness creep up her neck. "I have considered that, yes. Maybe I will."

He smiled gently. "Your father will be worried sick, you know."

At this, she finally lowered her head. "I know... but he sent me on a suicide mission. He even told me to win or die trying. I... I didn't like that. Didn't deserve it. He always acts like he knows everything just because he's five hundred years old and an immortal, but I don't think that's right. So, it's okay. Let him worry. He could use some heartache."

"And the rest of your tribe?"

"They can handle it. Besides, we barbarians hate holding each other back. They'll understand. And if I never make it back..." Her gaze darkened. "Then I died in the Forbidden Cave, hunted by delvers for protecting a guest of the tribe."

Jack's appreciation of her rose. If nothing else, Nauja was clear-cut and decisive. "Very well. In that case, we should get going. I suppose we already searched the ruins, in our own, special way."

Nauja looked around. "I suspect this kind of searching will become our staple."

"Heh. You know what? Our team has a brorilla, a barbarian, and a musclehead. Sounds like a recipe for fun."

"And death."

"Not if we can hit it hard enough." He laughed.

"What about that friend of yours? That Gan Salin?"

"Oh, he's the worst of us all. He's insane."

She rolled her eyes. "Great. Maybe we should try breaking that door after all."

Jack laughed again, accompanied by Brock.

"Let's get going," he said.

They only took a few steps before Nauja froze. Her eyes widened. "Wait! Oh, by the System, I can't believe I forgot to tell you."

"Tell me what?"

"While searching for you, I scanned some things. The statue, the wood in the ruins. And, well..."

She sounded equal parts worried and guilty, like it was a big deal.

"Well, what?" Jack asked.

"You might want to take a look for yourself."

"But the rules—"

"Trust me. It no longer matters. Just inspect it."

Jack was already worried, but he trusted her. He directed his gaze at a collapsed house and finally gave in to the urge of scanning.

Ancient Wood
A kind of wood only found in—

The screen suddenly crumbled, replaced by another.

WARNING!
ANCIENT ACTIVITY DETECTED. EXTERMINATION PROTOCOL INITIATED. THE NEAREST AUTHORITIES HAVE BEEN NOTIFIED. EXTERMINATORS HAVE BEEN DISPATCHED.

LEAVE THE AREA IMMEDIATELY. VISIT ANY HAND OF GOD
HEADQUARTERS TO RECEIVE THE APPROPRIATE BOUNTY. YOUR
DISCOVERY CODE IS DT3759FGD937RN.

ALL DETAILS OF THIS MATTER ARE NOW CLASSIFIED. SHARING
ANY INFORMATION WILL RESULT IN YOUR SWIFT
EXTERMINATION.

THANK YOU FOR CONTRIBUTING TO THE NEW WORLD.

Jack recoiled. The intensity of the System message was unlike anything he'd ever read before.

"Red, capital letters? Extermination? Bounty? Hand of God? What the hell is going on!"

"I have no idea," Nauja replied. "I don't know many things about the outside world. It almost sounds like there is a bounty on Ancients... but that should be impossible. The System was created by the Immortals to avenge them. It should be overjoyed at any sign of surviving Ancients. Why would it want to exterminate them instead?"

"The Hand of God is acknowledged by the System?" Jack asked, focusing on that part of the message. He shook his head. "I really have no idea what's going on anymore."

"We should go."

"Absolutely. I don't like this. The farther away we are from whatever is happening, the better... And let's not tell anyone about this. Just to be safe."

"Agreed. The tunnel is just behind that hill. Let's go."

Rushing over, they reached a stone door engraved with images of dinosaurs and fur-clad people, along with colossal sea creatures, dragons, and all sorts of large monsters.

"Not every part of this ring has dinosaurs," Nauja explained. Jack grabbed the door and pulled it—Brock took notes—revealing a dark tunnel sloping downward. "After you."

"Charming."

There were no torches here, but Brock grabbed some wood from the ruins behind them—not the scannable kind—and lit it up. He went first, followed by Nauja and Jack. The door slammed shut behind them, leaving the ruins undisturbed, silent, alone. Sacred. As they had been for eons.

————

Trial Planet was alone in a sea of nothingness, unattached to any stars, simply floating through the vastness of space. The only signs of life around it were two moons in orbit, each housing one station of the Hand of God. Nothing changed here. Ever.

On this day, space was ripped apart like a torn sheet. A small fleet of starships flew in through the rift. Ten were dark and needle-shaped, each an order of magnitude larger than the *Trampling Ram*. The last was white and even larger, shaped as the curve of a magnet.

These ships housed a flurry of activity. People dashed back and forth, all of them immortals. Each of the ten needle ships was commanded by a person clad in long white robes, to whom all nearby immortals showed great deference.

On the bridge of the largest ship stood a woman whose mere presence bent space. She was tall and lithe, middle-aged in appearance. White hair framed her pale face, and a white robe stretched from her shoulders to her ankles, but her physicality belied the gargantuan force that hid inside her.

The Dao flowed around this woman like a river around a rock. Reality shuddered where she looked, and all nearby immortals avoided her gaze, unworthy of even meeting her eyes. She exuded a feeling of purity, like everything was made cleaner just by being near her, but it was the kind of purity that could smother and extinguish everything else. Her eyes were narrowed at Trial Planet, clear, yet intense.

"We have arrived, Head Enforcer," a white-robed man said, falling to his knees behind her. He was her lieutenant, and he, too, was someone that the nearby immortals greatly deferred to.

"Trial Planet..." the woman said slowly, her voice like river water. "What an inconvenient place. Why am I here?"

"Head Enforcer, the protocol dictates that a B-Grade is always to lead the ext—"

"But I cannot enter that planet, can I?" She swiveled around to look at him, her eyes boring holes through his heart. "So my time is wasted."

The man hesitated. "Protocol is—"

"I am aware," she said with a sigh, turning back to Trial Planet. Already, the leaders of each satellite station were rushing over to meet her, but she was in no mood. Unfortunately, even B-Grades couldn't openly oppose protocol. She hid her discomfort, asking, "Do we have more information?"

"We only know they're somewhere inside the planet. Not too close to the surface, so we can rule out the second ring."

"Inform every Hand of God initiate inside Trial Planet to be on the lookout. Detecting the Ancient remnants is now our top priority. They are to scour their respective rings exhaustively. If they find anything, they are to back away and inform us without taking action. They should also ask around for unusual events within the last couple of days. Additionally, assemble a team of a hundred E-Grade initiates, give them the proper equipment, and send them into Trial Planet within three days. They are to search everything and not return until they find the Ancients."

"Do you mean we should spend a hundred tokens, Head Enforcer?"

"Did I stutter?"

The lieutenant remained silent, sweat forming on his forehead. "I hear and obey, Head Enforcer."

"As you should. Conveniently, the Animal Kingdom gave us those tokens just recently."

"Should we withdraw our members from the Garden Assault, Head Enforcer?"

She took a moment to calculate. "Keep our head team in the assault and withdraw everyone else. The extermination takes precedence," she decided, sighing again. "We will remain here until the remnants are confirmed exterminated, as protocol dictates. Arrange for one of the two moons to be evacuated and made into my meditation chamber."

"Yes, Head Enforcer," the lieutenant said, bowing deeply.

The woman with the Dao of Purity gazed at the planet, scowling deeply. "A waste of my damn time." She shook her head, then looked to the side as if remembering something. "Oh, and obviously, surround Trial Planet and get the proper equipment to deep-scan anyone who exits. The Ancients liked to leave power behind for their successors. If anyone got it, they won't escape our net."

CHAPTER FIFTY-TWO
VILLAGE RING

JACK EMERGED FROM THE TUNNEL WITH A FULL BREATH OF FRESH AIR.

"Ahh," he said in mock relief. "Nothing beats a good old desert."

The Village Ring, unlike what its name indicated, was not a village. It was a scorching desert striped with red and brown sand, complete with a large amount of sun mushrooms a hundred miles overhead, an arid climate, and a whole menagerie of fearsome monsters.

The ring's name came from the nine villages spread around its surface, each in its own oasis. These nine were, in fact, the only oases of the entire ring, and they were the main meeting points of cultivator teams throughout Trial Planet. People entered by themselves, crossed the second and third ring, and reconvened here, where they could interact with other cultivators or recruit them to fill in their missing team spots—in case someone died on the way.

This practice was so fundamental to Trial Planet that, even though the Hand of God spread the members of teams across multiple entrances to the second ring, they didn't separate them by too much, allowing them to reach the same village in the Village Ring. Hence why Gan Salin had been so confident they would reassemble here.

Of course, Jack and Brock didn't know all that. Nauja had informed them as they crossed the long tunnel.

"I always dreamt of the day I left my ring," she said, stepping out of the tunnel entrance behind Jack. "This is... almost dreamy."

"Wait till you see the good parts," Jack said. "This desert is a poor introduction. Don't you think so, Brock?"

The brorilla carried his Staff of Stone in one hand and wiped his forehead with the other. Though his short fur was well-suited for a desert climate, he was simply too low level. The temperature here was far higher than in any desert of Earth. The sand burned like coal, and the air shimmered from the heat. Moreover, the sun mushrooms glared from above, a large crowd of little suns, and there wasn't even a hint of a cloud to protect the poor cultivators below.

"From what I've heard," Nauja said, stepping to the front, "this ring isn't too dangerous. We should be fine as long as we're careful."

Jack nodded. "Fine by me. Any idea where that village is? The sooner we reach it, the better."

"Simple. See the columns?"

"Yeah." As in every other ring, the entrance tunnels were large stone columns that extended from the floor to the ceiling a hundred miles overhead. Obviously, they were visible from a large distance away. They towered in all directions, sparse but clearly present. The closest one—besides theirs—must have been a day's walk away.

Since this was the fourth ring, its surface area was much smaller than the entire planet's. As a result, not only were nine villages enough to cover the entire desert without anyone needing to walk too long, but the ring's curvature was easily visible. Jack caught the ceiling arcing in the horizon, the stone columns rising diagonally.

"There is no entrance near the villages," Nauja explained. "If we find the place where the columns are sparser, that's where the village will be. Can't miss it."

"Hmm." There were stone columns as far as the eye could see, stretching intermittently like middle fingers to the heavens. Looking more carefully, Jack spotted a suspicious absence of them around a spot to their front and left. "On the bright side, I think I got it," he said. "But it's far away."

"Yeah," Nauja confirmed, shielding her eyes. "Must be a week's worth? Maybe closer. I can't calculate distance well here."

"Neither can I. Don't worry about it."

"Shall we?"

"We shall."

And so, without any sort of ceremony, they left their stone column behind and marched on.

"You know," Jack said as an afterthought, "isn't the column we came from suspicious? If anybody maps these entrances to the exits above, they'll notice that our column doesn't lead to any known exit. With a bit more research, they'll trace it to the Forbidden Cave."

"I guess. But it's not that easy. Mapping entrances to exits requires precise coordination between two teams, one in each ring, and nobody has the time for that. Besides, it's not like they'd earn anything."

"What if anyone tries to climb up from here?"

"Not all entrances are accessible from below. If I had to guess, this one isn't, and nobody wants to climb up for a day only to reach a locked door and have to go all the way back."

That's how long it took them. The tunnel from the surface to the second ring was hollow, allowing Jack to cross it quickly with leaps. The rest of them weren't, forcing them to walk a hundred miles down— much more, if one calculated the slope. Even at a brisk jog—the equivalent of a pre-System human's run—it had taken them a day to reach this ring from the Ancient ruins.

As a bonus side effect, not only were they in a desert, they were also winded.

"Very well. Let's hope nobody takes a closer look," Jack said, throwing the column a final glance.

"Yeah..." Nauja agreed. "Let's hope so."

"Yes," Brock added his two cents.

And so, they cast into the desert. It was... dull. There was no terrain besides endless sand dunes. Moreover, the sand itself was annoying, as it had the bad habit of sometimes caving under their feet and forcing them to exert more effort. Other times, it was hard as a rock, throwing off their rhythm.

It was easy for one's attention to drift in the desert. To doze off. Thankfully, Jack had Indomitable Will, letting him remain razor-sharp even in this dull terrain—at the expanse of boredom.

He also took the time to go through the screens he'd received upon entering the desert.

Congratulations! Title "Second Ring Conqueror" upgraded to "Third Ring Conqueror!"
Efficacy of all stats: +10% → +15%

Village Ring Quest:
- **Make your way to the Space Ring in a team of at least three and at most five individuals.**

The 5% increase was a welcome bonus. Jack's strength was already pretty high, what with all the level-ups from the Enas trial and the extra, fused Dao Root—or what the System assumed was a Dao Root—with its sixty stat points. Add to that the now-fused Indomitable Will, which also gave sixty stat points, the Immortal Serum he'd consumed on Earth, which gave another fifty, and his perfect Dao Seed, which was a qualitative advantage, and his strength was beginning to snowball well outside the reach of a normal level 80 cultivator. Or, at least, so he hoped.

With any luck, he could now fight late E-Grade monsters equally, perhaps even peak ones.

Amusingly, that also made him stronger than Nauja. Probably.

She caught his weighing glance. "What are you looking at?"

"Nothing. Just admiring the only thing that moves in this damn desert."

"How can you be bored already? We've been here for, like, twenty minutes."

"That's nineteen minutes too long, if you ask me."

She laughed, more out of good mood than amusement. "Whatever, desert hater. This place may seem uninteresting to you, but it's the first time I've seen anything other than my jungle. Aren't you simply overwhelmed by all this?" She gestured wildly.

"All this what?"

"All this empty space!" She spun in a circle. "Look! There are no trees, no bushes, no dinosaurs. My eyes can see far away without climbing on the canopy! I have perfect awareness of my surroundings! It is so empty! So... *different!*"

Her voice almost culminated in an excited squeal before she pushed it back down, but Jack could sense her enthusiasm bubbling over. She was like a kid in an amusement park. It could have been adorable if not for her ripped body and big-ass longbow hanging on her back.

Still, he cracked a smile. This could have been me when the System came, Jack thought. If everything wasn't trying to kill me. Must be nice.

Then again, hadn't he felt this way when watching the stars from the bridge of the *Trampling Ram*? When he woke up in Pearl Bay, was teleported to the Belarian Outpost, or crossed half a galaxy to reach Trial Planet, with its ruined surface and multi-layered innards? When he met the giant forest and its insects, when he hunted dinosaurs and drank alcohol with barbarians in a picturesque valley in the middle of a lush jungle? When he stood in front of a God?

What a big world...

He drew in a deep breath, uncaring of the burning wind, letting it fill his lungs and expel the sadness. He was free, unfettered, adventurous. He was an explorer, a pioneer. Even the constant danger was more of a pleasant inconvenience than a terrible fate. His path was one of violence, now. In conflict, he felt alive.

And what a great feeling that was.

"You know, Nauja," he said, sliding up besides her, "the world is such a vast, wonderful place. There are oceans, mountains, deserts, jungles, forests, plains, cities. There are stars—giant balls of fire that can easily fit a thousand Trial Planets inside them—planets of all kinds, people of a million different species, all distinctly different, and yet equally mesmerizing. Have you heard of kovans? They're shaped like spinning tops, with four arms and one leg they hop on. Their planet's atmosphere is so dense that they can fly, and they feed on gas."

Her eyes widened. "Really?"

"For sure!"

"I've seen kovans before, but I never knew..." Her gaze darkened a bit. "Those are all cultivators though, aren't they? Delvers. Greedy, disrespectful, unethical bastards."

"I'm a cultivator too, aren't I?" Jack shot back, his smile gentle. "The world is full of assholes, but there are nice people, too. On the way here, I met a captain and his crew who toured the stars with only cama-raderie in their hearts. They accepted me as one of their own even though I lied to them—even though I had to." His gaze grew distant. He still didn't know what happened to the *Trampling Ram*. "I hope they're okay."

"And how do you find people like that?" she asked, letting her curiosity take the better of her. "All the delvers I've seen are..." She didn't finish her words, but her grimace was crystal clear.

"I don't know about delvers," Jack admitted. "They come from B-Grade factions, so they're a different breed... But there are all sorts of people out there. You just have to sift through the bad apples and keep looking until you find a good one. Bond with them, then keep going until you're surrounded by trustworthy, loyal, wonderful people."

She shrunk back. "That doesn't sound easy."

"It is not. But with a little bit of courage, a little bit of practice, and a bit of patience, you can make your world a beautiful place."

"I... I don't think I can."

"Everyone can."

"No, you don't understand, I—" She cut off, biting her lip and shaking her head. "Nevermind."

She stormed on ahead. Jack followed her with his gaze, surprised at her sudden change of mood, but didn't press the issue.

Brock, sensing Nauja's foul mood, grabbed her hand. She froze, staring at him, but then resumed walking, one barbarian and one brorilla, each drinking in the company of the other. Nauja's steps regained her spring shortly afterward, though a hint of bitterness remained deep in her eyes.

Minutes turned into hours. The terrain flowed on, one sand dune giving way to another. Everything looked the same. There were no landmarks besides the stone columns, but they were so big and so far away they seemed unchanging, as if they were walking but staying in the same spot.

It could be disheartening. The harsh environment also didn't help. Thankfully, Jack had been through worse, Nauja was busy being excited, and Brock didn't care too much, though he did occasionally ask to ride on Jack's shoulders. His bare feet couldn't handle the hot sand too well.

Unfortunately, they had neither an umbrella nor the spare fabric to make one, so they were forced to endure the scorching sun mushrooms.

Occasionally, they spotted monsters. They were rare but strong. Jack was the one to spot an oddly shivering sand dune, which they made a wide circle around. Once, they were attacked by a level 80 giant scorpion which simply burst out of the sand. Due to its ambush, the threat was far larger than its level would indicate, but Nauja saw it coming just in time and jumped away. After that, the battle was swift, bloodless—for them—and, unfortunately, level-less.

There were horse-sized scaled lizards hiding just under the sand, snakes slithering between the dunes, as well as round, brown ticks that camouflaged seamlessly into the desert. The weakest monster around was level 80, with the strongest—the snakes—ranged up to 124.

However, by far the biggest threat they saw was a colossal sand worm.

CHAPTER FIFTY-THREE
VIVI'S STRENGTH

Vivi soared through the sky. Her flame wings beat back the clouds as she rushed at top speed.

Usually, this kind of energy expenditure would be considered reckless and putting her at risk. Now, she had no time to care. Smoke rose in the horizon. The smoke of Ouagadougou—the capital of Burkina Faso. Her headquarters.

She sped through the air and over the walls. The people below shouted at her, but the wind stole their words. Her wings took her to the presidential palace courtyard, where a battle had taken place. Corpses were strewn everywhere. Men and women who used to be her most promising recruits now lay cold and lifeless.

She dropped to the ground, letting her wings dissipate as she took in the destruction. Her rage shimmered and burned, but she held it down.

"What happened?" she demanded.

A man approached her through the rubble. It was the lieutenant general who served as her advisor. He was limping. "The Ice Peak executives," he said. "They attacked while you were gone. We tried to fight back, but they were too strong."

Pain flooded her heart. Disappointment, regret, guilt.

The professor of the Bare Fist Brotherhood had advised her to tighten her defenses, fearing an imminent strike. Vivi had been unsettled. She compared herself to the other two leaders—the professor and Petrovic—and found herself lacking. Her people believed in her, wanted her to lead, but she didn't have the calculating skills that her opponent and allies did. She was a warrior queen.

She'd decided to play to her strengths instead of fighting a losing battle. Vivi took to the front lines, leading an elite squad, and had conquered two dungeons in the span of a day. Her insecurities had abated, filling her with confidence and satisfaction. Finally, she was doing something right. She was winning.

Until she wasn't. She'd left her capital weakened. The Ice Peak had been planning a strike, just as the professor warned, and Vivi had only made it easier for them. They took advantage of her absence to launch a sharp offensive on her presidential palace, slaying some of the elites she'd poured so many resources into before running away.

Nobody would admit it was the Ice Peak. They were in cold war, after all. This attack would be framed as terrorism, but everyone knew the truth. There were even icicles still melting throughout the destruction.

At the top of her palace, only a plain, broken flagpole remained. The red and green flag itself was missing, no doubt taken as a war trophy.

Vivi wanted to scream.

Instead, she reined in her emotions. She was a leader. Managing this disaster took precedence. Her own peace would come later.

"What's the number of casualties?" she asked her lieutenant.

"It was an inside job," he replied. His words were calm, steely, but his eyes let a hint of accusation show. Vivi didn't have the heart to confront him about it. "We lost thirteen elites, fifty high F-Grades, and a hundred middle ones. The enemy lost nine in total. Additionally, some in Ouagadougou died to the fires and wide-scale attacks of the offenders, while many were injured. We have managed to put out the fires, but a small portion of the city is temporarily inhospitable. However, the largest loss we received was in prestige. Our people are in shambles. They are filled with doubt. When I announced we were recruiting, not many showed up."

He gestured to a small kiosk by the side, where a battle-hardened woman sat on a chair with her arms crossed. People came to her in a trickle. Nothing like the rush that usually followed an enlistment opportunity to the prestigious Flame River.

I caused this, Vivi thought. She struggled to keep a straight face as the earth swam beneath her feet. *I'm ruining my faction and my country.*

"What should we do, Commander?" the lieutenant asked, throwing her a level stare. Challenging her.

She had to reply and reestablish her authority... but say what? What was the best course of action to recover from this disaster? The lieutenant had clearly handled most things already. The wounded were tended to, the corpses were being removed, and recruitment efforts were already taking place to restock their numbers.

Was she even necessary?

I am not a leader, she thought again, heart swimming in darkness. The people want me, but they are fools. I... Why would they even want me? What do they see in me? I am not as smart as the professor or as experienced as Petrovic. All I can do is fight. I truly want to help them, I would lay my life down for them all, but every decision I make is wrong. All I cause them is pain.

I am useless.

A ruckus came from the front gates. Belatedly, Vivi turned, finding a large crowd rushing her with elation in their eyes. Her guilt intensified.

Don't look at me like that. I did this. I do not deserve your love.

"Commander!" the first people cried out. "You're back!"

"We're safe now!"

"The commander is here!"

Their cheers were iron spikes in Vivi's heart. Why? she wondered bitterly. Why do you cheer? Stop. Blame me. Curse me. Just don't... Don't look at me like that...

For the first time in recent memory, tears threatened to come to her eyes. She quickly blinked them away. A small contingent of guards was blocking the crowd, politely yet firmly stopping them from approaching too closely. Vivi could still see their souls through their eyes, see the appreciation and belief they held in her, how they adored her.

It wasn't just her performance in the Tournament. Since her return, she'd ruled close to the people. She went to the market often, listened to their problems, and worked on solutions alongside them. She helped where she could. She personally apprehended the biggest troublemakers, roused the spirits of the people, pacified them, and reassured them that everything would be okay.

Vivi led from the front, and the people loved her for that.

But I don't deserve it, she told herself. All I can do is be there for you. I'm doing everything I can, but my best is not enough. Why do you still believe in me? You're dying!

Some of these people had lost friends and loved ones in this attack. She could see the rage in their eyes, the barely chained hatred, but those emotions weren't directed at her. They were aimed at the people who attacked them. The enemy.

"The people are expecting a speech, Commander," her lieutenant whispered, stepping beside her. "From you."

There it was again. That challenging tone.

Lieutenant General Shemarke wasn't a bad man. After Sadaka's passing, Vivi had chosen him as her closest assistant because of his principles. He was a strict, deeply kind, integral person. They were on the same page.

His challenge now wasn't because he yearned for power. He didn't want the seat of commander. He just genuinely doubted her ability, wanted to see how she would face this hurdle. If she didn't rise up to the occasion, she would lose his support, fair and square.

Vivi had half a mind to tell him to give a speech. Just that small thing would be enough to relinquish her authority.

If not for the fire in the eyes of those people. They had just suffered an attack. They'd witnessed their city burn and their protectors killed. They were in pain. If she left them too, betrayed their trust, they would truly lose all hope in the world.

No, she couldn't let that happen. She had to be there for them. Now was not the time to cower. It was time to act. She *had* to help them.

Vivi stepped forth and raised a hand. The people quietened in a wave that started from the front rows and spread to the back. She cleared her throat. She had no idea what to say, but she had to say *something*.

A thousand things crossed her mind. In the end, she just decided to address the elephant in the room.

"We received a loss today," she began, her System-enhanced lungs carrying her voice over the entire courtyard. She was surprised by the commanding tone she heard in the echo. "Detestable people infiltrated and assaulted us. I won't say names, but we all know who they are. They killed our warriors, set our homes ablaze, and terrorized our families."

Sounds of agreement came from the crowd.

Vivi was being torn in two. She was inside her mind, numb, weak, hearing the words coming out of her mouth like it was someone else talking. At the same time, she was giving a strong, confident speech.

"They only got away with it because *I* wasn't here. They didn't dare attack in my presence. They are cowards, backstabbers, calculating dicks."

More sounds of agreement, along with a bit of laughter. She wanted nothing more than to admit her fault and take the blame for everything, but that wasn't what these people needed to hear. They needed support. Encouragement. Something to believe in.

The details were better saved for her advisors.

"I know you are all pained by what happened today. So am I. In fact, I am burning with rage and sadness. I knew every single person who fell. I have chatted with them, walked with them, trained with them, listened to their problems like I listen to yours. My grief is terrible, and trust me, it will not abate until I make things right."

She became swept up by her emotions. Guilt was replaced by righteous rage and the deep desire to pay back the Ice Peak, to stop them from ever harming her people again. She might step down after today, she might be shamed—that changed nothing. Even as the lowliest of soldiers, she would fight.

Vivi flowed to the forefront of her mind, becoming one with the person who gave this rousing speech, sinking into the moment.

"They will not get away with this!" she thundered, full of fury. She projected confidence and leadership. The people's pain disappeared. Smiles blossomed on their faces, their spirits repaired, and hearts reborn from the ashes like a phoenix. "We are Flame River. We are Burkina Faso. When disaster strikes, we will not break. We will fight, we will rise, and we will strike back. Nobody can oppress us. Make no mistake; justice *will* be served, sooner or later, and I will be at the very front, fighting Alexander Petrovic for all of you. All of us. Death is nothing before our fire."

More roars. Vivi's voice turned louder.

"March beside me, warriors! Take up arms and fight. Tell your families that a life fought is a life well lived. You are all heroes, every single one of you. Rise with me and roar, fight for our lives, for what we believe in. We are Burkina Faso. We are Flame River. We are heroes. And we. Will. Not. Fall!"

The crowd's roar swept her like a fierce gale, blowing back her robes and hair. Vivi stepped against the wind and roared with them, her flames rising like a torch, flowing like a river. She threw her head back and unleashed a wildfire into the sky, a beacon visible across Ouagadougou, rousing the spirits of every soul who could hear their combined roar.

No attack could hold them down. They fell, but they rose again. They were warriors. Heroes.

The crowd streamed into the recruitment kiosk, so fierce they almost overwhelmed the woman presiding over it. The ones who remained met Vivi's eyes, nodding excitedly and stepping off with renewed vigor. Suddenly, the injured city was only a backdrop that made them stronger.

"Send more officers to the recruitment desk, Shemarke," Vivi said, turning to the lieutenant general. She was out of breath and sweating a bit, but that was fine. Her heart was on fire. She was so fucking happy that she'd helped her people.

The lieutenant stared at her, his gaze complex. He lowered his head. "Yes, Commander."

Vivi was taken aback. He relented? Where was the challenging tone from before? All she'd given was a rousing speech. She remained partly at fault for what happened. Why did he—

Oh.

Suddenly, it was clear. The lingering guilt clouding her mind receded like a pulled curtain, revealing reality for what it was.

She wasn't useless. The professor and Alexander Petrovic may be smarter and more skilled than her, but she had something they didn't: warmth. Fire. She led from the front, her back a beacon to the people. Her army was made of lions.

That was why the lieutenant relented. This was her power. The love she shared with her people, the fire she transmitted to them. Something that Petrovic, cold and calculating as he was, could never have.

There was a reason why she led the revolution that overthrew Burkina Faso's dictatorship. There was a reason why she led Flame River now. There was a reason why everyone believed in her.

The professor and I each have our own strengths, she realized.

"Shemarke," she called out. "Let the professor know that I will listen to her instructions from now on, okay? I will handle battle, she will handle everything else. Actually, you know what? Nevermind. I'll head there myself."

"Yourself?" He hesitated, his newly found faith shaken. "That's—"

"Trust me, Shemarke. I know what I'm doing. There are some things I must discuss with the professor alone. And not just her." Her brows fell. Knowing where her strength lay, she knew what she had to do. There was one weapon that their alliance wasn't utilizing, a strong card that, if available, could have averted this disaster *and* let her lead the army like the warrior queen she was.

Edgar.

Who refused to participate in the war and cultivated alone. Who let their people drop like flies when he could save them. What he lacked was fire in his heart.

And Vivi would give him just that.

CHAPTER FIFTY-FOUR
DESERT NIGHTS

THE SAND WORM WAS WIDE ENOUGH TO SWALLOW A HOUSE, AND LONG ENOUGH that they never saw its tail. It erupted out of the sand without any warning, biting down on and swallowing a scaled lizard that lounged on top of a dune. Thankfully, it didn't attack them.

Giant Sand Worm, Level 124 (Elite)
Giant sand worms infest the deserts of many planets. They use the Dao of Stone to swim through the desert floor, then burst up to devour their target before dissolving it in one of their many hyper-acidic stomachs. They detect prey through vibrations on the sand's surface, so try to avoid stomping.
They are also rare encounters. On planet Dune, immortals saddle and ride them, while their fighting pits are one of the planet's most profitable enterprises.

The worm snapped up the lizard and dived back down, raising a huge wave of sand.

"Rare encounters, it says," Jack said dryly. "Aren't we lucky."

"Extremely," Nauja added. "So. Light steps. Brock, sorry to say this, but you'll have to walk on your own for a bit. If that thing attacks us... Well, as we say in my tribe, na'ste'kala."

The worm did not attack them nor appear again, probably having traveled to some other area of the desert.

———

Night in the Village Ring reminded Jack of Earth.

As the sun mushrooms dimmed, each was left a silver glowing core, a fraction of what they used to be, and they were so tightly clustered that they resembled stars in the night sky.

On the ground below reigned silence. Nothing moved in the dim light. Only the wind remained alive, twisting and turning over the sand dunes, picking up sand to deposit later or lure upward to swirl it endlessly in the high currents.

The temperature had dropped sharply. In the span of an hour, it tumbled from scorching to freezing, making poor Brock shiver so hard they had no choice but to seek shelter. The desert didn't offer much in the way of that, but they did find a group of sand dunes clustered together. Before long, they were huddled in the small valley, covering themselves in the cool sand to resemble bedding.

They had no tents and no supplies. When they left the Tri Lake tribe, they expected only a short trip in the jungle. As if that wasn't enough, they decided to forgo lighting a fire to drive the cold away, not wanting to bring any undue attention after going unnoticed by that sand worm.

Thankfully, the desert wasn't completely empty. Cacti rose intermittently. Jack knew how to get water from them, so at least they had that covered. As for food, they had no choice but to starve. If it got too much, they could try eating the unknown desert creatures.

This was an inhospitable desert.

They alternated guard duty, starting from Brock, then Jack, then Nauja. The middle of the night was Jack's shift, and it found him perched on the tallest sand dune nearby, looking over the endless desert that stretched in all directions. Everywhere he looked, all he saw was sand and distant stone columns.

Yet, he couldn't suppress his excitement. They'd reached the fourth ring already. Just how far could they go? How strong could he get?

Could they conquer Trial Planet? Everyone said it was impossible... but how impossible could it really be?

"Hey," a low voice greeted him. He'd noticed Nauja approaching, of course, he'd just chosen to keep his eyes in the distance, unwilling to break his spell of awe.

"Hey," he replied, finally turning around. "I didn't think it was your shift yet."

"We have no clocks. Your guess is as good as mine," she said with a wry smile.

They stayed there for a while, sitting next to each other atop the sand dune in the middle of a desert in the bowels of a hollow planet.

"You can go back to sleep if you want," Jack said. "I'm not tired."

"Neither am I. How could I sleep when I'm... here?"

"Heh. Being E-Grade has its perks."

"It sure does."

Another moment of silence passed between them. Despite not knowing each other for long, going through life and death together brought people closer.

"About before—" Jack started saying, but Nauja cut him off.

"It's alright. You said nothing wrong. It was my fault." She took a deep, trembling breath, looking into the distance. For a moment, as Jack observed her pale, strong profile, she seemed almost vulnerable. Scared. "I have my own troubles. I don't want to talk about them yet, but there is no need for you to feel uncomfortable."

"That's fine. We're a team now. If you ever want to share anything, I'd be glad to listen. If you don't, I will stay by your side and support you anyway."

She threw him a surprised glance, as if taken aback by his words. "Thanks. That means a lot."

"It's only natural. The least we can do is be there for each other."

Now, it was her turn to gaze at his profile. "You are not like other delvers," she said, her tone questioning. "You are kind, straightforward, principled. When we were running in the cave, you didn't throw me at the pursuers to delay them. I have to admit, I was surprised."

Jack raised his brows. That possibility hadn't even crossed his mind. Had it crossed hers? Had she considered throwing him away to save herself?

"I wouldn't do that. Honestly, it didn't even occur to me."

"I know." Her gaze was piercing. "That's what surprises me the most. You have clearly seen your fair share of combat and deception, and you are clearly a hardened man, but at the same time, you are almost pure-hearted. How do you do that?"

"I guess... I just know who I am. I will not discount myself. I'll break through all obstacles in pursuit of my path, as a fist, until I either die or succeed. If I betrayed who I am, then I would be miserable. It's a fate worse than death. Honestly, I don't understand how everybody else can act like a dick. Do they not see that they are killing themselves?"

Nauja considered his words for a long moment. "Not everyone can think that way. Do you know what my tribe has noticed about delvers, Jack? They lie to themselves. A lot. They cling on to life with tooth and nail, and they double down on their weaknesses instead of fighting to surpass them. They do not understand the value of a good life, simply because they've never experienced it. They fear death and failure with all their heart, and in their attempts to avoid those, they end up hollow. They don't even realize that what they fear is already happening. They live through the very nightmare they sacrifice everything to avoid."

"Life is simple," Jack agreed, perfectly in tune. "Just... live. Be free. Stop living in fear, stop constraining yourself, unclench your heart, and dive into the world headfirst. So what if you fail? There are literally no consequences."

Nauja narrowed her eyes. "Are you still talking about delvers?"

"I don't know," Jack admitted with a sigh. "Sometimes, it feels like I'm the only sane person in the world, like everyone else is blind. It's so fucking simple. Why can't they see it?"

"Hmm... Everything seems simple from up ahead. But, from behind, the tiniest of steps can be wide gulfs. Don't begrudge the world, Jack. Give it time."

"I guess..."

They sat in silence for a while longer. The cold night wind brushed their barely-clothed bodies, but they were too strong to mind.

"Maybe this is why you have a perfect Seed," Nauja said. "You see things so simply, so clearly..." A chuckle. "Truly, you are like a fist. You don't even understand the extent of your gift."

"Maybe." His gaze was lost in the distance before he turned to her. "What's your Dao, anyway? You never told me."

"The Dao of Wind."

"Really?"

"Yes. What did you think?"

"Archery, maybe. Or the bow. Or dinosaur-hunting."

She chuckled. "I did follow the Dao of the Arrow in the F-Grade, but I made my second Dao Root, Wind, into a Seed. It wasn't even on purpose. It just happened one day... and I think it was the best thing that ever happened to me."

She raised a hand, and the sand around them rose with it. Gripped by a gale, it swirled around them, forming symmetrical spires that spun in all directions at once. It was a show of beauty that left Jack gaping.

"Why did you never do that before!"

"I didn't trust you at first. And then..." Her smile took on a mischievous hint. "I saved it for the perfect moment."

"Is this your perfect moment, then?"

She met his gaze. "To reveal my powers? Yes, it is."

He held it for a bit, then leaned back on the sand. Nauja smiled. "Tell me about the wind," he asked, closing his eyes.

"It is wild and free," Nauja said. Her fingers danced above her palm, twisting the sand into ever more elaborate patterns. It didn't matter that Jack had his eyes shut. She was doing this for herself, losing her heart in the simple-minded beauty. Without knowing it, her voice had dropped to a reverent whisper, pulsing with warmth. "It is unfettered, unblocked. It goes everywhere it wants. The wind is freedom, from the tallest peaks to the deepest valleys, and it is joy as it springs from the clouds and tours the sky. It is found in..."

She went on, forgetting herself as the sand danced around her, on a lonely sand dune in the middle of a desert. The silver starlight of the mushrooms struck her pale skin, making her glow like a goddess of the night. The flame in her heart was so strong and bright it illuminated even the darkest corners.

Jack lounged with his eyes closed, savoring the moment. His heart unclenched fully, releasing all the fear and worries it held inside, reveling in the here and now. His joy was pure and whole.

Like the wind, he was free.

———

Time in the desert passed quietly, serenely. Even monsters were very few and far between. They ran into one or two a day, and most were on the weaker side. That was a bummer, since Jack hoped to level up a lot here. Scorpions, lizards, snakes... They challenged anything they could get their hands on, so they could progress faster. After all, Jack was on the clock.

None of the battles were particularly difficult. During the journey, Jack got another two levels—and was probably close to a third one, but not quite there yet—while Nauja only got one. Unfortunately, the leveling difficulty spiked the higher you went, and being two people meant the System didn't consider their victories as impressive.

Brock couldn't participate in the battles, though he practiced, closing his eyes and walking on autopilot as he focused on expanding and deepening his Dao.

His level kept rising as he grew, both in strength and size. By now, Brock was level 45—and, thanks to his Dao, an Elite.

By the fifth day, they were approaching the area where the stone columns disappeared, where the village lay. However, they were also starving. They'd avoided eating uncertain meat so far, but even E-Grades felt hunger after five days, let alone Brock. Jack caught him frowning and grabbing his belly at times; he was a brave brorilla, a true bro.

Jack started keeping an eye out for edible creatures.

On the same day, they ran into something they'd never seen before. Brock spotted it. He'd stopped and raised his arms for seemingly no reason.

"What is it, Brock?" Nauja asked. Brock pointed at the next sand dune in their path, making low warning sounds.

Jack frowned and narrowed his eyes, seeing nothing. Then, he found it. His eyes widened. Nauja whistled.

A chameleon was plastered on the sand, its color altered to blend in almost seamlessly. It took careful observation to notice that the ever-present lines in the sand formed the outline of its body, but when you did, its shape was clear.

Giant Desert Chameleon, Level 123
Giant Desert Chameleons are solitary ambush predators. They blend

into the sand and lie in wait, often spending weeks without any movement whatsoever. When prey comes close, they strike hard and fast, using their tongues as their main weapon.
Despite their ambushing tendencies, they are also formidable fighters.

"It looks dangerous," Nauja said.

"And plump," Jack added.

"What?"

"I say we eat it."

"What!"

"What do you mean, *what*? We're all starving. We can give it a shot. I won't have any at first, so I can carry the two of you if something goes wrong."

"Bro..." Brock said, his voice filled with gratitude.

Nauja flashed Brock a look of understanding. "Okay. Want to do the tyrannosaurus trick again? Where you hide in ambush and I shoot it from afar?"

"I actually have a better idea," Jack replied, smashing his fists together. He hadn't fought seriously in a while. He was getting itchy—and he was far stronger than he used to be. "Let me handle it."

"Alone?"

"Yes." A wild, expectant smile crept on his lips. "Can you scout around a bit, make sure we're alone? I think this is a good chance to finally test my Life Drop."

CHAPTER FIFTY-FIVE
MORE ARMS, MORE FUN

JACK CRACKED HIS KNUCKLES. HE WAS EAGER TO FIGHT, EAGER TO UNLEASH HIS pent-up energy on this clueless monster.

Nauja and Brock stepped away, leaving him alone against the monstrous chameleon hiding in the sand, unaware they'd noticed it. Unfortunately, Jack wanted a fight.

"Come out!" he ordered, shooting a Meteor Punch from afar. The purple blow landed on the chameleon's back with an explosion that leveled the nearby sand dune, sending waves of sand dozens of feet into the sky.

The chameleon sprang into motion. Yellow eyes snapped open, each with two green irises in their midst, and each moving independently of the other. Its skin turned green, there was a ridge of spikes running down its back, and webbing was between its fingers, probably to help it glide through the sand.

It was the size of two horses put together, and it crawled over at a speed that would put any camel to shame. It reached Jack near-instantly.

Jack braced himself. He was going to test the Life Drop's power—his four-armed form—but first, he wanted to try out his bare self. The Ancient trial had given him eleven levels and a fused Dao Root. He wanted to see how he stacked up against this chameleon, a peak E-Grade monster.

When the chameleon reached a hundred feet away from Jack, its mouth cracked open, a pink tongue shooting out like a missile. It was the width of Jack's torso and long enough to reach him at this distance.

Thankfully, the monster's description had warned him of the tongue attack. It still came too fast, too early. He crossed his arms before his chest and felt like he was struck by a cannonball. He was sent flying back, piercing through a sand dune to stop at a second, flat against the sand.

The chameleon hadn't stopped. It was on him again, crawling over the tumbling sand with its tongue hovering in the air, waiting to strike like a scorpion's stinger.

Jack rolled aside, letting the tongue bury itself in the sand. It retracted like a spring before he could hit it. *This tongue is trouble*, he thought with a grimace.

He jumped up and faced the chameleon. He charged forth, having no advantage at range.

The monster didn't acknowledge his power. As he charged, so did it, tongue whipping all the while. It came at him from all directions, moving at blinding speed and with great force. Jack dodged valiantly. He ducked, sidestepped, or, for the more accurate attacks, Ghost Stepped away. Having tasted the power of this tongue, he didn't dare block.

The sand caved under his feet, but he simply pushed harder, letting the grains scratch his shins.

He was upon the chameleon in a blink, fists blurring as they shot out a flurry of blows. They landed on slick scales, denting them or sliding off. The chameleon tried to headbutt him. Jack leaped over the strike, shooting two Meteor Punches into the chameleon's neck and one behind himself—so that the explosions wouldn't push him into the air.

He landed in a crawl, jumped aside, then rolled under a tongue blow. He ducked low and sprang up with force, burying his fist into the chameleon's guts, raising the beast an inch off the ground. Jack felt his elbow creak.

For the first time, the chameleon felt pain. The moment it landed, it regarded Jack as an opponent rather than prey, adjusting its tactics. It stepped back and let its tongue take over, wielding it like a long mace.

The control it had over its tongue was frustrating. It could twist and bend midair, form into angles, and keep chasing Jack as he escaped.

At a distance, Jack was losing. He couldn't let that stand.

He Ghost Stepped twice in rapid succession, closing the distance. His fist smashed into its nose, breaking it with a sickening crunch and burying its head into the ground. Just as he pulled back to strike again, the body of the tongue shot sideways and hit him in the ribs, sending him flying.

Jack suppressed a groan. Something was cracked again, as it often was. That tongue was no joke.

He kept his cool. Meteor Punching the air to shoot back at the ground at a sharp angle, he turned and landed on his feet, then dashed for the chameleon again. The tongue shot out, a maelstrom of pink violence, but he had a sense of its patterns now. Like the tyrannosaurus, the chameleon was stupid.

He ducked under an attack and jumped over another aimed at his feet. He kept going, ignoring a feint, then took a grazing blow to the arm when that wasn't a feint after all. Cursing, he Ghost Stepped to the chameleon's face and again to arrive at its back.

He smashed a Meteor Punch down, making the monster croak and arc its back downward. He punched again and again, charging up each strike to make it a purple meteor. The explosions shook the sand, cracked the denser ground underneath, sank the chameleon in.

Its tail came from behind to swat Jack in the same ribs the tongue had cracked before. He flew away, already grimacing in anticipation of the pain soon to come... But it didn't. There was no feeling of cracked ribs straining to remain whole or digging into his innards. It was like his ribs hadn't been injured before.

What?

He remembered the skill upgrade he got when the Life Drop fused with his soul. The Dao of Life had increased his Indomitable Body's regenerative properties to "extreme."

He skidded into a landing and grinned. His cracked ribs had healed in a matter of seconds. Granted, the injury had been small, but such a speed of recovery...

It could make him unstoppable.

The chameleon slithered opposite him, pulling itself free of the sand where Jack had buried it. It was angry now, its eyes and tongue rapidly darting around. Despite taking three Meteor Punches head-on, it wasn't too injured.

Neither was Jack, but he was getting tired. Keeping up with the tongue required multiple uses of Ghost Step, which tired him out quickly. He had to admit that, if he fought the chameleon like this, he would probably lose.

However, this was still a large step-up from when he'd been completely overwhelmed by the tyrannosaurus. Now, he could keep up. He could protect himself. Fight it as an equal.

And he had more to give.

"Nauja!" Jack shouted. "Is it clear?"

"There's nobody around!" a voice carried over from a nearby sand dune, the highest around, and Jack grinned. Reaching into his soul, he lifted the barrier around the Life Drop's core, letting its energy flood him until it reached an equilibrium.

His form shifted, growing taller and wider. The chameleon shrank as he enlarged. The bare skin under his armpits itched, then ruptured to reveal two tubes of flesh and writhing muscle that quickly entwined around each other to form two extra, fully functioning arms.

The chameleon had frozen, inspecting him with confusion. It was considering fighting or fleeing. Jack felt the power course through his body, felt his strength rise rapidly. He could barely control his anticipation as he charged, each stomp shaking the desert.

It chose to fight.

The tongue blurred through the air, coming from his right. Jack raised two hands to block. The strike met his forearms next to his ears. It was heavy. The impact shook his body, pushing him to the side and forcing him to take a side-step to maintain his balance. His two right forearms protested under the pressure.

But that was all. One step. Before transforming, a head-on collision had sent him flying.

He grinned.

The tongue circled around and came at him again, this time from the left. Jack saw it. The pink whip was no longer blurring through the air. It was merely fast.

He leaned back, letting the tip of the tongue sail past his face, then reached out to hook its body under his elbow. It pulled, but he held. The two bottom arms grabbed the tongue, large fingers closing around the dexterous muscle, as Jack's upper arms grabbed it farther back and pulled.

The chameleon did not expect that. It stumbled, yanked forward by its own tongue, then hurriedly planted its feet deep into the sand and pulled back. It was frantic now, trying to escape.

But would Jack let it?

His two arms held on tight, their veins sticking out. His muscles were iron cords filled with power, his fingers were iron pliers, his body a boiling furnace. He pulled against the chameleon, dragging it into a tug of war with its own tongue. The tip flapped in the air and tried to strike him, but he used an extra hand—he had so many!—to trap it under his armpit, where it could do no harm.

He pulled, and the chameleon heaved. There was no Dao involved here, no skills. It was pure strength versus strength.

Obviously, Jack was losing. His greatest advantage against this beast was his Dao. His feet dragged through the sand, his fingers laxing and threatening to lose purchase.

However, no matter how strong the chameleon was, there was only so much force its tongue could handle. It cried out in pain. Jack felt the tissue under his hands begin to rip as the tongue was stretched beyond its natural limits.

The chameleon had to give way. It dug its feet out of the sand and rushed at Jack, hoping to surprise him. It failed.

The moment it stopped pulling, Jack got to work. He had so much tongue to play with. His four hands blurred through the air, tying it into tighter and tighter knots until he formed a large pink mass that only stretched thirty feet out of the chameleon's mouth instead of a hundred.

The chameleon reached him then, and Jack let go of the tongue and charged forth. Two meteors blazed on his right and two on his left. All four struck the chameleon's face, sending it flying. The explosions were larger than usual. So large, in fact, that Jack was almost blinded and deafened.

He reached the fallen chameleon in a blink and pummeled it. His every fist carried tremendous power. Even without using Meteor Punch, their force was enough to rupture scales, rip skin, and bruise tendons. The poor chameleon tried to resist, but its tongue was so tied up that it couldn't control it, and its limbs were far from strong enough to face Jack in his current form.

All it could do was lay there and take a beating.

Which made Jack feel bad. He was fine with hunting monsters to eat —such was the law of the jungle—but prolonging the fight would be very disrespectful.

With a sharp strike, he tore into its throat and ended it.

Level up! You have reached Level 83.
Level up! You have reached Level 84.

Thank you, brother, he mentally told the chameleon. You fought well.

Jack dusted himself off, allocating the new free points in Physical.

He couldn't help but admire his power. Before using the Life Drop, he was slightly weaker than the chameleon. Afterward... He almost toyed with it. He was stronger by an entire tier.

Just how strong am I? he couldn't help but wonder.

"Well done," Nauja said, arriving next to him.

"Yeah," he agreed. There was no point to further maintaining this form. He let it dissipate, returning to his normal size with the extra arms shrinking and disappearing.

"Wow," she muttered, eyes glued so hard to his body that he felt almost uncomfortable. "That was..."

"Impressive?"

"And brutal. I've seen people augment their bodies during battle, but nothing like that."

"Right?" he replied, smiling. He flexed his hands. "And that power... Oh, boy. That was something else."

"How long do you think you can keep it up? Indefinitely?"

"A few minutes, maybe. I can only draw a finite amount of power from the Life Drop, and it would run out eventually."

"Wow... So, wanna eat it? I'm starving."

"Yeah."

Belatedly, Jack realized that using the Life Drop—and fighting in general—was exhausting.

They then proceeded to make a fire, using the second torch head that Brock carried in his pocket, and roast the meat well.

The desert chameleon tasted as awful as it sounds, but at least it satiated their hunger. After five days of starvation, the taste hardly mattered. They wolfed it down like it was made of jelly.

With their bellies full and almost an entire chameleon left behind for the desert's critters—it really was too large—they set out toward the village again.

"How far away is it?" Jack asked, rubbing his belly. He burped.

"Not much," Nauja replied, looking at the cave ceiling. "But far enough that we'll have digested everything by then. Remember, we don't know what awaits us there, so we should be at peak form when we arrive."

"Right. Do you think that minotaur will be at the village?" His mind was still on his new powers—specifically, how he'd like to bury all four of his fists into Bocor's face for daring to slap Brock.

"Probably." She shrugged. "Only one way to find out."

CHAPTER FIFTY-SIX
THE VILLAGE

THROUGHOUT JACK'S WEEK-LONG JOURNEY THROUGH THE DESERT, HE DIDN'T forget about the Dao Soul.

Every second night, he entered his soul world instead of sleeping. The Dao Soul waited there, a mute copy of Jack that took childlike joy in fighting.

Here, the Dao came easy, but the System was cut off. He'd changed the terrain from a grassland to a desert, to better resemble his current environment. The only other difference from last time was the shining green beacon in the sky—the Life Drop—though Jack discovered he couldn't draw on its four-armed power here.

Every time he arrived in this soul world, he found himself enjoying it even more. His soul yearned for battle. For the thrill of the fight. He itched to pit himself against someone who could match him, to punch against a skilled opponent.

Copy Jack used the real Jack's Dao and fighting skills, while giving its own twist to them. Sometimes, it uncorked combinations Jack had never considered, utilizing the Dao in novel ways.

There was inventiveness in the way it thought. The Dao Soul wasn't a machine, but a nascent soul, a real living being. It wasn't as complete as an actual person, which was why it needed to leech off Jack, but the seed was there.

There was a time, far into the pre-System days, when Jack would play fighting videogames with a friend from high school. That was exactly how this felt. He pitted himself against the copy again and again, each trying to sharpen their skills while learning the other's patterns. They had to mix things up, try new maneuvers, new combinations. Most of the time, it failed horribly. But, sometimes, it worked, and Jack learned something new.

Of course, the greatest benefits had come from the very first time Jack arrived here, when many of his then-weaknesses were revealed. In the week through the desert, no skill notification arose from this training, but Jack felt his strength increase noticeably. Since he was unable to rely on the System in his soul world, he gradually developed his own understanding of Fistfighting, which he then confirmed with the System's assistance in the outside world.

Many of his skills felt on the cusp of evolving once more.

His Dao was also improving by the day. Unlike the outside world, his soul allowed him to use the Dao freely. He could even manipulate it outside his body, which was usually a domain reserved for D-Grades. As a result, he came into contact with insights that most people of his level never had access to. Through constant battle against the copy, he discovered more efficient ways to implement his Dao, slowly but surely approaching the skill with which the System guided his Dao when using Dao skills. He was still very, very far away—but he was moving in the right direction.

This process, too, put many of his skills on the cusp of evolving.

The Dao Soul wasn't the best tool to expand one's abilities, since it included no real danger or pressure, but it was perfect for stabilizing what he already knew. It could greatly accelerate the twin cycle of cultivation—expansion and stabilization.

Given Jack's deadline of one year, it was the best thing he could ask for. After the third night, he stopped sleeping altogether and spent every resting moment in his soul world, practicing against the Dao Soul. Copy Jack welcomed the challenge.

As a result, Jack was tired toward the end of the trip. His eyes had black bags under them, his body was sore, and only his Indomitable Will kept him from dozing off. He was slowly turning into a training maniac.

But he was improving fast.

Only on the last night, just before they reached the village, did Nauja convince him to sleep. They didn't know what they'd meet there; they had to be at their peak.

———

The oasis colored the heart of the desert, a splash of life in a wasteland.

Palm trees rose from verdant grass, swaying in the breeze. A small lake was in the middle, its waters crystal clear and inviting. Birds and little animals darted around between the trees, and cultivators, for once, weren't trying to kill each other.

The village itself sprawled around the lake with roughly fifty little houses, all picturesque and identical. They were made of light wood and resembled forest cabins, with logs sticking out at the end of walls and a flat roof above—unlike normal forest cabins, these ones didn't have to fear the rain.

People of all species walked or rested in their midst. There were about forty of them, each moving with the confidence of an elite. None of these people were simple. They had the status and strength to be granted a Trial Token, and they had made it through the second and third rings, crossed the desert, and reached the village.

Each was a prodigy of a B-Grade faction, on the level of the Integration Tournament's scions—or higher.

Jack saw feshkurs, a kovan, lycans, treants, insectoid people, creatures made of stone, others of wood. Some had wings, skin in all colors of the rainbow, or random assortments of limbs. They carried halberds, spears, swords, bows, maces, mallets, daggers, knives, machetes, staves, even guns. Many didn't wield weapons but instead radiated peculiar auras, their mere visage struck Jack's brain oddly. Others wore strange garments and held artifacts that screamed magic. One person was completely naked.

Their levels ranged from the late seventies all the way to 119. Undoubtedly, they had the strength to match.

Jack, Nauja, and Brock watched all that from a distant sand dune, crouched on its surface so as to not be seen.

"Look at all those people," Jack said. "They're so different."

"All delvers," Nauja replied with distaste. "Their exterior doesn't matter if they're rotten on the inside."

"Look. Our friends are there, too."

An easily distinguishable treant moved through the crowd, like the one they'd been chased by in the Forbidden Cave. There was no way to tell if it was the same treant from this distance, since all of them looked similar to Jack, but the woman who walked beside it sealed the deal. She was bald and clad in purple robes.

The minotaur's forces were here.

"We can't enter the village," Nauja said. "They'd chase us again."

"I'm stronger now."

"Stronger than all of them? *And* their allies?" Nauja raised a brow. "The minotaur wasn't even the top of the pack. He mentioned that he worked under someone, remember? A Lord Longsword. If they spot us, we're done for—or, at least, I am."

Jack grumbled. She was right, but they were tired and starving after a week in the desert. Poor Brock was the worst. He was wobbling and had trouble concentrating. Jack had carried him for the last half a day. Even the hat they'd fashioned out of a dead scaled lizard wasn't enough to spare him the scorching sun. Moreover, they sadly discovered that these lizards weren't edible.

Brock might have been a level 45 Elite beast, but even he had his limits, and they were fast approaching.

"We have to get some food," Jack said. "For Brock, and for us. Who knows what will be in the next ring?"

"Well, it's the Space Ring. I know some things, but... not if it has food. I... never thought to ask."

"You know who has food? That place." He pointed at a specific building in the village. It was a cabin larger than the others, with smoke wafting from a little chimney. Tables were arranged at the front for cultivators to eat, with two lycan waiters shuffling between them and the kitchen, where a single kovan used its four arms to cook three meals at once.

Many groups of cultivators were clustered around the tables, chatting merrily and gorging themselves on drinks and food that looked delicious even from this distance.

Then again, everything looked delicious after a week in the desert.

"There's still your friend, right?" Nauja asked. "That Gan Salin person. We can't enter the village, but he can. Maybe he can buy food for everyone."

"Not a bad idea," Jack replied. "The problem is, I don't see him."

Despite the colorful assortment of cultivators, Gan Salin was missing. Jack hoped he was just inside a cabin, out of sight.

"We are well ahead of schedule," he said. "We'd agreed on a one-month deadline to reach here. It's only been like, what, two weeks? He's probably still touring the second ring."

"Or dead."

"Not helping."

"Not trying."

Jack chuckled. "Let's wait a bit. Maybe he'll show up from one of the houses. If not... Well, good luck, Gan Salin."

"Na'ste'kala."

"You said that before, what's it mean?"

"An expression my tribe uses. It's slang for goodbye. Similar to the sound a triceratops makes when sad."

"Aren't you guys too few to have slang?"

She gave him a weird look. "What does our population have to do with anything?"

"Well, size matt—You know what? Nevermind."

"Can we get back to our starving?"

"Sure. If Salin doesn't show up soon, we could try other things. Maybe disguises? No, that wouldn't work. We could steal some food in the night, I guess, or pay someone to buy it for us."

"That last one sounds like a good idea. Even if the minotaur's told people to look out for us, I doubt any delver will care if we pay them enough."

"Okay. Let's wait a bit, and then we proceed with that plan. Afterwards... Where's the exit again?"

"Inside the village." She pointed at a small island in the middle of the lake, where a stone shrine stood out.

"Right. Perfect."

"We can try sneaking through. If we get as close as possible and then make a run for it, I doubt anyone will be able to stop us in time."

Jack nodded thoughtfully. "Okay. So, we wait a bit for Salin to appear, then get someone to buy food for us, then try to reach the exit tunnel."

Brock counted as an individual, thankfully—as had been revealed in the Barbarian Ring—so they matched the "at least three individuals" requirement for the Ring Quest.

"What are all these people waiting for, anyway?" Jack wondered. "Why aren't they going to the next ring?"

"There's an annual event sometime soon. The Garden Assault, when everyone works together to reach the depths of Trial Planet. I think they're waiting for that."

"Hmm... I guess none of them are in a hurry."

Jack looked at the village again. Those were a lot of people. A lot of potential enemies.

Of course, they could also try another village, but... There was no time for that. Even with his recent bonuses, his goal of defeating the C-Grade Planetary Overseer within a year remained near impossible.

The Integration had taken a month, his space trip two weeks, and his Trial Planet run so far another two weeks. Ten months remained until Earth's grace period was over... and Jack was still in the E-Grade. There were plenty of letters left to go.

Damn the alphabet.

At least, they had a plan now. Wait, pay, run. Simple and clean.

From between Jack and Nauja, Brock made monkey sounds and pointed.

"Hmm? What's that, bro?" Jack said, squinting.

A trio of cultivators had just thrown the scraps of their food at something behind the tavern. It wasn't visible from where Jack watched. *A stray?* he thought, then considered it better. *No. Those people are laughing. Why would they be laughing? Are they making fun of strays?*

Brock made monkey sounds again.

"We can take a look, ok bro?"

The three of them slid down the sand dune and made a wide circle around the village, taking in everything from a second viewpoint. A few minutes later, the area where the cultivators had laughingly thrown scraps at was slowly revealed.

Thick iron bars. A metal cage in the mud. And, inside it, munching on the bone of a chicken, was Gan Salin.

Jack groaned. "Oh, *come on*. You have got to be kidding me."

"Is that your friend?" Nauja asked, eyes wide.

"Yeah."

"Why is he in there?"

"I don't know." Jack was getting angry now. He and Gan Salin had their differences once, but the canine helped him escape the Animal Kingdom bounty hunters. They'd entered Trial Planet together. Maybe they weren't exactly friends, but they were a team.

And somebody was treating Gan Salin like trash.

Perhaps the canine had done something stupid and brought this upon himself—Jack wouldn't be surprised. But something told him this wasn't the case. Gan Salin was slightly insane, but he didn't come off as suicidal.

Why was Gan Salin trapped in a cage and fed scraps while people laughed at him? Who did this?

And what could Jack do about it?

"Change of plans," he said. "Night is falling soon. We'll sneak in and talk to Gan Salin. Rescue him if he's bullied. In the process, maybe we'll steal some food, too. I doubt the big guns will come after us over a couple of cold meals."

"Rescue him, how?"

"I can break the cage."

She raised a brow.

"What?" Jack replied. "I'll be quick. Then, we can run to the next ring before they have time to respond."

"...You're lucky to have me." Nauja sighed. "One of my Dao Skills can harden air in a bubble. It's nothing impressive in battle, but it stops sound. If I cast that around the cage, you can break it soundlessly. Then, we run."

"You can really do that!"

She shrugged. "It never came up before."

"Okay. Perfect. Then, that's the plan."

Nauja smiled. She hated the delvers on principle. Seeing them mistreat someone, anyone, she instantly identified with that person. Gan Salin being her potential ally only fanned the flames.

They lay on the sand as time passed. Eventually, the sun mushrooms above dimmed. They went from suns to stars, showering the desert in silver light. Day gave way to night.

Most of the cultivators withdrew to their cabins. They didn't need to sleep every night, but they had no need to stay awake, either. A few remained outside, positioning themselves in key spots and scanning the desert. They were careless, though. Some even sipped drinks from clay mugs. They weren't guarding against an assault from other cultivators, only the rare desert monster stupid enough to attack an oasis.

Jack, Brock, and Nauja slipped in like shadows. They crossed the sand dunes, not climbing over them, but following the valleys in between. The cold sand was their ally now, muffling their steps.

Before long, they were walking on grass, and the cabins loomed before them. Some were illuminated from the inside, firelight spilling from open windows. The palm trees rustled above, their leaves whistling lightly in the night wind, while the birds and little animals had returned to their nests to hide from the cold. Impressively, the lake's surface was gradually freezing over.

The tavern was still open, but only a couple of tables were occupied. They weren't serving food now, just drinks, and the raucous laughter of drunk cultivators filled the front of the building. They tried to keep it low, though. If their noise annoyed someone strong, they could end up beaten, or, even worse, like Gan Salin.

The three of them crossed the cabins in silence, darting from one to the other, always staying out of sight of the few lookouts. Before long, they made it behind the tavern, spying on the hardworking kovan bartender through a window. From there, Gan Salin was only a few steps away.

Canine, Level 61
Faction: Animal Kingdom
Title: Planetary Frontrunner (10)

Up close, he looked bad. His hair was messy and soiled, his clothes were dirty, torn in places. The remains of food lay at the side of his cage, stripped of every scrap of nutrition they ever had, while the mud under his wooden cage stank of piss. He was thinner than Jack remembered, looking weak and tired, and he was huddled against a corner, tucking his head into his chest and trying to sleep.

The sight struck a chord in Jack's chest.

"Psst," he said, crawling close to avoid being seen. Nauja and Brock remained behind in the shadows. Salin didn't respond.

"Psst!" Jack tried again, and this time, the canine raised his head. The hardness of his eyes gave way to confusion when he saw nobody. "Down here. On the ground," Jack whispered.

Gan Salin looked down. His eyes shone. "Oh, hey, Jackie," he whispered with a smile. "Long time no see, huh?"

CHAPTER FIFTY-SEVEN
TO THE RESCUE!

GAN SALIN WAVED AT JACK. DESPITE HIS TATTERED APPEARANCE, HE BEHAVED like everything was normal. He wasn't even deterred by the wrist-thick iron bars that separated the two of them.

"Salin," Jack whispered, "what the hell is going on?"

"I'm trapped," Gan Salin whispered back.

"I can see that, but why? What happened?"

"Oh, lots of things!" He got excited. "I somehow lucked out and survived through the second and third rings—by the way, did I mention that was almost a suicide mission for me? There is a reason nobody enters here at level 51. On the bright side, I got ten levels! Though you obviously did better. A shame. Anyway, my second ring was an icy tundra with roving packs of wild penguins, so I—"

"Salin!" Jack hissed, still keeping his voice low. "I'm not here to catch up. Get to the point."

Gan Salin crossed his arms.

"Wow. That's so rude. We haven't seen each other in two entire weeks, and you don't even wanna learn what I've been up to. Nice best friend you are."

"I'm not your—" He bit his tongue, starting over. "I can't believe I'm saying this, but I'm here to get you out. I'm risking my life. Just tell me the important things, please!"

"Risking your life? Oh!" Salin's eyes flashed. "That's right. I seem to remember there's a big bad minotaur in this village who's seriously pissed at you."

"How do you know that?"

"Guess who put me in here."

A moment of silence passed between them. The sounds coming from the front of the tavern, the laughter and conversation, only reminded Jack to hurry.

"I'm sorry," he finally said. "I guess this is my fault."

"Partially," Salin said. "Apparently, the Animal Kingdom wasn't happy I ditched the Hounds to team up with you. News got around and, ah, let's just say Bocor was not excited to see me."

"You know that minotaur?" Jack asked.

"We've met a few times. He's also a prodigy of the faction, but he belongs to an outside family, so he wasn't invited to Animal Planet much. Anyway, I came right to him the moment I reached the village. I thought, you know what? He's Animal Kingdom, I'm Animal Kingdom. In this foreign place, we should set our differences aside and work together! But no. He just threw me in a cage, like an animal, without batting an eye. Can you believe that?"

"I think I can." The minotaur hadn't struck Jack as the *kind* sort. "Did he mistreat you?"

"A bit." Salin's eyes glazed over, his smile taking on a bitter hue. "He was always bitter at the noble families. I can't blame him. He had the talent, but no matter how he tried, he was constantly ignored just because he didn't carry noble blood."

Jack's heart clenched a beat. "I can imagine."

"Yeah. When he had the opportunity to take it out on me, he was all too eager, you know? He even had an excuse: Since you and I came here together, I might know your whereabouts."

"A stupid excuse. We obviously weren't traveling together."

Salin shrugged. "It doesn't really matter, does it? Point is, you're here to rescue me. Can we get to it, please?"

Something in his eagerness to escape triggered Jack's perception. It felt like a momentary drop of Salin's joviality, letting the desperation seep out from beneath. Jack frowned.

"Did he torture you?" he asked.

Salin hesitated. "There's a limit to what he can do to me. Even as a criminal, I remain a member of the noble families."

"But?"

"...He did have a lightning wizard play with my cage a bit. The other cultivators found it hilarious. Nothing to worry about, though." He gave a wide, hurt smile. "I'm strong enough."

"I see." Jack's anger ticked up a few notches. Even reluctantly, Gan Salin *was* his friend now. "Did they feed you?"

"Isn't rescuing me more important?"

"No."

The canine hesitated again, but faced with Jack's resolve, he had little choice. "The tavern patrons sometimes throw scraps at me. Enough to keep me going. I didn't have much to eat in the desert, as you can imagine."

"He didn't give you a single meal?"

"No."

"And for water?"

"I dip my finger in the mud below and lick it. Sometimes. It's not pleasant for the stomach. On the bright side, Bocor made sure I had a good view of the pond, so I could fantasize about it a lot."

"And you can smell the tavern's meals all the time. And hear everyone else as they eat and drink and laugh."

"It's a privileged location for a cage."

Gan Salin was trying to joke, but Jack could clearly sense the pain underneath. The anger, the humiliation, the bitterness.

Jack clenched his fists and took a deep breath, beating down the fire inside him so it didn't spill out. Not yet, at least.

"Don't worry about me, Jack," Salin said. For once, his voice was earnest. "I'm fine. Just get me out of here, please."

He was playing it strong. Jack appreciated the gesture, but it did little to alleviate his fury. "Wait a moment," he said, making a gesture backward.

"Do you have more—" Salin kept speaking, but his voice was no longer audible. His eyes widened.

From the shadows, Nauja had activated her silence skill.

Being literally enveloped in silence was an odd feeling for Jack. He opened his mouth, but no voice came out. It was eerie, almost disturbing. His ears picked up a complete absence of sound, not even his own heart beating, though he could feel his body vibrating to the tune of his blood. Just like Nauja had promised, the sensation was deeply unpleasant.

In fact, it wasn't exactly silence. More like the air resisted the urge to vibrate, as if stuck inside a ball of effective sound insulation.

Salin frowned but gave Jack a thumbs-up. Jack wrapped his fingers around the iron bars of the cage, brought them to his chest, and pulled. His muscles went taut. The metal bent slightly under his grip, but no sound came. Jack pulled harder.

His veins were popping all over his arms. His eyes were bloodshot. He pulled with the strength of fifty grown men, but the metal kept resisting. These were thick bars, after all. They were designed so Gan Salin couldn't affect them.

But Jack wasn't Gan Salin. His veins throbbed as he pulled harder, refusing to be defeated, absolutely intent on bending these bars out of shape. His Dao of Power seeped into his Indomitable Body, fortifying and enhancing his muscles. His pulling intensified.

Gan Salin also tried to help, but his Strength attribute was lacking. Still, the effort was commendable.

Jack opened his mouth and roared soundlessly. Slowly, the metal bent under his fingers. Inch by inch, the two iron bars were pulled away from each other. Jack kept pulling. At some point, the metal was bent so badly that its resistance waned, letting Jack accelerate and part the bars completely.

When he stopped, he could feel his entire body shaking from overexertion, but he still heard nothing. It was even more disorienting than before.

He'd succeeded. A small hole was open in the bars, which Salin was already struggling to cross. He wiggled through it, pushing his shoulders to fit. It was just slightly too tight. His face was red, and his skin grated against the metal.

Jack wanted to help, but he was afraid he'd break something.

Eventually, Salin accepted that he just barely didn't fit. His eyes momentarily sharpened, his jaw set. His Dao Root of Resolve flared. With an abrupt motion, he smashed one shoulder into the metal, mouthing a silent cry of pain. The bone was dislocated, bent oddly through the cage, and he finally managed to slide through.

The moment he was out, he took a deep, trembling breath, then snapped the bone back into place. His grimace was harsh, sweat marred his forehead, but he was out and safe.

Jack felt the silence skill disappear. Sound returned, from the raucous laughter at the front of the tavern to the cries of nocturnal animals.

"Are you okay?" Jack asked, looking deeply at Salin.

"Better than ever." The canine forced a smile. "Thank you, Jack. Really. I appreciate it."

Jack smiled back. "Don't mention it. Now, let's—"

He froze. A person had just rounded the tavern, probably heading home to get some sleep. Unfortunately, they were in the way. This man was staring directly at them.

As if that wasn't enough, Jack recognized him. It was the fire mage who chased them in the Forbidden Cave, the one who'd screamed at Jack and Nauja about killing the ferretfolk.

Jack watched the man's eyes turn to orbs of confusion, then widen even further with anger. He'd put two and two together. Salin's broken cage and the canine himself were clearly visible.

So much for stealth, Jack thought.

The bald woman stepped out behind the fire mage a moment later, her expression mirroring his.

"Hey," Gan Salin said, raising his hands. "This isn't what it looks like. We're, um, eloping."

The fire mage took a deep breath, shouted, "Intruders!" and charged at Jack.

Which was a stupid decision. The man was level 72, one of the weakest cultivators in the village. He probably still thought of Jack as the weakling he'd chased in Forbidden Cave, but even then, Jack had only ran because there were a bunch of pursuers.

Even if the fire mage had inspected Jack now, he only saw a level 84 cultivator. The mage probably thought he could delay Jack until reinforcements arrived.

But Jack was not the average level 84 cultivator. Seeing the fire mage shout and charge, Jack's brows lowered dangerously. They had to run. This person was an enemy.

He charged too, using Ghost Step. His feet stomped on cobblestone. Suddenly, he was right before the enemy. The flames that just started pouring out broke against Jack's bare chest. The bald woman was too slow to react.

Jack's fist flared purple. Colors and sounds were sucked in. Jack's fist made contact with the fire mage's chest like a hurtling meteor.

The ensuing explosion rocked the entire village. A loud boom and a blinding flash covered the night as the man's body exploded, dying instantly. The strike was so strong that it carried behind the fire mage, striking the tavern wall and shattering it.

Wood splinters flew everywhere. Pipes on the inside were bent, pots and pans flew all over the place, fire spilled out from the kitchen to the ground, and the entire building creaked before starting to collapse.

Jack stood before the ruined corpse of the fire mage, fist still outstretched. The bald woman, who'd been ready to cast some spell, froze mid-action. She lowered her gaze, raised her hands, and slowly stepped back. The lycan waiter and two human cultivators—all under level 100—who just rounded the corner, startled by the mage's shout, also froze on the spot. They didn't dare approach. One of the two—a completely naked man—even started shivering.

"Mercy," said the lycan waiter, showing his open palms and arcing his back to push his belly forward—a habit deep in his genes.

Gan Salin gaped at the destruction, as did the kovan that was working inside the kitchen, his apron showered with splinters and dust. At least, this expedited Jack's plan of getting food.

There were more discreet ways to enter the kitchen than blowing up the wall. The plan was to sneak through the window, neutralize the cook-bartender, and steal anything they could get their hands on.

But things had taken another direction, and Jack didn't regret it. These people were all accomplices in Gan Salin's plight. They were the ones who laughed when the lightning wizard electrocuted him. They were the ones who threw scraps to humiliate him.

Yet, Gan Salin didn't complain. He simply endured the insults, sucking the bones dry to get nutrition, dipping his finger into mud and licking it to quench his thirst, smiling in the face of horrible mistreatment.

Jack was furious. He burned with rage. Since every plan would end up at a chase anyway, he might as well go scorched earth on this village. These assholes didn't deserve a tavern and nice food. Let them eat raw meat.

Besides, after the mage's previous shout, their infiltration had already failed. Now, it was a hunt. Urgent cries came from all directions, including the front of the tavern. Reaching the nearby exit tunnel was no longer an option.

Jack ignored the terrified crowd and rushed to the kitchen benches. Gan Salin followed a beat later. The ingredients—meat, vegetables, spices, and more—were neatly arranged in piles, and grabbing a sack, Jack filled it to the brim with anything he could get his hands on. Salin was grabbing water sacks from across the tables. He also found a small pile of credit cards, which he pocketed. At this moment, his excitement genuinely suppressed the signs of mistreatment on his face and body.

The bartender snapped out of his shock and ran for the door, screaming, at the same moment the chimney collapsed. The walls followed a beat afterward. Jack and Gan Salin were already outside, each carrying a bunch of sacks over their shoulders and running at the desert full tilt.

"What the hell did you do!" Nauja's voice reached him as she jumped out of the shadows, already sprinting.

Jack picked up Brock and hoisted him under his armpit, one arm carrying the brorilla and the other the sacks of food. Brock didn't make a single sound in protest. "What they fucking deserved!" he shouted back. "Less talking, more running!"

They broke into the desert, flying over sand dunes like they had wings. Thankfully, Gan Salin specialized in speed, so he could follow them—at least for a bit. Then, Jack would have to carry him, too.

Jack glanced back. From the moment he broke the tavern to now, only a few seconds had passed. With any luck, it would take time for the strongest within the village to realize what happened and come after them. By then, they could be miles away, far from anyone's ability to chase.

Getting to the next ring would be a problem. They could either circle back to this village and try to sneak through on the next night, or they could walk half a month to the next one. They had food and water now. It would delay Jack's timeline, of course, but he had the Dao Soul now. He could just spend that extra time stabilizing his recent gains.

Not like he had a choice, anyway.

The most he could wish for right now was escaping. With any luck, it would be doable. What kind of cultivator mastermind personally goes after vandals?

Unfortunately, luck had its days. As Jack looked back, he saw three figures leap over a sand dune, still far away but clearly on the chase.

One of them was the Animal Kingdom minotaur, Bocor. The other was a cold-looking woman in white robes who floated many feet off the ground, flying over the sand dunes without needing to follow the desert's terrain. And the third was a dark-haired man in tattered robes, whose sheathed sword was easily nine feet long.

This particular man was closing the distance so fast that he made the minotaur seem sluggish. It didn't take a genius to know that this was the Lord Longsword that Bocor served.

Jack cursed his luck.

CHAPTER FIFTY-EIGHT
FACING LORD LONGSWORD

JACK, NAUJA, GAN SALIN, AND BROCK RAN OVER THE SAND DUNES, HEADING AS far away from the village as possible. They thought they would be fast enough. Turns out, they weren't.

Lord Longsword's team was the first to crest the tall sand dune between the village and the desert, sprinting after them. Jack could see them clearly under the silver starlight. Longsword himself was at the front—at least, the person Jack assumed was Longsword—followed by the icy witch and the dickhead minotaur, Bocor.

Following them was a vast array of cultivators. In a brief glance, Jack spotted a blue-haired guy showered in lightning sparks, a lanky, pale-faced teenager riding a desert scaled lizard, a woman clad in a dark robe with a deep hood—

He turned back to the front. There were easily a dozen people there. No point observing them.

How the hell did Longsword move so fast? Jack wondered. If it was Rufus Emberheart in his place, he would lounge back and have an underling handle the chasing.

Turns out, not all young masters were similar.

"To be fair, you could have seen this coming," Gan Salin added helpfully, running side by side with Jack. "That was their favorite tavern in the entire village."

"It was the *only* tavern in the village."

"Did I say otherwise?"

"Less talking, more running," Nauja said, making Gan Salin turn to her.

"I'm Gan, by the way. Gan Salin. Though everyone calls me Salin recently. I don't know why."

"Nauja," she replied. She glanced at his outstretched hand, hesitated, then shook it quickly.

"Brock," said Brock, eager to participate in the conversation.

"Brock!" Jack exclaimed. "You can say your name now! Nice job!"

"Brock," Brock repeated proudly. Nauja and Gan Salin chuckled, while Jack braved another glance.

"Do you think they'll catch up?" he asked, still running. Lord Longsword himself was far ahead of the pack, gaining on them every second.

"Absolutely," Gan Salin replied. "I don't even know why we're still running. Perhaps we should hide in the sand and pretend to be lizards —though, really, I'm a canine."

Jack gritted his teeth. "What if I beat him off?"

"That's Lord Longsword. You can't even slow him down." Gan Salin focused on speed, not endurance, which was one reason why he could speak so casually while running. The other was his certainty of getting caught.

"You don't know how strong I've gotten."

"I know how strong that guy is. There's no way you can fight him."

"Oh yeah?" Jack struggled inwardly. "Watch me."

"Don't do this!" Nauja yelled at him.

"It's a terrible idea," Salin agreed.

"Bro," said Brock, his intent indecipherable.

"What choice do I have? He's almost here!"

Lord Longsword glided over the sand dunes, his feet barely discernable beneath him, each step carrying him a large distance forward. His tattered robes fluttered in the wind as his long dark hair was pulled back, revealing a sharp, clean-shaven, expressionless face.

No—was that a smirk of amusement?

There was no way they could escape. From everyone else, maybe, but not this guy. Jack made his decision. "I'll hold him off. It's me they're after, anyway. You guys keep running."

He stomped into the sand, arresting his momentum and turning around. In the same movement, he tossed Brock and the sacks of food he was carrying to Nauja, who caught them reflexively.

"Bro!"

"Jack!"

The sounds of feet dragging came from behind him, where his companions were running, but Jack couldn't spare the attention. He just hoped they kept going.

Lord Longsword was almost upon them. Seeing Jack stop, the hint of smile on his face grew an inch. He landed in the sand fifty feet away from Jack, then dusted his robes. The nine-foot-long sheath trailed behind him, its tip grazing the desert's surface.

From up close, there was a sense of playful arrogance to this man. The underlying assumption that he was far better than everyone else, and that he viewed them as a grown-up would view a bunch of kids. In this arrogance, at least, he resembled Rufus.

Human (Earth-74), Level 122
Faction: Wide Swirls (B-Grade)
Title: Wide Swirls Prodigy

"I commend you for—" he began, but Jack had no time to waste. If he could defeat this guy fast enough, maybe he could outrun the other delvers. They were a few seconds behind.

He charged in. A purple meteor blazed on his fist, ready to explode on that playfully arrogant face. He even considered using the Life Drop for a second but changed his mind. The Ancient voice had instructed him to keep it an absolute secret.

He flew within nine feet of Lord Longsword. The smirk on the man's lips flickered. His eyes narrowed like unsheathed swords.

Jack barely registered the movement. One moment, the nine-foot-long sword was in its sheath. The next, it was hurtling at Jack's face, coming sideways at tremendous speed. Before he even realized what was happening, his every instinct screamed to dodge.

Jack leaned back hard. The blade sailed over him, barely missing his nose, and he tumbled back-first into the sand.

"Your weight was too forward," Longsword said, shaking his head in mock admonishment. "Don't just charge like that."

Jack's heart was beating like a war drum. He jumped to his feet. Longsword held the blade at his side, nine feet of sharp steel, not in a hurry to swing again. But if Jack didn't escape fast, a dozen other cultivators would catch up.

He rushed in again. This time, he kept his body low. If the blade came, he planned to leap over it, catching his opponent by surprise—that was the only way he could win.

The sword cracked like a whip. Longsword simply turned his wrist, and the tip of the nine-foot blade hissed through the air like a baleful gale, reaching Jack near-instantly. Not only was Longsword fast, but the length of his sword—and its apparent weightlessness—further enhanced that. Jack already felt cornered.

He followed the plan. He leaped over the blade and somersaulted, noting how the metal curved by the air resistance under him. It was made of soft, flexible materials. Unfortunately, this knowledge was of little help.

With another flick of Longsword's wrist, the sword changed directions and leaped at Jack, aiming to bisect him. It was too fast. No sword should be able to move like that. The longer the sword, the harder it should be to wield. Longsword used his as fast as one might a dagger.

Jack Ghost Stepped diagonally and forward through the strike, landing on the sand and leaping off to punch Longsword. His fist blazed purple, drawing a narrow, fast arc.

At the last moment, Longsword's hand blurred. He slapped the strike away. The explosion burst to the side, leveling a nearby sand dune from the shockwave, as Jack found cold steel pressed into his neck.

He froze. He lost? Just like that?

A growl escaped Jack's throat, brutal and guttural.

"Eloquent. I like that," Longsword said. "Listen, little guy. I'm going to pull back my sword. Don't try to resist, okay?"

He did pull back. Even at this range, he didn't seem particularly afraid of Jack. A dozen cultivators landed around them.

Meanwhile, Jack was reeling. His mind was going through a thousand thoughts at once, trying to understand everything about this battle.

Longsword was a sword fighter. He used no extraneous Daos, none in this fight at any rate. He could manipulate the long blade with just a flick of his wrist, giving its tip extreme speed, like a whip. At the same level, how could anyone keep up with that? Jack's dodges had been more prediction than observation.

Did the others escape?

He looked back, only to find Nauja, Gan Salin, and Brock fifty feet behind him. They had their weapons drawn as if ready to assist Jack, but they stood still. Lines of smooth ice stretched through the sky, above Jack's head, and around his friends, ending in sharp tips aimed at their throats.

Jack realized what happened and groaned. They hadn't kept running. They turned around to help, but that was all the opening the ice witch needed for her magic to reach.

"You must be wondering," Longsword said, drawing Jack's attention. He caressed the handle of his weapon, already sheathed. "This is Featherlong. An Ancient artifact forged of extremely light, yet wickedly sharp metal alloys. One flick of my wrist is enough to sever a hill."

"When?" Jack growled.

"When was it made?"

"When did I ask?"

Longsword's smile faltered momentarily, then returned. From this distance, his eyes were like deep pools of brown, and that sense of playful arrogance was even stronger. It didn't escape Jack that the dozen cultivators, each a prodigy in their own right, stayed silent in deference.

"To be honest," Longsword said, "I didn't expect you to survive a single strike. Your strength is admirable for your level—you might even be Elite. Tell me: did you know who I was when you chose to fight me?"

"I had my suspicions." Jack was already captured. The best he could do was see where this guy was going. "I know that asshole." He jutted his thumb at Bocor, who snarled. "Works for a Lord Longsword. You're hella strong and have a long sword. It didn't take a genius."

"Hmm." Longsword cupped his chin. "Your personality is as I've heard. I have to admit I'm intrigued, Jack Rust. Your fighting skills are lackluster—"

Your mom is lackluster, Jack almost said before catching himself.

"—but you certainly have potential. I'll tell you what we can do. You have a little bounty with the Animal Kingdom, but my Wide Swirls are also a presence in the galaxy—and, unlike the Animal Kingdom, we accept outside disciples. Join my team. Swear an oath and devote your life to me for this Garden Assault. If you can impress me sufficiently, I might negotiate your protection in exchange for joining my faction."

The crowd did not expect this. Brows were raised, eyes widened. Bocor the minotaur was the most shocked of all. He quickly said, "My lord, the Animal Kingdom—"

"I am aware, Bocor," Longsword cut him off. "But subordinates are part of one's strength. I won't weaken myself to placate your faction. If this man impresses me, the Wide Swirls and Animal Kingdom might work something out."

"But—"

"Are you doubting me?"

His tone was calm. Yet it was enough to make Bocor bottle up his rage. "Never, my lord."

"Good. Now, what do you say, Jack Rust? Your strength has earned you a second shot at life."

Jack, too, was shocked. This had come completely out of the blue. *Join him?* he wondered. *Join a B-Grade faction?*

Honestly, he didn't really have a reason to refuse. There was no bad blood between him and Lord Longsword—though he instinctively disliked the man.

"You mentioned protection," he asked carefully. "If I may ask, would that extend to my planet, as well? We were recently Integrated, and I believe we rubbed the Animal Kingdom the wrong way."

"Planets are expensive." Longsword shook his head. "Every Wide Swirls disciple can bring up to three family members. I'll make that five for you."

Jack's heart clenched. *Five people...* He almost started counting before realizing that the people he had to protect were far, far more than five.

"And my companions here?" He motioned at Nauja, Gan Salin, and Brock.

Longsword cupped his chin. "The pet can be spared, but we'll kill the other two. The kovan whose tavern you ruined is my associate. I can't let such an act go unpunished."

Jack looked back, meeting Nauja's trembling stare. A moment later, she steadied. She was a barbarian. If she had to die, she would face death with honor.

"I would prefer not to—" Gan Salin tried to speak, but the smooth ice line that extended to his throat grew a bit, the tip drawing a drop of blood.

All this time, the ice witch stood a step behind Longsword and hadn't batted an eye.

"This is not a negotiation," Longsword said, noticing Jack's hesitation. "It is an opportunity for you. Many would give up their entire families to be part of a lord's team. Accept or I will hand you over to Bocor here, to treat you as he sees fit. I assure you; that is not a future you want to face."

Jack glanced at Bocor. The minotaur's face was torn between brutal glee and impotent fury. This was the same guy who'd slapped Brock in the Forbidden Cave. Part of the Animal Kingdom which bullied Earth.

What do I do? Jack thought desperately. *If I decline, he'll kill me and the others.*

If I accept, I will survive for a little longer, and I may be able to save more of my people down the line... but I can't surrender my friends. Plus, this guy is off. Everything he does feels a bit... too cold.

Goddammit. How am I supposed to make a choice like that? Is there really nothing else! What would a fist do?

Unfortunately, the essence of the fist was predicated on not losing. Since he'd already lost, all the fist could help him do was die. There was no way to fight his way out of this one.

But he was more than just a fist. Jack squeezed his brain dry for a solution, anything that could save him and his friends. He could feel their stares into his back. They relied on him.

And, as his brain was squeezed to the limit, it started spitting out random ideas. Most were stupid. But a few things made sense. Suddenly, the inklings of a plan were forming. A delicate manipulation that had a small chance of working, if executed properly.

CHAPTER FIFTY-NINE

ONE PATH TO SURVIVAL, A THOUSAND TO DEATH

"Your offer is tempting, Lord Longsword," Jack said, consciously relaxing his body and mouth. He even forced a small smile. The first step was to give Lord Longsword his respect in front of everyone. "How could anyone refuse? You are an unmatched prodigy. Honestly, after fighting you once, my respect for you is through the roof."

Longsword nodded. He assumed Jack was just complimenting him to make up for his earlier disrespect. Before he could say anything, Jack continued.

"Besides, I would have to be an idiot to let myself be handed over to that guy," he said, jutting a thumb at Bocor and laughing loudly. "Not only is he an asshole, he's also a weak asshole. Dying to him would make for an ugly tombstone."

Longsword frowned. "I acknowledge your intention, but you shouldn't insult my other subordinates. It is ungainly."

"Oh? I apologize, lord. I wasn't trying to insult anyone. I was just stating the facts. That person is, indeed, weaker than me. There is no shame in that, right?"

"I could destroy you with one finger!" Bocor bellowed. He was a minotaur, and bulls weren't known for their composure. Just as Jack had hoped, he was outraged.

"Of course you couldn't." Jack laughed again, latching on to this opening. "We both know you're the weaker party here. Wouldn't you agree, Lord Longsword?"

Longsword didn't reply immediately. Instead, his frown deepened. He wasn't an idiot. He could sense Jack was up to something; he just didn't know what. "Bocor is obviously stronger than you. What's your point?"

To an outsider, Bocor absolutely looked stronger than Jack. Not only was there a difference of thirty-one levels between them, but the minotaur was talented enough to be placed in Lord Longsword's team. He was far stronger than most people at his level.

In fact, Jack also suspected he was the weakest of the two, but he didn't have many options.

"He? Stronger than me?" Jack said, feigning surprise, even incomprehension. "My lord, I understand you have to speak up for your subordinates, but this really isn't proper. I've seen this minotaur fight. He is extremely weak for his level. In fact, his being part of your team is an affront to your great strength."

His hesitant words threatened to take back the respect he'd already given to Lord Longsword—in front of everyone. That would be awkward for the lord.

"Bocor is obviously not weak," Longsword responded. He was starting to get impatient, so Jack cut to the chase.

"I see. Well, I happen to disagree, and I wonder, do you enjoy gambling, Lord Longsword?" The cat was out of the bag, so he didn't leave time for anyone to interrupt his carefully crafted speech. "You mentioned before that subordinates are part of one's strength. How about you let me test this part of your strength, my lord? Let's make a bet. I'll duel the asshole and prove his incompetence. If I lose, I will gladly die for my disrespect, or join your team, or whatever you desire of me. But, if I win, you will let me and my friends go for now. You can hunt us down again in the next ring."

Brows rose all around. Even Jack's friends were surprised by this turn of events. Lord Longsword's eyes were narrowed, suspicious. "What are you trying to achieve?" he asked. Obviously, he didn't think Jack had a shot against Bocor, so he assumed there was something else at play.

"Nothing, my lord," Jack assured him. "No plans, tricks, or ploys. I am simply confident in my strength. If you are confident in your strength, too, and the minotaur is part of your strength, let me duel him." His expression hardened. "I refuse your previous offer. Go ahead and hand me over to the Animal Kingdom. In the process, why not offer a spectacle for everyone present, humiliate me, and showcase your subordinate's strength—if there is anything to show?"

Jack seemed confident on the outside. Inside, he was gnawing at all his fingernails at once. This was the only plan he could come up with: take advantage of Lord Longsword's playful arrogance to lure him into a seemingly impossible bet. Could Jack really beat the minotaur? He didn't know. But he believed his chances to be above zero. He'd grown a lot stronger since they last met, even faced a peak E-Grade beast almost equally.

Of course, that all hinged on Lord Longsword accepting this bet. Jack had already done his best. He had even used the lord's previous words to trap him. His only deficiency was that he had nothing to bet besides his own death, but there was nothing he could do about that. Revealing the existence of any secrets—like the Life Drop—would be the same thing as revealing the secrets themselves.

Lord Longsword cupped his chin. He still looked at Jack suspiciously, like there were more tricks lying in wait, but he couldn't find them—because they didn't exist.

However, his eyes held a hint of intrigue. Jack's heart lightened at the sight of it.

"Very well," he said. "Form a wide circle, everyone. Bocor, show no mercy."

The minotaur had the most bloodthirsty, sadistic smile Jack had ever seen. "Yes, my lord."

The cultivators made some distance, leaving a wide, empty circle in the sand for Jack and the minotaur to face-off. Bocor remained as everyone receded around him, solid as a boulder, staring down Jack while slowly grabbing his tower shield.

"I don't know what got into you," he said, "but I will enjoy this."

Jack wasn't paying attention to the minotaur, not yet. His eyes scanned the surroundings, taking in the cultivators. Lord Longsword stood at one end of the circle, accompanied by the icy witch—who still hadn't expressed emotion or said a single word. Nauja, Gan Salin, and

Brock were by her side, surrounded by smooth ice lines ending in sharp tips.

They watched Jack with hope. Gan Salin, with amusement.

"Hey, Jackie," he said, ignoring the ice that almost bore into his throat. "I don't know what you're planning, but go for it! I'm sure it will be fun."

"I'm planning nothing," Jack replied honestly. "I'll just kick his ass."

Somehow, Salin believed him. His face dropped. He turned his eyes —he would be impaled if he moved anything else—to Longsword. "Say, lord, normal battles are so last millennium. Could we consider something else instead? Perhaps a dance-off?"

"Shut him up," Longsword ordered. The ice lines wound so thick around Gan Salin's throat that even breathing was a struggle. When he swallowed, two shallow lacerations were drawn on his Adam's apple. He didn't speak anymore.

Jack drew his eyes from Salin to Nauja, who simply nodded, and then to Brock, whose eyes burned with passion. It warmed Jack's heart. The little brorilla didn't have the slightest of doubts about Jack's victory.

Around them, people were getting ready to watch the show. The bald woman from before glared daggers at him—probably still pissed he'd killed her two teammates, the ferretfolk and the fire mage.

The wizened treant was also there, the one with leaf magic, accompanied by a club-wielding woman and a robed individual Jack hadn't seen before—perhaps the invisible enemy from the Forbidden Cave?

Besides those, there were plenty of cultivators in attendance. More had arrived after Jack and Longsword started talking. A human with blue hair, white at the tips, through which ran blue sparks. A lanky, pale-faced teenager who rode a scaled lizard with a sneer on his face. A completely naked man. A kovan with a dirty apron and the most professional glare Jack had ever seen.

Not everyone's powers were easily discernible. There were plenty more who just stood there, clad in robes or armor, carrying sheathed weapons or odd trinkets. For a moment, Jack let his mind wander. What Daos could these people be following? The Dao of Victory? Of the Drunken Fist? Of Love, War, Sand, or Sky?

Maybe the Dao of Bad Breath? The Dao of No Clothes?

He couldn't wait to find out.

Then, relishing in this small respite, he took a deep breath and fortified his mind, focusing on one person: Bocor, the Animal Kingdom minotaur.

Jack had a bone to pick with this guy. Not only had he tried to kill Jack on multiple occasions, but he'd also mistreated Gan Salin badly, had slapped Brock. Jack still remembered the sound, crisp and clear. He was determined to get revenge—he just didn't imagine the time would come so soon.

Bocor stood opposite Jack, weighing him with his gaze. "Are you done sightseeing?" he asked, but Jack ignored him.

Minotaur, Level 115
Faction: Animal Kingdom
Title: Resilient

Meanwhile, Jack himself was thirty-one levels below.

Name: Jack Rust
Species: Human, Earth-387
Faction: Bare Fist Brotherhood (E)
Grade: E
Class: Fiend of the Iron Fist (Elite)
Level: 84

Strength: 350
Dexterity: 330
Constitution: 350
Mental: 50
Will: 80

Skills: Ghost Step I
Dao Skills: Indomitable Body III, Meteor Punch II, Iron Fist Style I, Brutalizing Aura I
Daos: Perfect Dao Seed of the Fist (late), Dao Root of Indomitable Will (fused), Dao Root of Life (fused), Dao Root of Power
Titles: Planetary Frontrunner (10), Planetary Torchbearer (1), Third Ring Conqueror

The four levels gained while touring the desert were a nice boost to his Physical stats. With all three working together, he would seem like a God to anyone in the pre-System era.

Unfortunately, his training with the Dao Soul through the desert trip hadn't yielded any tangible benefits, but he felt himself sharper, more aware of his surroundings and how the System channeled his Dao to use his Dao Skills.

Compared to other people of his level, he had two fused Dao Roots, a perfect Dao Seed, the Immortality Serum, an Elite Class, a third-tier Dao Skill in Indomitable Body, and the old reliable, Meteor Punch. The Life Drop was unfortunately off-limits for this fight. If he used it, he still wouldn't escape, and he would have revealed himself to the "great forces" the Ancient voice had warned him about.

He would have to win this purely on his own power.

The minotaur, on the other hand, no doubt had his own advantages. Elixirs, resources, fused Dao Roots, maybe an Elite Class or a perfect Dao Seed. Undoubtedly high-class training, all sorts of top-tier resources, and who knows what kind of equipment.

More than anything else, Jack had his fist and the resolve that, if he lost, he would die.

Simple and clean...

He licked his lips, finding them dry, and settled into a fighting stance. The minotaur's hulking body was eight feet tall, covered in bulging muscles hidden under a full set of plate armor that only left his face exposed, and crowned with sharp, twin horns. His face had thick, masculine features, his fur was a light brown, and his eyes were hateful little slits clouded with rage.

A large tower shield was in his hands, easily the size of a door and undoubtedly weighing ten times as much. When he stuck it in the sand before him, it sank easily until it hit a stone below with a hollow thud.

"In the name of the Animal Kingdom, are you ready to die?" the minotaur asked, reveling in his soon-to-come glory.

"Are you?" Jack replied, clenching his fists. The Dao coursed through him, filling him with power. His body tingled, his pores opened, his hair stood on end, a wild grin appeared on his lips.

He was ready.

Bocor bellowed and charged.

CHAPTER SIXTY

JACK VS. BOCOR

JACK'S WORLD SHARPENED TO A POINT: THE MINOTAUR. EVERYTHING ELSE FELL away. He entered combat. A battle he couldn't afford to lose.

Bocor closed the distance in less than a blink. His hooved legs carved the sand, parting it like air.

But Jack was also fast.

The sharp butt of a tower shield crashed where Jack used to stand. He'd jumped away, smashing a Meteor Punch into the minotaur's side. The ensuing explosion could fell a hill. Sand flew away in all directions, whipping the bodies and eyes of those watching.

When it settled, Jack was cradling his hand. A sharp pain ran from his middle knuckle to his shoulder, the result of the hard impact. The minotaur's plate armor was slightly dented but had easily withstood the strike. "Fool," Bocor said. "Someone like you could never break this armor."

Jack grimaced. Technically, blunt weapons—like his fist—were the best weapons against heavily armored opponents. But this was plate armor, and his hand was made of flesh. Until he broke the armor— which was nigh-impossible—it would distribute a good amount of his impacts across the minotaur's body, reducing the power of his strikes.

There was no way around it. He had to either strike the minotaur's face through his open helmet or keep pounding away at the armor. His hurt knuckle was already recovering, his Indomitable Body's magnificent healing properties set to work. While Jack's will remained whole, so would his body.

"I don't need to break the armor," he retorted. "I need to break you."

As Jack charged, Bocor brought the shield before his body. He bashed Jack, who sidestepped, then the minotaur swung the shield's sharp bottom. Jack rolled under the strike, finding himself before the minotaur, and punched out. He didn't use Meteor Punch—it hurt him more than the opponent.

His regular punches weren't anything to scoff at, either. They came densely, one punch following the other in a dance of violence. Jack smashed a straight into the minotaur's chest, a hook to his ribs, an uppercut into his jaw. Bocor's hands tried to clap Jack's ears, but he ducked, letting them clap each other, and charged up a fierce strike into his opponent's armpit.

Bocor grunted. It was the first sign of damage.

The shield came crashing down, forcing Jack to Ghost Step behind the minotaur and keep pummeling. His strikes bled into each other, but their effect was limited. It felt like punching a boulder. No matter how long you kept at it, all you achieved was to injure your own hands.

However, he'd made a great observation. He had the stats to face the minotaur. He wouldn't be steamrolled.

Suddenly, the air hardened around Jack. It became thick and slimy, like water, limiting his speed and strength. Every movement was now a battle against the pressure.

Bocor turned to face him, his glare ugly. "Welcome to the swamp, kid." He let go of his shield with one hand and slapped Jack, sending him flying to the edge of the circle. The lightning wizard there grabbed Jack—the grip sent a jolt of pain into him—and threw him back inside.

"There is no escape," Bocor said again, taking slow, purposeful steps at Jack. "You cannot harm me. You can run, but you are going down."

Jack's entire body was tense, his gaze hard. This guy was so frustrating to fight against. His whole being was designed to endure damage.

I have to strike his face, he thought. It was the only place where the plate armor wouldn't get in the way. Though, undoubtedly, the minotaur had more skills to protect himself, and the face was a difficult target to hit.

What are my advantages?

The minotaur was a cultivator. A scion of a B-Grade faction, like Rufus Emberheart. He had trained throughout his life, but how many real, life-or-death battles could he have experienced? Not many. And how many of them were against skilled, humanoid opponents? Probably very few.

Jack, on the other hand, had a wealth of experience. The Dao Soul by itself had made him adept in combat.

Brute strength wouldn't triumph here. He had to use skill. His hand closed around a handful of sand.

Jack felt the Iron Fist Style rev up inside him. The relevant knowledge came to the forefront. He was a Fistfighter, an expert. All his other skills were just tools.

With a roar, he stood and charged.

Bocor laughed and stood his ground. The air liquified around him again, making every move a struggle. Jack dived into it anyway. His ranged Meteor Punches could be easily blocked by the shield.

He dived, dodged, sidestepped, and rolled. It was harder now. The thick, slimy air inhibited him, but he pushed through. One punch under the elbow, another behind the thigh. He dodged a shield swipe, followed Bocor's backstep, and feigned an uppercut. In reality, he just opened his hand, shooting the sand he'd gathered into the minotaur's face.

Bocor released a cry of surprise. Jack had already jumped, dodging a blind strike to screw his fist directly into the minotaur's face from above. He felt bone groan under his knuckle, the collision of his fist against the ridge of his opponent's wide nose.

At the same time, it was like he'd punched granite. His knuckle ruptured. The minotaur's skin was even harder than his plate armor. At least it couldn't spread the damage everywhere.

Jack let the impact take him high, then twisted his body midair and punched again, a Meteor Punch with his entire weight behind it. Bocor had already raised his shield to block. Jack's hand met it with a crack. The shield was completely unmoved as he flew back, shooting a Meteor Punch into the air to accelerate his landing.

In this fight, mobility was his weapon. He couldn't afford to be stranded in the air.

The minotaur had recovered. His eyes were red now, steaming with rage, and blood trickled down his nose. "YOU!" he shouted, unable to muster more coherent words, and barreled forward like a loose train.

Jack welcomed the charge. He feigned to the left, letting the shield sail there without a target, then sidestepped to the right and planted a fierce punch right into Bocor's face.

Despite all the hardness and endurance his knuckles possessed, they were still fractured. The minotaur staggered, seeing stars as Jack pressed the attack. The Iron Fist Style flowed in his veins. He was one with it. His movements were fluid, smooth, clean, even in the mino- taur's aura skill.

His attacks weren't many now, but they were persistent. Each went after the minotaur's face, pursuing odd angles and timing. He mixed things up, adding feints, body slams, all mixed in with Ghost Steps. He was a machine of violence, a dance of mayhem tuned to the very edges of his skill.

Bocor avoided most of the onslaught. His face was a difficult target to hit, but thanks to Jack's persistence, a couple of strikes got through. To Bocor, it was a nightmare, like fighting a bee intent on stinging your eyes. His nose had gone from dripping to flowing blood, his lips were split, and his cheekbones were steadily caving in.

This was like fighting the rock bear all over again.

Bocor was rage personified. He was getting publicly beaten up. In front of his lord. The attacks didn't hurt him too much, but they wounded his pride. Yet, the more he gave in to rage, the more predictable he became. Jack was using all sorts of tricks, like a wild animal instead of a principled fighter. His moves weren't necessarily optimal, but they were unpredictable. Bocor wasn't trained to handle this.

As a result, his movements weren't practiced. They held clear patterns. Every time something worked, Bocor tried it again, only to find himself brutally countered. Jack had practiced against Copy Jack a lot. He knew how to read patterns and adapt on the fly.

Of course, Jack was regularly receiving hits. An armored gauntlet dug into his guts. A backfist met his face, the side of the shield crashed into his ribs, a headbutt broke his nose, a sharp horn slashed his shoulder.

Each time, Jack would fly back, slow down for a while. But his Indomitable Body would quickly heal him. Moreover, every time Jack landed a hit on the minotaur's face, his knuckles cracked. The pain was sharp, but Jack was beyond caring. His Indomitable Body only needed seconds to recover the damage.

Bocor may have been a tank, but so was Jack!

Nobody expected this. They witnessed Jack's attacking power and assumed he focused on Strength and Dexterity, that he was a strong but frail fighter. The first time he was struck hard, everyone thought it was over, only for Jack to stand up and keep fighting. The same thing occurred the next three times, until they got used to it.

The look of growing horror on Bocor's face fueled Jack, made him forget his aching stomach, his burning muscles, his leaden limbs. He was exhausted, but he was indomitable. His body would give up before his mind did.

Lord Longsword's expression hardened as the fight went on.

Stat-wise, Bocor was slightly superior. The same went for training and resources. Their Daos were comparable in power.

The deciding factor in this battle was skill. In this realm, Jack was clearly superior. Everyone could see it. It wasn't just the tiers of his Dao skills, either. Dao skills were mere guidelines. Jack was inventive. Experienced. He went above and beyond the skill's limitations, constantly improvising.

Strikes came and went, punches flashed, roars, bellows, rising sand, and the dull thud of skin on bone. Jack's skill in battle gave him the advantage, and his incredible tenacity helped him capitalize.

No matter how hardy he was, Bocor couldn't take a beating forever. He began to slow. His eyes were blurry, his mouth drawn into a permanent, enraged scowl, his moves subconsciously more defensive than before.

Of course, Jack also couldn't keep going forever. At some point, his body would just give out on him. The trick was falling *after* Bocor. He had to land a good strike.

Throughout the fight, he couldn't use Meteor Punch on Bocor's face.

Using the skill slowed his strike, and the openings he had weren't wide enough for that. He needed to find a better one.

So he stalked. Waited.

Until the scales of battle tipped in his favor.

He went from the underdog to an enigma. Nobody knew how long he could keep going, but they could all see his strength, his speed, his tenacity, experience, and excellent use of skills. Even Longsword's eyes held new light.

Until, at a certain point, Bocor crossed an invisible threshold. In the deepest recesses of his soul, he started believing he would lose. Jack sensed that change with his entire body. He saw it in the minotaur's eyes, his posture, his movements.

And, in that precise moment of hesitation, he *finally* used Brutalizing Aura.

It escaped his body with unrelenting force. It shimmered into the air around him and slammed into Bocor. The minotaur's eyes widened. The effect was immediate.

Brutalizing Aura worked by projecting the certainty of death into the target's mind. The feeling it invoked was like facing a natural disaster. Jack would kill them. There was no rage there, nothing to negotiate with. Merely a natural disaster that could only end in one way. It invoked a primal fear inside the target, something deep, ancestral, and uncontrollable.

Normally, it wouldn't work on someone as strong as Bocor. It was intended for use against crowds of weaker opponents.

However, throughout the fight, Jack had acted as a machine of death. He came for Bocor, fighting with overwhelming, inevitable skill. He persistently aimed for the face, a difficult target, and kept hitting it. No matter how many times he was struck, he always got back up and returned to the fight, hiding his exhaustion.

Bocor *knew* he was fighting a person, another cultivator, but Jack's incessant drive spoke otherwise. Slowly but surely, he'd cast a shadow on Bocor's mind. A shadow of terror, inevitability, and powerlessness, like he was trying to stop the sea waves.

Brutalizing Aura stepped precisely on that shadow, magnifying its effects. Everything Jack had done in the fight before culminated to this singular moment. Bocor was stunned.

A purple meteor flared around Jack's fist, imbued with all the resolve he could pour into it. He couldn't afford to lose. This was the only good opening he would get.

A ding rang into his ears.

Congratulations! Iron Fist Style I → Iron Fist Style II

"This is for Brock," he whispered, just low enough for Bocor to hear.

Color and light were sucked into his fist. The world went mute and dark, leaving only a shining purple meteor, beautiful in its deadliness. Jack swung with surgical accuracy. It went under Bocor's shield, between his outstretched arms, and right into the gap of his helmet, landing square against his face. The entire force of the strike focused on Jack's middle knuckle, which shattered on collision.

So did Bocor's face. It'd already taken a thorough beating. This meteor was the straw that broke the camel's back.

A blaring explosion was followed by a sickening crunch. Sand flew everywhere, obstructing the stars above. The dune under their feet was leveled. A strong wind flapped the clothes of all those watching, making them cover their eyes as Bocor's entire body flew back headfirst, passing right by Longsword to skid on the sand behind him.

Jack waited, arm outstretched. His shattered knuckles sent waves of pain into his body, but he ignored them—after the Life Drop's torture, this was nothing. His eyes were glued on Bocor's fallen body. His brain was still in combat mode, prepared to keep fighting until he collapsed. He didn't dare believe in victory. He couldn't afford to lose.

But Bocor didn't stand up. He remained on his back, hands sprawled to the sides, shield on the ground next to Jack where it had fallen, face bleeding into the ground. He wasn't dead, but he was unconscious.

For a few moments, there was silence. Everyone digested the impossibility they'd beheld. Someone had crossed a thirty-one-level gap, and won. Moreover, against an opponent that could also jump ranks to defeat those stronger than himself.

Everyone knew Bocor's strength. He was highly capable. How could he be defeated by someone at level 84?

The spectating cultivators all had their own thoughts. Suddenly, in perfect unison, everyone turned to Lord Longsword, including Jack and his captured friends.

Longsword hesitated. His eyes shined with fervor. There was desire there, like an enthusiast watching the newest sports car. It made Jack's skin crawl.

"Very impressive," Longsword said. "Even I didn't imagine you hid such strength. My interest in you is rekindled. What do you say, Jack Rust? Would you like to join my team? If you say yes, I'm willing to kick out Bocor. And, if you survive Trial Planet, I guarantee that I will ask my master to save you from the Animal Kingdom. I can even spare your friends here."

Jack took a moment to gather himself. He'd just escaped fierce combat. He was exhausted and tense. How long had that lasted?

He snuck a glance at Gan Salin, Nauja, and Brock, finding them standing in a corner. The ice lines around them had retreated.

"I appreciate your offer, Lord Longsword," he said. "Since I defeated the minotaur, I believe it is time to honor our agreement?"

"Of course! A bet is a bet," Longsword replied, unbothered by Jack's refusal. His eyes still glinted with excitement. "You and your team are free to go. Starting from the next ring, we'll be enemies again. You have until the morning before my team climbs down. However... I will be watching your progress with great interest. If you ever change your mind, just find me. I will make sure to save you something good from the Garden Ring."

"Thank you, Lord Longsword," Jack replied. He'd already released all his frustration in the battle. He didn't feel like being rude.

He also had zero intentions of ever joining Lord Longsword. Not only had his offer been shitty before Jack revealed his strength, but the way he treated his subordinates was terrible. He had publicly offered to kick out Bocor. Clearly, people were just pawns to him.

Jack wanted nothing to do with that sort of person.

"As a token of my appreciation, let me give you some tips before you go," Longsword said, his smile casual. "Your understanding of tactics is decent, but your movements are a tad unrefined. I would suggest working on your fighting style Dao Skill. Moreover, you might want to do something about that movement skill. It's good for now, but it doesn't mesh with the rest of your skills. I suspect it isn't even a Dao

Skill yet. If you don't find a way to evolve it soon, it will bottleneck your growth."

Jack narrowed his eyes. What Longsword said made sense... but they were enemies. Kind of. Even if he couldn't fight the other man right now, he refused to believe he still couldn't fight once he reached the peak E-Grade himself.

He couldn't just let Longsword lecture him.

"Thank you for your tips, Lord Longsword," he replied. "Allow me to reciprocate with a tip of my own. You might want to watch that wrist."

Longsword's eyes narrowed dangerously. "My wrist?"

"You move your entire sword with a flick of the wrist. If someone were to block the strike accurately, your wrist might snap. So, watch it."

"My sword is too fast for a perfect block. In any case, I know what I'm doing. You are in no position to lecture me." Longsword's eyes held a storm, which calmed just as fast, his casual smile returning. "I look forward to someone trying to snap this wrist of mine. Now, perhaps you've dallied long enough, Jack Rust. The Space Ring awaits you."

"Right. Come on, guys. Let's go," Jack told his friends. "We'll be heading to the next ring immediately. And we'll be keeping the food and water we got from the tavern. I don't suppose anyone disagrees?"

He scanned the crowd, but nobody stepped up. Even the kovan tavern-keeper, whose food and water Jack was now publicly taking after destroying the tavern, stayed quiet. He didn't dare meet Jack's gaze.

"Oh, and Jack," Lord Longsword said, almost as an afterthought. "If you decide to join the forces of any other lord after receiving my offer, I will be terribly offended. Okay?"

There was steel in those words. Jack kept them in the back of his mind but didn't pay too much attention. He didn't even know what it meant to be a lord. Was it a nobility title? A euphemism for very strong delvers? A moniker for people with long swords?

In any case, if the other lords were as rotten as this one, he didn't plan to ally with anybody.

"Thank you, Lord Longsword," he said again, turning to the village.

With nobody stopping them, and nothing left to settle on the fourth ring, reaching the center of the little lake and walking down to the next ring was as good as done.

Next stop... Space Ring!

CHAPTER SIXTY-ONE
DIRECTIONAL SHENANIGANS

"That was *amazing!*" Nauja said, walking excitedly next to Jack. "The way you tricked them... Genius! And here I thought you were a dumb meathead."

"You are literally a barbarian," Jack replied, but he wasn't annoyed. He was exuberant. Just now, he'd earned a great victory and secured the safety of himself and his companions.

Plus, he'd punished the asshole who slapped Brock.

"That was for you, little bro," he said, turning to the brorilla, who was walking with his back almost perfectly straight.

"Bro!" he replied, giving Jack a big thumbs-up. "Good!"

"Ohh! You're learning new words by the day now, aren't you? I can't wait until you speak to everyone."

Brock stood even straighter.

"I have to say, you've come a long way, Jackie," Gan Salin added, walking on Jack's other side. "Once upon a time, you struggled to beat even me. Now... Well, Bocor is a known prodigy in the Animal Kingdom. This victory of yours will make waves."

"Eh. They're already after me. How much worse could it get?"

"If your bounty gets any higher, even I may be tempted."

Jack glanced at him sideways. "You wouldn't do that. I just saved you."

"I'm *insane*. I can do anything."

Jack wasn't sure whether Gan Salin was kidding or not. In the end, it didn't really matter. "If you ever want a crack at me, just let me know," he said. "Now, can someone finally tell me what's the deal with that lord guy?"

The village was before them. It was mostly empty—everyone had rushed to witness Jack and Bocor's fight, and they'd stayed behind to honor Longsword's words.

It was a surreal sight. These flat-roofed forest cabins stood in the middle of an oasis, taking in the breeze. But nothing was as normal as it seemed. Did the delvers build these cabins, or had they always been here, like the barbarians, the Forbidden Cave, and the Ancient ruins?

To think that most of the galaxy's strongest immortals once passed by this normal-looking place...

"Lords," Gan Salin began explaining, "is the name we give to the strongest scions of Trial Planet. They are the movers and shakers. The literal lords of the rings."

"I see," Jack replied. "That's why Longsword was so strong."

"Yes. You've heard about Elite and King monsters, right?"

Jack raised a brow. "Some. Enough to know it's important."

"They're power classifications. Elite beasts are a tier stronger than regular beasts of their level. A low E-Grade Elite monster can battle middle E-Grade monsters."

"I know those, yeah."

"Well, King monsters are another tier higher. Kings are to Elites what Elites are to everyone else."

"Okay... And what does that have to do with anything?"

"The B-Grade factions use a similar system to assess the strength of their members. An Elite cultivator is one who can fight a tier above his strength. A King cultivator can fight two tiers above. Right?"

Jack's eyes narrowed. "And I suppose Lord Longsword is a King cultivator?"

"Exactly. Not just him; all lords are. Of course, there are differences between them, but the King level is generally the strongest that cultivators can get. After that, the difference in attribute points becomes too much."

"Hmm."

They passed by the ruined tavern, admiring the destruction they'd wrought—without consequences. Jack even considered taking some extra food, but they already had plenty. Brock was munching on a pack of bananas.

"Then, am I a King?" Jack asked. "I think I'm about as strong as a peak E-Grade beast, but my level is only 84."

"Technically, yes. That's why Longsword tried so hard to recruit you. Just keep in mind that things get a bit weird around the peak of each Grade. Since there is a large difference between a normal peak E-Grade and an Elite peak E-Grade, a normal beast could technically fall anywhere within that spectrum of power. So, if you see a beast at level 124, don't just go running. It could be much stronger than it seems."

"I'll keep that in mind," Jack said, nodding thoughtfully. "So, how many lords are there?"

"Right now? Three. They're gathered for the annual Garden Assault, where every strong cultivator works together to defeat the seventh ring's guardian."

"Cultivators work together? Without killing each other?" Nauja laughed. "I'll believe it when I see it."

"Oh, they kill each other, alright. They just pause for a moment to defeat the guardian."

"Is it that strong?" Jack asked. "I thought each lord was a King at the peak E-Grade. What could stop them?"

"A D-Grade guardian," Gan Salin replied seriously. Jack's smile faltered.

"Oh."

"Yep. Think of it like this: Elite is one tier above normal monsters—and cultivators. King is two tiers above. And the next Grade is three tiers above."

"That's—wait. So, the breakthrough to the D-Grade will increase my power as much as my entire rise through the E-Grade?"

Salin did some quick calculations and he beamed a smile. "Yeah! There's a reason we call those people immortals."

"Because they live long."

"That too."

"Man..." Jack whistled. "There's a long way to go... How will I ever make C-Grade in a year?"

"Oh, is *that* your plan?" Salin asked. "You won't. Okay? It's absolutely impossible. People take centuries to become C-Grades, and only one in a billion succeeds."

Jack frowned. "I've done impossible things before. Don't dash my hopes."

"Whatever you say, boss. Let's just focus on reaching the next ring for now."

"The Space Ring, right?"

"The Space Ring."

"Anything you can tell me about that?"

"Oh, many things."

Jack waited, but Salin didn't say anymore. He simply kept walking like everything was said and done. "So?" Jack finally asked.

"I can tell you things," Salin replied, "but I won't. Come on! Where's your sense of adventure? It will be a surprise!"

From the side, Nauja frowned. "The Space Ring is—"

"Shh!" Salin jumped in front of her, bringing a finger to his lips. "Don't tell him! He'll just see it in a bit, anyway."

She frowned.

"I'll see it tomorrow," Jack corrected him. "The tunnels between rings are fucking long."

"Not for the Space Ring." Salin winked. "Trust me. It's better as a surprise."

Jack and Nauja rolled their eyes. By the side, Brock was nodding in agreement with the canine. After all, he liked surprises.

They'd reached the lake in the center of the oasis. Due to the low night temperature, it was frozen over, letting them simply walk over to reach the little island in its midst.

There, they found a small shrine. It was a simple circle made of stone, with an obelisk rising thirty feet into the sky. A stone door blocked their way, carved with images of scorpions, sand worms, lizards, even creatures that looked like sand sharks. There were also many humanoid figures carved into the stone, depicted as living in houses similar to the ones in the village.

"This is the mystery of the Village Ring," Nauja whispered, tenderly touching one of the figures depicted on the door. "These people are shown everywhere in the desert. Yet, nobody has ever found them. The villages were empty when the first delvers arrived. What happened to them? Nobody knows."

"That's intriguing and all," Jack said, "but why is the door on the floor?"

He was right. This door wasn't placed on a vertical surface, as all doors should be. It was flat on the ground in the middle of the stone circle. It could have been a trapdoor, but its shape was like a normal door.

"Oh, this is part of the surprise," Gan Salin replied, giggling. "Come on, open it."

Jack frowned. "I'm not opening it."

"It will be fun."

"Nope, not doing it. You open it."

"But I know what's going to happen!"

"Can you stop acting like children?" Nauja said, rolling her eyes. She grabbed the door's handle and pulled it open. A passage was revealed, similar to the previous tunnels, except... vertical? It was like this tunnel was meant for people to walk on the walls, like ants.

Before Jack could say anything, an odd feeling came over him. He was disoriented for a second. Felt like he was tipping over. When he came to, he was standing in the tunnel inside the door like nothing was wrong.

He blinked. "What?" Looking back, the door was right behind him, placed against the wall, except he could only see sky through it. The path under his feet was placed properly, not vertically, as he'd seen before. As he peeked outside the door, he saw that the entire Village Ring had been tilted sideways. What used to be a door flat on the ground was now a door on a cliffside. "What?" he repeated.

"Surprise!" Gan Salin cried out, raising his hands. "Ta-dah! I present you, gravity!"

"Gravity?"

Jack looked around. His feet were steady on the tunnel that had seemed vertical from outside the door. From inside, where he stood, what seemed vertical was the Village Ring's ground.

"This tunnel warps gravity," Nauja explained. "Instead of pulling you down, toward the center of the planet, it pulls you sideways."

"It doesn't feel like I'm sideways," Jack said.

"It's all relative," she said. "Get used to the feeling. There's a bunch of this in Space Ring—or so I've heard."

"There is indeed," Salin agreed with a grin. "The Space Ring is very fun."

"Really?" Jack raised a brow. "Is that the word people use to describe it, or is it just you?"

"Well, just me, but I'm plenty. The others just call it impressive."

"No kidding." Jack glanced back to the Village Ring that had turned sideways. "I'm looking forward to it."

Like in every tunnel so far, there was a basket of torches at the entrance. Brock grabbed one, lit it with a snap of his fingers, and led the way. The rest of them followed.

Jack prepared himself for a long trek. Belatedly, he realized he'd forgotten to check the new skill he'd received after his fight with Bocor.

Iron Fist Style II: You have surpassed the limitations of mortal forms of combat. Your body is infused with the Dao of the Fist. Reality bends before the Dao.
The Iron Fist Style is the spine of its user. It allows you to combine all your skills, weapons, and resources, integrating them seamlessly into one fighting style.

The first paragraph had just been condensed a bit. As always, the real change compared to the previous tier of the skill was italicized.

Would you look at that, Jack thought. So it better integrates the rest of my skills. Is it because I used all of my skills while fighting Bocor? Or because I finally developed enough of them for Iron Fist Style to utilize?

I wonder what the next tiers will be.

In any case, it was a welcome improvement, the fruit of his hard training against Copy Jack. More strength was always good. Especially when he was hunted by Longsword.

The rest of the trip went by in silence, spiraling down and down the tunnel. However, the trip didn't last long. Only a few minutes of jogging later, light appeared at the end of the tunnel.

"What?" Jack said in surprise. "But we just came here." He squinted to see past the open door at the other side. Before he could manage, Salin pushed him from behind.

Jack tumbled into the door. He was assaulted by the same disorienting feeling as before. Gravity changed directions again, and suddenly, he found himself standing on gray stone, surrounded by colossal sun mushrooms that threatened to blind him. The door he'd just passed through was flat on the ground next to his feet. He saw Gan Salin, Brock, and Nauja walk on the wall like it was nothing, then stumble and rotate sideways as they crossed the door.

"We're on the ceiling of the Space Ring," Nauja explained after reorienting herself. "It feels like we're standing on the ground, but we're actually upside down. That's why the tunnel was so short. It only had to cross the few miles of stone between the two rings, not go all the way to the floor."

Jack wasn't really listening. He was captivated by the majesty of the Space Ring. It was absolutely surreal.

CHAPTER SIXTY-TWO

SPACE RING

THE SPACE RING PUT ALL PHYSICS JACK KNEW TO SHAME.

It was a vast expanse of space, stretching so far he couldn't see the end. The sun mushrooms pierced the darkness, illuminating little colorful bubbles, tiny compared to the vastness surrounding them, slowly floating through.

Jack could see a forest, a valley, an icy tundra, even an active volcano encircled by an archipelago of stone islands. It was like someone had uprooted pieces of the terrain, put them in bubbles of air, and sent them floating through Space Ring. The outline of each bubble was visible as a transparent, yellow-greenish veil, like a soap bubble reflecting the sunlight.

"What am I looking at?" Jack asked, lost in wonder.

"Behold, the Space Ring!" Gan Salin said proudly, stepping beside Jack and putting an arm over his shoulders. The other arm motioned widely at the view before them. "The only place in the galaxy where space is *inside* a planet!"

"But... How? And why? And what are those?"

"Those, my friend, are bubbles."

Jack glared, so Nauja took over explaining. "The Space Ring is the most fascinating place in Trial Planet. Every bubble you see contains a small biome, anywhere from a few feet to many miles in diameter. The bubble-ish border you see around them separates them from the void. Furthermore, each bubble has its own gravity, as do the ceiling and floor of this ring."

"How could someone make this?" he wondered aloud.

Nauja shrugged. "Nobody knows. Even B-Grades don't have this kind of power. And for whatever magic maintains this place to remain intact for a million years..."

She didn't finish her sentence, but the meaning was clear. Jack turned his eyes back to the floating bubbles. Each was tilted at a random angle, making it seem like there were a dozen different worlds floating through this space. Perhaps there were.

It was awe-inspiring.

On cue, blue screens flashed before Jack's eyes.

Congratulations! Title "Third Ring Conqueror" upgraded to "Fourth Ring Conqueror!"
Efficacy of all stats: +15% → +20%

Space Ring (1) Quest:
• Claim an Inheritance for any member of your team.

Space Ring (2) Quest:
• Complete the Space Ring (1) Quest.
• Slay an Elite space monster.
• Make your way to Labyrinth Ring.

Jack felt the familiar surge of strength through his body, using it to ground himself.

"Why do I have two quests?" he asked.

"Space Ring is actually two rings," Salin explained. "Don't ask me why. Maybe it's because of the size. In any case, the first quest will give you the Fifth Ring Conqueror title, and the second will give you the Sixth Ring Conqueror."

"Really?"

"But in exchange, Space Ring is twice wider than all others," Nauja added. "Two hundred miles of space and biome bubbles."

"And space monsters," he replied. "The quest said so."

"Yep, it's teeming." Salin nodded. "Anything from middle E-Grade to Elite and King monsters. There are D-Grade ones, too, though they never emerge from the dark areas."

"Terrific." Jack licked his dry lips. "The first step is to get one of those inheritances. I suppose they're the same things as the Trials you've mentioned before, Nauja?"

"Right. Inheritances are the rewards of Trials."

"Then, what are we waiting for? Longsword could come after us anytime now—even if he said he'd wait till morning. The deeper we are by the time he arrives, the better. And, Nauja... I assume you're coming with us, right?"

She blushed, the red striking on her naturally pale face. When they arrived at the Village Ring, she was still entertaining thoughts of returning to her tribe. She hadn't mentioned that since.

"Yes," she finally admitted. "This may not be the wisest decision... but I believe the will of my ancestors brought us together. I will come with you as deep as I can."

A shadow passed through her eyes. Jack saw it, but chose not to comment.

"I'm glad," was all he said, smiling warmly. He turned to the bubbles again. There was a large stretch of space separating them from the first one. "Any idea how we can get there? Last I heard, E-Grades couldn't survive space for long." *And Brock is still F-Grade*, he added in his thoughts.

He hadn't seen it at first, but there was also a bubble around them and the entrance tunnel. It wasn't big, just a few tens of feet across, but enough to let them breathe and walk freely.

"Are you blind?"

Salin pointed behind them, where a small basket was placed by the entrance tunnel. It contained familiar helmets, similar to the one he'd used on the *Trampling Ram*. Jack grabbed one, turning it in his hands, thinking back to the couple weeks he'd spent touring the stars with Captain Dordok and his crew. The helmet resembled a head-sized fishbowl.

I hope they're okay... he thought. He still didn't know how the *Tram-*

pling Ram's face-off against the Hounds had turned out. All he could do was hope.

"This is very handy," he said, referring to the helmets. "Trial Planet has it all figured out."

"Not Trial Planet," Gan Salin corrected. "The Hand of God. They're the ones supplying the torch baskets at every exit tunnel, as well as the helmets here."

"Really? How nice of them."

"Yeah... Otherwise, this ring would be ten times as difficult to cross."

"Say that again."

Jack put on his helmet, securing the clasp under his chin, and felt the familiar bubble-ish barrier surround his body, isolating him from the outside. The others did the same. Brock couldn't find a helmet small enough to fit him. The best he got was one that made him look like a child wearing his father's clothes, but at least the barrier worked just fine.

Brock was extremely excited. He'd never had a chance to enter space while on the *Trampling Ram*.

They leaped.

Jack pushed through the bubble headfirst, feeling only the slightest resistance. It was like surfacing from the sea. The next moment, he felt the subtle but distinct influence of space around him.

Some things could be felt even through the helmet's barrier. It was cold. Either whoever made this place had purposely imitated the cold of interstellar space, or low temperature was a characteristic of the extremely low-density void.

Jack's education made him bet on the latter.

Gravity had disappeared, too. Looking down—or where down used to be a moment ago—Jack saw the ground—which was actually the ring's ceiling—stretching far around him, its curvature discreet but clearly distinguishable. It was covered in sun mushrooms, only half of which were currently lit, radiating light so intense it made him look away.

On the other side stretched vast, deep darkness. Only the occasional bubble reflected the mushroom light, making them resemble small stars. No light came from the depths, where the inner side of the ring lay.

Brock was fumbling near Jack, slowly rotating around himself with growing panic. He had no way to control his flight.

Jack laughed—only he could hear the sound inside his barrier—and flew over, using small explosions of Dao to propel himself. He grabbed Brock and set him straight. The brorilla's grateful look was priceless.

Come to think of it, Brock can't expel Dao at the F-Grade, Jack realized. I'll have to carry him.

With a few quick hand gestures, he got Brock to hold onto his back.

Gan Salin was familiar with moving in space. He performed a couple somersaults before pointing and laughing at Nauja, who flailed around ineffectively. Her face hardened at Salin's mocking, and she pouted, but was unable to control her flight.

Then, her eyes noticed Jack flying over to save Brock. After a moment of experimenting, she got it, and managed to straighten herself. She then waved a fist at Gan Salin and angrily shouted something, but Jack couldn't hear her.

Despite her apparent anger, her eyes were filled with excitement. It was easy to forget that this confident, easygoing barbarian girl had never been outside her tribe before—and she went almost directly to the Space Ring, one of the most impressive sights in the galaxy. If she didn't short-circuit out of sheer awe, she would come to love traveling even more than she currently did.

On Jack's side, seeing her half-clothed body—she only wore fur around her privates and chest—floating in space was a contrasting feeling. His mental image was still that of Earth's astronauts, covered head to toe in bulky uniforms.

After some minutes of orienting themselves, the group set out toward the nearest bubble. Nauja turned out to be the fastest, followed by Jack, and then Gan Salin. Her Dao—Wind—was the most suitable for moving in space. Jack could make do with small explosions, and Gan Salin—

Jack actually had no idea how the canine was moving. He had to remember to ask.

Even the nearest bubble was several miles away, but that wasn't a problem. In space, there was no force slowing them down. As long as they managed to accelerate—which they could easily do—the distance would evaporate.

———

Vlossana fell to her knees. Her mouth hung open in abject horror. Her eyes widened and forgot to blink. Her face went pale.

The smoking ruins of her home lay in front of her, at the base of the hill. The manor was broken. The horses, dead. The servants' bodies piled up and still smoking from the fire. The garden was upturned and destroyed.

And all this, why? Because Jack Rust boarded their starship. Because the Animal Kingdom found out. They didn't care if Vlossana's father was an accomplice or not. Their semblance of proof was enough to conduct atrocities. To set an example.

This "example" was the destruction of everything Vlossana had ever known. She'd rushed over the second the *Trampling Ram* made it to the next port, but she was too late. Of course she was. All she managed was to witness the fatality with her own eyes, the heads of her relatives stuck on wooden stakes, the remains of the place she used to call home.

All her dreams, of leading her people to joyful, happy lives, turned into smoke and flew away, disappearing forever. Her life was ruined. So was her mind.

Not a soul was in sight to share her agony.

Vlossana raised her head to the sky and screamed. Her voice tore her own throat, but she couldn't feel it. She was lost in grief.

The Dao Seed of Joy inside her tried to lift her spirits. To feed her joy, as it always did. But there was no joy to be found here. No happiness. No warmth. Only death and ashes.

In anger, Vlossana turned to the only target she had—her own, persistent Dao—and cracked it down the middle, forsaking her path. It went quiet, and she remained full of sorrow, not even close to having vented.

All that dark energy amassed inside her, wound into a tighter and tighter ball, spreading over the large crack she'd inflicted on her Dao Seed—her soul—and filling it in. Drowned in darkness, Vlossana missed the notification sound, but she sensed the change.

In a mere moment, she developed and fused the Dao Root of Sorrow. It contrasted her Dao Seed of Joy, filling in its blanks. Together, the two formed a new entity, one she couldn't yet decipher, but one that was far more powerful than she used to be.

She surrendered everything to it. Anything to escape this feeling.

Vlossana's emotions fell into place. The empty shadow didn't disappear. It receded into her soul, becoming a dark presence that poisoned her thoughts and waited to be unleashed. Her joy covered it up, concealing it, her Dao Seed reduced to a thin, fake veil of joviality.

Vlossana wiped her eyes and stood. Her overwhelming sorrow had been transformed into a steady trickle she could endure—a trickle that would not heal with time. Then she walked away. There was nothing here for her anymore.

She didn't know what to do next. The nearest teleporter, where she'd just come from, was a day's walk away. She had time to think.

All she knew was that she had two enemies. The Animal Kingdom...

...and Jack Rust.

CHAPTER SIXTY-THREE
BUBBLE TERRAIN

JACK, NAUJA, GAN SALIN, AND BROCK HURTLED THROUGH OPEN SPACE, approaching a large number of biome bubbles. The curved, sun mushroom-filled ceiling was on their backs. It felt like a descent into darkness.

There were three bubbles near them. One was a wide grassland, maybe a mile in diameter. The second was a valley, complete with cliff walls on either side, while the third was a barren mountain peak, also a mile across.

Jack gestured at the three bubbles, asking, "Which?" They couldn't speak in space.

Gan Salin shrugged. Nauja also shrugged. Jack turned back to the three bubbles and chose the mountain peak—simply because it looked cool.

As they approached, more details became apparent. The mountain peak was a cone of bare stone, with rock fragments trailing under and behind it. There were weeds growing between the rocks, along with a single, stubby tree on the very top. Jack spotted no animals or other points of interest.

The mountain peak floated lazily through space, heading in the direction Jack perceived as right, and it was smaller than he'd originally assumed. Only a few hundred feet across.

No space monster attacked them. There was no hint of movement in the dark nooks of space, no sudden tentacle reaching to grab Jack's ankle.

They slid into the bubble with a popping feeling. The membrane bent by their pressure, then opened and let them pass before closing behind them. The four of them fell ten feet to the rock below, and Jack quickly removed his helmet to take a deep breath.

"Fascinating," he said, breathing out. "We're on a mountain hovering in space."

"Not really a mountain, not really space," Salin was quick to point out. "Buty fascinating, yes."

"Are you kidding?" Nauja spun around, greedily devouring the sight. "This is fantastic! I—It's the happiest day of my life!"

Salin stared at her, then turned to Jack. "Did she hit her head on the way?"

"She's just happy. She always dreamed of escaping her ring. For her, every new sight is an adventure."

"I see." Salin placed a hand on her bare shoulder. "Don't worry about it. I'm crazy, too."

She gave him a confused look. "I'm not crazy."

"Sure."

"What's that supposed to mean?"

"Is there anything here?" Jack asked, scanning the half of the mountain visible from where he stood. "Maybe there is a trial."

"This close to the entrance? No way." Salin shook his head. "This place gets visited often. I bet we won't find a single natural treasure, let alone a trial."

"Natural treasure?"

"You know, like Dao Fruits, or like that Fire Ice Lotus in the Integration Auction. Those things grow in most biomes, but the easiest to reach —and the most valuable—are already picked clean by cultivators. You'll have to go pretty deep to find anything."

"Oh... Then, are these early bubbles useless?"

"Pretty much." He shrugged. "But we can take a look. Who knows? Maybe everyone else missed something."

The four of them spread out to inspect the mountain peak. There wasn't much. It took them less than five minutes to search the entire bubble. Jack even broke the surface of the stone to look for hidden rooms underneath, while Nauja flew under the mountain peak to survey its bottom.

They came up with nothing.

The only point of interest was the stubby tree at the very top. It did radiate an aura of the Dao, but no apparent way to use it.

"Perhaps we should cut it down?" Jack asked.

"Oh, wow, and people call me insane," Salin said. "It's a *tree*. If you take a closer look, the aura of the Dao is focused on its branches. It probably produces fruits that hold special properties, but these things take time. We would need ridiculous luck to chance upon its blooming moment. Cutting down the tree would just ruin the treasure for everyone."

"Sounds exactly like something delvers would do," Nauja said.

"Not for zero benefit. What would you even do with its wood? Make an oar?"

"What if someone cultivates the Dao of Wood?" Jack asked.

"It doesn't work like that. If I pour my Dao into my fist, could you study it?"

Jack considered it. Salin's metaphor made an odd amount of sense.

"We'll find nothing out here," the canine said. "The aura of treasures is so thin that even space monsters are rare. If we want anything good, we'll have to head deeper."

"Why would cultivators leave the deeper treasures be?" Jack asked.

"Not on purpose. Each bubble you choose neighbors many deeper ones. As a result, the deeper you go into the ring, the more possible paths there are for you to take. The middle of Space Ring has thousands of bubbles, probably tens of thousands, and is teeming with space monsters. Even after a million years, this place isn't fully explored. And, even if it was, natural treasures regrow." He pointed to the tree. "If a bubble hasn't been visited in a few years, it usually has something interesting."

"What about Trials?" Jack asked, putting his helmet back on and securing the clasp underneath. "Do they regrow, too?"

"No." Salin smiled aggressively. "And that's the catch. Most of the weakest Trials never close—they are open to as many people as are interested, always. They don't offer anything too valuable, you see. But the good Trials... Those have finite resources. Only one or a few people can benefit from them before they collapse forever. It's why everyone pushes forward, deep into the darkness, looking for those elusive bubbles that promise greatness. It's also why Space Ring has the second highest mortality rate in all of Trial Planet. Cultivators are prone to greed, which gets them killed."

Nauja snorted. "Sounds about right."

"But... We *should* be greedy, right?" Jack asked. "If the best Trials are dangerous to reach, we have to risk it. Why come all the way out here to chicken out at the last minute?"

"That depends. For people like you, it's ambition. For people like me, it's greed." Salin smiled sadly. "Honestly, I'm already overperforming by reaching Space Ring. Someone like me should have died at the Barbarian Ring, or even the Giant Ring. At best, I should have taken the Village Ring's teleporter and returned to the surface. I don't belong here."

"Come on, man." Jack slapped his shoulder. "Don't be like that. You're a scion of the Animal Kingdom, remember? You were so promising they even sent you to Earth."

"Where I failed horrifically, and I've kept failing since... But I appreciate the cheering." He returned a bright smile, then put on his helmet. "Lead the way, boss."

Jack wanted to say more things. He wanted to encourage Gan Salin, talk him up a bit. But he also didn't want to lie. Salin was level 61. From what Jack had seen in the Village Ring, Salin may well be the weakest person in the entire Space Ring.

"Luck always plays a part," he finally said. "You're here now. And the opportunities we'll find will propel you to glory. Just keep your head up and don't die."

"I'll try."

Whether Gan Salin was cheered up or not—or even if he needed cheering up in the first place—Jack couldn't tell. His own helmet was already on. He grabbed Brock, who couldn't move through space by himself, ran to the edge of the mountain peak, and jumped out. The bubble easily gave way, breaking around him to reveal empty space.

Gan Salin and Nauja followed right after.

As Salin had mentioned, they now had another few bubbles to choose from, each taking them farther and farther away from the ring entrance. The horizon beyond was pitch-black darkness, an endless void where no stars were visible. It could stretch on forever.

The only source of light were the sun mushrooms behind them, whose glow steadily dimmed the farther one tread into the darkness, as well as the bubbles, which reflected the mushrooms' light like a series of small moons.

Jack's group headed ever deeper. The hours bled into each other. They crossed a number of bubbles—a grassland, a marsh, an odd, gas-filled landscape, and others—all invariably empty. The deeper into the ring they went, the dimmer the illumination grew, and they weren't even halfway to the other side—or so Salin said. Jack himself had no way to judge, as he couldn't see the other side.

In fact, with all the bubbles floating randomly in this three-dimensional space, and with each having its own gravity, it was easy to lose one's way. If someone wasn't careful, they could end up making circles around the circumference of the ring instead of heading deeper. The only anchoring point was the wall of light at the far back, away from which they kept heading.

They didn't discover any active Trials. The only one they found was a ruined cabin in the woods that exhibited an aura of the Dao so strong Jack could almost identify it. It felt like a lumberjack working away at a forest, one tree at a time.

The cabin was collapsed, though, signifying that it had already blessed as many people as it could. They had no choice but to move on.

Who created these Trials? Who gathered all these biome bubbles and put them into Trial Planet? How? Why?

Jack, of course, didn't know. Nauja didn't either, and even Gan Salin had no idea. In fact, he admitted that even the B-Grade factions didn't know much about Trial Planet—or, if they did, they didn't tell their junior members.

Regardless, every bubble they visited only served to enhance Jack's awe. The Space Ring was a masterpiece of unfathomable proportions. It was difficult to even imagine who could make such a thing. Even a God might have trouble creating this place.

On and on they trudged. From bubble to bubble, from the light into gradual, impenetrable darkness. They didn't meet any other people.

Space monsters began appearing after some point. They attacked with increasing frequency, but only one monster at a time. Nothing that Jack couldn't handle. The late E-Grade monsters were manageable with a bit of effort, especially with Nauja's assistance, whose arrows crossed space even faster than they did the air.

Whenever a middle E-Grade monster appeared—which was usually the case—Jack had Gan Salin go at it. The canine was strong for his level, as was every scion, so he could handle most of them. In the end, he even got a few levels for his trouble, rising to level 64.

Poor Brock was the only one who couldn't fight. Not only did he lack the strength to do so, but without a Dao Seed, he also lacked the means to propel himself through space. If he tried, the most he could achieve was flail ineffectively as he slowly floated through the void.

The moss-covered, ancient-looking Staff of Stone remained unused. Brock didn't complain—how could he?—but Jack felt growing sadness. His monkey bro hadn't been able to do much in Trial Planet. He must be feeling frustrated—useless, even.

Jack swore to help him as much as he could. Perhaps some natural treasures could increase his strength, at least by a bit.

All he could do was hope.

They lost track of time as they ventured deeper and deeper. At some point, as they stood inside a glacial biome, Nauja glanced back and raised her brows. "Look!" she said, pointing to the distance.

Looking back was hard due to the brightness of the sun mushrooms, but the distance dimmed the light. Jack obliged. As he did, he could barely make out a few small shapes, fighting in the backdrop of another bubble.

"What's that?" he asked, squinting.

"I can't make them out either," said Gan Salin.

"Yes," Brock agreed.

Nauja, whose senses were by far the sharpest, shielded her eyes with a hand and stared attentively. "It's Longsword. I can see him, the witch, and Bocor... They're fighting—I mean, annihilating—a horde of space monsters."

"They're here?" Jack asked worriedly. "Is it morning already?" The lord had promised his team would wait until morning to enter Space Ring.

"It probably has been for a while. They're way past the first bubble."

"I hope they don't follow us."

"I doubt they will. We're pretty far away. Longsword must have better things to do."

"I don't know... I did insult him a fair bit." Jack scratched his head.

"Well, at least they aren't on the same path as us. We didn't pass by that bubble. And we certainly didn't meet that horde. There are probably a dozen monsters there."

"I didn't even know there were hordes here with what we've seen," Jack said.

"There can be," Gan Salin said. "Space monsters are agitated by cultivators. If many of them enter the ring at once, monsters will gather like sharks to blood. In fact, hordes can get super-massive sometimes, to the point where even lords have to hide in bubbles and wait for them to pass."

"They can?"

"Totally. Well, not often, but I'll explain later. For now, the point is that there are many cultivators here."

Jack looked back to the faraway figures. "Seems like three to me."

"Longsword probably brought his allies over," Nauja explained. "It's the Garden Assault. It wasn't supposed to happen for a few days more, actually, but he probably grew impatient after everything that happened. If that's the case, there must be dozens of cultivators following Longsword, and the other lords could be here as well.

"The five of us—me, Rufus, and the others—were supposed to participate in this Garden Assault if *someone* hadn't destroyed us."

"Hey, you're the ones who invaded my planet."

"Does one of the other lords look like a young, tanned girl with the sun in her palms?" Nauja asked, looking at another spot in the distance. "And is she friends with a super fat guy?"

"Hmm? Yes!" Salin cried out in surprise. "How do you know?"

"Because they're right there."

"Oh. Well, we probably don't have to worry about them. That's Lady Priya, from—"

He trailed off, mouth gaping. The people Nauja had been talking about entered battle against another horde of space monsters. A massive golden palm appeared, so large that even Jack could see it clearly, to plow through the monsters. The fat man Nauja had mentioned was laughing.

And, in the wake of his attack, the girl struck. A terrifying explosion tore through the entire horde. A new sun was born.

CHAPTER SIXTY-FOUR
MEET THE LORDS

JACK AND HIS COMPANIONS COULDN'T SENSE THE AFTERMATH OF THE GIRL AND the fat guy's attack, but it must have been tremendous. The space monster horde had all but evaporated before them, sent flying by the giant palm or burned to cinders by the sun that erupted in their midst.

Thankfully, those people were so far away they were barely visible.

"As I was saying," Gan Salin continued, "that's Lady Priya of the Exploding Sun faction. One of the three lords."

"Exploding Sun?" Jack's ears perked up.

"Your master was part of them, correct?" Salin asked. "Then, I suppose these people are possible allies. We're in dire need of some."

"Right."

"The Exploding Sun are... less oppressive than the rest of them," Nauja added, hesitantly. "I could work with them."

"Or you could die," Salin probed her.

"I'm a proud barbarian. I am not afraid of death. What's that?"

Her finger was pointed far to the right of the Exploding Sun lady, something odd was going on. Jack had to squint to make it out. "Are the monsters fighting each other?"

"I don't think so," Nauja replied, staring intently. "It's like the space monsters are fighting a horde of... beasts? I think I see a bear. And a bird. Maybe an eagle?"

"Maybe they're animal-shaped space monsters."

"Or summoned beasts," Gan Salin intervened. Everyone turned to look at him. "If two of the lords are pushing into Space Ring, chances are, so is the third. And she's a summoner. That could be her."

"A summoner?" Jack asked, eyes wide.

"Did you notice a guy riding a scaled lizard back in Village Ring? An annoying-looking guy? That was a summoner, too. They use beasts to fight."

"It isn't common, but not too rare, either," Nauja added, her eyes hardening. "I've seen plenty in my ring. They like capturing dinosaurs."

"I can imagine..." Jack's voice trailed off. His eyes were still on the faraway battle between beasts and space monsters. In fact, calling it a battle was far-fetched. More like a slaughter.

The space monsters, their forms multicolored and easily visible, were ripped apart by the beasts. Before long, nothing was left.

"What faction is she from?" Jack asked. "This summoner lord."

There was a sinking feeling in his stomach. If she used animals to fight, could she belong to...

"It's not what you think," Salin said, chuckling. "The Animal Kingdom *is* animals. We actually despise summoners."

"Oh, thank God."

"However, the faction she comes from is even more terrifying. That's Lady Minerva from the Hand of God."

"I didn't know the Hand of God raised their own disciples," Jack said.

"Of course they do. They were formed to enforce the Star Pact, but that doesn't mean they aren't a real faction. They have businesses, headquarters, training planets, disciples, elders... All the good stuff."

"Then, are they the strongest B-Grade faction?"

Salin thought about it for a moment. "Yes and no. Technically, they possess the greatest military power, influence, and legal authority of all the factions. However, it's not like they can ever mobilize fully. To create the Hand of God, every other faction offered some people and resources. As a result, they all have influence on the Hand of God's internal processes, and the faction itself is a patchwork of several groups vying for dominance. If it ever went to war, there would be chaos."

"But it's already at war. Against the Black Hole Church."

"That's not the same. The Church isn't part of the Galactic Alliance. Just a bunch of strong lunatics."

"I see."

As Jack was leaving Earth, the Sage had revealed he belonged to the Black Hole Church. He'd also helped Jack a lot during the Tournament. Were they really lunatics?

Plus, Master Shol had told Jack that the Church worshiped the Old Ones—or something like that. The Ancient ruins where he'd found the Life Drop also had hints of people—the Ancients?—worshiping the Old Ones, which made little sense.

Could things be more complex than they seemed?

Jack almost laughed at himself. Of course they were. The Black Hole Church was one of the strongest organizations in the galaxy. They couldn't just be lunatics—it's just that, up there, everyone utilized propaganda.

Thinking of those matters reminded Jack that, at the very end of the Tournament, the Hand of God had turned a blind eye as the Animal Kingdom bullied him. Technically, they were his enemy.

He returned his gaze to the beasts, which were just finishing up the space monster horde. As a large monster tried to flank them, a burst of darkness swallowed it whole. When it receded, the monster was just flailing, shivering by itself in the darkness. The bear-shaped beast disposed of it easily.

"What was that?" Jack asked, referring to the darkness. It felt familiar, somehow.

"I can see the summoner. She isn't alone," Nauja said. "There are two people behind her. One of them unleashed that darkness we just saw."

"Right. So, they're strong."

"Of course they are."

Those Hand of God cultivators would probably turn out to be trouble.

Then again, maybe not. Jack didn't know exactly what happened between Galicia and Vocrich, and in any case, his enmity with the Hand of God was nothing before the hatred he shared with the Animal Kingdom. If fate made it so, allying may not be impossible.

Maybe he should look for a way to smoothen things between them. Having many powerful enemies at the same time was unwise.

"I'm surprised Lady Minerva is even here, actually," Gan Salin said. "I thought she would go bananas like the other Hand of God members."

"Bananas?"

"Little yellow fruit. Brock would love them."

Jack gave him an empty stare.

"Oh, maybe you meant, 'why do you say they went bananas, Gan Salin?' A few extra words wouldn't hurt you, you know."

"Just get on with it."

"Ugh." Salin grabbed his heart. "Whatever you say, boss. The Hand of God went haywire about a week ago. They spread all over the rings, asking strange questions and looking for something. It's the first time I've heard that happening."

Jack's heart clenched. "Strange questions?"

"Yeah. They asked if anyone had seen anything unusual in the last few days, if there were any suspicious people, things like that. Nothing that concerns us, right?"

That wasn't a rhetorical question. Salin may be partly insane, but he wasn't dumb.

"Of course not," Jack lied. "It's just odd. I wonder what's going on." He turned his gaze back to the distant battles, hiding his thoughts.

Are they looking for the Ancient ruins? he wondered. Probably. The System gave all sorts of red warnings. Goddammit. At least they don't know about me. And the voice in the trial said nobody can sense the Life Drop without special equipment.

This means I'm not in danger... right?

"By the way, not that I dislike peeping, but are we going to stay here long?" Gan Salin asked. "All of those lords are heading deeper as we speak. They might come this way."

"Right." Jack snapped out of it. "Let's run."

I'll just keep an eye out.

They left the glacial biome behind, jumping into the darkness. Space enveloped them. With every bubble they crossed, the light of the sun mushrooms dimmed until it was more twilight than blinding.

The Space Ring was enormous being comprised of two rings. Even in a straight line, they had to cross two hundred miles of monster-infested darkness. Despite that, the group wasn't beset by any hordes. Cultivators drew space monsters like moths to the flame, but Jack's group alone was too small a presence.

In that sense, they were lucky. Since most delvers had waited for the lords to start advancing for the annual Garden Assault, Jack's group was moving at the front by itself, almost stealthily. The other cultivators came as a stampede, raising the ire of every monster in this section of Space Ring.

It wasn't just the lords, of course. Each of them was followed by many teams, dozens of cultivators, who sought to participate in the Garden Assault.

As a result, Jack's team didn't have to worry about space monsters. The ones they met were few and far between, all handled easily by their team of four—effectively three—even if they were at the late E-Grade.

On the darker side, this meant fewer levels.

Over their first fifteen hours in Space Ring—thankfully, they had little need for sleep—Jack rose by four levels, to level 88. Salin got ten, stopping at level 74, and Nauja got two, reaching level 103. By that point, they were halfway through.

Space Ring was a tricky place. With all its bubbles, biomes, and trials spread around, it sounded like something that would take a long time to explore. In reality, the first half was picked clean. There were no natural treasures to find, no Trials to complete. Any trial still available was either low-quality or extremely niche.

Compatibility was a big concern when it came to Trials. They altered the cultivator, offering insights or assistance on a specific path. To someone cultivating a different path, this could actually be harmful. Even if you were on a compatible path, a low-quality inheritance could give you benefits that accelerated your current growth but became problems later on.

Therefore, just finding a trial meant nothing. You had to grasp its contents beforehand and decide whether it was suitable for you.

This was all insight that Gan Salin gave them on the way. Apparently, the first Ring Quest of Space Ring, completing a trial for any member of your team, wasn't easy.

Throughout their trip, the group had stumbled upon several Trials, none suitable for any of them. Most were empty, too, already claimed.

However, there were tens of thousands of bubbles. By now, the group had traversed dozens, carving out a path through space that was uniquely theirs. As they passed the halfway mark of Space Ring, they finally chanced upon a bubble that hadn't been visited in ages.

The air was dense here, rich in oxygen. A small hill rested in the middle of a grassland, with vines crawling all over its surface. Jack spotted a small rabbit chewing on the roots.

"Incredible," he said, staring at the little animal. "A rabbit. Here. How many centuries, how many millennia has its family spent in the darkness, in this mile-wide bubble?"

"Come here, little buddy," Gan Salin said, stepping forward. "Carrot noises. Carrot noises."

"What are you saying?" Nauja asked.

"Rabbits like carrots. Obviously, I'm making carrot noises to attract it."

"...I can't even begin to explain how stupid that is."

"Really? Then, why is the rabbit coming?"

The rabbit approached and sniffed them. Indeed, its family line hadn't seen cultivators for a thousand generations. They did not know to be afraid.

Nauja facepalmed.

Thankfully for the rabbit, Gan Salin didn't intend to harm it. He picked it up and hugged it, petting it between the ears. The rabbit seemed shocked. A moment later, it kicked its way out of his arms and rushed into a hole in the base of the hill.

"Okay, that was cute," Nauja admitted.

Salin smiled. "Animals indicate a healthy biome. Healthy means untampered. And untampered means riches for us. Hurray!"

He threw his hands in the air.

"Hurray," Jack followed half-heartedly. Brock did, too, but with great excitement. Nauja simply stared.

"Can we focus?" she asked. "Those lords are delayed by the hordes, but they're still after us."

"No worries. This deep in the ring, stumbling upon others is unlikely. If we run into a lord here, that's just bad luck. The next ring is where everyone will converge."

Since the bubbles were safe—space monsters couldn't enter, and there were no dangers inside—searching was quick and easy. It took the group only a few minutes to realize that the natural treasure here was the fruits of the vine. There were two of them, one on each side of the hill, radiating a strong, metallic life force.

They were red and pumped full of juices.

"Blood Dao," Nauja said, inspecting them. She plucked one off, holding it between her thumb and index finger. "Too bad none of us cultivates it."

"Look at the bright side," Salin said. "We can sell them off. I don't think they're strong enough for immortals, but they should fetch a good price."

These berries were similar to the Fire Ice Lotus that everyone had fought for during the Integration Auction. Perhaps not of the same quality, but still very useful. They contained naturally grown hints of the Dao.

"There's two of them," Jack said.

"Can I have one?" Nauja asked. "A tribe close to mine has someone with blood Dao. This could help them."

"Sure. Salin, want the other one?"

"Okay," the canine quickly agreed. "You get first dibs on the next one. We'll probably start finding things from now on."

"I hope so..." Jack said, turning to the darkness beyond. The light of the sun mushrooms had already dimmed to the point of moonlight on Earth. Even deeper into the ring, that gradually dimmed, to the point where the deepest reaches were completely dark.

The far side of Space Ring—the inner side—wasn't covered in sun mushrooms as the outer side was. That was where the greatest Trials and treasures waited, as well as the greatest dangers. According to Gan Salin, the darkness hid even D-Grade monsters.

The only exceptions to the darkness were a few distinct columns of light—the exits to the next ring. Each exit was surrounded by a small amount of sun mushrooms that projected a wide beam of light, like a beacon. That way, anyone wanting to reach the next ring could do it without braving the total darkness.

But that would mean losing out. And Jack didn't feel like losing out.

CHAPTER SIXTY-FIVE

THE DARKNESS AND THE FLARE

WITHIN THE FINAL ONE-FOURTH OF THE RING, WHERE THE SUN MUSHROOMS' light couldn't reach, fifty miles of pitch-black were crowded with the strongest, meanest space monsters around, and also treasures that nobody had accessed yet.

Jack, Brock, Nauja, and Gan Salin were currently skirting just outside its border. This area had biome bubbles that not many approached due to the danger. From this close up, Jack and his team occasionally caught glimpses of bubbles just inside, quickly assessing them to see whether any were worth risking for.

They had been exploring for two days now. They jumped from bubble to bubble, taking care of any attacking monsters as soon as possible to prevent them from piling up, and making good distance from the lords and their forces. According to Gan Salin, it was customary for a Garden Assault to spend five days in this ring, letting everyone reap the benefits they could discover, before progressing deeper.

However, exploring the Space Ring was more a measure of luck than skill or strength. The bubbles were simply too many. Their constant floating made mapping impossible. One had to go as deeply as they dared to increase their chances, then just keep searching.

The radius where Jack's team was currently searching was the optimal one. Nauja's gaze caught all bubbles within ten miles, and they also kept an eye on the darkness itself, where the best treasures and Trials might appear.

The monsters of Space Ring also had their own hierarchy. Some were elites. The weakest were peak E-Grade. According to Gan Salin, even meeting King monsters wasn't impossible. At least the D-Grade ones were so few and far between that running into them was highly improbable.

The stronger a monster became, the deeper inside it moved. The reason why was unknown—maybe they just preferred the darkness. Or maybe they were somehow trained to do so by whoever created them. After all, the density of space monsters here was far, far, *far* greater than in actual interstellar space.

The trip so far had been fruitful. Though they hadn't found a suitable trial for any of them yet—those things were stupidly rare—they had collected an assortment of minor treasures: berries with the Dao of Blood, herbs with the Dao of Life—that Jack kept for use later—a suspiciously sturdy rock, and even a little pebble that had a mouth and laughed whenever someone touched it.

The most precious treasures, like the laughing pebble, were even acknowledged by the System, letting Jack inspect them:

Ticklish Pebble
A pebble that laughs when touched. While possessing only minimal sentience, it is useful for cultivators pursuing the Daos of Laughter, Joy, or similar, as well as cultivators pursuing the opposite Daos, like Grief or Sadness.

Jack had kept this one, too, intending to gift it to Vlossana whenever —and if—they met again.

She's going to love it, he thought with a smile.

However, these treasures weren't too important right now. The greatest benefit was all the levels they accrued by fighting the space monsters.

Once again, Jack marveled at the efficiency of Trial Planet. Outside, people were willing to travel many planets away to find a late E-Grade monster. Here, they were common as dirt, letting everyone progress at unfathomable speed.

Jack was now level 89, Nauja was 106, and Gan Salin was 78. Their team's strength had taken a massive leap forward—and it had only been two days.

Of course, most of that was due to Jack being way stronger than his level indicated. In team fights, the other two benefited as well.

The only problem was that he'd stopped training much with the Dao Soul. After fighting constantly, he just didn't have the energy. Or the need. The Dao Soul's utility would shine when things slowed down.

On the third day, in one inconspicuous bubble—a forest biome that was unfortunately empty of treasures—Jack noticed something odd.

"Hey," he said, "is the light going down?"

Gan Salin's eyes widened. He'd been lounging on a log and singing, but he now shot to his feet. "Quick!" he said. "The flare is coming!" And he bolted off to the side of the bubble facing the darkness.

"The what?" Jack asked, already running after him. Nauja and Brock were a step behind, equally confused.

"The flare!" Salin explained while running. "There are two sets of sun mushrooms. When one dims, the other lights up, and there is a short moment in between when both are lit. We must catch it!"

"Catch it for what?"

Jack remembered how, when he first entered Space Ring, only half of the sun mushrooms were lit. In hindsight, it made sense. Sun mushrooms had their cycle of day and night, as the previous rings had shown, and even the creators of Trial Planet didn't want to sink Space Ring in total darkness.

Though they'd been here for two "days", those were standard galactic days. The mushrooms' cycle lasted more than that—around three days.

"The darkness!" Salin shouted, reaching the edge of the bubble and stopping. In the dim illumination that reached this bubble, the canine's outline was the only thing visible. The space beyond was completely dark—that was the border of darkness.

Jack's eyes widened in realization as he approached. The light kept dimming, down to half its usual intensity, submerging them in total darkness. Jack could see nothing.

And then, in a bright flash, it was day. The second set of mushrooms flared to life before the first was done dimming. For a moment, every single mushroom on the ring ceiling was lit, illuminating places that usually remained hidden.

The light washed over Jack, extending beyond. He caught a glimpse of what lay ahead.

Dozens of bubbles, each reflecting the light like stars. Humongous shapes floating around them like schools of squid, space monsters at the peak and Elite levels. Jack even caught a massive, serpentine creature lazily drifting back and forth. A King.

However, he only spared a glance for the monsters. His eyes were glued to the bubbles. This was the real prize. They had a moment of visibility. They could see far more of the dark area than ever before.

He inspected the dozen bubbles as the light dimmed. He caught a volcano, a cloud, a lake. His heart skipped a beat with each, quickly assessing them and deciding if any were suitable for him or his team. Most of the bubbles sported at least some degree of human activity—ruins, towers, houses—the telltale sign of Trials. Moreover, these bubbles were close enough to the edge that they could make a run for them should the rewards be worth it.

However, as he scoured them, his stomach dropped. Not a single one felt suitable. There was nothing visibly pertaining to insanity—or anything to do with the mind—the wind, archery, working out, or fist-fighting. And one by one, the bubbles were swallowed by darkness again.

Jack hardened his heart and decided that the cloud one might be okay. They could give it a shot. Clouds were close to wind, right?

Then, the light flashed again. Not all mushrooms had come on at the same time. A small percentage were out of sync, and as they activated, they overpowered the dimming ones to push the light a little bit farther than its previous limit.

It was momentary.

But enough for Jack to glimpse one more bubble. A stone palace. Ancient-looking. Covered in moss and vines. With engravings on its side, large enough that he could make them out from here. Various animals were depicted, along with glyphs whose meaning eluded him.

The light receded. The border of darkness returned to its previous radius, but just that glimpse had been enough.

Brock gripped Jack's wrist. He'd noticed it, too. Jack looked down, but he wasn't looking at the brorilla. He was looking at the Staff of Stone, tightly gripped in Brock's hand. The staff made of ancient, moss-covered stone, with animals and glyphs engraved on it.

Even the feeling they gave off was similar.

"Brock," Jack said, "I think we found your trial."

"Yes, bro," Brock responded.

"Which one, which one?" Salin asked excitedly, and Nauja stepped in to explain. Her sharp eyes had naturally caught the resemblance, too.

"Are you sure we should go?" she asked after explaining to Salin. "I know this seems like fate, but it's just a random staff. Just because they happen to look similar doesn't mean they're related."

"A random staff? What do you mean?" Jack asked. "Have you never inspected it before?"

"I—No. It's inspectable?"

"Of course. How could you not know?"

"Brock is using it. We can't scan things used by others. Quick, Brock, put it down and let us see."

"Huh." Jack didn't know that. He tried inspecting the staff while Brock still held it, and indeed, he got nothing. It made sense in hindsight.

Brock set his weapon down and took a step back, letting them have a look.

Staff of Stone, Life Weapon (D-Grade)
An Ancient weapon that utilizes the Dao of Density to adjust its weight, matching the wielder's strength perfectly. Its max density is suitable for anyone with up to 1000 attribute points in Strength. Carved and enchanted by Bozdom the Crafty.

"Woah, an Ancient artifact!" Salin cried out. "That's impressive! Where the hell did you find it?"

"In a random anthill in Giant Ring," Jack replied absent-mindedly. It was the first time he noticed that the "Ancient" part of the description was capitalized, indicating the Ancient race instead of just the age of the staff. The previous time he'd read this description, he didn't even know about the Ancients, so he naturally ignored the capitalization. Now, it was a wealth of information.

"You lucky bastards," Salin said, laughing. "Ancient artifacts aren't too rare in Trial Planet, but not common, either. I'm surprised you have one."

Brock picked up the staff and held it protectively.

"I take that back," Nauja said. "I didn't know the staff was an artifact. The two are clearly related. If the staff contains the Dao of Density, we can assume the palace has a trial related to a similar Dao. And since Brock is obviously well-suited for it..." She looked at the brorilla. "I guess we found our trial."

Jack was beyond elated. Brock's progress had been a thorn in his heart for a long time. Now, with a chance that could potentially skyrocket his little bro's power, there was no way they'd let it slip.

Maybe Brock would even form a Dao Seed.

"We still need to find a way over," Nauja said. "That bubble was very deep in. If we just rush it, we might be overwhelmed on the way."

"True," Jack said. "Then, what do you suggest?"

"Thankfully, I also paid attention to the temple. I saw its movement. It was heading slightly deeper and sideways, in that direction." She pointed to the intended path. "And guess what's there."

A pillar of light rose in the distance, starting from the inner wall of Space Ring and forming a lit passage into the bright area, bypassing the darkness. It was one of the light beams that led to exit tunnels to the next ring.

The creators of Space Ring didn't want everyone dying as they blindly crossed the darkness.

"That's not just a passage," Nauja explained. "It's also a way to infiltrate the darkness. I think we can use it for more than just getting to Labyrinth Ring."

"Or, as I like to affectionately call it," Salin added, "Labyring."

Everyone stared blankly.

"What? I found it hilarious!"

CHAPTER SIXTY-SIX
BRAVING THE DARKNESS

LIGHT SPEARED THE DARKNESS, ILLUMINATING A LONG, MILE-WIDE AREA. A bright path stretching from the middle of Space Ring to an exit tunnel leading to the next ring.

As Jack's group found themselves flying through the light, he was stunned and speechless. Just a hundred feet away, the darkness was impenetrable. It could hide the richest treasures or greatest dangers of Space Ring, and nobody would know.

Bubbles occasionally floated through the light, entering from one side and disappearing at the other. They weren't fast enough to be dangerous, just impressive. Unfortunately, since no one could see them coming, and they were pretty rare, being at the right spot to catch one would be very difficult.

The space monsters never entered this area of light, just like they never entered bubbles.

There were many light beams like this, scattered around the inner side of Space Ring. Each led to an exit tunnel. Just one more stunning sight of Trial Planet.

Jack watched the walls—where bright light met pitch-black darkness—to the left and right as they flew. He imagined monsters lying just beyond. Tentacles shooting out to grab him and recede into the darkness, where space muffled the screams.

His enemies' screams, that is. Because he would punch them.

The main reason why he stared at the walls was that looking ahead, toward the base of the light beam, was painful for the eyes. According to Gan Salin, there were a bunch of sun mushrooms in a bowl-shaped alcove, guiding their collective light into this single column.

Suddenly, Nauja raised her hand. Jack and Salin slowed down beside her. Their communication came as hand signals to make up for the lack of sound in space, along with what they'd discussed before leaving the last bubble.

Nauja pointed down, indicating that this was the place. Then, her face taut in concentration, she turned to face a wall of darkness. She raised her hand. The moment she dropped it, they would have to dash.

Into the unknown.

Jack gulped. He distracted himself by admiring Nauja's abilities. He couldn't even tell how far away the palace bubble had been, but she managed to calculate its precise trajectory at a single glance. Thankfully, she had a skill about that. It was supposed to be used in archery, but there was no rule against using it on space-traveling air bubbles.

Still, it was damn impressive.

Nauja's hand shook a bit. Jack almost took off before catching himself. Between his arms, he felt Brock stiffening.

Her hand dropped.

Nauja was the first to tear into the void. She expelled air Dao from her back, propelling her fast without a single glance back.

A brave woman.

Jack and Salin followed. One after the other, they dived out of the light and into the darkness. Jack rushed to avoid thinking about it.

The feeling was like plunging into dark, cold water. Besides the noticeable change in temperature, Jack immediately lost his sight. He couldn't even see Gan Salin anymore.

He also couldn't speak. Couldn't hear anything. Couldn't smell. Couldn't touch. He was all alone in infinite, monster-filled darkness, with Brock being his only company.

For a moment, he was petrified before his Dao Root of Indomitable Will protested, propelling him into action. Jack could sense the hints of the Dao of the Fist he'd left behind, using them to maintain his sense of direction. He shot forward.

This was a gamble. According to Nauja, the bubble would be close to them, just a minute's travel through the darkness. They just had to hope there weren't any monsters in between, but monsters generally avoided the light. It should be fine.

Faint light came from behind him in the form of the light beam, but everything else was black. The light blocked by some property of space that Jack wasn't sure was magical or scientific. Probably magical. Light was supposed to cross the vacuum without degrading.

The seconds flowed on. Jack's blood drummed on his temples, the cold vise of fear tightening around his heart. He was short of breath.

He thought he saw faint, lumbering shapes. A tentacle-shaped patch of black deeper than its surroundings. A giant eye, barely distinguishable and very close-by. A hint of Dao coming from his left.

He didn't know if he was imagining those or if they were true. Darkness had a way to claim the mind, to upset and terrify it, make it materialize its fears to fill in the absence of visual input. Jack was aware of how the brain had evolved to work in the darkness, but all that did was enhance what he already felt: the dark was dangerous.

Has it been a minute already? he asked himself. He didn't have a clock. All he could do was count his own heartbeats, estimating them to be sky-high, but that wasn't accurate.

The plan was to find the bubble within a minute. Whoever found it first—the three were slightly spread out—would unleash a bunch of Dao to inform the others. If no one did, they had to turn around and rush back to the light.

At the E-Grade, their ability to sense the Dao was there, but very limited.

A little bit more, he promised himself, acutely aware that the bubble could be anywhere outside of his path, and he could diving headfirst into a bottomless pit. He wouldn't even see it, just sense the faint Dao that the bubble structure itself exuded.

For the first time in a long while, Jack wished he hadn't lost his phone. It had a flashlight.

Something wet and elongated slapped him out of nowhere. Jack was sent off his path, letting out a scream that only he could hear, spinning head over heels in the vacuum of space. He punched out where the hit had come from.

A purple meteor bloomed in the darkness, illuminating nothing. It flew farther and farther away from Jack, showcasing just how vast the blind void around him was, before it slammed into something. Jack caught a glimpse of a purple shape, a squid with tentacles jutting out all over its body.

It thrashed, likely injured. E-Grade space monsters were barely sentient sacks of Dao, and Jack sensed the Dao escaping, leaking out of the squid where the meteor had struck. He could track it now. In the absence of all light, his Dao sense was clearer than ever.

He sensed another beacon light up nearby. A twisted knot that screamed of confusion, persistence, and single-minded ramming into what didn't make sense. Insanity.

Jack realized that he, too, must be such a beacon. He also realized that, if he could sense them, so could the space monsters sense *him*. By fighting here, he was summoning everything within several miles, and the first monster was already here. His blood ran cold. They had to hurry. There was no time to search for bubbles. They had to retreat back to the light.

The Dao of Insanity collided with the squid and lost terribly. The monsters here were at least peak E-Grades. This was a high-level area. And Salin was only level 78.

The canine had been flung back from the impact, away from the light. Jack hesitated for only an instant before going after him. There was no time to think. He simply followed his instinct.

Was the squid chasing? Definitely. Jack twisted to the left, releasing a meteor that crossed the darkness, barely missing the source of the Dao leak—the squid's wound—and dissolving into nothingness a few hundreds of feet away. He cursed and tried again. A Meteor Shower bloomed in the darkness, a shining beacon for anything hungry, and went flying for the squid. It responded too late. Its body was pelted, the meteors smashing into its squishy flesh and ripping it apart, leaving gaping holes and open wounds.

The squid thrashed, trying to cope with its injuries. Jack reached inside his soul, tearing away the veil that kept the Life Drop's powers at bay, and felt himself grow larger and stronger, two arms sprouting under his armpits.

With a loud roar that echoed in his ears, trapped inside the helmet's barrier, he exploded through the void and after the still-flying Salin, whose trajectory hadn't changed in the slightest. He must have been unconscious.

With the power granted by the Life Drop, Jack accelerated fast. He reached the canine and grabbed him, then turned toward the light. The squid was retreating. It was probably too injured to fight. Jack felt a hint of relief.

Then again, since when did space monsters retreat?

Jack's eyes went wide as he glanced around, but there was only darkness. Then, something blocked the light in front of him. He hurriedly blocked with three of his arms—the fourth held Brock and Gan Salin—barely enduring the strike. It felt like getting struck by lightning. His entire body shook and jittered. He was sent flying, barely managing to right himself.

The void blossomed with electric blue light. An eel the size of a bus swam directly for him. Its eyes were red slits filled with malice, while lightning arced all over its body.

"Fuck," Jack said.

Space Monster, Level 124 (Elite)
Experts speculate that, when large quantities of the Dao are left undisturbed for a long time, they can spontaneously coalesce into a Space Monster. While this is a very rare occasion—

He had no time to read the description—he'd seen it before, anyway. He focused on the monster's level and its Elite tag.

Going after the palace had been a calculated risk. But calculated risks sometimes backfired. Now, he had to fight his way through and hope to survive.

Jack's body erupted with power. His three Dao Roots were brought to the fore, blending with his Dao Seed of the Fist to unleash the greatest strength he'd ever revealed. The eel was almost blindingly fast, but his brain was processing things so quickly that he could follow its movements. The world had slowed down.

Power gathered in his arm, suffusing it. He let it rip. A blinding meteor exploded on the eel's nose and pushed it back. Jack's remaining two free fists also smashed out, each hitting the eel at full power.

It hadn't expected that. In its senses, Jack was weak. It had underestimated him.

Still, a few surprise strikes weren't enough to take down an Elite. This monster was far stronger than Jack's last real opponent, Bocor, had been. It absorbed the recoil and wound around him, seeking to entrap him in lightning. Jack kept punching. One meteor led to another until a shower was formed. The eel's slick skin made the strikes slide off, but their real purpose was to achieve momentum. Jack was propelled backward at absurd speed, escaping the eel's encirclement and flying into the darkness, toward the light. He'd managed to turn around the first time he hit it.

The eel pursued. Faster than he could ever be. It was upon him in an instant, opening its jaws wide and biting down. Jack smashed out above his head, altering his trajectory downward and barely escaping its jaws, which clamped shut right above him.

His entire body leaned into an uppercut. Unfortunately, as there was no ground to stand on, its power was limited. His fist dug into slimy, slippery skin. The eel's head jutted upward, but it wasn't too injured.

Right then, wind invaded the void. It was fast and straight, like an arrow. No—it *was* an arrow.

An arrow made of wind came out of nowhere to strike the eel, embedded deep in its eye. It raised its head and screamed a Dao-infused cry that resounded even in the vacuum, then swiped its tail at Jack, who Ghost Stepped out of the way. It took a lot out of him. That skill was best used on solid ground, and not with the weight of two others tagging along.

His Dao perception expanded. He tried his best to push it out as far as possible but felt nothing. Still, he'd seen the arrow's direction. He knew where it came from. It was sideways into the darkness. He kept shooting out punches to head that way.

Then, he felt it. A hint of the Dao, like a gentle breeze caressing his skin. Nauja was somewhere over there, no doubt unleashing her power as strongly as possible to make him sense her. Jack spared a second to focus.

She was moving. Slowly, smoothly, and laterally along the light beam. Why would she be moving that way?

Because she'd found the bubble.

That was the plan. Since they all moved at different speeds, whoever found the bubble would galvanize their Dao as intensely as possible to let the others sense it and fly over.

Jack oriented himself at Nauja. However, that moment of focusing on her had given the eel an opening. It jammed its head forward and headbutted him. A strong electrical current flowed through his veins. His entire body seized. All four fists clenched by themselves.

Thankfully, Jack's momentum was already going, and there was nothing to slow him down in space. He kept flying backward, further propelled by the eel's strike. The pain was burning him from the inside out, but he'd been through worse. He refused to yield. He forced his twitching muscles to obey. His Indomitable Body purged the lightning.

"AHHH!" Jack roared. Three of his arms blurred as he shot out another Meteor Shower, pelting the eel with his full strength. It weaved through the attacks, sliding them off its skin, but some struck true. One found it at the nose, another under its chin, one at the side of its tail.

Jack had his front toward the eel and his back at Nauja's presence, using his meteors to simultaneously keep the eel at bay and accelerate backward. Already, his speed was incredible, though he had no way to perceive it in the void.

Unfortunately, the eel was even faster.

CHAPTER SIXTY-SEVEN
REACHING THE BUBBLE

A SECOND ARROW PIERCED SPACE TO ACCURATELY LAND ON THE TIP OF THE EEL'S nose. Jack sensed the Dao of Lightning leak out. The eel shook its head and chased him with renewed effort. They exchanged strikes. He was on the losing end, but not by much. His punches caved its flesh almost as much as its lightning charred his, but he had the Indomitable Body and Life Drop's regenerative properties, and the eel had nothing. Its greatest weapon, the lightning's lingering effects, was countered by Jack's Indomitable Body.

Jack was losing, but the situation was growing more manageable.

Additionally, the closer he approached Nauja, the denser the arrows came. They pelted the eel like a second Meteor Shower, not particularly strong but exceptionally accurate. Nauja's marksmanship was impeccable—as she'd revealed, she could adjust the trajectory of her wind arrows mid-flight.

Many arrows still missed, but a few hit the mark. They distracted the eel, causing a small but considerable amount of damage. It couldn't slide off the piercing arrows like it could Jack's fists. Moreover, since the eel was physically larger than Jack, Nauja could hit it without worrying about hitting her ally.

Her strength may not have been on par with Jack's or the eel's, but this was the perfect situation for an archer to excel.

Jack was charred and injured. He'd been electrocuted a dozen times already. His regeneration worked overtime to combat the lightning, but the eel wasn't much better. It didn't regenerate nearly as fast. Its wounds accumulated until its attacks slowed down.

Being an Elite, it had a hint of intelligence. It could choose to retreat when things went south.

Jack was almost at the bubble now. His body was tattered, but he'd managed to protect his helmet—which was highly durable, anyway—as well as Brock and Gan Salin. Sensing the eel slow down, he hesitated.

He could keep going and escape inside the bubble.

Or...

Or he could try to kill the eel.

They had to kill an *Elite space monster* for the Sixth Ring Conqueror title. These monsters were found almost exclusively in the darkness. The eel was already heavily injured. When would he find a better opportunity than this?

Plus, this was his chance to gain so many levels.

Jack found himself letting go of Gan Salin and Brock. The bubble was slow, and his current trajectory was accurate. There was obviously no monster in between, or Nauja's arrows would have been intercepted, and neither Salin or Brock released any Dao right now. To the space monsters, they were invisible. Jack was certain they would reach the palace bubble.

He fully released them both.

Then, he turned around and started punching. His momentum lessened until it reversed. He was flying *at* the eel now, not away from it. Behind his back, the arrows kept coming.

The eel hadn't imagined Jack would return, but it charged him, undeterred.

There was a difference between letting prey go and cowering from a challenge.

Jack and the eel got entangled into a violent dance of punches and lightning. Teeth snapped. A tail swiped. Arms blurred in the light of sparks. Meteors blossomed on slick skin, each strong enough to demolish a hill.

Arrows rained from behind, some missing but a few hitting their mark. The eel leaked Dao from all over its body. Jack was exhausted but still regenerating. The crippling lightning had little effect on him now.

As the eel opened its jaws to bite down on Jack, he Ghost Stepped under it. When its upper jaw met the lower one, pushing it down, Jack smashed up with all his strength. His fist shone purple. The lightning was sucked in, then exploded. A hole was ripped clean through the beast's underjaw, into its mouth, and up from its snout. Dao streamed out like a broken dam.

The eel shook once, then its lightning began to dim. Jack felt the void get charged as so much Dao escaped. His skin was tingly. He braced himself for another attack, breathing heavily, but none came. The eel went still.

Finally, the notifications began to stream in.

Congratulations! You have reached Level 90.
Congratulations! You have reached Level 91.
Congratulations! You have reached Level 92.
Congratulations! You have reached Level 93.

He allowed himself a smile before reorienting on Nauja and rushing over. She wasn't too far away now.

He let the Life Drop transformation fade away. He also used Brutalizing Aura on the way, just to be sure, but it was unnecessary. Whether because they gave space to the eel or because of blind luck, there were no other monsters nearby.

Jack could make out light in the darkness. A torch illuminated the wall of a palace and the side of a courtyard, surrounded by a shimmering, transparent, green bubble. A pale-skinned archer with fur clothing over her privates stood at the very edge of the bubble, bow drawn and poised to shoot, while a young brorilla held up a torch and anxiously waved it from side to side. Gan Salin lay unconscious between them.

The archer lowered her bow when she saw him. A bright smile blossomed on her face.

Jack wanted to make a hero entrance. He tried to slow down, but he miscalculated. He flew into the courtyard at high speed and smashed into the wall beyond, collapsing a small, stone structure that could have been a garden shack.

He lay among the debris, sprawled out. "Ow," he said. Nauja burst out laughing.

"Hit your head there, warrior?" she asked.

"A bit." He rubbed the back of his head. His entire body was banged up after the fight. There was lightning in his veins, he had several deep burns all over, as well as deep purple bruises where the eel's tail had hit him.

His mood, however, was through the roof.

"Did you see that?" he asked. "We beat an Elite monster!"

"Yes!" she replied, equally excited. "If Father knew, he would be so proud."

Brock cheered, too. He twirled his staff in the air and hopped up and down, performing a brorilla celebratory dance.

"However," Nauja's voice carried a hint of warning, demanding Jack's attention. "You used the Dr—That thing, right?"

"...Yeah. Could you tell?"

"Could I *tell*? You *erupted* with the power of life! If I hadn't seen it before, I would have thought you got swapped with an immortal mid-battle."

Jack grimaced. "Was it that bad?"

"Let's just say it's good you made it back. This area should be teeming with space monsters any second now. You must have drawn everything in a ten-mile radius."

They all looked outside. Darkness. Nothing could be seen... but that didn't mean space was empty. For all they knew, they could be surrounded by space monsters.

Well, not yet, but they soon would be.

"Will they stick around?" Jack asked. "If yes, that could be a problem."

The bubbles followed a circular trajectory around Space Ring. It wasn't completely set, but Nauja estimated theirs would approach the border of darkness or a light beam within the next few days. Now that they were *in* the darkness, they could see the light outside just fine, so they would know.

That plan would be severely complicated by a bunch of space monsters following them around like hungry sharks.

"How am I supposed to know?" she asked back. "I hope not. We need a way to find them, if they're close. We can't sense them unless they're injured, in battle, or producing light like your eel."

Jack considered it. Gradually, his eyes hardened. "We'll think on that later. It's not like the monsters can enter the bubble. For now..." He turned to the palace walls behind him. "We have a trial to face."

From up close, the palace was even more imposing. Tall stone walls rose a hundred feet, narrowing near the top to end in sharp-tipped domes. The architecture was angular, with even the curvature of the walls presented as a series of small steps. Moreover, moss covered the surface of the stone, partly obscuring the many large engravings. Lions, elephants, cows... All sorts of animals were depicted on the walls, a colorless series of lines carved in stone.

"How long do you think it's been since this place was built?" Jack asked, losing his breath.

"Millennia," Nauja replied, her gaze wandering. "Maybe more."

"Maybe more," Jack agreed. He turned to Brock. "What do you say, little bro? Are you ready to get stronger?"

Brock gave a toothy smile. "Yes," he said. His grip was tight on the Staff of Stone, and his short fur was raised with excitement.

"Good. The faster you complete the trial, the faster we'll be able to leave this place, once the bubble approaches the edge. And, if it doesn't, we'll make it."

There was a second way to escape the darkness. Technically, Jack, Nauja, and Gan Salin could push the bubble toward a direction. It would be slow, and it would attract a whole bunch of monsters, which is why doing such a thing was only plan B.

"I agree," Nauja said. "Let's find the trial and get you started as soon as possible."

"What about Gan Salin?" Jack asked. The canine was still unconscious. That first space monster, the squid with too many tentacles, had gotten him good.

Nauja threw him one look and shrugged. "It's safe here. Let's just wait for him to get up. He has a healing skill, anyway."

Leaving Gan Salin to guard their belongings—mostly food and water, both from Village Ring and the various bubbles they'd visited on the way—the three of them headed deeper into the palace.

It wasn't big. The bubble only stretched two hundred feet from one side to the other, making it quite simple to locate the spot of the trial. In fact, the entire palace had a single room inside its walls: a spacious, empty courtyard filled with dead plants. A statue stood tall in its midst: a muscular man, intricately carved, raising a staff towards the sky. His features were hard, his gaze stony. He wore a mantle that reached his calves and a set of heavy armor that reminded Jack of ancient Chinese warlords.

The only oddity was his mouth, which seemed drawn into what could be a playful smile, but might also not be one.

"Hello, Mona Lisa," Jack said, reverently approaching the statue. Nauja threw him a questioning glance, then ignored him. Brock didn't even listen. His eyes were set on the statue's staff—an exact replica of the Staff of Stone.

"What are the chances?" Nauja said. "You say you accidentally found the weapon that corresponds to this exact trial. Are you hiding something, Jack Rust?"

"Bro!" Brock said, making an offended "what are you saying?" gesture at Nauja. She was stunned.

"I swear it's all true. We found the staff near a corpse in Giant Ring. This is just a large coincidence." Jack tilted his head. "Then again, we wouldn't be here if we didn't have the staff, would we? We would have just ignored the palace and chosen another bubble."

"Hmm."

But what could he say? To the best of his knowledge, it really was a coincidence. Therefore, he endured Nauja's suspicious glare and approached the statue. He found himself able to inspect it, and after a moment's hesitation, did so.

Trial Statue
A statue serving as the gateway to a Trial Planet Trial. Touch to enter.

"Fewer words next time, asshole," Jack grumbled. He didn't touch the statue, but he did approach enough to make out a small engraving at its bottom:

Ermedil Asantra. First General of the Low Sky.

"Well," he said, "no time like the present. Are you ready, Brock?"

The brorilla gathered himself and nodded.

"Let me warn you," Jack continued. "This will be difficult. The hardest thing you've ever done. You might die in there—and, if you do, I will be extremely sad. But you can survive, too. The trial will adjust to your strength. Try your hardest, and when you return, we will celebrate your triumph. Get stronger to fight by my side. I believe in you, bro."

Brock paused at that. He reached out to shake Jack's hand, then jumped into a hug. Nauja observed from a distance.

A moment later, Brock let go. He approached the statue, holding his staff with pride. He turned around to give a thumbs-up.

"See you, bro," Brock said, revealing two new words at the same time.

Jack smiled widely. His heart just about to break. Why was he this nervous? "Good luck, bro. I believe in you."

"Good luck, Brock!" Nauja cried out.

Brock nodded, touched the statue, and disappeared. His Trial had begun.

CHAPTER SIXTY-EIGHT
BROCK'S TRIAL

WHEN THE WORLD SETTLED, BROCK FOUND HIMSELF IN A LONG AND NARROW underground chamber. At least, it looked underground. There were no windows. He might as well be in a large stone box illuminated by a series of torches on the walls.

Said walls were covered in moss, like the outside ones, but the room's main point was the floor. Brock stood on a narrow ledge against one wall. A second ledge was against the far wall, with a closed door—the only door in the room.

Between the two ledges, the floor was about ten feet lower. Green, wooden poles rose sparsely from it, standing at about the same height as the ledges. At first glance, Brock got the instinct to jump from pole to pole to reach the other side. But there was no reason. The floor looked fine.

Of course, he would still jump on the poles, because it was more fun.

"Welcome, brave soul, to my Trial," a male voice boomed out. Brock jumped in surprise, almost dropping his staff, but there was no one around. He scratched his head in confusion as the voice continued unabated. "My name is Ermedil Asantra, First General of the Low Sky. My Dao is that of Force, but at the E-Grade, which Trial Planet is meant to test, I cultivated the Dao Seed of Density. Therefore, that is the Dao I will pass on to you!"

There was power in that voice. Deep, unshakable confidence, an edge that made Brock apprehensive. At the same time, there was also excitement. The voice spoke with a rush, like energy was bubbling from its throat.

Brock didn't get all the words. He got the point, though.

"I have composed a trial of three chambers," the voice bro continued. "The first chamber will test your balance, a necessary skill to master Density. You must make it to the other side by jumping on the tips of the bamboo poles. If you touch the ground, you will be eliminated and teleported out. I wish you luck!"

Then, it went silent. Brock scratched his head, squinting at the room ahead. He was already going to jump, for fun.

But Big Bro had taught him to be careful. Therefore, Brock decided to scout for traps. Reaching back, he grabbed a piece of poop and sent it hurtling through the room, crossing the hundred feet of space before landing on the other ledge with a dry *plop*.

No traps. Brock nodded to himself, deciding it was safe. Big Bro would be proud.

Therefore, tightening his grip on the staff, Brock jumped on the first bamboo—as the voice bro had called it. Landing was easy. However, the moment he did, the bamboo bent under his feet, leaning forward before swinging back again.

Brock made monkey sounds, almost losing his balance before steadying himself. He intuitively held his staff horizontally, helping him balance. The bamboo swayed, and even Brock's Elite F-Grade body couldn't handle this easily.

He rode the bamboo's forward swaying to leap to the next pole, which also began to sway. This time, he was ready. As it fell forward, he leaped again, crossing ten feet to land on the next one. He was prepared for it to sway again, so he leaned back. Unfortunately, this bamboo was treacherous. It remained steady.

As a result, Brock was falling backward. He windmilled his arms in the air to regain his balance, releasing worried monkey cries all the while, but he was too far back. As he slowly tipped backward, he pictured his big bro's disappointed face if he failed.

No. He was already dead weight. He couldn't fail here.

Brock's rotating arms moved faster like a whirlwind. He used them as oars, pushing the air back so fast that his tipping slowed. At the same time, he channeled the Big Thought in his heart. An entire line of muscles, from his heel to his butt, to his spine and neck, all clenched at the same time. His toes hugged the edge of the bamboo with all their strength, and with massive effort, he pulled himself straight.

He heaved a sigh of relief, wiping sweat from his forehead. Then, he narrowed his eyes at the rest of the poles.

This bamboo was crafty. But he refused to fail. He could do it. Like everything else, balance was a muscle, and he had the Big Thought of Muscle.

Focusing on his balance muscle, Brock jumped again, ready to respond to the pole. This one swayed. Brock was using his Big Thought now, controlling his body's muscles perfectly, so he wasn't fazed in the slightest. He leaped from this pole to the next, which did not sway. Brock took a second to steady himself, but he was okay. Like that, he kept going.

There were no other tricks to the bamboo poles. Some swayed, and some didn't. Brock reached the far ledge without a problem, landing right next to his thrown poop. He considered taking it with him, to not soil this place, except it had tricky bamboo. It deserved to be pooped.

He opened the stone door and entered the next room. This one was narrower, almost a corridor, and only ten feet across. There was nothing wrong with the floor or walls, but instead of a door leading farther in, a massive boulder blocked the exit, wide enough that it occupied almost the entire width of the corridor.

"Congratulations! Your balance must be outstanding! And if you flew your way across, well, flying requires balance, too!" the voice bro returned. Brock nodded gracefully, accepting the praise.

"Yes," he replied.

"This chamber will test your strength—the opposite end from balance. Both are required to master density. Starting now, you have one minute to lift the boulder, which is adjusted to your current level, and reach the final chamber. I wish you luck!"

Brock knew how long a minute was. Big Bro had taught him. But it was too little! This voice bro was stupid!

Frantic, Brock rushed to the massive boulder blocking the exit. It was wider than his two arms stretched to the limit, and it rose above his head. How was he supposed to lift it?

Thankfully, Brock had practiced at the forest gym with Father and the other bros. He knew how to lift. Holding the Staff of Stone in his mouth, he bent down and slipped his fingers under the rock. Keeping his back straight, he lifted with his knees.

Instantly, he felt the boulder's crushing weight. It was so heavy he could barely raise it a couple inches, and his arms were already burning. So were his thighs.

Again, the consequences of failure passed through his head. He would be left behind. He would have to abandon his big bro or pull him down. He would be useless. A burden. And his big bro would be disappointed at Brock's failure.

He did not want to be discarded. Failure was not an option.

Brock channeled the Big Thought again. He believed in the muscles of his arms and thighs, encouraged them to work harder. *Help me, muscle bros!*

Inch by inch, the boulder rose. Brock's neck muscles tightened, bringing him fear, but he used his bravery muscle to overcome it. Exhaustion crept in, tempting him to give up, but he used his resolve muscle to silence it. His vision started to waver, but he just flexed his eye muscles.

When his arms went numb, his waist was compressed, and his legs were on the verge of giving in, he reinforced all those muscles with the Big Thought.

The boulder finally rose to Brock's chest. Now, he had to pass under it.

With slow, small steps, he inched forward. He ducked his head under the boulder, transitioning its weight from his arms to his shoulders and neck, letting it rest there fully for a moment as he repositioned his arms to push up with his palms.

Thankfully, the forest gym practiced all sorts of heavy lifting.

Slowly and carefully, taking good care to maintain proper form, Brock rolled the weight over his shoulders until he was halfway through. Then, he simply let it roll away as he jumped to the other side.

He escaped the crash. Only the tip of the Staff was caught under the boulder, but Brock simply yanked it out.

His entire body burned, but he'd made it through.

"Congratulations! Your strength is surely outstanding! And, if you somehow cheated my trial, well, shame on you!"

The voice bro was here, as always, though Brock couldn't see him. Maybe he was hiding in the walls.

"You have proven your balance and strength, but density is more than its extremes. You must be able to transition between them and use them fluidly. Therefore, the final chamber will test your skill in combat. If you fail this trial, you will die. I wish you luck!"

Die?

Brock released a sound of protest before realizing it didn't matter. He wouldn't fail. But how sad would Big Bro be if Brock never returned? Would he even know what happened?

Such a thing was unacceptable. Brock ignored his burning body and channeled the Big Thought fully, ready to go all out from the very start.

This chamber was a fifty by twenty foot stone box. There was no exit, and the entrance was blocked by the previous boulder. The only other thing in the room was a stone statue which rigidly moved to face Brock—something that good stone bros rarely did. It wore a horned helmet and armor that cascaded over its body, similar to the statue on the outside, though the face was different.

This statue also wielded a massive halberd that took up at least half the room's width.

Brock prepared himself for combat. He twirled the Staff of Stone, settling into a stance with the staff behind his back. He charged out first. His Big Thought went into his legs, increasing their strength, pushing him from a run to a gallop.

The statue swung overhead. Brock raised his staff to block. The strike came hard. Brock shook, his knees buckled, his palms split, and his elbows groaned as they almost gave out. He barely held.

He twisted the staff to the side, letting the halberd slide its way across, then swiped it at the stone bro. The stone bro stepped back, dodging and retrieving his halberd. It came from the side. Brock jumped over it, focusing on his reflex muscles to grab onto the shaft midair, rotate with it, and swipe his staff at the stone bro from above.

Staff met horned helmet, making the stone bro look down for a second. Brock used that time to somersault through the air, using his strike's recoil to fly over the stone bro and land behind him. The stone bro swiped his halberd around, but Brock, expecting this, ducked under it. He swung low, swiping the stone bro's legs out from under him, then raised his staff and smashed it into the stone bro's neck from above mid-fall.

Brock jumped over the stone bro again, expecting a wild slash from the halberd, but it never came. The stone bro's neck had been broken by the previous strike. He now lay on the ground, lifeless, like all good stone bros should.

"Congratulations!" the voice bro spoke again. Brock wondered if he would finally exit his wall and come talk face-to-face like a real bro, but that wasn't meant to happen. "You have proven balance, strength, and skill. You have passed my trial! Again, congratulations!"

Brock nodded, gracefully accepting the praise.

"With this, you will now inherit an item that should help you master Density: the Pink Muscle Pill! I made it by combining the insights of my Dao Seed of Density and the Dao Root of Muscles."

Brock's mouth formed into an 'o'. He released a cry. This was no voice bro. He was a Dao bro!

Light flashed before Brock, and a pink pill the size of his pinky nail appeared in front of his face. He caught it as it fell and swallowed it.

The change was instantaneous. Brock felt the pill dispersing in his mouth before he even swallowed it. A breeze spread through his body, seeping into his every muscle and making it stronger.

And not just stronger, more durable, too. Brock was beyond elated. His entire body had transformed into a better version of itself. His muscles, from his toes to his biceps, had been through ten years of working out all at once.

He swung his Staff of Stone, marveling at how precise his control was, how explosive his movements. It felt like he could do anything.

He couldn't wait to show his big bro.

"Red muscles are explosive; they have great strength but can only work in short bursts. White muscles are weak but can work for long periods of time. The Pink Muscle Pill will transform all your muscles into pink muscles, which can release explosive strength momentarily or weaker strength over longer periods, depending on what you need.

"This happens by altering their interior density to perfectly accommodate both states—a feat that is normally achievable by long, grueling training. As a Dao pill, it works on all sorts of physical beings, regardless of body structure. In short, this pill will enhance your combat strength significantly, making you far more versatile than you currently are. Moreover, by meditating on the new properties of your muscles, you can gain insights into Density."

The voice suddenly grew downcast.

"Unfortunately, the Pink Muscle Pill is all I can leave you. I do not possess the strength to impart you with a Dao Root or the rank to leave my actual insights in this Trial Planet. Even the weapon I used up to the early D-Grade, my prized Staff of Stone, has been stolen from me by Alta'zed the Almighty! If you ever run into him or his descendants, you should fight to get it back!"

Brock proudly beat his chest. This Dao bro had nothing to worry about. Brock's strength was so great that he'd already retrieved the staff!

"With that, my trial has concluded. I have great hopes for you, brave soul. Perhaps one day you will reach the heights I have and be able to lead armies of immortals against your enemies, claiming glory and power! Laugh and prosper. Never give up. And, most of all, I wish you luck! Farewell."

"Thanks," Brock replied.

Instantly, space warped around him. Brock felt a lurching in his belly and found himself standing before the statue again, just in time to see it collapse and disperse into dust.

Unfortunately, he only had time to give his Dao bro a hasty nod before looking around. The entire palace was shaking. His friends were shouting.

Brock scowled. He had only left them alone for five minutes. How had they managed to screw up already?

CHAPTER SIXTY-NINE
MEET THE KRAKEN

Jack was lounging on a rock when Gan Salin woke up. He coughed, then shakily raised his upper body. "What happened?" he asked.

"Space monsters," Jack replied. "But we pulled through. Are you okay?"

Salin's eyes were piercing. "Did you save me?"

"It was nothing."

"He fought off an Elite monster while carrying you and Brock," Nauja said, stepping into the courtyard. "Hardly *nothing*."

"I appreciate that," Gan Salin said. While he seemed earnest, he was perplexed, like he expected Jack to let him die.

"No problem."

"Where are we?"

"The palace." Nauja gestured up and around at the mossy stone walls, then out into the darkness. "Brock went into the Trial already. With any luck, he'll succeed before the bubble approaches a light beam again."

"Are Trials that long?" Jack asked, looking for light beams spearing the darkness. They were far away.

"Some are," she said. "We can't know. Just have to wait."

"I hope he's okay."

Jack was worried about Brock. He'd seen the brutality of these Trials himself, and now his little bro was in one. All alone.

He didn't even care if Brock succeeded. He just wanted him to return safe. In the three minutes since the brorilla touched the statue and disappeared, Jack's heart had been filled with doubts. Was it a bad idea? Should he protect his little bro instead of sending him into a death battle? Power could come even without Trials, it would just take longer.

No, Jack quickly chided himself. Brock has chosen this path himself. He does not want to be left behind, even if there's danger. The way of the bro is to respect that.

But this didn't abate his worries. To escape them, he turned his mind to other matters.

"How is the darkness, Nauja?" he asked the barbarian girl. She'd just made a round near the palace to check for monsters. "Did you spot anything?"

She pursed her lips. "See for yourself."

The palace was illuminated by a bright torch, courtesy of whoever made this bubble. They had lit it up and placed it in a central spot. Now, Nauja walked over and picked it up, holding it against the edge of the bubble, illuminating the darkness.

Tentacles slithered outside the light. Colorful, squirmy bodies.

"Still there, huh?" Jack asked.

"Still there. They're sticking to us like fleas to a velociraptor."

"We're trapped in a bubble in the darkness, surrounded by hungry space monsters?" Gan Salin asked. "What a nice morning."

"Maybe they'll go eventually." Jack shrugged. "Besides, I doubt they're hungry. More like curious."

"About us?"

"Yeah."

They'd decided not to tell Salin about Jack's Life Drop. He was a tentative ally, not to mention an insane one, and this was a subject that demanded absolute secrecy.

"Makes sense," he replied. "We're all they've seen in who knows how long. If I were a space monster, I'd stick my nose to the glass, too."

"Thank God they don't have noses."

"And, for your information, they do get hungry. Not in the same way we do, but they have this urge to consume our Dao and grow stronger—

but only if we're around the same level. According to legend, the progression principles of space monsters is what the Immortals based the leveling of the System."

"Interesting."

"I just wish they'd leave us alone," Nauja said with a sigh. "If they decide to stick around permanently, we're going to be in trouble."

Gan Salin stood up. "Just watch. I got this."

He reached down to grab a mossy rock—fallen crumb off the walls —and flung it into the darkness. It popped through the bubble and hit a tentacle before ricocheting off into space. The monster didn't seem to register the impact.

"That's right!" Salin shouted, waving his fist. "Get the hell out of my yard!"

Jack smiled. Then, to his absolute surprise, the monster shook before bolting away at top speed.

"...What?"

"Uh... Told you I got this."

Nauja moved the torch around, illuminating a small horde of space monsters that were hurriedly running away. "What is going on?" she asked.

"I'm scary, obviously."

"I really don't think that was you, Salin," Jack said, standing up. "Space monsters have sharper Dao perception than we do. It could be that—"

His words trailed off. His eyes widened. Something was coming from below, far under their feet, deeper into the darkness. Something whose Dao shone like a sun. And it was fast.

"Fuck," he said.

Large, white tentacles rose around their bubble. These were nothing like the previous ones. Each tentacle was the size of a space monster, and they were solid, like actual flesh instead of strung-together Dao. Moreover, they gave off a sense of finality. Of death. Whatever this was, its Dao was well-defined and stable, unlike every other space monster Jack had ever met, with one exception: the green crocodile that Captain Dordok had fought.

"It's a D-Grade!" he said with rising panic. No wonder the other monsters had run off. This was the boss of the area!

"Okay, this is bad," Salin said. "Maybe it doesn't eat canines?"

"Stay calm," Nauja ordered, stretching her hands. "It's probably curious to see what drew all those monsters together. It can't reach us here. We're safe. We just have to wait for it to go away."

They still couldn't see its body, but it must have been enormous. The tentacles rose all around the bubble, twitching through the void in search for something.

"We're safe," Jack repeated, more to convince himself than reassure the others. The monster below them blared in his Dao perception like a sun to the face.

"How is it here, though?" Salin asked, perfectly calm. "The immortal monsters almost never leave the inner wall of Space Ring."

"No idea," Jack replied, but he was lying. He knew why this monster was here. Because he'd used the Life Drop, erupting with Life Dao. It was sought *him*.

He and Nauja exchanged only a glance.

The tentacles looked around a bit more but didn't find anything. The power of the Life Drop was now safely withdrawn inside Jack's soul, and even the space monster's D-Grade perception had no way of infiltrating that.

They could only watch as the tentacles grew increasingly frustrated. Its fury emanated in waves, suffusing the void and stretching outward. Being so close to an upset D-Grade monster was unnerving. It was only the bubble's protection that helped them maintain composure.

At some point, the monster would realize it'd lost its target and move on. It had to. Right?

A moment later, Jack felt its frustration surge to a peak. He seized up, wondering what was going to happen.

The tentacles touched the bubble. For a moment, Jack froze, but the bubble held, not budging in the slightest. However, it didn't repel the monster. One tentacle after another wrapped around the bubble, dark suckers sticking to its surface, as the space monster got a good hold over it.

Then, it started to move. Jack saw the light in the distance—the bright area of the ring—recede. He couldn't believe it. The monster had grabbed their bubble and was pulling it deeper. At the same time, more space monsters were flying away around them. Dark shapes crossed the void, heading in the opposite direction. When the D-Grade monster passed close to them, Jack could see them contort and twitch in fear. Some were even expelling part of their Dao to get away faster, blindly and desperately escaping to the light. More than once, Jack felt an explosion of random Dao near them, an unlucky monster getting too close to this enraged giant.

"We have to get out of here!" Nauja shouted, snapping out of her fear. The darkness around them was deepening by the second. Thankfully, space monsters used their Dao perception to hunt, not their eyes, or the flaming torches would have drawn in everything.

"But how! We—"

"There's no time!" Nauja cut him off. "We have to try and leave now, while it's distracted by the bubble. It doesn't know we're what it's searching for. We must run and hope to escape in the other monsters' panic. If it drags us even deeper, we'll never have a chance to escape again! We'll never make it back up!"

"They aren't just panicking," Salin said, still calm. "Remember how I mentioned super hordes before? This is how they start. A D-Grade monster rises from the depths, terrorizing the E-Grade space monsters in a large radius, which begin to flee in panic. Other monsters see the fleeing ones and instinctively follow. The panic spreads as a chain reaction until there are thousands of monsters running away toward the outer side of the ring, a large wave that doesn't stop until it hits the far wall."

"What does it matter?" Nauja said. "We have to go *now!*"

Jack gritted his teeth. "Brock is still in the Trial."

Nauja warred on the inside until her mind was made. Then, she crossed her arms, not saying a word more.

"I guess we're waiting," Gan Salin said. "In the meantime, wanna hear more trivia about space monsters? Did you know some of them can procreate, if they have the right Daos? My faction actually has a level farm with procreating space monsters. Funky place. Never been there, but I hear their sex is, uh, disturbing."

"What are the chances Brock will come out quickly?" Jack asked.

"No idea," Nauja replied. "And Jack, I know you don't want to hear this, but we'll know if he fails. Either he'll come out, or the statue will echo like a gong."

Jack gritted his teeth. "He won't fail."

"Then, we'll just have to wait. I'm a barbarian. I would rather die than abandon a friend."

"Space monsters are mostly purple at the E-Grade, but they have all sorts of colors and forms later on! It's usually animals, but I've heard of one shaped as a ship. There's a famous B-Grade space monster that wanders the galaxy as a continent-sized whale. People say it has an entire civilization in its stomach."

Jack tried, but he struggled to enjoy Gan Salin's fun facts.

The void was still flying past them, several times faster than they could achieve by themselves. It had only been half a minute.

"Do you think—"

Congratulations! Title "Fourth Ring Conqueror" upgraded to "Fifth Ring Conqueror!"
Efficacy of all stats: +20% → +25%

Jack moved instantly. He bolted inside, finding Brock standing by the crumbling statue, perfectly safe and sound. He held his Staff of Stone in one hand and gaped as he looked around, at the many tentacles hugging their bubble. He said something in monkey.

"Good job! I'm proud of you," Jack said as fast as he possibly could, then grabbed Brock under an arm, put helmets on both their heads, and ran back outside. It took him exactly three seconds.

Nauja and Gan Salin didn't waste any time, either. By the time he returned, they were both ready to go.

"You know what we could use?" Salin asked, picking up a piece of old but steady rope that held a torch to a wall. "Space monster reins. Since we're riding the space horde, we might as well do it in style."

"Just go!" Nauja shouted.

The darkness was still receding around them. Panicked space monsters were flying everywhere.

They jumped out.

CHAPTER SEVENTY

SURFING A TSUNAMI OF SPACE MONSTERS

SPACE MONSTERS WERE UNIQUE CREATURES. THEY WERE FORMED BY DAO THAT stuck together, the fundamental properties of the universe given shape and form. When that happened, sentience was developed, but most monsters only remained at the E-Grade, their infancy.

As a result, they were driven by two primary instincts: progress, and survival. Progress came from devouring other creatures that cultivated the Dao—usually cultivators, or sometimes compatible space monsters. Survival was more complex, and being barely sentient, what space monsters did was blindly follow what other space monsters were doing. If they saw one moving with purpose, they followed it. That was how monster hordes were formed.

At the same time, this sort of instinct could have unintended consequences.

In the densely crowded environment of Space Ring, once enough monsters got to stampeding, there was no stopping them. More monsters took note and automatically started making haste as well, spreading the panic like a wildfire in dry grass. A massive horde could form swiftly, with dozens, hundreds, or even thousands of space monsters all rushing over each other to escape... something. They didn't know what they were running from, nor did it matter. Everybody else was doing it, so they followed.

The super horde that formed on this day was the result of an event chain accidentally started by Jack. When he activated his Life Drop to fight the electric eel, the eruption of Dao was so strong that it caught the attention of a D-Grade space monster slumbering in the bottom of Space Ring. That monster rose to investigate. However, as the Life Dao had disappeared, it focused on the closest special occurrence it could sense—the gathering of space monsters around a specific bubble.

The D-Grade monster didn't know what was happening there, but it had the intelligence—albeit barely—to connect the dots. It concluded that a high-quality, life-related treasure had matured inside that bubble. Such a treasure could be invaluable to this monster, since it cultivated the Dao of Death. Therefore, it grabbed the bubble and pulled it to its lair in the inner wall of Space Ring, where it could investigate at its leisure.

However, the monster's arrival and subsequent frustration terrorized the nearby space monsters, sending them into a frenzied escape. In its retreat, it also squashed some of them to quell its rage, further fueling their panic. Such a monster could create large waves. It wasn't long before every E-Grade monster in the region, from peak to King, was in motion, heading out of the darkness and into the light, where the poor cultivators had no idea what was about to happen.

———

Jack, Nauja, Gan Salin, and Brock emerged from their fast descending bubble into a void that brimmed with activity. Behind them, the mossy palace floated in a bubble wrapped by large, white tentacles. They barely caught a glimpse of the massive creature below, dragging the bubble ever deeper.

It was a white squid the length of a skyscraper. A space kraken. The entire palace was like a toy to it.

Thankfully, the kraken didn't pay them any attention. It descended at great speed, disappearing in the darkness as the palace's torches went off one by one.

Unfortunately, the kraken wasn't the only monster here. More and more of them surged out of the depths, frightened out of their minds by the kraken's appearance and anger. Jack glimpsed dozens of them in the bubble's dying light. The weakest were peak E-Grades, and the strongest was a King monster that resembled a dark blue rhinoceros.

All those monsters were surging toward Jack, Brock, Nauja, and Gan Salin. They barely caught a glimpse of all the monsters before the final torch in the palace went out, and they were sunk in absolute darkness.

For a moment, there was stillness. Jack hovered quietly, like the approaching horde was only a dream.

Then, something crashed into them, and the group was flung forward. They didn't try to fight back. They let the flood take them, doing their best to align with it and stay alive. Their only saving grace was that the monsters, in their haste to escape, did not try to eat them.

Jack's world was filled with bursts of all kinds of Dao. He was almost overwhelmed. His mind focused on his friends. Wind, Insanity. Brock, he was carrying.

There were dozens of Daos erupting out of everywhere. Shapes bumped into him. The monsters felt an urge to come together, leading to a tightly clustered pack in complete absence of light.

Jack finally felt a mind-turning burst from the side. He rushed over, hoping to not get tackled by a monster, and found Gan Salin.

He was struggling. Already, he was in dire straits, his bursts of Dao erratic. Two monsters surrounded him, not trying to kill him but accidentally swatting him with their tentacles while he was trying his hardest to survive.

Jack couldn't see the battle, but he could perceive parts of it.

He sensed Salin erupt with speed as he dashed at Jack. Suddenly, he was flung aside—probably batted by a loose tentacle. The strike was hard, but Salin wouldn't give up. He forced himself to remain conscious and doubled down on his original trajectory, once again rushing toward Jack.

He was struck away again, but he persisted. He would try the same thing again and again until it worked.

Jack arrived. He swept by Gan Salin's side, falling in line next to him to protect one side. The canine stopped struggling as much.

Wind came from another direction. A gale blew through the monsters, finding its way next to Jack. The three of them formed a nucleus surrounded by strong space monsters, pushing against all sides to avoid getting crushed. There were bodies all around them, now. They weren't cramped, but the monsters were so large, fast, and strong that, without sufficient space to dodge, Jack's team would be squeezed into paste.

They were practically fighting blind-folded. Jack's perception was overwhelmed by Dao eruptions. He swatted away a tentacle and dodged another. A monster rammed into them headfirst while both of Jack's hands were busy, but Salin was there, using his signature move, Five Star Grasp, to slap the monster straight in the head and make it curve around them. Nauja was covering their other side, stopping a variety of monsters from assaulting them.

All the while, they sped forward, in step with the horde. If they slowed down even in the slightest, they would be overrun and stomped to death.

On all sides, space monsters were zipping for the light. More and more surged up from the depths of the darkness like an unstoppable tide.

The monsters deeper down were generally stronger than those in shallower parts. Therefore, they were also faster. As all monsters began heading in the same direction, with the faster ones behind the slower ones, they gradually squeezed together, forming a dense layer of monsters all moving together in blind panic.

It was in the center of that layer that Jack's team had accidentally wedged themselves.

Jack's entire mind was focused on survival. He lost track of time. At some point, he realized the light was fast approaching.

To the horror of everyone in Space Ring, the super horde emerged and continued unabated. Cultivators pointed in shock and ran away at top speed. Space monsters watched on with confusion before their instincts kicked in and they, too, joined the horde.

Bubbles and cultivators were swept by the horde, taking them along in their mad rush for the far wall.

Jack could finally see again. The monsters surrounding them were a snake—he'd confused its tail for a tentacle before—and a gorilla with tentacles for arms. Both peak E-Grades.

Now, their group could fight better. They coordinated. Jack flew aside, exploiting a break in the unintended space monster offense to assist Gan Salin. The canine jumped back, taking on the flank he was more suited to covering, letting Jack smash a bunch of meteors into the monsters behind them.

An arachnoid Elite monster shot out a white substance at him. An arrow of wind pierced and drove it away, pinning it to another space monster. There, the substance hardened and bound to its victim, gluing itself to its appendages until the space monster slowed down so much it was swallowed up by the horde, torn to a dozen pieces as the rest of the monsters clawed their way through.

Jack looked to the side. Gan Salin used all his strength to smack away an errant tentacle. Another was rising behind him, so Jack shot over a meteor. Salin spotted that, cursed in his helmet, and leaned back, letting the meteor sail over him and smash into the tentacle, saving him.

Right after, Salin pointed behind Jack, letting him twist around another projectile—a horn-like appendage? Nauja arrowed a monster about to reach Salin, and the canine attacked at the same time, slapping it away twice.

Gan Salin was grinning. Though his life was on the line, he was clearly having fun.

Through a gap in the monsters, Jack took a quick glance around him. It was chaos. The entire ring, everything he could see, was in chaos.

By the time the first monster emerged from the darkness, an entire army followed, dozens of high-level ones. The spread of the super horde didn't stop. More and more monsters joined the dance. Soon, they'd created a horde so massive it swallowed bubbles, pulling them along simply by momentum, like forest animals running away from a wildfire.

This entire side of Space Ring was swept up. Any cultivator unlucky enough to be traveling between bubbles was drawn into the horde, struggling to save their lives. Anyone lucky enough to be in a bubble stayed there, holding on for dear life as the world tumbled and turned around them.

And at the very head of the super horde was a small team riding the wave. By staying there, instead of buried inside the body of the horde, they could survive. It was like surfing a tsunami.

They were gradually getting away from the darkness and heading back to Village Ring. At the same time, the squeezing around them got more and more intense.

Trying to escape through the horde would be very difficult. The monsters changed positions all the time, and one mistake would be enough to get them crushed.

All they could do was ride the tide and try to survive in the ever-increasing pressure. Moreover, all these attacks slowed them down, and they had to constantly expel Dao from their Dao Seeds to stay up to speed. Their endurance wasn't infinite. Eventually, they would run out, and they would fall into the horde.

This can't go on! Jack thought. We must find a way to use less energy.

It wasn't just the sides and flank. There were monsters above and below them, everywhere the eye could see, pressuring them so hard that they had to give it their all just to stay afloat.

Jack looked back, trying to find a solution, and crossed eyes with Gan Salin. The canine smiled brightly like he'd been waiting for this moment. He reached to his belt and recovered the old, steady rope he'd taken from the mossy palace, giving it a couple test tugs.

At the time, Jack had thought Salin was joking. As it turns out, he might have had a point.

I can't believe this, Jack thought, reaching out. Salin gave him the rope. Jack let the canine hold off the monsters for a moment as he looked for a suitable target.

There. Right below them was a rhinoceros-like space monster. A King. And being a King also meant the other monsters gave it a wide berth. It was perfect.

Jack dived down, using a series of Meteor Punches to approach the rhino. He quickly passed the rope around one of its horns.

It was surreal.

The rhino ignored him, not even bothering with his small existence. Every other monster was running away, filling the rhino with urgency.

Jack's rope was now tied around the rhino's horn. He gave it a tug to make sure there was no problem. The rhino, bursting with strength as it was, didn't even slow down. He gestured at his friends, who rushed to join him, letting two monsters clash where they used to float.

Jack held onto the rope for dear life. There was barely enough space for the three of them—Brock was holding onto Jack's back.

Finally, they were somewhat safe. No monsters would attack the rhino, even by accident, and there were no other Kings around. Moreover, it didn't seem to mind giving them a ride. For now, they could take a breather.

Which let Jack gaze ahead, where the horde was headed. Poor cultivators rushed to reach a bubble before the wall of space monsters reached them first. A bubble swept to the side, pushed along by all the monsters behind it. Two cultivators were inside, pale-faced and shaking like leaves—one was the lizard-riding man from Village Ring.

Looking into the distance—and shielding his eyes from the sun mushrooms—Jack saw another bubble in their immediate path. It was a sandy coast.

Suddenly, three cultivators jumped up from the coast, voluntarily exiting their bubble. It was like they hadn't noticed the approaching super horde. Jack prayed for their poor, stupid souls.

Then, those cultivators started running in parallel with the horde, but slightly slower. They let the horde approach them and slowly merged into it, matching the speed of the frontrunners. Coincidentally, they happened to arrive very close to Jack's team. He, Brock, and Gan Salin were staring like they'd seen a ghost.

One of the new cultivators erupted with lightning, charring a monster in front of him and making room for his team to burst in. Another swung a mallet larger than her torso, smashing it into the void, expelling Dao from its business end, and propelling the entire team forward. The third member just watched, content to be carried around by the other two.

In the blink of an eye, this new team of cultivators reached Jack's rhino and flew beside it.

Long time no see, Jack, said the Sage telepathically, with a full smile that showed off his yellow teeth. *Care to share the ride?*

CHAPTER SEVENTY-ONE
A SPICY REUNION

JACK COULDN'T BELIEVE HIS EYES. HERE, HOVERING IN THE MIDDLE OF A SUPER horde in Trial Planet's Space Ring, was the Sage.

What the hell?

"You aren't even going to say hello?" the Sage said again. His telepathy was coming in handy.

"Hello," Jack responded numbly.

The Sage looked almost exactly as Jack remembered him. Tattered clothes, dirty hair, and an equally dirty brown backpack on his shoulders.

However, there was something more this time. A feeling Jack couldn't put into words, like their two souls were faintly resonating. He'd never sensed something like this before. It was highly peculiar.

Judging by the Sage's slightly narrowed eyes and discreetly puzzled expression, he must have felt the same. He seemed equally perplexed— or, perhaps, it was all in Jack's mind. He looked behind the Sage, to find Dorman Whistles.

The young man had changed a lot. He held two pitch-black daggers with bright blue streaks, like they'd been struck by lightning. His slanted eyes were focused and serious, piercing, inspecting Jack with mild surprise.

Jack scanned them both, starting from the Sage.

Human (Earth-387), Level 100
Faction: Barren High (C-Grade)
Title: Planetary Torchbearer (10)

Human (Earth-387), Level 107
Faction: Barren High (C-Grade)
Title: Planetary Torchbearer (10)

The third member of their team was a djinn. However, she wasn't a merchant, like Ar'Tazul or Ar'Karvahul. She wielded a mallet whose business end was larger than her torso, and her dark hair was caught in twin ponytails that highlighted her blue skin and strong, brown eyes.

Djinn, Level 124
Faction: Barren High (C-Grade)

"What are you doing here?" Jack asked through the Sage's telepathic connection. He didn't know whether to feel joy or caution. These guys were part of Barren High now? What had they been up to since he left Earth? What was happening back on his home planet?

"Exploring!" the Sage replied, his smile bright. "But perhaps our talk should wait until we're in a safer place?"

Jack remembered they were riding a rhino-shaped space monster at the head of a super horde. He looked around, finding Gan Salin stunned, but also amused. If the Sage and Dorman wondered why Jack and Gan Salin were traveling together, they didn't show it.

Maybe they knew already. The Sage was, well, a sage, whose prophecies had come true multiple times.

Come to think of it, didn't they jump into the horde to find us?

Jack gave a thumbs-up to Salin and Nauja, informing them that these people were allies, then turned back to the Sage. *"Lead the way."*

The Sage's smile widened. "Sharp as ever. Follow me."

He let the rope go. So did Jack and everyone else. The rhino under their feet immediately began to move away.

Then, the Sage dove. Dorman, the djinn, and Jack, with Brock clinging to his back, followed without losing a beat. Salin and Nauja hesitated for a single moment before moving along.

They were heading directly toward the arachnoid monster from before. Just before they arrived, a reindeer-looking monster rammed into the arachnoid from behind, sending them both careening forward. The Sage calmly slipped into the gap like he'd expected this to happen.

For the next few minutes, he led them slowly but steadily out of the horde. To anyone else, this task would be near impossible. The Sage made it appear effortless.

At times, he would dive into certain death, only for whatever monster was in his way to randomly move aside. Other times, he would stand still like waiting for a bus. Then, when the timing was right, he would dash into the monsters, which miraculously formed a path for him to cross.

The rest of them followed quickly, afraid of being too far behind.

The seemingly impenetrable, stampeding horde of space monsters was nothing before the Sage's predictive powers. Before long, they had escaped the dense head of the horde and were at the outskirts, where the space monsters were sparser and individually weaker. The Sage led them through convoluted paths in the void before approaching a bubble. It contained only a large disc of bare stone with a bit of moss on its underside, and it was far enough from the center of the horde that the monsters had time to go around it, not sweeping it along.

They all dove fluidly into the bubble, reaching safety, then watched the monsters gallop through space all around them.

It was a breathtaking spectacle. Hundreds of space monsters moved together, sweeping bubbles and cultivators alike without a care in the world. Not everyone had a Sage to help them. Any cultivators caught in the horde, even at its outskirts, had no choice but to go with the flow, rapidly retreating to the outer wall of Space Ring, from where they would have to make their way back to the inner wall—if they survived. It was a huge setback.

Even lords had to give way to the horde. In a bubble far, far away, Longsword was huddled with his team, letting the storm pass. Priya, the Exploding Sun lady, was caught mid-space by the horde's outskirts. She took the head-on approach. Suns blossomed on her hands, detonating space monsters by the dozens. The fat man beside her used large, golden palms to split the monsters as a rock may split the waves, while the third person in their group, a captivating woman with long hair, simply held up a palm at the approaching monsters, and they wordlessly curved past.

In a distant place of Space Ring, the horde was stopped by a group of beasts, each summoned by the Hand of God lady. A wall of darkness rose next to the beasts, swallowing any space monster stupid enough to enter.

Gradually, the horde turned from a raging river into a tame stream, then a trickle, before eventually abating. It was past them now. All they could see were the monsters' receding backs as they dashed toward the outer wall of Space Ring. Upon reaching that wall, they would break like the tide on a beach. Only then would they realize there was no danger behind them and return to their original spots, signaling the end of the super horde that had upset at least a third of Space Ring.

A breathtaking, unique phenomenon.

However, Jack had more to consider than the super horde. He turned his gaze away, meeting the Sage's calm eyes. Everyone removed their helmets.

"I'm a good guy now," Salin said quickly. "Please don't try to kill me again."

Dorman raised a brow. "Be quiet, dog." Clearly, he still held a grudge.

Nauja's hand reached for her bow. "Careful how you speak to my friends, boy."

Instantly, the two groups of three were facing off, tension brewing.

"Calm down, everyone," Jack said, raising his hands. "We're all friends here. No need to argue."

"Take it easy, Dorman," the Sage added, pointedly glancing at the young man. Dorman nodded, crossing his arms. "It's a pleasure to see you again, Jack. Gan Salin."

"Likewise. And thank you for helping us with the horde. What are you doing here?"

"We are promising members of Barren High now. How could we miss the Garden Assault?"

"Jack," Nauja said, "care to introduce us?"

"Of course. I was just so surprised I forgot to. Nauja, these people are the Sage and Dorman, friends from my home planet. Guys, this is Nauja, an ally from the Barbarian Ring."

"It's a pleasure to make your acquaintance, Nauja," the Sage said softly, beaming at her. "We have great respect for the natives of Trial Planet. Meeting you here is an honor."

She seemed taken aback. "Thanks."

"And this is Poppy," the Sage introduced the last member of their team, the djinn. "She is the star disciple of Barren High, focusing fully on battle."

Poppy, blue and barely four feet in height, nodded.

"Introductions done," Jack said, "what have you guys been up to? Last time we met, the Animal Kingdom was trying to kill us all."

"Nothing much. Certainly less than you," the Sage replied, laughing charmingly. "We left Earth-387 shortly after you, recruited into Barren High on the recommendation of my master. We trained there for some days before taking the opportunity to join this Garden Assault. What about you?"

"I disguised myself, boarded a starship heading to the Belarian Outpost, then was assaulted midway by the Animal Kingdom's Hounds. Thanks to Gan Salin, I somehow escaped and made it to Trial Planet. One crazy adventure led to another, and here I am."

The Sage burst out laughing. "Classic Jack. I knew we'd find you here, of course, but I still feel great joy to see you safe and sound."

Jack smiled, though it didn't reach his eyes. His relationship with the Sage was complicated. Not only did he owe the prophet several favors from their time on Earth, the Sage had also revealed that he belonged to Black Hole Church, the galaxy-wide terrorist organization. They were laughing and greeting each other now, but there was an entire layer of communication that went unspoken.

Was Barren High, the highly prestigious prophetic faction that not even the Animal Kingdom dared to offend, involved with the Black Hole Church? Would the Sage try to cash in any of Jack's favors on behalf of the Church?

Finally, the question Jack chose to ask was: "Do you know what's happening on Earth?"

The professor was there. So were Edgar, Vivi, Harambe, and everyone else. He had no way of knowing anything before he got a hundred million credits to buy the telepathy function for his faction, but he was always worried.

"I don't know much, I'm afraid," the Sage replied, shaking his head. "The Bare Fist Brotherhood and Flame River are currently at war against Ice Peak. Everyone is working hard to clear the planet's F-Grade dungeons and get ahead in power while sabotaging the enemy. The conflict isn't at the point of all-out battle yet, but true war could break out at any moment."

"I see."

The Forest of the Strong would be safe, no matter what. Sparman was guarding it, and he had the power of a D-Grade. There was no way anyone on Earth could combat him.

Jack wanted to know more, but this was all he would get. Therefore, he refocused on the present. The Sage had sought him out—for a reason.

"And what brings you here, Sage?" Jack asked directly.

"Ah, straight to the point. Is it alright with you if we speak privately?"

Jack glanced behind him. "Of course."

He followed the Sage to the other side of the stone disc that made up this bubble biome. Dorman also came along. So did Brock.

On the way, Jack still sensed that peculiar resonance with the Sage, something originating from deep inside his soul. It was faint enough to be just his impression, but also solid enough to be real.

How odd.

"Allow me to be forward with you, Jack," the Sage said, turning around when they reached the other side. He kept his voice low so the ones left behind—Nauja, Salin, and Poppy—couldn't hear. "I want to invite you into the Black Hole Church."

CHAPTER SEVENTY-TWO

HISTORY

Jack didn't respond right away. He savored the words. "Invite me into Black Hole Church?"

"Yes," the Sage replied. "You already know I'm part of it—though I hope you've kept this information safe. Dorman is one of us, too, as are many people across the galaxy. And we want you."

To the side, Dorman nodded.

"Isn't the Black Hole Church a terrorist organization?" Jack asked, crossing his arms.

"That's what the Hand of God says. In truth, we are the good side here."

"How so?"

The Sage smiled. "Because the galaxy—and the wider universe—is a palace of oppression. The offspring of misunderstanding, built on a foundation of irreversible disaster. We fight against the tyrants, hence we are deemed criminals."

"That's a lot of words to make no sense."

The Sage burst out laughing. Jack reminded himself that, despite his appearance, this was a deeply charismatic man. He had to keep his guard up.

"What do you know about the Immortals, Jack?" the Sage asked.

"Not much. I know they made the System and were robots created by the Ancients." Nauja had told him as much in the Forbidden Cave.

"Correct. Why did they create the System?"

"To defend against the Old Ones."

"In more detail?"

Jack frowned. He felt like he was being tested in school, but gave the Sage the benefit of the doubt. "The Old Ones destroyed the Ancients. In revenge, the Immortals created the System to start a crusade and push them off."

"Aha," the Sage said calmly. "You do know some things. That's good. Means I don't have to overload you with information. But not everything is as you've heard."

Jack raised a brow. "Oh?"

"I will explain. However, I am limited in what I can reveal unless you join us, so please bear with me."

"I'll try."

"History, you see, is written by the victors. Many times, the truth is twisted... There were three main groups once: the Old Ones, the Ancients, and the Immortals. After the Ancients were destroyed—which wasn't as simple as you may think—the Immortals indeed created the System and launched a crusade against the Old Gods, pushing them to the fringes of the universe, outside System territory. However, the crusade did not manage to kill a single Old God.

"You must remember, now, that the Immortals were created for the sole purpose of defeating the Old Gods. That was their core directive, and it remains so until today. As a result, their System is a menace to the world. You have felt its malice first-hand. It pits all living creatures against each other, uncaring about the number of sacrifices and mountains of pain. Its only purpose is to create strong soldiers against the Old Gods—and damned be everything else. That is quite the terrible ruler, wouldn't you agree?"

Jack considered it for a moment. "This makes sense."

After all, he had seen how the Integration worked. It was a meat grinder that killed a billion people to create one strong immortal. So far, everything the Sage said was in line with what Jack knew.

"I'm glad," the Sage continued. "For some people, that is fine. But not for us. The Black Hole Church is an organization created to dismantle the System, slay the Immortals, and restore peace in the universe. This perpetual war we are embroiled in is a remnant of the Immortals' programming, which is stuck now, since the Ancients are gone. Someone needs to put them down."

"Hmm." Jack narrowed his eyes. "But the System is meant to protect us from the Old Ones, right? The gods you worship. If the System falls, won't the Old Ones, I don't know, annihilate us as they did the Ancients?"

The Sage's face wrinkled into a sad, bitter smile. "As I said, that was not as simple as you believe. The Immortals have twisted history to their benefit. I cannot reveal much yet, but believe me when I say the Old Gods mean us no harm—or, at least, any harm they inadvertently cause us will be far less than what the System does on a daily basis. Between the Immortals and the Old Gods, the latter would be far kinder rulers—if they even bothered."

"Hmm. I don't know. You're basing a lot of things on stuff you're not telling me."

"That's why I warned you. Unfortunately, I cannot explain fully. I do not expect you to believe me today. I am just planting the seeds of true knowledge in you because I believe you are a man of integrity. If you keep what I told you in mind, you will eventually discover clues that I speak the truth."

"Then, you're considered terrorists because everyone else obeys the System? Why would they do that, if it's so evil?"

"Because they have power. The harsher a system, the kinder it is to those at the top."

"Okay. You still haven't explained why you worship the Old Ones. From what you said, even if they aren't evil, they are neutral at best, right?"

"Correct. But we don't worship all Old Gods. We worship Enas. The God trapped in the black hole. He is the one who views us mortals kindly and helps us. He is the one who harbors deep hatred for the Immortals and what they've done. If He is ever released from his prison, He will march with us. His power will twist the System and give us the strength to fight the Immortals on equal ground. Without him, our war is a lost cause. Their armies are simply too powerful."

"So you want to release an Old One from his eternal prison."

"Right."

"You know how that sounds. It's sketchy as fuck."

"I am aware. As I said, I do not expect you to simply trust my words. After you leave Trial Planet, travel a bit. Ask around. See what horrors the System has inflicted on all worlds, and try to find proof of the Black Hole Church's purported evil. They accuse us of things we have not done to twist the world against us, but all their supposed evidence crumbles before the wise eye. It is only meant to trick the naive and foolish."

"...Okay. So you guys want to dismantle the System, which is an evil thing imposed on the world by unfeeling robot overlords. And to do so, you want to release a kind god from his eternal prison, where all the other neutral gods unjustly placed him?"

The Sage smiled. "Precisely!"

"Listen, man. I know you're trying really hard to make sense, but this all sounds very questionable. I don't really distrust you, and I won't reveal what you told me to others, but you understand my hesitation, right?"

"Of course! Take as much time as you like. If you ever find yourself agreeing with us, our doors will be open."

Jack nodded. "Is that all you had to say?"

"More or less. I will be eagerly awaiting your response. In the meantime, we can help each other. Trial Planet is a dangerous place—and the greatest danger is other cultivators. If the opportunity arises, let's save each other."

"Wouldn't you know already, Sage?"

"Hah. My eyes are not what you believe, boy."

"Fair enough." Jack chuckled.

"Any last questions before we head over?"

Jack thought about it. He looked to where Dorman stood without a care in the world. He clearly knew about all this beforehand. Brock also waited calmly by Jack's feet, trusting his big bro to parse through all the complex information.

As for Salin and Nauja, they were conversing with Poppy at the other side of the disc. Salin was gesturing animatedly, probably explaining something nonsensical.

Jack was dying to ask why the System was hunting down all

remnants of the Ancients, as had been revealed in the Ancient ruins. Even if everything the Sage just said was true, it still didn't make any sense. Unfortunately, asking that meant revealing his connection to the ruins, and that wasn't a risk he was willing to take.

At the very least, he *knew* there were secrets. Things were not as they seemed. Maybe they weren't as the Sage said, either, but at least Jack knew there was more than met the eye... somewhere.

"Just one question," he finally said. "What's the deal with you, Sage? You were in cahoots with the Church since very early on, weren't you? They were the ones who fed you information about the Integration Auction. There's no way you prophesied everything at the F-Grade."

The Sage simply smiled, not revealing anything. Jack continued.

"You never told us about your Integration experience, either. I suppose they helped you. But why? How did you reach them—or they reached you—so early on? Was it dumb luck? Did their starship land next to the bench you were sleeping on? But, if you were a random person off the streets they picked to train, how did you become strong enough to fight on par with the rest of us? Why do you have such an odd, powerful Dao? There are so many coincidences surrounding you, Sage, and I know nothing about you. Not even your real name."

The Sage smiled like there was a joke only he could see. "If I had a name once, it is now void. All I am is the Sage. As for how everything happened..." He winked. "I cannot reveal it yet. If you join us, then I will tell you."

"Heh. Are you saying it's a deeper secret than what you already revealed?"

"What I revealed was a history lesson. You cannot act on it. On my story, perhaps you could. No need to take chances."

"I guess." Jack chuckled. From the very first time they met, the Sage had been a walking enigma. Now, even after growing tremendously and reaching the Space Ring of Trial Planet, Jack was stunned to realize that this man was even more enigmatic.

He was very curious to know the truth—but not enough to join an organization he knew next to nothing about based on an outlandish conspiracy theory.

"I appreciate the offer," Jack said. "I promise to think about it."

The Sage clapped. "Good! Now, let's head back. I sense that Poppy is about to turn our canine friend into dog paste."

They quickly returned to the others. As the Sage had said, Poppy—the twin-pigtailed djinn with the large mallet—was glaring at Gan Salin with her arms crossed. The canine, on the other hand, insisted on explaining why painting herself green would be better than blue.

"It's camouflage!" he protested, opening his arms wide. "Picture this: You can hide in forests, in swamps, in the defecations of someone who ate too much spinach. Where can you hide if you're blue? The sky? You are not a bird. The sea? You're not a fish. Clearly, being green is the better choice."

"I will not paint myself." Poppy's voice was high-pitched, like a child's.

"But why? If you just—"

"Salin," Jack said good-naturedly. "Let the poor girl alone. Nobody will paint themselves for you."

"I—Bah. Fine. But when you're in a forest and have nowhere to hide, don't say I didn't warn you."

Poppy narrowed her eyes. "I won't say that."

"Are you guys done chatting?" Nauja asked. "If so, we have a ring to explore. Trials to find."

"I have a suggestion about that," the Sage said. "I sense you already found a Trial for... at least one of you. Brock, right?"

Brock nodded before anyone could stop him.

"The fates of the rest of you do not lie in Space Ring. Labyrinth Ring and Garden Ring hold greater Trials than here, and I predict that all three of you"—he pointed at Jack, Nauja, and Gan Salin—"will find something there. Don't waste your time searching the stars. Reaching Labyrinth Ring before the lords holds far greater value."

Jack considered it. Trials aside, this was a great place for leveling up, but he couldn't just focus on that. Fighting the same enemies repeatedly would only stunt his growth. He had to keep exploring and delving ever deeper, reaping as many levels as he could in the process without slowing down.

Ever forward. That was the way of the fist, and the way of cultivation.

Nauja frowned at the Sage. "Are you saying we should forget about all the Trials here?"

"To find something better later. Remember: No Trial at all is better than a bad Trial. You should take the best you can."

She bit her lip in thought—a habit she probably didn't notice. She turned to Jack. "Can we trust him?" she asked directly, not caring about insulting the Sage.

Jack tilted his head to the side. "He did just help us. If the horde dragged us to the far wall, we'd need several days to make it back here. Plus... we're old friends. I trust his prophecies."

"Then, fine. Let's do as he says and go directly to Labyrinth Ring. What do you think, Salin?"

Gan Salin jolted up, surprised she considered him. "Sure. Let's go where it's most fun."

"It's not like there's much left to see here." Jack shrugged. He turned to the Sage. "I presume we'll travel together in the next ring?"

"Not quite."

Jack raised a brow. "No?"

The Sage laughed. "We can go *to* the next ring together. But the Labyrinth Ring is a peculiar one. Everyone is split up as we enter, so there is no guarantee we can find each other. Let everyone pursue their own luck, and we can meet again when the Garden Assault fights the labyrinth guardian. And don't worry—you and Brock are considered spiritually bound, so you'll probably go together."

"Oh," Jack said. "I didn't know that. Then, sure. Have you also completed the quests of this ring? To find a Trial and defeat an Elite monster?"

"We have."

"Great. Then, let's go. The Labyrinth Ring awaits."

"Labyring," Salin corrected him. Everyone stared. He crossed his arms and said, "Well, I still find it hilarious!"

CHAPTER SEVENTY-THREE
CRACKING ONE'S SOUL

THE SUPER HORDE WASHED OVER THIS SIDE OF SPACE RING, CAUSING widespread confusion and casualties. Several cultivators were overrun. A few were swept up but managed to make it out alive. Most were already in bubbles or found one in time. Even the lords mobilized, exerting their fearsome powers to rescue themselves, their teammates, and many of their followers.

In the end, the horde broke against the far wall, sending disproportionately strong space monsters flying everywhere. It was chaos for a day. When the monsters realized there was no danger, they receded back to the darkness, officially ending the super horde like nothing had happened. The only lasting evidence of this event would be the many bubbles that were swept by the horde into the outer wall, ripe for the taking and easy to access.

As a result, the smartest cultivators spent another day exploring those bubbles, hoping to find something useful. Unfortunately, not many were from the darkness, but there was still treasure to be found.

All of this was no longer Jack's business. Following the Sage, his team traveled to the nearest light beam and dove into it, piercing the darkness. Given the absence of space monsters and the confused state of cultivators, there was nothing to stop them.

The source of the light beam was as Gan Salin had described. A bowl-shaped rock formation filled to the brim with mushrooms, focusing their light ahead like a powerful headlight.

It was so bright, in fact, that they couldn't stare directly. The last part of their journey was made looking sideways. By the time they reached the base of the light beam, Jack was horrified. The inner wall of Space Ring was just a hundred feet away, behind the light. That was where the strongest monsters of the ring, like the D-Grade kraken, awaited.

He had never been happier to have light.

Their group flew into the base of the light beam, landing in its center. Most of the brightness instantly dissipated. There was a patch of rock twenty feet across that was empty of mushrooms, letting them finally open their eyes.

Right in the middle of that empty patch stood an iron pedestal.

"What's that?" Jack asked, approaching it.

"The entrance to Labyrinth Ring," the Sage explained.

"It's not a door."

"It's a teleporter."

"A what?"

"A teleporter. Like the big ones you're used to, but far smaller and with shorter range."

"Wow..."

Jack wasn't even that surprised. After Space Ring, with its bubbles floating in space and the hordes of space monsters, simple teleportation devices sounded almost homely.

"Any last things to say?" Jack asked. "You know, something to warn us about, or what we should do in the labyrinth?"

The Sage cupped his chin. "Hmm. There are monsters, obviously. Strong ones. This is the last hostile ring of Trial Planet, so the challenge is hard enough that even lords may fall—if they are careless. Besides that, the labyrinth contains dungeons, which contain Trials."

"Dungeons, huh? That brings back memories..."

"Be careful, though. These ones are designed to challenge people who have made it this far. They're far nastier than the ones on Earth."

"But they contain great rewards!" Gan Salin spoke up. "One of my ancestors got his Berserker's Axe here, and I hear that even one of my faction's B-Grades once found their luck in Labyrinth Ring."

"With danger comes opportunity." Jack nodded. "I know the concept."

"Then, there isn't much else to talk about," the Sage said. "We will be split up as soon as we touch that pedestal. Challenge a dungeon if you're up for it, avoid the monsters if you aren't. Ally with anyone you find—getting through the labyrinth alone is dangerous. And remember to follow the colors—the darker the walls, the deeper in the labyrinth you are. Let's all reconvene at the guardian's gate."

"Wait." Jack raised a hand. "You said to ally with anyone we found. But before, you said we should hurry to get here before the Garden Assault does. Who are we supposed to ally with? Each other?"

"The labyrinth is large enough that we probably won't find each other. But don't worry. The Garden Assault isn't as united as you think. There are benefits to entering the labyrinth quickly, so there will be plenty of cultivators already inside. The reason we enter quickly is that, right now, those people will also be desperately looking for allies. If the entire Garden Assault enters, your group will be ostracized."

"Hmm. Okay, then. Let's say our goodbyes and get going."

"Of course. We'll go first."

The Sage, Dorman, and their djinn ally, Poppy, simply walked up to the pedestal and touched it. No goodbyes, no kind words, no nothing. In the next moment, they vanished.

"...I bet they have a way to find each other," Nauja said.

"If they do, good for them. They weren't obligated to share."

"Maybe they're just crazy," Salin said.

Jack laughed. Then, he gave his friends a warm look. "Listen, guys. We're all strong now. We may be split up in there, but I believe we'll all pull through. Just focus on staying alive. We'll meet again at the end of the ring."

"You silly bastard," the canine said with a big smile. "I'm not strong. I'll probably die."

"You're inventive and decisive. I believe you'll make it."

"Well, if I was afraid, I would have teleported out at the ring entrance, wouldn't I?" Salin said.

Space Ring was one of Trial Planet's exit points. If one scoured the outer wall, there were many teleporters leading outside the planet. Many people rushed there as soon as they got the Fourth Ring

Conqueror title. Salin, even with his relative weakness, never even considered it.

"I will try my best. If I die, I die," Nauja said, her head held high. "That is the barbarian way."

"And so will I," Jack said.

"I'm not worried about you. With your strength, you can easily protect yourself—and Brock, since you'll probably be together," Nauja said.

"You heard what the Sage said. Even lords can fall in this ring, if they aren't careful, and I'm no lord." He smashed his fists together. "But I sure as hell don't intend to fail. If there are monsters, I'll just get a few more levels."

Salin laughed. "Ah, there's the Jack we all know and love. Always ready to punch stuff. Anyway, this sentimental stuff makes me feel awkward. Wanna go?"

The four of them exchanged a look, knowing it was possibly the last time they'd see each other. "Let's," Jack and Nauja said together.

"Yes," Brock agreed. "Bros."

Jack cracked a bitter smile. "Bros," he agreed, as did Gan Salin and Nauja. Salin wrapped them all up in a group hug. They laughed.

"See you," Jack said.

They touched their hands to the pedestal at the same time. With a violent tug through space, they disappeared.

———

Jack stumbled from the middle of an inter-space void onto a stone floor. It was a corridor of brown, dusty stone, with a height and width of nine feet. It instantly felt claustrophobic.

The air was stuffy. The corridor turned sharply to the front and back of Jack, at ninety-degree angles, and lit torches hung intermittently on the walls, dense enough to illuminate the labyrinth but sparse enough to leave deep shadows between them.

Jack's eyes surveyed everything—mostly because there wasn't much to see. He chuckled. "Holy shit, Brock. This place is—"

And then his heart dropped, because Brock wasn't there.

———

Edgar watched Vivi pace through his room with purpose. Her steps were solid, and her entire body exuded authority, confidence.

He, on the other hand, was just sitting on a chair with his arms crossed. "I appreciate you giving the leadership of the alliance to the professor," he said, "but if you think that's going to change my mind, you're mistaken."

"It's not a bribe," Vivi retorted. "I am fit to lead from the front, and she is fit to lead from the back. That's all there is to it."

"I understand."

"Then—"

"No." He shook his head. "I'm not fighting."

He expected her to argue fiercely. In truth, his heart had been aching all this time, and his enhanced brain had already ran a hundred scenarios for how this conversation might unfold.

To his horror, Vivi chose the path he feared most. She sighed.

"I understand how you feel, Edgar. And you're right. You have already contributed greatly to our cause, both during and after the Tournament. If you don't want to fight, I cannot force you." Another sigh as she plopped into a second chair, ignoring the neat stacks of paper piled around her. "But, Edgar... We are dying."

He wanted to interrupt and say something. The more he let her go on, the more right she would be. He didn't want her to be right. Fighting a war, using his magic to inflict harm on others, would break his heart into a hundred pieces.

It would be nothing like the Integration Tournament.

He found nothing to say. Not fast enough.

"Just yesterday, the Ice Peak assaulted my headquarters in Ouagadougou while I was away. They killed my citizens and soldiers. They decreased our battle power, crumbled our morale, and tore a wound into our flesh."

Edgar flinched. She didn't have to be so vivid. His high intelligence pictured the scene, the mutilated corpses, the stench of war, the screams. It came as natural as visualizing his magic. He couldn't stop it.

"That all happened because I was away," Vivi continued. "The Ice Peak has me in a headlock. If I stay in my headquarters, my people will be fighting a losing battle in the dungeons. If I go with them, my headquarters will be vulnerable. There is nothing I can do before one of my lieutenants gets strong enough to hold the fort, and that could take a long, long time. They don't have the titles we do. They aren't planetary frontrunners."

Edgar gritted his teeth. "Evacuate everyone," he said. "Bring them here. We have Sparman. He—"

"You already know that's impossible. Why suggest it?" Her gaze was piercing. "I could evacuate my elites, but that would mean leaving everyone else to Petrovic and the Animal Kingdom's mercy—a quality they lack."

"You can—"

"I can do nothing." She shook her head, and the pain in her voice made him unable to retort. "We cannot win this war without you, Edgar. I know how difficult it is for you to fight. I know how desperately you don't want it. I know, because I am also a Mental cultivator. I feel every scrap of pain I cause. I'm aware of every mother crying because I killed her son. But, Edgar, I cannot let that stop me. If I don't fight, my people will die. It will be *their* mothers crying. My mother.

"I am carving up my soul to save the ones who believe in me, and I implore you to do the same. When everything is over, half the people will be dead. You get to choose whether it will be me, you, Margaret, Harambe, everyone you've ever known and loved... or the enemy, who sold out our planet to the Animal Kingdom to save themselves."

She stood, letting her flame-painted cape flutter in the small room. Edgar saw she was upset. Her tight jaw and narrowed eyes. Her calm voice was only a facade. On the inside, she was burning.

Her words came from her soul. How could he possibly retort?

Vivi approached the open window and grabbed its edge. "What I'm trying to say, Edgar," she set one foot on the window sill, "is that you have the choice to protect your friends or let them die. You cannot avoid it. Sitting idle is also a choice. And I expect you to make the right one."

She jumped out, not looking back, falling from the second story. She rose back up, carried by flame wings. Edgar watched until she disappeared in the horizon.

She left him miserable. His heart was about to break in half. His soul was in deep pain.

He understood what she was saying. But his Dao... It wasn't one of battle. It was magic. Beauty, wonder, dreams. It was supposed to be a breathtaking "wow," an escape, what he felt as a child reading his favorite book. Using it to cause harm wouldn't just pain him deeply; it would injure his Dao, dilute it, stain it, refuse it.

He only understood this after the Integration Tournament, when he finally had time to look deep inside himself. Back then, he'd just been doing what others told him to, even if he hated it. Now, he understood that battle was not his path. And yet...

Why does it have to be me? he lamented, burying his face in his palms. Why is the world like this?

Who knew that so much beauty could bring so much pain?

He loved magic. If there was no war going on, he would be the happiest man in the world. It's all he ever wanted.

But there *was* a war going on. He had to make a choice. And, between the bubbling pressure inside him and the terrifying pressure from outside, Edgar felt crushed.

And from the pressure came a spark. And the world opened its eyes. And Edgar sunk into his soul, meeting the breathtaking, wonderful, indescribably beautiful essence that was magic.

His breakthrough began.

CHAPTER SEVENTY-FOUR
LABYRINTH RING

THE LABYRINTH CONTAINED A WHOLE LOT OF NOTHING. TORCH-LIT CORRIDORS AS far as the eye could see. Turns after turns after twists and bends. Dead-ends. Brown stone in all directions. Forks and intersections every two minutes.

It was driving Jack mad. Even his newest title didn't help.

Congratulations! Title "Fifth Ring Conqueror" upgraded to "Sixth Ring Conqueror!"
Efficacy of all stats: +25% → +30%

Labyrinth Ring Quest:
• Defeat the Guardian.
• Make your way to Garden Ring.

However, what drove him even madder than the labyrinth itself was worry.

Brock is somewhere out there... Without me. Jack's heart was strangled by black snakes as he ran, making turns and bends and twists. *Please be okay. Please be okay.*

The labyrinth wasn't supposed to split the two of them. They were bound spiritually. Even teleportation worked on them at the same time. So why?

Jack didn't know. All he could do was endure his fear and run, hoping to catch a sound, any sound, so he could follow it. Alas, all he heard was his own footsteps, endlessly stomping against the stone.

"BROCK!" he shouted. So what if there were monsters in the labyrinth? By now, he could take most of them. Even if an Elite showed up, he could activate his Life Drop and hope for the best. It might draw even stronger things, but there was nothing he could do about that. If there was a God, the labyrinth monsters would lack the space monsters' acute Dao perception.

And if a King showed up...

Well, Jack had to risk it. Brock wasn't even at the E-Grade. If any monster noticed him, he was instantly dead.

Name: Jack Rust
Species: Human, Earth-387
Faction: Bare Fist Brotherhood (E)
Grade: E
Class: Fiend of the Iron Fist (Elite)
Level: 93

Strength: 395
Dexterity: 375
Constitution: 395
Mental: 50
Will: 80

Skills: Ghost Step I
Dao Skills: Indomitable Body III, Meteor Punch II, Iron Fist Style II, Brutalizing Aura I
Daos: Perfect Dao Seed of the Fist (late), Dao Root of Indomitable Will (fused), Dao Root of Life (fused), Dao Root of Power
Titles: Planetary Frontrunner (10), Planetary Torchbearer (1), Sixth Ring Conqueror

Trial Planet had been kind to Jack. Fruitful. His level had risen meteorically, reaching almost the high E-Grade, and his skills and Dao Roots had vastly increased in potency.

Unfortunately, there was nothing in that status screen to help him locate Brock.

How big could the labyrinth be?

Surely, not too much. This was the seventh ring already. They had to be pretty close to the planet's core.

If every ring is around a hundred miles wide, and there are two rings under me, I'm at a radius of two hundred miles. The surface of such a sphere...

Jack did some quick calculations, and the result made him pale. *Five hundred thousand square miles! That can't be right...*

From what he understood, there was only one guardian. The labyrinth had to be small enough that the cultivators could walk there no matter which entrance they used.

Maybe the rings get smaller. Maybe I'm in a radius of... What's the best case? Ten miles?

Even ten miles came up to a surface area of over a thousand square miles. There had to be something better. There was no way people were expected to travel a thousand miles through such crampy, winding stone corridors. They would die of thirst before even reaching the guardian.

Regardless, Jack's result was that the labyrinth was large. Perhaps not as unfathomably large as he calculated it, but still highly expansive. Finding Brock here would be like searching for a needle in a haystack.

Jack's heart dropped, his steps slowing. *Where even am I?* he wondered, looking around. *Darker walls lead to the guardian. Got it.*

Maybe Brock would run into other cultivators and manage to ally with them. All Jack could do was travel to the meeting point—the guardian—and hope for the best, while mentally berating himself all the while.

Harambe trusted me with his son, and I went and lost him. Idiot.

Jack's mood was at an all-time low. He itched to bury his fist into a wall, and he would have, if he wasn't afraid of the corridor collapsing on his head.

Which is why he was pleasantly surprised to see a monster round the corner.

It was an abomination—a monster of bone and scrawny limbs. It had a vaguely humanoid shape, except its entire body was bleached white and made of bones twisted around each other like a beanstalk.

Bone Sentinel, Level 124
A creature made to endlessly wander the Labyrinth Ring's corridors and fight intruders. It possesses low Mental and Will attributes, as well as low speed, but outstanding strength and durability. When a Bone Sentinel slays an enemy, it either absorbs their skeleton into its own or raises the skeleton as a new Bone Sentinel. Therefore, their numbers are self-replenishing.

Knowing that defeat would let this monster spin his own skeleton into a monster didn't at all abate Jack's fighting spirit.

"Come here, fucker," he said, cracking his knuckles. "I will break all your bones and feed them to you."

If the Bone Sentinel understood his words, it didn't show it. Instead, it raised two hands tipped with sharpened bone claws. A thick white tail followed it around the corner, lined with teeth and ending in a human skull.

Jack let it approach. After facing Copy Jack and Bocor, its movements came across telegraphed. When it got within nine feet, he crouched into a stance, Ghost Stepped into its guard, and smashed a Meteor Punch into its chest.

Bone shattered under his knuckles. The monster's body caved under the strike. The explosion carried on inside its body, shattering its innards and sending shards of bone flying out of the wound.

Still, the monster held. The bony tail slithered past Jack and raked his thigh, carving a bone-deep wound with the skull's teeth. Jack grimaced, pushing past it. Such pain was nothing compared to the Ancient trial.

He charged, catching up with the monster before it even hit the far wall, and smashed out another Meteor Punch. It tried to block with crossed arms to protect its chest, a grotesque sight of gnarled bone that made Jack's stomach lurch, but it was unable to block his full-power strike.

Bone shattered. The walls shook as the monster crashed into them, leaving a finger-deep impression on the stone, then collapsed in a broken heap.

Level up! You have reached Level 94.

Jack stood over it, panting. He'd received another slash to the ribs as he obliterated the monster, but nothing too deep. He could already sense his regenerative powers stitching his skin together, regrowing his muscles and tendons.

It was pretty disturbing, actually.

As he observed the broken monster, his fear for Brock intensified. These things would cut the brorilla into ribbons. If the labyrinth was filled with them...

I need to keep moving, he thought.

Endless corridors after endless corridors. Jack didn't know if he was moving in the right direction. The walls were supposed to darken as one approached the guardian, but he couldn't spot any differences. Was he just moving in circles?

At the next fork, he tried to turn by ninety degrees and keep going as straight as possible. After a while, the walls got just a touch darker. Or maybe it was just his impression.

Hours passed.

Throughout the journey, Jack discovered a few interesting things. There were crab monsters patrolling the corridors—little blue things that reached up to his knee. However, they were weak. Far too weak to challenge anyone with the ability to make it here. And they skittered away whenever they saw him.

Why?

Stone-eater Crab, Level 56
Crabs that subsist entirely on stone, which their unique digestive system can metabolize into water and nutrition. For that reason, they are often found deep beneath the earth, living in large communities that, over centuries, hollow out rock formations.

Jack failed to see what a stone-eating crab added to this labyrinth. Eating the walls? On the bright side, he didn't care, either.

He only ran into one more Bone Sentinel. The rest of the living creatures he met were all blue crabs, and even those only appeared once every ten minutes, roughly. For the most part, the labyrinth was despondently empty.

That was a good sign. With a little bit of luck and caution, Brock could maybe avoid everything.

Jack also hadn't met a single cultivator. He hadn't heard or seen signs of intelligent life. It was like he had his own, private labyrinth.

After defeating a crab—to see if something would happen, but nothing did—he used one of its pincers to carve a capital J on the walls. He then put the crab down and promised not to kill another—they hadn't attacked him, and they were so low-leveled they barely even gave him any experience.

It was one of those times when things randomly came into context. The black wolf he'd fought tooth and nail against at the Forest of the Strong was weaker than these crabs. It was a stunning realization. Sometimes, he just failed to understand how quickly and how far he was progressing.

To the current him, the black wolf would be almost comically slow. To a normal human, these little blue crabs would be fast as lightning. Maybe their little pincers could snap clean through a limb.

Jack didn't know how long he spent alone in the labyrinth. It could have been six hours. It could have been two days. His throat was getting parched—Brock had his supplies—and the walls were discreetly getting darker. By now, he was pretty sure they were several shades darker than when he first started exploring. He was on the right track.

Wandering became mindless. He simply jogged ahead—at the speed of a pre-System human's sprint—taking one turn after another.

When another cultivator appeared, he almost didn't register them. Then, his eyes widened, and his thoughts screeched to a halt, as did his feet.

"Jack Rust," said the other person. "What a coincidence."

"You have got to be kidding me," Jack said.

CHAPTER SEVENTY-FIVE
FROM PRESSURE COMES THE SPARK

NAUJA STUMBLED INTO A WALL. STILL REELING FROM THE AFTEREFFECTS OF teleportation, she leaned on it.

Deep inside, she was excited. It was finally time to explore alone. To venture on her own power. To prove she was worthy. A primal urge rose inside her, the urge to—

"Oh, hey. Fancy seeing you here."

Nauja's excitement deflated.

"What?" Gan Salin said, standing behind her. "Are you not happy to see me?"

"Do you want the honest answer?"

"No. The good one."

Jack's friend, the Sage, had mentioned they would probably be split up. This *was* a split. But it was the most annoying one possible.

Nauja sighed. "Let's set some ground rules. If you speak nonsense, I will cut your tongue off. Okay?"

Salin wasn't even fazed. "Oh, come on. That's clearly a bluff."

"Wanna try me?"

"Sure."

She glared at him. He smiled radiantly. Nauja clicked her tongue and turned around. "Just keep the crazy to a minimum."

"As always."

Done with the annoying canine, Nauja inspected the place they were in. Crampy corridors of brown stone. Torches on the walls. No sound besides theirs.

"I think we're alone," she said, keeping her voice low. She groaned inwardly. If Father heard her shouting in hostile territory...

No. Mistakes happen. This is why I'm here. To learn and train alone.

"How big do you think this place is?" she asked.

"At least two."

"Two what?"

"Two bigs. Square bigs, to be precise. Wait—that's called wides!" He slapped his forehead. "I'm a genius!"

Nauja shut her eyes and took a deep, trembling breath. This was going to feel like an eternity.

———

Brock found himself in a place of crampy brown corridors. The bends at his front and back were waiting, yawning maws of death just out of sight.

The very first thing he noticed was that he was alone. Everyone was gone. Even Big Bro.

A pit opened in Brock's stomach. He thought he was falling. Next thing he knew, he was leaning on a wall.

Big Bro was gone.

He always knew this day would come. But not now. It couldn't be now. He was trapped in a place where he shouldn't be. Everything here could kill him instantly. Big Bro protected him. With Big Bro gone...

What would happen to Brock?

The little brorilla gathered himself, extinguishing the rising panic. He then raised his head and took a long, deep breath, flexing his lung muscles to draw in as much air as possible. It was stuffy and smelled stale—like bad bread.

Then, he forced a massive exhale, relaxing at the same time. His fear remained, but his mind was back.

The wise bro had said Brock and Big Bro would go together. Clearly, that was a mistake. Therefore, Brock had to make do with what he had.

He was alone. There was no way back. He had to find Big Bro before whatever prowled these corridors found him. What was the best way to go about it?

As a young brorilla, barely a few months old, Brock wasn't the brightest. However, the brain was a muscle. By flexing his Big Thought, he forced himself to think strong, going beyond his natural limits.

When he stopped, the plan was made.

They'd agreed to meet at a place called the guardian's gates. To get there, they had to follow the darkest walls. Brock would head over stealthily. Making noise might draw Big Bro, but monsters were far more likely to be near. After all, if this place was small, it wouldn't be a labyrinth.

If he ran into other people in the meantime, he would join them to protect himself. That was his best shot at staying alive.

Brock opened his eyes and nodded. He had a plan.

Would it succeed? Probably not. Chances were, he would die very quickly. Nobody would ever find his corpse, Big Bro would be very sad, and Father would be disappointed.

But if that happened, so be it. Brock would just do his best.

On the bright side, he had food and water. Since he felt useless, he volunteered to carry everything. Dog bro and girl bro had taken their shares before entering the labyrinth, but Brock still had Big Bro's share.

The labyrinth was about to face its greatest adversary: a small brorilla wearing red pants, carrying two bags of food and an Ancient artifact called the Staff of Stone.

Squaring his jaw, Brock started walking. Slowly, silently, and ever carefully. He could not afford to relax.

———

Nauja peered behind a corner. Nothing.

She motioned for Salin to follow. The only sounds reaching her ears were their muffled footsteps and the occasional crack as Gan Salin broke off a chunk of bread to gather the crumbs. He was spreading those on the ground behind him.

"Can you stop?" she asked, gritting her teeth.

"I told you, I'm a genius," he whispered. "Some good people on

Jack's planet taught me this. If you are lost, just leave a trail of bread-crumbs behind you."

"How is that helping?"

"I'm not sure, to be honest. Perhaps Jack will get the clue and follow us? It's supposed to help us find our way back, but ah, I don't think we want that."

For the tenth time in half an hour, Nauja resisted the urge to smack him.

"Just break the bread more softly. I almost jump every time."

"Just hear more softly."

She whirled around. "Listen here, you—"

She froze. At the end of the corridor behind Gan Salin stood a white creature of terror. Bleached, entwined bones, the skeleton of a human twisted ten times around itself by a forest giant.

The sense of wrongness brought her to full alert even before the System's screen did.

Bone Sentinel, Level 124

She was level 107. Salin was at 79. This creature out-leveled them greatly, and most importantly, this terrain didn't favor them.

The Bone Sentinel stared at them. Not moving. Just staring.

"Salin," she said quietly. "I want you to turn around slowly. Don't panic."

He obliged. Seeing the high-level terror before them, he said, "Holy shit, is this guy ugly."

Perhaps the thing had ears. Perhaps it was just luck. Whatever the case, the monster chose that exact moment to charge, jaws hanging open in a silent roar and bone-tipped claws rending the air.

"RUN!" Nauja shouted, bounding away from the creature. They weren't equipped to fight it in such narrow space. They had no one to block its assault. Gan Salin was too low in level, and she was built as a ranged fighter.

At least, the monster was slow.

Nauja found herself sprinting through the corridors, making one blind turn after the other. It reminded her of the time in Forbidden Cave, when she and Jack escaped the minotaur.

Her bare feet stomped against the stone floor, and the wind blew on her back, pushing her forward. It did the same to Salin, helping him keep up. The canine was fast, thankfully, though he lacked endurance.

The monster made no sound. Only its stomps were any indication it was still chasing. Nauja braved a glance back. With a body like that, it was a wonder it could even run. Being slow was natural.

Her glance also revealed Gan Salin breaking the bread and throwing its crumbs on the ground at an accelerated pace.

"What the hell are you doing?" she thundered.

"Marking our way back!"

"Back to *what*!"

"I don't know yet. To be honest, I didn't even expect to reach this—"

They stomped into an intersection of four corridors. Another bone monster spotted them from one and charged after them. Nauja grabbed Gan Salin's collar and darted sideways, cutting off his words as they rushed into a different corridor and kept going.

"Keep your mouth shut," she hissed through gritted teeth. "There are more of them."

This time, Salin complied without a word.

Outrunning one monster wouldn't be a problem. They were significantly faster. But if there were more at every corner... Well, then they would die.

And the walls were ever so slowly getting darker.

———

Despite his best efforts, Brock was troubled.

He was being stealthy. When approaching a corner, he always peeked out before proceeding. At intersections, he stretched his ears at every possible path before deciding. He didn't make a sound, always keeping an ear out for footsteps.

He'd heard a few, occasionally. But when he hid near an intersection to watch who produced them, he only saw a horror of twisted bones, like a rose that was all thorns.

He ran away.

These creatures were easy to avoid. Their footsteps were audible, if one paid close attention, and they weren't too common.

But there were more than just the horrors of bones.

Brock spotted blue crabs that reached his waist, just roaming the corridors and eating small pieces of stone off the walls. They kept the walls perfectly straight, only taking care of tiny outcroppings or puking liquid stone to fill in little dents on the ground.

These creatures didn't feel like monsters. However, they always attacked Brock on sight. Since they were vastly stronger than him, he had to run away. At least they were slow, their movements rough and stony.

He managed to outrun the first crab that chased him but lost a bag of food in the process. He also lost his way—though that didn't matter too much. He remained equally lost.

This could not continue. The crabs were too many. Every few minutes, he would discover one and have to backtrack. If he was chased and forced to run blindly again, he might end up sandwiched by another crab or, even worse, a bone monster.

He did not want to be caught by those. He witnessed one eating a blue crab. The sight was brutal and gruesome. When the bone monster was done, not even the crab's shell or blood was left.

Brock was feeling trapped. Like the walls were closing around him. He kept running into dead-ends or monster-infested corridors. He circumvented all those, but his escape routes were cut off one by one, and soon, there would be no path left. The enemies he'd bypassed could arrive behind him at any moment. And he was crossing the large labyrinth with slow, tiny steps.

At this rate, even if the monsters didn't catch him, he would run out of water and die before he even made it a few miles in.

Immense pressure threatened to smash Brock. On one hand, he had his responsibility toward Big Bro, Father, Mother, and everyone else. If he died here, he would make many people very sad.

On the other hand was his responsibility to himself. He didn't want to die. Not here, alone and trapped in bare corridors. Not to faceless bone monsters. He wanted Big Bro. Mother. Father. *Anyone.*

He was scared. The monsters closing in from all directions became a mental bind around his mind, bit by bit increasing the pressure. He fought to remain sane, to flex his bravery muscles and retain control of himself, but it was difficult. The fear was overwhelming. The helplessness was wearing him down.

Panic was rising again, the only response his body could muster to the pressure.

This was all happening because he was weak. He had only ventured this far because of Big Bro. Without his protection, Brock was nothing.

Why? Why did it have to be like that? Why did he have to be *weak*?

He was born weak. He was smaller than the other brorilla children. His muscles were less defined. That was why Father kicked him out of the pack—though Big Bro insisted that Father had acted out of love.

He'd grown stronger by Big Bro's side, but he remained useless. Ever since they came to this weird place, Brock had achieved nothing. He'd always been carried and protected by Big Bro. If this continued, then sooner or later, he would be cast out again. Maybe forced to return to his pack as a loser. Nobody would accept him.

There was a clear line between survival and death, victory and defeat, triumph and uselessness. It was called strength.

But his muscles were too small. He tried his hardest, but it was never enough. The Big Thought promised him strength, but it, too, abandoned him, betrayed him.

And yet, if there was one thing that could save him now, it *was* this Big Thought. It had given him most of his strength. To get even more strength, he just had to make it bigger. A Bigger Thought.

Brock was surrounded and overwhelmed. He almost broke but didn't. And from the pressure came a spark. The Big Thought called to him. And Brock dove into it.

To make it bigger.

CHAPTER SEVENTY-SIX
MAKING FRENEMIES

JACK'S EYES TRAVELED FROM THE TIP OF THE LONG SWORD, DOWN ITS LENGTH, to its handle, and up to the sharp brown eyes that hid under dark hair. A tattered cloak drifted behind this man, its edge almost touching the floor, and his brows were raised in amusement.

Human (Earth-74), Level 122
Faction: Wide Swirls (B-Grade)
Title: Wide Swirls Prodigy

Minotaur, Level 115
Faction: Animal Kingdom (B-Grade)
Title: Resilient

"Jack Rust," he said. "What a coincidence."

Jack clenched his fists, instantly entering battle mode. His eyes narrowed as they took in Longsword's form, as well as Bocor, the minotaur, whose gaze burned with hatred.

"Longsword," he said, ignoring Bocor. "Fuck."

"Looks like fate wants you dead, Jack Rust," Long replied, laughing. Bocor took this as a sign of aggression and drew his tower shield, approaching Jack with the intent to battle. His position was expertly chosen. He could easily intercept any of Jack's attacks without inhibiting those of Longsword.

Not that the lord needed any help.

Jack's brain worked quickly. Bocor hated his guts, and he'd offended Longsword last time they met. Then, the lord had declared they would be enemies starting from Space Ring.

What kind of shitty luck is this!

He gritted his teeth, calculating his odds. He had very little confidence in beating Longsword, even though his strength had increased significantly since the last time they fought. Plus, Bocor was here.

On the other hand, if he ran, he still couldn't escape. Longsword had demonstrated his speed when he hunted Jack's group through the desert of Village Ring. Bocor was slow. If Jack ran, he could split up his enemies, forcing Longsword to fight alone. Then, if things went Jack's way, perhaps he could—

Thinking time was over. Bocor was upon him, his horns almost scraping the ceiling and his tower shield blocking most of the corridor. He moved from side to side, revealing openings through which Longsword could thrust his sword.

Jack crouched and prepared to leap back. Ghost Step was only a thought away.

"Wait a moment," Longsword said. Bocor froze. Unwillingness flickered in his eyes before he stepped aside like a good grunt, making room for Longsword to approach Jack, who could run away at any moment.

"Don't run," Longsword continued. "It would change nothing and lose us all precious time."

Jack's eyes narrowed further. "Aren't you going to attack me?"

"I am considering it."

There was haughtiness in that voice—deep and masculine, carrying a sort of brutality. At the same time, it hid great intelligence, along with an almost playful edge.

Longsword was strong, imposing, charming, and intelligent. Coupling that with high-end training since childhood and a natural talent for the Dao, he really did seem to have everything.

Although, Jack *was* good at punching stuff. "Consider it faster."

"Why the rush?"

"Because your witch could be flanking me as we speak," Jack said.

The ends of Longsword's lips rose a bit. "She was split from us. A shame, really, but not even Bone Generals can catch her. She'll be fine."

Jack waited in silence.

"How about we relax and have a little chat?" Longsword asked, raising his hands. "We are all lost in here. Fighting each other would be a waste."

"I thought we were enemies."

"We can be, if you want. But our enmity will last very little, and it will end with your head far away from your shoulders."

Jack crouched deeper, ready to escape at a moment's notice. "What do you want?"

"You."

"Explain."

Longsword leaned in just a hair. "Have you considered my offer at all, Jack?"

"Working under you?"

"Yes."

Jack's mind spun again. He hadn't considered it. Joining Longsword seemed like a bad idea after seeing how coldly he treated Bocor, one of his closest followers. Even now, the minotaur was sitting by the side, steaming from all orifices but not daring to speak up. Longsword hadn't spared him a single glance, like he was little more than furniture.

Jack speaking his thoughts right now might be a deadly mistake. For whatever reason, Longsword still seemed willing to negotiate. If the other choice was death, perhaps Jack could pretend to think about it until he could escape.

The Dao of the Fist reveled in headfirst collisions, but it had nothing against deception.

"Of course I've thought about it... but I hesitate," Jack said. Tipping his hand too early could only end badly. He wanted to scout Longsword's intentions and see where this was headed.

After all, he followed the Dao of the Fist. Deception was fine, but betrayal and dishonor were entirely different matters. Jack couldn't swear loyalty as a lie, not even to save his life.

"I can see that. I have a proposition for you," Longsword said. "Join me for this ring. Just the labyrinth. Afterward, you can go your own way. We don't even have to be enemies—though we probably will be."

"Sir!" Bocor couldn't contain himself. "That's—"

"Silence," Longsword said without even turning around. Bocor bit his tongue. It must have taken all his willpower and then some. Jack could see veins popping under his fur.

"Why?" Jack asked.

"Because I appreciate your value," Longsword replied. He sounded honest. "You possess great strength and titles. If you reach the peak of the E-Grade, you will probably possess the strength of a lord. Comparable to mine."

"So you want to keep me close."

"Ideally, I want to recruit you. You are a rogue cultivator, and you've made powerful enemies. An agreement between us is something we could both benefit from."

Jack was beginning to sense there would be no battle here, but he remained on guard. "And if I leave after this ring?"

"Nothing ventured, nothing lost. It's a gamble. Your perception of me is probably skewed. If we travel together for a few days, if you come to understand how things work in the galaxy, I believe you may have a change of heart. That will be a great boon to me and my faction. If not... Well, I won't lose much, to be honest. A King-tier rogue cultivator won't matter in the grand scheme of things, especially since the Animal Kingdom will take care of you in short order."

"They can try."

Bocor's head almost exploded from suppressed anger.

"This is the best offer you could ask for," Longsword continued. "I could kill you. Yet I offer you a chance to not only live, but also enjoy my protection for the duration of this ring—and I get an extra helper for any trial we find. Any other lord would demand your absolute loyalty in exchange, but I understand that someone with your Dao would die before yielding. Therefore, all I ask is a *chance* to change your mind."

Jack had to admit this sounded good. Longsword wasn't stupid. He understood Jack's potential and offered a deal that worked for both of them.

Could he actually be decent? Jack wondered. Whatever the case, he had to respect Longsword's adept handling of the situation.

"You got me," Jack said, slowly straightening his body. If Longsword wanted to attack, there was no need to go through all this. "I have to admit. I expected you to be more..."

"Thoughtless? Arrogant? Overbearing?"

"Something like that, yes."

Longsword laughed, a deep, booming sound that came directly from his stomach. "You will find, Jack Rust, that most people are as complex as you. Nobody reaches the top by being an idiot."

Jack found mirth rising inside him, but he kept it down. At the end of the day, this man was more an enemy than a friend.

Another downside here was that Jack had planned to kill as many bone monsters as possible in the labyrinth to level up. The presence of Longsword and Bocor would greatly affect the experience he got from each monster... but there wasn't much he could do about it. Any way he looked at it, teaming up here was the best way to go about things—among other benefits, it was the fastest way to find Brock.

Besides, leveling was already slow. A couple extra levels would matter far less than any benefits he got through a temporary team-up.

Not to mention that he was completely lost by himself.

"So, what now?" he asked.

"Now, we keep walking. The darker the walls, the closer we are to the guardian."

"I've been wondering: just how big is this labyrinth?"

"Oh, very. Hundreds of square miles filled with winding paths. Reaching the guardian from here should take us days. Maybe a week."

"Then I have to endure this for a week?" Jack asked, motioning at Bocor, who glared with every fiber of his being.

Longsword turned to his follower. "I know this is difficult for you, Bocor, but bear with it. At the end of the day, you and Jack have no personal enmity—and, if you do, you were the one who started it. Perhaps this is doing your faction a favor."

Bocor growled. "The Animal Kingdom doesn't take losses."

"So it says, but you'd be surprised. Now, how about you accept my judgment and rein in your emotions?"

Longsword's words were spoken calmly and with a smile, but they contained unshakable confidence. Bocor had no choice but to relent.

Longsword gave Jack a side glance. He probably expected him to walk forward and extend a handshake to Bocor. Jack didn't do that. Neither did Bocor. In the end, Longsword simply shrugged.

"Do you know the way?" Jack asked.

"We have a compass," the lord replied, revealing an intricately carved piece with three needles in three concentric circles.

Jack's brows rose. "Huh. I never considered that."

"You couldn't find one, anyway. Trial Planet is too messed up. Thankfully, being part of a B-Grade faction comes with a lot of perks." He winked.

Jack chuckled. "Too bad I'll never find out."

"You certainly will, one way or another. Now, let's go. With any luck, we'll find a Treasure Trial on the way." Longsword beamed a smile at Jack. "That is why you entered the labyrinth early, is it not?"

"I did that to avoid you."

Longsword laughed again. "Well, I believe you'll find there is more to this labyrinth than mere stone walls. This ring contains Trials, like Space Ring, though not all of them are Dao Trials. Treasure Trials are not tailor-made to their creator's Dao, some will simply give you treasures that can be useful to anyone. Unlike Dao Trials, you can enter as many of them as you like. They're one of the main allures of Labyrinth Ring, as they're easier to complete."

"The plan is to get as many as possible then?"

"They aren't that common. Finding even one is considered lucky."

"I see. Because Trial Planet has existed for so long that most of them are taken already?"

"Oh, not at all. Labyrinth Ring changes every few months. The paths move around, and new Trials appear in the place of old ones. They contain highly valuable rewards and are hard to conquer, but they are also very few."

Jack tilted his head. "Then, shouldn't everyone be rushing to get them? I heard that the Garden Assault waits a few days in Space Ring."

"That's the agreement, yes. But there was a super horde, and many teams rushed to the labyrinth, so I just came along. Let the other lords take their time. What are they going to do? Tell me off? I will have the rewards of at least one Treasure Trial, and they will have the moral high ground. Guess what wins in a fight."

Jack couldn't prevent the ends of his lips from rising. "I guess that's one way to look at it."

"Of course. As I said, I'm not an idiot."

"Do you also have a way to locate other people, not-an-idiot?" Jack hadn't forgotten about Brock. Finding his brorilla remained his number one priority. Everything else could come after.

Longsword shook his head. "Sadly not. If I did, Eralda would be here, too. She's my ice witch, by the way."

Jack looked down, then up again. "I understand."

He never expected things to go this way. That he would be split up from Brock, then travel and make deals with his enemies. That Longsword would turn out to be terrifyingly enterprising.

The moment the lord turned away, Bocor gave Jack a dirty look. Clearly, the grudge between them was nowhere near settled, but Jack didn't care too much.

"Hey, Bocor," he said, making the minotaur's dirty look intensify. "I know we don't like each other, but it looks like we'll be traveling together for some time. Keep it in your pants or you'll just be annoying to everyone. And, by the way, I beat you when I was level 84 and you were level 115. Now, I'm at 94, but you are still at 115. Do the math."

Bocor's face split into a predatory grin. "But guess who got a Trial in Space Ring, dipshit. If you want me to tear you a new asshole, I'm ready anytime."

Jack turned to face Bocor squarely.

"No fighting." Longsword raised his arms. "The Trials of Labyrinth Ring are no laughing matter. We will need to be at full power. If you want to settle your differences, do it in Garden Ring."

Jack held Bocor's stare for another moment. He wasn't going to look away first.

The minotaur turned his eyes after a moment of inner struggle. "Yes, sir," he said darkly. "Garden Ring, Jack Rust."

Jack snorted. "Sure. Garden Ring." He didn't know what that ring was, but it almost sounded nice.

CHAPTER SEVENTY-SEVEN
EDGAR'S BREAKTHROUGH

EDGAR FLOATED IN NOTHINGNESS, SUSPENDED BEFORE A MASSIVE SAPPHIRE sphere. His eyes watered. It was the most beautiful thing he'd ever seen.

The sphere was light blue, with little stars glistening inside. It was made of a material like starry silk. The outer layers flowed around the sphere, while the inner ones stayed still. Clouds of colors floated within, occasionally merging with each other or splitting to create new combinations.

A magical sight.

Edgar tried to draw a deep breath, only to realize he had no body. Well, he did, but not a physical one. Though it looked like him, he realized that here, wherever here was, he was a floating orb of light, and the physical form was only a mantle he chose to clad himself in.

He got rid of it at once. His body was part of him, but this glowing orb... This was the *real* Edgar. The closer to the truth he was, the better.

He knew what was happening. This was the inside of his soul. He was breaking through.

Excitement flooded him like water pouring out of a broken dam. His worries and fears washed away in the stream of power. He wasn't useless. He hadn't taken a wrong step. His breakthrough had just been a matter of time—and the right circumstances, as he observed. High pressure was the catalyst to forming a Dao Seed. Perhaps not the only one, but a catalyst nonetheless.

His first instinct was to note it down. But, as his attention rose to the sapphire sphere, he was captivated again.

This was magic. His magic. His dream. He had to succeed.

The Dao Stabilizing Pill he'd gotten from Ar'Tazul activated in his stomach, where it had waited for weeks. A warm stream passed through his veins, calming him.

He could feel the Dao calling. The sphere meant to merge with him, become one whole entity of vast, breathtaking power.

Edgar jumped right in.

Brilliance surrounded him on all sides. He had no eyes, yet he saw. No ears, yet he heard. Giant mountains of gold. Floating islands over the sea. Animals made of stars and solar gasses. Humans of glass, their heart shining orange, and a giant, benevolent eye with three tentacles trailing behind it.

Edgar knew not who he was. The essence of magic was distilled into his body, filling his mind with power and wonder.

One moment, he was a bearded old man. As he gently raised his hand, the sea rose with it, and as he brought his cane down, the waters split as if by heaven's sword. Then, he was a winged woman surrounded by light. One smile was all it took for the earth to mend under her feet, wiping away the wounds of war. He was a barefoot child, cradled in an alley between buildings, with the heavy rain cascading over him and making him shiver. Magic erupted from his body, washing away the pain and fear, bringing warmth he'd never felt before.

A flash of pain snapped his attention to the present. The Dao around him was an angry tide, every part rising to seek his attention. With a second flash of pain, a ring of light spread from his body, calming the Dao where the two met.

Edgar was shaken. He'd almost lost himself to the visions. If not for the Dao Stabilization Pill, he would have failed.

But the first hurdle was past. Edgar was the master of himself now, and he couldn't stop excitement from sparking all around him, a wild exhilaration rising from the depths of his soul. It was just him and magic now. A private lesson, with the universe itself as the tutor. He would sink into the wells of knowledge that were his deepest dreams.

He opened his arms and let the Dao flood him. His mind remained whole, an impregnable fortress, but the essence of magic filled his body to the brim. It spoke to him; sought to take him over. Sought to battle him.

But Edgar corrected it. His magic was not made for battle. It was made to awe, to inspire, to create.

He sensed the misalignment inside him. This was his magic, but it was not the very essence of his being. He was not perfectly aligned with his Dao.

Then again, he didn't need to be. Let the rest of his soul wash away, let the impurities forever hide themselves in a treasure chest under the ocean. This was the path he wanted to walk. This was the life he chose to lead.

This was the Edgar he chose to be.

His mind shattered into a thousand pieces. It remained whole, but each piece faced a different vision, a different scenario. Edgar saw the three people from before and nine hundred and ninety-seven more—one thousand visions, no more and no less.

In each was a creature—be they human, animal, or strange beings he knew nothing of—work their magic. This time, he wasn't them. The vision was a script he could tamper with. He could sense how things were going to turn out, and in every vision, he chose to alter the course of history.

Where the bearded old man split the sea to let his people pass, Edgar forced the waters to bend the knee, saluting the man's effort. Fish danced. A few children behind him laughed.

When the woman smiled and mended the earth, Edgar made flowers rise from the ground. One came up to her nose, blessing her with its fragrance. The angel's smile turned warmer.

Where the child erupted with magic, banishing the cold and fear of rain, Edgar willed the clouds to disperse, letting a brilliant sun dominate the sky, the herald of a new day.

In every vision, Edgar followed his heart to change the world. He found himself laughing. All the awe, beauty, and childlike wonder he created came back to encompass him, suffusing his soul until it was ready to burst.

The visions went away. Edgar was left with a body of magic, a soul bursting at the seams. His smile was warm and his eyes sparkling. He let himself stand, taking a deep breath to stabilize his new Dao Seed.

He then opened his eyes to find a different world. A world where he was one step closer to the person he dreamt of being.

Edgar waved his hand, and a gentle breeze escaped from the window and flew around the humans, gymonkeys, and brorillas working in the forest. Where it passed, flowers bloomed in the grass, and the creatures of the forest were tickled.

He waved his other hand, and the messy papers and notes across his study rose, arranging themselves into neat piles deposited on the desk.

The last hints of excess magic, left behind by his breakthrough, were expelled through a slow exhale, which cleaned the room of dust, polished the walls until they shone, and summoned a little spectral monkey dancing in their midst. A final, small gale met the door, swinging it open just as an old lady was about to knock it from the other side.

Edgar raised his eyes. "Hello, Professor."

"Edgar?" the professor said, her eyes widening. She took in the changes, then inspected him. She began to shiver. "Edgar!" she cried out with excitement. "You—"

"I broke through," Edgar said calmly, inspecting his own hand. Physically, nothing had changed. But everything else had.

"That's incredible! You finally did it! You are the first E-Grade on Earth!" The professor was wild with joy. She rushed in to hug him, expressing her deep relief. The lack of an E-Grade had been pressuring them hard. Now, that issue was no more.

However, Edgar did not respond with the same enthusiasm. Still with a smile, he gently pushed her away. The professor frowned and tilted her head at him—but even her prodigious powers of understanding weren't enough to see through his intentions.

"What's the matter?" she finally asked.

"I did break through," Edgar repeated. His smile turned bitter. "I hold great power, but it is not as you hope. Magic is not a weapon. Not my magic. It is a tool of beauty, a device of wonder, a medium of joy."

He could see the professor's heart fall. So did his.

"But, Edgar, if you don't fight..."

"I know."

He pursed his lips. His new Dao Seed was still crying out in joy, relishing in the powers of creation he'd been granted. Yet his heart cried salty tears, because it knew that things were as the professor said. If he did not fight, the people he loved would die. Beauty would lose, and mediocrity would reign. But what could he do, if he wielded great power that was not a weapon?

"My magic is one of peace," he repeated, every word weighing on his soul, "but even roses have thorns." He closed his eyes. The weight of his decision was heavy, too heavy. He was choosing to defile the most beautiful thing in the world, there just wasn't any other choice.

"Just once," he said, and the professor's gaze turned perplexed. "Just once, I will strike out with this power of mine. Just once, will I ruin that which is beautiful. I will tip the equilibrium for your armies. If we fall after that... Then, let it be fate. I will die in a field of flowers."

"Edgar..."

"I will be off, Professor," he said. His body levitated, easily pulled by the strands of the elements around him. It was almost effortless. As he reached the window, he turned to her again, smiling warmly through his pain. "And when I return, prepare a celebration for me, okay? Bring the children. I will give them a show they will never forget."

"Edgar..." Her voice trailed. Why did she look so sad?

Only when his tears touched his lips did Edgar realize he was crying. So be it. He shook his head, letting the tears fall. Even in sadness, there was beauty.

"I will be quick," he said, turning to the horizon. With a pull of the world's strands, he flew away, picking up speed as he headed to the other side of the forest, where they had parked their starship. It wasn't anything spectacular, just the cheapest they could find, but it was plenty for inter-continental travel.

He waved away the guards, entered the shuttle, and took off. Steering this thing was beyond easy. The clouds split around him as he raced to the northeast faster than most planes could.

There was time until he reached his destination. Hours. Until then, he decided to inspect his System notifications.

Congratulations! Dao Root of Magic → Dao Seed of Magic (early)

. . .

Congratulations! F-Grade → E-Grade
Congratulations! Your body has been infused with your Dao, taking
on its attributes.
Intelligence +20
Wisdom +20
Charisma +20
Free stat points per Level up: 2 → 5

Level up! You have reached Level 50.

Congratulations! For being one of the first ten cultivators on your
planet to develop a Dao Seed, you are awarded the Title: Planetary
Torchbearer (10).

Planetary Torchbearer (10): A Title awarded to the first ten
cultivators to develop a Dao Seed in an Integrated planet. A sign of
great potential, marking the owner as a person worthy of the
Immortal System's assistance.

Efficacy of all stats +10%.

Edgar chuckled. He'd theorized many things about the E-Grade. Finally, he was about to find out everything. And most importantly, what Class he would get.

Class Upgrade available. Please choose your new Class:

Elemental Adept
Elemental Adepts are Mental cultivators who specialize in controlling

the nine elements. Their greatest strength is their adaptability, and they exceed in battle scenarios where they can use clever tactics to outwit their enemies.

Arcane Body (Elite)

Most wizards choose to specialize. Arcane Bodies do not; they maintain an affinity with all types of magic. As a result, their battle power is limited, but they boast great utility and adaptability.

"Magic is the very fabric of reality, the driving force of the cosmos. Why limit ourselves to just one corner?"

It saddened Edgar that all the System cared about was battle strength. Was his magic flawed? Was he an outcast? A pariah?

That line of thought evaporated as quickly as it had come. He knew what he felt. Magic *was* supposed to be used his way. Everyone else either compromised, got it wrong, or simply didn't see the world as he did. In any case, his use of magic was the one that fit him best.

Being offered two Classes was pretty normal, from what Ar'Tazul told him. In this case, the choice was clear. The first Class, Elemental Adept, was obviously meant for battle, which put it out of the question.

Elemental Adept was also the Class his master had encouraged him to pick. In fact, most of his training during the Integration Tournament had been meant to unlock this Class. Unfortunately, Edgar had other priorities now, and any lingering doubts were extinguished by the other Class being Elite.

"Arcane Body," Edgar said aloud, tasting the words. He smiled. "Not bad."

It wasn't perfect, but it was meant for him. Perhaps he'd get choices closer to his Dao at the D-Grade—if he ever reached it.

Edgar chose the Arcane Body Class. Immediately, the Class Selection screen disappeared, replaced by a few new ones:

Congratulations! You are now an Arcane Body (Elite).
Congratulations! Mana Manipulation (III) upgraded into
Spontaneous Magic (II).
Class Skill unlocked: Mana Sight (I).

Edgar's world was filled with colors. He could see the strands of magic now! And they were everywhere!

He had to stop and take his time parsing through all the new information. Excitement filled him all the while.

This skill was revolutionary!

Thankfully, Edgar's Mental stat was off the charts. He rearranged his mind to adapt to his new skill, then went on his way. He could feel a Dao Vision at the back of his mind, eager to jump out and present itself to him, but he kept it at bay for now.

When his job was done, he would return to learning. Now... Now, he had to fight. Once.

Dark thoughts filled his mind for the rest of the trip, warring against the joy of breaking through and all the possibilities of his new powers.

Eventually, Edgar reached a world of ice and cold. He hid the starship far away from his destination and flew over the clouds himself for the last few miles. When he descended, he found his target.

Half-buried into a glacier were the headquarters of Ice Peak. A place devoid of E-Grades.

He was going to destroy it.

CHAPTER SEVENTY-EIGHT
BESTIES

"Hey, Nauja, check this out!" Salin held up a blue crab, moving its pincer from side to side. "It says *hi*."

"Salin, put the poor thing down."

"But it's happy. It's waving."

"*You* are waving."

"Fiiine." Salin reluctantly placed the crab on the floor. It skittered away, disappearing behind a turn. "Goodbye, little one!"

"Can you focus for half a second?" Nauja snapped. "You'll attract the bone monsters. If an Elite shows up, we won't be able to escape."

"Oh, don't worry about it. If worse comes to worst, you don't have to run faster than the bone monster, just faster than me. Which you can." He gave her a bright smile. Nauja rolled her eyes—there wasn't much she could retort to that.

They had only barely managed to escape the two bone monsters previously chasing them. Thankfully, the monsters were very slow for their level. Almost like they'd been designed to be escapable.

Of course they were, Salin replied to himself. It makes sense. Hah.

"What?" Nauja asked.

"What, what?"

"You were nodding."

"To myself. I'm thinking smart stuff."

She glared suspiciously. "Do I want to know?"

"Probably not."

"Thank the System."

Salin liked this girl. She always responded to his craziness, letting him go on for longer. Maybe she saw silence as a form of weakness.

In any case, Salin was having great fun. Much better than staying on that silly backwater planet or, even worse, in the uptight Animal Kingdom.

Then again, the Animal Kingdom has female canines. Hmm...

Nauja snapped up a hand. He froze. Nauja was plastered on the wall, peeking from a corner with sharp eyes. He knew what this meant. A bone monster.

Which was pretty silly, in Salin's humble opinion. Why bone monsters? Were they supposed to be disturbing and birth horror in the minds of labyrinth delvers? But they were so slow, even *he* could outrun them. Hell, he was pretty certain he could slip right past one if he had to.

These monsters were more like overblown annoyances than lethal predators.

Couldn't the makers of this place install, I don't know, larger crabs? Crabs are scary. And cool. They can even wave!

Nauja, her body still taut like a drawn bow, lowered her hand. "It's gone," she whispered.

"Good. I was totally paying attention."

There were times when Salin wondered if she would snap. Nobody was watching here. She could dispatch of him quick and easy, and leave his body for the crabs to feast on. Maybe his twisted skeleton would rise in the future to haunt these empty corridors, a reminder of his inescapable mortality and sheer fucking stupidity.

But it wouldn't be stupidity if she didn't snap, right?

An icy moment later, Nauja resumed walking. Salin decided to take five minutes of silence. It wouldn't do for her patience to run out. He needed her in top shape to keep playing!

Not that he couldn't converse by himself, but *he* wasn't as easily frustrated. Plus, he always expected what he'd say next. Speaking with others was much more fun.

The five minutes of silence turned into ten, then twenty. Salin found himself enjoying the mindless wandering. He imagined himself as a bone monster, haunting the labyrinth in eternity, feeding on blue crabs and careless cultivators.

"Boo," he moaned under his breath. Much to his disappointment, Nauja didn't respond. "Boo!" he repeated, slightly louder.

"I can hear you," she replied through gritted teeth.

"Oh, okay. Just making sure."

"You know, your stupidity will get you killed one day. For real."

"But will it be *this* day? Probably not."

"It might if you keep pushing me."

"You wouldn't do that. You love me."

"I barely even like you."

"Aha! So you *do* like me. In that case, allow me to apologize for my overflowing charisma, As we belong to different species, I'm afraid we cannot procreate." Salin resisted a cackle at her silence—even her non-responses were fun! "Speechless, are you?"

"Mercy, please. For the love of the System, just keep your mouth shut."

"Okay."

Yep, Salin was having a lot of fun. This was his favorite ring yet! Much better than the village one, where he was mildly tortured.

At the end of the day, he wasn't a mean individual. He decided to cut back on the insanity, for the sake of Nauja's mental health and his physical one.

The hours flowed. Gan Salin and Nauja kept traveling through the labyrinth, heading ever deeper. The walls around them gradually took on a darker hue of brown—whether by luck or Nauja's skill in navigation, they were heading in the right direction. And, as they did, the bleached bone monsters became even more terrifying.

There was a monotony to the journey. A monotony that began to exhaust even Salin's vast reserves of witty remarks. Hour after hour, day after day, they walked through crampy stone corridors. It felt like they were standing still. Like they were trapped in an endless illusion.

The only breaks to the monotony came when they stopped to eat and drink—they had their supplies when they were teleported—as well as when they encountered bone monsters. Those were intense moments. Most of the time, Nauja would hear or see them one corridor in advance, letting them wait the monster out.

Other times, the monster would round the turn before them, spotting them. Then, it was always a chase backward, through corridors they'd already explored, which had the lowest probability of housing more monsters. After they escaped the bone monster after them, they could retrace their steps and keep going.

In these instances, Salin's breadcrumbs were *actually* of assistance. The twin loaves he'd stolen from the village tavern had long gone bad, but they were good for marking their path. However, even they didn't have endless crumbs. Salin was running out, so now he was only dropping one in every intersection.

To alleviate the boredom, he told Nauja stories of the outside world. She absorbed them wide-eyed, like a sponge drank water, and Salin was happy to see his friend excited.

He told her of the Animal Kingdom constellation, of the ninety thousand inhabitable planets they ruled. He explained how stars worked, the gas clouds in which they were born and the massive explosions in which they died—some of them. He told her about black holes, space monsters, the nine B-Grade factions, the Hand of God, and the galaxy's inner workings. He bragged about the exploits of his ancestors—a part that got her especially excited—and the wars of the Animal Kingdom. The myriad species that made up their constellation.

In return, Nauja shared stories of her life in Barbarian Ring. She described their way of life, hunting in the morning and dancing by the fire at night. She explained how the various tribes of Barbarian Ring cooperated to maintain the balance, how they divided their territories and organized hunting trips deep into the jungle. How they sometimes exchanged members, and how young barbarians were allowed and even encouraged to travel the ring before settling down and getting married.

She even explained her tribe's methods to raise triceratops— keeping the secret parts out.

Overall, it was an interesting trip. On Salin's side, he was impressed by Nauja's previous way of life. It felt like someone grabbed his eyes and forced them open. He had spent his entire life in the high-intensity environment of Animal Kingdom, spending most waking hours training and fighting.

Earth-387 was the first place where he could relax. Now, Nauja spoke of something similar, yet even better. Salin still wanted to train hard and become strong, but there was an argument to be made for relaxing occasionally, letting the stress slide off you like water in the shower.

Though Salin started to notice how there was always something holding Nauja back. A shadow behind her eyes. A mental barrier. He didn't know what it was, nor did he ask, but he could clearly sense it. It made him wonder—and worry.

Deep down, Salin cared.

As the days passed, and the walls became darker, the labyrinth grew more dangerous. The bone monsters appeared at increasing frequency. Once, Nauja even spied an Elite monster behind a turn, clasping her hand over Salin's mouth to prevent him from making the slightest peep.

Bone Lieutenant, Level 124 (Elite)

A creature made to endlessly wander the Labyrinth Ring's corridors and fight intruders. Originally a Bone Sentinel, this monster has absorbed enough cultivators to fully augment itself by one level, evolving to a Bone Lieutenant.

It possesses low Mental and Will attributes, as well as low speed, but outstanding strength and durability. When a Bone Lieutenant slays an enemy, it either absorbs their skeleton into its own or raises the skeleton as a new Bone Sentinel. Therefore, their numbers are self-replenishing.

Compared to the normal bone monsters—the Bone Sentinels—this one was far bulkier. If the others were like twisted humanoid skeletons, the lieutenant was more like a heavyweight wrestler turned to bone. Additionally, it had clear facial features, with serrated knife-like canines stretching up from its mouth like a boar's tusks.

Salin didn't see all those, but Nauja described it after. Thankfully for them, the monster didn't spot them—thank the System for its lack of a nose—and went on its merry way to slaughter innocents.

They waited several extra moments to make sure it was far away.

"Shit," Nauja said after the monster was gone. "That was scary."

"We're approaching the core of the labyrinth, huh?" Salin replied, chuckling. "Look at the bright side. We're closer to the end."

"Our end or the labyrinth's?"

"Both."

They laughed. It helped melt the tension.

"Let's go," Nauja said. "And, from now on, we stay quiet. For real."

"Yes, boss."

The hours kept passing, but they were tenser. Any bone monsters they met were striking white against the dark walls. The blue crabs were harder to spot now.

Until, at some point, the tunnel they were following opened up.

"Is this the guardian?" Nauja asked, looking around.

"I don't think so," Salin replied. "A Dungeon, maybe. Or a Trial."

"A Trial?"

Gan Salin swept his eyes around the room. It was an ancient-looking temple, longer than it was wide. Light gray stone made up the walls and ceiling, with polished white marble as the floor. Despite this place being in the labyrinth, there was not a single speck of dust to be seen, as if everything had been cleaned recently.

Flames burned on large plates across the side walls. Bow-wielding stone statues stood at attention between the fires, evenly spaced, while the area between the entrance and far wall was left empty. This emptiness didn't come across as simplistic—instead, it created a sense of awe.

At the far end was another statue, larger than the others and made of marble. It depicted a woman clad in leather armor, with a mantle fluttering behind her. She held a bow, half-drawn, with a thin arrow made of black crystal balancing on the string.

The most impressive thing about this statue was the motion it was in. Though the marble itself was still, the woman was carved in such a way that she appeared to be mid-fight. Her hair was flying, her mantle fluttered behind her, her legs were bent, and her fingers were in the middle of drawing her bow.

It was as if someone had taken a female archer, asked her to strike a pose, conjured a strong wind to blow at her, then snapped her into stone. She was beautiful, too. Her features were sharp enough to be attractive, but there was a hardness there, a strictness.

Nauja gasped. Salin shared her sentiment. This was a Trial related to archery. It was perfect for her.

"Salin—" she started saying, but he cut her off.

"I know. Go."

She smiled and rushed into the temple. There were no traps in Trials. Nothing to be afraid of. As they approached, Salin scanned the statue, confirming what he already knew.

Trial Statue

A statue serving as the gateway to a Trial Planet Trial. Touch to enter.

Nauja was already looking at a small inscription under the statue. "Hey, Salin!" she called out. "What does this say?"

"Hmm?" He took a look, raising a brow. "Veheil Maestro Cir. The sun killer."

"Sun killer..." she muttered. Her hand rose to touch the inscription, then she lowered it again. "I have never even seen a sun."

"Well, what are you waiting for?" Salin replied, a smile playing at the ends of his lips. "Just go already."

"But you..."

"I'll be fine. Trial areas are usually safe from monsters. And, even if they aren't, I can escape. Unless I get unlucky and an Elite waltzes in here, in which case, na'ste'kala."

She chuckled. This was a phrase of her tribe.

"I'll try to be quick," she said.

"Just don't fail."

"You got it. Thank you, Salin."

"No problem."

With a final, heartfelt nod, Nauja touched the statue and disappeared. Salin was left alone in the empty temple. The weakest cultivator of their team, and the one who still hadn't found a suitable Trial.

He looked around at the still statues, the calm flames, and the silent corridor beyond.

"And now what?" he asked. He then sat down and started carving on the marble with his nails.

CHAPTER SEVENTY-NINE
LORD LONGSWORD

JACK OPENED HIS EYES, GLANCING AT THE DANCING BONFIRE BEFORE HIM.

He was still inside the labyrinth, it was just ridiculous what kind of resources people like Lord Longsword got. He had his own *bonfire*, fuel-free and foldable enough to fit in his pocket.

Despite the homely light, there were still dark brown walls around them. Stone under their feet. Monsters lurking just around the corner.

Jack scowled and stood, eager to stretch his feet. By the side, Bocor was lying on his back, sleeping like a log, while Longsword meditated cross-legged. On the slightest hint of Jack's aggression, he would stand and draw his sword in the blink of an eye.

Though Jack was technically their ally, they didn't trust him to keep watch alone.

He paced back and forth, keeping his footsteps light on the stone. The flames illuminated his bare chest and toned muscles, his dark hair, his deep eyes. The deadly fists he carried.

The torches on the wall were extinguished. Longsword insisted that his bonfire was more atmospheric and brought better results when meditating. It was true—though the bonfire's calming effects were induced through the specially crafted incense stick in its center, not the brightness of its flames.

Jack sighed.

What am I even doing... Is this what they call sleeping with the enemy?

It was already their second day together. After Jack agreed to join Longsword and Bocor for this ring, they'd traveled in relative silence. Jack was tense. So was Bocor. Longsword, on the other hand, was cheerful. Despite his rugged exterior and tattered mantle that might indicate a silent person, Longsword was always quick with small talk. He was witty and had his way with words, as well as a smile always tucked away, ready to be released at the first opportunity.

Lord Longsword wasn't just a strong swordsman. He was a charismatic man, a calculating, approachable genius. Despite his doubts, Jack found himself enjoying his talks with Longsword. The lord always knew the right thing to say, making awkward silences seem like a distant memory. He had interesting and well-thought opinions on everything under the sun, and his sharp comments, humorously phrased, often provoked Jack into deep thought.

Of course, Jack wasn't an idiot. Throughout their many talks—not like they had much else to do—he kept his cards close, not revealing anything Longsword could use against him. The lord, on the other hand, seemed like an open book. He freely shared information about his sect and techniques, and even offered to give Jack battle training, though Jack refused that.

He still wasn't convinced. As pleasant as Longsword was, he was clad in a clear veneer of arrogance. Bocor was ignored. When Longsword addressed him, it was mostly to avoid seeming too distant. Obviously, this grated on the minotaur, who acted calm but boiled inside. Jack could see it clearly. So could Longsword, he just didn't care.

Jack kept his guard up.

What I wouldn't give for Brock, Nauja, or Salin...

He sighed again.

"What's the matter?" a cheery voice came from behind him. "Fruitless meditation? Or, perhaps, something more private?"

Jack turned to find Longsword still in a meditative position, but with his eyes open and a cocky grin on his lips.

"Something like that," he replied.

"Me too. Becoming an immortal is so difficult. Who would have thought?"

"Everyone?"

Longsword laughed. "I guess. But perspective changes when you're high up. For most, becoming an immortal is a pipe dream. For me, it's the bare minimum."

"Are all lords so arrogant?"

"We are all so skilled."

Jack sat down, resting his back against the cold stone wall. "Doesn't it ever irk you?" he asked, letting his head fall back. "That you are so above the world. Most people—billions of them—work their whole lives to achieve what you were born with, and still fail. They will never reach your level, no matter how hard they try. Doesn't that seem... unfair?"

"What is fair, then?" Longsword replied. "Would it be fair for everyone to have the same things? Would it be fair for everyone's efforts to be equally rewarded? Or should they be judged based on their results?"

"It's just an uneven fight. You were born with everything. Some people don't even have food, let alone high-end cultivation resources."

Longsword thought for a moment, then shrugged. "There isn't much I can do about that. I could disperse my faction's resources to the world to give everyone equal fighting chances, but what's the point? The people with talent and hard work would still rise. I cannot distribute my talent to the people, nor my devotion to cultivation, and certainly not the mental fortitude it takes to rise above the masses."

"But doesn't that irk you?" Jack insisted. "Exactly that. Rising above the masses. Doesn't that make you feel... I don't know, like you're making some sort of mistake? Like you're putting them down by daring to be above them? Doesn't it make you feel bad?"

"Not at all." His eyes twinkled, but the hard line of his jaw made it clear that the next words would be spoken seriously. "I was not raised with such considerations. Perhaps you were, given your grassroot origins at an unintegrated planet, but these are merely feelings left over from when you were weak. As the person below, it is natural to view the ones above you with scorn and identify yourself as *against them*. It's a coping mechanism."

Jack narrowed his eyes in thought.

"Again, those are leftover emotions," Longsword said, leaning against the wall with a straight back. "You are at the top now. In time, you will realize that being better than others is no sin—that you should not be ashamed of having power. Instead, it is something to take pride in, and use it to better place yourself in the world." He let his words sink in, then added, "After all, you are the living proof that anyone can rise if the proper conditions are met."

"Not necessarily. I was lucky, too. A person can have all the talent in the world, but if they aren't born in the right circumstances, there is nothing they can do."

"I guess. But children are a continuation of their parents' lives. It is fair for the children of successful people to start high, as is the opposite. If you do well in life, you help your children start at a better place than you did—and don't forget that talent is often hereditary. If you're born at the bottom but with great talent, maybe you won't reach the top, but you will certainly give your children a much better starting point."

"Shit, man. You aren't holding back at all, are you?"

"Am I wrong?"

"Maybe. If I'm being honest, that's a pretty brutal way to look at the world, not to mention unfair. How about you chill and think about it some more?"

In the face of Jack's cutting words, Longsword simply laughed. He was not the least bit bothered. "That's what I like about you, Jack: your directness. Yes, it is a brutal way to see things, but it's how I've been raised. The world is brutal. And whoever sees that goes farther than those who don't."

"I don't necessarily disagree with you... but goddamn is that a way to put it," Jack replied. He didn't particularly like the way Longsword saw things. It was too... cold. Too uncaring.

Longsword shrugged. "There is nothing wrong with disagreeing, my friend. We are different people, naturally, we have different opinions. But let's stop here for now. Going too far out of our comfort zone can be counterproductive. Change happens one step at a time, be it yours or mine."

"Right," Jack said. "Just so you know, you have some messed-up opinions."

"It's how you know they're true!" Longsword laughed rowdily—so rowdily he might have awoken Bocor. "I want a break from meditation.

Failing consecutively can be... disheartening. How about you join me in bonfire-gazing?"

"Fine by me," Jack replied. He didn't feel like speaking with Longsword more, but he, too, wanted to take a break. That's why he had been stretching his legs before. And he couldn't just sit by Longsword and ignore him. "What are you meditating on? Trying to break through?" he asked. "You're already at the absolute peak of the E-Grade, right?"

"Absolute peak is a bit of a stretch, but yes, I am." Longsword settled down near the bonfire, making himself comfortable. His cloak covered the floor behind him, amassing dirt, and his legs were crossed near the edge of the fire. His nine-foot-long sword rested on his knees, ready to be drawn at any moment. "I have already fused all my Dao Roots, but there is still a gap between maturing your Dao Seed and sprouting it as a Dao Tree. A mental leap, if you will, that combines all of your under-standings into a singular entity. Obviously, the more Dao Roots you have fused into your Seed, the more difficult this final step becomes."

"And you've fused many?" Jack asked, fishing for information.

"A good few. It's the eternal dilemma. The more power you reach for, the more difficult it is to claim. It's why many star disciples get stuck at the peak of the E-Grade for decades, or even forever. In fact, there is already a person from my generation in the Wide Swirls that has become an immortal. She only had one Dao Root, of course, but that was a good thing. She knew her limits. Right now, funnily enough, she is stronger than me."

"So you're trying to... further fuse all your insights into one?" Jack asked.

Longsword threw him a glance. Through narrowed eyes, he undoubtedly spotted Jack's complete lack of information, and chose to assist. "Not an insight. A system of thought. A philosophy, if you will. A way of life and thought that perfectly combines all your understand-ings, defining your own, personal path through the Dao. It defines your life henceforth. Forming and cementing a path like this is the path to immortality, but it is also damn difficult."

He sighed in frustration, lost in his thoughts. "That is what we lords use Trial Planet for. The Garden Ring contains all sorts of wondrous treasures. The best ones can help us form our Dao Tree... and it is those treasures we kill each other for." He then snapped out of it. "Of course, that doesn't concern you. You are far from the peak of the E-Grade, where those treasures would be used, and you are also far from the power you need to contest for them. Don't worry, though. There are many precious treasures in Garden Ring. With my assistance, you could lay claim to some of the best."

"Only if we're still allied in the next ring."

"True." He smirked. "But I don't see why not. It's not like I'm asking for much, and we're getting along just fine, aren't we?"

Jack chose to simply shrug in response. The more he observed Longsword, the more conflicted he became. This was clearly a great cultivator and a superficially pleasant companion. But, under all his gifts, was he actually a decent person?

Jack wasn't sure. "You keep mentioning Garden Ring, but that's only the eighth ring, right? What about the ninth?"

"The Final Ring?" Longsword laughed. "I know what you're thinking, Jack, but get it out of your mind. Conquering that ring is completely impossible—even for lords. The Garden Ring is the best we can get."

"So even you, an ambitious lord, aren't even considering it?"

"I told you, it's impossible."

"Why?"

"Oh, you'll see. In fact, it's so impossible that many believe it's only meant to beat us down—a final exercise in humility, if you will. A lesson that no one is infallible."

Jack scowled. "That's so disappointing..." *But I'll still take a look*, he added mentally.

"I know," Longsword replied, smiling sadly.

Jack didn't say anything more, and Longsword's mood must have soured, because he returned to meditation a few moments later. So did Jack.

Not that he was actually meditating. He was just diving into his soul world and fighting Copy Jack, increasing his battle ability and sharpening his Dao usage at the same time. With all that practice, Meteor Punch already felt on the cusp of evolving again, and Jack had great plans for it.

He'd fused two of his three Dao Roots—though one wasn't really a Dao Root, and it had fused itself. That was enough to get a grasp of how the progress worked. Fusing a Dao Root meant integrating its Dao with his Dao Seed's. Essentially, it meant the complete fusion of the Dao Root into one of his Dao Skills—that's how it had gone the previous two times at any rate.

So far, both of his fused Dao Roots had gone to enhancing Indomitable Body, which wasn't bad. The combination yielded an incredible skill. His body's regeneration was off the charts, and its durability was also impressive.

However, Jack thought that was enough for defense. His remaining Dao Root was that of Power, and he knew just the skill to fuse it into.

Good old Meteor Punch.

CHAPTER EIGHTY
BROCK'S BREAKTHROUGH

BROCK FELT LIKE HIS EYES WERE OPEN FOR THE FIRST TIME. HE SAW HIS SOUL. IT was beautiful.

His inner world was a gaping nothingness peppered with floating leaves. It felt crampy and impossibly expansive at the same time, like space had lost all meaning.

Brock floated in the middle of this world, gawking at the endless leaves.

"Bro..." he muttered.

Right in front of him hovered the Big Thought. It was a flexed bicep, an arm that extended from the shoulder down and must have been working out for decades. The skin was missing, allowing Brock to observe its clean musculature. Every muscle was impeccably defined, bringing a sense of awe that he'd never felt before.

Not even Father had such muscles. Not even Big Bro.

He felt an urge to bow to this flexed arm. To show his belly, declaring subservience. But, at the same time, something held him back. This was *his* soul. This arm was *his* Big Thought. Why would he submit to something that was his?

That would be very un-bro-like.

Squaring his jaw, Brock adopted a bodybuilder stance, showing off his gruesomely worked-out muscles. He brought his arms above his head and flexed them. He then clasped his palms behind his back, also flexing. He was challenging the big arm for dominance.

The big arm accepted the challenge. It flexed harder—and, in an instant, Brock's entire world was covered in muscles. In power. He released a monkey cry as muscles drowned his world, and out of instinct, he flexed harder. Veins popped all over his body. His eyes went bloodshot.

The arm wasn't content to just sit there and be challenged. It attacked. Brock felt fear cloud his senses, but he responded with his bravery muscle. Immense pressure surrounded his body. His every physical muscle twitched as it was pulled apart, their tenacity put to the test. Brock was in excruciating pain. He yelled, but by then, it was already over, and Brock remained whole.

After all, he followed a rigorous work-out routine that spanned his entire body. A good bro didn't leave weaknesses.

The arm redoubled its efforts. It transported Brock to a world of forests, where several highly-muscled brorillas flexed their hardest. He was like a dwarf amongst giants. The brorillas stared at him, waiting to see his performance.

Brock felt the judgment in their gazes. He was small—smaller than all of them. His muscles, though strong, weren't as impressive. It was like being in his pack all over again.

His bottom lip began to quiver. His arms flopped to the sides. He was too weak to be here. He did not belong. They would mock and cast him out, like Father had done.

The brorillas around Brock liquified, combining into one, large brorilla.

Father.

Harambe.

Brock shrunk before his father's gaze. The large brorilla, the leader of the pack, stared him down, expecting something. But what? Brock had tried so hard, but he wasn't grown yet. He wasn't as big as the other brorillas. Perhaps he never would be.

Brock opened his mouth and almost made submissive monkey noises. Almost.

At the last moment, he held himself back. Why was Father doing this? He'd already kicked Brock out. What more did he want? How could he expect Brock to be even stronger than he currently was? He was trying his very hardest!

A veil was lifted from Brock's eyes. Indeed, he had tried his hardest since leaving the pack. He followed the teachings of the brorillas to work out and act as a bro would. He dutifully followed his big bro, and though he made a few mistakes, he learned from them and never repeated them. Brock was doing everything he should.

What more did Father want?

Whatever it was, Brock couldn't give it. Father, the biggest of bros... was wrong to stare. His brain muscles had made a mistake.

Brock shook from the realization.

The world blinked before his eyes. His father's accusing stare melted along with the big brorilla himself, revealing the large arm again. It was a brorilla's arm, obviously, just without fur and skin. And perfectly sculpted.

Brock narrowed his eyes. Something was wrong here. Whatever was happening felt disjointed. The hand was the Big Thought representing Muscle, but his father... What did his father have to do with that?

What was Brock missing?

The arm flexed again. Pressure showered Brock, enveloping him. The little brorilla flexed his muscles, but his thoughts were incomplete. Yes, he had the strength to resist. But what was he supposed to do? What was the path forward?

How long did he have to persist for?

Weights appeared around his wrists and ankles. Dumbbells stuck to his fingers, and a weighted bar fell on his shoulders, urging his knees to bend. Brock maintained himself, instinctively coming into form.

His entire body shook. Every muscle taut to its limit, but the pressure remained. Nothing changed. He was doing something wrong.

No. He was just doing *nothing*. That was not the bro way. That was weakness. Passivity.

Brock had made many sounds in his life. He'd laughed and mocked others, screamed, yelled, and thumped his chest. Even said human words. At this moment, as rage and shame at his own mental weakness flooded Brock, he made a new sound. He roared deeply.

Brock fueled his muscles with resolve and pushed them further. At the same moment they ruptured, the weights were thrown off, breaking against the walls of his soul and leaving him free.

The world shattered around him like glass. Father appeared again, his gaze just as accusing as before, but Brock only snorted. He got into a bodybuilding stance and flexed his muscles. They weren't large. But they were strong. That was the purpose of muscles. To have *strength*. Not to be big.

Despite how Father narrowed his eyes, Brock was no longer a child. He met his father's gaze head-on and shook his head.

You are wrong, he said.

His father's eyes shot wide and he prepared to charge. Brock stared him down. When his son stayed his ground, Harambe's body lost its strength. Old age passed through its eyes, then elation. Harambe nodded, and the vision dispersed, leaving behind only darkness with floating leaves and a large arm sculpted with muscles.

And there was more. Lines were visible around the nothingness, throbbing muscles on the walls of Brock's soul, and he could feel that each of those were his. He was reclaiming his soul. The big arm was his, too, no matter how much it tried to control Brock's soul.

The arm noticed Brock's rebellion and was enraged. It clenched its hand into a fist and swung at him. Brock saw Big Bro's spirit in this fist, but he did not buckle. He did not cower. His big bro was a righteous bro, and what this hand was doing was wrong. It needed to be taught a lesson.

The large fist flew at Brock's face like a swinging log as large as his entire torso.

Brock raised an open palm. As the large arm approached and he stayed his ground, it gradually shrunk to the size of his own fist. He grabbed it in his palm and wrapped his fingers around it, stopping it.

"Bro," he said, shaking his head. "No."

The fist resisted, seeking to press on. Brock clenched his fingers, digging them into the fist and shattering it. With a violent shiver, the arm reformed, watching Brock like a snake in the bush.

It wasn't an enemy; just an unruly bro. Like a child. And Brock was no longer a child.

Having overpowered the fist, he approached it boldly. Its pressure now broke against his muscles like a hollow tide. The arm clenched its fist again, ready to fight to the end.

With the brightest smile on his face, backed by undeniable strength, Brock stretched out an open hand. "Bro."

The hand hesitated. A moment later, its fist slowly unclenched, revealing an open palm. Slowly, as if in fear, it grabbed Brock's into a handshake. Brock shook it, reconciling his muscles with his soul. "Bro," he said, nodding, and he felt the big arm return the favor.

He knew the truth now. The hand wasn't his nor a tool to use, but neither was he a vessel for it to conquer.

They were bros. And he was the big bro.

The world's borders opened before Brock's eyes. His entire soul shivered, and his mind split into a thousand pieces. Each found itself observing a different scene of people—either humans or brorillas—interacting. In every scene, Brock was both an observer and an actor. It was a peculiar feeling.

He observed, then took charge. Every situation was borderline unbro. He slowly but firmly grabbed the scenes and set them straight. Every single one of them. It was a piece of cake. The correct decisions came naturally, as if emanating from his heart—as if he'd swallowed the rulebook that all good bros had to follow.

He'd learned about this rulebook. It was one of the brorillas' most sacred entities, a fountain of knowledge that only the greatest of bros could master.

The legendary Bro Code.

Surge swelled inside Brock. His knowledge and understanding were tested, and he prevailed every time. Before long, the thousand visions were all resolved, and Brock was back in his soul—everything had changed.

The large hand waited quietly in the corner. It wasn't hovering in space anymore, it was now firmly planted into his soul walls, spreading its muscles around his soul and making it stronger. Brock felt the change, and how everything about him was stronger now. Every muscle, both physical and mental, were enhanced like he'd been working out for ten hours straight.

That also wasn't the biggest change. His soul was no longer a dark void. It was now lit with clear, bright light, and on its brown walls were lines and shapes. They weren't letters of any language. They were repre-sentations of the unspoken rules that made up the world's greatest book of conduct: the Bro Code.

And Brock could read them.

The Bro Code had become one with his soul, fused perfectly. Though, perhaps that wasn't its real name now. Yes, it was the Very Big Thought of Brohood. Through contesting the large arm—the Big Thought of Muscles—Brock had directly conceived and merged with his soul the Very Big Thought of Brohood. In the same fell swoop, he'd also fused the Big Thought of Muscles into his soul, too.

Brock allowed himself a moment of unrestrained pride and elation, sensing that what he just achieved was monumental.

He opened his eyes in the real world, shocked by the changes in his body. He had become inconceivably stronger. The Big Thoughts were part of him now, flooding his every nook and cranny, enhancing him way beyond what was physically possible.

Only the Staff of Stone in his hand remained perfectly weighted. A confusing matter, but Brock couldn't bring himself to care. He was just so happy. He was no longer weak!

The brown corridors now seemed inviting. He dashed through them, restless to meet an adversary and test his might. It didn't take long. Three corridors down was a blue crab, pinching tiny stone outcroppings off the walls and eating them.

Brock skidded to a halt, staring the crab down. The crab watched him attentively, hesitating between attacking or running. Brock smirked and hooked his finger at it, inviting it forward. He'd already decided that this crab bro would be his sparring partner.

The crab made up its mind. It attacked.

A few moments ago, just this charge would be at the limits of Brock's perception. Now, it was almost slow. He didn't even need his staff.

Brock let the weapon fall, electing to meet this bro in bare-armed combat. He leaned away from a pincer, letting it clip his rib fur, then smashed a fist into the crab's face. The crustacean flew back, landed feet-first into a wall, and jumped at him again.

Brock growled. Punching was his big bro's area of expertise, and

Brock wanted to walk a path of his own, lest he end up trapped in Big Bro's shadow. What should he do?

He jumped over the crab, which barely reached his waist. The pincers closed around empty air. Brock planted his palm on the crab's head, following its rotation to land behind it. Before the crab could understand what was happening, Brock had wrapped his hands around its body from behind and raised it above his head, leaning back and planting its head into the floor with all the power he could muster.

The stone floor shook. The crab made a pained sound, its shell slightly cracked from the impact.

Brock's face was split by a massive grin. He couldn't wait to show Big Bro how strong he'd gotten.

He jumped upright, ready to go another round, but the little crab had had enough. Deciding Brock was more than it could handle, it turned sideways and sprinted away.

Brock let it. After all, it wouldn't do for him to bully this little bro.

Then again, what other fate awaited this crab? It would keep on eating stone until one of the bone monsters—the monsters that Brock knew how to avoid—devoured it. That was no life for Brock's sparring partner.

That was no life for anyone, actually. Someone had to step up for the crabs.

With a few quick steps, Brock caught up to the little crab and stopped it. It didn't fight back, appearing resigned to its fate.

Brock shook his head. We have a lot of work to do, little bro. But don't worry. Big Bro Brock is here!

CHAPTER EIGHTY-ONE
THE TREASURE TRIAL

Jack, Longsword, and Bocor stood before a dark cave mouth.

"Well," the lord said, "guess we found something. What do you think, Jack?"

"I think it's a cave, and I also think I can't see in the darkness."

Bocor snorted. "Are you afraid, little man?"

"Don't worry," Jack replied with a smirk. "I know my way around caves." He wasn't angry. This cave was too nostalgic for that. After all, his entire journey had started in a little cave in the Greenway Natural Reserve.

This one, as it seemed, wasn't too different from his. As they transitioned from the labyrinth's straight-cut, well-lit corridors into jagged cave pathways, carrying their own torch that Longsword had fished from his bag, their path was almost immediately cut short.

Only a few feet into the cave stood what looked like a mirror. An oval wooden shape embedded into the wall, as tall as a grown man and as wide as the three of them side by side. Its surface was covered in glass, but that was where the similarities to a mirror ended. Through it, Jack could see not himself, but a small cavern filled with treasure.

There were weapons and sets of armor, all intricately carved and covered in jewels. A mound of gold coins at the back reached up to Jack's knee. There were fist-sized jewels on small pedestals. And, at the very end of the small cavern, a small gray orb rested on a red velvet pillow. The entire arrangement of the room seemed to point at that orb, as if everything else were merely a warm-up before the real treasure.

Jack tried to scan it, but either he couldn't do so through the mirror —maybe it was a window?—or the item wasn't scannable in the first place.

But why was there a mirror-like window between them and the treasure?

Just as Jack had thought, the mirror's surface flowed and undulated. The shapes inside it warped, turning from treasures in a cave into glass apparatuses and round faces, with desks, white robes, and a blackboard at the very end. Jack, to his absolute shock, found himself staring at one of the labs he used to teach in Northeastern University, separated only by a mirror and a few months of extreme change.

"What the hell?" he asked.

"Are you seeing what I'm seeing?" Longsword asked, equally surprised.

"Yeah. But I mean... Do you even know what that is?"

The lord gave him an odd look. "Of course I do. It's where I grew up."

"You grew up *there*?"

"My lord," Bocor said. "Forgive my disrespect, but that is impossible. Someone of your stature would never set foot in this gambling den."

"What?" Jack asked.

"What?" Longsword asked, equally confused. "What exactly do you see, Bocor?"

The minotaur frowned. "Drunks, card cheaters, and scum of the earth. Bottles, dirty tables, standing beds, smiles, all arrayed under the statue of a grape-holding satyre."

Jack took a second look. Still, all he saw was the lab. *Am I hallucinating?*

"Oh," Longsword said, squinting at the mirror's top. His eyes brightened. "Oh!"

Jack followed the lord's gaze, but all he saw was the mirror's wooden case.

Mirror of Origins
Unlike conventional mirrors, this one does not show the current self.
Instead, it is an elaborate device that shows the observer a scene of
their past, which they can experience and relive as soon as they step
through the mirror.

"Oh," Jack repeated.

"We are all seeing different things," Longsword explained. "I believe this is a Treasure Trial."

"So, what do we have to do?" Jack asked.

"If I had to guess? Walk through the mirror, resolve whatever vision appears, then step into the treasure room and take everything."

"Hmm," Jack said. "Did we all see the same place before the mirror activated? A small cave with treasures and a prominently placed gray orb?"

"I did," Longsword replied. Bocor nodded, too.

"So, that's the real treasure room."

"Most likely."

"Okay..."

Jack cracked his neck, staring at the laboratory in the mirror. There was a bit of nostalgia there. Surprisingly, only now did he realize that he hadn't thought about his past days at all since the Integration. He hadn't missed them in the slightest.

Talk about good life choices... I guess I really didn't like it that much.

"Should I go first?" Jack asked.

"No."

That was more decisive than expected. Jack turned to Longsword and raised a brow. "Why?"

The lord frowned at the mirror, considering his options. "Let's go all at once."

Jack's brows rose higher. *Why?* he considered again. It took him a moment to follow Longsword's train of thought.

They didn't know how long this Trial would take. How exactly does one cross a mirror? There was a chance it would be instant, but it could also leave them stranded for unknown periods of time. In other words, any trial taker might become vulnerable.

Therefore, Longsword didn't want to go first, in case Jack—or Bocor —took advantage of his vulnerability and assassinated him. At the same time, he also didn't want to let Jack lead, because whoever went first would also enter the treasure room first. If Jack was that person, he might sweep a few trinkets into his pockets, with nobody being the wiser.

Then, why not send Bocor first, as a test subject? Jack wondered. There was only one reason: Longsword didn't trust Bocor, either. In that case, the only solution for Longsword would be for everyone to enter the mirror at the same time. Provided he completed the trial first, he would not be vulnerable or prone to losing treasure.

For the first time, Jack realized they were three men all on guard against each other.

"Very well," Jack said.

Jack stood beside Longsword, and Bocor was on the lord's other side. Longsword held his head high, hand hovering around the handle of his sword.

"A small clarification, gentlemen," Longsword said before they entered. "As the strongest person here, and as the leader of our small group, I get the lion's share. Agreed?"

He turned to stare directly at Jack, who met his gaze.

Jack expected this. He wasn't happy about it, of course, but there was nothing he could do, either. Longsword *was* the strongest person around. If he wanted the lion's share, he could take it.

Although, if this were Jack's group, they would have shared everything equally.

The fact that Longsword was so proactive in demanding more dropped his standing in Jack's opinion.

"Agreed," he replied, making sure to let his dissatisfaction show. The lord didn't seem to care.

"Of course," Bocor confirmed.

"Good!" Longsword clapped, recovering his jovial self. "Then, let's get to it. On three. One, two... three!"

Jack dived into the mirror. Through the corner of his eye, he noticed that Longsword waited an extra half a second to confirm that both Jack and Bocor had entered. Only then did he enter himself.

In the next moment, Jack found himself in the lab he used to teach.

"Ah, Mr. Rust," a few students said, noticing him. "Welcome, sir."

Jack nodded at them absent-mindedly. He was busy marveling at his surroundings. Everything was as he remembered. The faint smell of glue, the sunlight streaming in through the windows, the stale air. A picture of his late father, Eric Rust, sitting on a tall shelf—this was Jack's lab, mostly, so he had the right to decorate it.

He looked down at himself, finding the white robe he was so familiar with. The gloves, the lab glasses around his neck, the hair net. Even the students were ones he recognized.

Most importantly, his body had reverted to his weak, pre-System self. There was no Dao to be found.

It really was a jump to the past, a punch in the gut. *What am I doing here?* Jack wondered. The difference in life quality was staggering. He was instantly drowned in the feeling of emptiness that pervaded most of his life, the dull routine that slugged his days. He remembered the existence of bills, rent, and loneliness. The weight of being forced into a life where he spent most of himself just to make ends meet.

It wasn't *bad*. Not really. Many people had it worse. It just wasn't the kind of life he was meant for.

Compared to the sheer joy of his post-Integration life, this place didn't feel like home at all. It was... unfulfilling. Which was odd, really. Here, he had bills. In the System world, he had interstellar empires chasing after him and the future of Earth on his shoulders.

How come he preferred the latter so clearly? Why did danger feel like his natural environment?

Was I always crazy? he wondered, then smiled. I believe yes.

Jack wanted to open the window and jump out onto the grass, lay on it and take deep breaths. He wanted to feel the sun on his skin, to relax without having anything to do, to go say hi to his mother.

"Mr. Rust?" a student said, interrupting his daydreaming.

Jack reoriented on the present—at least, what the present looked like. "Right," he said, walking to the front of the lab. "Remind me, guys. What are we going to do today?"

"Extract banana DNA, sir," one student said.

Jack nodded. It had only been less than three months since the Integration. He remembered how to do something as simple as that. "Right. Let's get started, then."

He wanted to go out and enjoy a day in this world. But, at the same time, there was something nostalgic to teaching this class. He didn't want to betray his past like this. Let the lab pass.

Visions like this were about making the right choice, and Jack's instinct hadn't failed him yet.

Two hours went by slowly, yet quickly at the same time. Jack didn't do much. He simply observed his students, occasionally giving them pointers, correcting their technique, or giving out instructions for the next phase of the experiment. For a one-time thing, this wasn't too bad.

Only toward the end of the lab, when he'd already spent more than an hour there, did Jack start to get worried. What if this *was* the real world? What if the System and everything else were just particularly vivid daydreams? What if he really was stuck here forever?

He suppressed that fear.

When the lab was over, Jack made sure all the equipment was properly cleaned and stored. When the last student left, politely wishing him goodbye, he turned off the lights and walked through the door.

And he was in a cave filled with treasure. He almost stumbled from the instant transition before regaining his bearings. He felt the massive strength coiled in his body, ready to be unleashed. The Dao in his soul; a powerful, revving engine.

He was back.

Before the smile even formed on his face, he looked around—he was alone in the treasure room. Longsword wasn't there. Neither was Bocor. There was nowhere to hide.

Jack was the first out.

His eyes fell on the object that was clearly the most precious. A gray orb on a red, velvet pillow. He could sense that it was scannable, but he didn't read its description. There was no time. Another thought was flashing in his mind, an urge so pressing he didn't bother squeezing it.

Longsword is an enemy. We both know that, and not stealing from the enemy is stupidity, he thought, approaching the velvet pillow. *I wouldn't have done this if he trusted me, but since he didn't... Well, it's a different story.*

Of course, if he took the gray orb, Longsword would know. They'd all witnessed the treasure room before the mirror activated.

But Jack had an idea. Because, in the hidden pocket behind his left thigh, rested an outwardly similar gray orb, except far less valuable. One called the Ticklish Pebble.

With a swift movement, Jack switched the orbs, sliding the new one in his secret pocket and withdrawing his hand.

"What are you doing?" a voice came from behind him.

CHAPTER EIGHTY-TWO
TRICKING A LORD

"What are you doing there?"

The voice startled Jack. He turned around, still standing before the gray orb—the one he'd replaced with the Ticklish Pebble. "Lord Longsword," he said with a nod. "You made it out."

"Were you trying to steal that orb, Jack?" Longsword did not seem amused, just disappointed. His hands were crossed behind his back, and the nine-foot-long sword dragged behind him and into the mirror's surface. He took the final few steps to dislodge it.

"I wouldn't dare," Jack replied. "Plus, I'm not stupid. You saw the orb before the mirror activated. If it was missing, you'd be suspicious."

"Then, what are you doing there?"

"I was curious."

"Curious enough to reach for the orb?" Longsword had caught Jack right as he retrieved his hand after swapping the true orb for his pebble. Thankfully, as Jack stood between the orb and the mirror, Longsword hadn't seen his hand's trajectory.

Jack smirked. "Oddly enough, yes. Just inspect it, and you'll know why I tried to touch it."

Longsword frowned. He took a couple steps to approach. Jack could feel the lord's entire body tense, only a thought away from drawing his sword and swiping it through Jack's midsection.

That didn't happen. Instead, Jack only saw the lord's brows crease as he inspected the pebble.

Ticklish Pebble
A pebble that laughs when touched. While possessing only minimal sentience, it is useful for cultivators pursuing the Daos of Laughter, Joy, or similar, as well as cultivators pursuing the opposite Daos, like Grief or Sadness.

He'd intended to save this for Vlossana, but... Obviously, he had to set priorities.

"You were trying to... tickle this pebble?" Longsword said flatly.

"Precisely."

Longsword seemed torn between disbelief and ridiculousness. He slowly raised a hand to touch the pebble.

"Hihi," a small voice came from under it. Longsword pressed his fingers harder. "Hihihi!" The snickering was louder now, as if someone was desperately trying to hold back their laughter. Visibly hating his life, Longsword grabbed the pebble and raised it, turning it around to reveal a little mouth etched into its bottom, complete with stone lips and a stone tongue.

The Ticklish Pebble couldn't contain itself any longer and burst out laughing, spitting stone flecks on Longsword's hand. He tossed it to the ground. The pebble rolled to a corner, where, untouched by anyone, it stopped laughing.

"Are you toying with me, Jack?" Longsword asked, his frows deeply furrowed. "If yes, it is a terrible idea."

"I didn't choose the treasure, lord," Jack replied. Only his impending doom stopped him from bursting out in laughter. "It's not my fault that whoever made this place was in the mood for jokes."

Bocor chose that exact moment to step out of the mirror, panting and looking slightly intoxicated. That intoxication melted away like snow in spring as he met Longsword's glare. "Sir!" He snapped to attention, scanning the room, noticing the empty velvet pillow. "That's—"

"A joke, that's what it is," Longsword rumbled. He must have been very expectant of this treasure. It was the first time Jack saw him break character. "A fucking joke by some fucking idiot."

Thankfully, he wasn't looking at Jack when he said that. He suspected nothing. How could he? No matter how intelligent he was, what kind of madman would assume Jack had a similar gray orb in his pocket and managed to swap them in time?

Not to mention my poker face was great, Jack thought with pride and a large amount of relief. His split-second decision to take the orb had been a calculated risk, but calculating the danger and tasting it up close were two very different things.

Bocor didn't understand what was going on, but he didn't speak again, unwilling to provoke Longsword's ire. He kept scanning the room until they landed on the out-of-place pebble rolled up against a corner. He bent down to pick it up.

"Don't touch that!" Longsword thundered. Bocor froze mid-crouch and quickly drew back his hand.

"Should we get to splitting the treasure?" Jack asked. "There's so much of it. The jewels, the weapons, the gold, the grand Ticklish Pebble..."

Longsword's glare landed on him like the smite of thunder. He was deeply pissed.

"Sorry," Jack apologized, realizing he'd gone too far. "I was only trying to lighten the mood."

"You find this funny, don't you?" Longsword demanded. Jack didn't reply—he didn't want to lie, nor could he say that he found this hilarious. Longsword continued unabated. "You rejoice in my frustration, is that it? You know you couldn't get the treasure, so you're happy that it's trash."

"That isn't the case," Jack replied, frowning. "Plus, any treasure this deep in the labyrinth should have a use. The Ticklish Pebble might hold secrets."

"Is that so? Keep it, then. Let it be *your* share of the treasure. I'm sure the crown jewel of this trial is more than enough for an underling's share."

Jack's frown deepened. Longsword was just bullying him now. They were surrounded by actual treasure; giving it up for a funny pebble was a terrible deal.

Longsword was in a bad mood, so he was punishing Jack's unruliness and cutting his losses at the same time. That wasn't proper conduct. He was basically cheating Jack out of his share.

Of course, Jack had already gotten the actual treasure, but Longsword didn't know that. He was just being a dick.

"That's unfair," Jack protested calmly.

"I set the rules here, and I find it fair. You will take your pebble and be happy with it."

Jack's body tensed. He was the Fiend of the Iron Fist. The champion of his planet. Could he stand being treated like this, even if the alternative was death?

The only thing helping Jack's mood was that he'd cheated Longsword first. In truth, he was the winner of this trial—how could gold and jewels compare to a real treasure? Though he didn't have time to inspect the gray orb, it had to be something good.

In that light, Longsword was just throwing a loser's tantrum.

Jack still considered fighting and dying for this insult. It took a significant portion of his willpower to keep that from happening.

His Dao didn't control him. *He* controlled *it*. And dying like this would be really stupid, especially when he was the real winner here. A fist was an unstoppable force that never looked back—but punching a wall was just stupid. One had to time his punches right.

Still, Jack promised himself he'd repay this insult later—preferably tenfold.

Bocor looked at Jack with open mockery. Thankfully, that was an insult he could return immediately.

"What are you looking at, cow?" Jack asked, snorting. "Jealous that I get to at least exchange words with your master?"

Bocor's face soured, going through several shades of red. "My lord," he said through gritted teeth, turning to Longsword. "Jack Rust is an unruly fellow. Even after traveling together for this long, he hasn't agreed to join you. How about we take care of him right now? My Animal Kingdom will remember this favor."

Jack glanced at Longsword. On the inside, his Dao was revving up, and he was ready to draw on the Life Drop's powers at a moment's notice. He couldn't fight Longsword, but with the Life Drop, he had a chance to escape. The mirror was right there, and from this side, it only showed the cave mouth they originally entered.

And, if that didn't work, Jack was prepared to lay down his life to at least strike Longsword once—and kill Bocor.

Everyone boiled in tense silence. Jack was ready to bolt. Bocor was ready to try and stop him. Longsword looked up with his eyes half-closed, calculating.

"I will not intervene in your faction's conflicts," he said. "Jack Rust was disrespectful just now, but he has already paid for it by giving up his share. That is enough."

"My lord! He is a wanted mortal, nowhere near the level of a confli—"

"Shut your trap, Bocor," Longsword barked. "You understand nothing. This man has a relationship with the Lady of the Exploding Sun, and I need her help to stand up to the Hand of God in Garden Ring. I will not involve myself in your faction struggles, and you will stay your hand until we reach Garden Ring, as I said. If you want to die after that, it's your business. Am I clear?"

A relationship with the Lady of the Exploding Sun? Jack thought. He'd only ever seen her from afar—once. Does she know Master Shol? And how does Longsword know?

Silence fell. Bocor was clenching his fists so hard they turned white. "Yes, sir."

"Good. As for you," he turned to Jack, and his voice softened. "I want you to know that conflicts like these happen all the time when treasure is involved. It is natural for people to get angry and lash out at each other—though a person of my stature really shouldn't do so. What just happened doesn't make us enemies. It is just the natural way of the world. If you are ever the strongest in the party, I fully expect you to act with similar authority, and I won't say a word if I'm slightly mistreated."

Jack was conflicted. He didn't expect such a change of heart the moment Longsword regained his composure. On one hand, what he said made sense. On the other... Whenever Jack was the strongest, he never mistreated anyone, nor did he lose his temper unjustly and act like a spoiled child who'd lost his favorite toy. That wasn't natural or the way things worked. It was bullying.

At the very least, he had to acknowledge Longsword extending an olive branch. There was even half an apology included in his words. As time went by, Jack got more and more convinced he didn't want to be this man's ally, let alone underling, but he had to admit that Longsword wasn't completely gone.

He was a multi-layered, intelligent, charismatic man. Too bad he was also a dick in disguise.

"That makes sense," Jack replied non-committedly, tempering his Dao and urge to argue. It was nice to resolve conflicts nonviolently for a change.

"Good. Let's get to splitting the rest of the treasure. Bocor, I will take two-thirds, and you will take one."

"Yes, sir." Bocor didn't seem to mind this split. It was probably what he expected—maybe even more, judging by his suspiciously narrowed eyes.

The rest half an hour was spent with Longsword picking out his share and placing it in the bag that hung from his belt—which, apparently, was larger on the inside. It easily fit all those weapons, armor, and golden coins despite looking barely large enough to fit a water canteen.

Jack had even seen Longsword retrieve a portable bonfire from in there. It was called a "Space Bag." Because it had extra space.

Scions sure are privileged...

Bocor didn't have such a bag. Thankfully for him, Longsword took all the larger items, so the minotaur was able to stuff everything else in his bulging backpack. The thing was the size of a small fridge. It looked almost funny against Bocor's rough exterior and full plate armor.

The rest of the trip went by quickly. They were close to the guardian's gates, with the labyrinth corridors now almost pitch-black. As a result, not only did traversing them hurt Jack's eyes and threatened his sanity, but the bleached-white bone monsters were exceptionally striking against the walls.

There were also more of them.

To his benefit, their group was made up of three strong cultivators, so none of the monsters posed a problem. The one time they ran into a Bone Lieutenant, the Elite version of bone monsters, Longsword personally took to battle and dismantled it. Even the crampy corridors, where his nine-foot-long sword barely fit, didn't seem to bother him.

His strength was impressive. Jack would need his Life Drop to eke out a victory against this Bone Lieutenant, but Longsword made it seem almost trivial.

Throughout the journey, the mood of the group was slightly more chilled than before. Longsword's jovial banter had died down, and Bocor's glares toward Jack had become less "I want to kill you" and more "I hate you."

Jack didn't mind. He'd decided not to ally with these people, and he wasn't the type to cozy up to them for future benefits. He responded politely to Longsword's chatting, but that was it.

Truthfully, even peacefully traveling with them was more than he hoped for.

The worst part was that he still couldn't inspect the gray orb. He was too afraid someone would spot it and connect the dots. He didn't even dare sneak a peek when nobody was looking, afraid of any hidden observation skills they may have. All he could do was feel it with his fingers, but it was just a smooth gray orb, cool and soft to the touch.

The wait was unbearable. It was right there in his pocket!

At least the occasional battles helped him level up, all the way to level 97—a small but important enhancement.

En route, he kept practicing against Copy Jack whenever he got the opportunity—essentially every time they stopped to rest. He could feel his Meteor Punch and Dao Root of Power grow closer to each other. He had already comprehended both to a good extent and was working on their fusion. All he needed now was a spark of inspiration.

Unfortunately, that spark could only come through battle, so he was forced to wait.

Two days later, the sound of voices reached them from deeper in the labyrinth. The corridors opened up to reveal a small plaza and large, bronze gates.

They had reached the guardian.

CHAPTER EIGHTY-THREE
NAUJA'S TRIAL

NAUJA APPEARED IN A DARK CORNER, INSTANTLY ON GUARD.

There was little she could make of the surrounding space. Everything a few feet away from her was darkness. There could be anything out there.

However, Nauja was a trained warrior. She crouched and directed her eyes slightly downward, away from the torches above. The better acclimated to the darkness her sight was, the earlier she would see attacks coming. At the same time, she focused on her hearing and made her breathing silent, keeping an ear out for any sign of incoming projectiles. Her bow was already drawn, with an arrow of wind gathering on its string.

How should I proceed? she asked herself.

As it turned out, she didn't have to. A short moment after she appeared, the room burst with light. Lines of torches lit up on the walls, gradually illuminating a long, narrow chamber. Bare stone walls surrounded her on all sides. She stood on a narrow ledge at one end of the long room. Ahead of her ledge lay a seemingly bottomless chasm.

There was nothing on the other side of the chamber. No ledge, door, or windows anywhere. Just her, her ledge, the torches, and the abyss. Everything else was bare stone.

Nauja wasn't used to enclosed spaces. In the Barbarian Ring, she was either in her hut or in the jungle, and this sealed room was even worse than the labyrinth. The stuffy air she only just noticed and the absence of any windows or doors pressured her deeply, making panic rise in her chest.

She fought to push it down. This was not her home. The outside world was dangerous and alien. She had to keep a level head for as long as she was here. Make her tribe proud.

And now what? she thought. A second look around the room revealed nothing. *What am I supposed to do?*

"Welcome, trial taker," a voice boomed. No form appeared; the voice came directly from the walls. It was feminine, spoken with authority and seriousness. "My name is Veheil Maestro Cir, a Planet Breaker of the Crimson Cloud faction."

Nauja's body seized. A Planet Breaker. That was... so strong. The equivalent of the B-Grade. An impossibly distant realm.

Wait. She called herself a Planet Breaker. That's the name my people use!

Before she could consider this further, the voice continued.

"On the behest of my faction head, I am leaving behind an inheritance for the future generations. I shall transmit upon you my greatest Dao Skill, the Sun Piercing Arrow. This is the technique that earned me my position as Faction Elder and my moniker: Sun Killer."

A moment of silence. Nauja didn't respond, understanding this was a voice projection, and that the person who made it was probably long dead.

"However, the Sun Piercing Arrow will not be transmitted to the unworthy. To succeed in my trial, you have to prove your archery, my skill's prerequisite. You will be presented with a series of targets on the far wall. You are to hit them all unerringly. If one arrow hits the wall, you will be expelled from the trial and banned from re-entering. If you use means other than archery, you will be executed for disrespecting me. You may use any archery-related skills you possess."

Nauja gulped. This woman, Veheil Maestro Cir, did not come across as patient. "Yes, Elder," she replied with a slight bow, more to compose herself than to placate the voice projection.

"You may begin," the voice finished, then faded away.

A stone basket flashed into existence behind Nauja. It contained exactly thirty-three arrows, each forged of iron, with steel tips and tails of crimson feathers. Before she could stop herself, Nauja walked over to the arrows and picked one up. It was heavy—it felt more like a weapon than any arrow she'd held before.

The sound of popping air drew her attention to the far wall. Nine targets had appeared there—red circles the size of her head, each with a color gradient that started red at the periphery and ended at a white dot in the center.

The nine targets were arrayed in three rows of three, a perfect square. This task didn't seem too difficult—the far wall was only a hundred feet away, and Nauja was a high E-Grade archer.

There was no time limit, either.

Her gaze returned to the arrows. From what she could tell, she didn't *have* to use them. Her wind arrows were an archery-related skill. However, this was an easy shot, and these arrows were too well-made to ignore.

She nocked one on her bowstring. It was far heavier than her wind arrows, or even her normal, wooden ones—not enough to encumber her, but enough to pull her shot down. Shooting straight would take a lot of strength.

Thankfully, strength was an archer's staple.

Nauja pulled her bowstring as far back as she could manage. She could feel her bow strain under the tension, but it was made from the heart of an elder treant, able to handle even the full strength of a peak E-Grade archer. The bowstring itself was nine tyrannosaurus hamstrings entwined tightly around each other.

This bow had taken her father a week to forge.

Its ends curved a bit inward as Nauja pulled, aimed, and released. She shot a bit higher than usual, just in case. The iron arrow pierced the air, shrieking as it flew. It embedded itself in the middle target almost instantly. Surprisingly, it didn't pierce too deep; the entire tip disappeared, but the body of the arrow was fully visible.

The target was made of very hard wood.

Nauja kept this information in mind—if she shot too weakly, the arrow might not even stick to the target. Good thing she used these heavy arrows instead of her wind ones.

Grabbing another eight arrows, she quickly hit all visible targets. Besides the first one—which she hit halfway between the outer edge and the center—all the rest hit bullseye. It was an easy shot for her; nothing more than a warm-up.

The moment she struck the ninth target, they all disappeared, only to reappear in pristine condition, with the arrows missing. However, they weren't stationary now. They hovered just before the far wall and moved around at high speed; some went right and left, others up and down, yet more diagonally or in a circle.

The trajectory of each target was set, as was its speed, but they were fast. This was a far harder task than the previous one.

"We're getting started, huh?" Nauja said, unable to keep a smirk from emerging on her face. She aimed for one of the targets. She took a moment to clearly observe its trajectory. She calculated its position, taking a practice shot with no arrow on the string. She got it right.

Then, she nocked an arrow and smoothly hit the target.

She did the same for the other eight. These shots weren't easy, but they weren't too hard, either. Since she could take her time, she managed all nine without breaking a sweat, though she was no longer hitting dead-center. One of the arrows hit close to the edge, making her curse.

The nine targets disappeared.

When they reappeared, again in pristine condition, Nauja frowned. They were still moving in set trajectories, but this time, their speed wasn't constant. They went slower and faster at set intervals, but not at the same places of their trajectory every time. The periods of their spatial and speed fluctuations weren't the same.

Nauja bit her lip in concentration. This was going to be difficult—and, even worse, there were fourteen arrows remaining in the basket. Since she wasn't supposed to miss a shot, it meant this was not the final test.

But she could do this.

She pulled the string without an arrow, observing the first target. She took her time. A minute later, when she felt she had it down, she did a practice shot. The result was unclear; it might have missed. Nauja tried again and again until she was confident she would succeed. Then, nocking the arrow, she observed the target, stilled her breath, and took the shot.

It hit halfway between the center and the edge.

Nauja released her breath. She could do this.

For the rest of the eight targets, she always took her time, between one and ten minutes per shot. She wanted to be sure. Some were more difficult than others, too—the one moving in a circle was the trickiest of all.

All the while, she kept imagining the results of a single miss. She would have to go out there and tell Gan Salin she'd failed. She would have to tell her father that she squandered the one opportunity she had to get stronger.

But an archer needed a clear mind. She kept the thoughts away with all the strength of her will and made the shots.

Thankfully, she got them all—though she almost missed the circle one.

Nauja released a deep sigh of relief. The targets vanished, and when they returned, there were only four of them, but they were ridiculous. Not only was their speed seemingly random, but so was their trajectory. They were crawling along the far wall without rhyme or reason, making random turns at random intervals.

Nauja was speechless.

How the hell am I supposed to hit those! she cried out inwardly, not daring to speak her thoughts aloud. The voice hadn't seemed easygoing. Who knew what hidden fail-safes were installed?

She bit her lip in thought. If the movement of the targets was random, she would have to rely on luck. After all, even though her arrows flew fast, there was still an interval between firing the shot and landing it. If the target just randomly moved away during that interval, if it accelerated or slowed down hard, it could cause her to miss. Even her wind-guiding skill, which could slightly alter her arrow's trajectory, could do little at this short distance.

She really hoped their movements were not completely random. Therefore, she set her sights on one target and began observing it.

A minute later, it still seemed random.

Three minutes later, still random.

Only after ten minutes did she get a sense of the target's movements. There wasn't a pattern, per se. It was more like... a combination of several patterns. Like the target was an animal; its movements were random, but not *too* random. Moreover, each target was moving in slightly different ways; one was erratic, like a rabbit, while another was more purposeful, like a triceratops.

There were two ways to shoot an animal in the jungle. The easiest one was waiting for it to stay still, but these targets never stopped. The second way was to try and identify when the animal was in a set trajectory, then predict and shoot it. For example, an animal running away from a predator was predictable—it would just follow the most direct route away.

Unfortunately, these targets weren't animals. They weren't going to run away from anything. How could she know when they'd fall into a pattern?

Nauja persisted—patience was an archer's friend.

She watched the targets for half an hour, trying not to memorize their patterns, but rather get a feel for how they moved. Instinct was a powerful force. One that was often overlooked.

Nauja opened her mind, and when the half hour was past, she kept watching—observing. She had all the time in the world. No matter how bored or frustrated she got, she wouldn't give up on this opportunity.

At one random point, it struck her. The targets weren't completely random; they chose their paths *in relation to each other!*

When that clicked, everything began to make more sense. One target was a predator; it usually moved *toward* the other three targets. The others were prey; they liked to move close to each other, and prioritized escaping the predator when it closed in.

Nauja's eyes flared with realization.

Of course, her task remained difficult. These patterns were nowhere near easy to see. The targets still moved erratically and almost unpredictably. Even when she focused on just one of them, she couldn't predict its movements. But she could see the driving forces now. She could calculate when the target would change directions because of the predator's nearby presence—as well as where it would head: in the exact opposite direction.

Nauja played the game for a while. She kept trying to see the patterns. She didn't need to predict everything; just the split-second after she shot, at any moment she wanted. She could do this.

Keeping her eyes on the target, she reached for an arrow and nocked it. She was holding still in complete concentration. Her eyes were taking in the movements of all four targets, focused on one.

There!

She released the arrow before realizing what she was doing. Panic overtook her in the split-second when her shot was in the air. Had she rushed it? Should she have waited longer?

Time slowed down. It seemed like she was going to miss. Then, the target abruptly rushed aside, directly into her arrow.

She hit dead-center.

Nauja released another deep sigh. This trial brought immense pressure... And it wasn't anywhere near over. She couldn't afford to relax yet.

She returned her attention to the targets. The arrow sticking out of one of them didn't seem to change their patterns. That was good. Nauja focused on another. Ten minutes later, her eyes flickered, and she released her shot.

It hit the target near the edge.

One hour later, all four targets were cleanly pierced through, even the predator, which had been the most difficult. Nauja was sweating all over. There was an element of luck in this trial. If there had been more targets, she might have missed the fifth or sixth shot.

Thankfully, she'd succeeded.

Nauja hadn't mentioned this to Jack or Gan Salin, but she was actually a pretty good archer. She was by far the best in her tribe. Even in the surrounding tribes it was hard to find someone who could meet her shots. She always came first in all contests.

Even the arrow-wielding delvers were defeated by her, with the exception of one man two years ago, who was a lord.

That this Trial pushed her to her limits spoke volumes about its difficulty.

Even after shooting all four targets, Nauja didn't allow herself to relax. There was still one arrow in the basket. The trial wasn't over.

She waited for the last target to appear, but none did. After a while, she began to wonder whether the trial was completed already, but the voice didn't speak.

What is happening?

Suddenly, a creeping suspicion entered her mind. She focused on the far wall and squinted, running her eyes over its entire surface.

There. Right in the center of the wall was a tiny white dot. A target only the size of her fingertip, a hundred feet away.

The final test.

Are you kidding me!

She wanted to call out the Trial's ridiculousness. This was clearly a joke. How was she supposed to hit something like that? She was barely able to see it!

Even when she hit the other targets dead-center, it wasn't *that* dead-center.

And yet, the final arrow waited in the basket, and the voice was not speaking up. Left with no choice, Nauja grabbed the arrow and nocked it. The shot was unfairly hard, but not impossible—after all, she was nearly an immortal.

Unfortunately, mock shots wouldn't help with this one. Neither would observation or patience. This was a test of pure archery skill. All she could do was aim and shoot.

Nauja half-pulled on the string and focused. She let her breath die out. Her world narrowed to a point. The Dao of Archery flooded her mind, making her one with the bow, and the Dao of Wind rose in the space between her and the target, ready to guide the arrow precisely to its destination.

Nauja took a deep breath. She blinked to clear her vision. Her entire body went taut and still, like a statue, as her eyes pinpointed the dot that was her target.

She loosed the arrow.

And missed.

CHAPTER EIGHTY-FOUR
SUN PIERCING ARROW

THE ARROW TIP HIT THE STONE A FEW MILLIMETERS TO THE RIGHT OF THE target, embedding itself in the wall. Nauja froze in her stance. Her mind struggled to believe this.

She didn't actually think she would miss. She'd convinced herself she would succeed. And yet, reality was merciless. She had missed.

Wait! she pleaded mentally. The edge of the arrow tip grazed the target. That might be enough.

Unfortunately, the rules of the trial were clear. Any arrow that touched the wall would mean disqualification.

Nauja felt such hatred, both toward herself and the creator of this trial, that she wanted the earth to open up and swallow her. How could she look anyone in the eye after this?

She had tried so hard!

"Thirty-two out of thirty-three," the voice boomed. She sounded dissatisfied. "Disappointing... but, since we need *someone* to succeed every few years, it is barely acceptable. I will distribute a weaker version of my skill to you, trial taker. If you fail to use it properly, nobody will ridicule me. And, if you somehow rise to the skill's level in the future, you may be able to evolve it to its original strength. Farewell."

Nauja took some time to process what she heard.

I—

Before she could think any further, her world transformed. She was no longer in a stone chamber in Trial Planet. She now hovered over the tip of a mountain, high above the clouds of an unknown planet.

For the first time, Nauja saw real space. She was paralyzed. The stars felt so immeasurably far away. Two suns burned bright in the sky, and the sheer emptiness around her made her dizzy.

She had never felt happier in her life.

Under her feet, a woman stood on the mountaintop. She wore leather armor and had long, flowing, sapphire hair. Her eyes were purple, her skin tanned, and she held a dark purple bow in her hands, as if made of crystal. It had a white bowstring with runes carved all over its length, so tiny Nauja almost couldn't see them.

Saphira, Level ??? (B-Grade)
Faction: Crimson Cloud (A-Grade)
Title: Planet Breaker

The woman aimed her bow at one of the two suns and pulled it. An obsidian arrow was nocked on the string, an object so heavy it drew in Nauja's gaze and curved the world around it.

The woman aimed, still as a statue, and shot.

The moment her arrow was loosed, Nauja felt a terrifying suction at work. The entire world was pulled to the arrow. As it flew, everything, from the air to the clouds, was tugged along. This arrow was ripping off the world's Dao, absorbing it for itself, using it to clad itself in ever greater power.

It wasn't growing weaker with distance, as normal arrows would. Instead, it was growing stronger, a multicolored outline manifesting around it like a mantle, until the arrow itself was just the core of a much larger, ever growing power.

Nauja saw it disappear into the sky, a comet heading upward, directly into one of the two suns. As she took a second look, her eyes widened. That wasn't a sun. It was a large orange bird, clad in flames and exuding such extreme light that her eyes had mistakenly took it for a sun, not daring to stare at it directly.

She couldn't even use the System to inspect it.

The bird cawed, and the world shook. Space trembled. The mountain under the woman crumbled, leaving her floating on thin air. Some of the arrow's mantle was ripped away from the bird's cawing and intense flames, but over half of it remained, and it stabbed into the bird with cataclysmic force.

The world exploded in colors. The force didn't impact Nauja, who was only there to watch the vision, but something else did. Suddenly, she was ripped away from the vision and tossed far back, interrupted before she could see the explosion's results.

The voice had mentioned a lesser version of the skill. This must have been it.

Nauja was blasted out of the vision and into her body, finding herself lying on cold stone with an intact statue beside her and the deep sound of a gong in her ears.

"Are you okay?" Gan Salin said, kneeling over her. "Don't worry about failing. Look! I carved our faces into the stone!"

She took a moment to respond. "What?"

"Our faces. Under your butt. Look."

She looked under herself, only to find a surprisingly accurate rendition of her face on the stone floor. Salin's face was right next to hers, making a grimace. If she wasn't still reeling from the vision, she would have admired his stone working skill.

"What?" she repeated.

Salin's voice was full of excitement. "So, how was it? Difficult, obviously, but was it scary? Inspiring? Did you get anything before failing?"

"I... I didn't fail. Not exactly."

"Really? Then, why is the statue still standing? Was it not a single-person trial?"

Usually, high-level Trials allowed only one person to claim them. When that happened, the trial statue would collapse to show that the trial was no longer available, but the one behind Nauja was still standing.

The barbarian recovered enough of her mind to respond properly. "I didn't succeed, but I didn't fail, either. I got a lesser version of the skill left behind in the statue."

"A skill? Ohh, that's great! What does it do?"

"It..." She frowned. "I think it allows me to shoot an arrow that gets stronger as it travels instead of weaker."

"Sounds useful!"

"Yeah. I saw the trial creator use it to shoot down the sun."

"The sun!" Salin's eyes grew wide as saucers. "What Grade were they?"

"B-Grade. But it wasn't really the sun. Just a very bright bird."

"Bright as in, smart?"

"Bright as in bright."

"So, the sun was a bird."

"No, there was an actual sun too... I think. I didn't look at it, to be honest, but it was probably the real sun."

"How do you know that if you didn't check?"

"Because I know it, okay?"

"Okay. So, the vision taught you that suns are made of bird."

"No."

"Then, birds are made of sun."

"Salin."

"What? Your answers are confusing."

"You are asking confusing questions."

"I'm just trying to understand. And why did the trial creator want to take down the sun? That sounds really bad for anyone under it."

"Again, it wasn't the real sun... and, I don't know why. I guess they were enemies."

"That's a stupid enemy to make. It's literally the sun."

"It's literally *not* the sun. And that's none of your business. Can we focus on this awesome new skill I got?"

Salin opened his mouth to say something more, then paused. "It sounds amazing! Can I see?"

Nauja smiled. She was so excited. Maybe she didn't have the complete skill, but it was the signature skill of a Planet Breaker! It was about time someone shared her enthusiasm!

"I can't use it yet," she admitted. "But I got the vision! If I just meditate on it, I will get the skill, sooner or later. And then, I will be able to shoot large dinosaurs from far, far away. Father will be so proud." *If I ever see him again*, she added mentally. Every cultivator could only enter

Trial Planet once in their lives. If she left the planet to see the world...
She would never be able to come back.

That was the sad reality that had been chasing her ever since she left
her tribe. The dilemma faced by every barbarian who chose to delve.
Nauja tore her mind away. She would consider it when the time came.
Who knows, maybe she'd die in the meantime.

In any case, this was her moment of triumph. She wouldn't let
anything cloud it. Not even the looming, heart-breaking decision.

"Should we get going?" she asked, standing up. Salin politely
extended a hand to help her, which she used—barbarians had manners,
too.

"Yep. We should have a head start. If I miss the fight between the
Garden Assault and the guardian, I will regret it for the rest of my life."

"Is it that spectacular?"

"Oh, you have no idea. It's probably the only time in your life that
you'll see E-Grades standing up to a D-Grade—and not losing terribly."

Her eyes sparkled. The strongest people around... She *had* to see
them fight. "Then, what are we waiting for?"

"Nothing. Let's go!"

Salin jumped and punched the air, with Nauja following after him as
they exited the temple. They were back in the crampy corridors now, but
she didn't mind. Her mood was at an all-time high. Nothing could ruin it.

"Wait," she said, raising a hand. "Do you hear that?"

"Hear what?"

"That." She focused on her hearing. "It's like... a landslide?"

Salin raised a brow. "Does it sound like something we should get the
hell away from?"

"Oh, absolutely."

They bolted. However, there was a limit to how fast they could cross
the labyrinth. There could be bone monsters hiding anywhere. They had
to tread cautiously.

Soon, the sound after them intensified so much that even Salin
could hear it clearly. An avalanche of pebbles may have very well been
raining on the stone floors—or perhaps a centipede of bone was
marching their way. And, if there was a bone centipede, it could only be
the bone monster version they had yet to meet: the King one.

By that point, it was too late to be cautious. Nauja and Gan Salin ran at full tilt, making some distance from the source of the sound, which was apparently chasing them.

Generally speaking, Labyrinth Ring didn't have dead-ends. Most of its paths connected to others, making for a confusing terrain where you had no idea if you were moving forward, backward, or in circles. To navigate it, people usually needed either Nauja's sharp eyesight, which could detect the miniscule changes in wall coloration, or a device like Lord Longsword's compass.

Occasionally, however, the labyrinth did house dead-ends. And, as luck would have it, it was at exactly such a dead-end that Nauja and Gan Salin ran into.

They both screeched to a halt.

"Fuck," said Nauja.

"Shit," said Salin.

They turned and prepared to run again, but the sound was too close now, approaching fast. Before they knew it, whatever was chasing them sounded like it was just behind the corner, ready to tear them apart. They could no longer escape.

They exchanged a look. "I guess this is the end," Nauja said with a small smile, drawing her bow. "Traveling with you was... not terrible. It's an honor to die by your side, Gan Salin."

"Same," Salin replied, putting on his clawed gloves. "It was about time, to be honest. I've lasted longer than I thought I would. At least nobody will miss me back home."

"Don't say that!" Nauja's eyes went wide. "I will miss you. Jack and Brock will. And certainly your family."

Salin chuckled. "You don't know my family... but thanks. I appreciate it."

That was all they had time to say before the abomination rounded the corner. It was a flood of hard blue, with shells and pincers sticking out haphazardly, and a thousand little legs moving the flood from underneath, while bone shards trailed on the ground behind them.

Wait. Were there little muscles on the crab arms that held those pincers?

Between the skittering crabs walked a young brorilla, reaching just above Nauja's waist. Seeing them, his eyes brightened. "Stop," he commanded, and the crabs froze. The brorilla then looked up at Nauja and Gan Salin, who were equally frozen. "Hello, bros."

"Brock?" they both said at once. Brock nodded.

"Yes. Brock. Little bros, hi."

The crabs all waved in unison. Nauja gaped. Gan Salin started laughing uncontrollably, until he ended up rolling on the floor.

"Brock!" he cried out. "I fucking love you, dude!"

CHAPTER EIGHTY-FIVE
INTRODUCTIONS

BROCK WAS PRETTY PROUD OF HIMSELF. HE'D SAVED HIS LITTLE CRAB BROS.

Dying to bone monsters all the time just wasn't good. Therefore, Brock had gathered them up and taught them how to defend themselves.

First came training. He taught the crabs how to raise their pincers, not to snip pebbles off the walls, but to defend themselves against predators. After all, even though they were far weaker than the bone monsters, they had much room to grow! Since Brock had taken over as their big bro, he couldn't just let them waste their potential.

Then came grouping up. By themselves, the crabs were too weak. No amount of training would let them defend against the bone monsters— at least, not in any reasonable time frame. However, they were also far more than their predators. Just touring the corridors alone was stupid.

Starting from the first crab—the one he wrestled into little brohood —Brock ventured into the corridors to find more of them. He was followed by an ever rising number of obedient crabs. Every time they met a new one, his little bros would convince the new crab that Brock was their big bro. Brock's little squad grew until it was nowhere near a squad anymore—hundreds of crabs rushed over each other in their haste to receive the teachings of their big bro.

Brock held lectures and work-out sessions. He had the crabs lift and spar against each other. He had them run up and down the corridors and walls. He taught them how to fight as a group, separating into smaller squads to surround their predator, burying it under sheer numbers. Even how to send out one crab as bait to lure the bone monsters into ambushes. Finally, he also taught them how to scout for approaching bone monsters.

They weren't bad bros. In fact, they were excellent. Obedient, smart, and thirsty for knowledge. They made him so proud.

The crab training took one day. When Brock was done with them, the crabs had evolved from harmless crustaceans to hardened veterans. They had scouts, hit squads, and battle formations. They could hatch proper plans, protect their own, recruit and train new crabs, and gradually expand throughout the stone corridors.

They were set to conquer the labyrinth, forever banishing the bone monsters. Brock had started a war.

But it was war against oppression, so it was fine.

After the bro bootcamp was over, the crabs accompanied Brock to the guardian's gate. They knew where it was, obviously, and took him there by the fastest route.

En route, they also defeated two bone monsters! Brock was so proud.

And then, completely accidentally, they ran into Girl Bro and Dog Bro! Brock had so much to show them. He'd gotten much stronger and had trained all these little bros.

They seemed surprised, which was odd, but Brock didn't give it much thought. He also noticed they were scared when he first found them. They must have been having a terrible time in the crab bro labyrinth. Thankfully, Brock was here now. As their big bro—he was Big Bro's first little bro, so he had seniority—he would protect them.

After Girl Bro and Dog Bro joined his group, Brock led everyone to the guardian. Nothing much happened in the meantime. Any bone monsters were assaulted and overrun by crabs, with their bones taken along as war trophies.

Soon, the walls were pitch-black, and the sound of faraway voices began to reach their ears. Brock raised a hand. "Stop," he commanded, and all the crabs came to a halt.

Big Bro had taught him to think before acting. Now, as much as he wanted to introduce these little bros to their Big Big Bro, he knew it would be a bad idea. There were more people up ahead. Strong people. If anything went wrong, his little bros would be in trouble, and he would have dragged his big bro into it as well.

That shouldn't happen.

Brock waved goodbye to his little bros. Manly tears sparkled in his eyes. They had grown so much—they didn't even need him anymore.

He shook the pincers of each and every one of them, then wrapped them into a group hug. Finally, he waved as the crabs disappeared around the corner, off to conquer their little corner of the world and manifest their full potential.

They grew up so fast...

"Nauja," Dog Bro said, "I think we just witnessed a fate-turning event for Labyrinth Ring..."

"I don't even know what to say anymore..." Girl Bro shook her head.

Brock knew why Girl Bro was lost for words. She did not understand the concept of bro yet. Neither did Dog Bro. But, as their big bro, Brock would make sure they understood. It was his duty.

After all, if he could handle a hundred crab bros, why not Dog Bro and Girl Bro?

———

When Jack entered the chamber, it felt like surfacing out of water. He hadn't even realized how confined the labyrinth's tight corridors had become.

The guardian's gates were a set of giant bronze doors. Each rose a hundred feet, all the way to the ceiling of the stone chamber, taking up the entire far wall. Torches dotted the other walls in regular intervals, forming a grid that stretched over the entire chamber.

The chamber itself was round in shape—save for the straight far wall. Twelve exits led back into the labyrinth, leaving a hundred-foot-radius, empty circle in the midst, where cultivators gathered in anticipation of the battle.

There were around a dozen people present—though none of the other lords. Jack scanned them all. Most were at or near the peak of the

E-Grade. They wore mainly armor or flowing robes that didn't obstruct movement, and they belonged to all sorts of species and factions.

One of them was the ice witch that belonged to Longsword's team. She was speaking to someone else, but broke off when Longsword appeared and came to greet him. Besides her, Jack saw a genderless stone golem, a snakeman, a humanoid woman with draconic features, as well as a man with gills and fins. The rest were all humans.

Of factions, he finally learned some more B-Grade ones. The stone golem belonged to Titan Mountain. The draconic woman, to Dragon Valley. The merfolk, to Deep Sea Shrine.

With the Animal Kingdom, Wide Swirls, and Exploding Sun, he now knew six. Three to go.

The moment Jack, Lord Longsword, and Bocor entered the chamber, all conversation hushed, and all eyes turned to them.

"Lord Longsword," a few people said, approaching and nodding deeply.

"My friends," Longsword greeted everyone, laughing and shaking their hands. "I'm glad to see you made it. Did you have any luck?"

A few people had smiles on their faces. Others, presumably the ones who hadn't found a trial, looked disappointed. It seemed that the labyrinth wasn't too generous.

Suddenly, he felt out of his depth. The cultivators who made it here were the galaxy's cream of the crop. These were talented scions of B-Grade factions, disciples of high-level cultivators, or otherwise privileged prodigies.

Jack, in comparison, was just... Jack.

Alone as he was, without Brock, Gan Salin, Nauja, or anyone else, he felt vulnerable. Like he didn't fit.

These cultivators all had a carefully crafted upbringing. They socialized like nobles. Longsword joined their "dance," laughing and chatting in groups, moving along like a social butterfly. These were all powerful people, and their interactions were an intense, jovial procedure that Jack had trouble following.

Even Bocor joined them, not forgetting to throw Jack a final glare. Longsword, on the other hand, just ignored him. He had realized by now that Jack was never going to become an ally.

Jack was left alone. Though he had arrived with Longsword, the others saw how the lord paid him no attention, so they followed suit.

"Hello." A woman approached him, in direct spite of his previous thoughts. Her smile was bright. "My name is Leafborn."

Human (Earth-74), Level 119
Faction: Wide Swirls (B-Grade)
Title: Sixth Ring Conqueror

She was from the same faction as Longsword, but speaking to Jack meant she and the lord were on bad terms. Everyone else took note of that.

"I'm Jack Rust. Nice to meet you," Jack replied politely.

Funnily enough, Jack had been in such settings before. Back when he was a PhD student, he often saw professors interacting with each other, and he engaged in these social settings himself every time he attended a conference. Those times were very similar to what he now saw—except these people had their PhD's in fighting, not science.

Though, wizards may qualify for science, too.

In any case, Jack did not enjoy this very much. There was joy to be found in these social dances, which is why they occurred, but he now followed the path of the fist. Convoluted matters didn't fit him.

Therefore, he simply remained polite and tried to make friends.

Leafborn, the human woman who'd first approached him, introduced him to the stone golem and the snakeman—who seemed like a nice person, in spite of all fantasy stereotypes against his species.

Jack made polite conversation, keeping some distance. He wanted to make friends, but he didn't want to get swept up in anyone's political games. The conversation still taught him a lot of things about the universe and its peculiarities—along with how unusual it was for someone so recently Integrated to get this far.

Thankfully, he didn't stay there for long. Soon after Jack's group, another group arrived at the chamber: the Exploding Sun lady's.

Again, everyone paused. Some went over to greet her, while others returned to their conversations. Jack approached her, too, as did Lord Longsword.

"Priya," Longsword said with a beaming smile. "You are fast."

"Not as fast as you," she replied. "Getting in early has its benefits." She was a woman in her twenties, with tanned skin and white strips wrapped around her wrists, like those a fighter would wear. She wore a red flowing robe that left her fit arms exposed, and her eyes were sharp as she took in Longsword.

Beside her was a fat man with a large smile, who instantly created a friendly impression in Jack's mind. There was also a captivating woman with long silver hair, whose eyes pierced Jack like a moon beam. All three were humans of the Exploding Sun faction.

"This is Jack Rust," Longsword introduced Jack, mentioning him directly for the first time since arriving. "We met in the labyrinth, and we helped each other make it through."

"Jack Rust?" Priya's eyes focused on him. "Why is your name familiar?"

"During my Integration, a member of your faction became my master. Master Shol. I believe he was a deacon?"

Her eyes lit up. "Ah, of course! Brother Shol has spoken about you. It's impressive that you made it here, Jack, but don't worry; I will protect you from here on out."

"Thank you, but I believe I can protect myself," he replied. Her kind eyes turned intrigued, and her smile didn't falter, but grew.

"So be it, then. I look forward to fighting by your side."

Inwardly, he heaved a sigh of relief. On the outside, he smiled confidently. "Likewise."

"And let's have a chat later, okay? There will be plenty of time."

His smile widened. "Sure." He looked forward to hearing about the Exploding Sun—and his master. With any luck, they might even help him save Earth.

Raucous laughter came from the side as the fat man approached. "What a brave brother!" he shouted, stretching out a hand. "Let's get along, brother Jack. The name's Chotu—Chotu Malhotra. And the beauty here is Kareena." He motioned at the long-haired woman, who raised a brow at him.

"I can introduce myself, Chotu."

"Blame me for wanting to help."

"In any case, I'm Kareena," she said. "It's a pleasure to make your acquaintance."

"The pleasure is all mine," he replied.

"Have you heard anything about Minerva?" Longsword asked Priya. Minerva was the Hand of God lady. "If you're here, I assume..."

"She should be arriving soon," Priya responded. "We ran into her in the labyrinth, actually. It should be any moment now."

On cue, three more forms appeared from the side corridor. All three wore black, and all were peak E-Grades from the Hand of God, but they belonged to different species.

At the front walked a tall, slender woman with pale skin, thin features, and dark hair that reached below her shoulders. Her black gown reached her ankles, and there was a certain gravitas to her steps, like she commanded the very earth she walked on, along with everyone's attention.

Longsword and Priya approached her at once to exchange greetings.

Following Lady Minerva were two people; one was a tall, slim man with light green skin, who had the ears of a deer. He wore a long, brown robe, while his eyes were slightly farther apart than a human's.

Dryad, Level 124
Faction: Hand of God (B-Grade)
Title: Sixth Ring Conqueror

Jack was intrigued, but his attention was stolen by the second follower of Lady Minerva.

This was a pale-skinned man with black eyes, clad in a formal black suit that seemed completely out of place in Trial Planet. To Jack's surprise, he knew this man, all the way from Earth.

He was Vocrich, the Hand of God representative on Earth, the one who hosted the Integration Auction and later turned a blind eye to the Animal Kingdom's excessive bullying.

"Shit," Jack said.

After the initial surprise, he realized that Vocrich being here made sense. He was at the peak E-Grade, had never revealed a Ring Conqueror title, and had good standing with his faction, since he was sent to oversee Earth's Integration. He had probably secured a good reward after selling out Jack, too.

Come to think of it, Nauja had also mentioned the Hand of God having someone with darkness powers in Space Ring.

The two of them locked eyes. If anything, Vocrich seemed more surprised than Jack himself, and walked over to meet him.

"Jack Rust," he said, looking him up and down. "Seeing you here was the last thing I expected."

"Yeah. I'm not dead yet. Surprise."

"It is." Vocrich smirked. "And I have to admit, your progress is superb. If we didn't have a rule against accepting wanted criminals of any B-Grade faction, I might have invited you into Hand of God."

"I would refuse," Jack replied with a smile of his own. "You left me to die at the end of the Tournament. I thought you were supposed to observe the rules."

Vocrich frowned. "That was business. What fool expects the rules to actually be followed?"

"Yeah, I know now. Doesn't mean it's right. Just to be clear, I don't hold too much of a grudge, but... Well, a little bit. I believe an apology would go a long way."

Vocrich laughed. "You know, you are actually the reason I'm here in the first place. The business deal I made with the Animal Kingdom gave me the capital to join Lady Minerva's team—and, if not for some unforeseen circumstances, we would have a lot more Hand of God members here."

Jack looked around. Besides the three of them, he actually couldn't see anyone from the Hand of God.

He also had a sneaking suspicion that the "unforeseen circumstances" were him entering—and revealing—the Ancient ruins. Gan Salin had mentioned that the Hand of God members in Trial Planet started asking strange questions right about then. Given the gravity of the System's announcement, it wouldn't surprise Jack if the Hand of God had pulled most of their people from the Garden Assault to focus on finding the ruins.

"I'm glad my near-death helped you, Vocrich," he said.

"Me too, my friend. Let's stay out of each other's way, okay?"

"We'll see."

With a final smile, Vocrich walked away. He actually seemed to be in a good mood—the polar opposite of Jack's.

Guess I'm enemies with two lords already. Nice. At least the Exploding Sun people seem nice.

"Your attention, everyone," Lady Minerva spoke up. Her voice was light, intense, and faintly bored, as if addressing these cultivators was a chore. "Since all lords are present and we have enough people, we will move to fight the guardian immediately. It will take some days for a new guardian to be created, so anyone who arrives here later will have the opportunity to enter Garden Ring as well."

Everyone murmured in agreement. Jack, however, had a thought.

"Excuse me," he asked, raising his hand. "This might be a given for everyone else, but I suppose we will all fight the guardian together to get the Seventh Ring Conqueror title, right? In that case, will the people who arrive later get it as well?"

Lady Minerva stared at him for a moment before responding. "Everyone present will assist in taking down the guardian. Even we lords cannot handle it ourselves—though we will weaken it for you. As for anyone who arrives later, no, they will not get the title. Entering Garden Ring is more than enough for them."

Jack hesitated. That meant his friends, who weren't here yet, would miss out. However, he couldn't exactly ask everyone to wait, could he? Especially since the majority of this group were either neutral toward him or enemies.

Then at that moment, one more group entered the chamber from behind Lady Minerva. It was Gan Salin, Nauja, and—bless the gods and all that was holy—Brock.

Jack felt such relief at seeing his brorilla safe and sound. Brock gave him a thumbs-up while Gan Salin waved intently.

Jack turned back to the lady. "Nevermind," he said. "All good. Let's fight."

CHAPTER EIGHTY-SIX
FIGHTING AN IMMORTAL

THREE SETS OF HANDS WERE PLACED ON THE DOOR. THE THREE LORDS WERE ALL human, scrawny in size and smooth of skin compared to the colossal constructions of bronze, aging back to antiquity and seemingly unmovable.

They swung open smoothly and soundlessly, like they had been pushed by a giant. After all, opening the door was not the guardian. The thing behind it was the guardian. They crashed against the walls with a loud bang that made everyone jump, flooding the guardian's antechamber before streaming into the many corridors.

Another large chamber was revealed. This one was not empty.

A rectangular room, around a hundred feet tall, another hundred wide, and three hundred long. An ancient, dusty air suffused it, like it had been centuries since it last opened. Six thick, stone columns were spread around its length in three rows of two. A wide red line was painted on the floor, leading from the entrance to the far end of the room, where the antechamber's light did not yet reach.

Torches lit up on the walls. They started from the entrance and stretched to the far side of the room, arranged in orderly lines, suffusing the room with light. A throne was revealed at the back. And, sitting on it, was the king.

Bone King, Level ??? (D-Grade)
The final evolution of Bone Sentinels. As it defeats its victims and adds their skeletons to its own, a Bone Sentinel gradually increases in size and power until it breaks through.
A Bone King is the apex of that process. It has devoured thousands of E-Grade skeletons, enhancing its body until it lost any resemblance to a person. It possesses extreme strength, durability, and dexterity. It usually cultivates the Dao of Bone.
This particular Bone King is the Guardian of this Trial Planet's Labyrinth Ring.

The Bone King was a gargantuan monstrosity sitting on a throne of bare stone. From the waist up, it was a humanoid skeleton, only ten times the size. Just its palms were the size of Jack's body, ending in sharp claws another half as long. Its face was humanoid, and red flames burned in its eyes, and its teeth were far sharper than they had any right to be, more like an animal than a human. Its skull was topped by a circle of sharp bone appendages—a crown of bone, befitting its name as Bone King.

From the waist down, the King's body was that of a snake. Endless bones made up a slithering tail the girth of an ancient tree, long enough that it could wrap around the base of the throne twice.

The King sat on its throne with its head resting against a palm. As the torches around it flared to life, shedding life on its ugly visage, the red flames in its eyes flared back. The King raised its head, and an undeniable aura of an immortal spread around the room, easily overpowering the Daos of everyone present.

Jack stood in a line with everyone else behind the three lords. Before the force of the Bone King's Dao, he felt as brittle as a leaf, fighting just to keep the spark of his Dao alive.

The three lords were taking the brunt of the pressure. They stood tall before this almighty enemy, weathering its storm with the weight of their souls. They truly were strong, these lords—the very best E-Grades the galaxy had to offer.

But their opponent was a D-Grade. There was an undeniable,

unbridgeable chasm between them. Thankfully, the lords were three, and they had the support of more than a dozen other cultivators, each at least at the peak E-Grade level of power.

The King observed the cultivators. When they didn't collapse to its pressure, it slowly stood. Its tail uncoiled, half resting on the ground and the other half supporting its massive upper body. It's Dao intensified.

Jack gulped. There was pressure to that Dao. Not just in depth, the nature itself was pressing against them like the lid of a coffin, burying them under the crushing weight of their own deaths.

The Dao of Bone.

It was about death. About the end of everything. At the same time, it was hard and sharp, a truth hidden under layers of lies. Brutal.

That was all Jack could glimpse of the thing's Dao. Its finality brought to mind his own Brutalizing Aura—a skill that would never work on such a superior opponent. He brought up his status screen, which he hadn't seen in a while, to get courage.

Name: Jack Rust
Species: Human, Earth-387
Faction: Bare Fist Brotherhood (E)
Grade: E
Class: Fiend of the Iron Fist (Elite)
Level: 97

Strength: 410
Dexterity: 405
Constitution: 410
Mental: 50
Will: 80

Skills: Ghost Step I
Dao Skills: Indomitable Body III, Meteor Punch II, Iron Fist Style II, Brutalizing Aura I
Daos: Perfect Dao Seed of the Fist (late), Dao Root of Indomitable Will (fused), Dao Root of Life (fused), Dao Root of Power

Titles: Planetary Frontrunner (10), Planetary Torchbearer (1), Sixth Ring
Conqueror

Level 97.

According to what Longsword had told him en route, this creature
was at the very bottom of immortals, a fledgling compared to true cultivators. The difference between 97 and 126 seemed small—but it signified an ocean of power.

If Jack faced this monster alone, he would surely perish. Even the
Life Drop could only prolong his death by a couple instants. Thankfully,
he wasn't alone. He wasn't even the frontline.

"Is everyone ready?" Lady Minerva, the lady from Hand of God,
shouted. Her simple-looking leather belt shone. Three shapes jumped
out of it, materializing from light into creatures. One was a yellow-
furred bear the size of a buffalo. Another was an eagle, whose wings
ended in sharp tips. The third was an ancient-looking turtle whose shell
was wider than a dining table.

"Prepare yourselves!" Longsword shouted, drawing his nine-foot-
long sword. He looked tiny compared to Minerva's beasts, but his
towering aura eclipsed theirs. His sword aimed at the ceiling. "This is
your chance to make history! This is the time when mortals kill
immortals!"

The cultivators behind him roared in response. Jack couldn't see
Longsword's face, but he knew the man was grinning.

Lady Priya of Exploding Sun didn't speak. Her open palms were
suddenly clad in fire and light so bright Jack had to look away. Their
power was enough to shake the air, coloring it yellow.

The Bone King stepped off its throne, signaling the start of the
battle.

Priya, Longsword, and the three beasts charged at once. That was
the plan. They would go first to weaken it, so the other cultivators could
attack without dying before even getting a single hit in.

The Bone King fell low. Its upper body was now parallel to the
ground as it slithered forward at great speed, becoming a blur like a
moving train. Its sharp claws opened wide to tear the lords apart.

It fell on them hard. Claws flashed. Bone glistened in the torchlight.

The clang of metal on bone filled the room, along with the beasts' roars and cries.

In that brief instant, Jack caught Longsword's sword meeting a claw head-on. Priya blocked its other hand, burning like a sun between its fingers. The turtle jumped into the King's mouth, sharp teeth rending its shell, while the bear and eagle fell on the King, striking with all their might. The bear smashed a paw into its side, cracking a layer of bones. The eagle carved a long line into its back, sending bone shards flying, but the King was made of many, tightly packed layers of bones. These attacks weren't enough to bring it down.

All those things happened in an instant. Time seemed to freeze as Jack observed everything. Then, the world returned to motion.

Longsword was sent flying. He smashed hard into a column, sending a cloud of dust into the air. Before he could recover, the Bone King came after him. Longsword jumped. He used his sword to climb the column. The King climbed with its tail around it, claws tearing deep grooves into the stone. Longsword reached the top and leaped into the void. The King jumped and bit down on him. The eagle swooped in from the side and picked up Longsword, barely saving him from the King's jaws.

This battle was not easy. Everyone here was risking their lives, including the lords. But what cultivator wouldn't?

The King landed on the ground and leaped to the side, aiming at Priya. She flew back like an arrow. Suns blossomed on her palms, and she threw them at the King, who took the strikes like they were nothing. To Jack, it looked like she was throwing bombs.

Longsword descended from above, released by the eagle. He fell with his sword pointed down and pierced clean into the King's back, eliciting a scream that threatened to burst Jack's eardrums.

The King swatted behind him. Longsword jumped away, then pulled back his sword and used it as a lever to pull himself to the ground, dodging yet another swipe.

The bear rammed into the King, shoving it aside. Both lost their balance. The King stumbled before its tail coiled around the bear, squeezing it tight and keeping it in place. It turned and prepared to strike.

Priya was there, arriving like a shadow. Twin suns blossomed in her palms, growing in size until they were larger than her body, then she slammed them into the bone.

The explosion was deafening. The released heat was enough to burn the skin of any normal person, even where Jack was standing. Bones flew everywhere. An inhuman scream came from the flames as a claw of bone tore through them, splitting the fire like it was water. Priya had already dodged.

A gaping hole now lay open on the King's side, but it wasn't enough. The claw completed its motion, tearing into the bear, and cutting through its rock fur like it was nothing. The King's palm slammed against the bear's back as the five claws tore into its body, destroying its insides.

The Bone King then grabbed the bear from the inside, raised it into the air, and tossed it at the entrance, where every other cultivator waited.

They scattered like flies. One guy got clipped and flung at a wall. The bear's large body rolled on the floor through everyone, spraying blood and innards before colliding with the far wall and staying there, unmoving. It was already dead.

A cry tore through the battle. The eagle and turtle were angry at the loss of their comrade, laying into the King with wild abandon and little regard for their lives. Lady Minerva's belt shone again, and a new beast appeared. This one was a white wolf, which jumped into the fray.

The Bone King roared. The sound shook the stone columns and rocked the labyrinth. Its Dao burst out at full power to sweep everyone, making them falter. In that split-second, its jaws bit at the turtle again, cracking and denting its shell. It wouldn't last another blow.

The King's claws swiped at the eagle, but it managed to recover from the stun and barely twisted out of harms way.

Longsword was there again. His sword cleaved halfway through the King's body, cutting through bone like it was butter. The King roared, losing some control over its body, but its tail came swinging from the back, slamming into Longsword and sending him flying into the stone throne.

Priya flashed next to the wound Longsword had opened. Her palms became suns that slammed into the broken bones, infiltrating the Bone

King's body and incinerating it from the inside. The King roared as it burned.

Again, it tried to hit her, and again it missed. Priya dodged two strikes, moving in ways that defied gravity and common sense, then hurriedly retreated and kept her distance, panting.

The wolf was there. It fell on the King jaws-first, grabbing hold of its spine and refusing to let go. The King squirmed and tried to reach behind it, but couldn't. It then crashed against a column, dislodging the wolf, and backhanded it away right as the eagle swooped by, carving yet another deep line into the King's short throat.

The King tried to roar, but its voice came broken.

"Now!" Minerva shouted from the entrance.

Jack and everyone else—with the exception of Brock, who was too weak to participate—had been waiting for that signal. They rushed in. Jack's adrenaline spiked. His body was on fire. His skills were at the tips of his fingers, just waiting to be unleashed.

The King roared again, a caricature of its former, mighty sound. Despite its large size, it had been injured.

Its Dao, however, remained whole. It was like a blade hanging over Jack's neck.

He charged.

CHAPTER EIGHTY-SEVEN
FELLING THE BONE KING

A claw came Jack's way. He barely Ghost Stepped away, the sharp bones carving into the stone floor. His fist shone purple. He unleashed a Meteor Punch at the arm as it recovered, but all his explosion did was break the surface bones. There were many layers underneath.

How can I be so weak! he thought, eyes wide. I may not be at the Elite level yet, but I'm stronger than peak E-Grade monsters! Is this all I can do?

Yet, the harsh reality was right in his face. Compared to the lords and the Bone King, he had a long way to go. He couldn't even use his Life Drop.

"Grab its arms!" Minerva shouted from the entrance.

The other cultivators around Jack sprang into motion. Magic flew everywhere. Explosions filled Jack's ears. Light blinded him.

Keeping tabs on the Bone King was all he could do. He charged with a roar, channeling a Meteor Punch.

The fat guy from Exploding Sun—Chotu—suddenly turned golden and gigantic. He grabbed one arm of the Bone King, struggling to keep it to the ground. The turtle fell on him as well, as did several other Physical cultivators.

The King tried to tug its arm free, but the cultivators' combined pressure stopped it for an instant—enough for the eagle to fly in its face, carving it up with its talons. The King roared. The wolf jumped on its back again, tearing through bones with its strong jaws, as Priya flashed under the King's belly and slammed a sun into it. The explosion raised its entire body by an inch.

Longsword flew back into the battle, holding his ribs with one hand and swinging with the other. His sword cleaved through the upper-left part of the King's face, cutting it clean off.

The King, realizing it was losing, went berserk. Its body erupted and thrummed with power. It threw everyone off its arm, then cleaved around wildly. Priya and Longsword dodged. Many others were not as lucky, cut into ribbons or shattered by the King's attacks. Jack himself had to Ghost Step away, narrowly escaping certain death.

Green power filled the air. The long-haired woman of Exploding Sun —Kareena—and the dryad of Hand of God both raised their hands, releasing life magic. It swam into the injured bodies and healed them, giving them the strength to fight again. Even Longsword's ribs were repaired.

Of course, those who'd died could not be saved.

The moment the healing magic was activated, the Bone King snapped its head that way like it smelled anathema. The healers were already running as the King's tail slammed into the ground and propelled its upper body forward, ramming through some cultivators and sending them flying.

Jack was one of them. He felt a colossal impact against his crossed arms, then the world spun until a stone column brought him to an instant halt. He fell to the ground, groaning and unable to stand. His ribs were broken. Through the corner of his eye, he spotted the King rampaging. It was trying to reach the healers while everyone else was taking the opportunity to pummel it.

A sun smashed into its head and exploded inside. The wolf tore its spine apart. Longsword cleaved at the base of its tail, and the eagle was swooping by, forgoing caution in favor of damage.

But the King, being a D-Grade monster, was not completely stupid. With a sudden halt, it raised its hand into the air, grabbing the eagle mid-flight and crushing it. No healing magic could bring it back.

It threw the eagle's body into the healers as if mocking them, causing them to jump aside and give an opening. It ignored that opening to spin around itself with its arms extended, maiming anyone who didn't react in time.

That was a lot of people.

Chuto, the golden giant, had no time to dodge. He used his open palm to block the strike—an impossible endeavor. He was propelled back in a straight line, crashing against a wall hard enough that the crack of his bones was audible over the din of battle. Priya screamed and jumped at the King, her entire body radiating intense light and heat. She smashed into its head like a smite from the heavens, unleashing an inferno that charred its bones black.

The King tried to roar again, but its voice was long gone. All it managed to do was open its mouth in a silent cry. A new beast flew in there—a sparrow smaller than the previous eagle, but also faster. It lodged itself into the Bone King's throat and started cutting around wildly with its claws and sharp wing tips. The King tried to chomp on it, but the sparrow was too far back. The King clawed at its mouth, but Longsword cut off its hand before it could reach.

It then swiped at him with the other hand, ignoring the sparrow, but the turtle and wolf attacked it at the same time, tipping it over and making it crash face-first into the ground.

In the blink of an eye, everyone was on top of the Bone King. Magic filled the air. Powerful strikes cracked bone. Colors abounded. All the elements had gone haywire. Darkness expanded around the King's head, cutting off its eyesight.

Jack had recovered. His prodigious regenerative powers had stitched his ribs together. He jumped into the battle, hovering over everyone else and unleashing a Meteor Shower on the King's back, digging deeper and deeper even as it squirmed under them.

With a final push, the King raised its body, throwing them all off. It faced the ceiling and roared—and, in its moment of defiance, Longsword's sword cleaved through its neck from behind, severing it.

A head of bone crashed onto the stone floor, its jaws closing one final time. The red flames went out. The colossal body collapsed slowly, rolling forward until it lay slumped and motionless.

Level Up! You have reached Level 98.

Level Up! You have reached Level 99.
Level Up! You have reached Level 100.

Silence pervaded the chamber. Then, a massive cry of triumph. Everyone yelled at the same time, celebrating their lungs out.

They had killed an immortal.

———

Jack waded through the battle's aftermath. He saw bodies strewn about —some of the galaxy's brightest geniuses, fallen in their quest to glory. The iron stench of blood filled the chamber. Broken bones crunched under his feet—all that remained of the D-Grade Bone King.

Healers toured the bloody chamber, helping the few wounded that remained. It was toward one such healer that Jack paced, slowly, absorbing the destruction around him.

Violence was ugly. But it was his path.

His steps brought him to a stone column, against the base of which leaned a man with canine tendencies. "Salin," Jack said in greeting. "Are you okay?"

"Hey... Jack."

The canine had received a backhand from the Bone King, which almost shattered his entire body. Only the long-haired woman's fast reaction had saved him. Yet, despite the excruciating pain he undoubtedly experienced, Salin looked ready to laugh. His lips were crooked into a smirk with one eye closed. All the pain in the world couldn't touch him—or so it seemed.

"Thank you," Jack said to the healer still tending to the last of Salin's wounds. She was Kareena, the woman with long silver hair who was part of Lady Priya's team.

"Don't mention it," she replied, not taking her eyes away from Salin. "In battle, we are all brothers and sisters. This is the least I could do."

Jack nodded. Right then, a small shape dashed before him, then stopped and extended a fist. Jack smiled and bumped it. "What's up, Brock?"

"Bro," Brock replied, giving Jack a thumbs-up. That carried all the meaning in the world.

Jack had seen Brock before the battle began, but he remained over-joyed. His little bro had broken into the E-Grade! That was terrific! Not to mention the army of crabs he'd reportedly amassed.

Nauja followed right behind Brock. As an archer, she'd remained near the chamber entrance during the battle, so she was safe. "Nice fight," she commented. "That move of yours was flashy."

"Meteor Shower? Thanks. It's my strongest one."

"I'm also working on a new skill. I tried to use it during the battle, but... I don't quite understand it yet."

"The one you got in the Trial?"

"Yes."

"It will come. I've experienced two Dao Visions so far. One was harder than the other, but both gave me insights. It's just a matter of time."

"I guess. I just can't wait!" She smiled radiantly. Jack smirked back. He was stupid to worry.

"What did you say it's called? Arrow that Cuts the Sun?"

She scowled. "Not even close. It's Sun Piercing Arrow."

"That's what I said."

"Not even close! What kind of name is Arrow that Cuts the Sun? First of all, it doesn't make sense, and second, it sounds terrible. Arrows don't even cut. Even a child could think of a better name."

"Whereas Sun Piercing Arrow is an artistic masterpiece."

"Whatever, Mr. Meteor Shower."

Jack laughed. From the side, he could practically sense Salin's urge to say something stupid. Too bad his chest remained caved in, making every word a struggle.

The battle against the Bone King had been bloody. Four of the twenty-three participants had perished, along with two of Lady Miner-va's beasts, and many more had been injured—so many that it took the healers hours to patch up their most grievous wounds. In the meantime, everyone else conversed with their companions, took in the battle and its aftermath, and prepared themselves for what was essentially the Final Ring of Trial Planet: Garden Ring.

Unlike every other ring, Garden Ring was more a reward than a trial. The cultivators who made it there could just walk around and collect treasures, enter Trials, or pursue other benefits. Of course, there *was* danger if you wanted the very best rewards, but most were content with what was freely offered.

The greatest danger in Garden Ring was other cultivators. When presented with such wealth, disputes arose easily, and nobody stopped people from killing each other. Even the three lords and their teams would be slaughtering each other for the greatest treasure—as Longsword had told Jack during their journey.

Just like the Integration, Trial Planet was designed to be a massive meat grinder. Many people died or failed, but those who proved their worth received enormous benefits.

In light of the next ring's circumstances, the rapid socialization had dwindled after the battle. Everyone knew they were finally at Garden Ring. The person they befriended today might be the one to kill them tomorrow.

The bodies of the fallen were buried in a corner of the antechamber. The hard stone that made up the floor was nothing for these strong cultivators. A massive rock was placed over the common grave, announcing the names of the fallen to those who would come next.

As Jack learned, the labyrinth cleaned and restored itself between batches of cultivators. The labyrinth itself was actually a small part of the entire Labyrinth Ring, constantly rolling around its surface to reveal new walls, corridors, trials, monsters, and throne rooms. Meanwhile, everything outside the current labyrinth's bounds was magically restored to its original state.

In other words, this grave would disappear soon. But the action still mattered, for everyone knew it was only luck that they weren't the ones in the tomb.

Then, led by the three lords, everyone walked to a small passage behind the Bone King's throne. It was short—only thirty feet in length —and led to an empty pedestal. It was a teleportation device like the one that transported them to Labyrinth Ring, except made of bronze instead of iron. That meant the teleportation wouldn't be random.

The lords and their teams were the first to touch the pedestal and wink away. More groups followed, while Jack was content to take his time. In the end, only he and his group remained.

Jack reached for his hidden pocket and retrieved the gray orb he'd taken from the labyrinth's Treasure Trial. He hadn't dared inspect it before, even when out of range, afraid of anyone in Longsword's team having an advanced perception skill. Now that the lord had warped away, he had his chance.

"What's that?" Nauja asked.

Repeat Exploding Orb, E-Grade
This orb can hold enough power to match the all-out attack of a peak E-Grade cultivator. When thrown with force, it explodes on impact, instantly releasing all the power it has accumulated. The orb itself is unharmed from the explosion. Its inner formation absorbs power from its surroundings, refilling its reserves over the next thirty System hours. It is then ready to explode again.

Huh. That's useful.

"An item I got in the labyrinth," he explained. "But keep it a secret, okay? I kind of stole this from Longsword."

Gan Salin raised both brows, while Nauja nodded. "Sure," she replied. "Good job."

"Thanks. What do you think about it?"

"That's a very strong item," Salin replied. "Explosive orbs aren't too uncommon in the galaxy, but they have limited utility because they're one-use items. I have never heard of one that can be used repeatedly. It's a very cost-effective item in the long run. I bet it can be sold for a stupidly large amount of credits."

"Really? Is it worth selling?"

"Depends. If you have someone at the F-Grade or early E-Grade that you want to protect, this item is a godsend. It can basically save their lives once a day. If not... Then, yeah, just sell it when we're out of here."

"Hmm. Do you want it, Brock?"

The brorilla shook his head. He then mimed that such a strong fail-safe would limit his future growth—let alone the un-bro-ness of relying on such an item.

Jack had expected that. For now, the orb would remain a strong weapon in his possession, and he would reconsider after leaving Trial Planet. He just had to be careful—if Longsword saw it, he would understand he had been tricked.

"Let's go," he said, re-pocketing the orb. "If we take too long, people will get suspicious."

Holding Brock from the shoulder—just to be sure—Jack laid his hand on the bronze, and space warped around them.

When he recovered, he quickly looked around. This was the eighth ring of Trial Planet: Garden Ring.

Where everything would be decided.

CHAPTER EIGHTY-EIGHT
GARDEN RING

GARDEN RING WAS A PEACEFUL PLACE. A WELCOME CHANGE AFTER THE FOREST, the dinosaurs, the village, space bubbles, and the labyrinth.

Grasslands stretched as far as the eye could see, interspersed with the occasional small tree or bush. Grass blades swayed in the wind, dancing to its silent tune, and the faraway fences resembled farms.

Of course, that was only from afar.

Garden Ring was a grassland dotted by gardens. The cave ceiling here was only five miles high, with the now-familiar sun mushrooms growing in regular intervals, and the ring itself was a sphere so small in radius that its curvature was clearly visible in the distance.

There was no danger to the grassland or the gardens. Garden Ring was the reward for everyone who'd made it this far. The grassland was meant to let the cultivators relax and cultivate in peace, while the gardens held rewards that one could claim either freely or by passing certain tests—but nothing dangerous.

Each garden held its own, unique rewards. They were surrounded by tall wooden fences and filled with light mist, not letting the cultivators peek in, but they had gates with the garden's name clearly visible. The closest one to where Jack appeared after teleporting was named Herb Garden. The next was Beast Garden. According to Gan Salin, there was also a Dao Garden, a Body Garden, a Mind Garden, a Soul Garden, a

Magic Garden, a Weapons Garden, a Tools Garden, a Spirit Garden, and a Knowledge Garden. The last and most precious of them was Trial Garden.

Twelve gardens in total, each tens of square miles in size. Together, they occupied half of Garden Ring.

Besides the gardens and the grassland, there were two unique locations. One was where Jack's group appeared, a stone circle on the ground with a pedestal in the middle. That pedestal served as both the entrance and the exit of Garden Ring, teleporting everyone outside when they touched it again.

The second unique location was a closed door that stood a hundred feet away from the stone circle. It was twice as tall as Jack, with a bare wooden surface. Behind it, lay nothing. It was just a door standing on the grassland by itself.

"What's that?" Jack asked.

"The ninth ring," Salin said. All of them had teleported together this time. "The Final Ring."

"And it's just... there? No labyrinth to cross? No trials to pass?"

Salin laughed. "The Final Ring is easy to access. However, it is impossible to conquer."

"Oh?" Jack raised a brow. Right then, System screens popped up.

Congratulations! Title "Sixth Ring Conqueror" upgraded to "Seventh Ring Conqueror!"
Efficacy of all stats: +30% → +35%

Garden Ring Quest:
• **Lay claim to the current Top Treasure: Dao Sprouting Pill.**

"Oh," Jack repeated. "No need to reach the next ring this time."

"There's no point. As I said, the Final Ring is right there."

"Right. And conquering it is impossible?"

Salin nodded. "The Final Ring is the smallest of all. Just one room. One battle. Achieve victory, and you will make history in the galaxy... Too bad it's impossible," he added, spotting Jack's interested look. "You'll see. Someone will face it soon enough."

Jack looked around. They weren't alone on the stone circle. Everyone had teleported. The three lords stood with their two followers. He also saw several other teams of cultivators talking amongst each other in hushed or excited tones. Only the Sage's team was missing—either something had happened to them in the labyrinth, or they just hadn't made it in time to face the labyrinth's guardian.

Everyone present was sneaking glances at the Final Door.

"What's going on?" Jack asked.

This time, it was Nauja who explained. "Delvers have a tradition for this ring. When they arrive, one of them will cross the Final Door and face the Final Guardian."

"Really? So they just sacrifice someone?"

"There is no danger to their lives. The Final Guardian doesn't kill anyone, as long as they're respectful."

"I see." Jack looked at the three lords, wondering which one of them would step forth.

"Not them," Salin intervened. "The Final Guardian may not kill the challenger, but getting publicly beaten up is still humiliating. The lords won't stain their reputation. Traditionally, it is always one of their followers who—"

"Trial Planet has been a hell of a ride!" a voice boomed out among the cultivators. Bocor's. He stepped out of the pack, walking directly to the Final Door. "My strength may be insufficient to conquer this planet, but I will never be satisfied unless I give it a shot. Let I, Bocor Aximar of the Animal Kingdom, face the Final Guardian and bring glory to my faction."

"Of course it's him," Nauja whispered, rolling her eyes. "Like he'd lose a chance to humiliate himself."

"Humiliation is temporary, but power is forever," Jack replied. "Even if he can't win, fighting that guardian could be a beneficial experience."

Salin shrugged. "Eh. There's a difference between a fight and a stomp."

"Is it really that strong?"

"I told you, it's impossible even for the lords. For Bocor... Well, you'll see."

As Bocor approached the door, everyone looked over. His horns reached slightly over the doors halfway mark, and even his wide shoulders seemed small compared to its width.

Bocor put his hands against the double door and pushed. It opened soundlessly. The terrain behind it wasn't the grasslands. Instead, a throne room was revealed, similar to the labyrinth guardian's but far grander. Chandeliers hung from the ceiling, lit candles were stuck to iron columns, and a warm red carpet stretched from the entrance to the end of the room, where a man sat on a golden throne.

As Bocor stepped into the room, the man slowly opened his eyes. He looked like an old human, what with his white beard and wrinkled skin. However, there was an edge to him. His beard was sharp and trimmed, his eyes piercing. He donned a set of iron armor, like a medieval knight's, complete with a red cape, a helmet that only left his face exposed, and a red cape that stretched behind him and over the top of the golden throne.

"Another challenger," he muttered as he stood. His eyes were fixed on Bocor, but more with criticism than interest. "Another unworthy child. Why must you remind me of our descendants' weakness?"

"Greetings, Elder," Bocor said, bowing low. "I am here to receive your teachings."

"All you will receive is a good beating."

Salin leaned to Jack's ear and whispered, "The Final Guardian is always like that, even when lords challenge him. Do you see now why they don't want to face him?"

Jack didn't reply. Even though he was looking at the Final Guardian through the door, it felt odd, like there was a very thin gauze between him and the room. Though the door remained open, Salin had made it clear that only one person could enter at a time—and, as Jack snuck a look around the door, there was only grassland.

Is it a wormhole? he wondered.

Additionally, he couldn't scan the Final Guardian—or Bocor, now that he was inside the throne room.

Brock must have felt equally baffled. As everyone had crowded around the door to watch, he raised a hand and gently prodded the opening. Something stopped him, an invisible wall. Intervening in this battle really was impossible.

Suddenly, the Final Guardian hefted a mace. His cape billowed in an unseen wind. The chandeliers rocked on the ceiling, and the candle flames flickered. An invisible force spread throughout the throne room, suffusing it so hard that a hint even leaked out of the Final Door, showering the world in its might.

Jack held his breath. That was the power of the D-Grade. The Final Guardian was an immortal.

And they were supposed to beat him in single combat?

In the span of a single moment, the guardian had gone from a strict old man to an unsurpassable existence. He towered at the far end of the room like a king. Across from him, Bocor's legs shook. It took all he had just to keep his shield up. The pressure he was facing was undoubtedly far greater than what Jack sensed.

"You challenge me, but you cannot even withstand my presence?" the guardian said, his voice dripping with disappointment. "Begone, child. Go play with your friends in Garden Ring. Go waste the treasures we left behind."

Holding up his shield was all Bocor could do. Jack watched with rapt attention, straining his eyes to catch every movement.

It didn't matter. The Final Guardian stepped before Bocor so fast that it resembled teleportation. Jack only saw afterimages.

The steel mace sailed into the shield. It looked effortless. The guardian was clearly holding back.

And yet, Bocor's feet left the ground, his shield dented inward until it met his ribs, and then he went flying back through the door, above the crowd, into the grassland beyond. He rolled for a while before stopping. His tower shield sported a massive dent. So did the front of his plate armor, like he was a tin can struck by a train.

He wasn't dead, but his pained bellows struck home how fierce the guardian's attack had been. That was the power of an immortal.

Jack looked back at the Final Door. It slammed shut, with only the guardian's dismissive expression as a parting gift.

The healers rushed at Bocor, fixing the damage before it killed him. Jack, meanwhile, turned to Gan Salin.

"What the hell was that?" he asked. "Do we really have to beat an immortal in single combat?"

"If you want the Ninth Ring Conqueror title, yes. But it's impossible. The Final Guardian is at the D-Grade. No mortal can defeat him."

"But then, why have this trial in the first place? There has to be a way."

Salin shook his head. "There's nothing. The factions have been cracking their heads over this for a million years. They've searched everything there is to search but come up with nothing. The only way to beat the guardian is to become strong enough to fight a D-Grade in the E-Grade."

"Is that even possible?"

"Of course not."

"Are you sure?"

Salin hesitated. "Look. Lords have strong titles, three fused Dao Roots, and perfect Dao Seeds. Despite all that, they can only survive for a few seconds against the Final Guardian. Even those legendary existences with four fused Dao Roots—only a handful of whom have appeared in the galaxy's history—were unable to beat the guardian. I really don't see how anyone could be stronger than them in the E-Grade. So yes, it's impossible."

"...That's just cheating."

"Hey, don't blame me. I just repeat what I've been told." Salin shrugged again, then smiled. "I know what you're thinking. If you want to face the guardian, you can go at it. He won't kill you. Just keep in mind that everyone gets a single opportunity to challenge him. If I were you, I'd save it for when you're about to leave Trial Planet, when you're at your strongest. Who knows? By then, you might be good enough to earn something off this experience."

Jack looked up. "I guess..."

Bocor was healed by now. He was currently punching the inside of his armor to straighten it, while his dented shield was strapped to his back again. Everyone else had turned their eyes away from the Final Door and were chatting in groups. Even the lords were huddled up, pointing in a certain direction.

Jack threw the Final Door a last glance before turning to Salin again. "What are they talking about?" he asked, motioning with his head at the lords.

"The Trial Garden," Salin replied. "Remember the Garden Ring Quest? It mentioned a Top Treasure. There is only one of those at any given moment, and it is hidden in Trial Garden. The lords and their followers will head there soon."

"Hmm. Wait. Can they all get the treasure at the same time?"

Salin winked. "That's the cool part. No, they can't. They will work together to get past the dangers of Trial Garden, then backstab each other near the end to get the treasure for themselves. It's pretty exciting."

"Really? They seem friendly to me."

The lords were currently discussing spiritedly with each other, like old friends hatching a plan.

"They are, for now," Salin said. "But they all know they'll be killing each other soon. This is just lords being lords."

"Hah. I guess."

Jack's thoughts refused to leave this be. The three lords would be fighting each other to gain the Top Treasure of Garden Ring and the title of Eighth Ring Conqueror.

Those sounded like nice things and he wanted them, too. After all, to defeat the Planetary Overseer of Earth in one year, he had to fight for every scrap of power he could possibly get.

Could he participate in their battle? Or would he die instantly?

"Salin, how exactly does this work?"

"This?"

"The hunt for the Top Treasure."

"Oh. The lords and their followers will go to Trial Garden. It's a big thing filled with traps and other dangers—the only dangerous place of Trial Garden. It also contains better treasures than the other gardens, even excluding the Top Treasure. But its Trials are difficult. They'll work together until the end, when they will fight each other in a big brawl. Other people can join them too, helping to get past the traps in the hopes of getting their scraps—the other treasures of Trial Garden."

"Hmm..." Jack still stared at the three lords, who seemed to have come to an agreement. "And everyone else?"

"Everyone else will be touring the other eleven gardens. There's no danger, and everyone has a good chance of getting some treasures. They aren't as precious as the ones in Trial Garden, but they're much safer— unless another cultivator kills you, of course, but you know how that goes. It happens to the best of us."

"Right. So, I can either play it safe and get slightly inferior treasures, or risk Trial Garden for a chance to get better ones."

"Pretty much."

"Why didn't you lead with that? It isn't even a choice."

Salin laughed. "I suspected as much. In any case, I'm not coming. My current strength is just too weak—if I came along, I would just have to ride on your shoulders again, and I don't want that. Plus, your sagely friend said my fortune was deeper than Space Ring, and it wasn't in Labyrinth Ring, so it has to be somewhere around here. I will search and find it!"

He was all smiles. Reaching this deep in Trial Planet was a dream come true for him, especially after the Animal Kingdom hadn't even given him an entrance token.

"I'll stay outside, too," Nauja added. "Barbarians are no free-loaders. I will stay here, where I can hunt for treasures with my own strength."

Jack nodded at them. "For the record, I don't see any of you as free-loaders." He didn't try to persuade them into coming, seeing their point. In their place, he might have done the same.

After all, the best growth came not from having the most precious resources, but by fighting for yourself with no one to rely on.

"Very well," he continued. "Then, I guess it's just me and Bro—"

Brock, however, shook his head. "No."

Jack looked on in shock. "No?"

"No."

The brorilla then embarked on a miming journey as he described his intentions to Jack.

"Are you saying you want to stay out here and gather resources?" he tried.

"Yes."

"That you understand you are the little bro, so you would rather help out here than burden me in Trial Garden?"

"Yes."

"You're not a burden, Brock."

Brock shook his head. He pointed to his bicep, then mimed it being small.

"You may not be strong enough yet, but you will be, soon," Jack said. "Don't underestimate yourself."

Brock frowned in disapproval. He mimed some more things.

"Oh," Jack said. "There's no need to worry because you know exactly what you're doing? That bravery is not the same as stupidity, which would be the case if you came to Trial Garden? That you want to chase your own fortune?"

Brock nodded.

Jack scratched his head. "I see. Okay then, bro. I understand. Sorry for doubting you."

"No problem," Brock replied with a monkey grin.

Jack smiled wide at Brock's rapid growth with language, he also wanted to say many more things. If he was in Trial Garden and Brock was alone outside, he wouldn't be able to protect him. What if another cultivator attacked him? What if something bad happened?

But he understood. If he always protected Brock, the brorilla would never grow. Sometimes, you had to let others walk by themselves, even at the risk of falling. That was the true path to growth.

"Very well," he said again, extending a handshake to Brock. "Then, I'll see you on the way out."

"Yes, bro."

Brock shook Jack's hand. They exchanged a glance. He waved goodbye to the other two, as well. Then, Jack turned and walked toward the group that was gathering around the lords.

CHAPTER EIGHTY-NINE
MAGIC AT WAR

EDGAR HOVERED HIGH ABOVE THE ETERNAL GLACIERS.

Below him was a flurry of activity. Buildings were etched in the ice, half-buried into the glacier and half-exposed to the freezing air. A snow-covered expanse spread as far as the eye could see, interrupted only by the sea in the distance. Emaciated polar bears sat in a massive steel cage, waiting to be fed or sparred against.

Between all that walked a large number of people. Some were dressed heavily, like Alaska's Inuit. Others wore laxer clothing, just a jacket or coat—these people had high enough stats that the Siberian cold didn't touch them. There were men and women, all humans, either training or meditating.

The headquarters of Ice Peak resembled a palace dug into the glacier —it was actually the F-Grade Dungeon, Iceberg Palace, that they'd conquered. Originally occupied by mermaids, merfolk, and ice spirits, this place was now filled with humans, from its wide courtyards to the several stories dug into the ice, to the impeccable sculptures that dotted its balconies. Fountains lined the front, with statues of mermaids holding vases from which dripped water.

It was a scenic place that struck Edgar's chord for beauty. Only the knowledge of its inhabitants' cruelty kept his mind in line. After all, the

mermaids and merfolk that once occupied this place had been exterminated. It was a hollow memory, a beauty on the shoulders of which rode
cruelty.

Nobody had noticed Edgar yet. Though there were anti-aircraft
weapons and radars on top of the glacier, he was not an aircraft. He was
flying by himself. At best, he would register as a large bird.

A particularly destructive large bird. He had just broken through to
the E-Grade. Everybody below him was F-Grade.

Edgar clenched his jaw. The people far below were humans, just like
him. Perhaps they had been coerced into working for the Ice Peak;
perhaps they had done nothing wrong yet; perhaps this place was all
they had ever known. Could he fault them for the war currently taking
place? Not necessarily. Not all of them. Did they deserve to be eviscerated?

Edgar didn't know. But he had to save his own. If left alone, these
people would kill his friends. He had to kill them first. Just this once.
Just to tilt the balance, so everyone else could handle it, because Edgar
sure couldn't. Even now, his stomach was turning, his vision was
fading, and a voice in his head screamed at him to stop.

All he wanted was to get away. The voice in his head grew louder
and more demanding. Leaving this place was all he could think about.
His heart was beating fast. He was panicking.

But he'd made a promise. Just once. He had to do this.

Edgar suppressed his rising fear and dove for the glacier. The wind
screamed around him. A shield of air blocked most of it, keeping Edgar
safe, though his control was faltering as his mind was occupied by
panic.

Blue sparks appeared on his fingers. They were beautiful; a spectacle
to watch, enough to fill one's heart. They carried the power of hopes
and dreams and wonder.

Edgar unleashed them in a beam that struck the ground, melting
the ice and upturning the snow. People screamed. Everyone looked up
to find a wizard hovering above them, attacking without warning.

Edgar's hands shone again. He took his newfound powers and channeled them into destruction.

The steel cage shone brilliantly and began to melt. As the bars disappeared, emaciated polar bears stepped out—each at around level 30, and starving. They growled and fell on those nearest, tearing them apart and covering the snow in blood.

Arrows of pure magic formed around Edgar and shot down. Each had unerring aim—with his intelligence, guiding all of them at once was a simple matter. People were skewered. Blood sprayed everywhere. Between the arrows and the bears, the people of Ice Peak had nowhere to escape. Unable to respond appropriately at such short notice, they were swiftly ground down to corpses. Even the strongest amongst them fell.

But Edgar knew that the bulk of the Ice Peak's forces were inside the palace. It stretched deep into the glacier, enough to house thousands.

There could be children there. There could be innocents. Civilians. Prisoners.

Edgar almost hesitated. The horror of what he had already done, and what he was about to do, weighed on him terribly, squeezed his soul so hard he wanted to puke.

The polar bears, consumed by hatred for their mistreatment, abandoned their victims and rushed into the palace. Edgar heard the screams of confusion mount into horror. The sound of flesh being torn by jaws and metal striking ice—or maybe he imagined those, as he was too far away.

He wanted to leave, but the rampaging polar bears drove home that he'd already committed to this destruction. It was happening. He had to see it through.

Just once.

His hands shone green. Vines rose from the ground, growing quickly until they dug into the glacier's most brittle parts. Chunks of ice began to fall. He used his magic to directly wrestle the ice apart. He showered the front of the palace with cyan orbs of arcane magic that exploded on impact.

The beautiful shrines and statues shattered. Columns were demolished. Courtyards were marred, balconies broken. Under Edgar's bombardment, the air was filled with a heavy cloud of snow and stone shards, and the palace groaned under the pressure. From inside, the screams kept mounting. The people of Ice Peak didn't know what was happening—killer polar bears rampaged through the halls while someone bombarded them from outside. They were in hell.

Edgar's vines hadn't stopped advancing. They grew around the glacier and into the palace, slowly but steadily strangling it. The ice began to shake. More chunks broke off. Edgar could also see the roof of the glacier from where he flew, and he saw parts of it collapsing inward, burying whatever lay under them.

It was utter destruction. Mayhem. Lives were lost by the second. And yet, Edgar pressed on. He buried his own mind and heart as he pressed the attack, hurting the Ice Peak as hard as he could. He sent animated ice statues within. He formed large mallets of arcane power to strike the glacier's roof, forcing it to collapse in places and detonating the anti-aircraft weaponry. He sent arrows of magic raining in through every door, every crack, and every window.

He closed his ears to the screams and kept attacking. Some of those screams were his. But he knew, deep inside, that he did not deserve to scream alongside the people he was slaughtering. Their pain was far greater than his—so why did his suffering feel so gargantuan?

Edgar's attack on the Ice Peak headquarters lasted for only one minute. By then, his mana reserves were dwindling, and his heart could no longer take it. But it was enough. The palace lay broken, half-demolished. Hundreds had been killed. The military force of Ice Peak had been deeply wounded.

When commanding voices spread through the palace, gradually restoring order, Edgar was so happy. He had to leave now. Even as an E-Grade, he couldn't battle the entirety of Ice Peak—especially now, with his mana mostly exhausted.

People shot out of the debris. Humans faster and stronger than the previous ones. Elites. The sound of gunfire filled the air. Bullets flew past Edgar, a rare few colliding with his arcane shield and bending it. Magic came at him, too—spikes of ice that he had to struggle to avoid.

But he could fly. He gradually rose higher until they couldn't reach him. A man with majestic wings of ice broke through the destruction, filled with righteous fury—Alexander Petrovic—but Edgar was already running away.

A scream came as Alexander rushed after him, his ice wings flapping furiously through the air, but he couldn't catch up. Even exhausted,

Edgar was an E-Grade now, and not even a weak one. His speed was incomparable to Alexander's, who still hadn't broken through.

The bird of ice stopped chasing after some point, and Edgar kept flying. He wasn't even sure he was going in the right direction. He couldn't be. His vision swam in tears, and his heart was cracked by wrenching pain, digging into it as his vines had dug into the glacier.

What have I done? was all he could think as hills flowed under his feet and ice gave way to sparse greenery. *I'm a monster.*

He had committed slaughter. It was in the service of war. In the service of his people. He would be celebrated back home.

But it was a slaughter.

His magic, a conduit of wonder, had been used for death and destruction. The flowers and vines that brought life had collapsed a glacier on the heads of its inhabitants. The brilliant arcane orbs had been used as bombs. The thousand forms of his magic had been reduced to arrows, which he shot in through every opening he could find, hoping to claim as many lives as possible, cause the maximum amount of pain.

Edgar screamed, and the sky echoed, but the remaining ice and growing fields underneath did not respond. Neither did the birds, which only ran away. Edgar was alone with his guilt and crushing pain. Nobody could help. Nobody could understand. The world was cold to him, as he had been cold when he slaughtered the Ice Peak.

"Never again!" he screamed at the top of his lungs, uncaring about the razor-sharp, icy wind that jammed into his throat. He had dropped his shield. He didn't care about the pain—he welcomed it. Deserved it. After what he had done, this cutting wind was the least he should endure.

If only war could be solved by one man's suffering.

"Never again!"

He cut through the clouds at full speed, the air booming around him. He had to resummon his shield at some point, or he would be too wounded to return.

He didn't stop to sightsee and he never looked back. He simply darted through the sky, a brilliant comet as he rushed to the west, where his starship waited. It would take him back to the Forest of the Strong. To Valville. To home.

There were hours of flying between them. Edgar only wished it could last longer. He needed the time.

After all, he was now a hero. The alliance's first E-Grade. The one who struck a crucial blow to Ice Peak. He would be celebrated, and he couldn't cry during that. Regardless of how he felt... he had to smile.

CHAPTER NINETY

THE EXPLODING SUN'S
OFFER

GARDEN RING WAS THE SMALLEST RING OF TRIAL PLANET, BUT IT REMAINED hundreds of square miles in size. As a result, the Trial Garden was some ways off the entrance.

The three lords, their followers, Jack, and the most ambitious of other cultivators broke into a jog. Of course, at their speed, a jog was about as fast as a pre-System human's sprint. Everyone else remained behind to seek their fortune in other gardens. Brock gave his big bro a thumbs-up from afar, which Jack returned. Salin waved. So did Nauja.

Jack didn't let himself get swallowed by sentimentality. There was plenty of time before they reached Trial Garden, so he adjusted his jogging to arrive beside Lady Priya and her team.

"Hey," he said.

"Hello, brother!" Chotu—the jovial fat man who could turn into a golden giant—smiled widely. Kareena, the silver-haired healer, nodded in his direction.

"Hello, brother Jack," Priya said. "Enjoying the jog?"

Jack laughed. "At this point, I've had enough working out for my entire life. Thank the System this is easy."

"True. I guess running without being hunted is a rare thing nowadays."

They shared a smile. "I wanted to talk to you about my master," Jack cut to the chase.

"Brother Shol."

"Right. Is he okay? Last time I saw him, his spiritual projection was torn apart by the Dao of a C-Grade. I hope that didn't hurt him."

"Oh, of course not. Don't worry. That kind of spiritual projection is minimally tied to its creator. At most, it gave him a light headache."

"I see. That's a relief."

"He did speak a lot about you," she added, narrowing her eyes. "Said you were a prodigy. A talented man put through the right circumstances. A future prospect of our faction."

"Master Shol really said that?"

As far as Jack could remember, Master Shol had been very light on compliments. He just kept pushing Jack as far as possible.

"He did. I'm guessing he wasn't as expressive around you, but that's just because he takes being a master very seriously. He's usually a pretty easygoing man."

"Are you sure we're talking about the same person?"

She laughed. "People change depending on the one across from them, Jack. Don't be surprised."

"I'll try."

A minute of silence followed. Finally, Priya said, "Have you considered his offer? About joining our faction."

Jack almost broke his stride. "You're direct, aren't you?"

"Of course! That's the way of the Exploding Sun."

"Mine, too," Jack said, saving time to think about it. Had he considered Master Shol's offer?

Actually, did he even have an offer?

Back in the Integration Tournament, Master Shol had spoken with his own master, an elder of the Exploding Sun. She—his master—promised to take in Jack and help protect Earth from the Animal Kingdom, but only if he won the Tournament.

Which he did... Then the Hand of God pressured the Exploding Sun to back off. Shol defied his master's orders to protect Jack, which ultimately ended with his spiritual projection getting destroyed by the Planetary Overseer.

"I didn't think I had an offer, actually," Jack finally replied. "Last I heard, it was canceled."

"Really? I don't know the details, but Shol was quite adamant about it when he spoke to me, and his spiritual projection was already destroyed by then. In fact, he insisted that I should try to recruit you at any cost if we met in Trial Planet."

"He said that!"

"Sure did."

"Still... Sorry to insist, but I have to ask. It was my understanding that your faction had received pressure from"—he lowered his voice to a whisper—"the Hand of God, to let me go."

Her dark hair flapped over her shoulders as she ran. "As I said, I don't know the details. I'm guessing the circumstances changed at some point. After all, you're in Garden Ring with the power of a peak E-Grade and still many levels ahead of you. Any faction would go to great lengths to recruit you now. Whatever the Hand of God offered us before, it is probably too little in comparison to your current potential."

"I see. So Master Shol meant that, if you find me here, I'll be good enough to recruit."

"Probably. I can always contact the faction to ask. I just have to go through one of the communication elders to do that, and, ah... That won't be fast."

"You can contact your faction from here?"

"Of course. Everyone can. Doesn't your faction have telepathy?" Seeing Jack's empty look, she continued, "Probably not. In any case, faction telepathy allows you to communicate with others from the same faction. It works on a limited number of individuals, of course, but I was given a spot as our representative in this Garden Assault."

"I see..."

He'd almost forgotten about that. In the faction shop, telepathy cost a hundred million credits. He had to buy it and talk with the professor. Find out what was happening on Earth. Give them a hand.

Was he or was he not the faction head, goddammit?

"So," Priya continued, "knowing you have a standing offer, what do you think?"

Jack, being the cautious person he was, considered it for an entire three seconds. "If my previous deal with Master Shol still applies, where the Exploding Sun protects my planet, then sure."

"Great," Priya said. And, just like that, Jack had promised to join a faction. "I'll have to ask to be sure of that, of course. I'm guessing the elders will want to see your performance in this ring before committing to protecting an entire planet. That would be... expensive." She grimaced. "If you want my advice, just keep excelling, and everything will be fine."

"That's what I plan to do."

Jack didn't know how to feel. Relieved? Hopeful? Overwhelmed? Or doubtful?

This was not the first time the Exploding Sun promised him protection. Last time, they took it back. Who was to say they would deliver this time? If the Animal Kingdom and Hand of God just offered them more things in return, maybe the Exploding Sun would turn a blind eye to Jack's plight—*again*.

At the end of the day, all he could depend on was himself. If the Exploding Sun helped him, it would be because he brought them enough benefits to make it worth their while.

For now, he would stick to his guns. Grow stronger as fast as possible, still aiming to defeat the Planetary Overseer before the end of Earth's grace period. That way of thinking had benefited him thus far, and it would help him in all possible ways going forward.

All the Exploding Sun's offer achieved was to make him less desperate. It was a welcome breath of fresh air.

And yet, Jack realized there was something missing. Yes, his first priority was saving Earth and his people, and the Exploding Sun's offer was a positive thing in regards to that. Then, why did he feel disappointed, deep inside his soul? Why did the thought of laying back, of saving the Earth without personally defeating the Planetary Overseer, leave him unfulfilled?

With shame, he realized he *enjoyed* what was happening so far. The mad rush for power. The despair. The danger. The exhilaration.

Am I addicted to chasing power? he wondered, gazing deep inside himself. And, if yes... is that bad?

He didn't know, but when was power a bad thing? His mind was set the right way. He wasn't greedy, arrogant, or exploitative of others. He didn't neglect his responsibilities. He just wanted to become stronger. Was that a greedy thing to seek?

His thoughts returned to their previous conclusion. He would keep the Exploding Sun's offer in mind while still trying to become as strong as possible. If things worked out, great. If not... he would return to Plan A and defeat the Planetary Overseer—or die trying.

"Oh, and by the way," Priya said, snapping him out of his thoughts. "I don't have the rank to invite you to the sect, obviously. That will have to wait until we exit Trial Planet. There is a deacon with us—she can invite you."

"Oh! Then, is Trial Planet surrounded by immortals?"

"Right now, yes."

"Not just any immortals!" Chuto added from the side. "The Hand of God is going crazy for something. Can you imagine they summoned an entire fleet of starships?"

"A fleet of starships?" Jack asked, trying to conceal his worry. He knew what the Hand of God was going crazy for. The Ancient ruins. The Life Drop. And, by extension, him.

"Oh, yes. And not just any old fleet, either. They have ships filled with immortals. They've ordered all their cultivators inside Trial Planet, except for Lady Minerva's team, to scour the rings for something. Otherwise, the Hand of God would outnumber all of us on this ring. I hear they're even using deep-scanning equipment to search anyone exiting the planet!"

"Chuto," Priya chided him, frowning, but he only snorted.

"What? Everybody knows that. And besides, brother Jack will belong to our faction soon. What's the harm in sharing a little gossip?"

"There's always harm in sharing gossip," she retorted, motioning with her head toward the Hand of God group. Everyone was in close vicinity, so Chuto's words were definitely overheard.

"Hey, you're the one who said we should make friends. What better way than harmless chatting?"

"You don't have to be a clown to make friends..."

Priya and Chuto must have been good friends, because they embarked into a small argument that lasted for a while. Jack, however, wasn't paying attention. His face was calm, but his mind was racing.

Deep-scanning equipment... They search anyone who exits Trial Planet...
His heart was beating fast. Can they find the Life Drop?

The voice had mentioned that nobody could sense the Life Drop without special equipment. Well, *someone* had special equipment. That sucked. Unless the Hand of God decided they'd found everything there was to find, or unless they abandoned the search, Jack was a sitting duck.

When exiting Trial Planet, everyone teleported to one of many set points on the surface, where Hand of God starships were usually waiting to transfer them to the teleporters leading farther inside the galaxy. In other words, there was no way for Jack to escape unseen.

Can I walk all the way to the surface? he wondered. He'd entered from a massive staircase on the surface, and there wasn't anyone waiting there. Not all entrances were exits. *What other choice do I have?*

If this deep-scanning could find his Life Drop, teleporting out would be a problem. If it couldn't, and he was caught sneaking through Trial Planet, they would suspect him, which would also be a problem.

What to do...

It was a worrying dilemma. Thankfully, it was also a future dilemma. For now, Jack's goal was simple: enter Trial Garden with the lords and secure as many advantages as possible.

"Jack," Priya spoke again. He pretended to have been focused all along. "Factions aside, every lord has a quota of two followers, and I have fulfilled it already. If you want to join Trial Garden, you will still have to do it as a treasure hunter."

"Right. Of course, I understand. And what exactly does that entail?"

"Following us around. You help where you can, and you also take some risks that we and our followers want to avoid. Basically, if something is dangerous, you do it."

Jack raised a brow. "Like a meat shield?"

"Exactly."

"That doesn't sound like treasure hunting."

"You get great treasures in return. We—the lords—are only interested in the Top Treasure, and our followers will be rewarded by our factions. Treasure hunters get every other treasure found inside—and there are a lot of them."

"We essentially risk ourselves for treasure."

"Sounds more like treasure hunting now, doesn't it?"

Jack fought to keep the smile from rising on his lips. "Got it. So, our relationship does not extend inside Trial Garden."

"Sadly, yes. If everyone played favorites amongst the treasure hunters, it would be chaos..."

"Fine by me. I don't plan to die."

It wasn't just fine. It was perfect. Jack had long set his sights on that Top Treasure. If Priya wasn't going to be his ally, he didn't need to feel bad about taking it from under her nose—if he managed.

Though the truth was, he remained under-leveled. He lacked the strength to battle the lords, and it was highly unlikely that he would level up twenty-five times inside Trial Garden.

Given those, emerging victorious and getting the Top Treasure was a tall task... Maybe even an impossible one. He also had to survive *after* taking the Top Treasure, because the lords wouldn't be happy. Still, he could take a look at things. If his chances looked too dim, he wouldn't just throw his life away. Suicide by lord wasn't how he wanted to go.

However, who knew how things worked in Trial Garden? Maybe the Top Treasure could be claimed through more than battle strength. Maybe there would be a sort of contest between them all. That made sense, because Jack could hardly see the factions sending out their top disciples to duke it out until only one remained alive.

That all goes to say, Jack would be ready. If an opportunity presented itself, he would make sure to be in the perfect situation to utilize it. If there was a chance, he would seize it.

Moreover, this wouldn't be a simple battle of strength, because he couldn't stand against the lords yet. He would have to use his brain—and all the research he'd poured into his almost-PhD might finally come in handy!

He couldn't be half-hearted about this. While they journeyed through Trial Garden, he would try to identify everyone's strengths and weaknesses, their patterns, along with anything that could be exploited.

One might say this approach didn't fit the Dao of the Fist. But they would be mistaken. The Dao of the Fist had nothing against trying one's best to prevail in a tough situation. Besides, going into battle unprepared was hardly commendable.

Jack couldn't just punch his way out of this one. For the first time since the Integration happened... He would need an actual plan.

The prospect made him giddy.

"Look, brother!" Chuto called out, pointing in the distance. "We have arrived. That's it: Trial Garden."

CHAPTER NINETY-ONE
TRIAL GARDEN

A MIST-FILLED GARDEN STRETCHED IN THE DISTANCE. IT WAS SURROUNDED BY A thick metal fence long enough that Jack couldn't see its end on either side, and so tall that it more resembled castle walls than fence. In its midst, right where they were headed, stood a hundred-foot-wide opening with the words 'Trial Garden' written on a plaque over its top.

"Wow," Jack said. "That's a big garden."

Unfortunately, there was nobody to reply. Brock, Nauja, and Gan Salin had left to explore other gardens. Lady Priya had made it clear they wouldn't be allies inside the garden, so he respected that and didn't walk beside her team. Longsword treated him coldly after the previous rejection, and Bocor was a downright enemy.

Besides those, Jack knew nobody. Well, he did know a few people from the labyrinth guardian antechamber, but the Wide Swirls woman who first approached him was missing. The rest of the group were present, but none was particularly responsive to Jack's chatting, so he lay the matter to rest.

He didn't *need* company, anyway. It was just pleasant to have.

The garden's entrance was even more impressive from up close. Light mist began almost exactly at the gate, spreading inward and denying visibility.

"Attention, everyone," Lady Minerva said, raising a hand. The other lords had let her posture as a leader—whether because of her personal strength, backing, or both, Jack didn't know. "We will now enter Trial Garden, one of Trial Planet's most mystical locations. You are all expected to follow our commands to the letter and without objection. In return, you take all treasures except the Dao Sprouting Pill. Anyone who disagrees should leave now. You can still find fortune in other gardens."

The crowd of cultivators glanced at each other, but no one moved. Besides the lords and their followers, there were nine people present, the galaxy's cream of the crop. Since they had come all the way here, they obviously wouldn't change their mind.

"Good," Minerva said, turning to the gate. "Then, we enter... and may the System help us."

Jack fought down a smirk. He expected something more... inspiring. A rousing speech, perhaps.

Regardless, they entered. One by one, they walked into the mist, letting it slither around them until it swallowed them altogether.

There was a chill to this mist. It felt dangerous, as if insisting they should exit and pick another garden. At the same time, this mist was rife with energy. Jack could feel it pressing against his skin. Elemental bursts, flourishing life, bone-chilling death, bundles of emotions that passed over him like cold currents.

All they managed was to rile him up.

Light flared from up ahead. Lady Minerva had lit a torch of spectral white flame with a body of rune-carved steel. Though this mist was undoubtedly magical, so was the torchlight, forcing it to recede by a few dozen feet in every direction. Their surroundings were still covered in rolling white, but there was now a bubble of visibility wide enough to fit all of them.

"Much better," Lady Minerva said. "Guide?"

A person stepped out of the crowd. He was a man with pale blue skin, fins, and gills—a merfolk.

Merfolk, Level 123
Faction: Deep Sea Shrine (B-Grade)
Title: Seventh Ring Conqueror

"Present, milady," the merfolk said in a dignified, yet oddly soothing voice. "Allow me to divine the way forward."

"Please do."

The merfolk walked at the front of the procession and started advancing slowly. Jack caught a glimpse of his closed eyes and constant murmuring.

Why do we need a guide? he wondered. Does this garden change every time, like the labyrinth?

He had no one to ask, so he just stayed silent and kept walking.

Trial Garden was a large place. Since they were now walking instead of jogging, it took them a while to reach the first point of interest. Nothing happened in the meantime. They were constantly surrounded by mist, so Jack had no idea what their surroundings looked like. For all he knew, they could be walking on a thin strip of land with ocean on either side, or in a perfectly empty garden.

Suddenly, the guide paused. A moment later, he opened his eyes and said, "There is a trap ahead, lords."

"Finally," Longsword replied. "Slow trot, everyone. Let's scout."

Their pace slowed to a crawl. Five minutes later, a shape emerged from the mist. It was a wall, blocking the path ahead and extending to either side farther than their light could reach. It also stretched higher than their light. In the middle of the wall was a ten-foot-wide, ten-foot-tall, and thirty-foot-long tunnel that led directly to the other side.

"A formation," Lady Minerva said. "Priya, I believe you have a formation master. This one is for you."

"Kareena." Priya beckoned, and the silver-haired healer stepped forth.

"Of course, my lady," she replied with a light bow.

Jack had no idea what a formation was, let alone a formation master, but a few discreet inquiries later, he found out.

Formations were basically trap-puzzles. Formation masters, in turn, was just a fancy name for the people good at these puzzles. Apparently, they had to study thick tomes full of solved formations, so they could memorize their patterns and have an idea of what to do when faced with unknown ones. The greatest formation masters could solve every formation ever created—or so insisted the draconic woman who fed Jack this information.

Kareena was nowhere near a true formation master, but she was good enough for Trial Planet.

At the behest of her lady, Kareena approached the opening and began scrutinizing it. Jack, curious to see what a formation looked like, did the same.

The tunnel wasn't as simple as it appeared. The walls were riddled with irregularly-spaced tiny holes—very suspicious for a tunnel. The floor was completely covered in a series of stone squares with three-foot-long sides, arranged in nine rows of three.

If this was a puzzle, Jack could easily tell what was going on: they had to cross by stepping on the right squares, or they would be riddled with... darts? Indiana Jones often faced dart traps. Why would this be any different?

There were also shapes drawn on the squares. They resembled animals, but no two were identical. On the twenty-seven squares, Jack spotted twenty-seven distinct animals ranging from ants to octopi to lions to things he didn't quite recognize.

"Why can't we just fly over?" he asked. Any one of them could easily clear a thirty-foot-long jump. The ceiling was high enough, too.

"Because we aren't suicidal," Kareena replied. "Formations are meant to be solved, not bypassed. At least, not easily. Teleporting to the other side would be fine, but trying to fly across would probably end with you dead before you even crossed the middle point."

"What if I'm fast enough to dodge the darts? Or durable enough that they can't pierce my skin?"

Kareena's frown deepened. "I'm trying to work. If you have more questions, please bother someone else."

That wasn't a very nice thing to say. Then again, Jack had probably insulted her expertise. *Whatever*, he concluded.

A few minutes passed. There wasn't much for Jack to do, so he settled on watching the squares. He tried to find patterns—and succeeded, too. The problem was, he found many.

For example, every line of squares had exactly one bipedal animal. However, every line also had exactly one quadruped animal. There were winged ones every two lines, and fish every three.

In fact, the more Jack watched, the more patterns he discovered, realizing that the point of the puzzle wasn't to find the pattern—it was to decide which patterns had priority. He admitted that he had no idea how to do that. Which was a good thing—becoming a formation master would mean reading thick tomes, which would take away from his punching time. He liked his punching time.

Kareena also struggled. Half an hour later, she finally said, "I think I got it." Jack couldn't tell whether she was confident or not, but he really didn't mind, either. It wasn't like he'd be the one to—

"Perfect. How about you volunteer, Jack Rust?" Longsword's voice came cheerful. "You seemed very interested in that formation. Maybe crossing it would give you some insights, the first step to becoming a genius formation master!"

Jack was not at all intrigued by the possibility. He didn't want to be a guinea pig. "I don't particularly feel like studying formations."

"Nonsense. I'm sure this will do you good," Longsword insisted.

Next to him, Bocor sported an ugly smile. Jack frowned and was about to respond when Priya spoke up.

"As treasure hunters, taking risks like this is your responsibility. This is what you signed up for. Now, go ahead and walk the tiles. Don't worry; Kareena is a very capable formation master."

Jack wanted to cry. Damn be the minutia of *rules*, Priya was supposed to be his ally in the end, and she was sending him into a trap as a guinea pig.

Then again, he'd known what he was getting into. Everybody else seemed to think this was normal, too.

"Fine," he agreed. His gaze lingered on the tiles. "How strong are these traps, anyway?"

"Most of them can threaten Kings," Longsword replied. "But don't worry. I'm sure you're going to be fine. It isn't like formations have one of the highest failure rates between traps."

Jack glared at him. Longsword gave him a dashing smile. "What are you waiting for? Go already."

Jack cursed inwardly. He felt a bit cheated, and not at all ready to brave a formation. However, he was already this far. He couldn't step back. He just had to trust Kareena.

"Start by stepping on the tiger," she instructed him. Everyone took several steps away. Jack cursed again. At least his Indomitable Body was very resilient. Even if things went wrong, he might survive.

He stepped on the tiger. He sensed the tile give slightly under his foot. Nothing happened.

"Then, the pelican," Kareena said. Jack took a breath and stepped over, tightening his body to defend against incoming darts. Again, nothing happened. "The prislow next," Kareena said.

"What's a prislow?" Jack asked back. There were two animals in the next row that he didn't recognize—a seagull with tentacles and a worm with three heads.

"...The bird with tentacles," Kareena replied, and Jack stepped on it. Nothing happened.

The rest of the twenty-seven lines went like this. Every time, Jack thought he was a goner, but Kareena had, indeed, found the right pattern. Even after he stepped on the twenty-seventh line and then out of the corridor, he remained safe and with zero darts hanging from his skin.

"Phew," he said, exhaling a massive sigh of relief. The rest of the cultivators started crossing, following the same tiles he had—all cultivators of this stage had excellent memory—but Jack's attention was quickly drawn to an item resting on his side of the corridor, just next to the opening, so it wasn't visible from the other side.

It resembled a snowball hanging from a vine. He scanned it.

Snow White Globe
A fruit of the Quasi-Elemental Vine, the Snow White Globe contains intense elements of frost. Consuming it can greatly benefit ice-oriented cultivators.

Short, sweet, and simple.

"You can take it," a voice said behind his ear. Jack turned to find Priya, who had been the first to cross. She was smiling. "It's your just reward for braving the formation. And don't think we were bullying you before. Formations are dangerous, but this is only the first trap we meet, so one of the easiest to solve. And Kareena really is a great formation master."

"Hmm. Alright," Jack replied. Now that he'd crossed the corridor safely, it did seem like a good thing he was chosen. After all, he'd gotten a treasure! He hung the fruit on his belt and waited for everyone to cross.

When all was said and done, the guide took to the front again, and the group continued into the mist, venturing ever deeper.

CHAPTER NINETY-TWO
THE SEAL HOUSE

THE TREK THROUGH THE MIST REMAINED SLOW. THIS TIME, JACK DIDN'T MIND. Better to be careful than take a wrong step when there were traps everywhere.

Everyone else had also fallen silent. The first trap had driven home just how dangerous this place was. Jack had survived, but the next person might not—and it could be any of them.

As for the lords, they were also preparing mentally. Everyone knew they would fight each other soon.

The merfolk guide stopped, then turned sharply to the right. Everyone followed wordlessly. Five minutes later, a barren hill appeared before them.

It was small, barely thirty feet in height, but steep, rising from the ground like a dropped boulder. On its front was a cave opening leading into the darkness.

"I believe we should pass through there," the guide said.

Longsword raised a brow. "Through there? I don't see an opening on the other side."

"It should appear after we enter."

To Jack, the guide didn't sound too confident. Everyone else must have felt the same, because Lady Minerva suggested sending in someone to check. The draconic woman was the unlucky one.

To her honor, she didn't talk back. One slow step after another, she approached the cave and basically crawled through the opening. A moment later, she was lost in darkness. There must have been magic at play there because, despite everyone's heightened senses, they couldn't see inside the cave.

"Are you still alive?" Longsword called out.

"Yes," a small voice came from inside. The draconic woman—her name was Maylin—didn't dare shout, in fear of awakening whatever may be in that cave.

Longsword snorted. He reached for his space bag, took out a yellow orb, and tossed it into the cave. The moment it touched the ground, it erupted with light, like a sun had been born. The draconic woman screamed in surprise.

Jack held his breath. The woman in the cave froze, her eyes darting around looking for danger.

There was none. It was just a cave.

"Couldn't you do that before she entered?" Jack asked.

"Someone had to volunteer first. Otherwise, who would get the loot?"

Jack was left speechless. That had to be the dumbest thing he'd ever heard—even though no retort came to mind.

The orb remained lit, showing a small cave that resembled an abandoned home. The walls were carved into almost straight lines. There was a door-shaped opening on the far wall, though Jack couldn't make out what lay beyond it. The walls curved as the cave stretched to the right, outside their line of sight.

"Do you see any other openings?" Longsword asked.

The woman inside recovered. She seemed a bit braver after nothing jumped at her, and she scanned the surroundings, even taking a couple steps away from the entrance.

"This is a house," she shouted. "There is an opening to the right, leading to the bathroom... I think. The door at the back leads to the bedroom. There is a bedframe rotting in there."

"Well, that explains the smell," Longsword replied, keeping his voice low. He then shouted, "So, no exits?"

"None! No treasure, either. Oh, wait—there is a lever!"

"Pull it."

"No!" the guide shouted. "Don't pull it yet!"

Everyone looked at him questioningly.

"Some mechanisms can only work once. We have records from previous Garden Assaults," he explained. "If she pulls the lever and another opening is revealed, this one might close. We'll be stranded here and have to find another way around—a far more dangerous one than this."

"There is a stone slab above the entrance," the draconic woman shouted from inside. "It can be used to block it, as the guide said."

The lords exchanged a glance of a thousand words. "We should face-check the trap," Lady Minerva said dryly. "That doesn't sound prudent."

"It's all we can do sometimes," the guide explained. He seemed nervous.

"And you're sure it's not a trap?"

"We can never be sure... but I believe that's our way forward."

The lords looked at each other again. "If we cannot trust our guide," said Priya, "who can we trust? I say we go."

"You would gamble your life away like that?" Minerva challenged her.

"Everyone else is doing the same. I don't mind taking a risk. And besides, the guide will be there with us. You can bet he's not lying."

"I agree with Lady Priya," Lord Longsword said. "Maylin already checked for traps. If that's the way forward, all we can do is follow through."

"Very well," Minerva responded after a moment's hesitation. "Let's go."

Nobody asked for the opinion of anyone else. The lords were the leaders here, and their word was law. Jack didn't disagree with them, either. They would all go in together. What were the chances of the entire Garden Assault getting exterminated?

Two by two, the entire group filtered into the cave, all eighteen of them. It was crampy. The smell of rot pervaded Jack's nostrils, coming from the far room, and a quick glance revealed the rotting bed frame the draconic woman had mentioned.

He could see that, besides the bedroom and bathroom, there was only the main area of the cave. It was the size of a living room with only a single, rotting meditation mat as furniture—which did not trigger the System's scan, so it was not a treasure. Very suspiciously, a thick slab of stone hung above the cave opening as if glued to the ceiling.

There was no way any E-Grade would miss that—could a trap be that obvious?

Besides those, the only point of interest was a lever on the side wall, where you couldn't see it from outside the cave. It was large and made of iron, seeming completely out of place with the rest of the cave, as if it had been added later.

"Right," Longsword said, eyeing the stone slab. "We must pull the lever."

"Yes, my lord," the guide replied. Lady Priya, who was closest to the lever, reached up and pulled it down.

The entire cave shook. The stone slab crashed to the ground with a massive bang. Then, everything calmed down as the shaking stopped.

No new opening appeared.

"...Did we fall for the most obvious trap ever?" Priya wondered aloud. All glares turned to the guide.

"I..." he said, his voice almost a whisper. He was frantically looking around. Still, no opening. "We may have made a mistake..."

"You imbecile!" Bocor growled. "You doomed us all! My lord, please allow me to slay this disgrace."

Many others seemed to share his sentiment.

"Calm down, Bocor," Longsword said. "We aren't dead yet. Maybe there's a way out."

"The lever isn't going back up," Priya said, pushing at it. "I'm using my full strength, but it isn't budging."

"Let's try to lift the boulder," Minerva suggested. "Priya, Longsword, come here. Every Physical cultivator, too. Give it a shot by yourselves before I summon giant beasts in an enclosed space."

A bunch of people approached the stone slab, including Jack. He tried to grab it from below, but it was deeply pressed into the floor, and its edge was so straight that there was no room for his fingers to wiggle in. He tried digging under it, but it was impossible—the floor here was made of magically enhanced rock, as was the slab.

When even Longsword's sword failed to scratch the floor, the slab, or the walls, everyone was stumped.

"Let's grab it from the side and try to tilt it upward," Jack suggested. "If we can raise it even a bit, we can pop our fingers under it for a better grip."

They tried what he said. Unfortunately, not only was the stone's hardness enhanced by magic, but so was its weight. Even with everyone using their full strength, it didn't budge. A few tests later, they realized that even pushing it to the side was impossible. The slab was completely immovable.

"I don't like this," Lady Minerva said, eyeing the cave. "Keep searching, everyone. There has to be a way. I refuse to believe this trap would make us die of thirst."

They set to it. These were eighteen very bright people. They checked everything there was to check. The lever, the walls, the floor, the ceiling. Even the inside of the bathroom and under the bed frame.

Nothing.

Jack thought that, if he died like this, he would go to the afterlife feeling extremely stupid.

Ten minutes later, Longsword was about to let Bocor go to town on the guide, who was shriveled up in a corner, probably feeling terrible.

Jack refused to give up. He had a planet to save. He couldn't fail because of a big stone. He returned to the slab and kept inspecting it, probing its every side for an opening. How would he deal with an immovable object?

When was the last time he'd faced such a thing?

The door leading to the Ancient ruins had been similar. It was far heavier and sturdier than its physical appearance indicated. Back then, he had to pour his Dao into it. He tried the same here, scouring the stone with his perception in search of Dao vacuums that even an E-Grade Dao could infiltrate.

His eyes widened. "Hey!" he shouted. "I got it!"

Everyone turned to him. "Speak!" Longsword commanded.

"Spread your spiritual perception to the rock. Focus on the center of the side facing away from the opening. Do you feel it?"

A moment later, the eyes of the lords lit up. "What's that?" Minerva asked.

"I believe it is a—" Jack almost revealed what it was before realizing this was dangerous. The lords were very experienced people. If they didn't know what a Dao vacuum was, maybe it was something very uncommon. It could draw a connection between him and the Ancient ruins. "A... hole," he said. "I don't know what it is, exactly, but I can push my Dao inside."

"Interesting," Minerva muttered, stepping up. "How did you discover this?"

"I just got desperate and scanned everything very carefully. Anyone would have found it, given time."

"But you did. Good job."

"Thank you."

Jack glanced at Vocrich. The vampire had obviously come along in Trial Garden, though Jack made sure to ignore him. This time, even the vampire had to nod at him.

Maybe he hadn't saved their lives, since they would've found it eventually, but he had saved them from growing fear. The exception was the guide, who sweated profusely as he bowed deeply in Jack's direction.

The lords took their time inspecting the rest of the stone slab, but there was no vacuum besides the one Jack discovered.

"I believe we just have to pour in our Dao," Lady Minerva said.

"Maybe a specific type of Dao is needed," Jack said quickly. "Better safe than sorry. Why not try with earth or stone-oriented Daos first?"

Lady Minerva nodded at him. "Very well. Let's do as Jack says."

Jack felt like he'd just been praised by the teacher. A feeling he immediately squashed. He was an equal to these people. If he just got a few more levels, and a little more insight, he would become a lord himself.

Plus, if he wanted to defeat the Planetary Overseer, he couldn't be subservient to E-Grades. Not to mention how the Dao of the Fist was unyielding.

They tried pouring earth-related Daos into the stone slab. It sucked them up like a sponge would absorb water. Before long, the cultivators with these Daos started sweating.

"It's a bottomless pit," one of them—the stone golem—said. "I get the sense that we aren't even filling it up."

"Maybe it's an issue of quality rather than quantity," Longsword said, and poured in a sliver of his Dao. "Oh! It absorbs my Dao of the

Sword as well, and I can sense it filling up a bit. It's not meant for a specific Dao, then. It looks like we just have to pour large quantities of high-quality Dao into the slab."

"What kind of cruel trap is this?" Priya wondered. "If you're not a lord, are you supposed to just wait here and die of thirst?"

"Not just a lord," Longsword retorted. He'd kept feeding his Dao into the stone, and by now, he was sweating, too. "I cannot fill it up by myself. Can my fellow lords help?"

"Trial Garden is not a game." Minerva sighed, placing a hand on the slab. "Some traps can threaten even immortals. We need to be careful."

Priya placed her hand on it, too. Three streams of energy flooded the cave. Even the little parts that weren't absorbed by the boulder were enough to rock the world and make Jack feel dizzy. He had to muster his own Dao to resist. Some others were not as lucky—he caught the draconic woman stumble.

A moment later, the lords retrieved their hands. "Done," Minerva said, a sheen of perspiration on her pale forehead.

At once, the cave shook again. The slab began to float. Inch by inch, it rose over the ground. Jack, Longsword, Bocor, and every other Physical cultivator reached under it and started pushing up, just in case.

Whether they helped or not was unclear, but the slab rose. Everyone rushed out into the light. The last person to exit was Longsword's ice witch, who picked up the yellow orb Longsword had thrown in at the start—the only source of illumination they had in the cave.

When they exited, everyone looked back. The cave remained just as they had found it. The stone slab hung over the entrance, the lever had been lifted to its original position, and it seemed dark and empty.

And yet, it was one of the deadliest traps around.

"I saw the back of the slab as it rose," Lady Minerva said. "There was no vacuum on the outside. It can only be opened from the inside. If Maylin had pulled the lever before everyone entered, she would have been stuck there forever."

The draconic woman was sweating in terror. She thanked the guide for insisting everyone should go in—forgetting he'd been the one to lead her there in the first place.

"There was no reward," someone noticed.

Indeed. Though they'd resolved the trap, no treasure appeared. That was unusual. Most traps had a reward.

"Could there be another way to solve this?" Minerva wondered. "Well, if anyone wants to go in and give it another shot, be my guest."

No one did.

"Sorry about that, Maylin," Longsword said. "It happens."

"It's okay," replied the draconic woman, who was excited just to leave this place with her life.

"Let's keep going," Minerva said, laying a hand on the guide's shoulder. "And, Farfer... Be more careful from now on, okay?"

"I will try my absolute best, my lady," the guide replied, bowing deeply. His fish-eyes were wide open.

Leaving the cave behind, they marched into the mist. This time, they were even slower. The guide was double-checking every decision he made, but nobody complained.

Ten minutes later, they were still walking through the mist when a voice came from behind them. "Excuse me, hello."

CHAPTER NINETY-THREE

EARTHEN UNIRABBIT?

"HELLO, EXCUSE ME," A VOICE CAME FROM THE MIST BEHIND THE CULTIVATORS, making everyone jump. Magic was held at the ready. Weapons were drawn.

Out of the mist walked three people. A middle-aged man with rackety clothes and a wide smile, a young, Asian man with two black daggers on his belt, and a djinn woman with twin ponytails and a large mallet.

"Sage?" Jack said.

"Do you know these people?" Lady Minerva asked, not letting up her readiness. The sparrow from before hovered over her shoulder, ready to attack. "If not, they could be illusions or transformed monsters."

"I know them, yes. I met them in Space Ring. Everyone, these people are the Sage, Dorman, and Poppy."

"Pleased to make your acquaintance," the Sage said, smiling broadly. "The lords, followers, and treasure hunters, I presume."

Slowly, everyone let up. Lady Minerva unsummoned her sparrow, but not before Jack could scan it.

Diamond Winged Sparrow, Level 124 (Elite)
A little bird with the ability to move at supersonic speeds without

breaking the sound barrier. Its wings are tipped with diamonds, and its tenacity is superb, giving it great attacking power on top of its speed.

If all of Lady Minerva's beasts shared the sparrow's strength, each could defeat Jack by itself, or at least pose a great threat. And she had revealed five already.

It was a sobering thought.

"The pleasure is all ours," Lady Minerva replied. "How did you find us in the mist?"

"I dabble in divination myself, honored Lady Minerva. I saw the best path forward and followed it, hoping to run into you. If you don't mind, I could use my paltry skills to assist your current guide, as compensation for joining this assault late."

"Wait," Longsword said from the side. "This doesn't check out. How did you get past the animal tile tunnel? The cave trap?"

"Ah, the tunnel was simple. You left footprints on the correct tiles. As for the cave trap... I'm afraid we didn't run into anything like that."

Everyone looked at their feet. The ground of Garden Ring wasn't sterilized, it was a grassland. Of course they left footprints. Plus, Jack himself remained barefoot. Nobody had offered him shoes that could withstand his explosive strength.

Wait. If they didn't go to the cave trap... Jack resisted the urge to smirk. Paltry skills my ass. The Sage is better than our guide.

In all honesty, the Sage felt unfathomable. From the very first moment they met, the Sage seemed to have everything under his absolute control, even when D-Grades and C-Grades were involved. If he couldn't guide them perfectly through Trial Garden, Jack would be a bit disappointed.

Many eyes turned to the merfolk guide, sharing the same suspicion Jack had. In response, the merfolk's eyes tightened. "Of course. Any help would be great," he replied simply. "With you confirming my calculations, I will be able to guide everyone safely through the mist."

After all, he was here as the guide. He couldn't just let go of his position—especially after it had been shaken by the cave trap.

"Of course, of course. I would be happy to lend a hand as needed," the Sage said, showing no intention to fight for the position of head guide. That pacified the merfolk. A few quick introductions later, the Sage's group joined them, and everyone advanced together.

"Where are your friends?" Dorman asked, walking next to Jack.

"They went to other gardens. I'm the only one here."

"I see. That was probably the right call."

"Yeah."

Dorman was now level 117. Since the last time Jack saw him, he had advanced by ten whole levels—all of them in Labyrinth Ring.

Jack had no clue where Dorman's current strength lay. He remembered how they'd sparred to a tie during the Integration Tournament. Afterward, Jack had broken through first and defeated Rufus Emberheart, but each had gone their own ways since then. Now, Dorman was higher-leveled.

Can I still beat him? Jack wondered.

"It's a shame you weren't in time to fight the guardian," he said. "The Ring Conqueror titles are no joke."

"Oh, don't worry about it. We have our ways." Dorman seemed nonplussed.

Jack grinned. "You've taken to the Sage's mysteriousness, haven't you?"

"Hah. It comes with the territory. You know what I'm talking about."

"Yeah..." On the plus side, Jack had company now. And old friends were the best kind of company. "How has life been treating you, Dorman? We didn't really catch up in Space Ring."

"I've been pretty well, to be honest. The Barren High didn't spare any expense in training me. I met plenty of strong fighters—even my master was invited over to help me. You remember her, right? The cloud worm."

"Hmm, kind of. The worm that moved like lightning and spoke telepathically?"

"That's her. She taught me all sorts of stuff... and Trial Planet helped me a lot, too. I got a ton of levels."

"Same here."

"You seem a bit low, though..." Dorman gave Jack a side glance. "You're twenty levels behind. If you don't work hard, you won't be able to fight me."

"I can still take you."

"Oho. Wanna try?"

"You bet."

Of course, fighting now would be a terrible idea for many reasons, but Jack kept it in mind. They had to spar again at the first opportunity. It could even give him the final spark of inspiration he needed to fuse his Dao Root of Power.

And what sort of fist would back down from a challenge?

The mists of Trial Garden were light and swirling, hiding all sorts of dangers. The next trap they ran into required someone to dive into an empty rabbit barren and pull a bunch of colored levers in the right order —or get buried in that barren forever. This time, a treasure hunter who was also a formation master was sent in, and he thankfully succeeded on the first try.

The hours passed. Their path turned more jagged as the merfolk guide confidently led them, while the Sage was content to follow and nod in agreement.

At some point, the two guides slowed down. They looked from side to side, then at each other. The merfolk made to move to the left.

"Not that way," the Sage said. "Something is intervening with your divination. That is the wrong path."

The merfolk frowned, repeating his calculations. A moment later, he replied, "I don't think so."

"I am pretty certain."

"How do you know?"

"I can divine it."

The merfolk's frown deepened. If the Sage could divine what he couldn't, then there was a clear gap in ability between them—and the merfolk had fought hard to remain in the lead position.

"You are confused," he finally said. "Our next destination is to the left. Nothing could intervene with my divination without my knowledge—and, if something could, there is no way you would find it."

"As you prefer," the Sage replied calmly. "However, we should be careful. At the first sign of trouble, we stop and send a treasure hunter to investigate."

Jack was very glad to not be the next treasure hunter in line. The merfolk nodded.

"And, on the way there..." the Sage continued, his face unreadable, "let me take us through a roundabout route. I promise that nothing bad will happen."

The merfolk narrowed his eyes. "Why?"

"You'll see. Just let me. It will be the same thing—we'll just walk in circles for a little while. If you feel any danger, just stop me anytime. And, if my caution turns out to be unneeded, I will freely admit that I was wrong."

Cryptic and mysterious as ever. Still, Jack trusted the Sage. If he wanted to lead them through a roundabout route, he must have his reasons.

"Wouldn't that make us lost?" a treasure hunter chimed in. "What if we can't find the way back later?"

"I guarantee that nothing bad will happen. If it does, you can freely take my life, and I won't complain one bit," the Sage replied smilingly. "Besides, you always have another guide to find the way back, right?"

Everyone else looked at each other and shrugged. Not trusting your guide was a great way to die. They glanced at the merfolk.

"Very well," the merfolk finally replied. He clearly seemed insulted, but also confused. In any case, no matter how convoluted Sage made the path, he could always find his way back—and perhaps, deep in his heart, he wasn't as confident in his guidance as he showed.

They veered left. As the Sage had said, he led them through a turning, twisting path, constantly changing directions. Jack could sense they weren't covering a lot of distance, but he didn't know divination—surrounded by mist, he lost his sense of direction.

Half an hour passed. Jack was now completely lost. Suddenly, a voice spoke in his mind. "*Greetings, cultivators.*"

Everyone froze. "Did you..." someone began, only for someone else to finish, "Yes. We all heard it."

"What is that?" Jack asked.

"*I am Drevil Kastermonf, a familiar left here for the worthiest of formation masters. Advance and lay eyes on my form.*"

The group looked at the guides. The Sage glanced at the merfolk, who shrugged. "Treasure hunter," he said, "off you go."

The stone golem valiantly walked into the mist. A moment later, his voice reached their ears. "It's safe."

Everyone walked up to him. The mist thinned a lot here, revealing a ten-foot-wide circle. Runes and symbols made up its periphery, their meaning unknown and forms mystical. A curtain of shimmering wind stretched over the circle, forming a transparent dome.

A creature stood inside the otherwise empty circle. It resembled a rabbit, except with one horn on its head and vivid green fur. Jack tried to scan it, only to come up with nothing. Whatever this circle was, it blocked the System's inspection.

The moment Kareena laid eyes on the rabbit, she gasped.

"Do you know what that is?" Lady Priya asked her.

"I do," she replied. "That's an Earthen Unirabbit. One of the most sought-after spiritual companions for formation masters and Mental cultivators. They can grow up to the D-Grade. This must be a baby!"

"The silver-haired girl is correct," the rabbit's voice rang in everyone's minds. *It was cheerful and quick, coming in bursts of many words. It really did fit a rabbit. A formal-speaking rabbit.* "I have been trapped here for the worthy... but approach with caution. Hear the rules of my trap: the one who releases me will become my master, either to command or sell me. If you make a mistake, however, hellfire will rise from the magic circle to burn you. Brave my cage at your own risk."

Spiritual companions could bring their cultivator many benefits, from stat improvements to insights. But not every animal was fit to become a spiritual companion. Brock, for example, wasn't, which is why Jack had never seen a tangible increase in his stats.

He was, however, an excellent bro.

Actual spiritual companions were very rare and very valuable. Even Jack could tell the value of a D-Grade one was astronomical—especially when you could raise it from a baby.

A few cultivators, including Kareena, approached the circle and began inspecting it. After all, the rabbit had made the rules clear. Whoever released it would become its master. It was a race.

Not everyone approached. Many people knew they couldn't match Kareena or the others in formation solving speed, so they didn't even bother. The merfolk's face beamed with pride.

"See that, Sage?" he asked. "I discovered such a valuable prize. We would have missed it if we listened to your hesitation. You should not let fear cloud your judgment."

"Indeed, an Earthen Unirabbit is a very valuable creature," the Sage replied, nodding. "However, answer me this: are Earthen Unirabbits capable of telepathy?"

The merfolk adopted a confused look. "What are you talking about? Yes, they are. All immortals are."

"But look at its horn. The horns of Earthen Unirabbits grow with their Dao understanding. This one only has five spirals—it clearly hasn't reached the D-Grade yet. It shouldn't be able to communicate telepathically, let alone manipulate the threads of fate to lead you here."

The merfolk's face was paling by the minute. "What are you saying?"

"I'm saying that everyone should get away from that thing. Now."

As the Sage spoke, many things happened at once. The rabbit jumped toward the formation's edge, transforming into a humanoid with gray skin, bat wings, red horns, spikes on its spine, and long, sharp ears. Its clawed arm then enlarged as it swiped at the cultivators through the circle.

Echidna Devil, Level 124 (King)

A creature manifested from an extremity of the Dao of Law. It is compelled to always keep its word, but it also gains extreme power against anyone who breaks their word to it. Therefore, it enjoys luring cultivators into craftily-worded contracts and deals that end up with it having the upper hand.
This particular Echidna Devil has lost most of its power due to the clauses of a past contract.

None of these cultivators were stupid. Hearing the Sage's words, they'd already jumped back. One of them, however, hesitated for a moment too long. The devil's claws moved impossibly fast, grabbing him from the back of the neck and pulling him face-first at the circle.

The cultivator rammed into the shimmering air like it was a physical wall. He gasped in pain. The devil screamed—its hand steaming where it came into contact with the shimmering air.

"Stomp on the circle! Stomp on the circle and pour your Dao into it!" the devil roared desperately, its voice taking on a magical tone that brooked no disobedience. Jack felt a supernatural urge to follow its instructions—which he suppressed.

Apparently, the captured cultivator didn't. His leg rose to stomp down. In the same instant, the tip of a long sword pierced into his neck from behind, ending his life instantly. The leg lost power and plopped softly on the ground, not disturbing the circle's symbols, let alone pouring any Dao into it.

Longsword calmly retrieved his sword, having averted a disaster. The devil roared and withdrew its hand, letting the corpse tumble. It then cradled its steaming hand against its chest. It was badly burned.

The devil's face remained wicked, even as it warped in pain.

"Smart human," it shouted in a rough voice, like its throat was parched. "Too smart. Suspiciously smart. Release me quickly, or I may reveal your secret to everyone. I promise to run away without harming any of you."

CHAPTER NINETY-FOUR
TEMPTED BY A DEVIL

THE DEVIL'S WORDS WERE SCARY, YET INTRIGUING AT THE SAME TIME. WHILE everyone reeled from the revelation of the rabbit's true identity, the sharpest cultivators turned to the Sage. He only smiled.

"Reveal whatever you want, devil. I have nothing to hide."

The devil looked him in the eye. Its wrinkled gray face, with black eyes and sharp teeth, took on a calculating look. In the end, it didn't reveal any secret—either because it didn't know and was bluffing, or because it chose not to.

"What bad luck is this... For Earthen Unirabbits to still exist, and for me to run into someone who knows so much about them," it lamented. "I have been trapped here for a long time, mortals. A very long time. Release me, and I will assist you in getting the Top Treasure or anything else you want. We can make a contract on your terms entirely, as long as I get my freedom. I'm desperate."

"Devil contracts are terrible ideas," the Sage informed everyone. "It's best to let this one rot here for eternity... but, of course, this is your decision to make, my lords." He gave a slight bow to the lords.

For the first time, Jack sensed hostility in the Sage's words. Did he have something against devils?

Then he realized that he, too, felt hostility. It was a feeling that came from deep inside him, stemming from the Life Drop that fused with his soul. The devil felt... wrong. Appalling. Like it went directly against everything the Life Drop represented.

He suppressed that feeling. He was the one in control, not the Life Drop. The sense of wrongness remained, but it was weaker now.

What is a devil? he wondered, keeping in mind to ask the Sage later. And what manner of creature is compelled to always keep their word? How does that even work?

The lords looked at the devil, then each other. "It's not worth it," Lady Minerva said.

"Agreed."

"Agreed."

Thankfully, they were smart, experienced people. None of them would complicate things without reason.

The devil hissed.

"It really must be desperate," Dorman said. "Devils are supposed to be composed, but this one is steaming at the seams."

Jack laughed. "I would be desperate, too, if I was trapped in a circle for eternity. Anyway, it's as the lords said. Best to let this one go. I've heard enough stories on Earth to not trust a devil."

As he said that, he realized something. If this devil had been trapped here since the creation of Trial Planet, it must have lived for over a million years. Just how strong was it before losing its powers?

"How about this?" the devil tried again. "I promise to serve whoever releases me for a thousand years. No hidden clauses, no questions asked. Short of harming or imprisoning myself, I will do anything."

No cultivator responded.

"On top of helping you get the Top Treasure, I could become your familiar and help you defeat the Final Guardian," the devil tempted them again. "Even with my powers sealed, I'm far stronger than any mortal of this Grade."

That definitely tempted people. Even the lords narrowed their eyes, trying to see through the devil.

"Still a terrible idea," the Sage cautioned. "False creatures like this are not to be trusted. A thousand years later, it will have found a way to restore its powers, and it will kill or enslave you and your entire factions. Taking this risk is absolutely not worth it."

"But if you refuse me and someone else releases me, your lives could be forfeit much sooner," the devil insisted. "Think about it. Even if you aren't tempted by this Trial Planet's greatest rewards, you can't possibly take the risk to leave me here. Any one of you could backtrack later and release me, then use me to slaughter the rest of you and emerge as a king."

That made a bit of sense. Even Jack was tempted. His plan was to scrape up as many resources as he possibly could, then reach the C-Grade within a year. To achieve such an impossible goal, impossible measures would be needed.

Everyone had their hopes and dreams. Doubtlessly, the devil's words tempted many.

"How do we resolve this?" Longsword asked, turning to the other lords—and the Sage. "That thing is right. If we just leave it here, anyone can rescue it later. We cannot guarantee that nobody will be tempted."

"Hmm..." Minerva and Priya seemed deep in thought, but neither had an idea.

"It's easy, too," the devil continued. "Just wiping one of these runes or infusing the formation with your Dao will be enough to release me. Any one of you can do it with the snap of your fingers."

"This is troublesome, indeed." The Sage nodded sagely. "How about this? On the way out, I can lead us through a convoluted path, just as I did on the way in. We'll end up where we started, on the right path, and nobody will be able to retrace our steps and reach this place."

Jack was floored by the Sage's foresight. Even the lords were. He'd predicted all this and taken them here through a complex path that nobody could retrace. If he also led them out in another roundabout manner, reaching the spot from where they'd started, nobody would be able to rediscover the devil's location—besides the two guides. If someone felt tempted and ran back later, they couldn't find the devil. Even on the way back, they wouldn't pass the devil's location again, so nobody would have an opportunity to do anything. For all intents and purposes, the devil would be forever lost to everyone besides the Sage and the merfolk guide.

The lords looked at each other and nodded. "Sounds sensible."

"Fine."

"Excellent! Nice suggestion, Sage," Longsword said with enthusiasm. "I have to admit, you have surprised me pleasantly many times already. Is your Barren High open to a disciple exchange?"

The Sage laughed. "I will have to ask my master, Lord Longsword. In the meantime, I commend you for your wisdom. All three of you were able to resist the temptation. That is no small task."

"Of course! What kind of idiot would let themselves be swooned by a devil?"

Everyone knew that was an exaggeration. Many people would be tempted by power. Mortals, lords, even immortals... Desire could over-power wisdom, and temptation was the downfall of many. Jack didn't for a moment believe the lords were as steadfast as they showed. One or more of them were probably tempted—and, if not them, some of the other cultivators present. The only thing stopping them was the pres-ence of the other lords. There was no need to risk everything for uncer-tain benefits.

"Fine," the devil's voice sparked with bitterness and deep hatred. Despair, even. "Walk away, little mortals. Soon enough, one of you is going to release me. And then, they will have everything."

Nobody responded to the devil. The Sage led the way out, with the three lords holding the rear, and soon enough, the magic circle was lost in the mist again. Everyone breathed a sigh of relief—but the disaster that had almost occurred remained on their minds.

For Jack, the presence of the devil took a much longer time to disap-pear. The sense of wrongness and repulsion still lingered in his heart like a burning coal pointed toward the devil, a primal urge to slaughter and destroy it. No, it didn't come from his heart—it originated from a specific part of his soul. The Life Drop.

What does this mean? Jack wondered. Does the devil have a special connection to the Dao of Life? Or to this Life Drop specifically?

Unfortunately, he currently knew too little about these subjects. He couldn't ask anyone either, just in case he revealed something about the Life Drop so he simply filed the issue away for future reference.

The Sage led them through a complex, winding path, back to where they'd started, where the merfolk had first sensed the devil and advised everyone to head over. They stopped following a roundabout route and kept walking deeper in the garden. Eventually, they were so far away that even Jack's odd feeling dissipated. The devil was now unfindable. They were safe.

As long as they kept an eye on the Sage and the merfolk, who could definitely return at any time he liked.

"Hey, Sage," Jack asked when they were far away, "what exactly are devils?"

"Creatures of extremity, that's what they are," the Sage replied with distaste. "The natural state of the world is a balance between chaos and order. Each of us contains a mixture of both these elements, as does every Dao, animal, cultivator, plant, or space monster in the universe— that is the wider path of Life. Devils, however, are unnatural. When a Dao is pushed to the extreme and one of those components vanishes, there appear beings that should never exist. They are anathema to all life and should be exterminated on sight, if the circumstances permit."

"You sound passionate."

"As everyone should be. No good can come from the extremes— avoid them at all costs. Just think about that devil. It lacks the fundamental ability to go against its word. Does that sound natural to you?"

"Hmm," Jack replied, nodding. There wasn't much else to say on the subject, but he felt this information was important, so he stored it safely inside his mind.

Over the next couple of days, Jack learned they were treading a narrow path between grave traps. The constant turns the Sage made weren't random; they were dodging the areas of highest danger, resolving only the tamest of traps the Garden had to offer.

Still, they ran into plenty. Some traps were formations, like the first one had been. Others were trickier. One involved a walk through a maze of stacked cages. Each cage contained a sleeping animal, and the faintest sound was enough to stir them awake, sending them into a frenzy that awoke every other animal in the maze—including a few Kings that were uncaged.

Thankfully, the maze was small, and the two guides led them through before anyone was harmed.

The Sage was at the front, confidently leading them. After failing to recognize the devil and almost dooming everyone, the merfolk guide had retreated behind the Sage and didn't dare make a peep.

The deeper into Trial Garden they journeyed, the harsher the traps became. Not every treasure hunter emerged unscathed. One lost his arm to a propeller of blades. Another died when Kareena failed to solve a formation. Thankfully, she succeeded on the second try—and the treasure hunter that tested that one was scared beyond his mind.

Overall, though, they remained safe. They had journeyed fairly deep and would be arriving to the core of the Garden soon, where the Top Treasure awaited. On the way, they'd run into ten traps—enough that Jack's turn had come again. Thankfully, he emerged unscathed, and with a body-related treasure to boot.

It was a small vial containing the Muscle Throbbing Juice. The moment he rubbed it on his arms, he felt his muscles begin to throb as they gradually rose in power. He got thirty points in Strength from that. Not bad at all.

Level: 100

Strength: 450
Dexterity: 425
Constitution: 425
Mental: 50
Will: 80

The mist thickened, increasing in density until the sphere created by Lady Minerva's spectral torch was just barely wide enough to fit all the cultivators.

"Be careful, everyone," the Sage said. "We must be appro—"

Suddenly, the mist disappeared. Jack had to blink a few times to understand what he was seeing. They'd stepped out of the mist and into a large dome-shaped space. Mist surrounded it in all directions, but the other side was hundreds of feet away.

Everyone came to a slow stop. Lady Minerva deactivated her torch, which was no longer necessary. "Welcome, everyone," she said, "to the core of Trial Garden."

"Woah," Jack said, and for good reason. The most impressive thing about the dome of clean air inside the mist was... another dome, just inside it. Thirty feet ahead was a transparent dome of green energy, similar to the one around the devil. Inside that was yet another dome, this one blue and flickering. Five more domes spread between the culti-vators and the center of the place, which housed a single, crooked tree that was roughly Jack's height.

That tree seemed small and ancient, as if completely devoid of energy and at the end of its life. Yet, from its branches hung a single fruit —a blood-red apple shining with such intense life energy that Jack's blood boiled. He felt like a superhero. Like his chest and mind were both inflated, and everything about the world was clear.

The sensation passed after a moment, but the awe remained.

"Is that..." he began, but didn't need to finish the thought. That fruit, hidden behind seven separate formations, was the Dao Sprouting Pill. The Top Treasure of Garden Ring.

The one that, according to Longsword, could help one reach the D-Grade.

————

The professor walked into the forest, whistling all the while. She was in a great mood. Edgar had broken through and was going to attack Ice Peak. Things were finally looking up.

They had to celebrate.

She burst into a clearing. Once upon a time, a goblin tribe used to stand here. Now, there was only the High Speed Bush... and a robot.

Sparman lay on the grass, hands behind his head and enjoying the sun. The professor still didn't know *how* a robot could enjoy the sun, but it was certainly possible.

"Sparman!" she called out. The robot raised his head and sighed.

"Get away," he said.

"I need you for a moment. Can you help build a stage? Edgar broke through, and we need to celebrate."

Sparman scowled. "I was ordered to protect the forest, not become a carpenter."

"It's for protection. If we don't have a stage, our morale will drop, we will lose the war, and the forest will *die!*"

She could see the robot try to go against its directives. She watched its inner struggle as, slowly but surely, it rose from the ground and paced in her direction. "I hate you," he said.

"Thank you."

"But I hate my directives even more."

"That's good to know."

Sparman gave the clearing a final, longing look.

"Don't be like that," she said, slapping its shoulder. It was harder than a diamond. "You can be back here tomorrow."

"Whatever. I guess this beats staying deactivated for years between Integrations."

The two of them headed for the headquarters together. Sparman was complaining all the while, but the professor didn't mind.

She strongly suspected that Sparman was lying. His core directives didn't force him to help her with chores if she just called it "protection" and pulled her reasoning from the air.

He just didn't want to admit he enjoyed it. She'd seen how his face looked every time he helped build stuff, spar against the brorillas, or teach the children about the galaxy.

At times, even a steel block of a face could express warmth.

You big softie, she thought with a smile. *Of course you help with chores, because that's what family does.*

CHAPTER NINETY-FIVE
SPREADING BROHOOD

Brock walked into a garden laden with mist. It was thin enough that he could see through it.

Animals lumbered all around him. He spotted deer drinking from a pond, squirrels jumping from branch to branch and gliding to the ground, a large, gray, scaled beast resting on a hot stone. Each of those animals was at least as strong as him.

Brock could not read the letters above the entrance, but he'd heard others call this place, "Beast Garden." It felt perfect.

He was alone, too. Dog Bro and Girl Bro had gone in other directions, as had most of the other cultivators. Which, again, suited him perfectly. If there were other people around, they would be envious of the great treasures he would undoubtedly secure.

The problem was, where could he find those? The garden was expansive in all directions. Searching for treasure would be like searching for a pine tree in the forest.

Thankfully, the way of the bro had an answer for all cases.

Brock walked up to the deer and greeted them politely. He then asked for directions to treasure. The deer bros, after staring at him, angled their heads in a certain direction. One of them mimed something tall, then touched a stone with its horns.

Brock and the deer didn't share a language, but bros didn't need to speak to communicate!

"Thanks, bro," said Brock. He fist-bumped the deer before continuing.

As it turned out, the garden animals were very friendly. Anytime Brock asked for directions, they showed him the way forward. Some were even polite enough to make small talk—in mime language. Brock was a good bro, so he was polite and friendly back. Before long, the animals here had become his friends. A squirrel treated him to a nut, and a chimp hanging from a tall branch handed him a fruit with a smooth skin. The moment Brock took a bite, he found it was overflowing with juices—which made him dizzy in a pleasant way.

He also discovered there were plenty of treasures here. Not all animals pointed to the same one. Brock decided to take them one by one. When an animal gave him contrasting directions to the others, he would mime "high" and "stone." The animal would then exclaim in understanding and point him to... wherever he was headed.

A few hours later, Brock finally reached his destination. A tall stone obelisk emerged from the mist. It was surrounded by shorter stone slabs, erected to form a ring around it.

Brock entered the ring of stone, looking around him in wonder. These stone slabs were huge! Who had set them up?

Then again, Big Bro could probably do it. Soon, so would Brock.

"Welcome, young one," a feminine voice rumbled. Brock looked around. A figure walked out of the mist—a large beast, three times as tall as Brock and many times as long. It walked on all fours, had the body of a lion, the wings of a bird, and the face of a human woman. Her eyes were clear and deep, so piercing that Brock thought they were cutting right to his soul.

He didn't mind. His soul had nothing to hide or be ashamed of.

He could also see a set of fierce fangs lining her mouth—the kind of fangs that could easily tear a brorilla apart. Moreover, he could sense that this creature was far stronger than him. It was similar in strength to the strongest cultivator bros he'd met in this place.

"Hello," Brock replied. "Me, Brock."

The creature's sharp fangs warped to resemble a smile. "Welcome,

Brock, to the Misty Stone Ring. I am a sphinx by species and Eterazel by name. You can call me whichever you prefer."

"Okay."

"I am pleased to see you have manners," the sphinx said, relaxing slightly. She walked to a stone platform before the obelisk and lay on it, crossing her front legs before her massive body. "You would not believe how many disrespectful cultivators I have to eat every season. They are all "give me this" and "give me that," and all sorts of rude comments. Distasteful, don't you think?"

Brock considered it. Going to another person's home and being greedy or rude wasn't nice. Therefore, he nodded.

"Good. Now, Brock, I see you are no cultivator, but you are not a creature of this garden, either. Am I right to assume you have come here for my treasure?"

"Yes."

The sphinx's sharp fangs warped into a smile again. A bone was revealed on the stone before her, like it had always been there but Brock had failed to notice. It smelled very tasty.

"This is the Sphinx's Bone," the lion-eagle-woman bro said. "Sucking its marrow enhances your body, mind, and soul. It is most effective on those not already strengthened by the System—that is, beasts like you and me."

Brock nodded. That sounded very good.

"However, if you want this bone, you have to answer three questions of mine first. Do you want to try?"

Brock nodded.

"Be careful, though. If you fail, I might eat you."

Brock nodded again. If this bro wanted to eat him, she could do it anytime. Therefore, answering her questions came at no cost. Even though he wasn't very smart, he hoped his Very Big Thought of Brohood would lead him to the right answers.

"Very well." The sphinx further relaxed, lowering her body until her jaw touched the stone. "The first question: what life do you dream for yourself?"

Brock took his time to ponder. What did he dream about, really? Following his big bro to the ends of the world? Helping all his bros lead better lives? Spread the legendary Bro Code to the clearly clueless culti-vators? Rejoining his pack and working out with them?

It was all of those... partly.

Having realized his answer, Brock started expressing it. He couldn't say it with words. He resorted to miming—which, despite his profi-ciency and practice, was a particularly hard endeavor. It took him more than a minute just to get it out, let alone all of the sphinx's clarifying questions and follow-ups.

The sphinx, however, did not lack patience. The two of them embarked on a conversation that lasted around half an hour, with Brock trying to get his point across as clearly as possible and the sphinx striving to understand every word of it.

In the end, the answer that Brock settled on was something like, "I want to act as bro as possible. Be faithful to my path. Lead a life that is enjoyable and beneficial to the good people around me. Make all the brave choices, laugh a lot, and let the world guide me where I am needed most. That is the life I dream. What about you?"

The sphinx nodded. "Excellent. Then, second que—Wait. What did you say?"

Brock pointed at her again.

"Me?" the sphinx's eyes widened. She pulled her head back a bit. "Why are you asking me? I am the one asking the questions."

Brock shrugged, then mimed that it was the polite thing to do. Besides, she seemed like an interesting person, so he was interested in what she had to say.

The sphinx was clearly flustered, losing her words a bit. "I—Thank you. Um, what life do I dream about... This, I guess. What my mother, grandmother, and all my ancestors did before me. I stay here and ask questions to the cultivators, then either eat them or reward them based on—Ahem. Nevermind."

"Oh," Brock exclaimed. He then asked the sphinx if she ever dreamed of leaving this place and exploring the wide world.

"It never occurred to me," she replied. "I have a purpose in life. I just... stay here and wait, mostly. It's great, if a bit lonely. I don't interact with the other animals much."

Now, it was Brock's turn to widen his eyes. He asked if she had no friends—he called them bros, actually, but the sphinx understood "friends."

"Not really," she responded. Suddenly, she seemed a bit bashful. "The other animals are afraid of me because I eat them sometimes. My relatives are all in different places. I usually just stay here and try to come up with better questions—but no answers. I handle questions only. Garden policy."

Brock didn't know what those last words meant, but he found it sad that the sphinx just wasted away her years here, all alone and broless. He suggested that he could be her bro, if she wanted.

"My friend?" Her face reddened visibly. "I... I have no friends."

Which was why Brock suggested becoming one.

"Okay then... Yes, I guess. Yes, we can be friends. I... I don't see what's so bad about that. I would like to have a friend." She seemed confused a bit. "But I still may eat you later, okay? Rules are rules."

Brock nodded. Inwardly, he thought that she could benefit from eating fewer potential friends, but preferred not to say that out loud. Or mime it, in any case.

"Then, second question, littl—Friend Brock. What is your greatest fear?"

Brock didn't need to consider it, this time. He mimed that his worst nightmare was being weak, alone, and abandoned by all his bros.

The sphinx nodded. She was starting to get the hang of Brock's miming, which made communication easier.

"Finally, third question: What animal walks on four feet in the morning, two in the afternoon, and three in the evening?"

Brock was stumped. Unfortunately, this was not something his Bro Code could help with. He thought deeply about the riddle. He considered all animals he knew. Unfortunately, nothing even came close—he had never heard of an animal growing more or fewer legs as it grew.

Finally, he shook his head.

"You don't know?" the sphinx replied, inching closer. Her fangs filled Brock's vision. "Are you sure?"

"Yes."

"Aha! So you failed a question!"

Brock nodded. He then mimed the question of whether she was going to eat him.

"Well, no," she replied, pulling back. "I naturally cannot demand that everyone knows this random riddle. My questions are meant to test people's integrity. Sphinxes can smell dishonesty. If you tried to trick me at any point, I would eat you. Since you didn't... Well, you succeeded. Congratulations, Friend Brock! You passed my test. The Sphinx Bone is yours."

Brock pumped a fist into the air. He had never once doubted his success. The path of the bro never went wrong.

Out of curiosity, he asked what the answer to the last riddle was.

"The Egalitarian Tripede," the sphinx replied. "I don't expect you to know it. It's a pretty rare animal. Although, many cultivators try to claim that the answer is humans, for some reason. It makes no sense. Humans don't grow any extra legs, and if I wanted to mean the phases of the day metaphorically, I would just say so. I think it's just a rumor one of them spread after failing my riddle. I know who it was, too; I should have eaten her. Too bad she was respectful. Pretty girl, too. Her hair was nice."

Brock nodded. He also didn't see how humans had four legs, then two, then three. Cultivators could be coocoo sometimes.

He approached the sphinx. She expected him to pick up the bone. Instead, he walked past it to shake her paw.

"I—What?" she said, absent-mindedly letting her paw be shaken. "Are you not afraid that I will eat you?"

Brock was pretty sure she wouldn't eat him.

"But everyone else is."

Good thing Brock wasn't everyone else. He laughed and indicated that he'd enjoyed their conversation. He then asked if she wanted to leave this place and travel with him, since she was clearly unhappy here. But she would have to promise not to eat everyone.

The sphinx got even more flustered. "I—Thank you for your offer, Friend Brock, but I cannot do that. I am happy here. This is how sphinxes live. We guard places and ask riddles. We really don't enjoy traveling."

Brock considered it, then nodded. Everyone had their preferences. He still mimed that she should try to find friends nearby. Even if she didn't like leaving her Misty Stone Ring, she could invite them here to spend some quality time together. He also suggested that maybe not eating everyone would help her make friends.

"That is not a bad idea," she agreed thoughtfully. "I don't know why it never occurred to me before. Okay. I will try."

Brock nodded happily. Another successful bro intervention. It was incredible how many people needed a good bro to show them the way.

Thankfully, he was here.

He then grabbed the bone and inspected it. It was a bone. How was he supposed to suck its marrow? Should he just break it?

"You can twist its top," the sphinx suggested. Brock did as she said and found that, indeed, the top was easily twisted. It popped off like a cork, revealing a thin line of red marrow. He brought it up to his mouth and sucked.

Instantly, thick liquid filled his mouth, and intense life energy flooded his entire being. Everything from his toes to his soul were strengthened. Brock's muscles contracted and hardened, becoming like iron cords. His mind sharpened and the world came into focus. He even felt his soul grow by a bit.

In just a moment, he'd gotten much stronger than before. It reminded him of the pink pill he swallowed in the Trial—which, in turn, reminded him that he still had to think about the Big Thought of Density.

Hopefully, he would find some time later. For now, he had to get as many treasures as possible, both for himself and his other bros.

"There's something more," the sphinx said, hesitating. "Wait here!" She rushed into the mist. When she returned, a small pouch hung from her mouth, which she deposited at Brock's feet.

He made a questioning gesture. This pouch resembled a closed lotus flower, and it was filled with a sort of white powder.

"This is called Beast Growth Powder," the sphinx said. "A cultivator of the past tried to bribe me with it after failing my test. I ate him, of course, but I kept the powder. I never discovered how to use it, so it remained in my lair... until now."

Brock mimed whether she had tried to eat it, as she liked doing to anything else.

"Of course not," the sphinx replied. "It is powder. Who eats powder?"

Brock considered it for a moment, then nodded. It made sense. He then asked why she was giving it to him.

Suddenly, her face reddened a bit. "We're friends now, right? Friends are supposed to exchange gifts... right?"

What! Brock quickly mimed that he couldn't accept this. He had no gift to reciprocate!

"It's okay," the sphinx replied, smiling in her particularly carnivorous way. "You became my friend and gave me advice. Take this as a token of my gratitude."

Refusing any longer would be un-bro-like. Brock accepted the powder, sticking it in his pocket. Maybe Big Bro would know how to use it.

"Thanks, bro," he told her. She made an awkward happy expression —her mouth was used to poising threateningly, not smiling.

"I thank you, Friend Brock. You were a welcome break in my mundane life. I wish you all the best."

Brock nodded. He shook her paw again—a motion as awkward as the first time, but letting that stop him would be un-bro—then waved goodbye and turned to leave. He really wished she would find some friends—but, in the end, it was her choice. Good bros should help people achieve happiness by their own strength, not handhold them into it.

He hadn't taken two steps outside the stone circle when two beasts landed to his right and left. One was a frog the size of a person, with yellow skin and green eyes. The other was a desert lizard reminiscent of the ones he'd seen in Village Ring.

Brock paused. Each of these beasts was much stronger than him. What was going on?

"I got you," a voice came from up ahead, as a humanoid figure walked out of the mist.

CHAPTER NINETY-SIX

TO SAVE ONE'S BROS

Turning, Brock found a human approaching. He was a tall, lanky, young-looking one with an evil glint in his eyes, like a kid about to bully his shortest pack-mate. Brock rummaged through his memory. He'd seen this person before. It was the guy that had been present when Big Bro fought the minotaur in the desert, riding the desert lizard that was now on Brock's other side.

"Hello," Brock responded. "Can I help you?"

This was an expression he'd specifically tried to learn. He found it cool.

"Oh, you can speak," the young man said. "Even better, then. Hand over your treasures."

Brock showed his empty palms, indicating that he had nothing.

"Don't lie to me. Jack Rust has no pockets, and he treats you very well. You must be holding on to *something*. Hand it over."

Ah. This was a clever path of thought. It was also wrong, but incidentally, Brock did happen to have some treasure with him. It was the Beast Growth Powder that his newest friend had just gifted him.

Of course, Brock didn't feel like handing it over, but the alternative was pretty clearly death, which would make many people sad. An interesting dilemma.

Hmm... Brock thought, channeling his inner bro to find the best solution.

Thankfully, it was unnecessary. The young man began to float over the ground. The reason was the sharp talon that had hooked his hood. Eterazel the sphinx stood behind the man, ogling him with distaste. The young man, on the other hand, paled like he'd seen a ghost. His two beasts froze.

"I—The sphinx!" he said in a high-pitched voice. "You are not supposed to leave the circle!"

"Another foolish rumor. It's not that I can't, it's that I don't want to," the sphinx replied. "But you are threatening Friend Brock. Friends are supposed to help friends..." She turned to Brock with a hint of hesitation in her voice. "Right?"

Brock nodded. "Yes. Thanks."

"No problem, Friend Brock."

The young man paled even further. "What are you going to do me to me?" he asked in a squeaky voice.

"Eat you, of course. There is only one destination for people who annoy a sphinx: her stomach."

The young man screeched. Brock no longer felt particularly scared of him.

"No," Brock said.

The sphinx looked over. "No?"

"No."

Brock then reminded her that she should try to eat people less.

"Right..." the sphinx said, clearly dissatisfied. "Then, what should I do with him? All I know to do is eat people—or ask them questions. Should I start asking?"

Brock shook his head, pointing at himself.

"*You* want to ask the questions?" The sphinx raised a brow. "Very well. It's quite unorthodox, but I'll allow it."

"Thanks."

Brock turned to the young man, who still hung from the sphinx's talon. His summoned beasts remained frozen. Brock made a questioning gesture.

"I am Squirrelborn of the Wide Swirls faction," the man said. "A high E-Grade tamer. These are my beasts, Long Tongue and Desert Walker."

Brock nodded. There wasn't much he wanted to learn from this man —but a good bro never let opportunities pass. He fished the lotus-shaped powder pouch from his pocket, pointed at it, then made another questioning gesture.

"What that is?" the man said. He inspected the powder with his eyes, then exclaimed, "D-Grade Beast Growth Powder! Where did you get that?"

Brock shook his hand to indicate that was none of Squirrelborn's business, then mimed that he would like to know how to use this item.

Seeing a sliver of hope, Squirrelborn hid nothing. "We tamers use that on our tools. You can apply it on the business end of a fishing hook, a taming circlet, a bird catcher... Anything, really. It attracts beasts and lowers their defenses, letting you easily capture them. Its odor is addictive to most beasts, too, so they are more obedient afterward."

Brock nodded. He did not quite enjoy what he heard. This person talked like beasts were tools to seduce and manipulate. That was not the bro way.

He asked—in mime—if that was all. In that case, he would just bury the powder so it wasn't a threat to all animals.

"Well..." The tamer hesitated. A shake from the sphinx evaporated all his doubts. "You can also eat it!" he added hastily. "It can greatly enhance a beast's body, which is why it's called Beast Growth Powder... but that's a huge waste! Nobody uses it like that anymore! It's far more efficient as a taming aid. Even if you don't want to tame beasts, you can just sell it and get beast enhancing treasures that are significantly more effective than just eating the powder."

Brock exclaimed in glee. That sounded better. Eating the powder would be better than burying it. Plus, selling it was a no-no. Such a thing should just cease to exist.

He also didn't forget to shoot a raised-brow-smirk at the sphinx. Apparently, she'd eaten everything *except* this powder. She looked away, embarrassed.

The summoner must have noticed Brock's intentions because he suddenly panicked. "Wait!" he said. "That powder is extremely valuable. If you sell it to me, I promise that my faction will reward you greatly! I'll even give you anything on my person immediately! You can have my beasts if you want, too! This powder can help me reach the peak E-Grade, or even become an Elite! Please don't waste it!"

Brock's dislike of this person grew by the minute. Purposely slow, and always maintaining eye contact with the unpleasant tamer, he brought the lotus-shaped pouch to his mouth and poured in all of the powder.

"No!" the tamer screamed. "Please don't waste it! Sell it to me! I'll give you anything!"

Brock ignored him and started chewing. It had a sweet flavor. A bit too sweet for his taste, but fine overall.

The tamer made a wordless cry. His eyes almost popped out, and he was so frustrated that he even coughed up a mouthful of blood that marred his robes.

Brock ignored the squirming man. In fact, he even purposely slowed down his eating speed so the tamer could enjoy this sight for longer. Then, after Brock finished his meal, he burped to show that he enjoyed it.

The tamer's frustration was so great that he coughed up another mouthful of blood. "You... You wastrel! How dare you! That's... That's such a waste! A disgrace to all tamers! Do you know how many beasts I've given away trying to get such a thing?"

Again, Brock ignored him. The sphinx did nothing, content with letting him handle this.

A rush of strength flowed through Brock's body. For the second time in a few minutes, his muscles contracted and became stronger. He was pretty sure he could strangle a tree now.

But he wasn't done. Having finished the powder, he turned to the tamer's two beasts and raised a brow as if asking, "Really? You follow this guy?"

The frog and lizard hesitated. Their eyes went to their tamer in fear. Brock was having none of that. He reached up and slapped the young man to display his dominance, then turned to the two beasts and mimed that they should not follow such a person. They deserved to be free, not slaves.

The two beasts obviously wanted to be free, but something was stopping them. Brock felt his words—which contained the Very Big

Thought of Brohood—wrestle against something implanted in the beasts' minds.

He turned and slapped the tamer again—harder, this time.

The resistance disappeared. Brock let the spirit of brohood seep into the beasts through his words, helping them escape the tamer's control. Suddenly, their eyes lit up. They shook their heads and looked over themselves in confusion, then at Brock in gratitude.

Finally, they glared at their summoner with extreme hatred.

Brock nodded. One more case of brohood helping the world. Really, why couldn't everyone just be good?

He then pointed at himself. "Follow me," he meant. "You are clearly distraught. I will show you the true way."

The two beasts, realizing that Brock was weaker than them, weren't keen to do so. But only for a moment. Their gratitude and relief won over, and they inclined their heads at him, recognizing him as their big bro.

Brock nodded. This was good. He had more bros now.

In fact, looking at how happy these beasts were and how this man only saw them as tools, a new plan formed in his mind. He wouldn't just hunt for treasure. First, he would try to find as many tamers as possible and rescue their beasts. He had seen a couple more entering Beast Garden. He could also recruit some native beast bros to help—the young man who'd approached him was one of the weakest cultivators around, so it made sense that the beasts of the others would be even stronger than these ones. He might need some extra muscle.

After miming his plan to his new bros, he found them in perfect agreement. The sphinx, sadly, shook her head.

"I will not join," she said. "I appreciate your intentions, Friend Brock, but I am a sphinx. I have no desire to leave my circle."

Brock nodded. Joining him would be more bro-like, but if the sphinx wanted to stay here, he wouldn't insist.

"Um, excuse me," said the tamer, who had been ignored for the last few minutes as the animals communicated through miming. He had mostly recovered from his previous outrage, too—or, more probably, he was just hiding it. "Can I go now? You already took my beasts and wasted the most valuable treasure I could ever get. There's nothing left for me. Can I please have your mercy, oh great monkey lord?"

Brock considered it. He mimed whether the cultivator had any more beasts.

"What?" the young man said. After the sphinx relayed the question, he replied, "No. These two were already the most my soul could handle."

"He is speaking the truth," the sphinx confirmed.

Brock nodded. He considered letting the man go. He then concluded that being a bro did not mean being stupid. Mercy was good, but too much of it could be harmful.

Therefore, he suggested to the sphinx that, while eating others was generally not a good practice, this man was not a potential friend. After all, she had to eat *something*.

"Really?" Her voice was full of elation. "Thank you, Friend Brock!"

The tamer somehow understood Brock's miming this time. He unleashed a panicked scream that contained hints of a soul attack, but everyone present could easily weather it. Beast tamers were highly specialized. Without their beasts, they were almost harmless.

In any case, this particular tamer's attack was interrupted by the sphinx's sharp jaws snapping shut around his throat. She chewed his head and swallowed it.

"Much better," she said, blood still dripping from her jaws—and erupting as a fountain from the headless corpse she held. "I told you; cultivators can be so disrespectful sometimes. Anyway, thank you for your advice, Friend Brock. I will return now, to recover from all these friendly interactions and lick the blood from my fur. Best of luck with your quest! Just remember that not all tamers are tyrants—some are friends with their beasts. Those ones are not bad."

Brock smiled, shook her paw, and walked away. As the sphinx returned to her stone circle, dragging her meal along for later, he went in the opposite direction. The frog and lizard followed him.

He didn't know where the other tamers had gone, but *someone* must have seen them. He'd just ask around and recruit native bros, too. Then, after rescuing all the unlucky beast bros and punishing the slave drivers, he would try to collect as many treasures as possible, both for himself and his bros.

He had two missions now, and he would see them both through!

CHAPTER NINETY-SEVEN
REALIZING TRUE POWER

TRIAL PLANET HAD NINE RINGS. GARDEN RING HAD TWELVE GARDENS. AND Trial Garden, the most dangerous but rewarding of those, had a core guarded by seven different formations, one behind the other.

In the System's world, numbers were everywhere—though, if these particular numbers had any mystical meaning attached to them, it flew right over Jack's head.

The entire group paused as they came into sight of the garden's core. A lone tree stood in the middle, with a single, blood-red apple hanging from its branches. Seven concentric domes of color surrounded it, each a formation barrier that shimmered with power. Even the mist had receded from this area—a tribute to the formations' power.

"We have arrived," Lady Minerva said breathlessly. Her eyes were glued to the tree, barely visible through the formations, and the apple on its branches. As were the eyes of the other two lords.

They had come a long way to reach here, having traveled through seven rings of Trial Planet, defeated an immortal labyrinth guardian, and overcome a series of deadly traps.

Except only one of them could claim the prize. Only one could have the Eighth Ring Conqueror title, and most importantly, the Dao Sprouting Pill. Jack didn't know what exactly that was, but he could see the limitless desire in the lords' eyes.

He leaned toward Dorman. "Hey," he asked in a low voice, "what exactly does that apple do?"

"The Dao Sprouting Pill?" the young man replied in a whisper. "Supposedly, it helps a peak E-Grade consolidate their Dao and grow their Dao Tree, reaching the D-Grade."

Jack nodded. "I see. So it speeds up the process?"

"Not just that. The more Dao Roots one has, the stronger they are, but the harder it becomes to breakthrough. Since the lords have fused three Dao Roots each, breaking through isn't guaranteed. Even if they succeed, it could take them years or decades, which cuts away at their D-Grade cultivating time. Essentially, they're in an all-out gamble. Either they'll reach the top of the world, or they'll end up mediocre... and this pill is a shortcut over the greatest hurdle."

"I see. Meaning they'll stop at nothing to get it."

"The title of this ring is good, of course, but the pill itself is the real reward."

"How does the System know who got the pill, though? Is it the first person to touch it?"

Getting Garden Ring's Top Treasure was the prerequisite to getting the Eighth Ring Conqueror title. However, when traveling through the labyrinth, Lord Longsword had told Jack that only one person would get it.

"Exactly. Whoever touches it first will get both the pill and the title—and, by agreement between the factions, the battle ends there. Which means the moment the final formation falls, or even before that, the lords will be battling each other. That's why they're so tense."

Jack looked around. Each lord team was gathered aside, talking over their plans. The final bits of joviality had evaporated. Now, everyone was at war. Faces were stern, eyes were hard, fingers twitching.

Jack's mind was also racing. To defeat the Planetary Overseer, he had to take the absolute best road to power. Yet, from what he understood, becoming an immortal was a long, difficult process.

He needed a shortcut. And here, right in front of his face, was a legendary treasure offering just that. The problem was the existence of three super strong cultivators between him and the treasure.

He wanted to join the battle for the Top Treasure. He wanted to face-off against the lords and defeat them, gaining the power he needed to save his people.

But he couldn't.

Jack had done his homework. He'd carefully observed the lords and their followers in Trial Garden—and even before that. He had seen how they spoke and acted, dissected their personalities for weaknesses he could exploit.

There were some. Bocor, for example, hated Jack's guts. He would be easy to bait into action. The ice witch always remained by Longsword's side, if possible. Longsword himself was prideful and arrogant—and also kind of a dick. He knew Jack would never join his faction, so he wouldn't mind killing him if the opportunity arose.

Lady Priya was a direct individual. She would not employ underhanded means. Chuto was eager to battle, so he could be lured into what he thought was single combat. Kareena used soul attacks, which Jack hoped to resist with his Indomitable Will.

The Hand of God team was the most difficult to deal with. Lady Minerva was a calculating and cautious individual. Moreover, she didn't really care about her summoned beasts, so they couldn't be used against her. Vocrich knew Jack, and they were already enemies, sort of... but he was too cold-blooded. Jack didn't feel confident in tricking him in any way. As for the dryad, she usually remained by Minerva's side and wasn't particularly strong, but her healing powers were phenomenal. When a treasure hunter got a deep slash on his thigh facing a trap, she cured it almost instantly.

The point was, Jack knew the lords and their followers. He'd watched and cataloged them. He had cards to play. What infuriated him was that his cards didn't seem enough. Despite having done his homework and actually invested effort in securing as many advantages for himself as possible... he still came up short.

Will I really have to give up the Top Treasure? he thought, gritting his teeth.

He didn't lack understanding, Dao Skills, or titles. The only thing he lacked was levels. He was at 100. The lords were all around 124. With each level representing five stat points, those were a hundred and twenty points of difference. He couldn't overcome that against the most talented people of the galaxy.

He gritted his teeth harder. Throughout Trial Planet, he'd struggled to grind levels. He had risen by forty-five since entering—a tremendous amount! But he had been chased out of Giant Ring. Been ambushed and forced to escape Barbarian Ring after only hunting a tyrannosaurus. The desert of Village Ring had been relatively empty, and the space monsters of Space Ring had been too few and far between—or too strong to hunt consistently. Even in Labyrinth Ring, bone monsters had been rare occurrences, not letting Jack rise by much. As if those weren't enough, he was always on the clock, for one reason or another.

Finally, Garden Ring was... almost empty.

Trial Planet was a treasure trove of experience and levels, and Jack had already gotten a ton of them, but there was a limit to how much he could grind when everyone was after him.

When all was said and done, he was just too damn under-leveled.

He had good titles, yes, but so did the lords. They were the prized children of B-Grade factions with a million years of experience in the System. They definitely had a way to feed their disciples the right titles. Against them, Jack was not at all optimistic of his chances.

Perhaps he could exchange a blow or two, but winning would be very difficult without using the Life Drop—which he absolutely couldn't reveal, especially with the Hand of God snooping around. Given the Exploding Sun's standing offer, the risk just wasn't worth it—even if it meant giving up on the Top Treasure.

Can I sneak through? he wondered. *If the lords are busy fighting each other, maybe I can just rush to the fruit... But that requires them being idiots, which is not the case—well, except for Bocor, maybe.*

"Don't even think about it," Dorman said with a smirk. Jack looked up.

"Think about what?"

"Greed is the downfall of cultivators, Jack. You are strong, but you're missing a few levels. Stay out of this."

Jack frowned. "You handle yourself, and I will handle myself."

"As you wish. I just warned you in good faith. If you die, that's on you."

"Yeah... I'm just anxious. I appreciate the warning."

Dorman nodded.

Jack really did appreciate the warning, but he didn't plan to heed it.

Dorman had just explained how the battle for the Top Treasure worked. The moment someone got it, everybody stopped fighting. Therefore, if Jack made it to the treasure, he would be fine.

He would keep an eye out during the battle. If he saw an opportunity, he would go for it. If not... Well, then, there was nothing he could do. He didn't possess the strength to fight for the pill fair and square—and he had no followers, either. The lords had two each.

"We are ready to start, everyone," Lady Minerva's voice cut through the whispers. Everyone turned to look at her. "Formation masters, please gather around me. You are to begin working on the formations immediately. Everyone else, please wait patiently, and do not leave this core area of the garden. Anyone spotted leaving, especially in that devil's direction, will be executed."

A wave of murmurs and nods followed. Jack nodded in agreement. Devils were best left untouched.

Three people approached Lady Minerva. One was Kareena, the silver-haired healer from Lady Priya's team, who was also a formation master. The other two were the draconic woman and the merfolk guide, who apparently also dabbled in formations.

The three of them settled down outside the edge of the outermost formation and began observing it. Occasionally, one of the three would make some observation aloud, to which the other two would nod or object. They soon sunk into their spirited research.

Jack admired them. All he could see of the outermost formation was a shimmering barrier of swirling green, emerging from a circle of mystical symbols on the ground.

What would happen if I wiped at those symbols with my foot? he wondered. Of course, he didn't suggest that. He knew better than to doubt the formation masters by now.

After the first ten minutes of observing, he grew bored. He looked around. Everyone was still huddled in their teams or alone, cultivating as they waited for time to pass.

Well, when in Rome...

As even the Black Hole Church people were cultivating, Jack sat down and did the same.

The world gradually disappeared around him. He was now on a grassy field, with a white sun dominating the sky and three stars slowly orbiting it. The sun was his Dao Seed of the Fist, while each of the stars represented a Dao Root—Indomitable Will and Life were fused already, tiny tendrils connecting to the sky around them. Only the Dao Root of Power remained unfused, a hovering dark blue orb.

Jack focused on exactly that orb. Since breaking through to the D-Grade wasn't currently possible, and neither did he want to develop any more Dao Roots, fusing his existing one was all he could do. Well, either that or sparring against Copy Jack.

As he thought of that, Copy Jack materialized before him. It was an exact replica of himself, down to the hidden pocket under his left thigh, with one glaring difference—Copy Jack always sported a wide, excited smile like a child discovering the world.

"Hey, Copy Jack," Jack said. "Wanna fight?"

The copy grinned even wider and nodded. Jack laughed. He had to admit that even this battle lust was an exact copy of his. He, too, was looking forward to sparring.

The Dao flared around him. A purple aura covered his body, focused around his fists. The powers of Life and Indomitable Will surrounded him, shielding him from harm. Since they were fused into his Dao Seed, they, too, were purple.

The only chromatic dissonance was the dark blue color shining on his knuckles—it was Meteor Punch, which he was using through the Dao Root of Power. He wanted to use this skill as the medium to fuse the Dao Root, making Meteor Punch stronger in the process. These two fit like peas in a pod.

And he was so damn close. Had been for a while. All he was missing was a final spark of insight. He could feel it brewing just outside his awareness, eluding him.

Normally, practicing against Copy Jack wouldn't bring about that flash of inspiration. It was the kind of thing that only appeared in actual battle.

However, the real deciding factor wasn't battle, but pressure. And Jack felt pressure right now. He wanted to go after the Dao Sprouting Pill, but he didn't have the power. Perhaps fusing this Dao Root would mean the difference between life and death. He needed to succeed before the formation masters were done.

He hoped this time pressure, along with the persistent feeling of powerlessness, would be enough to push him over the edge.

"Come," he said. Copy Jack, his Dao aura and colors identical to Jack's, charged.

They knew each other now. Had fought hundreds, maybe thousands of times. Soon, they fell into a familiar dance. Punches led to blocks, to dodges, to dashing, and back to punching. Jack jabbed thrice. The third was a feint, leading to an uppercut. Copy Jack saw through it and dodged, leaning aside to throw a cross into Jack's face. Jack let the force of his uppercut carry him forward, parrying the cross with his shoulder and back fisting Copy Jack in the face—back fisting counted as a fist attack.

Copy Jack flew but righted himself. He ducked under Jack's blow and planted a fist in his abdomen. Then, Copy Jack stepped forward and prepared a wild haymaker. Jack expected it to be a feint—so it smashed into his nose like a meteor from orbit, flaring blue with the Dao Root of Power, and threw Jack back so violently that the soul world warped to help them remain close-by.

Jack stumbled. His twin fused Dao Roots worked together to repair his nose and face structure. "Nice one," he said with a growl. He jumped back into the fray. They kept exchanging blows, with no one really getting the upper hand.

Jack came to the realization that this wasn't working. He wouldn't fuse his Dao Root like this. All he was doing was practicing his battle awareness.

He had no time to waste. He had to lean into that feeling of powerlessness, somehow. The final understanding was locked inside it. But how?

With a spark of inspiration, he strangled the Dao flow to himself. It was now a trickle rather than a stream. Instantly, his power was reduced.

Copy Jack raised a brow but complied. He came in with fists blazing. Jack tried to fight back, but he was too slow, too weak. Copy Jack was dominating now. His punches struck like mallets, his arms blurred at the limits of Jack's perception, and his defense was unbreakably rock-solid.

It took everything Jack had to remain standing. Powerlessness creeped into him again. He didn't like this feeling. He hated it. It reminded him of the times before the System. He had no control. He was suffocating.

Yet, he did not yield. He kept restraining the flow of his Dao. His defense was broken, his attacks were useless, his eyes couldn't follow the copy's punches. Jack was toyed with like a toddler.

And yet, he kept rising. Again and again, he threw himself at Copy Jack, only to fail miserably. Every failure only reminded him of his weakness. Every painful punch he received emphasized his helplessness. The power difference between them was just too much, and Copy Jack was too skilled. There was nothing Jack could do. Absolutely nothing. He even resorted to less dignified tactics, throwing dust at his opponent's eyes or distracting him with odd movements. He tried to receive a punch on purpose just to throw a weaker one himself. He just wanted to land one strike.

Everything failed. Before absolute power, all tricks were useless. Jack could do nothing. His weakness was a purposeless hole, a bottomless abyss in his chest. He felt lost and alone. Small.

Copy Jack threw a Meteor Punch. Jack's chest caved in, his ribcage shattered, and his body was almost broken in half. Regeneration took hold quickly—he couldn't die in this place—but the feeling of weakness was even stronger than before, almost swallowing him entirely.

His entire existence was predicated on power. If he was weak, he couldn't do battle. He couldn't use his fists or stand up for anything. He was useless. Helpless. Alone. Despondent.

Only a tiny part of Jack remained now. Everything else was blanketed by mute despair. This small, remaining part was the one focused on progress. It was the part forcing him to repeatedly throw himself at this inevitable suffering, analyzing his feelings.

He kept at it for hours.

Weakness seeped deeply into Jack's psyche. After a while, he felt true fear. Was this experience against his Dao? Was he harming himself in the name of progress?

And yet, he kept at it. He took the risk. Deep despair drove him. The undeniable urge to obtain more power. The reasons why he fought passed through his mind—so many faces, so many fears, a deep desire —until he was just a weak, tired, little man. Another Meteor Punch came at his face. Finally, he almost gave up. The deep confidence he always felt wavered, and he knew he couldn't resist Copy Jack's fist. It filled his entire world, a power far greater than anything he could muster.

The tiny part remaining of Jack shone. *Now!*

His Dao returned at full force, flooding him with power. He felt like a god. At the same time, the copy's Dao flow was strangled, becoming a fraction of what it used to be. The situation was reversed. Copy Jack's Meteor Punch faltered. Suddenly, it was laughably weak and slow. Jack simply slapped it aside.

Such a punch could never touch him. He held absolute power now.

For a single moment, the sensation of crushing weakness and overwhelming power coexisted in his mind. He felt the strength brewing in his fist, but he also saw it from the copy's eyes. He saw his strongest punch from the other side.

He was no longer the one facing an unstoppable god. He *was* the god, watching himself through the eyes of the weak. And his punch was so undeniably powerful. Only through weakness came true understanding of power.

Jack smashed out. It was a Meteor Punch stronger than any other, fueled by the mirror image of the helplessness that he knew his opponent was feeling. It was absolute. Jack had never felt more certain that his strike would land and decimate.

Finally... This was true power.

The copy tried to block but was blown away. The Meteor Punch tore through his crossed arms and chest, drilling a hole straight to the other side. The copy's body flew away, spiraling out of control and into the distance.

Of course, he couldn't die, either. The soul world warped, and the copy was standing before Jack again, safe and sound. But Jack remained in his after-punch stance. He hadn't moved. Understanding was flowing through his brain, filling it. Everything clicked together, and Jack laughed at the sky.

"I got it!" he shouted. "I finally got it! Thank you! Thank you, Copy Jack!"

The copy smiled and nodded. Both were panting—not from physical exhaustion, which they couldn't feel here, but from a spiritual one.

Jack turned his gaze to the sky. The dark blue star was shivering. Slowly, tendrils extended out of it, connecting to the surrounding sky and pumping its essence out. The star lost its color, but it was stronger than ever—the dark blue was fused with the purple of the sun, the vastness of the sky.

Jack felt so happy and relieved. He also felt deeply exhausted. He didn't even know how long he'd meditated for.

"I have to go," he said with a big smile. "Thanks again, Copy Jack. See you soon."

The copy waved, and Jack opened his eyes in the real world, finding himself surrounded by figures, some sitting, some standing.

"Hey," Dorman said. "Took you a while."

Jack didn't reply. He only had eyes for the screens hovering before his face; especially the very first one.

Congratulations! The Dao Root of Power had been successfully fused with your Dao Seed.
Strength +20
Constitution +20
Will +20

CHAPTER NINETY-EIGHT
A SUSPICIOUS GIFT

Congratulations! Meteor Punch II → Meteor Punch III

Meteor Punch III: When meteors fall from space, they cause exponentially more damage than their size would indicate. Your punches can carry the same effect. Overdraw your body's potential and combine it with your Dao of the Fist to unleash a devastating attack. Shoot out your punch like a meteor.

That's... Jack reviewed the description. He took a second and a third look at it. There were no italics. Did this mean there was no change?

Pulling up the description of Meteor Punch II, he confirmed they were identical.

What the fuck?

Was the upgrade so small that no changes were needed? Or...

Jack summoned the power of a Meteor Punch, not throwing it, just holding it in his fist. A few cautious glances were directed his way, but Jack was only paying attention inward.

He gasped.

Not only was there a new stream of Dao enhancing his fist—the Dao of Power—but his conscious control over the Dao had also increased after using it extensively in the soul world. The System didn't need to handhold him as much anymore, so it could focus more on empowering him.

The feeling of the current Meteor Punch reminded him of the very first time he got the skill. Back then, it used to be an overpowering, overwhelming strike that annihilated his opponents in exchange for exhausting him and breaking his hand. He'd grown a lot since then, until he was able to freely use the skill, but this also meant its relative power went down.

Now, the overwhelming power had returned. Holding the Meteor Punch at the ready felt like holding a live grenade. It was like a demon had infested his fist, struggling to unleash itself. Or like he'd strapped a racing car engine to his wrist. The moment he punched out, it was very likely his hand would be mangled.

The power of his skill had gone way, way up, returning to the one-hit killer it was always meant to be.

"Woah," was all Jack could say. He was beyond pleased. This felt not only appropriate for an evolution of Meteor Punch, but also like a very handy last resort. If he was ever cornered, he could just throw a Hail Mary. Additionally, it synergized well with his third-tier Indomitable Body and its extreme regeneration abilities. Even if his wrist was broken, it would recover, as long as it wasn't completely shattered.

As for the inevitable pain... Well, it came hand in hand with power. Jack was used to it.

The only downside was that he'd lost the ability to use Meteor Punch for smaller reasons. Meteor Shower was temporarily unavailable, too. But it was a trade-off Jack would make any day of the week.

He couldn't wait to test it out.

"Hey," a voice came from beside him, demanding his attention. Dorman had opened his eyes and was squinting at Jack's closed fist. "Are you preparing something?"

"Just testing. I upgraded a skill."

"You did?" Dorman's eyes widened slightly. "Congratulations!"

"Thank you."

"Just congratulations?" a second voice came from somewhere behind Jack. Turning, he found the Sage's smiling form approaching. "Not many people can reach the third tier of a Dao Skill in the E-Grade. This is stunning work! Well done!"

Jack let his own smile blossom. "Thank you, Sage. I'm trying my best." Of course, he also had Indomitable Body at the third tier, but there was no need to reveal everything. Instead, his eyes narrowed. "Wait. How did you know that?"

"I'm a sage. Knowing stuff is what I do."

Jack's eye-narrowing intensified. *Did he just trick me?* he wondered, but the Sage's expression was inscrutable. *Well, whatever. Not like I can do anything about it now.*

"How long was I meditating for?" he asked, turning his gaze toward the center of the area, where the lone tree stood surrounded by seven formations. To his surprise, only three formations remained active. The outer four had disappeared, leaving only circles of blackened symbols on the ground. Kareena and the other two formation masters were currently sitting just outside the edge of the fifth formation—a transparent orange barrier. Two of them were inspecting the symbols on the ground, while Kareena was observing the barrier itself.

"A day, roughly," said the Sage. "You became kind of an attraction. If you were planning to hide your breakthrough, you should reconsider."

"A day!"

No wonder he suddenly felt thirsty! He'd spent an entire day meditating. It hadn't felt nearly as long.

Wait, he thought. *Does time flow differently in my soul world? No, I didn't notice any discrepancies the previous times. Then, how did I lose track of time?*

"Don't fret," the Sage said again. "It happens. The higher you rise, the longer meditation takes, and the more time loses its meaning."

"I guess... But we're almost at the tree."

"That, we are."

"What if I had meditated all the way until the end? Until someone took the fruit?"

"It's a pill, not a fruit," the Sage corrected him. "And, yes, that could happen. In that case, we would make sure you're undisturbed. Fusing Dao Roots is not easy."

"But I would have missed the finale."

"You would have missed the waiting, too," Dorman said with an irritated groan. "Not everyone can break through at will. And let me tell you, sitting still for an entire day is annoying."

The Sage laughed. "Patience is a virtue, Dorman. Look at the bright side. They're almost done. Only two formations left."

"Three."

"Two."

Dorman raised a brow. On cue, one of the formation masters exclaimed something. The three of them quickly embarked on a spirited conversation while the one that had exclaimed pointed at a few of the symbols by his feet. A moment later, the other two nodded, and the person who exclaimed reached down to touch the base of the formation.

The barrier dispersed.

The formation masters stood up, dusted their clothes, congratulated each other, and moved to sit by the next formation—a curtain of swimming shadows.

"Is there anything you can't predict, Sage?" Jack asked.

The Sage smiled proudly. "Many things... but I can also predict many. Divination is a powerful practice."

"Maybe I should learn it as well," he joked.

"You could if you wanted to. I can sense a strong affinity to life inside you."

Jack raised a brow. "Does it require studying thick tomes instead of punching stuff?"

"It requires studying the world."

"Right. And I suppose being all cryptic and mystical is a trick of the trade?"

"Oh, yes. It's rather mandatory."

Jack laughed. "Maybe another time, Sage."

"Maybe another time." The Sage smiled back. Suddenly, his line of revealed yellow teeth turned crooked, and his eyes took on a calculating hint. His voice lowered in volume. "By the way, Jack... I can sense that your Dao understanding is particularly strong. If you don't mind sharing, do you happen to have three fused Dao Roots?"

Jack hesitated. He did have three fused Dao Roots, and he did owe the Sage a few favors, but just revealing his strength like this...

Whatever. I do owe him.

"Yes," he replied.

"Hmm. In that case, you're on the same level as the lords. Maybe even slightly stronger, given your Integration titles. If not for your low level, you may have been able to contend for the Dao Sprouting Pill, a shortcut that would greatly help you save Earth."

Jack narrowed his eyes. "Why are you rubbing salt on my wounds, Sage?"

"That's the wrong question. Reasons are the easiest things to find. Try again."

Jack did plan to contend for the pill, if possible. If he wanted to defeat the Planetary Overseer, he needed all the power he could get. However, the offer of the Exploding Sun still stood. He wasn't too desperate anymore. If getting the pill was a suicide mission, he wouldn't do it.

"What are you trying to say?" he asked. He also noticed that Dorman's eyes were narrowed as he looked at the Sage.

"Since we are mostly aligned, the stronger you are, the better for us. Incidentally, I happen to carry a highly condensed experience ball. I could exchange it for that Snow White Globe you got from the animal tile formation at the start of the garden."

Jack crossed his arms. "First of all, how do you know that? You weren't even there. And second, why would you do that?"

"I told you. Our interests are aligned. As for knowing about that little treasure... Well, as I said, I'm a sage. Knowing stuff is what I do."

His yellow-toothed smile was wide and full of meaning.

"Sage," Dorman's voice came sharply from the side. "What are you doing?"

"Trust me, my friend."

"Trust you? We're supposed to—" Dorman cut his words short, glancing at Jack. "Can we have a moment?"

"There is no need," the Sage replied, raising an open palm. "I will need you to trust my judgment."

Dorman's eyes were spewing fire. His inner struggle was apparent, but he relented. "Fine," he said, crossing his arms, still boiling on the inside.

Jack had no idea what was going on. Was that experience ball valuable to them?

"Why would you offer me that?" he asked. "If you need the experience ball, I don't want to take it."

"On the contrary, it's completely useless to us now. I was just carrying it in case we didn't level enough in the previous rings, but we did. So, why not exchange it? In fact, I have to warn you that your Snow White Globe would go for a far higher market price than this experience ball."

Jack's confusion increased. He glanced at Dorman, who was still glaring suspiciously at the Sage. "Then, why..."

"We have our own thoughts," the Sage replied, still smiling. "Helping you here is a small change of plans, that's all. So, what do you say? Wanna exchange?"

Jack almost opened his mouth to ask something, then stopped himself. Any further questions would get him nothing. Moreover, he clearly knew too little to decipher these people's intentions. All he could do was consider the Sage's suggestion.

Am I getting tricked, somehow? he wondered. If he suddenly got a bunch of levels, that would put him in the run for the Top Treasure. There were high chances he would battle the lords, with all the consequences and risks that brought.

Would the Sage benefit from that?

No matter how hard Jack thought, he got little. The only possibility he could come up with was that the Sage planned to contend for the pill himself, and he would benefit from the chaos of an extra challenger added to the mix, but that was far-fetched.

Another possibility was that the Sage foresaw Jack killing one of the lords or getting killed himself, and that would somehow further the Black Hole Church's interests. But, if that was true, there was nothing Jack could do about it. He'd just have to be careful.

And he *did* want that experience ball. A lot. It would negate his greatest weakness against the lords and greatly help him further his own goals. All the plans he'd made, which were just on the verge of fruition, would suddenly become possible.

Even if he accidentally helped the Sage, that wouldn't be too bad, as long as he didn't harm himself. After all, the Sage had assisted him on plenty of occasions. Jack still owed him a bunch of favors.

What a crafty deal... he thought, sweating. Is the Sage a devil?

"Don't think too hard, Jack," the Sage spoke up. "There is no ploy. I have nothing against you. I genuinely just want to see you get stronger because I predict that, in the long run, your strength will benefit us as well."

There was no free lunch in the world. But there were good deals. And, though Jack didn't feel that the Sage was completely honest—or as selfless as he claimed—he decided this was a deal worth taking.

More power was a good thing. If something bad happened down the line... he could only blame himself.

"Deal," he agreed.

The Sage smiled. "Great! Here." Angling his body so that it hid what they were doing, he dug a hand into his robes and pulled out a pinky-sized jewel that radiated soft, multicolored light. Jack grabbed it and stuffed it into his secret pocket.

"Aren't you afraid that one of the others has a skill to detect things without seeing them?" he whispered.

"They don't," the Sage replied.

Jack grimaced. So much for hiding the gray orb even when Longsword wasn't looking. He reached for his belt and unhung the Snow White Globe, handing it over to the Sage.

"Thank you," the middle-aged man replied, inspecting the globe before sliding it in his robes.

I should make a visible pocket, Jack realized. The Sage already knows of the secret one's existence, but now I have to either store the experience ball— jewel—on my belt where everyone can see it, use it, which I don't want to do yet, or put it in my secret pocket, revealing that I have one. After all, they will notice my missing Snow White Globe. I wouldn't have given it out for free.

"How many levels will that thing give me?" Jack asked.

"Plenty. But use it at the last moment. Surprise is a useful weapon."

"Of course."

Jack's mind was already spinning. Everything came under new light now. With all the effort he'd invested into researching the lords teams, and this jewel as the final drop...

He could fight for the Top Treasure!

CHAPTER NINETY-NINE
THE LAST FORMATION FALLS

JACK POCKETED THE EXPERIENCE BALL—JEWEL, ACTUALLY—AND WAITED.

Not much later, Lady Priya approached him. "Hello," she said, greeting both Jack and the Barren High people. "Congratulations, Jack. The elder has confirmed my previous words. As long as nothing goes wrong, you will be accepted into our faction after Trial Planet. However, the protection of your planet will be decided at the end of its grace period. Is that fine with you?"

Jack nodded somberly. Until the Exploding Sun actually promised to protect Earth, he would treat them as unreliable. Too many things could go wrong in the following months. Besides, there was the problem of leaving Trial Planet. The Hand of God was still scanning everyone that exited. If they discovered his connection to the Ancient ruins, who knew what would happen.

"Sure," he replied. "Does that make us allies now?"

"Not yet. For the duration of the Garden Assault, we will remain unrelated, as the rules dictate. Please don't attempt to help me later, or we will both be put into an awkward spot."

"Understood." Jack had no such intentions. The exact opposite, in fact. Since they were unrelated, he wouldn't feel bad about going after the Top Treasure himself.

Priya narrowed her eyes. "In any case, I didn't mean to intrude. I will see you after the assault, Jack. Stay safe."

"I will try my best." He smiled slightly. He didn't mean to be cold; it just happened. Considering they were going to be opponents soon, that wasn't a bad thing. "Thank you for your concern, Priya. I'll be sure to repay it after exiting Trial Planet."

She gazed deep into his eyes. She clearly felt there was something more, but in the end, she didn't manage to see through his words. "Sure thing," she replied, then walked away.

Jack watched her leave with a sad smile. The Exploding Sun's administration had sold him out once, but their people had been nice to him. Master Shol, Priya, and her team had all been friendly and helpful. Good people.

If this were a couple months ago, he would have hesitated to go directly against them for the Top Treasure. Now, however, he understood how things worked in the galaxy. Kindness wasn't the foundation of relationships. Strength was. As long as he didn't kill anyone, going head-on against the Exploding Sun wouldn't lower their opinion of him. If anything, they would pursue him even harder, since he would have proven his strength.

"You've grown, Jack," the Sage commented from the side. Jack felt the rare emotion in his voice.

"I had to," he replied. Sighing, he dropped his head back, gazing at the swirling mists above. His voice was sad as he spoke. It carried a hard edge. "But I guess... this isn't too bad. What better environment than a battlefield for a fist to thrive?"

The Sage smiled without responding. Dorman looked at Jack with new eyes, inspecting him again.

A few moments later, the formation masters were agitated. They were discussing animatedly while pointing at the magic symbols on the ground. Kareena and another formation master—the merfolk guide—seemed to disagree on something. Finally, she and the third formation master took a few steps back, while the merfolk reached down to touch the symbols.

A terrifying explosion shook the garden. Flames shot high. The heat was scalding. A shockwave rolled over the ground, wiping the previous formations out of existence and impacting the resting cultivators, tossing them back into the mist.

Jack had no time to react. He was thrown like everyone else, consumed by the chilling mist that rose in temperature as it absorbed the explosion's heat. Thankfully, he was at the edge of the blast. He'd only been knocked away a hundred feet and the flames only licked his skin.

After making sure he was fine, he rushed back to the core area. Most of the flames had already dissipated when he emerged into the mist-less space—they had nothing to burn. The Sage and Dorman, who had been resting beside him, were also fine. More people were returning, having suffered mild to no injuries.

There were three exceptions, however. Kareena and the other formation master that had retreated sported heavy burns. Their skin was red and bubbly where the explosion had crashed into them head-on, and their screams replaced the previous eerie silence. As for the final formation master, the merfolk that had been next to the exploding formation... Only a pile of ash and burned scales remained where he used to stand. Not even his clothes had survived. He was already dead.

Kareena flared with green power as her wounds began to recover. Slowly, her burnt skin was shed, and new, rosy skin grew in its place. She'd survived worse and would recover.

The other formation master—the draconic woman—was treated by the dryad that accompanied Lady Minerva. She, too, would survive.

"What the hell just happened?" Jack asked.

"These formations are no joke," the Sage replied. His clothes and hair were disheveled, but he looked completely uninjured. "At point-blank, even immortals would be burned to death. We are lucky the previous five were resolved successfully."

"Say that again..."

This garden as a whole was no joke. They'd started with eighteen people. By now, three had died, and one had lost an arm. Even with the addition of the Barren High team bringing them up to seventeen, they had a fifteen percent death rate, and the Garden Assault wasn't over yet.

Even for Jack himself, this was the third time he came close to death. First with the animal tile trap, then with the imprisoned devil, and now this explosion. He didn't even count the cave in which they were sealed for a while.

And all those happened despite him being very close to the apex of power for E-Grades. Trial Planet really pushed people to the limits—it was like a second Integration.

The remaining cultivators recovered from the shock. One person took the fallen formation master's remains to bury beyond the mist. The others settled back down to meditate, while Kareena and the other formation master, despite their shaking, approached the final formation shielding the scrawny tree and the Dao Sprouting Pill.

"Are deaths so common?" Jack wondered aloud, noticing how little people seemed to mind.

"Trial Garden is a very dangerous place," the Sage explained. "Even entire groups like our Garden Assault have disappeared in the past. A few deaths here and there are nothing."

Jack hadn't known that. After everything he'd seen so far, he didn't struggle to believe it, either. If it had been the first formation that exploded, the one that reached almost to the edge of the empty area, their entire group would have been decimated.

Then again, if all formations were this dangerous, they would have camped farther away.

Finally, however, only one formation remained. A milky white barrier that radiated a Dao of Softness—but Jack knew better than to underestimate its lethality. The moment that formation fell, an all-out brawl between the three lords and their teams would commence. They would tear each other apart to reach the Top Treasure first. Even killing each other wasn't unexpected.

Jack inspected them. Longsword was sitting cross-legged with his sword on his lap, but his eyes were open. He was taking deep breaths, sharpening his edge. The ice witch and Bocor flanked him, ready to pounce at any moment.

Priya was standing, closing and opening her hands. Every time she opened them, blue flames flickered on her palms. Chotu, the jovial fat man, was bouncing from foot to foot beside her with a wild smile. As for Kareena, she was one of the two formation masters working on the formation.

Lady Minerva had an entire side of the core area for herself. She had already summoned her three beasts—the wolf, the turtle, and the sparrow—each of which was an Elite at the peak of the E-Grade. The dryad had finished treating the other formation master and stood beside her lady, with arms crossed and eyes glowing green. Vocrich also stood by Lady Minerva, his dark suit flickering like it was made of shadows. He caught Jack's gaze and winked with a cocky grin, ever the charmer.

Every treasure hunter had retreated to the very edge of the area, where they would be safe. They were Jack, the Barren High people, and five other treasure hunters.

The tension was mounting. Nobody was speaking. The lords were preparing for battle. Even surrounded by a blanket of mist, you could hear a pin drop.

Jack had his mind on the experience jewel. As soon as the time was ripe, he would crush it and erupt with power, hopefully reaching the level of a lord or at least close. At the same time, he kept an eye on the Black Hole Church team. Though they'd helped him, they remained unfathomably enigmatic. It wouldn't surprise him if the Sage or Dorman had lord-level power.

"You aren't going to fight, are you?" he whispered low enough that only the Sage could hear.

"If we were, we wouldn't have helped you."

"Good. Can I have two of you guys as helpers? The lords all have some."

The Sage smiled. "No."

"I thought so." Jack laughed, drawing a few odd looks, but he was beyond caring.

"Nervous, Longsword?" Priya asked, eyeing the swordsman. "I can see you shaking."

"In your dreams," he replied, laughing freely. "The pill is mine. Just make sure your unskilled formation master doesn't die by herself. She already fucked up once."

"On the contrary—she never did."

Sparks were flying. The three lords were removing their metaphorical gloves, jousting at each other with words. They no longer cared about etiquette. Any pretense of friendship was gone, leaving only enmity.

"Are you both so scared that you need to talk?" Lady Minerva asked.

Longsword laughed again. "Are you so scared that you want to shut up?"

"She just knows she's too stupid to debate," Priya added.

Minerva laughed. They all smiled, doing their best to project confidence. After all, the more confident the lord, the harder their followers would fight. "Everybody knows who's the strongest lord," Minerva said. "And if they don't, I'll just prove it."

"You? The strongest?" Longsword retorted. "That's a big word for someone who needed two attempts to reach the E-Grade."

Minerva's eyes narrowed. A hint of her fighting spirit leaked out, making her three beasts look up aggressively. "Wait and see, failure of the Wide Swirls. That's what they used to call you, right?"

Longsword's brows fell. His hand slowly moved to his sword handle.

"Losing your composure so early?" Priya mocked him. "No wonder your mother is so embarrassed of you. I heard she didn't even accompany you here herself."

"At least I have two parents."

Priya went white as a sheet. Her hands snapped open, the flames in them flaring. She did not retort, and the other two lords didn't continue speaking. Their resolve was clear. They would kill each other, no holds barred.

Jack watched the exchange with raised brows. The battle hadn't even started yet, but he could sense its brutality. These guys didn't even hold back with words—when they fought, someone was bound to get massacred.

The minutes crawled by. Jack focused on the sound of his breathing.

At some point, Kareena and the other formation master exchanged a few words. They nodded at each other, seemingly agreeing on something. Then, Kareena stood up and walked to Priya's side, preparing to battle. Her silver hair glowed faintly. Her eyes turned deeper.

The lords glared at each other, affirming their resolve. Nobody spared a glance for the treasure hunters. They didn't even register anymore. They weren't supposed to participate in what was going to happen.

Then again, why are they so certain? Jack wondered. Anyone else could be planning to steal the Top Treasure, too.

Before he could further advance his thoughts, the other formation master stood up. She looked around her, realizing she was standing at what would soon be the epicenter of a massive conflict. She gulped.

Then, without any fanfare whatsoever, she pointed a finger at the mystical symbols. The formation trembled. For a moment, everyone held their breaths. Would it explode?

The formation fell. The tree of the Dao Sprouting Pill was laid bare. And the lords sprang into action.

CHAPTER ONE HUNDRED
LORD-LEVEL SLAUGHTER

THE MOMENT THE FINAL BARRIER FELL, THE LORDS UNLEASHED THEIR PENT-UP fighting spirit, and their teams followed a beat later, roaring out war cries.

Chaos descended.

Chotu turned into a golden giant and collided with Bocor, who barely held his ground. The ice witch sent vines of ice to grow around Vocrich, whose darkness devoured them. Kareena's silver light extinguished the darkness, letting the ice vines penetrate Vocrich's defenses. He twisted away, suffering several nicks and cuts. The dryad's healing powers focused on him in the next moment, healing him.

After smashing a palm strike into Bocor's chest and sending him flying away, Chuto laughed. He took a step forward to stand before Longsword, an unmovable golden giant. Before him, Longsword seemed tiny. Yet, when he slashed out, the Dao radiating from his sword filled the air.

"Out of my way!" he shouted. Magic enhanced the blade as it bit into the giant's palm, which he'd raised to defend. Golden blood spurted out. The sword cut halfway through the palm. It was stopped, however, and Chuto only laughed as Kareena's silver light healed his wound.

"You aren't getting past me!" he shouted in defiance. Longsword snorted.

Behind them, near the crooked tree that held the Dao Sprouting Pill, Priya was clashing against Minerva, who rode her white wolf into battle. Each gave it their all, not letting the other near the fruit.

A palm strike that carried the sun landed on the wolf's side. At the same time, the sparrow flew through Priya's defenses, diamond wingtips slashing her skin open. Suddenly, Minerva's turtle fell from the sky and landed before the Exploding Sun lady, cutting her off.

Priya's eyes shone. "You can try!" she growled. The temperature rose drastically. Flames shot out of her orifices, forming a radiant ball of fire around her. Flame tongues licked Priya's surroundings, focusing on the turtle's shell and boiling it alive.

The turtle screamed. Its stubby legs emerged and carried it away, letting Priya storm through. The sparrow chirped and made a wide circle, no longer daring to approach her.

A man of shadow then stood in her path. "Going all out already?" he asked. His tuxedo unraveled into countless shadows, hugging his skin tightly and revealing the scale armor underneath. The shadows expanded into a sphere around him, submerging the world into cold darkness.

"Hmph. So what if I go all out?" Priya replied proudly. "You cannot stand against me, Vocrich!"

The ball of fire rammed into the darkness. They warred for a moment. Tongues of flames and tendrils of darkness wrapped around each other, snuffing themselves out. Soon, the flames gained the advantage. Vocrich could not beat Priya... but he could hold his ground for a little while. He could delay her.

Priya shouted. Her flames intensified, but she still needed some time to get through. Minerva was free to advance on the fruit.

Seeing this, Chuto, the golden giant, stepped aside. Lord Longsword darted past him, swinging his blade through the air and shooting out a long black streak directly where Minerva was headed. A whip of green energy came from the side like an enraged vine, clashing with Longsword's slash head-on. The vines were sliced in half, but the slash was sent off-course, veering into the ground and carving a wide swath of earth before dissipating.

Longsword screamed in outrage, still too far away. In such a fast-paced battle, even a hundred feet could seem like an unbridgeable chasm.

Minerva's followers had delayed the other two lords. She had a clear shot at the tree. Already, she was rushing there atop her wolf, her dark clothes striking a contrast against its white fur.

The Dao Sprouting Pill was within grasp.

"Stop right there!"

Two different powers merged together and came at Minerva from the front, forcing her to stop and dart aside. Kareena and the ice witch stood side by side in front of the tree, cooperating in the face of a common enemy. One's eyes shone silver and the other's white as both unleashed the full extent of their power on the lady.

Even though they were standing beside the tree, followers were not allowed to touch the fruit. Only lords held that right.

Tubes of ice grew from the ice witch's fingertips. They kept growing through the air, pushing their spike tips forward, lengthening while their body remained stationary. Soon, they formed a net that closed in on Lady Minerva. Kareena's ponytail began to float as a silver halo materialized around her head, resembling the brilliance of a full moon. Minerva winced—she was suffering a soul attack.

The wolf, however, was not. It jumped to the side and ran away, narrowly escaping the ice net. The tubes unraveled, each chasing the wolf like they had a mind of their own. They were tipped with sharp spikes and grew rapidly, filling the space where they passed.

But the wolf was an Elite E-Grade beast. It jumped between the tubes, dodging their sharp ends and forcing them to circle around. It stepped on their bodies, frozen in place as they were, snaked between them, and leaped over them. The ice witch hurriedly abandoned these tubes, forgoing their floating properties and letting them crash to the ground, as new ones shot out of her shoulders.

But she was too late. The wolf had leaped into the air, heading directly for the crooked tree.

A golden giant jumped before it. One palm was wide open and drawn back, shining brilliantly. "Stand down!" Chuto shouted and smashed the wolf.

It had nowhere to dodge. The palm fell on it like a mountain, neutralizing its forward momentum and nailing it to the ground like a spiked volleyball. A pained cry came from the wolf, which struggled to stand back up.

Minerva wasn't there. She had recovered from Kareena's soul attack as Chuto's palm came crashing down, and she jumped over the palm, flying into the air. Chuto looked upward. His entire golden body shone brightly enough to blind her, but she only closed her eyes. Her hands were stretched upward.

But Minerva could not fly. She was defenseless.

The ice witch's sharp-tipped tubes arrived then, growing from below her like a bamboo forest.

The sparrow flew over Lady Minerva. It grabbed her by the wrist and pulled her along, clearing the spikes and passing over the golden giant. She was directly above the tree now. The sparrow dove.

A black slash carved the ground as it headed her way. A green whip rose again—the dryad's power—but it wasn't enough. The black slash cut right through it, maintaining over half of its power as it crashed into Minerva. It was so fast that even the sparrow couldn't help her dodge in time.

Minerva was flung backward like a ragdoll. She turned three times around herself midair and spat out blood. Green healing energy surrounded her, and she instantly regained her bearings.

Just in time, too. Bocor had taken to the air, attempting to spike her into the ground with his tower shield like the golden giant had spiked the wolf. Minerva sharply turned her head. Before Bocor could look away, they had crossed eyes.

He practically frothed at the mouth. His Dao crumbled. His shield lost its strength, and his body began to fall without ever striking out.

To add insult to injury, Lady Minerva landed on his chest feet-first and used him as a platform to jump to the ground, sending him flying away.

Jack didn't see what Minerva did next, because all hell was breaking loose around the scrawny tree. Longsword's blade clashed against Priya's palm. A sun erupted, sliced in half by a dark line. The point of impact detonated. Flames and sword slashes flew everywhere, random discharges of energy that could rend the ground and slice the mist.

Neither were blown back. They couldn't fly, either. They stayed close to each other and kept exchanging strikes as they fell. Palms fell like boulders, and Longsword's sword moved like a snake. Despite its length, which made it inconvenient for close combat, it had a sharp blade more threatening than Priya's bare palms.

Suns blossomed and were diced apart. Black slashes melted before the sun. The air shimmered around them. Longsword's tattered cloak billowed like it was caught in a hurricane, and his long hair floated behind his face, making him look demonic.

Priya's entire body glowed with heat. Her tanned skin had taken on a reddish hue, and her palms were glowing white like hot iron. Every time she clashed against Longsword's blade, sparks flew, and a wave of heat spread in the direction of her attack.

Longsword couldn't pierce her bare palms.

While the two were embroiled in combat, their followers clashed below, each wrestling for control of the tree's immediate area for when the lords landed. The ice witch filled the air with sharp tubes, which wobbled and fell apart where Kareena's silver aura shone. Chuto's golden radiance was overshadowed by Vocrich's long mantle of shadows. Since Bocor remained unconscious, the vampire had come to even the playing ground until his lady arrived. He couldn't let any of the other two lords claim the fruit.

From the time the barrier fell to now this all happened in the span of three, maybe four seconds. Jack's jaw threatened to drop at the level of battle he was watching. Everybody here was extremely strong, a genius in their own right, matching Rufus Emberheart in ferocity. They had excellent battle awareness, too. He struggled to find mistakes in any exchange he witnessed, and everyone reacted appropriately to all situations, making it hard for anyone else to find an opening.

Before he knew it, Jack's blood was boiling. This was it. This was the level he aspired to reach. The highest plain he could stand on. The very summit of power. These people were his opponents.

Battle lust flooded his mind. His fists sang with the Dao, and an oppressive aura billowed out of him, raising dust, upsetting the mist, and drawing everyone's glances despite the heated battle at the very front.

Jack was watching a battle of demi-gods. He didn't know if he could fight against them, but he wanted to try so very badly. His lips wouldn't stop grinning. His skin wouldn't stop shivering.

He was overwhelmed by a desire to battle. To prove himself. To test his might.

There was no sense waiting anymore. He reached into his pocket and crushed the experience crystal. An aura of power flooded him harder than he'd ever felt before. His state of being rose meteorically. His battle lust was heightened into ecstasy by the many level-ups.

Level up! You have reached Level 101.
Level up! You have reached Level 102.
Level up! You have reached Level 103.
Level up! You have reached Level 104.

...

Level up! You have reached Level 123.
Level up! You have reached Level 124.

A cascade of levels. A cascade of blue screens. A battle of epic proportions before his very eyes, and the ticket to greatness at the tips of his fingers. What better time to be alive? What better way to live?

In just a moment, Jack had reached the peak of the E-Grade. There was even a bit more energy which dissipated as his body refused to accept it.

He didn't even know how many stat points he had available. He didn't care. It didn't matter. With a thought, all of them went to Physical, split equally between Strength, Dexterity, and Constitution. There was no time for finer calculations. The battle for the Top Treasure could end at any moment. He had to join now.

Amidst the battle, everyone glanced in his direction. Even the lords ceased their exchange of blows for a moment. Priya's eyes widened. Longsword's narrowed. The golden giant, wrapped in shadows as he was, laughed. "Come!" he shouted, and his voice shook the air.

Jack's blood had been replaced by lightning. He'd never felt such a surge of power before, except for the time he'd absorbed the Life Drop. In a single moment, he had transformed. He spared a look for his screen, simply to admire the numbers.

"Here I come!" he shouted.

And, with a laughing roar, jumped into the fray.

Level: 124

Strength: 590
Dexterity: 545
Constitution: 565
Mental: 50
Will: 100

CHAPTER ONE HUNDRED ONE
JACK JOINS THE FRAY

JACK JUMPED INTO THE FRAY WITH A LAUGHING ROAR. HE COULD FINALLY SEE THE lords' movements clearly. Longsword's slashes were readable. Priya's suns were no longer instant. The ice witch's tubes were slow.

He'd finally done it. He was strong enough. He could fight these people head-to-head, and he wouldn't give up this opportunity for anything in the world.

Yes, he was a battle maniac. But so what?

Priya and Longsword exchanged another strike. Both used the momentum to fly back to their respective camps.

"Jack Rust!" Longsword growled through gritted teeth. "I knew I should have stopped you."

"Don't do this," Priya warned.

"Too late!" Jack shouted. He was barreling forth like an angry bull that could no longer be stopped. "My apologies, Priya, but let's fight! Let the strongest cultivator win!"

Even battle maniacs had a brain. In this case, Jack had a three-step plan to get the Top Treasure.

One, showcase his battle lust so nobody would suspect he was holding back. After all, lords were the apex existences in Trial Planet. Who would imagine that a random punching guy now had the same level of power?

Two, hide his real strength. Although he suspected he could fight lords, he would pretend to be just an elite.

Three, erupt with his full strength the moment he found an opportunity and seize the fruit—the Dao Sprouting Pill.

Very simple. One-two-three. Couldn't go wrong, right?

Jack bounded into the fray with fists swinging and a wild smile. The lords exchanged a glance as Kareena and the ice witch, who had been clashing for a while, angled their battle to intercept Jack.

"Bring it on!" he shouted.

Suddenly, his world was filled with ice and purity. Sharp-tipped tubes grew around him like snakes whose bodies never moved, only lengthened. A sickening silver aura crashed down on his head, seeking to purify his mentality and turn him into a vegetable. One was a physical attack, the other a soul one. Moreover, both fought each other for ground as they enveloped Jack, and he was lost between them.

Both Kareena and the ice witch were elites. Their strength was nothing to scoff at. A few moments ago, Jack would have been overwhelmed by either of these attacks and been forced to defend with all his might.

However, the present and the past were two very different things. He was strong now. Very strong. He just had to hide that.

"Ah!" he screamed as the ice tubes circled him like vultures. They grew at him, and he barely dodged, letting two nick his sides. He smashed a fist into a tube's body so they couldn't entrap him, watching it crumble from end to end. The ice sought to surround him, growing and attacking from all directions, as the silver aura melted it in real time. It melted Jack's soul, too. He could feel his strength fading away like snow in the oven.

It was a very unpleasant feeling, similar to when he suppressed his own strength in the soul world to comprehend weakness. For the same reason, he wasn't flustered. He forced his Indomitable Will to stand down, letting the silver erode his soul. He let the weakness creep in. Let himself stumble.

An ice tube pierced into his thigh. He groaned as he punched its body, shattering it, where a bloody hole was left on his leg. He struggled to walk. His regeneration was hindered by the silver aura, too.

To all watchers, Jack looked to be in dire straits. Longsword and

Priya tsked as they turned back to each other and recommenced their battle. Both seemed convinced that Jack Rust wasn't a major threat, just an annoyance.

Of course, tricking them wasn't that simple. These people were all highly intelligent. Even if they thought him weak, they wouldn't just forget about him.

But he could work with that. Every step he took was a victory.

Meanwhile, Lady Minerva had abandoned her wolf and now rode a hulking hippopotamus—also an Elite beast—which stomped through the battlefield to reach the fruit. The sparrow flew over her shoulder, and the turtle was approaching from the side, ready to intercept whoever tried to stop the lady. The dryad rode the hippo, too, just behind Minerva. She would heal the beasts and make sure they kept fighting.

The battlefield was a swiftly changing environment. Chuto was locked in combat against Vocrich. The clash between Kareena and the ice witch had reached a climax, not letting either disengage, and Jack was trapped between them. Longsword and Priya were fighting each other near the fruit, unable to approach without revealing an opening. Sun-clad palms met the long blade. Suns were torn apart. Dark slashes were immolated.

As Minerva made a mad rush, surrounded by beasts and backed by a healer, the other two lords exchanged a glance. At the same time, they turned and charged to intercept her.

The turtle threw itself in the way, blocking Longsword's slash with its shell. The sparrow flew at Priya, maneuvering around her palms to strike from behind. Its burnt feathers and the turtle's cracked shell were repaired by the dryad as the hippo barreled forth unstoppably.

A sun and a blade crossed before it. The hippo groaned as a deep wound was cauterized on its forehead, and it was forced to slow down, but it remained a formidable threat. The sparrow kept circling Priya at blinding speed. One mistake would end with her throat torn. The turtle stubbornly remained before Longsword, blocking as many of his slashes as possible.

The three lords were finally embroiled in an all-out battle. Minerva seemed to be the superior one, but the other two were working together to keep her at bay. They were exchanging time for the blood of her beasts, of which she had a lot. Obviously, they were winning. Two lords against one and an Elite was just too good of a matchup.

As their battle mounted, and everyone was busy fighting their own opponents, Jack saw his chance.

He roared, unleashing more of his strength. The silver aura was held at bay for a moment as Brutalizing Aura erupted from his body, sapping the ice tubes of their strength. He put his head down and charged like a bull, smashing punches in front of him to clear the way. He Ghost Stepped, too. Amidst a shower of ice shards, he escaped the battle between Kareena and the ice witch, who couldn't follow this time, lest they expose themselves to their opponent.

He remained injured, at least on the surface, so he didn't seem like much of a threat. However, he was now much closer to the fruit. Someone had to stop him.

Chuto and Vocrich growled at the same time. Chuto smashed a golden palm into the shadows, banishing them and sending them flying toward the central lord battle, where Vocrich could assist his lady and balance out the battle. The golden giant had to stop Jack, so he conceded this advantage.

He turned and charged at Jack. "You caused me a lot of trouble, brother!" he roared, laughing. "But I just have to beat you fast enough. Let Chuto, the golden giant, measure your strength!"

Jack grinned wildly. All that stood between him and the fruit was this man, who the rest were convinced could stop him for a good while, if not beat him soundly.

Step two, hiding his strength, was complete. Now... it was time for step three. Reveal it.

A golden palm fell toward Jack. For the first time, he felt the pressure. He was standing up to the full might of an Elite. His knees wanted to bulk. His neck tingled, and his hair rose. But all those were remnants of the past. Fears left over from when he was weak.

The palm was large enough to cover the sky, easily as wide as he was tall. It fell on him like a tumbling cloud. Jack clenched his fist and felt the power brewing inside. His Dao was singing. It'd been suppressed long enough. Now, it was time to fight. Time to punch. Time to battle!

The golden palm's radiance disappeared. Time slowed. All sound and color were sucked under the massive palm, where a single clenched fist shone purple, a meteor about to crash. It pulsed with incredible power. Even Jack didn't know how strong this new Meteor Punch was.

The world held its breath. Jack stepped hard and smashed out with all his power, forgoing defense. A single purple fist in a world of darkness, illuminated the way forward.

And the world exploded. Color and sound erupted from the point of impact. Everything shook.

The golden palm was broken. Chuto's gigantic body was sent flying, blood spurting from his mouth, like he'd been struck by a moving train. Jack's feet had formed craters on the ground, but he still stood. His hand was shaking. The knuckles were cracked. Exhaustion threatened him for a moment before the feeling of overwhelming power returned.

He stood there, with his fist outstretched, as the golden giant rolled to the ground a hundred feet away. His previous wounds were closing at increased speed until he was good as new.

Everyone had fallen silent. The battle had paused. Every eye in Trial Garden was aimed at Jack Rust, who had just proven he could stand on this stage. The greatest stage.

He was a lord.

Longsword's gaze became serious. Priya's, elated, but also conflicted. Minerva's, calculating. All three of them now viewed Jack as an equal. For the first time, they genuinely took notice of him.

And Jack couldn't stop his smile from spreading. His hand regenerated. The cracks closed. His expended stamina didn't return, but he still had plenty. He could easily shoot two or three more Meteor Punches, if needed.

He raised his head at the sky and laughed.

"I am here!" he shouted. "Fight me, lords! May the strongest win!"

He didn't know how he stacked up against them. Their Daos were of a similar caliber as his. So were their titles, probably, but he had no followers, while each of them had two.

Most importantly, he was too close to the fruit. Nobody expected him to get past Chuto so quickly. This was the opening he needed.

Strength gathered in his legs. He shot out. Ghost Step flashed, carrying him forward. Everybody tried to react, but they didn't have time to stop him. The fruit was his.

In the lord battle, Longsword's eyes hardened. He stopped

defending against the hippo. Instead, he jumped into the air and crossed his arms, letting the pink head smash into him with all its strength. He went flying so fast and so hard that he spat out blood. Yet, midair, he rotated and reoriented his body. He was flying at Jack. He'd been hit on purpose to make it in time.

Jack Rust could not be allowed to get the pill.

Longsword crash-landed and jumped up. He was close to the fruit. If he just defeated Jack, he would get it. At the same time, Minerva redoubled her efforts. Flanked by Vocrich and the dryad, they were swiftly overwhelming Priya, who had fallen at a great disadvantage but didn't even have time to disengage. Chuto spat blood and stood back up, rushing to help his lady, but even he could only delay the inevitable. They were just outmatched, and Kareena was locked in another combat.

If a winner appeared between Jack and Longsword, that person would get the fruit. If not, Minerva would.

Jack focused on his opponent. Finally, he could face this lord on equal ground. "I've been looking forward to this," he said, cracking his knuckles. "Come, Longsword. Let's see how you fare without impossible stats."

"See, and die," Longsword retorted. His black blade split the sky. It swung around like a whip and flew at Jack tip-first. Like the last time they'd met, his skill with the blade was superb. He wielded it as naturally as his arms.

Unlike last time, Jack could keep up. And he, too, took pride in his skills.

He leaned back, letting the blade sail over his nose. He ducked and charged. He couldn't fight Longsword at long range. Up close and personal was the way to go.

Longsword was no joke. He jumped back, accelerating his slashes. The world was filled with dark blades that reached for Jack's neck. He felt the pressure mounting. It was more than he expected. Just like the time he fought Rufus Emberheart, he felt suppressed, his power and skill matched to their very limits.

There was a certain feeling to fighting like this. It was completely unlike any other enemies he'd faced. Completely different from the many monsters he'd slain and opponents he'd stomped. Rufus then and Longsword now challenged him on equal footing. They were pushing him to the very edge by pure skill. Striving to prove themselves better than him. More capable.

If he lost now, it wouldn't be due to a lack of stat points or experience. He would simply lose because he was inferior. His pride as a warrior was on the line. The skills in which he had devoted everything were tested on Longsword's blade.

And it was exactly this kind of battle that made Jack's blood boil, that filled his veins with steel, that awakened his wildest, most primal instincts.

Time slowed to a crawl. His mind accelerated to the max. His Indomitable Will cut away all distractions, and his Dao Seed erupted with power, beating to the tune of his heart. Jack was not a human anymore, but a machine made to destroy and triumph. To conquer with his fists.

He'd always wondered about his Class name. Now, he understood. It wasn't random. The System knew exactly what it offered him.

Because, in this moment, when Jack's barest self was revealed, he *was* the Fiend of the Iron Fist.

An aura rolled out of him. It filled both ground and air, making everyone frown. The weakest people present had sweat on their brow. Longsword remained unaffected.

"Show me your worst," Longsword called out. His eyes were narrow and calculating. His mind was cold and his heart on fire. Like Jack, he was a born warrior, and the two met chin-to-chin.

"I won't show mercy," Jack replied.

His fist met the blade head-on. Color and sound disappeared. A purple meteor was the only thing left. It exploded against the tip of Longsword's blade, meeting its tremendous strength directly.

The earth was blown apart under their clash. Dust and wind flew everywhere. A shockwave erupted, making Longsword's hair and cloak billow. Jack, on the other hand, wore nothing but his pants, and his hair was short. There was nothing to billow. He was a mass of pure, ferocious power.

It was exactly at this moment that Bocor woke up from where he lay unconscious. It took him a long while to comprehend what he was seeing. When he did, his jaw dropped. He still gathered his shield and rushed to rejoin the fight.

Both fist and blade were pushed back. Their powers were roughly equal. If anything, Longsword had gotten the best of the exchange, but only by a tiny bit. It wasn't enough to overpower Jack.

That lit a fire in the swordsman. If he just beat Jack here, before Minerva could defeat Priya, he would get the fruit. He would win.

He charged again.

Jack seemed to panic. He bit his lip—a motion he'd picked up from Nauja—as if desperately trying to come up with something, anything. He reached for his secret pocket and took out a gray orb, flinging it at Longsword to scare him. At the same time, he made a run for the fruit, gambling it all.

Longsword snorted. Idiot, he thought. In your panic, you forgot that I was there when you took this. It's the Ticklish Pebble. Only an idiot would be scared of it.

He ignored the coming pebble and closed in on Jack, ready to slash at his exposed back. After that, he would easily get the pill and the title. Triumph was so close he could taste it.

Except for one thing: this wasn't the Ticklish Pebble.

The Repeat Exploding Orb exploded in Longsword's face. He had no defenses. The full force of a peak E-Grade explosion struck him head-on, and even as a lord, he was injured. He screamed. Blood erupted from his mouth and he was flung away.

Everyone watching failed to comprehend this. It made no sense. Longsword had just ignored a coming projectile. Of course he'd been hit. What an idiot.

Most importantly, Longsword had been the only thing standing between Jack and the blood-red apple—the Dao Sprouting Pill.

"No!" Minerva and Priya screamed at the same time. Longsword was on the ground, roaring in impotent fury. This time, he couldn't make it. Everyone else was busy fighting elsewhere. For the second time, Jack had punched through much faster than anyone anticipated, proving his brains in addition to his brawn.

He dashed the final few feet, reached the tree, wrapped his palm around the apple-looking thing that was the Dao Sprouting Pill... and cleanly tore it from the branch.

He had the Top Treasure.

CHAPTER ONE HUNDRED TWO
BULLIED BY A SORE LOSER

JACK'S HAND WRAPPED STEADILY AROUND THE BLOOD-RED APPLE—THE DAO Sprouting Pill. It fit in his palm snugly.

The moment he touched it, the world went silent. Everyone around him paused mid-fight and gaped. Longsword glared with intense hatred.

Congratulations! Title "Seventh Ring Conqueror" upgraded to "Eighth Ring Conqueror!"
Efficacy of all stats: +35% → +40%

Final Ring Quest:
• **Defeat the Final Guardian of Trial Planet. Reach the apex.**

The appearance of the next quest was a bit odd. He wasn't at the Final Ring yet. Then again, accessing it was so easy that he might as well be.

However, Jack didn't have time to consider titles and rings. He was surrounded by a large number of powerful, furious individuals. All battle had ceased, and all eyes were glaring at him.

"Jack Rust..." Longsword said, gritting his teeth. His gaze alternated between Jack and the Dao Sprouting Pill like he couldn't comprehend what was happening. "You..."

"I played by the rules and won," Jack said, calmly pocketing the fruit. It barely fit in his secret pocket, which wasn't secret any longer. *I really should get a normal pocket. Reaching for the back of my thigh is awkward.*

"You did *what?*"

"I won," he repeated assuredly. He stared right at Longsword. "The rules of this battle state that once someone gets the fruit, it's over. The title is already mine, anyway. That said, if you still want to duel me... I'm right here."

He expected Longsword to meet his challenge with hard words. Instead, the man laughed. Still covered in blood and burns from the Repeat Exploding Ball, he made for a gruesome sight.

"The rules!" he shouted. "*The rules*, he says. What do you know about rules?"

Jack got a bad feeling. "Is that not the case?"

"Oh, it is, absolutely. It's even written in the Star Pact: Once the representative of a B-Grade faction gets the Top Treasure, the battle is over. Everyone will honor that. So, tell me, Jack: just which B-Grade faction do you represent?"

Jack pursed his lips. He glared at Dorman. The young man had previously explained the rules to him, but neglected to mention—or forgot, or didn't know—the "representative of a B-Grade faction" part. Now, he only shrugged.

It suddenly made sense why all the other treasure hunters were content to simply watch.

Shit, Jack thought.

"He belongs to my faction," Lady Priya intervened. Her gaze was stormy and conflicted, but her words were steady. "He represents the Exploding Sun."

"Bullshit," Longsword retorted. "He isn't even part of your faction. And you know damn well that each faction can only have one lord."

Priya fell silent.

"This was an honest mistake," Jack explained. "I misunderstood."

"Who cares? You got the title. It's gone now—for all of us. Even if you hand over the pill, it changes little."

Despite the rough situation, Jack didn't really intend to surrender the pill. He'd fought hard for it. Earned it. "Listen," he said. "I know how little your factions care for the Star Pact. I've experienced it first-hand. No matter what the law says, this pill was placed here by the creators of Trial Planet for the worthiest to claim, and you cannot deny that I won it fair and square. I joined this battle openly. I fought you to a draw and proved my strength. I emerged victorious because I played my cards better than everyone else. Do you really think, deep in your heart, that I don't deserve this? That you deserve it more than me?" He fished his treasure out of his pocket and held up the apple.

He also glanced at Minerva, gauging her opinion. She seemed hesitant. After all, this pill didn't belong to one of their factions. It belonged to Trial Planet, a place open to everyone in the galaxy. Even if the law stated that only someone from the B-Grade factions could claim the pill, that was a law they had come up with. The truth was, Jack had indeed won this contest. Grouping up against him because he had no backing would be the behavior of a sore loser. A dishonorable thing to do in public.

On the other hand, he did pretend to be just a treasure hunter before, or he would have never made it here. And, at the end of the day, everyone wanted the fruit. What was honor before power?

Everyone besides Jack and Longsword were deep in thought. This situation was unclear.

Longsword laughed again. "Victory and deservedness has nothing to do with this. You came here like a thief, rode our tails to this core area, and snuck into our battle to emerge with the pill. You ruined our chance to advance quickly. For one of us, you ruined our lives. How are we supposed to split the pill now?"

Jack's brows fell. "I earned this. You knew I was coming for the pill, and I beat you fair and square. I have every right to claim it."

"Oh yes, fair and square," Longsword said, picking up a gray orb. He turned it in his hand, inspecting it from all sides. "A Repeat Exploding Orb, I see. A fine treasure. This is the real reward of the Treasure Trial we entered together, isn't it? The one I was supposed to get. You swapped it with the Ticklish Pebble before I emerged from the trial."

"So what?" Jack replied. He didn't try to deny anything. "You were going to get that treasure by bullying me with your higher level. I just used quick thinking to bully you first."

"Spoken like a true thief!" Longsword laughed. He raised the tip of his sword to the sky. "Greedy, honorless scum. You are a fine little parasite, Jack. Your one deception led to another. If not for the trickery you played around this orb, how could you beat me now? How could you get past me?"

"By punching you in the face."

The temperature seemed to drop. Everyone else watching the altercation mutely, widened their eyes by a crack. Longsword stared at Jack as if struggling to grasp the height of his confidence.

"Hand over the pill, Jack, and stretch out your neck so I can cut it. Give yourself an honorable death, at least."

Jack smiled. Finally, Longsword was speaking his language. "You really are just a bully, Longsword. A sore loser used to getting his way. I joined this competition openly, and just because I have no big daddy behind my back, you think you can bully me? That I should stretch out my neck for you? Hah! A death at the hand of trash like you could never be honorable. Both my head and the pill... if you want them, come get them."

Jack returned the treasure to his pocket and clenched his fists. Brutalizing Aura rolled out of his body in waves, galvanized by his will to fight.

Faced with Jack's cutting words, Longsword laughed back. "Oh no, you don't deserve a fair fight! You don't deserve the honor of dying in a duel. You will be slain like a dog on the street, crushed and helpless."

"Oh yeah? By you and what army? I don't see any other lord willing to stoop to your level."

It was a fine effort. However, Longsword's grin widened. He turned to Minerva. "Hand of God! This man broke a clause of the Star Pact right in front of you. What is the appropriate punishment?"

Lady Minerva hesitated before making her decision. When she opened her mouth, she uttered a single word: "Death."

The moment she said that, her three beasts and Vocrich started pacing around Jack, seeking to entrap him. Bocor and the ice witch were already there, taking up one side each.

Lady Priya met Jack's eye and shook her head. She wouldn't help.

Chuto, releasing his golden giant form, sighed sadly. Kareena looked away. And the Sage, who had given Jack the chance to fight, only shook his head.

"Sorry, Jack," he said telepathically. *"I didn't know the Star Pact's exact phrasing. We can't fight all these people. You're on your own."*

Jack gritted his teeth. There wasn't even time to blame anyone. If he hesitated for a single second, his escape would be cut off. He was deep in unknown territory, surrounded by enemies, and he'd just earned their ire.

I must survive. No matter how hard they push me down, I refuse to yield. The thought came unbidden, filling his entire being. He felt like he did back in the Forest of the Strong. The time when an earth bear had chased him through the forest came vividly to his mind, until he could even remember the smell of its musky breath and the sound of its hooves stomping on the soil.

This time, there was no bear, but the killing intent surrounding him was almost palpable. These people were going to kill him. He couldn't fight them. He had to escape.

The world slowed as he prepared for battle. The time for words was over. The time to act was nigh.

The other cultivators tensed up, sensing Jack's resolve. Everyone blurred into action at once. All these strong people, who'd been fighting each other before, now turned on Jack. Even if he used the Life Drop, which would cause him endless trouble in the future, there was no way he could win here.

His skin tingled, his legs were filled with power. "Fuck me," he muttered.

And he ran.

"Stop him!" Longsword shouted. Everyone was on him instantly. Shadows flew. Ice tubes grew everywhere. A sparrow flew in faster than sound itself, a hippo charged unstoppably, and a black blade fell from the sky.

Jack ignored everything. This wasn't about victory or minimizing the damage. It was about making it out of the encirclement alive.

He focused on the weakest link and let the sparrow slice his back like a whip, let the tubes dig into his flesh, let the shadows hug and burn his skin. Only Longsword's blade he dodged, Ghost Stepping to the side at the last moment possible and suffering only a cut to the thigh.

Still, he kept running. With his three fused Dao Roots, there were two things that Jack was good at. One was durability and regeneration. His body could take the punishment. Skin and tissue already regrew where he'd been cut, and his body kept moving despite the many wounds. Thanks to his Indomitable Body and two defensive Dao Roots, he could survive.

His other strength... was pure offensive power.

Jack arrived before Bocor, who'd steadied his tower shield and was ready to block anything. If he could stop Jack for just a moment, everyone else would catch up. Unfortunately for Bocor, he was the weakest cultivator present. He wasn't even an Elite.

Jack pulled his fist back. All color and sound was sucked in. The world trembled. The air shimmered around his fist. All that remained was a bright purple meteor, heading directly for the minotaur's shield.

"MOVE!" Jack roared.

Bocor bellowed. He dug his shield into the ground and put his shoulder behind it, doubtlessly activating every defensive skill he possessed.

When the punch landed, the world exploded. A terrible shockwave pushed everyone back and made the sparrow spin. The ground was upturned, the wind burst into a gale. Bocor's shield went flying, as did the minotaur himself, spitting out blood. His entire body took to the air, plate armor and all, as he instantly lost consciousness. His shoulder, which had been propping up the shield, was dislocated.

Jack blew through the defenses without slowing in the slightest. Even his broken wrist was only one injury upon many. His back was burning. He could sense blood flowing down his spine. His left leg faltered every few steps.

He roared and ran. More attacks fell on him—a parting gift. Even burned and flayed, he made it through. He burst out of the encirclement and sphere of attacks like a train emerging from the mist, and he kept running at top speed, with his head down and his entire being focused on just going faster.

His path led straight for the treasure hunters—to the path where they'd come from.

"Stop him!" Longsword shouted, flying after Jack. Now that the latter had increased in level by so much, they were similar in speed.

Thankfully, none of these treasure hunters were stupid. Most were weaker than Bocor. Who would dare stand in Jack's way after seeing what he did to the minotaur?

As for Sage, Dorman, and their teammate Poppy, there wasn't even a question.

"*I will protect Brock*," the Sage told him mentally. It was a welcome thought, because Jack didn't know if he could do that in his current state. A welcome repentance for pushing Jack into the fire.

The treasure hunters stepped over each other to get out of Jack's way, who bulldozed through like a hurricane. He dived into the mist headfirst, with the Top Treasure in his pocket and the galaxy's greatest mortal cultivators on his heels.

In his despair, Jack's plan was simple. Retrace his steps through the mist, go through the traps he already knew how to solve, and exit Trial Garden. By then, he would have hopefully left his pursuers in the dust, which would allow him to pick up Brock, Nauja, and Gan Salin, and escape Trial Planet altogether.

If he still hadn't lost his pursuers by then... he would just turn and fight, and damned be the consequences. These guys were just bullying him. He would rather fall in battle than abandon Brock and run away by himself. Plus, if all went to hell, he could resort to the Life Drop—it might give him a tiny chance of victory.

The mist filled Jack's vision. Even the sounds of footsteps and roars behind him came muffled. Could he outrun them while accurately retracing their path through the mist?

Even with his System-enhanced intelligence and all the titles enhancing its efficacy, he wasn't sure. But he had to try. Because, if he failed at any step, the only viable alternative was death.

CHAPTER ONE HUNDRED THREE
MAKING A DEAL

JACK DASHED THROUGH THE MIST, HOPING HE WAS MOVING IN THE RIGHT direction. Half his mind was occupied with sprinting at full tilt. The other half desperately tried to retrace the path. A third, smaller part was constantly thinking, *fuck-fuck-fuck-fuck*.

There were objects in the mist. A boulder here, a plant there, a mound the other way. Little things that had been completely insignificant on the way in now served as waymarks for his memory to work off of. His field of sight, however, was pitiful. Barely nine feet ahead. His only saving grace was his Dao perception, which had evolved along with his levels and could now scout the environment up to thirty feet around him, if he kept it constantly active. Which he did, despite its energy consumption, because what choice did he have?

Angry stomps and roars came from behind. Longsword and the ice witch, along with Vocrich, the dryad, Minerva, and most of her menagerie were after him—only the turtle had been left behind, as it was too slow.

Longsword could match Jack in combat by himself. Minerva was probably even stronger, and there were also the followers. This wasn't a fight he could handle.

Jack followed the path of the fist. It meant he was proud and unyielding, not that he enjoyed punching walls. Turning to fight now would just be lord-assisted suicide—better to take the pill, run away, breakthrough, then return to pay them back ten times over.

Besides... there was no shame in running away from unfair battles. Especially when he had nothing to lose by running.

Fuck off, you bullies! he screamed inwardly, darting to the left as a large rock entered the range of his perception. His mind worked in overtime, trying to come up with a solution on top of all the other tasks it juggled.

Many things had worked together to reach this point. He'd revealed his previous trick—stealing the Repeat Exploding Orb—to Longsword. Dorman had omitted a critical part of the rules when explaining them. The Sage had given him the experience jewel and mis-predicted the result of Jack's actions. When he finally got hold of the fruit, this death hunt was already bound to occur.

This was all very suspicious. Did the Sage and Dorman plan this? It sounded far-fetched, but with the Sage's divination abilities, it was more than possible. The more he considered it, the more obvious it seemed that he'd been set up. Which left one all-encompassing question: why? Why would they do this? What did they stand to gain?

Jack wrangled his brain and came up with nothing. He couldn't focus on that right now.

Fuck those guys, he concluded. If I survive, I'll fucking punch them in the face! At least they promised to protect Brock... If that's even true.

Survival was a bleak possibility. Just as Jack cut to the left, the dark outline of a blade slashed through the mist beside him, smashing into the stone and searing it in half. Longsword wasn't holding back. Even on Jack's Indomitable Body, those things would hurt.

The most annoying opponent, however, was Minerva's Diamond Winged Sparrow. It possessed extreme speed, far faster than Jack or any of his pursuers. It'd already jumped at him twice, each time trying to tear some tendon or blind him. At least it was weak, and Jack had the reflexes to punch it if it came from a bad angle. It was forced to lurk at the edges of his perception and wait for an opening.

A patch of ground before Jack's feet turned slightly darker. He instantly jumped up, dodging the shadow hand that sprouted from the ground to catch his ankle. As he was airborne, the sparrow swooped in, slashing a deep line on his cheek. He turned his head at the last second, barely shielding his eyes.

Jack cursed under his breath. The sparrow disappeared in the mist, farther than he could perceive, and he landed smoothly, not breaking stride. The wound on his cheek closed, and the blood evaporated. His Indomitable Body and Dao Root of Life—the Life Drop—were a killer combination.

Unfortunately, everything had a price. His regeneration allowed him to withstand the occasional attack, but it sapped at his stamina like crazy. He was panting already, and it hadn't been a minute since he started running. At this pace, he'd run out of energy soon—let alone outrunning his pursuers.

I have to do something, he thought. Tossing the Dao Sprouting Pill into the mist came as an idea. It might distract them. However, that would mean losing the pill, the only reason why he was running to begin with.

The other idea was to activate the Life Drop and face everyone in epic combat. Unfortunately, even with the Life Drop, he would probably die going against two lords at the same time, let alone their followers. Maybe doing both things at once—throwing the pill and then activating the Life Drop when fewer people were left—would work... That was such an ugly solution.

He would keep it as a last resort. Maybe they had far less stamina than him, or they would turn back, afraid of losing their way. In the end, the longer he ran, the more people would run out of stamina and stop chasing, leaving him fewer cultivators to face when he inevitably turned and fought them. With any luck, they would already be exhausted from the previous battle.

Suddenly, two stacks of cages appeared in Jack's perception. His eyes widened. He instantly dived between them, coming across a maze with walls of stacked steel cages. All sorts of beasts slumbered inside them. The moment he set foot in the maze, his stomps woke them up, and they began to rise and howl, awakening their neighbors as a chain reaction that spread across the maze.

Jack remembered this place. It was a trap they'd run into on the way.

Back then, they had found a way through it by being deathly silent and having the two guides divine the best path forward. Now, neither of those options were available. Jack had no option but to stomp through.

On one hand, he remembered the way. The maze wasn't particularly large, and it was full of easy waymarks—the caged beasts. On the other, there were King beasts loose in the maze. One of those might appear in his way, since they'd all wake up soon.

Jack darted around the first corner and heard his pursuers enter. The beasts were making a cacophony that had no equal. Howls, chirps, screams, roars, growls; all sorts of animals were contained here. It was a wondrous place—and also one that deeply pained Jack's heart, seeing all these wonderful animals trapped.

Unfortunately, both the previous time and now, he lacked the ability to do anything about it. He promised to return if he ever found the opportunity.

One corridor gave way to another. The cages bled together. Jack was just running, doing his best to follow the safe path.

Before he knew it, he was out, thanking all the stars in the sky that no King beast had come to face him. His pursuers weren't as lucky. A colossal roar split the mist and threatened to burst Jack's eardrums. Sounds of combat came from behind him, followed by the screams and shouts of cultivators.

Jack breathed a sigh of relief. For once, he'd gotten lucky. Perhaps the beast would slow them down enough for him to escape.

Before he even finished the thought, another roar came through the mist, this one laced with deep pain and fear. They'd already beaten it.

Jack set to running again, cursing his luck. At least he'd earned a second. His feet thundered against the soil. The surroundings zoomed by. His breath came in uneven rasps. The sparrow stalked him still, attacking whenever it saw a fraction of an opening.

Once, Jack's backfist clipped its wings, but all he achieved was to make it slightly more careful.

Blades still flew at him occasionally, shadows tried to entrap him, ice tubes grew at him whenever he made sharp turns. The hippo's roar shook the entire garden. Lady Minerva was eerily silent.

Between dodging all these attacks, remembering the way, and

maintaining top speed, Jack's mind was stretched to its limit. Only the Dao Root of Indomitable Will kept him alive, maintaining his focus razor-sharp. In contrast, his pursuers only had to follow him.

What if I veer off the right path? Jack wondered in a moment of panic, only to beat down the idea. He'd witnessed the deadliness of Trial Garden first-hand. This wasn't a place for E-Grades. Any random trap might end him before he even had the chance to scream.

But I have to do something!

The seconds flowed on. Before he knew it, Jack had already sprinted the distance it'd taken them days to walk. Most traps were already resolved, thankfully, so he could just walk right through them. Unfortunately, there wasn't anything he could activate to hinder his pursuers.

Suddenly, as he charged forth, something new invaded his perception. No—his psyche. It was a deep distaste, a disgusting, gut-wrenching feeling of wrongness. It was so strong and sudden that it almost made him trip.

What the hell is that! he wondered. It took him a second to remember. He knew this feeling. He'd experienced it only a couple days ago, when they ran into that trapped devil. Back then, he'd noticed he was the only person feeling this way—which made sense, given that it originated from his Life Drop, for some reason. He'd also noticed that the feeling persisted for a long time, serving as a sort of compass to the devil's location.

After the devil, the Sage had taken them through a path so needlessly convoluted that nobody could retrace it, returning them to the right path. He'd done the same as they approached. As a result, nobody besides the two guides could find the devil again.

But Jack could. For whatever reason, he had a devil compass inside him.

He eyed the mound before him. The way to the garden's entrance lay to the left. However, his devil compass led him to the right.

He veered right, diving headfirst into the mist. Devils were bad news. And right now, he needed a miracle.

He sensed his pursuers hesitate. They remembered the right path, too, and knew he'd wandered off. They also remembered that they'd met the devil somewhere around here. Undoubtedly, a thousand thoughts went through their minds, but Jack couldn't hear them. If all went well, they would just drop the chase.

They chose to follow. He could hear their footsteps and shouts, sense their attacks and evade them. Everyone remained on his tail. They wanted that pill too damn much.

Jack felt the deep repulsion grow stronger. His strides shortened as he crossed unfamiliar terrain. The distance to reach the devil was actually much closer than anyone might assume. The only risk was the possible existence of traps in the straight line between Jack and the devil, but the distance wasn't too great, and the garden's traps weren't too densely packed.

Suddenly, a presence appeared in Jack's mind. It hovered there, as if watching him from a distance. Jack's spine tingled. Thankfully, he knew how to speak telepathically, as long as the other person opened the connection. *"I will release you! In return, help me escape my pursuers, and never try to harm me, my friends, or my family in any way! I'm giving you a good deal here, so don't try to cheat!"*

This last sentence was the best Jack could do. In his present state, coming up with a waterproof contract was simply impossible.

Manic laughter rang in his mind, along with a deep, seething voice. *"DEAL!"*

The mist opened before him, revealing a twenty-foot-wide circle of magical symbols, with the air shimmering above them and a devil trapped in their midst. It remained an ugly, repulsive creature. Spikes ran down its spine, horns grew on its head, and its hands ended in long, sharp claws.

For a brief moment, Jack wondered whether he was fucking up. Unfortunately, the choice was already made. It was either this or dying to Longsword. He just had to pray.

He punched the air, shooting a stream of Dao at the magic symbols on the ground. It wasn't a Meteor Punch, just a weak Dao expulsion, like the ones he used to move in space.

The symbols shook. The shimmering air shone purple, then evaporated like a burnt sheet. The devil stared at Jack like he couldn't believe it.

"I'M FREE!" it roared. Dark power rose around the devil like a tide.

Jack felt like he was suffocating. The System may have called the devil a King E-Grade creature, but its power was stronger than anything Jack could currently muster. He realized that, if the devil attacked him, he might not survive more than three hits.

But it wouldn't... right?

The devil jumped at Jack. He ducked, cursed, and prepared to defend. The devil's leap turned into flight. It shot over Jack's head, into the mist behind him. Jack's eyes shone as he followed the devil. If it attacked his pursuers, he could help it finish them off.

Screams rang from the mist before he even came within range. An explosion of energy cleared the surrounding mist. Jack spotted Longsword recovering from being sent flying, the hippo lying on the ground with a deep, lethal-looking gash across its belly, and Minerva running away. The ice witch was nowhere to be seen—perhaps she'd turned back, too exhausted to contribute to the chase.

Of course, the difference in power between this devil and the lords wasn't as great as it seemed—they'd just been ambushed and too slow to react.

In the blink of an eye, the devil appeared before Vocrich and cut off his head. There was nothing the vampire could do. He simply died, all his shadows melting into thin air.

"Vocrich!" Minerva shouted.

The devil didn't spare Vocrich's body a second glance. It kept going, reaching the dryad that hid behind the vampire. "Die, you cursed life-wielder!" it shouted, pinning the dryad to the ground. As she screamed, the devil dug both hands into her chest and tore her in half like a pillow. Blood and entrails flew everywhere. The dryad, despite all her healing powers, died instantly.

Jack froze momentarily at the brutality.

"There, I helped," the devil said, pulling back its hands. Its savagery seemed spent on the dryad, and it now sported a wide smile. "Have fun, kids. Thanks for freeing me!"

Then, with a final shout of mad joy, it flew into the mists and disappeared. It was heading in the opposite direction from the garden entrance.

Jack remained frozen, this time in surprise. He glanced at Longsword, who was glaring back full of hatred. "You are dead," he said, voice dripping hatred.

"Shit," said Jack. So much for freeing the devil.

Thankfully, the assault had scattered the pursuers, giving Jack a clean view of the way he had come from. Without a second thought, he started running again, and everyone chased with renewed hatred, leaving the bodies of Vocrich and the dryad, along with the hemorrhaging hippo, to rot in the mist.

CHAPTER ONE HUNDRED FOUR
UTTERLY HUMILIATED

AFTER JACK DISAPPEARED INTO THE MIST, FOLLOWED BY LONGSWORD, MINERVA, and a few of their followers who were determined to get the fruit, everyone else was left in an excited silence. They struggled to comprehend what happened. At the same time, they were brewing with excitement.

To these people, what Jack had done was the equivalent of a particularly spectacular suicide.

As whispers spread, debating the how and why, only two groups of people remained somber. One was the Exploding Sun team, who were equal parts disappointed and puzzled.

The other team was the Barren High. Dorman glared daggers at the Sage and quickly pulled him away from the other treasure hunters, while Poppy remained behind, seemingly nonchalant but actually making sure nobody overheard.

"I trusted you," Dorman whispered, "but they're all gone now. Explain. Why the hell did you give up the Dao Sprouting Pill to Jack Rust?"

The Sage gave Dorman the all-knowing smile he always did. "Ever since Space Ring, I have sensed something odd about Jack. He developed a strong affinity to the Dao of Life. That means he's on our side, and though my fate reading is blurry, I predict that securing his friendship will be more important in the long run than getting the pill."

"But it's the whole reason we came here!" Dorman hissed. "You needed that pill. You can't just throw it away on a whim!"

"I don't *need* it. My immortal breakthrough will come regardless. The pill would just facilitate the process, but waiting a few extra months is no big deal."

"What about the Final Ring? You were supposed to challenge the guardian after getting the eighth ring title. Now what?"

"Yes, we'll have to skip that part. But it's all worth it. Most Dao inheritances are useless to me, and the treasures here are only useful up to the D-Grade at most. If my gamble works out, Jack Rust will be much more beneficial in the long run. Plus, he benefits too, so we sow good karma."

Dorman grumbled. "The greatest treasures of Trial Planet, and all you have to say is, 'we'll have to skip that part...' How is Jack going to escape, anyway? You said not to help him. How are you so sure?"

"That part of fate was easy to read." The Sage laughed. "He will be pushed to his very limits but escape with the pill. He will then wander the galaxy for a few months, surviving all sorts of ordeals, and reach the middle or late D-Grade before requesting our help to deal with the Planetary Overseer. It will be a hard few months for him, but he will grow a lot."

"I guess..." Dorman's gaze darkened. His voice hid doubt. "But, Sage, if you didn't need the pill... Why not give it to me?"

For the first time, the Sage's gaze turned earnest. A bit regretful, even. "Divination is all about calculation, my friend... To be honest, you don't need it either. You have superb talent. Becoming an immortal is a hurdle you will surpass sooner or later, just like me."

Dorman sighed and leaned back. "I trust you, Sage..."

"As you should! In fact, I—" The Sage's head snapped to the side, looking in the direction Jack had escaped in, and his eyes widened. "How!"

Dorman tensed. "How what?"

"Jack found the devil! That's—How did he do that? There was no fate path leading there!"

"The devil? Should we..."

"We should, and right now! There is no time to waste! We can't let it escape!"

Both dashed in the direction of the mist. "Lead the way, Sage!" Dorman shouted. "Poppy, we're running!"

The djinn fell in step. The three darted into the mist, disappearing at a speed that left everyone else stunned. Even Priya, the Exploding Sun lady, raised a shocked brow.

"How did this happen, Sage?" Dorman asked, blue sparks flying where his boots touched the ground.

"His affinity to life must be even stronger than I anticipated!" the Sage replied. As he ran, a green aura wrapped around his body, and his feet smashed against the soil like mallets. "But that's... How? There shouldn't be any treasures that strong in Trial Planet! Did he get one before coming to this place? But where? This was completely outside my predictions!"

"So even the great Sage can be stumped at times," Dorman said, laughing.

"This is no laughing matter, Dorman! I lost track of fate! I don't know what will happen to Jack now. I don't know how he escaped my sight. And, worst of all, that devil will be released. We must contain it *now*!"

The mists parted as they crossed through at top speed. The Sage led them in a straighter line than the one they'd followed on the way in, minimizing their travel distance. They dodged all traps, save for a few they had already solved on the way in.

They made record speed. Before long, they appeared in an empty area which the mist was slowly reclaiming, with dim magic symbols etched on the ground. The corpses of Vocrich, the dryad, and Minerva's hippo lay nearby, but the devil was nowhere to be seen.

"This is bad," the Sage said, lines creasing his brow. He looked around, then closed his eyes. A green halo appeared around his head, a million tiny lines that squirmed around and all fit together in a chaotic pattern that made Dorman's head hurt. A moment later, the Sage's eyes snapped open, and he dashed in a certain direction. "This way!"

Dorman and Poppy followed a step behind.

The Sage's eyes sharpened. Gone was the easygoing old man, and born was the warrior. He leaped into the air, galvanizing his Dao to the fullest. The power he exuded blew away the mists, revealing an area several hundred feet in diameter. In its very midst was the devil, sitting cross-legged and meditating. The moment the Sage appeared, its eyes opened, full of surprise and urgency.

"Leave me alone!" it shouted, jumping to its feet.

The Sage was already above it. He raised an open palm. The surroundings burst with life, a green aura blanketing everything. As it touched the devil, it screeched like it had been burned and raised its arms to defend.

The Sage slapped his palm down. "Die, you foul beast!"

The impact shook the entire garden.

———

Jack was exhausted. His legs were made of lead. His mind, of slog. Dodging the incoming attacks became harder and harder. His Indomitable Will could only handle so much concentration. Even finding the right way was difficult now.

His pursuers remained on track. Longsword bounded after him, long sword in hand and swinging with abandon. Minerva had summoned a new beast to replace the hippo—a boar, which wasn't too suitable for this zigzagging chase. She must have finally ran low on beasts.

Jack couldn't see her, but he imagined her. Pale-skinned and clad in black clothes, riding the boar with rage in her eyes. Because of him releasing the devil, Minerva had lost both her followers and an Elite beast. She must have been *pissed*.

Jack was rapidly running out of options. Running to the devil's location and then back to the right path had used up much of his stamina. Already, black spots covered the edges of his vision. Even if they didn't catch up to him, he couldn't go on much longer.

He still hoped they would run out of energy first, but he wouldn't bet on it. Minerva's boar was brand-new. Longsword only had to focus on running, not finding the way and dodging attacks like Jack. He also didn't have to regenerate his wounds all the fucking time.

The sparrow endlessly pestered Jack, slashing open shallow

wounds. It must have been ordered to do so by Minerva. His regeneration could easily handle those, but it cost him stamina.

Jack could not outrun these people. He could not fight them either. He had nowhere to hide.

Was he a goner? Did he have to hand over the pill and beg for his life?

He would never do that. At the end of the day, Jack followed the path of the fist. No matter how many people depended on him, he would rather turn and fight to the death than surrender, cripple his path, and hope for mercy.

He was almost ready to do that, actually—turn around and fight to the death. There was no salvation in sight. He was already mentally apologizing to Brock for leaving this life early when something familiar entered the range of his perception.

It was a large boulder, standing up from the ground like a small hill. One of its sides had an opening. It was the cave they'd been sealed in shortly after entering Trial Garden. The one that couldn't be opened from the outside.

Jack latched on to this ray of hope like a drowning man would latch on a floating plank. If he rushed in and pulled the lever, they couldn't get to him. They could guard the entrance, of course, but for how long? He had the fruit now. Supposedly, it could let him breakthrough to the D-Grade. He could cultivate with it inside the cave, then come out once he'd broken through and wipe the floor with all the so-called lords.

Suddenly, he saw survival.

The problem was, he'd slightly lost the way due to his exhaustion and imperfect memory. The cave was far to his right, at the edge of his perception range. If he tried to dash there, the lords could catch up and stop him.

But maybe they couldn't. And Jack found comfort in the simplicity of that gamble. If he just punched them hard enough, he would make it to the cave and hopefully survive. If he wouldn't, it would be a battle to the death, anyway.

That was his language.

His feet stomped against the ground as he slid to a halt. He darted sideways. The sparrow fell on him but missed. A series of outlines instantly appeared through the mist—Longsword, Minerva, and her beasts. The only other pursuer was the ice witch, but Jack didn't see her outline.

He was ready.

Besides the Life Drop, which he decided to keep as a final resort, he went all out. The adrenaline returned energy to his body. His pores opened. His breath deepened. His mind sharpened. His clenched fists were wrought in purple aura, slapping away the mist as they began to suck in the essence of the world.

He grinned. This battle would end in a flash. One second of all-out battle.

What more could he hope for?

The moment the first shape emerged from the mist, he fired a Meteor Punch. It detonated on the boar's face. Flesh and bone shards flew everywhere. The boar roared, then veered to the side and toppled over. It wasn't dead, just seriously injured. So was Jack. His hand bone was cracked down the middle, and his regeneration sucked greedily at his remaining energy to repair it.

Lady Minerva, who'd been riding the beast, jumped. Her body arced through the air. Her belt shone, the boar dispersed into motes of light, and a new creature appeared next to Jack. It was a red, horse-sized octopus sitting steadily on the ground—and it flared in his Dao perception harder than her other beasts had. Minerva landed on its head.

"Surrender!" she ordered. "That pill is mine."

This octopus must be her hidden ace, he realized, but there was little time to care. The octopus slapped down with three of its tentacles. He Ghost Stepped out of the way, closer to the cave entrance, then turned and shot a Meteor Punch on its body.

The explosion rocked the mist. The wind whipped Jack's face and pulled at his short hair. The shockwave flung pebbles off the ground.

The octopus made a pained sound. A bloody bruise was visible in the center of its body, but it remained whole. That was fine. Jack's goal wasn't to kill it. He just wanted to unbalance it. Its tentacles could reach the cave entrance, but he had time to sneak through before it recovered.

The only problem was that Longsword stood right in front of the cave entrance. He was an intelligent man. He'd seen through Jack's plan right away and placed himself in the perfect spot to thwart him.

One silver lining was that all this running managed to exhaust the ice witch, who was nowhere to be seen.

A malicious grin played on Longsword's lips as he held his sword horizontally, ready to swing. "You brought this upon yourself," he said, reveling in Jack's dead-end. "You deserve this."

"Sure I do," Jack replied, stepping heavily before Longsword and readying a Meteor Punch. "Because I will survive."

He roared. His fist became a beacon of purple in a dark world. A herald of destruction. A carrier of power.

Longsword slashed. His nine-foot-long sword curved through the air like a whip, meeting Jack's fist with its very tip, where it was strongest. Steel and flesh collided. Color and sound returned to the world. A massive explosion cracked the stone and peeled the ground. Jack felt the shockwave on his chest. Longsword's tattered cloak billowed so hard it left his shoulders, flying into the cave mouth behind him.

For a moment, they remained frozen in their stances, neither willing to give ground. They pushed with all their might, pouring all their energy into their strikes. Both roared; a clash of masters.

This clash proved identical to their previous one, in the battle for the Top Treasure. Back then, it had been a draw, which is why Longsword tried the same thing now, investing fully in the attack. He wasn't afraid of losing the exchange, and he didn't need to win, either. If he just delayed Jack, Minerva's octopus would catch up, and they would overwhelm him.

However, he missed something. When Jack grabbed the Dao Sprouting Pill, his title had been upgraded to Eighth Ring Conqueror. He'd gotten an extra 5% efficacy in all his stats. This made him slightly stronger than in their previous clash.

And, in a battle between masters, every little thing matters.

Jack's fist pushed back the sword. An inch led to a mile, and he overwhelmed Longsword. With a crack, his wrist snapped. His sword flew back. The remnants of the explosion smashed right into Longsword's chest, shooting him backward into the rock, which didn't budge in the slightest. He took the entirety of the impact. He groaned as all air was pushed out of his lungs, plastered as he was with his back against the stone, then landed wobbly on his feet.

Jack hadn't budged. He glanced at Longsword's broken wrist, then winked and said, "I warned you."

He dashed into the cave. Longsword, however, wasn't done. His eyes bulged like they were about to pop out, both from humiliation and rage. He didn't even register the pain. Jack had cheated him, tricked him, and now overpowered him head-on. He was three to zero. By all accounts, he was simply superior!

And Longsword couldn't take that. He couldn't lose like this.

With a massive bellow, he overdrew on his Dao Seed. Cracks spread across it as Longsword forced his body to move before it was ready, forcing his Dao to circulate and lash out. He grabbed his sword with his other hand and slashed out.

He just needed to delay Jack for a split-second. Outrunning this blow was impossible. Jack would have to defend, the octopus would catch up, and he would lose.

Jack flung something at Longsword. It was a gray orb. Longsword instantly recalled the terrifying explosion from last time. In panic, he hurriedly stopped his strike midway, further injuring himself, and pulled back his blade to defend.

The pebble touched his blade and harmlessly slid to the ground.

"Hihihi," it snickered. It was the Ticklish Pebble.

Longsword froze. He couldn't believe this. In his entire life, he'd never felt more humiliated than in this moment. His entire body erupted with rage until all his previous injuries were aggravated and he spat blood. He stomped at the pebble, but it was a magical item, and he only managed to hurt his foot.

He was so furious that he couldn't even speak properly. "JACK RUST!" was all he managed to scream.

Jack met his glare with a smirk from inside the cave. If Longsword had carried on with his attack, Jack would have been forced to use the Life Drop or die, trapped between two lords.

Thank God he's an idiot.

Jack rose his hand to grab the lever and pull it down. The stone slab above the entrance crashed into the ground, sealing the cave. The last thing he saw was an octopus tentacle rushing his way a fraction of a second too late, along with Longsword who was frothing at the mouth in anger and humiliation.

The slab cut off the cave from the outside world. Sealing Jack in darkness.

CHAPTER ONE HUNDRED FIVE
IMPOSSIBLE?

IT WASN'T JUST LIGHT THAT WINKED OUT. ALL SOUND FROM OUTSIDE disappeared as well, and all Dao perception was blocked by the walls.

Jack stayed still in absolute darkness, panting heavily. He remained exhausted from the chase and battle. He still couldn't believe he was safe. Maybe Longsword would barge in at any moment, angrier than anyone had ever been. Jack was ready to unleash his Life Drop and fight to the death.

Only after a few long moments, when nothing disturbed the silence of the sealed cave, did Jack accept that he was safe—for now. He breathed a deep sigh of relief. He'd escaped with the Top Treasure. He'd gotten the Eighth Ring Conqueror title. Everything had worked out.

Except for the fact that he was sealed in a lightless cave, maybe forever, while Brock was out there with his enemies.

The thought pained Jack's heart. There were times in one's life when you had to make the hard choice. When you had to trust your bros, treat them as equals, and not shield them from everything.

If he always had to worry about his enemies turning back to retaliate against his friends and family, he would never do anything. In this case, Brock was nowhere even close to the action. He was off doing his own thing. Jack's enemies had no reason to go after Brock—if they did, they would just be dishonorable and petty to no benefit.

Therefore, Jack chose the only path that could lead to victory: seal himself, breakthrough, and return to take care of things. As for what would happen outside in the meantime... he could only hope.

The highest expression of brohood was not being afraid to risk each other. That was also the way of the fist. Not simply ahead. But taking the truly strong path.

Thinking up to that point, Jack put the outside matters out of his mind. All he could do was focus on the present. He was sealed in a cave, with the task of breaking through as soon as possible.

How long will it take? he wondered. The darkness and silence were crushing. They applied a unique weight on his soul. *Is this how prisoners feel in isolation?*

It wasn't pretty. Not at all. He could already feel his sanity threatened. How was he supposed to cultivate in these conditions? Could he even break through?

Wait! I still haven't scanned the fruit!

Amidst the previous, exciting battle, he'd completely forgotten about this. Reaching for his secret pocket, he quickly took out the pill and scanned it.

Dao Sprouting Pill

A pill designed to assist the sprouting of a cultivator's Dao Tree. Each bite cleanses the cultivator's spirit and heightens their Dao sensitivity, allowing them to comprehend it more efficiently than usual. If the cultivator attempts to sprout their Dao Tree under this pill's effects, the pill's energy remnants place them in a state of artificial enlightenment, greatly assisting the breakthrough.
Unlike similar pills of lower quality, consuming the Dao Sprouting Pill carries no drawbacks.

The pill resembled a blood-red apple and had even grown from a tree. Jack failed to see how this was a pill, but it wasn't like he cared much. If the System wanted to call it a pill or a shoe, that was its problem. All Jack cared about was breaking through—which, it seemed, this pill would help him achieve.

And then, he would be an immortal. His chest inflated with pride.

But what if I fail? he couldn't help but wonder. Breaking through to the D-Grade is supposed to be much more difficult than to the E-Grade, and I've cultivated for such a short time... What if, even with the pill's assistance, I'm still not ready?

Will I be trapped here forever?

He had a deadline to catch. Defeat the Planetary Overseer and reclaim Earth within a year, or at least find allies who could do it for him. He also had to find Brock and make sure he was okay—as well as let him know that he, too, was okay.

Even if it doesn't work, I have to wait long enough to ensure that Longsword and the others have left... But will I even be able to exit?

The anxiety ate away at him. Three lords had worked together to unseal this place before. Could he do it by himself if he didn't break through?

Tentatively, he approached the stone slab and placed a palm on its surface. It was cool and smooth, as if cut with a single slash. Closing his eyes, he sensed for the Dao vacuum, found it, and slowly poured in his Dao. He didn't want to open it by accident, just check how difficult it was.

As time passed, his brows creased. He poured more and more of his Dao-clad energy inside the stone, but not much happened. The vacuum was filling up way too slowly. From the time he started to when he ran out of energy, only a fourth had been filled.

Granted, he was already tired from the battle and chase before, but he estimated that, even at full power, he could barely fill up half of this vacuum. As if that wasn't enough, the vacuum constantly leaked energy to its surroundings, meaning he couldn't take his time to recover before continuing. He had to fill it up in one go.

Which, at his current level, was clearly impossible. Even the Life Drop couldn't assist much here—it would at most let him reach 70% of the vacuum's capacity.

Jack didn't let this realization bring him down. He already planned to break through. By then, he would certainly have enough energy to fill up this thing. If he failed...

It's okay. Pressure helps with breakthroughs, he comforted himself, already sweating—and not just from exhaustion. He was trapped in a dark, sealed cave. He didn't even have food and water. If he failed to break through, this place would become his grave.

———

Longsword slammed the pommel of his sword against the stone slab and roared in outrage.

"It won't budge," Minerva said from the side, eyeing the entire small hill. "You already tried, Longsword. Calm yourself."

"How can I possibly stay calm?" Longsword thundered. "Did you not see what he did?"

Minerva gave him a deep look. In truth, she didn't need to say anything. Longsword already knew that this was all a result of his own incompetence. Getting tricked by Jack once, through unlucky circumstances and the use of an unknown treasure, was one thing. Getting tricked twice by a treasure he already knew existed... That was just his fault.

If only I hadn't pulled back to defend... he thought for the thousandth time, gnashing his teeth. Victory had been in his grasp before he completely threw it away. Even thinking about it made him feel sick, angry, and humiliated.

Unfortunately, there was no medicine for regret.

"What's done is done," Minerva said, leaning against the side of her Elite boar. "Let's focus on our next steps."

"Right," Longsword agreed. He passed a hand through his long, dark hair, trying to calm himself. "Jack Rust is trapped inside. He chose to die with the pill rather than give it to us—what a frustrating idiot."

"You have to admire his resolve, though. Sealing your own grave is not an easy feat."

Longsword glared at her. "Don't rub salt in my wound."

"I won't lie, either. You made a mistake. It happens. Get over it."

Longsword debated striking her. Perhaps he could get a sneak attack in...

What am I even thinking? he chided himself. She's right. I need to compose myself... But she doesn't understand how I feel. She has never been humiliated before. Neither had I, until...

Another burning stake through his heart. Another blue pit at the bottom of his stomach. He grimaced.

"Are we sure he's trapped?" he asked. He yearned for Jack to get out. If he didn't personally strike him down, he may never recover from this hit to his pride. His confidence would always have a hole—and a nicked sword was a poor sword.

"You sensed that Dao storage thing as well as I did," Minerva replied. "It takes at least two lords to fill it up. Even if he has some treasure that can temporarily enhance him, it will never make him double as strong. There is no way he can lift the stone slab."

"Hmm..." Longsword thought back to Jack's face as he pulled the lever. His eyes were hard as he said, "I will survive." Forcing down the hatred that sprang in his soul, Longsword examined those memories. "He didn't look like a dead man. More like he had a plan."

"Could he know another way out of the cave? Hmm. I remember that, when we exited this cave, we found no treasure. No reward. Maybe there is another way to resolve it which we simply didn't find."

Longsword shook his head. "I spoke to the merfolk guide afterward. Traps like these don't usually have a reward. The cave itself is the reward. They are the cultivation chambers of ancient immortals, meant to isolate them from the environment. Cultivating in there is more efficient than outside, which I suppose for whoever made this place considered it a reward... but not for us. E-Grades can't even pull the door handle of an immortal's cultivation chamber. For the same reason, there is no other way to exit. Why would someone need a backdoor to their cultivation chamber?"

"Makes sense." Minerva nodded. "Then, if Jack Rust thought there was a way out, what could it be? Did he misunderstand something about the cave?"

Both considered it. Longsword came to a realization that made his loss to Jack seem even worse, and his face paled. "I think I know. He must be planning to use the pill to breakthrough inside the cave."

Minerva raised both brows. "No!"

"Think about it. He was just Integrated a few months ago. He doesn't know anything about cultivation. He didn't even know the rules around the Top Treasure."

"Surely he's not *that* ignorant," she insisted. "Not only is it extremely difficult to become an immortal, even if he could do it, it's impossible to break through inside Trial Planet. The very essence of this planet forbids that, in the same way immortals cannot enter. There is no way he doesn't know that."

"I hope you're right. Maybe he hopes to get an extra Dao Root and escape? But that's crippling himself. He will never become an immortal."

"Plus, it still wouldn't be enough. One Dao Root doesn't double one's power."

"Right."

Again, they fell silent. A few moments later, Minerva said, "Nothing comes to mind. I think he really did choose suicide to keep us away from the fruit. What a headstrong man."

Longsword grumbled. "Let's search around the hill. Maybe there's another way to enter or exit, despite what the merfolk said. We can't rest until we're certain he's trapped forever."

"Very well. Let's do that."

Over the next hour, the two of them searched every nook and cranny of the rough hill. They scanned every inch for Dao vacuums. They tried to break everything. They even dug under the hill to find a way in, but it was all one big boulder. It was magically enhanced, too, so they couldn't chip a single pebble despite using their strongest attacks. Moreover, the stone slab was completely immovable and impenetrable.

When the rest of the group finally arrived, including Priya and the Sage, who looked like he'd been through a battle, the two lords were forced to call it quits. There was no way to enter or exit the cave besides the obvious. They even asked the others if they had any ideas, but even the Sage and the formation masters shook their heads.

The Sage said, "In all honesty, I hadn't predicted this. I really don't see any way he can exit. No matter what line of fate I inspect, all show Jack dying in there."

"Speaking of," Minerva said, "you were the one who gave him an experience jewel, weren't you?"

He smiled, showcasing a line of yellow teeth. "It was an honest exchange. I got a Snow White Globe! If he later used the jewel to harm your interests, that has nothing to do with me."

She gave him a deep look, then nodded slowly. He kept his smile up throughout. "There is one final thing we need to inspect," she finally said, turning away from the Sage. "Jack Rust has a pet beast. Perhaps they have a special way to communicate or transfer energy, which would allow him to exit the cave. Let's take a look at that brorilla."

"Of course," Longsword replied, grasping his sword's handle. "Just a small, harmless look."

CHAPTER ONE HUNDRED SIX
KICKING AN IRON WALL

TWO PEOPLE WERE RESTING OUTSIDE THE ENTRANCE OF BEAST GARDEN, SITTING cross-legged and sipping from a gourd that seemed to never run out. Mist rolled behind them, occasionally revealing the shapes of bushes, trees, or resting, lumbering figures. Gan Salin was describing his adventures in Mind Garden, adding quite a bit of flair.

"And then—bam! The snail overlord couldn't handle my impeccable reasoning and toppled to the ground. There was foam in her mouth, too —I think I gave her insanity."

Brock laughed, sipping from his gourd. "Nice, bro!" he said.

Salin puffed out his chest. "Of course it was nice. As if genius could compare with insanity!"

Each person could only access one garden in Garden Ring. If they tried to enter a second, they would find themselves blocked by an invisible barrier. Therefore, both done with their gardens, Brock and Salin rested together while they waited for Jack.

The reason they chose to wait at the entrance of Beast Garden, and not Trial Garden, was that Nauja was still in the nearby Weapons Garden, standing on a hill and shooting arrows at another. From where they sat, they had a good view of her mostly fruitless efforts to master the Sun Piercing Arrow.

They'd already waited for several hours when shapes appeared in the distance. Both their attentions zeroed in to find a procession of humanoid figures, led by a black-dressed woman and a man wielding a long sword.

"Where's Jack?" Salin asked, scanning the procession. Brock's face tightened. Before long, the group had approached within shouting range. "Hey!" Salin yelled at them. "Did you guys forget Jack?"

"Hello, my canine friend!" the Sage shouted from just behind the leaders. "You can say that, yes."

Salin heaved a sigh of relief. Brock only nodded, like this was natural. His big bro couldn't die.

It was only when the lord group reached them that they realized they seemed battered. Longsword, who walked at the forefront, had a head of messy hair, blood smears on his face and clothes, and seemed paler than usual. The Sage was unhurt, but his shirt sported a long tear down the middle. Several people were absent, too, including Vocrich and the Hand of God dryad. And Jack, of course.

All the treasure hunters were gone, as they no longer had a reason to stay.

The Sage walked ahead to explain the situation.

"I'm happy to see you both in good shape," he said with a smile. "Our excursion, however, wasn't bloodless. We lost several members. As for our common friend, he is currently trapped in a sealed cave of Trial Garden. It is unknown whether he can escape or not."

"How did that happen?"

"He was running away from me." Longsword stepped forward. He was in a terrible mood. His usually composed eyes hid twin storms, and his posture indicated that he was ready to cause trouble. "Jack Rust broke the rules of a Garden Assault to steal the Top Treasure. He then ran away like a coward, released a devil to stop us, and sealed himself in a cave to escape our pursuit."

Brock snorted as he stood. "No," he said. Big Bro was neither a thief nor a coward. If he took the treasure, it was fair. If he ran away, it was not out of cowardice.

Of course, his miming fell on blind eyes.

"Are you doubting me, monkey?" Longsword asked.

"Yes."

"Good. Good! That makes things easier. We know you are his spiritual companion. Speak! Do you have a way to communicate with him or transfer him energy?"

Brock snorted and did not respond. He refused to be intimidated by an enemy.

"Well, have it your way." Longsword smirked. "We don't actually need your permission. Minerva, could you please use your tamer skills to deep-scan this beast? Then, everything will be made clear."

"Of course," she replied. "But I need it immobilized and within arm's reach."

"That's easy." Longsword stepped forward, only for a lean man to stand before him.

"Hey, do you think I'm invisible?" Salin said.

Longsword's face contorted with disgust, as if a middle E-Grade standing up to him was an insult. He wouldn't even soil his hands by acting personally. "Not invisible, *weak*. Bocor."

"This is not a good idea," the Sage intervened calmly. "I would advise you to stop."

Everyone ignored him. Having been summoned, Bocor stepped threateningly toward Gan Salin. "Move, or I'll make you."

"Hah. Give it a try, bitch."

Bocor growled. He made to attack.

Suddenly, the mist behind Brock and Gan Salin parted. They'd been sitting with the mist only a few dozen feet behind them. Now, that same mist contorted and bent like it was blown at by a dozen giants. One shape after another emerged.

The largest creatures were a lion with a mane of fire, a giant gorilla with four arms, and a millepede the height of a horse. These three were elites at the peak of the E-Grade. Nine more beasts followed, each at least at the high E-Grade. The desert lizard and frog, that Brock had rescued from the first tamer, were included.

All glared at Longsword.

Everyone in the lords' group gaped. Even Bocor, who had been about to attack, froze mid-step. "What the—"

"Bros!" Brock said in elation. He looked at Longsword sideways and wagged his finger. "No. Bad bro."

"Brock is our bro," said the four-armed gorilla, crossing his arms in two sets of two. His glare was hard. "You mess with him, you mess with us."

Longsword's face was trembling. Not only had a bunch of beasts appeared out of nowhere to challenge him, but Brock even wagged his finger! Everything was so damn nonsensical and frustrating when Jack Rust was involved.

At the next moment, he remembered he was a lord and kept his composure. "Minerva?" he said. Unfortunately, she was even more troubled than him.

"I have no idea," she said. "Not even I could command all these beasts. I think they are here of their own volition."

"What are you staring at, pipsqueak?" asked the gorilla. "I already told you, you can't mess with our bro. Beat it."

Longsword was incensed. First, Jack Rust had defeated and humiliated him. Now, some random beasts were insulting him, and he was struggling to even touch Jack Rust's *monkey*, an Elite beast that was only level 81! He didn't know if he should shout or cry.

How did I go from the top of the world to... this?

This Garden Ring had been the worst experience of his life. He refused to take it anymore. His eyes quickly ran over the people behind him. Bocor and Eralda—the ice witch—were with him. Minerva was at his side, but she had no followers left. Priya was against him, but would she actively fight him just to protect a monkey? As for the Sage and his two followers...

There was something about this man that put Longsword on edge. Unconsciously, he already regarded the Sage on the level of the lords, even though the latter had shown no indication of power besides his outstanding divination.

The Sage's gaze warned Longsword to be cautious. So was Priya's.

However, if he stepped back now, what would remain of his honor?

"That's right," Gan Salin said, "put your tail between your legs and run. Even lords cannot stand up to the Brotherhood!"

Longsword had considered running away. Not anymore. He met Bocor's eyes and nodded slightly. The minotaur bellowed and raised his tower shield to slam it down on Gan Salin's head—with Bocor at level 119, the two of them had a forty level difference, so it should be quick.

"Keep my lord out of your dirty mouth!" he bellowed.

"I don't even like men!" Salin said. He jumped to the side, dodging the first attack as Bocor prepared to unleash a second.

Many things happened at the same time. A sharp sound came from the distance—it was sharp yet drawn-out, like someone was sucking at the entire world with a spiked straw. Before Bocor could react, an arrow was approaching his head at incredible speed, clad in a mantle of multi-colored energy. In fact, the more it traveled, the stronger and faster it got!

On a distant hill, Nauja's face glowed with satisfaction. This was the first time she successfully used a Sun Piercing Arrow. Pressure did help one break through.

Bocor couldn't react to this arrow, but Longsword could. He made his decision in a split-second and swung his long sword to intercept it. Lightning flashed. Blue light washed over him. A young man with slim features stood before Longsword, blocking the strike with his two obsidian daggers—Dorman Whistles.

The arrow kept going. It struck Bocor in the ribs and unleashed a piercing explosion into the minotaur. His plate armor shook, barely saving his life. Waves of piercing energy still ran over him, slicing open his skin. He flew sideways like a ragdoll, rolling on the ground until finally slamming down the base of his tower shield to stop himself.

Longsword's eyes narrowed. His sword had been blocked by a random follower of the Sage. That was an insult. He jumped back and swung again, properly aiming at Dorman this time. The sword cracked through the air like a whip. Dorman's daggers were even faster. The young man accelerated so rapidly it seemed unreal. Lightning coursed through his entire body and raised his hair into spikes. His twin daggers shone with lightning-shaped veins and crashed at Longsword's chest from the left and right simultaneously, like a centipede's fangs.

Longsword had to abandon his strike and fall back, taking only a scratch to the chest, which was still enough to send a lightning burst through his body. He lost his breath and struggled to right himself. "What—"

Dorman grinned. "If you were at your best, you could fight me... but you're injured now. Step back."

Longsword's eyes widened.

At the same time, a van-sized boar came at Dorman from the side, charging him headfirst. It was Minerva's summoned beast, an Elite at the peak of the E-Grade. Dorman didn't even look in its direction. The head of a mallet appeared before the boar, meeting its forehead with pure strength. Bone cracked and split. The boar's tremendous charge was stopped like it'd crashed into a steel wall, and it bounced back, dropping to the ground and not standing again. Poppy landed lightly on the ground, holding her mallet like nothing had happened.

The moment Bocor recovered from the Sun Piercing Arrow, Salin was already on him, five fingertips glistening like diamonds. "Five Star Grasp!" he shouted. Bocor bellowed and barely managed to reposition his shield in time. He blocked well. But there was no time to block the stone staff that flew at his cheek, slapping him so hard that two teeth flew out and his entire body spun around itself once and fell to the ground.

He didn't lose consciousness, but he was momentarily dazed. Brock put the Staff of Stone back on his shoulder and smiled. "Revenge," he said.

"Damn right," Salin agreed, high-fiving the brorilla. They grinned at each other.

All these things happened in the span of a single second. Everyone was still reeling when the legion of animal bros moved forward as one, ready to crash into the lord's group.

The Sage raised his hands. Green energy seeped out to heal both Bocor and Longsword, making all their wounds disappear like they were never there in the first place.

"Let's not escalate, everyone," he said calmly, smiling. "What's done is done. How about we all go our separate ways?"

GAN SALIN'S INSANITY

THE ANIMAL BROS HESITATED, GLANCING AT BROCK FOR HIS OPINION. AFTER thinking on it, the brorilla nodded. Bocor hurriedly stood and stormed away, bottling his humiliation as he waited for Longsword's instructions.

However, all three lords were frozen. Even Longsword had forgotten that he'd just been pushed back and humiliated yet again. There were more important matters at hand.

Both followers of the Barren High team had just demonstrated the strength of lords out of nowhere—and they weren't even the leaders of their team.

What the heck!

Even Priya, who hadn't participated in this fight, laughed bitterly. Only now did she understand just how doomed this Garden Assault was. Even if Jack Rust didn't emerge out of nowhere to take the Top Treasure, the Barren High team would have. They certainly possessed the strength. All three of the lords thought they were the main charac-ters... but, in truth, they never stood a chance.

"Who are you?" Minerva asked, staring at the Sage. He smiled.

"Just an old man who likes making friends."

"Of course you are," she replied, giving him a deep look. "And you represent the Barren High, yes?"

"So it seems."

"Then tell them to hide their allegiances better. The Hand of God does not take well to insults."

The Sage's mouth widened, a yellow-toothed grin full of hidden meaning. "I have no idea what you're talking about."

"Of course you don't." Another long look later, she turned and walked away. "I already got everything I can. I'm departing Trial Planet. Good luck, everyone."

Longsword wasn't as quick to let the matter drop. When the shock of revelation passed, he realized that he'd once again ran into a wall. This Garden Assault was a disaster. He hadn't even found a Dao Inheritance for himself.

In the span of a few hours, he had been mocked, tricked, outsmarted, defeated, and intimidated. What *lord*? He was just a peasant!

How would he ever live down this failure?

And for all those, one way or another, were due to one person. "Jack Rust..." he muttered, gritting his teeth. There was no one he hated more than that man. Everything happened because he chose to spare Jack Rust back in Village Ring, thinking he could recruit him—even if he didn't, how much could a middle E-Grade affect things?

Unfortunately, there was no medicine for regret. Longsword had lost wholly and decisively—in everything. At his present state, he couldn't even beat the lightning-dagger-wielder, let alone the Sage, the djinn with the mallet, or the army of beasts.

Bile rose so high inside him that he almost puked. Only the intense despair to protect his last shred of dignity allowed him to swallow it back down.

"I will remember this," he said, eyeing everyone present. Mercifully, nobody responded—besides Brock, who gave him the finger. Longsword pretended not to see it—the most painful moment of his life. He turned around, and without another word, walked to the pedestal that could teleport him out of Trial Planet. Bocor followed, equally brimming with fury and not daring to look back.

"A shame," Dorman said, sighing. "I was looking forward to a good fight... Next time, I guess."

Priya walked up to Gan Salin, Brock, and the Sage, who were

standing close together. "I won't ask what is going on here," she said with a wry smile. "I thought Jack Rust was gone forever... but, after everything I've seen today, I believe he'll somehow make it out alive. Take this."

She tossed a medallion at Brock, who grabbed it out of the air. It was slightly larger than his palm, made of bronze, and depicted a sun in the middle of exploding.

"If Jack does make it out, give him this," she said. "It allows him to contact our faction. If not... Well, you can keep it. The Exploding Sun would welcome a brorilla as talented as yourself."

Brock inspected the medallion. He tried to bite it, but it proved too hard. He shrugged and slipped it in his pocket. "Okay," he said, extending a hand.

Priya shook it with amusement. "I'm sorry things had to go this way. I suspect I couldn't change anything even if I tried. I wish you and your, uh, big brother, the best of luck."

"Me too!" Chuto added from the side, roaring in laughter. "What a man he was! And you too, brother Brock—I look forward to training alongside you in the Exploding Sun courtyards."

Brock nodded politely.

"If there is nothing else, we will be going now," Priya said, eyeing the Sage. "I suspect I'll hear more about you soon."

"You never know," he replied playfully, "because you're not a sage. I wish you reach immortality, Lady Priya."

She seemed taken aback. "You too," she replied, then turned around. "See you all."

Chuto and Kareena followed her after bidding their goodbyes. Only Brock, Gan Salin, the Sage, Dorman, and Poppy were left—along with Brock's bro army and Nauja on the distant hill, who was now shooting Sun Piercing Arrows in a different direction.

"As embarrassing as this is to say," the Sage confessed, "I actually have no idea what is going on with Jack. I cannot tell you if he will escape or not—he has already surprised me multiple times. His fate is one that even I cannot read—not yet, in any case."

"He will," Gan Salin said confidently. "Imagine if, after all this, he just dies in a random cave somewhere."

The Sage laughed, then described what really happened with Jack, along with the specifics of where he was trapped. "We won't be sticking around," he finished. "There is urgent business in our headquarters, and the road to immortality is too long to wait. What about you?"

Brock pointed at the ground. He was certain that Jack would find a way to survive. He would stay and wait for his big brother—besides, he had many things to think about, like the Big Thought of Density. Not to mention that staying here would give him more time to spread brohood among the beasts of Beast Garden.

"I'll stay, too," Salin said. "I'm in no rush to return. Plus, I think I'm still wanted by my faction. Whoopsie."

"I think they'll forget about it rather quickly when they see that Seventh Ring Conqueror title you have," the Sage replied smilingly. "And I suppose your archer friend will stay, too?"

"Probably. She's never left this planet. A few days won't make a difference."

"In that case, I commend your friendship. If I'm being honest, I would rate Jack's chances of survival pretty low... I am familiar with the trap he's in, and I don't see any way he could escape, given his current strength. But who knows? He has already proven himself beyond my sight. Maybe I'm wrong."

"For sure you are. Jack wouldn't die in some random cave," Salin insisted. "Well then. If you're going, let us walk you to the pedestal."

"It would be our honor."

After bidding a temporary goodbye to Brock's beast bros, who felt uncomfortable leaving Beast Garden for extended periods of time, the five of them walked to the entrance of Garden Ring, making small talk along the way. Everyone who'd left earlier had hurried, and they were already behind the horizon of this ring's sharp curvature.

When they arrived, Dorman eyed the giant, solitary gate in the middle of the grassland but didn't walk over. It was clear that, with his current strength, he didn't think he stood any chance against the Final Guardian.

"Can I have a moment with you, Sage?" Salin asked when they reached the pedestal. The Sage, whose hand was already gliding over it, paused.

"Certainly," he replied.

"Sage," Dorman said, but the old man only shook his head.

"I'll be fine."

Dorman stared at Gan Salin for a moment, who only shrugged. "We'll be waiting outside," he said. Both he and Poppy touched the pedestal and disappeared. Brock, too, walked away to give them privacy after bidding his goodbye to the Sage.

"What is it, my friend?" the Sage asked, turning to Gan Salin. They were alone now.

Gan Salin's face was hard. His smile, a fake one. "You're a Sage. Wouldn't you know what I have to say?"

"I do."

"Heh... but your predictions are not always correct, are they? Back in Space Ring, you said we shouldn't dally there because all our fates laid deeper inside. Jack found his. So did Nauja. But I... No matter how I searched Mind Garden, there was no Dao Inheritance suitable for me. In this trip to Trial Planet, my first and last opportunity to make a difference, I failed to find an inheritance—a benefit even greater than the titles." He fell silent for a moment. Seeing that the Sage didn't respond, he added, "Tell me, Sage. Did I do something wrong? Did you get it wrong? Or..." His eyes darkened. "Did you lie to me?"

The Sage gave Salin a sad, tight smile. "You already know the answer."

"I want to hear it."

He sighed. "I apologize, my friend, although I know an apology now means little. I did lie to you. My faction has vested interest in Jack's future, so I guided events in a way that would maximize his benefits. I knew that, if you didn't leave Space Ring quickly, he might miss out. In truth, the Trial meant for you was in Space Ring, just a few hours away from where we met."

"I see... So you wasted my potential to help Jack."

"I did. And, while it is sad, it was a decision I had to make for the larger picture. I had to sacrifice you and betray your trust. I am sorry."

Salin sighed deeply, throwing his head back. "You have balls to say that to my face... Aren't you afraid I'll lash out at you? You're only a Soul cultivator. At this distance, a surprise attack from me could end you."

"I know you wouldn't. After all, I am a Sage—a gift and a curse, somet—"

Salin's hand emerged from Sage's back. It was bloody—and, between its five shining nails, rested a still-beating heart.

"That's the cool thing about insanity, Sage," he said, pulling his hand back with a wet splash. "It's unpredictable."

The Sage toppled backward. His eyes remained open in shock and disbelief. He couldn't comprehend what happened.

Salin stepped back and looked at the body with sadness. "You may have been a good man, but you ruined my life."

All at once, green winds filled Salin's vision. They radiated a force of life so intense that he had to shield his eyes and move away. He felt his entire body grow alive in a way he'd never experienced before. It made no sense.

"Divination is a path of Life, and Life is Balance wrapped around Chaos," a voice came from inside the green winds, which were tussling and turning like ribbons. "When either element is pushed to the extreme, you get entropy... A concept outside the realm of life. How could I forget such a simple rule?"

The winds disappeared, sucked into the body of the Sage, who stood whole like his heart had never been ripped out. A green halo stood over his head, and a heavy pressure bore down on Gan Salin's heart. Only the Sage's pale face and slight panting indicated any sort of exertion.

Gan Salin was stunned. He'd clearly just killed the Sage. Not even D-Grade healers could repair a torn heart. Jack's regeneration, which everyone hailed as extreme, didn't even come close to this.

This didn't make any sense. It was insanity.

"How!" Salin asked, more in shock than fear.

"Like everyone, I have my secrets," the Sage replied. There was a hint of strictness in his smile, the threat of a storm thinly veiled. "You tried to kill me. Should that go unpunished?"

"I mean, you started it."

"I did." The Sage's green halo disappeared, and the pressure in Gan Salin's soul melted. The Sage turned away. "While your intentions were clear, you caused me no real harm. I, on the other hand, had good intentions but harmed you greatly. All bad karma has been resolved. After this, we are even. Are we not?"

Salin nodded, surprised he wasn't dead yet. "That makes sense."

"Good. But, Salin... The road of entropy is not one you want to walk.

As you advance, you will grow deranged and disastrous to everyone around you. Eventually, your friends will become enemies, and someone will have to end you. Don't choose that path. Water down your wine. Add a Dao Root of Order to your Dao Seed, so you can freely walk the path of insanity without fearing entropy. Add balance to your chaos. That will be enough."

"I... will consider it. Thanks."

The Sage turned and gave a tight smile. "No problem." Then, his hand pressed on the pedestal, and he was gone.

It was right then that Brock arrived, having run over from where he stood the moment he sensed Salin's attack and the green winds. "What?" he asked.

"I have no idea," Salin replied, still reeling. "But I think the Sage gave me a good idea. Oh, well. Jack is still in his cave, and who knows how long he'll stay there. What do you say we drink some more, then cultivate?"

Brock glanced at the ground, where drops of crimson blood glowed unnaturally against the grass, then at Salin's smiling face. "Sure," he said.

CHAPTER ONE HUNDRED EIGHT
CLOSED DOOR CULTIVATION

JACK WAS ALONE. IN THE DARK.

There was no source of heat or light in the cave. Nothing flammable, besides his clothes and hair. Even if he snapped his fingers hard enough to create sparks, all he achieved was a momentary respite from the darkness, a hollow light that accentuated the walls and floor of his prison.

He had to escape. He had to reach the D-Grade.

Jack knew some things about cultivation now. Rushing headfirst into his most difficult breakthrough yet would be a fool's errand. He needed to prepare as best as possible—work on his Dao until the only thing left to do was break through.

Thankfully, he had time. He sat down, closed his eyes, and began to meditate.

The first few days passed easily. Though the darkness bore a crushing weight, Jack's heart was as stable as a mountain. He sat cross-legged in the center of the main room, closing his eyes out of habit, and focused on his breathing. The loneliness didn't daunt him. Neither did the stakes. There was only him and the Dao.

He made some progress. Sinking into his soul world, he practiced against Copy Jack, finetuning his new Meteor Punch a little. He got a sense of where the skill's limits lay, as well as exactly how much energy it required—turns out, he could use it up to five times before exhausting himself, provided that he let his hand regenerate in the meantime.

It was exceptionally strong, too. Not enough to dent the reinforced cave walls, but strong.

Despite cultivating for days, Jack didn't feel his inspiration running dry. Throughout Trial Planet, he'd been running a lot and meditating little. He amassed a large amount of experience that he had to slowly unravel.

He didn't feel any sort of enlightenment, either. There was no spark of inspiration that would allow him to spontaneously break through like he had for the E-Grade. He just had to work hard, like his life depended on it—which it did.

Due to his strong body, thirst wouldn't kill him easily. He could go for a few weeks if needed. Therefore, he resolved himself to wait as long as possible in order to maximize his chances of success.

But the darkness was hard to endure. As was loneliness.

By the second day, Jack had explored every nook and cranny of this place. There wasn't much to see. The main room was completely bare, save for a rotten meditation mat in the very center that he'd moved aside. The bedroom had a rotten bed frame and an iron stool. The last room was the bathroom—nothing but an alcove in the rock with a three-foot-deep hole leading nowhere. At least this part was blissfully empty.

Besides those few things, all that existed was smooth rock, and the immoveable lever and stone slab.

And Jack.

He didn't feel there was anything more to discover, but he kept trying. No matter how deeply he sank into cultivation, he always awoke, and every time he did, he remembered the darkness. Standing up and walking around became an increasingly frequent habit. Feeling the walls was a relief—it meant there was no danger. He hadn't been magically transported to another darkness. This was *his* darkness.

On the fourth day, he discovered one extra thing in the cave: a tattered cape, bunched-up in a corner. It wasn't falling apart like everything else, though Jack knew the reason. He was the one who threw this cape in here. On his final clash with Longsword, when he finally overpowered him, the shockwave had been strong enough to send the swordsman's cape flying. As he'd been standing with his back to the cave mouth, it ended up here.

Jack chuckled to himself. "What luck," he muttered, estranged by the sound of his own voice. "It's just me and the cape of my enemy. Maybe I'll call it Wilson."

By the ninth day, he started to feel unwell. Dark thoughts sprang in his mind unbidden. His throat was parched from thirst, and his stomach protested from hunger. The cold solitude had seeped deep into his soul, infecting him with a fear he couldn't shake. Even when he succeeded, it always came back, slightly stronger than the last time.

Of course, this strange fear wasn't that much of a problem by itself. Given his strong Will, he could easily endure it. The problem was that it obstructed his cultivation sessions. At times, he would be deep in meditation when a sudden surge of fear would shoot him awake.

There were times when he would suddenly shout out and punch the rock. Not due to creeping insanity, just to vent. With nobody watching, Jack could allow himself small respites.

He even went as far as to prop up the cape against a wall and speak to it at times, to relieve the loneliness.

As the days passed, Jack felt himself degrading. He was growing dirtier, since there was no water. Slimmer, too. His hair was disheveled, and his facial hair had grown erratically, but he had no heart to groom it. Not that he could, anyway—there was nothing sharp here, and his hair grew more durable along with his body. Normal razors would dull before he was even halfway done.

His mental well-being was also suffering. The irrational fear was now permanently nested in his chest. There were many times when he was certain he saw red eyes in the darkness. He sensed a hot, musky breath on his shoulder—the black wolf's from the Forest of the Strong. Once, he thought he heard the cries of Rufus Emberheart as he pummeled him into paste.

"This sealed chamber is not a nice place," he told the cape on the wall. By now, most of his thoughts were made aloud. "I wonder how strong immortals are, for them to find peace here. Or maybe they don't stay for over a week per session. Will I turn into Gan Salin if this goes on?"

Despite his troubles, the one thing that didn't degrade in the slightest was Jack's resolve to break through. He would not die here. He could not. He would survive.

Every time he sank into meditation, the Dao lay before his eyes, an infinite blanket he could traverse with tiny steps. It was woven out of power, and life, and resolve, and the deepest essence of the Fist. It was as large as a desert, with its dunes and valleys, with every grain of sand being its own star.

The sheer enormity of this task frightened Jack. It made him despair. And yet, he trudged on, day after day, thought after thought. He compared his insights and contrasted them. He passed them through a fine-toothed comb, looking for the tiniest imperfections and contradictions.

Just because he'd fused his Dao Roots didn't mean he understood them perfectly—just enough to see where they fit into the greater picture of his Dao Seed. And, if each Dao Root was an enormity, comprehending their infinite combinations was an unfathomable task. How was he supposed to find a solution that perfectly satisfied the Fist, Indomitable Will, Life, and Power in every possible scenario?

There was some inner balance to be found, but it was so elusive and incorporeal. As he analyzed every insight he possessed, the tiniest mistakes could cascade into gaping holes. Sometimes, one imperfection meant the entire insight had to be scrapped.

What was the Fist? What did it mean to have Indomitable Will? What was Life? What was Power?

How did they all fit together?

Over time, Jack realized why almost every immortal had only one Dao Root. The complexity rose geometrically with every extra one. It was like adding an entire new axis to the universe.

As the days passed, he grew more and more uncertain of his success. His resolve didn't waver, but he understood the height of his task better. It could take him years. No matter how talented someone was, and no matter how many good opportunities they had, some matters simply couldn't be forced.

His only hope was that, when he ran out of time and used the Dao Sprouting Pill, it would be enough to let him break through, even imperfectly.

He didn't actually know much about this breakthrough.

To become an immortal, you had to take your Dao Seed as the basis and combine it with your Dao Roots, forming a system where the roots supplied meaning and energy to the seed to let it grow. If you could form a solid enough understanding, the world would resonate with your Dao, sprouting it into a Dao Tree.

However, even the tiniest imperfection could have a huge impact on your tree's stability, just like one hair-thin crack could ruin an entire sword. Small mistakes could lead to the entire thing crumbling and your Dao remaining stuck forever, with a broken tree piercing its center like a blade through the heart. The blooming tree reduced to nothing but a little flower, making you the weakest of immortals who could never progress.

Jack knew these things because Salin and Nauja had told him while traveling, but he had no real frame of reference. What was a "tiny mistake?" How high was he supposed to reach? Was his current understanding even remotely close to good enough?

And, most importantly, would the bare minimum of a Dao Tree satisfy him? He had dreams. He had a planet to save and the peak of power to pursue. He was far ahead of the pack, a lord who reached this height in an incredibly short amount of time. He had the blood of a God in his soul.

He didn't want to just break through. He wanted to achieve a Dao Tree as robust as possible, so he could continue to dominate and grow stronger like he had so far.

Yet, would he have the choice? His decisions had led him to this cave, where he had to rush his breakthrough or die.

"Do I regret it?" he asked himself. Every time, his eyes shone, and a strong breath filled his chest. "No. I followed the path of the fist here, and I will follow it to the end, because it gave me a life worth living. If I die or break my path, so be it. It will just signify that I was never meant to reach higher."

This sort of resolve was the core of his Dao. He didn't look back. He charged ahead with roaring laughter, fighting until he fell.

As for when that would be... Who knew.

However, as the days passed, Jack's condition worsened. His body slimmed until he was a husk of his previous self. His throat was so parched he could barely speak. The thirst was strong enough that even he, for all his willpower, teetered on the edge of collapse.

By this point, he was sitting in his own filth. And yet, his eyes were as bright as stars, and a faint purple aura shimmered around him with every breath. If one only took a quick glance at the current Jack, they would not see a man, but a clenched fist.

He lost track of time. Even his previous estimations had only been based on instinct. It could have been two weeks or three—he couldn't tell.

And there came a time when his eyes sprang open, and despite his pain, they were filled with unyielding resolve. He had cultivated as much as he could—any longer, and his body would grow so weak that it would impact his breakthrough. His time was up.

Now.

A hand reached for the side, where he'd placed the Dao Sprouting Pill. He could sense it in his palm—an apple rife with life, pulsing with the power of the Dao and its infinite permutations.

Jack closed his eyes, though it made no difference, and bit into the apple. He lost his breath as the flavor fired every neuron in his brain at once.

His breakthrough had begun.

WHAT IS THE DAO?

JACK BIT INTO THE DAO SPROUTING PILL AND ITS JUICES RAN OVER HIS TONGUE.

Almost instantly, he felt the world screech to a halt. His eyes opened wide. Colors spread through the darkness until they filled it, then kept going. Shapes and geometric patterns materialized, floating haphazardly through the air, breaking and reforming at random, each bringing Jack new inspiration.

The small part of his mind that remained sober thought this resembled the hallucinogenics of Earth. Except, those didn't work for cultivation. If they did, everyone would be an immortal already. They were just random neurons firing. This one, however... This was the real deal. What he was seeing wasn't visions. It was the Dao.

Jack was becoming one with the world. The environment around him unraveled, turning from rock and air to currents of the Dao, vibrating and oscillating as they wound around each other. The Dao was everywhere. It was the fabric and moving force of the universe, what gave everything meaning.

And it wasn't just particles—or maybe it was, but also so much more than that.

For the first time, Jack realized that the Dao was alive.

It was a laughing gale and a stubborn stone. It was carefree water and hungry fire. The Dao was the spirit of the world split into infinite tiny pieces, and each piece took on a form suited to its mentality. That was why understanding mattered. If the Dao was alive and had feelings, even the barest hint of sentience, it made sense that understanding it would allow you to resonate with that part of the Dao, even going as far as to make it cooperate with you.

Maybe even suck it inside your soul and make it a part of you.

Jack's eyes were opened. For the first time, he saw the true essence of the world. This was the Dao. Like a million tiny fairies, each capricious in their own way, sentient yet elementary in their intelligence.

Then, what did it mean to cultivate the Dao? What did it mean to absorb it inside you and form your own understanding of the world?

It meant to condition your inner world. It meant to invite in the Daos that suited you and teach them how to work together without flaws.

In the F-Grade, you contacted the Dao and resonated with it in small parts, letting tiny quantities inhabit your body and make you stronger, faster, smarter. You let them transform you in accordance with your desires—with your Dao.

In the E-Grade, you pulled in more. You resonated with more facets of the Dao, broadening the spectrum of the world with which you could interact. You pulled it in and expelled the irrelevant Daos from your body until your inner Dao composition became so attuned to your soul that you could control it with your will, the same way an oarsman controls the water.

And, in the D-Grade, you consolidated the Dao inside you to such a degree that you turned into a beacon of power. In the sea of diverse Dao, which was so sparse and chaotic as to be powerless, you became a dense mass of power guided by the will of a human. By forming a complete system of understanding and assimilating your inner forces, you became a part of the Dao. Then, its high concentration inside you allowed you to dominate your surroundings, which lacked a will of their own.

Jack felt breathless. So *this* was how the Dao worked. Come to think of it, Master Shol had once explained something similar, but Jack hadn't understood it then. How could he? Without experiencing reality first-hand, as he was doing now, it was like trying to teach a blind man what the color red looked like.

Hearing about something and actually experiencing it were two different things.

But now, Jack knew. He understood what it meant to break through to the D-Grade, how and why he could achieve it.

Then, what were the meanings of roots, seeds, and trees? Where did that imagery fit into the larger picture? What Jack saw now looked nothing like plants.

He didn't ponder that too much. The effects of the Dao Sprouting Pill wouldn't last forever. Whether the plant stuff was imagery produced by the System to facilitate understanding, or whether it was some higher concept of the Dao that he was unable to grasp, it mattered little.

The Dao knew how to break through. All he had to do was follow it —and hope his understanding was strong enough.

Good thing this state brought clarity.

Jack dove deep into his own body. He found his soul. Finally, he knew what it was: simply the lump of Dao that subscribed to his own will. The core of his conscious existence. Without it, he was nothing but flesh and bones. With it, he was a person—a cultivator.

No wonder it didn't have a physical substance.

Jack observed his soul. When he'd reached the E-Grade, it had become one with the Dao of the Fist. Now, he was it, and it was him. His entire existence was built around a lump of Fist.

Throughout his cultivation journey, he'd added more Daos to the mix. Indomitable Will and Power were there—parts of the Dao that had been with him since the F-Grade. Life had been added later—the Life Drop, a sphere that contained titanic quantities of Dao compressed to the limit of possibility. Jack gasped. For the first time, it felt like he had a nuclear bomb strapped to his heart.

Only now did he realize the significance of this Life Drop. It had no will of its own, but its sheer quantity was so large that it resonated with all the Life Dao around him, letting him control it even without fully understanding it.

He had no idea how this could be achieved—a concept so advanced that considering it right now was simply a waste of time.

Belatedly, Jack realized that he actually hadn't comprehended any new Dao Roots while in the E-Grade. *Huh.* Still, he let the thought flow away. He had a job to do. He wasn't here to ruminate.

Forming a complete system of thought... Let's see.

There were a few Daos inside him. How could he merge them into one homogenous whole, in such a way that they were perfectly aligned with each other?

The Fist would be the core. The other Daos would simply be feeding into it, refining its edges and turning it from a concept into his own, personal interpretation.

Jack started preparing. As if in a distant world, he sensed himself take another bite of the Dao Sprouting Pill. Under its effects, everything was made so much clearer, the world returning to its essence.

He had to break through.

In a trance, Jack grabbed the Daos with his will and started weaving them together. He placed the Fist in the very center, plugging in the others where they best accentuated the Fist. Contradictions spawned almost instantly. Every move he made sent ripples across the board, striking a dozen different spots and weakening them. It was like trying to weave a delicate fabric with fingers as fat as water bottles.

Jack gritted his teeth and pressed on. He had to find a way. His understanding wasn't perfect, but he had to make it and iron out the imperfections.

Even with the clarity provided by the Dao Sprouting Pill, working with four concepts at once was impossible. There were gaps in his weave. Holes and bumps. Places where something was needed but he had nothing, and places where he had too much and needed little.

This clearly wasn't working.

He switched his mental image. He was no longer weaving the Daos together but treating them like three-dimensional puzzle pieces. The Fist was his centerpiece, a rod-shaped object with bumps and holes. The other Daos were sheets he could wrap around his centerpiece, each with their own holes and bumps. To achieve a perfect breakthrough, he had to fit them together perfectly to form a smooth shape—the trunk of his Dao Tree.

Once again, the result was imperfect. There were holes he couldn't close. Bumps he couldn't cover. The Daos he had were finite, and there just didn't seem to be a perfect combination. The trunk he was forming was ugly and uneven.

Jack felt despair creep in. Was his breakthrough doomed to fail? Even if he succeeded, would he end up a mediocre immortal destined to stagnate in the D-Grade? This terror gripped his heart like an iron vise. He despised his own weakness. He didn't want to be trapped, to stagnate. He wanted to grasp his fate and use his strength to obtain freedom.

A mediocre immortal was still an immortal. He would still be able to fight until he fell, as the Fist and his soul dictated. He could lead a happy, fulfilling life.

So why did mediocrity feel like a curse? Why did powerlessness scare Jack more than death?

However, the dice were cast. All he could do now was shoulder on and try his hardest to make this breakthrough work. If any problems cropped up later, he would find a way to deal with them.

He kept on with his puzzle-solving, fitting the pieces together as well as he could, jamming them in where he could do nothing else.

Suddenly, out of nowhere, thunder rumbled in his soul, a sound strong enough to reach him even in this pill-induced trance. The Dao around him flew into disarray. His puzzle was broken. Everything was chaos. His breakthrough had been interrupted—thankfully, he had still been at the early stages, so no harm was done.

Jack snapped awake. This didn't feel like a natural phenomenon. Had someone attacked him?

However, sweeping his surroundings with his perception revealed nothing. The Dao was slowly recovering from the disarray, but there was no hint of anyone present. Jack still felt suspicious. He knew what he'd sensed. Someone or something had deliberately interrupted his breakthrough.

Who could it be? And why?

The trance was still in effect. Jack's mind drifted as he tried to focus on mundane matters, but he forced it to attention.

Who could do this? he wondered.

Nobody. There was no way an E-Grade cultivator could mess with the Dao in this way. Some treasure? Possibly, but there was nothing in his vicinity. Even if there was, why would it happen right at that moment? Was it a hellish coincidence?

The Final Guardian?

That was an immortal. Jack didn't know the limits of its power—perhaps it could detect his breakthrough and stop it. But why? It was supposed to be just a testing tool of Trial Planet.

Wait. Did Trial Planet itself interrupt me?

Immortals weren't allowed in Trial Planet. Lords were considered the apex existences. So, why would the B-Grade factions not send in someone at the very precipice of breaking through? They could enter as E-Grades, break through, then dominate the entire planet. Even the Final Guardian, who had never been defeated, wouldn't be that difficult.

There was only one reason why all these didn't happen.

How could I have missed this? Jack thought, overcome with despair. Trial Planet itself doesn't let us break through. No cultivator can become an immortal here. We are forced to deal with the Trials at the E-Grade, or the entire system would break.

Wait. Then, what about Nauja's dad? He's an immortal.

Maybe Trial Planet only stopped delvers? Maybe breaking through was possible, just more difficult? Maybe there were other conditions to be met?

He did not know. The fact was, his breakthrough had just been interrupted, and looking down, half of the Dao Sprouting Pill was already gone. There was no time to waste. He only had enough for one more attempt.

What if Trial Planet just stopped him again?

But did he have another choice?

I do! he realized. In this state, with my powers of understanding through the roof... I could try to comprehend another Dao Root. Coupled with the Life Drop, maybe it would be enough to let me escape this cave. And then what? Breaking through with four Dao Roots would be even more difficult. My path would be cut short.

Nothing else came to mind. Jack had two options: attempt to break through again or try to develop a fourth Dao Root.

If he tried to break through, Trial Planet—or whatever—might stop him again. Then, his Dao Sprouting Pill would be wasted, and he would probably die of thirst soon. Even if he succeeded, he could sense that a perfect breakthrough was currently impossible. At most, he would become an average immortal, and he would progress no further.

On the other hand... If he developed a fourth Dao Root, Trial Planet wouldn't stop him, and he would become stronger than lords. He would dominate the E-Grade. In return, breaking through in the future would be almost impossible. He would be biting off more than he could chew.

But almost impossible wasn't the same thing as impossible. Indeed! Why not develop a fourth Dao Root? Jack could bite off as much as fit in his mouth. If he couldn't chew it, that would only be the result of his own weakness. If he could, not only would his path not be cut off, but it would instead become even grander.

After all, there had been people in the history of the galaxy who broke through with four Dao Roots. If they could do it, why not him?

Aim for the top or die trying. Punch high. Fight until you fall. Was that not the path of the Fist? Was that not what Jack preached?

Suddenly, he opened his mouth and laughed out, letting the harsh sound echo against the cave walls. So what if his dried throat was torn from the effort? So what if the air was stale, and ingesting it made him want to puke? So what if he was cornered into a life-or-death decision?

So what? He was Jack Rust! He followed the Dao of the Fist! Since when was he scared of a challenge? Since when did he choose the easy road?

How had breaking through with only three Dao Roots even crossed his mind?

All thoughts of breakthrough, all weaving and puzzle-solving were tossed out of the window. Jack would double down and form a fourth Dao Root. He would aim for the very top. And, in the future, he would just work hard to succeed.

He'd made his decision.

Now, which Dao Root?

CHAPTER ONE HUNDRED TEN
HOLDING UP THE SKY

JACK REMAINED IN A TRANCE. A THOUSAND THOUGHTS CROSSED HIS MIND IN A single instance, each reinforced or repelled by the Dao in and around him.

What significant insight did he have that was not yet a Dao Root?

His resolve to reach the top? He had that. His understanding of how power shaped the world and weakness was a curse? He had that, too. An understanding of life? That was also a Dao Root, though in a round-about way.

What other feeling or concept was deeply rooted inside him?

Fear.

The thought came unbidden. But why? How?

He was trapped in a sealed cave. There was no light. No sound. He was alone, and he might die here without ever seeing another face. His loved ones would never know what happened. Brock might wait outside the cave for who knows how long.

And that dark solitude bore heavy on his soul, a crushing weight that would sooner or later drive him to insanity.

Of course, Jack had the resolve to escape. His Dao wasn't one to sit and accept its fate. He was fighting, not giving up in the slightest.

But what if it was someone else in this cave, and not him? In fact, there was no cave. The cave didn't matter. What mattered were the feelings of fear, powerlessness, and despair. They could make a man kneel, give up. And he understood these feelings because he'd experienced them for who knows how long already. He was deeply steeped in them.

Then, for this new Dao Root, is there a skill I could—

His thought process skidded to a halt. His eyes shone. Once again, he laughed, uncaring about the pain that tore his throat.

Of course he had a skill to couple with his new Dao Root—Brutalizing Aura! The one that came from his Fiend of the Iron Fist Class.

Oh, System! he cried out mentally. You knew. You always knew! Or is this fate?

So be it. If I am a fiend... Then let me become the greatest fiend to ever live!

He buckled down. His mouth opened wide and took a big bite of the red pill. Jack dove into a trance that unraveled the world into the Dao, but it was even more intense than before.

He had all the emotions. The resolve. The understanding. He had the perfect pill to help him.

Perhaps using the Dao Sprouting Pill just to get a Dao Root was overkill, but Jack couldn't care less. He set his mind on these feelings of weakness. He used the awareness provided by the pill to dissect them, inspect them, experience them to their deepest limit. He let them invade and pervade his soul. He let himself sink into despair. He let powerlessness flood his being.

The process reminded him of how he'd fused the Dao Root of Power. Back then, he had restrained his power and fought Copy Jack again and again, until he comprehended power from the side of the weak. Then, he reversed the situation and used that understanding to glimpse his own power through the eyes of a weak opponent, thus comprehending how Power could fully augment his Fist.

But why skip that weakness? Why use it only as a springboard to comprehend power? If he could inflict this weakness on his opponents, if he could infect their minds and hearts with it, would his strength not rise in comparison?

To comprehend power, one must comprehend weakness. Jack had already walked this road. He just hadn't realized it then.

Weakness itself was a concept. One that could enhance his understanding of the fist. After all, to truly understand his fist, he had to see it from all sides—and weakness was the feeling one got when they faced its business end.

Jack saw himself from outside his body, and this vision superimposed itself on seeing himself from the inside. All the dark feelings he'd suppressed while inside this cave erupted at once. For a moment, he fell into the darkness. He screamed in utter anguish.

And then, he snapped awake, and he was more lucid than he'd ever been. The last bit of the Dao Sprouting Pill was gone from his palm. The last bit of darkness had vanished from his soul, contained within a black orb that hovered orderly around his fist. It was no longer a parasite, but a weapon for him to use—a truth of the world he could finally see.

It felt like he finally acknowledged a missing piece of himself.

It wasn't just a Dao Root, either. Under the miraculous effects of the Dao Sprouting Pill, Jack had gone one step further. He hadn't just developed it. He'd fused it, too.

Congratulations! The Dao Root of Weakness had been successfully fused with your Dao Seed.
Mental +20
Will +40

Congratulations! Brutalizing Aura I → Brutalizing Aura II
Brutalizing Aura II: The fear of death is one of the most primal instincts of all living creatures, *as is crippling weakness*. You have learned to project your Dao and intent in a way that targets these fears, amplifying them and paralyzing all weaker targets in a wide range around you.
Additionally, the fear of your enemies feeds into your own power, enhancing you as you affect more and stronger enemies with Brutalizing Aura.

That was an intriguing skill. Jack even had the feeling that it wasn't just the Dao Root of Weakness that participated in this upgrade, but also the Dao Root of Power.

In any case, pondering this skill would come later.

He drew a deep, trembling breath. His eyes opened to find darkness, but it was no longer an enemy. Just a grim reality. As the last of the trance dissipated, Jack looked at his status screen. He now had a new Dao Root, Brutalizing Aura had been upgraded, his Dao Seed was indicated as *peak+*, and his Physical sub-stats were almost at six hundred points each.

He couldn't help but wonder if there was any other E-Grade in the galaxy with stats like his. There probably were. Somewhere. Maybe.

At the very least, he stood at the absolute highest level amongst mortals. He no longer possessed the weakness he'd just comprehended.

Jack smiled sadly. He could sense that this Dao Root had changed him, somehow. Grounded him. His path remained the same, but he now understood better his hurdles and impact. His effect on the world.

His heart was a bit heavier, but his resolve was incomparably more corporeal. As was his power.

Slowly, Jack stood up. His perception ran over the cave, clearer than ever. He could see everything, but nothing new. The walls were as solid as before. Longsword's cape remained propped against the far wall. The stone slab still stood before the entrance, challenging him.

And, finally, that was a challenge he would accept.

Perhaps his body wasn't at its strongest, but his Dao was. Unless he somehow progressed even further, he would never have a better chance of lifting the stone slab. And, if the lords were still waiting outside... he would just fight them as he was. An extra Dao Root was a great leap in power. He could easily take on Longsword now.

Belatedly, Jack realized that the devil he freed before must have been around this level.

He took another deep breath, the stale air almost familiar. He mentally bade it goodbye, as he did to the cape, and stood before the slab, reached inside his soul, and tugged at the Life Drop.

Power flooded him. His bones rumbled as he grew a foot taller. His skin burst open under the armpits as two new arms jutted out as ribbons of flesh that wove together. An ocean of life coursed through him, enhancing him in body, mind, and soul.

He was at the absolute strongest he'd ever been. It was almost euphoric—but, with his new Dao Root of Weakness acting as grounding, he remained unchanged by this rush.

Jack placed a hand on the back of the stone slab. He sensed the vacuum. Like an army of horses, his Dao galloped in. It felt like a raging river through his veins. It was stunning.

The rushing power's quality increased its effectiveness. Slowly, the Dao vacuum began to fill up. Ten percent. Twenty. Thirty.

Jack remained there, still as a boulder. The energy was still leaving him. Fifty percent was filled. Seventy. Eighty.

He was growing exhausted. He tore at every scrap he could find to push even more energy into the slab. If he failed now, he would likely die. He had neither another Dao Sprouting Pill nor the insights to comprehend a new Dao Root, let alone break through.

Ninety percent. The vacuum was so temptingly close to full, yet a small part of it remained empty. Jack had scrapped up every iota of Dao energy in his body. Some still ran through the connection, but it was too little. It would come close to filling the vacuum but fall short.

Despair was born in his heart. *No!* he thought. *I cannot fail here! I must succeed!*

With such a strong stream of power between himself and the vacuum, he no longer needed to touch it directly. With a roar, he tried to dig his fingers under the slab. It was hard. The floor was unbreakable to the current Jack, as was the slab. But the vacuum was the seal that kept it down. With it almost filled, the slab could budge a bit.

Jack roared again. All four of his hands dug underneath, struggling to find purchase. It shook a bit, rising half an inch. One finger succeeded. Then another. The more he got, the easier it became. With better grip, he could lift harder.

Jack snuck all twenty of his fingers under the slab and had lifted it an inch. Its back was against the entrance wall, so lifting it from one side lifted the whole thing.

Veins popped on his forehead. He was running short of breath. His entire body protested. His back was cracking. His calves were burning. Even with the vacuum filled at ninety-five percent, this stone slab was too heavy.

But he had to lift it.

He gritted his teeth so hard they almost broke. He didn't care about the pain or burn. All that existed was him and the slab.

A couple more inches. Its speed of rising was almost torturous. But Jack pressed on. His fingers got a better grip. The higher he raised the slab, the faster it became. Its magical resistance waned. His stance got better.

Eventually, it was so high that Jack could sneak a shoulder under it. Then another. He felt like Atlas holding up the sky. His entire face was red, his eyes bulged, his teeth were gritted, his body screamed at him to give up, but he pressed on.

The energy he'd poured into the vacuum began to dissipate. From ninety-five percent, it fell to ninety-four. The slab's weight increased. Jack had to succeed quickly. His shoulders were compressed under the stone, but he rooted his feet in the ground and summoned all his strength, uncaring that, if he failed, the slab's unbearable weight would crush him into paste.

His palms met the stone. He managed to draw in a breath. He could see the light outside—it was almost blinding.

"AHHHH!" Jack screamed, pushing at the slab with every scrap of power he could muster. His calves buckled. He got cramps everywhere. A couple muscles were torn. He ran out of power.

But, just for a moment, he'd pushed up hard. And that was enough to break the resistance. The slab passed an invisible barrier and lost all magic, becoming just a regular slab of stone—heavy, but nothing Jack couldn't handle. It shot up like a missile, smashing into the roof and staying there, hovering over the entrance like it always did. The lever rose as well.

Jack fell to the ground, his regeneration drawing on the last bits of his energy to repair his broken tendons. He couldn't stand yet, but he couldn't care less. His lips were drawn into a wide smile. He didn't even feel the pain. Fresh air and light were all he could sense.

He escaped the cave. He was free—and stronger than ever.

Jack Rust was back.

CHAPTER ONE HUNDRED ELEVEN
THE FINAL CHALLENGE

JACK WALKED OUT OF TRIAL GARDEN ONE STEP AT A TIME. IT WASN'T EASY—HE was dehydrated and completely exhausted.

The mist parted before his feet. Slowly, he made it to the animal tile formation, which now felt like it was so long ago. He stepped on the right animal tiles, still not knowing how they were deduced.

From there, it was a straight line. Step after step, the mist thinned, and the towering garden gate appeared before Jack. Only now did he realize that it was over. That he had truly escaped. It was hard to contain his emotions.

Many questions he'd ignored suddenly returned to his mind. Where were the others? What had Brock, Salin, and Nauja done while he was trapped? Did they know? Had the lords sought revenge and killed them? Had the Sage kept his promise to protect them?

All those thoughts whirled around inside Jack's mind, faster than he could process. If needed, he could use his Dao of Indomitable Will to suppress them, but he didn't. He'd already done that in the cave—now, it was time to let them be. Let his heart experience the uncertainty of life, which gave everything meaning.

Before he knew it, he was anxious. The darkest possibilities went through his mind. His heart climbed to his throat. If something had happened to Brock...

The mist cleared. Finally, Jack could see outside Trial Garden. An expansive grassland filled his gaze, curving out of sight. The sky was covered in bright sun mushrooms, and a colossal fence rose to the far left—the Tools Garden, one of the other gardens of Garden Ring. The air smelled of grass.

A single brorilla stood before the entrance of Trial Garden. He was busy doing push-ups with a large boulder on his back, sweat dripping all over his toned body. He was so focused on the exercise that it took him a moment to detect Jack.

Jack's heart swelled with relief. "Brock..." he muttered as loudly as his parched throat could manage. Only then did the brorilla realize someone was there. He turned his head, and spotting Jack, his eyes widened, and he froze so abruptly that his arms buckled. The next moment, he jumped up, tossing the boulder away, and rushed to Jack.

"Broooo!" he shouted.

Jack became intimately aware that he was swimming in his own filth. It'd been several weeks since he last took a shower. "Wait, Brock, don't—"

Brock didn't care. He fell on Jack and wrapped him in a tight hug, then took a step back, inspected him with care, and stretched out a hand. "Bro!" he repeated, smiling so widely that Jack thought his jaw would unhinge.

He smiled back, shaking Brock's hand. "It's good to see you, bro. I'm so glad you're safe."

———

"A beast army!" Jack exclaimed between biting a banana and chewing on a potato. After discovering Brock, he had quickly bathed in a lake near the ring entrance, then rushed to where their food pile was—the beasts of Beast Garden had been very accommodating.

"You should have seen Longsword's face," Gan Salin said with a laugh. "He was so fed up."

"It wasn't just the army!" Nauja chimed in, poking Salin's side. "Tell him about my arrow."

"And Nauja made an incredible shot with her new arrow!" Salin complied. "She hit Bocor right in the ribs from... How far away was that, again?"

"Two miles," she added proudly.

"From two miles away! You should have seen it, Jack. That arrow was stealing the world's energy as it traveled, like a... a... a sticky arrow! But it was growing faster and stronger, too. A large lance of power had formed around it."

"It's called the Sun Piercing Arrow," Nauja explained proudly—though it wasn't the first time she told Jack about this skill. "At its strongest, it can even fly to the sun and pierce it! Of course, *my* arrows can't even go ten miles before breaking, but uh, it's something."

"For sure it is," Jack agreed. "That's a very impressive skill. I'm sure all the dinosaurs in the jungle will be terrified."

"Right," she replied, losing a bit of her enthusiasm.

"Have you guys considered what you're going to do after here?" Jack asked.

The canine spoke first. "I think I'll return to my faction. They won't attack me anymore, given my achievements in Trial Planet, and they can help me push my strength to a new level. Now that I have the Seventh Ring Conqueror title, I'll be in favor."

Jack nodded. "I hope it works out for you, Salin. And, if we clash on Earth, I will try to show mercy."

"Hah. That's only if you get the chance! I won't always be weaker than you, you know."

"I look forward to seeing that."

"I have thought a lot about it," Nauja said in a heavy voice. Everyone lost their joking mood and focused on her words. Jack even put down his banana and potato. "This journey through Trial Planet has helped me so much. I got a great Dao Skill, and I leveled up from 99 to 107—which would have taken me years if I hadn't joined you. Most importantly, I tasted adventure, and I will never be able to forget it."

She took a deep, trembling breath. "If I leave Trial Planet, I will never be able to return... but, if I stay, what am I to do? Return to my tribe, get married, and spend the rest of my days tending to triceratopses or hunting in the jungle? Never to experience the real world again? I don't want that. I... I want to adventure. To explore. To see the world and fill my eyes with its sights. To find out what a sun looks like, or space, or the myriad planets, with their plants and animals and people. To feel the wonder of the universe. To find out what happened to my ancestors—the Ancients. To pierce the sun."

She raised her eyes, and they were filled with warm pain. Tears sparkled at the edges. "I don't want to leave my tribe behind, but that is not how I'm meant to live. The Barbarian Ring will kill me slowly, day after day. I have decided to follow my heart and be happy. And, if that means abandoning everyone I know..." She set her jaw. "They can handle it. So can I. We are barbarians—we are strong. If I threw away my happiness just to be with them... they wouldn't want it. Father wouldn't want it."

Jack smiled warmly. "I admire your resolve, Nauja. I think you're doing the right thing. And you can always find someone on the outside to pass a message to your father, let him know you're alive and well. Maybe you can even exchange letters through the delvers."

She laughed. "Maybe we could. I hadn't considered that."

"Plus, you won't be alone out there!" Salin said. "I'll be your friend. Jack and Brock, too, and who knows who else. You can come with me to the Animal Kingdom, or back to Earth-387, or wherever you want. The world will be an oyster, and you will be its pearl."

"I suppose so." She sniffed, wiping at her eyes with a smile. "Thank you. From the bottom of my heart, I truly, really thank you. If I hadn't joined you in this journey... I fear I would forever remain trapped."

"Having you along was an honor," Jack said. "You were great help."

"Of course I was. I'm a barbarian!"

"What about you, Jack?" Salin asked. "What are you going to do?"

He leaned back on the grass. "Hmm. I still need to save Earth. I think I will visit the Exploding Sun first, see what they have to say, and if they can help. Pay my respects to Master Shol, as well. Then... I don't know. Wage war against the Animal Kingdom? Sounds like a great way to level up."

Salin laughed. "That's the most laidback declaration of war I've ever heard."

"You don't believe me?"

"Oh, I absolutely do. If you became an immortal, even the Animal Kingdom would have to take you a bit seriously..." He grinned. "I just look forward to it. One man against a multi-planet empire with several

B-Grades holding the fort. And yet, why do I feel that you can make it?"

"Because you're crazy." Jack laughed.

"Oh, yes. I forgot about that for a second."

They also had to find a way to escape the Hand of God deep-scanning, or at least hope his Life Drop didn't trigger it. Jack hadn't mentioned anything yet. They would have time to consider this issue later.

"Before doing all those, however," Jack said, his eyes turning serious. "There is one last thing I want to do here."

"Do you mean..."

"Yes." He turned his gaze to a lone wooden door in the grassland, seemingly leading nowhere. Jack knew that wasn't true. Behind that door lay the final and hardest challenge of Trial Planet: the Final Guardian. An immortal. The ninth ring, which no one had conquered before.

When Jack first arrived here, the Final Guardian was an unsurpassable existence. However, he'd grown a lot since then. He now had four Dao Roots, the Eighth Ring Conqueror title, and the Life Drop. He was confident that, amongst all the mortals of the universe, he was ranked at or near the very top. If someone stood a chance against the Final Guardian, it was him.

But could even the strongest mortal beat an immortal?

"You are welcome to watch," he said, eyeing the Final Door with a heated, battle-ready gaze. After all, he had been through thick and thin with these people. They'd waited for him for almost a month. He trusted them—even the insane Gan Salin. Showing him the Life Drop was a risk he was willing to take. "I'll finish eating and rest for a few hours to recover to my peak strength, as well as practice a bit with my new Dao Root. When the sun mushrooms brighten again... I will challenge the Final Guardian of Trial Planet."

Salin laughed, biting into a turkey leg. "Of course we'll watch. I can hardly wait. Though, I have to say, I've never heard of a mortal beating an immortal before. Don't get your hopes up."

"If anyone can do it, I believe it's Jack," Nauja retorted. "I wouldn't miss that fight for the world."

"Bro," Brock said, and gave Jack a thumbs-up and a bright, confident smile. "Good luck."

"You've learned a lot of words recently, haven't you?" Jack asked.

Nauja laughed. "He's at the E-Grade now. It's only natural that his mind is more advanced. Wait until he reaches the D-Grade—he might be able to speak as well as the rest of us."

Jack nodded. In fact, Brock's progress was astounding. Even though Jack himself was growing stronger at breakneck speed, Brock wasn't falling behind. If anything, he was slowly but surely closing the gap.

Will there be a day when we fight side by side? he wondered, pride surging in his chest. You are an excellent bro, Brock.

Brock winked as if sensing Jack's thoughts.

The rest of the meal went on with pleasant conversation and exchanging stories. Jack's heart filled as fast as his stomach. The darkness of the cave was now a distant memory.

As soon as the sun mushrooms dimmed, the group lay on the soft grass under the star-lit dome that served as this ring's sky. They kept chatting for a while until falling asleep. Jack couldn't remember the last time he was so relaxed. Maybe back in the Integration Tournament? Or even further in the past?

When he woke up, the mushrooms were still dark—the day and night cycle in Trial Planet was longer than on Earth. Jack spent the next few hours meditating, sharpening his edge against Copy Jack. He practiced with the upgraded version of Brutalizing Aura, finding that its effects were no longer constrained on only weaker opponents. Stronger ones were less affected, of course, but it was a very useful change.

When Jack opened his eyes, the sun mushrooms had just brightened. He was at the peak of his power, bursting at the seams with so much energy that the Dao curved around him like a tight sheet would curve around a heavy ball. His friends were awake, too, giving him looks of encouragement.

"It is time," he said, standing up. "Let's go."

They bade goodbye to the animals of Beast Garden. They walked to the Final Door, standing alone on the grassland. Jack placed both palms on its surface. It was wooden and rough, like an ancient tree turned to door. He took a deep breath, solidified his resolve, and pushed.

The doors swung open, revealing a bright hall and a knight on a throne. An immortal.

Jack stepped in.

CHAPTER ONE HUNDRED TWELVE
CHALLENGING THE FINAL GUARDIAN

JACK ENTERED THE THRONE ROOM, AND A BREEZE PASSED OVER HIS SKIN, LIKE he'd been caressed by a curtain of wind.

He took a deep breath. The air was fresh here—strong, almost verdant. Even breathing this air heightened his senses and brought out his body's full potential. Torches lined the walls, gold-trimmed stone columns were arranged uniformly across the rectangular hall, and a red carpet stretched from the entrance to the throne, where an old knight sat with his eyes closed.

Soon after Jack entered the room, the knight's eyes opened.

"Another challenger," he said with a sigh. "Let's see, will it be an unimpressive hatchling, or a slightly less unimpressive weakling?"

"How about a proper opponent?" Jack replied from across the room. He infused his voice with his Dao, making it echo against the walls like a struck gong.

The knight laid eyes on Jack. He took his time, his lips rising slightly. "Finally, someone with real skill. Four roots, correct? Not bad, not bad at all. You are still too weak to face me, unfortunately, but at least you're not a waste of resources like most of your compatriots."

Unlike his previous words, the guardian seemed amenable. He even smiled at Jack. Seeing this, Jack also took a mental step back and became respectful.

"Not compatriots, senior," he answered. "I come from a planet that was only recently Integrated. Actually, most of the people who made it to this ring wanted to kill me."

"And I see they failed."

The guardian rose from his throne. He was like a normal human in size, except clad in iron armor like a medieval knight. A simple mace was strapped to his belt, and his helmet was open, revealing a slightly wrinkled, white-bearded face. His brown eyes remained hard and radiated Dao. Meeting them took all of Jack's willpower.

"I outsmarted and defeated them," Jack said. "A twist of fate later, I developed my fourth Dao Root to escape a trap, and I emerged as the victor of this Garden Assault."

"Garden Assault, eh?" said the old man, his lips quirking. "I remember a time when young cultivators made it here regularly, not once a year, as you do now. The labyrinth guardian isn't that strong... Has the world degraded that far?"

"Degraded? How long have you been in here, senior?"

The old man waved his hands. "It doesn't matter. However... An Integration, you say..." His face revealed sadness, a hint of regret. "I suppose it does work. Throw a billion mortals into the meat grinder to create a handful of powerhouses. Such a waste of life."

"Isn't Trial Planet the same, senior?" Jack asked. "A meat grinder to make the strongest rise?"

"Hardly comparable. The people who enter Trial Planet choose to do so, fully aware of the risks involved. An Integration is forced onto ignorant weaklings."

Jack considered the old man's words, then said, "I am Jack Rust of Earth-387, cultivator of the Dao of the Fist. Can I have your name, senior?"

"I care not for your name or Dao. You are an interesting break in my monotony, young mortal, but I only have ears for those capable of defeating me. As for my name... Well, defeat me, and you'll find out."

"That's more like it." Jack laughed and smashed his fists together. "Then, shall we begin?"

"You do not have the strength to fight me. Four roots and a perfect seed are not enough. Leave now, before I humiliate you and kick you out."

"If you don't try me, how will you know?"

The old man stared into Jack's eyes, the pressure enough to give him a slight headache. Then, he grabbed his mace and took a step forward. "So be it. A beating is a good way to learn."

The two of them were separated by several hundred feet of empty space. Yet, the moment the knight dashed, that distance closed almost instantly. Jack barely had time to cross his arms and defend.

However, this wasn't the casual strike that the knight had once used to strike Bocor. This was a real one.

Jack was flung away. His bones cracked. The attack was strong enough to be unstoppable, and he flew all the way until he crashed into the wall above the entrance—the still-open door from where Brock, Salin, and Nauja watched him.

The wall cracked only slightly under his back. Jack took the brunt of the impact, and he landed before the entrance, barely keeping his balance.

"Is that enough?" asked the knight.

"Heh," Jack replied. "I'm just getting started."

He reached inside himself and tapped into the power of the Life Drop. Suddenly, energy flooded his body. His veins were overrun with molten iron, his bones turned to steel. Jack groaned as he grew a foot in height and two arms under his normal ones.

He hadn't forgotten to use this form before. He just wanted to feel the power of an immortal head-on. To take a strike with his normal strength and see just how far apart they were.

A lot, as it turned out. But the Life Drop brought a considerable increase in fighting power. Even if Jack couldn't win, he could at least fight.

Now four-armed and pulsing with barely contained energy, Jack set his gaze on the knight. He looked at him dead straight. His body radiated intent to battle, and his muscles bulged in anticipation of the destruction they would wreak.

"Come," he growled in a slightly deeper voice. "Let's fight!"

The knight, meanwhile, was gaping. His old eyes had gone wide as saucers. "That's—You have been chosen! You carry *His* legacy! This is—Unbelievable! It's still alive! The torch still burns!" He broke into laughter, loud and clear. "Thank you, young man, thank you! Even if you cannot defeat me, the hope you have given me today is the best gift I've gotten in a million years."

"I want to ask you many things," Jack said, "but I want to beat you first."

"Don't think I will go easy on you. If anything, I absolutely won't let you cheat."

"I never dreamt of that. Come, old man. I'll kick your ass."

"Old man?" the knight's lips rose again, this time wildly. "I'll make you eat those words, boy."

"Hah. Try me!"

Jack laughed and charged. He fell deep into battle. This was it. The culmination of his journey so far. The greatest opponent he ever challenged. The greatest stage he ever stood on.

Victory would open the doors to greatness. Defeat would forever consign him to weakness. There had been people in the past who could beat this old man, that much was clear. If Jack couldn't match them now, he would never surpass them, and the top of the world would be forever closed off to him.

He had to win. For his people, his planet, his Dao... and, most importantly, for himself.

To grab his fate with his own two hands, he needed power. This was the defining moment. He had to succeed.

Jack balled all four fists. A purple aura trailed him like he was a meteor himself—a manifestation of his overflowing Dao. As he charged, he resembled more a thrown fist than a man.

"Come!" the knight shouted, his eyes narrowed; finally, he took Jack seriously. He fell into a stance, with his mace to the side and his body diagonal. Jack didn't recognize the stance, but it didn't matter.

An immortal had taken him seriously. This was... extraordinary!

Jack reached the immortal. His fists flared like beacons. Color and sound were torn apart as they were sucked in four different directions at once, and the Iron Fist Style filled Jack's body, guiding him to unleash the most of his potential.

Seeing the four Meteor Punches headed his way, the old man smashed out. His mace swung through the air in a perfect arc, seeking to break all four fists at the same time. Its head smashed into one fist, breaking its bones. For the second, it fractured them. The third stopped the mace in exchange for an injury. The fourth fist remained untouched. It flew through the air and exploded on the old man's face, breaking Jack's hand as he sent the knight flying.

Jack didn't even register the pain of his four injured hands. He'd just blown away an immortal. He could do this. He could win. All it took was a perfect Dao Seed, extraordinary titles, four fused Dao Roots, and a gift of the gods.

The final shred of doubt inside Jack was extinguished. He had so much power—for the first time, he believed maybe he could win. His Dao roared like a revving engine, and all four of his roots operated at full power. He was overflowing with energy, a boiling furnace about to explode.

Life Dao flowed into his hands, healing them. The Life Drop's energy in Jack's body decreased by around a third—though its actual reserves were near limitless, the energy Jack could draw into himself was not. The more he drew, the harder it became. He had to utilize it effectively.

No more head-on clashes, he thought, still drunk in satisfaction. *Let's fight smart.*

The knight stopped himself midair. Using the power of flight, which all immortals possessed, he hovered there, looking at Jack from above. Besides a bloody nose that was already healing, his face seemed unhurt from the strike.

"Tremendous power!" he acknowledged. "But will it be enough?"

"Only one way to find out."

"Hah. Of course!"

The knight dove down. His speed remained tremendous, but Jack could glimpse it now, mere shadows and afterimages that indicated where the next strike would come from. He leaned back, letting the mace sail before his face. The wind pulled his now-longer hair back, threatening to overturn him. Jack steadied himself. The Iron Fist Style guided him, and his experience from fighting Copy Jack helped, too.

The knight swung again. The mace came diagonally from below. Jack twisted around it, adapting to the wind he knew would come, turning to deflect while he threw a punch at the old man's face. The knight followed the momentum of his mace to reposition, turning and smashing a kick into Jack's abdomen, nailing him into a distant column.

Jack lost all air in his lungs. The knight was on him instantly. Jack barely managed to duck before the mace crushed his head into paste, denting and cracking the entire column.

He was livid. This old man wasn't playing around. If that attack had landed, Jack would be absolutely dead!

"Getting cold feet?" the knight said, jumping back to avoid Jack's punch. "The world is violent, boy, and this is a battle. If you cannot handle it, go home."

"Handle it? I *am* violence, old man. So what if I die? At least I will have followed my path!"

The old man grinned. As he stared him down, Jack realized he was loving this. He loved that the old man was really trying to kill him. That he wasn't holding back. That either of them could die at any moment.

The fear, the adrenaline, the tension... They reminded him of the time in the Forest of the Strong. The dungeon that defined him. The experience that forged him into his present self. That helped him become who he was always meant to be.

This was Jack's place in the world. Facing down an enemy with his life on the line. It was perfect.

His eyes must have conveyed all these thoughts, because the old man laughed. "I respect your resolve! I will try my hardest to kill you. Come!"

The world became a battle. Jack's vision closed in on his opponent. Time slowed. His entire body was pumping Dao and power. He was an unstoppable machine of Fistfighting.

He was the Fiend of the Iron Fist, and he would destroy this arrogant old man.

Brutalizing Aura oozed from every pore of his body. Jack felt the world warp around him as it struggled to accommodate his Dao. His resolve and killing intent took on a physical form and smashed into the old man, whose only reaction was to narrow his eyes. But Jack saw the momentary conflict. He saw the hint of his aura taking root.

At this moment, he'd started a second war with the old man, this one on the level of their willpower. What was more absolute? Jack's intent to kill his opponent, or the old man's confidence?

After being upgraded, Brutalizing Aura could work on opponents of similar strength to Jack, just to a limited extent. That was fine. A few tiny gaps was all he needed—gaps he could plug with his fists.

The old man slowed by a hair. Faced with Jack's fiendish assault, he actually adopted a defensive stance. Fists rained. Every strike enough to level hills and dent steel. Jack became a force of nature as he tore into the old man, who defended with all his power, using the body of his mace to intercept the punches. Clearly, his strength was superb. As was his skill. But so was Jack's. He hadn't spent tens of hours fighting Copy Jack for nothing.

Jack dug deeper. His four fists flowed out like the waves of the sea, carrying the ferocity of a falling mountain and the sharpness of a gale. The fists rotated in their attacks. When one retreated, another was always there. To his surprise, Jack discovered that the Iron Fist Style— his Fistfighting Dao Skill—had already adapted to the four fists he wielded. His attacks formed a constant stream that gave the old man no room to breathe, let alone fight back.

Jack could fight an immortal head-on.

"Enough!" the knight shouted, letting a punch through. Jack more sensed than saw the incoming attack. He abandoned his own strike and ducked right as the mace swung where his head used to be, its strength and speed taken to a whole new level. "If you want to fight above your weight," the old man said, his eyes spouting flames, "then so be it!"

A storm was born. The air whipped Jack's face. His hair was pulled in all directions. A tremendous pressure fell on his soul, trying to suppress him, and all four Dao Roots had to work in tandem with his perfect Dao Seed to resist.

This was no longer just a mace-wielding old man. A silver aura erupted from his body, filling the hall like the domain of a god. It was intangible, yet made of steel. The world was dyed silver. Jack almost lost control of his Dao before wrestling it back, but it remained contained in the very edges of his body.

His body was his domain. Everything else was the old man's. The entire hall was under his control.

"This is the power of an immortal, boy," the old man said, his silver hair floating in an invisible wind and the head of his mace radiating a steely light. "You are worthy of facing it. Adapt or die!"

CHAPTER ONE HUNDRED THIRTEEN
MASTERING ONE'S DAO

THE OLD MAN STRUCK. JACK JUMPED TO THE SIDE. THE WORLD RESISTED HIS movement, seeking to constrain him, but he used his physical strength to escape.

The ground where he used to stand was destroyed. The mace head landed like a real comet, exploding the stone that made up this hall's floor. The red carpet was torn apart. Stone shards flew through the air. The shockwave pushed into Jack's ears and took his breath. His eyes widened.

What kind of power is this!

There was no way he could block that, whether he had four arms or a hundred. Immortals could control the world around them. All the Dao in the hall was under the old man's influence, helping him while obstructing Jack.

This... This was just unfair! How was he supposed to fight with such a disadvantage?

The old man didn't give him time to think. The mace fell again, and Jack had to retreat. Every strike brought disaster. The hall was torn apart. Craters formed in the ground, cracks ripped into the walls. One column collapsed after being broken in half—thankfully, they seemed unnecessary, as the ceiling could magically support itself.

Jack escaped with all his power as the old man chased him,

smashing out unstoppable strikes with every swing like it was nothing. Evading was all Jack could do. Staying to fight would mean instant death. The old man was an angel of steel, destroying everything in his path to get to Jack.

As if that wasn't enough, he was flying! Jack had to run around while the immortal could just glide, attacking from all sorts of angles that Jack wasn't used to.

What can I even do! he asked in panic, leaping away from a strike that broke the ground under his feet. He landed on the side of a column and pushed away just in time to avoid the mace that shattered it. He tumbled on the ground, pressed against the throne, jumped on the ceiling, then back down.

The old man was always there, just a step behind. His strength was extreme, but his speed was only on par with Jack's, letting him just barely escape every time.

"Is running all you can do?" the old man taunted as he gave chase. "The entrance is right there. Escape if you want to live! Give up!"

A fire burned in Jack's heart. He would not escape. He would not give up. He would defeat this immortal and chase the very peak of power.

But how?

He wrung his brain dry to come up with a solution. There had to be something he could do, some way to combat this domain of steel the old man had unraveled.

Suddenly, a realization lit up in his mind. As he activated the aura, the old man had said, "Adapt or die!"

What did that mean? How was Jack supposed to adapt?

The mace fell next to his head, interrupting Jack's thoughts. The shockwave of the attack flung him into the far wall, but he also expelled part of his Dao mid-flight to accelerate himself. After all, he couldn't fly. If the old man caught up, it was over. The faster he reached a surface, any surface, the safer he would be.

As Jack expelled his Dao, the domain assimilated it. He saw the process clearly. His purple aura—the Dao of the Fist—could only resist for a few seconds as all the surrounding Dao took on a steely hue and bore down on it. In the end, surrounded by enemies on all sides, that small amount of his Dao was defeated and assimilated.

Fireworks went off in Jack's brain. In that fraction of a second, he understood what he had to do.

The moment he landed, a purple aura flared around his body. It was nothing compared to the old man's domain—just a candle before the sun. And yet, it was *his* candle. It defined an area where the Dao of the Mace couldn't reach. A pocket of freedom in the old man's domain.

An inch of purple now surrounded Jack's skin.

Of course, this wasn't easy to do. Mortals couldn't control their Dao outside their bodies, just expel it. In contrast, the old man clearly could. His Dao Domain constantly ground against Jack's aura, reducing and destroying it as it tried to reach his body. It was like using snow armor to protect himself in a burning oven.

Jack's response was to expel even more of his Dao. It was a crude solution. A good portion of his energy was wasted every second just to keep the domain at bay. He had to constantly expel more and more Dao, rapidly dwindling his reserves.

But, as crude of a solution this was, it remained a solution. The old man was strengthened from the domain, but Jack was no longer restrained. It was progress.

All he had to do was win before he ran out of energy.

"Laughable!" the immortal cried out. "You cannot do it!"

"Watch me!" Jack roared. He stopped running. Instead, he charged. One good strike of the mace could end him, but it was either this or run until he lost.

The old man laughed and met Jack's charge head-on. He swung. The moment his mace met Jack's aura, its strength waned slightly, but it remained super-charged. Jack dodged, letting the strike demolish another column behind him. He punched out. A purple meteor flared in the silver air flickering for just a moment. It couldn't draw in the colors and sounds, but it didn't need to. All it had to do was explode.

The punch found the old man's gut. It detonated on his armor, making him gasp as another punch met his chest, sending him backward. Jack followed. He couldn't afford to delay. This aura he had would last only a few seconds. He needed to end this.

Besides, if the old man was flung around, he had no time to fly.

Jack roared as he punched. Four meteors were born on his fists. Four purple stars. The old man pulled up his mace to defend.

Their clashes echoed through the hall. Walls broke. Columns fell. The carpet was reduced to shreds. The throne was shattered. Jack and the knight were two streaks of light, one purple and one silver, chasing each other at speeds a normal person couldn't even follow.

Their every clash ended with someone flung away, and the other always followed. The old man had no intention to draw things out. He wouldn't exploit his Grade advantage. If he did, he wouldn't deserve to be an immortal.

Both opponents were fully submerged. One clash followed the other in an endless dance. Time stretched until each second became an infinity. The room, the watchers, the stakes, everything disappeared, and all that remained was a battle to the death.

Two of Jack's fists met the old man's jaw, throwing his head back and eliciting a groan. The mace met Jack's calf, breaking his leg and tossing him through a column and into a wall. The old man arrived without missing a beat, ignoring the pain of his broken jaw to strike fast. Jack, whose calf had already regenerated, leapt aside, letting the mace sail an inch from his face to strike back. Two of his fists met the old man's side. The other two, his chest. He flew diagonally away, passing through a collapsing column from before and into the ceiling.

The old man's regeneration was nowhere close to Jack's. The strikes added up. In the end, it was a contest of endurance. Would Jack's energy run out first, or would the old man succumb to his injuries?

Jack flashed through the air, reaching the ceiling. His fist drew a purple line through the room as it rose like an upward meteor. The old man spat out blood, roared, and ignored Jack's fist to smash the mace into his chest.

Jack expected that. He expelled some Dao to move sideways, launching his Meteor Punch away from his hand, letting it sail alone through the air to smash into the old man's chest, nailing him deeper into the ceiling. Jack himself landed to the old man's right, then pushed against the ceiling to throw himself at the ground before gravity took over.

The old man did the exact same thing, and suddenly, they were falling side by side. Their trajectories intersected in the very middle of the hall. All hell broke loose.

Jack sensed his energy reserves dwindling. Already, he was running on fumes. There was barely a second before he was exhausted and the old man's domain snuffed him out like a candle.

The old man, on the other hand, was bloody and injured. Bruises covered his body under the armor, which thankfully wasn't very effective against blunt weapons, and he sported several internal injuries. There was definitely something broken, too. His face was warped in an expression of permanent pain, his movements far slower than before, and his attacks weaker.

So were Jack's, though not by much. His regeneration could hold the fort.

As they intersected midair, falling sideways into each other, Jack knew this was the moment. There was no more time. This would end— *now*.

Meteors flared on his fists. A bit of the silver domain was drawn into them, assimilated into the purple. He smashed out. So did the old man, and Jack was ready. He released his Brutalizing Aura at full power, pulling out all the stops. If he failed, it would be over, but it didn't matter, because he wouldn't fail. He would win.

The old man grimaced as the aura hit him. For a fraction of a second, his attack grew hesitant. Jack used that opening to slap away his mace-holding hand, making the attack miss as he buried two Meteor Punches into the old man's body. One fit perfectly into the open helmet.

The old man was spiked downward, but Jack wouldn't let him escape this time. He used his fourth hand to grab onto the armor's edge, pulled along by the power of his own strike. They crossed the room together and smashed hard into the floor, further cracking it. Jack gasped. His entire body was protesting from lack of energy, but he didn't back down. He had no time to.

The old man remained conscious. He pushed Jack, flying to stand opposite Jack, roared, and smashed out. Jack used his trump card— Ghost Step. This skill wasn't a Dao-imbued one, so it hadn't been too useful lately. At Jack's current level, three or nine feet was nothing.

However, when kept as a hidden ace, it was perfect for exchanges like this.

The old man's mace sailed through empty air as Jack appeared behind him, smashing a full-powered Meteor Punch into the back of his helmet. The old man's head rocked. Somehow, his neck didn't break. He didn't fall unconscious, either. He absorbed the strike and followed the momentum of his previous attack, swinging around himself to attack Jack, who was in no position to dodge. He was forced to meet the strike head-on.

The old man noticed this and his eyes shone silver. The entire Dao Domain retreated instantly, diving into the mace head, which shone brilliantly like a silver moon. An ocean of power pulsed in that mace. This strike clearly contained all the remaining power of the old man, and Jack had no option but to face it.

"FALLING STAR!" the old man shouted, his mustache marred with blood. This was his strongest attack.

Even though it was his best attacking skill, his actual power had decreased since the start of the fight. He was heavily injured, and had just extinguished his own domain. The strength he could channel was limited—at best, this strike reached the ones he'd used when he first activated his domain.

There was only one thing Jack could do.

Attack.

There was relief in that realization. Glee. His entire being was aligned. His soul was one piece.

Jack readied all four of his punches. Purple flared brightly on them all, more than ever before. This would be the final blow. They were both going all out. He poured every scrap of energy he could muster into his fists, dividing it equally, birthing four meteors that burned through the air and blazed through the Dao.

Since the domain was gone, these meteors weren't weakened. Color and sound fell into them like they were black holes. The air screamed as it was ripped apart. Before these meteors, nothing could survive.

And Jack had four of them.

All four punches smashed forward at once. His Dao flared like a brilliant purple sun.

In the singular spot between the two opponents, all four punches met the glowing silver mace at the same time. Both Jack and the old man roared in defiance.

The explosion was blinding and deafening. Jack felt his world burn. His bare chest was seared from the heat. He thought he'd died.

A moment passed in which he'd lost all his senses.

When his vision recovered, he saw a silver mace flying alone through the air to land against the far wall. The old man before him stared incredulously as his entire hand was missing, disintegrated from the massive explosion. Jack's hands were absolutely mangled, too, but he was used to that. They would recover.

Belatedly, he realized that the floor was black under their feet, and a large black X was seared across the ground, stretching from their location in the middle of the room to each of its corners—it was the outline of the two-pronged explosion. However, the lines were far wider on his opponent's side of the room. Most of the energy had been pushed that way. Jack had won the exchange.

He raised his eyes to see the old man toppling to the ground. He lay there, limbs spread and staring at the ceiling, unable to move. Only then did the mace land on the floor, far away.

Jack could barely stay standing. The pain was impossible. So was the exhaustion.

But all those were overshadowed by the realization of one simple fact: He had won.

CHAPTER ONE HUNDRED FOURTEEN
THOUSAND ESSENCE FLOWER

Jack panted over the Final Guardian's body. His legs wobbled and his mind swam. Not falling over was the most he could do, but it didn't matter because he *won*!

"YES!" he shouted, raising a fist to the sky. That action unbalanced him, and he fell on his butt. The Life Drop's metamorphosis was already reverting, and he was so devoid of energy that even his regeneration didn't kick into effect. A screen appeared before his eyes:

Congratulations! Title "Eighth Ring Conqueror" upgraded to "Ninth Ring Conqueror!"
Efficacy of all stats: +40% → +50%

The rush of stats returned some power to Jack, who barely managed to get back on his feet. He first looked at the once glorious throne room. Half the columns had been demolished and lay in debris. The walls, floor, and ceiling were filled with craters and cracks. Thin stone dust covered the floor. And, of course, part of the room was blackened where the final explosion had spread.

It was utter mayhem. So utter, in fact, that Jack momentarily marveled at how he participated in a battle of such ferocity. After all, this room wasn't made of simple stone—before developing his third or fourth Dao Root, he wouldn't have even been able to scratch it.

He looked outside. Through the still-open wooden door that had thankfully avoided the explosion, three sets of eyes stared at him with intense pride and joy. Brock was jumping up and down, unable to contain himself. Gan Salin was bragging about something to Nauja—knowing him, it was probably something along the lines of "I made that kid." As for the barbarian girl, her eyes were starry and filled with wonder. At that moment, she truly admired Jack as a fellow warrior.

He smiled and waved at them.

Finally, he directed his gaze downward, at the old man's still body. *Did I kill him?* he wondered. The iron armor was undamaged, and his helmet cover had fallen over his face, so Jack couldn't tell. One hand was missing from the wrist, and his mace still lay across the hall.

Suddenly, motes of silver light rose from the floor. They surrounded the old man's body with blinding brilliance, forcing Jack to avert his gaze. When the light dimmed, he looked back to find the old man standing before him again, whole and well.

"Well done," he said in a voice full of emotion. He didn't seem to mind that he'd lost. "Well done, child... Well done!"

"Thank you, senior," Jack replied, bowing with a smile. "It was a great battle."

"Indeed! That transformation you used, and expelling your Dao to counteract my domain... Superb! I have to admit, losing for the first time in a million years feels much better than I thought it would."

Jack smirked. "Has nobody else defeated you, senior?"

"Nobody. There were some who came close, but..."

Through his exertion, Jack forced himself to focus. "But how can that be? I know I'm stronger than most, but we're talking about an entire galaxy's worth of geniuses over a million years. How did I, a random guy who just got Integrated, do something that all those couldn't?"

"The winning path seems simple to the winner, but only through the eyes of the losers can you tell the difference," the old man said. "True, there were others with four Dao Roots and a perfect Dao Seed before—what we call perfect mortality, or perfect foundation. But how many of them had titles as good as your Integration ones? How many were as experienced in life-or-death battles? How many had the good fortune of stumbling upon one of the rarest and strongest items in existence?"

"That's true, I guess..."

"At the end of the day, young man, don't think too hard on it." The old man smiled. "You made it. That's what matters. Celebrate a little!"

"Hah. I already shouted out before, you were just too dead to hear me."

"Dead? Please. This is just a proxy body. My real strength is far above the D-Grade. Even if I let you hit me for a thousand years, you couldn't even bruise me."

Jack laughed. When not fighting or condescending, this old man was actually rather pleasant.

"Shall we proceed to the Final Ring?" the old man asked. "You can take your spiritual companion along, if you want to."

Jack pointed at the door. "What about my other friends?"

"They cannot come, unfortunately, unless they defeat me. But I can notify them when you teleport out of Trial Planet, if you want, so you can all exit at the same time."

"That would be great. Thank you, senior."

"Not a problem at all. Now..."

The old man raised a hand. Jack felt the air coalesce in a line above his head, and Brock started floating. "Bro!" he shouted in panic and tried to punch the air, but Jack only laughed. The brorilla floated smoothly through the door and entered the throne room.

"See you soon, guys!" Jack shouted at Salin and Nauja. "You'll be notified when I teleport out, so we can all leave together."

"Okay! Have fun with your friends. Just remember to return before bedtime!" Gan Salin shouted back as the door swung closed on his face.

Jack, Brock, and the old man were left alone in the throne room.

"Could we have your name now, senior?" Jack asked.

The old man laughed. "You did defeat me. I suppose you can."

Jack's surroundings melted away like they were just a dream. He found himself on what resembled a tiny planet in the center of the world. Six sun mushrooms hung on the ring ceiling, around a mile away, each in one cardinal direction. The ground underfoot was a sphere barely a hundred feet in diameter.

And yet, the power of gravity here was astonishing. Even with almost six hundred points in Strength and a combined +75% efficacy from his titles, Jack found himself straining to stay on his feet. The dense air deposited Brock on the ground, but a thin silver barrier appeared around him, helping him to withstand the increased gravity.

"What is this?" Jack asked.

"The Final Ring," the old man replied emotionally. "The core of Trial Planet. My home."

A little wooden cabin was visible in the distance—which, given the tiny sphere's curvature, wasn't more than a few dozen feet away. Besides that, only grass covered the ground, swaying gently like it wasn't under mountain-crushing pressure.

"This is no house," Jack said. "It's a prison!"

He couldn't imagine living in such a tiny place for a million years. However, the old man only laughed.

"My cabin is larger on the inside. I am also not restrained here—I am actually the spirit of Trial Planet, so I can see and hear everything that happens inside it."

"Really? Then, why were you surprised by my transformation?" Jack asked. He remembered that, when he used the Life Drop, the old man's eyes had gone wide as saucers.

The old man gave a wry smile. "Well... Almost everything. Some spaces are isolated, for both my sake and theirs. Besides that, this planet is my body and world. Saying I am trapped here would be like saying you feel cramped in your own body."

Jack's eyes brightened. "So, you're the spirit of Trial Planet. What does that mean?"

"It means I control this place. I am responsible for the smooth operation of everything: the resetting of Labyrinth Ring every few months, the reactivation of traps, managing the monster population, restocking the treasures, keeping immortals out of this planet... Everything. You asked for my name, but I do not have one—if I do, than it is Trial Planet. You can also call me Spirit, if you so wish."

"Senior Spirit, then," said Jack, recalling Master Shol's lessons on galactic etiquette.

"Bah, that's much too formal. You're my only guests in forever. Just call me Old Man Spirit."

"Then why—" Jack took a deep breath. "Okay. Old Man Spirit it is."

"There you go." Old Man Spirit smiled. He still wore his iron armor, and his mace had returned to his belt at some point. He turned to Brock. "And I suppose this brorilla is Brock, correct?"

Brock nodded and reached out for a handshake. Bemused, Old Man Spirit complied. Watching a knight and a brorilla shake hands was quite a funny sight.

"Now, before we get to your rewards, do you have any other questions for me?"

The thought of rewards intrigued Jack—just what treasures could the Final Ring hide?

Before that, he did have a few things he wanted to ask. Old Man Spirit was a powerful, ancient existence that knew about his Life Drop secret. Finally, he had someone to give him actual information.

"Can you tell me about the Old Ones, senior?" he asked.

Old Man Spirit raised a brow, growing cautious. "What exactly do you want to know?"

"Many things, actually, but the most important is... what exactly happened between the Old Ones, the Ancients, and the Immortals? I've heard that the Old Ones killed the Ancients, and so the Immortals created the System to defeat them. Except, I've also seen evidence that the Ancients *worshiped* the Old Ones, and that the System itself is hunting down any Ancient remnants. All those things together don't add up. What really happened?"

Old Man Spirit didn't reply immediately. His eyes were narrowed, like he was thinking. "I am limited in what I can divulge. Even if I wasn't, however, I wouldn't tell you. You are still too weak to partake in those secrets. When you become strong enough, you will naturally know."

That told Jack nothing.

"Is there nothing you can tell me?" he insisted. "I may be too weak right now, but I still interact with all those forces. The System wanted me to report something to the Hand of God. The Hand of God is looking for the Life Drop inside me. The Black Hole Church is trying to recruit me, but I know *nothing* about them. Can you guide me even a little bit?"

"No."

"Come on, Old Man Spirit. Please!"

The old man nearly huffed—nearly. "I am limited in what I can reveal, due to a Dao Contract I have signed to keep some secrets. However... If someone is chasing you, you naturally want to stay away from them, right?"

Jack's eyes narrowed. "Right. I want to stay away from the people who are chasing me."

"Of course. That's a sensible choice to make." Old Man Spirit nodded. "And, if somebody wants to become your friend, isn't it rude to decline?"

Jack tried to interpret these words. If he understood correctly, Old Man Spirit was telling him to stay away from the Hand of God and join the Black Hole Church.

Which made sense. The Hand of God was after him, and the Black Hole Church had helped him on multiple occasions. Still, it was nice to get confirmation.

"Okay," he replied. "I think I understand, senior. Thank you."

"Not a problem."

The issue was, Jack still had no idea what was going on with the Old Ones, the Ancients, and the Immortals. He didn't know what connections the Hand of God and Black Hole Church had with those groups.

On the bright side, he didn't need to bother. He should be friends with the Church and run away from the Hand of God—simple.

"Speaking of that," Jack said. "If, hypothetically speaking, the people chasing me had surrounded Trial Planet and were deep-scanning anyone who exited... would they find anything suspicious on me?"

This was the most burning question in his mind. The Ancient voice had warned him that if anyone discovered the Life Drop, terrible things would happen. Since the Hand of God was here, and they had "deep-scanning equipment," could he even leave Trial Planet?

Old Man Spirit seemed to share his concerns. His gaze darkened. "Hypothetically speaking, that would be terrible. You would not want those people to find you."

That was the last thing Jack wanted to hear.

"Is there a way to avoid them?"

"Not unless they're idiots. Trial Planet isn't that big. Even if I teleported you to a random point on the surface or one of the two moons, they would find you easily."

"Shit." Jack gritted his teeth. If there was no way out, what was he supposed to do? Die? "Couldn't you teleport me farther out? Even in the middle of space. I could get a helmet and—"

"And go where? Do you have any idea how long it would take you to reach any planet from the middle of nowhere? Not to mention they would still find you. My powers cannot teleport a mortal too far." He sighed. "Listen. You carry the inheritance of my creators. I don't want you to be captured... but there really isn't much I can do."

Jack wrung his brain for a solution. "Don't you have a teleporter? I was transported across half the galaxy before. If you have one, I could go directly back to my constellation."

"I do not. Normal teleporters don't work inside my planet. The best I could do was use some of the energy of Trial Planet to forcefully teleport you away, but that would put tremendous strain on you. Before becoming an immortal, enduring it is impossible."

"What if I did become an immortal?" Jack asked. "I'm close, right? What if I meditated and broke through?"

"You are not close at all. Becoming an immortal takes years of experience, even for the most talented of cultivators... but I guess that's all we can do. I, too, have sensed the hypothetical forces surrounding my planet. They will certainly catch you if you teleport outside. The only way is for me to send you far away, and for that, you need to first become an immortal."

"Then—"

"It is not a problem." Old Man Spirit shook a hand. "You can cultivate here. It will be a bit boring for you, but if you work hard, you should be able to break through within a year or two."

"A year or two!" Jack gaped. "Senior... You may not know this, but I'm in a hurry. I must return to my planet within eight months from now and defeat a C-Grade Planetary Overseer, or at least secure someone who can protect me against them. Otherwise, everyone I know will die. I cannot spend a year here. Isn't there a faster way?"

Old Man Spirit gave him a level look. "I was not aware of that. In other words, you have to leave my planet within seven months at the latest, and the only way to do that is to become an immortal."

"Right. I've used a Dao Sprouting Pill before. If you can give me something similar, I can try to break through faster."

"A Dao Sprouting Pill would not be enough. Even if I had another, it is meant to help someone already on the precipice of breaking through, not someone like you who's still a ways away..."

"Then, some other treasure. You mentioned I get rewards for defeating you, right? Isn't there anything that can increase cultivation speed?"

The old man hesitated. "There is, actually... but you shouldn't use it."

"Why?"

"Because it's too dangerous."

That was music to Jack's ears. Since when was he afraid of a little danger?

"I can handle it," he said.

"You don't even know what I'm talking about. Don't get ahead of yourself," the old man said sternly.

Jack realized he'd rushed it a bit. "Sorry. Could you tell me more about this treasure?"

Old Man Spirit sighed. "I suppose I can. You see, I do have a treasure that can help you break through in time. In fact, let alone eight months, it can let you break through in one day."

"One day!" Jack's eyes went wide.

"Yes... but, of course, that would come at a price. Take a look."

The old man waved his hand. An item floated before Jack. It looked like a flower with a yellow core and white leaves, each painted with mystical swirling patterns. Even looking at it made Jack dizzy, like the mere sight of this flower activated some hidden switch in his brain.

"This is the Thousand Essence Flower," Old Man Spirit explained. "It has absorbed the essence of a thousand immortals and their Daos. When consumed, it temporarily links your mind to that essence, greatly expanding your ability to comprehend the Dao. It would be like having a thousand immortals debating the Dao with you—given your perfect and decently solidified foundation, it would allow you to instantly break through and become an immortal."

"It's *that* powerful?" Jack's eyes widened.

"Yes. In fact, not only will this flower let you break through immediately, it will also ensure your Dao Tree is as robust as possible, not harming your foundation in the slightest."

Despite all these strong words, Jack's gaze darkened. This flower sounded too good to be true. The catch, whatever it was, had to be equally tremendous.

"And the downside?" he asked.

The old man smiled sadly. "With danger comes opportunity, but the reverse is also true. Treasures like this are actually *too* useful. As a result, the Dao frowns at their usage. Have you ever heard of a tribulation, Jack?"

"I have not."

"With the assistance of such a powerful treasure, anyone could reach the D-Grade—that breaks the rules of the Dao, which state that only the worthy may advance. As a result, the Dao will inflict a tribulation on you—a test, if you will. If you succeed, you will be deemed worthy, and using this treasure to save time will be acceptable. If you fail, you die, and your Dao is shattered. Tribulations are not easy. They are a particularly feared form of deadly torture. If anything, breaking through the normal way is significantly easier."

Jack ran over his choices—there was only one. As long as it was a test, he was confident he could pass it.

"I can handle it," he said. "Give me that flower, senior. If I can save time by just enduring a tribulation, of course I'll do it. In fact, this is exactly what I was looking for."

"I don't think you understand how perilous tribulations are."

"Do I have another choice? I cannot spend a year here, and there is no way to exit safely before becoming an immortal."

"It is a great risk. Cheating the Dao is harder than it sounds."

"I understand, senior, but I must do this. Besides, you said that the tribulation is a test. Given my power, do you think I would fail?"

The old man looked him up and down. "Not necessarily... Keep in mind that a tribulation tests more than your power. Regardless, this is your choice to make. The Thousand Essence Flower is one of the treasures I would offer you—you can have it."

The flower floated toward Jack, who gently grabbed it by the stem. From up close, its fragrance was intoxicating. Every whiff activated parts of his brain he didn't even know he had.

"Besides this flower, what other treasures could I have chosen, senior?" he asked curiously.

"You can only have one treasure, as per the rules. However, your other choices would have been a starship that can travel at incredible speed and give you insights on the Dao of Space, as well as a one-use weapon with the power to instantly kill anyone below the B-Grade."

"What?"

That weapon could just get rid of the Planetary Overseer directly. However, Jack didn't think about it too much. Even if he chose such a thing, he wouldn't make it back to Earth before the end of the grace period—and, by then, there would be many more immortals present than just the Planetary Overseer.

Besides, the flower could contribute directly to his personal power —the one thing he could always rely on. External assistance, like weapons, were not trustworthy.

"Since you chose this flower, I would suggest using it to break through immediately," the old man said. "Becoming an immortal in Trial Planet is forbidden, but that rule doesn't apply here. There is no need to wait, either. You already have everything in order. Just rest to recover your full strength, meditate for a few minutes, and when you feel ready, eat the flower to break through."

Jack raised a brow. "Eat the flower?"

"Of course," the old man replied seriously. "How else did you expect to consume it? By sniffing it in?"

"I thought—Nevermind. Who am I to disagree? Eating the flower, it is."

"Perfect. You can even use my personal meditation spot for your breakthrough. I wouldn't normally allow that, but..." He smiled widely. "I really look forward to the Dao Tree you develop, boy. And I hope you survive."

"So do I," Jack replied honestly.

The old man led Jack and Brock to a place on the other side of the tiny planet. It resembled a park kiosk with only a meditation mat placed in its very center. Sitting down, Jack felt like he was using the meditation mat from back in the Integration Tournament. His mind felt unnaturally excited, like he was in the middle of some grand inspiration.

With a knight and a brorilla watching him, Jack sat down, closed his eyes, took a deep breath... and meditated.

CHAPTER ONE HUNDRED FIFTEEN
BREAKTHROUGHS

GAN SALIN WAS BREATHLESS AS HE WATCHED THE BATTLE BETWEEN JACK AND the Final Guardian. He struggled to believe he was at the same tier as these guys. Their speed, their strength, their skills, their control over the Dao...

This was a level he could never, ever reach. At this moment, he completely and utterly submitted.

The battle carried on, and Salin's excitement only grew. He had never heard anything about that four-armed transformation. Plus, expelling one's Dao to counter an immortal's Dao Domain... Who did that!

When Jack won, Salin could no longer restrain himself, and his jaw fell so low it almost hit the floor.

"Wow..." he muttered breathlessly. A mortal had defeated an immortal. The unbridgeable chasm had been bridged. His friend, Jack Rust, had done the impossible. "Wow."

Nauja recovered from her surprise first. "Hey," she told Salin, "not a word about his transformation, okay? To nobody. It's a huuuge secret."

"Okay," he agreed absent-mindedly. "What the hell was that?"

"Damn me if I know. He's just Jack. How did he become so strong!"

Soon after, the immortal was reformed, Brock was taken inside the room, and Jack promised they would be notified as he teleported out, so they could join him. Then, the door closed, and Gan Salin with Nauja were left alone in the grassland.

However, while the throne room was sealed, Salin's mind was still on the battle. He felt deep pride for his friend—and also a hint of envy, which he couldn't deny but could suppress. It was natural. Everybody felt like that when their close people succeeded—the trick was to let that feeling flow without affecting you. It was a trick he'd been forced to learn.

But now, for the first time, that pride he felt for Jack had awakened something else inside him. A fear. Why?

He dug deeper into that feeling.

He really enjoyed spending time with these people. Jack, Nauja, Brock... He considered them his friends. Now that Jack advanced into the Final Ring and Salin was left behind, what was he afraid of?

That he would be abandoned. That his friends would cast him aside due to his weakness. That he would be driven back to the Animal Kingdom, where nobody cared about him—and, funnily enough, returning there had been his plan all along. Perhaps that was a mistake. Maybe he should stick with these guys. They wouldn't abandon him. Even if they did, it wouldn't be due to his weakness.

The Sage's words jumped to his mind.

The road of entropy is not one you want to walk. As you advance, you will grow deranged and disastrous to everyone around you. Eventually, your friends will become enemies, and someone will have to end you. Don't choose that path. Water down your wine. Fuse a Dao Root of Order to your Dao Seed, so you can freely walk the path of insanity without fearing entropy. Add balance to your chaos. That will be enough.

These words had sounded reasonable then. They still did. The truth was, even the insane had feelings. Gan Salin didn't want to lose his friends... If he kept walking this path of pure insanity, he would sooner or later harm them, or betray them, or act in ways that bothered them. It didn't matter how much he liked them. Insanity was randomness. Maybe he would reveal Jack's secret on a whim, even after receiving the latter's trust.

Was the Sage right? Did Salin have to angle his path in a way that would allow him to remain loyal to his friends?

The Sage had mentioned a Dao Root of Order. That went against

Salin's teachings from back in the Animal Kingdom, but he now realized there was another path besides being a crazed suicide warrior.

He would alter his path. Not completely—after all, he enjoyed his insanity. Just one Dao Root, as the Sage suggested. A root that would ensure he never lost track of what mattered most. A guide to hold the reins of his insanity.

What would it be? What life did he envision?

Somewhere deep in Gan Salin's blood, an ancient instinct awakened, one hailing from the days of his canine ancestors. He remembered Jack's battle—that was a friend whose level he could never reach. A man he admired.

Salin lowered his head, sinking into cultivation right where he stood. Nauja said something, but he was too engrossed to listen. Insights and understanding flickered inside his mind as a new, blue Dao Root took root in the insanity.

He'd developed the Dao Root of Loyalty. He would follow Jack and never betray him—nor anyone else.

For the first time, Gan Salin had the sense that things would be alright. The world was finally looking up for him. Even though he hadn't found a Trial in Trial Planet, he'd gotten an extra Dao Root, leveled up from 51 to 79, attained a new, more solid path, and most importantly... made friends. *Real ones.*

He had bros now.

Gan Salin opened his eyes, and they were filled with new light. Ignoring the screens that popped up in his vision, he turned to Nauja and said, "Fuck the Animal Kingdom. I'm going back to Earth."

———

Alexander Petrovic stood in the ruins of the Iceberg Palace's left wing. Chunks of ice lay everywhere. Blood stains were frozen on the ground. A hand stuck out from under a single, large ice block that had fallen from the iceberg ceiling.

Alexander grabbed its edge and violently tossed it aside. Under it, the crushed corpse of his son was revealed.

"Vladimir..." he muttered, voice trembling. "Why?"

"Because this is war," a person said from his side. It was an E-Grade lycan merchant, the representative of the Animal Kingdom in Ice Peak. "This man was not innocent. He fell in battle."

"He was my *son*," Alexander rumbled, raising his voice to the lycan. "Am I meant to treat him like a normal soldier?"

"I didn't mean that, Commander," the lycan replied, bowing slightly. "War brings casualties. The longer it goes on, the more people will die, and some of them might be dear to you. Choosing to not rely on the Animal Kingdom is a worthy ambition... but, even if you can win this war without us, this is the price."

Alexander fought hard not to slap this man in the face. Instead, he turned his eyes to the ceiling, where light was streaming from a hole.

For the duration of this war, he'd repeatedly refused the assistance of the Animal Kingdom. It would not come cheaply. If he accepted, higher tax rates and generally stricter conditions would be applied on Earth as soon as the grace period came to an end. They would strangle the people into poverty.

Alexander didn't want that to happen. He planned to dominate Earth—under the flag of the Animal Kingdom—so he wanted its people to be as prosperous as possible.

However, the war did not end as quickly as he anticipated. The Bare Fist Brotherhood and Flame River had played their cards well. To this day, three months after the start of the war, they resisted and held their ground. If this carried on, they would just be dragged into a world war that would decimate the entire planet.

And he might lose. After all, his enemies now had an E-Grade cultivator, and he did not.

He tried to maintain some semblance of mercy in his soul. Now, he felt the pressure, and it was heavy. He could no longer afford sentimentalism. He had to be cold.

Clenching his jaw, Alexander looked the representative in the eye. "Fine," he said, standing over the corpse of his son. "Tell the overseer I accept her conditions. Send us help, and I will oppress the people of Earth for you."

The lycan nodded so that his smile couldn't be seen.

Right then, Alexander sensed something. A new strand of ice was born inside his soul, cold and calculating. He'd just suppressed his grief to make a callous decision. As soon as he came under pressure, his heart had frozen over, eliminating all emotions to achieve a harder edge.

The Dao sensed that, and it finally acknowledged him. Finally, he saw the path he would follow. The path of True Ice.

"I will break through immediately," Alexander said, advancing to his chambers. "Take care of Vladimir's body. My previous message remains unchanged, but I will not wait. That man killed my only son." His eyes narrowed, his gaze a storm. "The moment I break through, I will destroy him myself."

———

Brock watched his big brother sit cross-legged and close his eyes, preparing for his breakthrough. He noticed that the air felt alive here, brimming with energy and understanding. His head was clear, and his heart felt serene enough to comprehend the world.

Watching his big bro's significant moment was important, but a good bro knows to set priorities. And right now, in this place, he had a great chance to finally tackle a thought that had bothered him for a while: the Big Thought of Density.

He could already feel its essence in his muscles and the way they clenched. It was just that, every time he tried to consider it, something was always missing. A spark of inspiration, like the final hurrah of strength when you lift a particularly heavy dumbbell. Something to make the whole thing click.

As he sat there, where the Dao was far denser than normal, that something clicked.

Therefore, with a joyful cry, he took a seat on the soft grass and used his bro powers to comprehend the Big Thought of Density.

CHAPTER ONE HUNDRED SIXTEEN
THE DAO OF JACK RUST

JACK SAT CROSS-LEGGED AND PREPARED HIMSELF. SLOWLY, THE WORLD FELL away, leaving behind only him, his resolve, and the Thousand Essence Flower.

He had to succeed. To brave the risk and break through. This was it. After this moment, he would either rise to the top... or fall to hell.

A little more time passed. Jack's resolve strengthened to its limit, though there really wasn't much space to go—he was already as hyped as he could be. His mind calmed down like a still lake, giving him a clear view of his soul—the Dao Seed of the Fist—and the four Dao Roots that were one with it.

After today, these would not be inheritances of some greater Dao. It would all be his own, personal interpretation of the world—a Dao that belonged only to him, Jack Rust.

Deep breaths. His chest rose and fell, filled with the verdant Dao that suffused the air of this place. He'd rested for two hours beforehand, so he had already fully recovered from the battle against Old Man Spirit. He was at his absolute strongest. There was no better time.

Jack did not open his eyes. Brock and Old Man Spirit were nearby, watching him. The increased gravity bore down on him, agitating his body and drawing out its potential. The breeze was peaceful, and the air filled with power.

He opened his mouth and swallowed the Thousand Essence Flower.

It was like an explosion went off in his stomach. He lost his breath and almost toppled from his seating position. Instantly, his mind and soul were overwhelmed by understanding.

This was nothing like his previous experience with the Dao Sprouting Pill. The pill had given him increased awareness, like a psychedelic medicine that ripped away everything else to expose the purest form of the Dao. It was useful, but at the end of the day, it was something that only enhanced his own power.

The Thousand Essence Flower was completely different. Nothing new was revealed. Instead, a thousand wise fairies had been unleashed in his bloodstream, probing and understanding everything. He opened his soul and let them in, at which point they started inspecting his Dao.

Jack didn't wait for them to finish. He immediately started his breakthrough. He fell into his soul world—it was completely barren this time, a limitless dark expanse with a single purple sun and four bright stars surrounding it. Motes of light also hovered everywhere—the spirits of a thousand immortals, here to assist him.

Jack took a deep breath. He raised his arms like a god—which, in this space, he kind of was. The sun shuddered. The stars flickered and changed their trajectories. The motes of light pulsed with excitement, realizing what was happening.

Who am I? he finally asked the question. His Dao rose to the task. So did his soul. The motes of light helped him, pooling their minds together with his to help him jump to the right conclusions.

Jack saw a vision of himself before the System. He was moving forward in life but staying at the same spot. There was little sense of progress or fulfillment. The world was a mundane, gray prison, and he was powerless to do anything about it—both in mind and body.

That powerlessness was expressed in his Dao of Weakness. It was his past, and the future of his enemies.

When the System arrived, he broke those shackles. He fought for his life, and it was hard. Many times, he almost died. Many more, he almost wished he had, but he always pressed on. He saw every threat as an opportunity to grow, and slowly but surely, he carved out a place for himself in the Dungeon, Forest of the Strong, with his Indomitable Will as the chisel. From then on, no matter what dangers assaulted him or how desperate the situation was, he always relied on that will and never buckled, never hesitated, always charged forward with roaring laughter.

That was his Dao of Indomitable Will. The cornerstone of his strength.

Through Indomitable Will, he gained power—and, with it, the ability to direct his fate. After escaping the Forest of the Strong, he was no longer weak. He was qualified to take the reins of his life and the world. To stand at the very front and make everyone else revolve around him. To impose his will. Even after the Integration Tournament, when he arrived at the genius-filled Trial Planet, he still exercised that power and always took the initiative, until he outgrew everyone around him and conquered the previously impossible peak. He dominated the world.

That was his Dao of Power. The state he would always be in, until the day he died.

And, around all those, stretched the Dao of Life. It was a blanket that framed everything. It was chaos wrapped in order, like the evolutionary race of animals on Earth. The strong won and directed the world, the weak felt pain, and there was no rule beyond survival.

The world of cultivators was close to that state. Laws and rules mattered little before unsurpassable strength. The weak had no right to speak, only the mercy of the strong. These ideals weren't just, not by modern standards. Nor were they something Jack enjoyed, which is why he avoided bullying the weak. But they remained the purest representation of life, before it was constrained by laws. A chaos of struggle, framed by the order of everyone's desire to survive. To deny this way of life would be to remain weak.

That was the Dao of Life. The only Dao Jack hadn't fully comprehended before, but finally understood after spending countless hours meditating on it in the sealed cave, and with the assistance of the Life Drop. Even if the Dao Root of Life hadn't been forced on him, his current insights would be enough to obtain and fuse it.

And, of course, at the core of everything stood the Dao of the Fist. The path which he followed, which gave him everything else. He hadn't always known about the other Daos—but the fist had been with him from the very start; his guideline, his weapon, his resolve.

Jack couldn't see it, but a purple hurricane was rising around his body, a focal point of energy. The more it revolved, the larger it grew. Brock stared with wide eyes. Old Man Spirit smiled.

Jack remained completely focused inside himself.

He had always been a fist. Maybe that is why, before the System came, he felt so trapped. Why he thrived now. Why he loved this world, despite its pains and troubles.

The fist was the center of his existence, the life he aspired to live. When following that path, he was happy beyond the shadow of a doubt. His chest filled with warmth. There were no doubts in his mind, no lingering regrets, no second thoughts. He was simply happy— fulfilled.

Of course, the fist didn't apply everywhere. That was where the rest of his Daos came in. Indomitable Will was the very foundation of the fist—the body of the iceberg that always remained below the surface, and without it, the tip could not exist. Power was how his inner fist was expressed in the outer world—the result of his actions, and what dictated whether his fist or the enemy would break first. Life was the field he played at—the true, unbreakable rules of the world that gave everything meaning. Finally, weakness was his past, what birthed and accentuated his fist, as well as the state of the enemy when he stood before them—it completed his understanding of the world, not just himself.

These four Dao Roots gathered around his fist and perfected it. Turned it from a path into a complete understanding of the world, a system of philosophy through which everything could be expressed. It was a viable way to see the complete spectrum of reality. A partial understanding that would never break. A lens that would never come short. One of the many irrefutable Truths.

A truth that belonged completely to Jack.

He snapped out of his thoughts, returning to his soul space, which was no longer dark. His Dao Seed, that floating fist, shone brilliantly. Purple light now covered every inch of this space. The four Dao Roots, which were previously shaped as stars, were bathed in that light. They began to elongate.

From dots in space, they turned to lines, then widened. Before long, they were fingers, each a different color. They came together and wrapped around the Dao of the Fist, which had turned into a finger shorter but thicker than the rest—the thumb. All together, the five Daos formed a complete hand, and then they slowly clenched.

Five fingers to make a fist.

The shape solidified. It was the realest thing Jack had ever seen. He could only watch in awe as this spectacular occurrence was happening inside his soul. There was no longer a sun or stars. All that existed was a colossal fist—it had a purple thumb, and fingers that were each silver, blue, green, and black, all with a slight purplish hue.

His Dao Roots had wrapped around his Dao Seed to form a complete understanding, a system that would never add or lose anything. The fingers clenched further, eliminating any gaps. The process was complete. From now on, if this understanding was even slightly imperfect, there was nothing Jack could do—it would forever remain that way. On the other hand, if it was perfect, if it really was a complete understanding of the world... he would become an immortal.

The motes of light cheered. Their job was done.

Suddenly, the giant, multicolored fist thumped. It became real, like it finally came to the fore—so real that it couldn't possibly exist just inside his soul.

A new force suddenly opened a door to let the infinite wonders of the universe in. A stream of power came from nowhere and smashed into the fist. Now, Jack was just a watcher.

This stream was not the tribulation Old Man Spirit had mentioned —it was a natural part of this breakthrough. The universe had sensed someone was forming their own Dao, but it couldn't permit an incomplete Dao to exist. It had to make sure Jack's was up to the task.

This was a similar situation as the thousand visions he had to resolve when he reached the E-Grade, except far harder. The thousand visions back then had only been a small test, like a professor giving an exam to her students. This one was the real deal, as if every professor in the world was peer-reviewing a student's paper.

There weren't just a thousand visions. They were infinite—or, at least, far more than Jack could count. The universe summoned its power to pit Jack's new Dao against every possible scenario in existence. If it couldn't properly respond to any of them, if it had the slightest imperfection or inner contradiction, the universe would not accept it, and Jack would never become an immortal.

What's worse, Jack couldn't do anything about it. This was just the highest powers in the universe scrutinizing his Dao. All he could do was watch with his heart in his throat.

With the assistance of a thousand immortals, at least he could hope that the end result was perfect.

The stream of power intensified. Every Dao out there lent a part of itself, creating its own little test for Jack's Dao. His soul was suddenly awash by every color in existence, and the awe was so strong that Jack barely resisted the urge to kneel. The colors also reached the motes of light and instantly extinguished them—as that happened, Jack felt anger building in the colors, as if the existence of these motes of light was an insult. Like he was cheating.

Time lost its meaning. Jack had no idea how long this process took. Eventually, however, the stream of power began to dim. It went from a torrent to a river, then a trickle, before it was finally extinguished.

Jack held his breath as he stared at his Dao, looking for the slightest crack.

But there was none. His Dao survived the onslaught and remained whole. It passed the test. The universe had acknowledged it as worthy of sitting on the highest throne—to become a completely new Dao on par with all the minor Daos of the world. From now on, people could cultivate the Dao of Jack Rust.

Jack felt extreme joy. He wanted to scream and shout, to cheer and celebrate, to pump his hands in the air.

Except, something was wrong. His breakthrough wasn't complete. He hadn't reached the D-Grade. A thin layer separated his Dao from fully coming into existence, like it was held back by an invisible force. He couldn't even access its powers anymore.

Yet, the breakthrough *should* be complete. The test had already occurred. Which could only mean one thing.

Jack opened his eyes in the real world. He witnessed the remains of a purple hurricane dissipating around him, as well as the excited eyes of Brock and Old Man Spirit just beyond. However, he didn't smile yet. He looked up at the ceiling of the Final Ring, where, despite all impossibility, a storm was brewing.

The tribulation was coming.

CHAPTER ONE HUNDRED SEVENTEEN
ENDURING THREE STRIKES

EVA SOLVIG, THE B-GRADE COMMANDER OF THE HAND OF GOD'S FLEET AROUND Trial Planet, was meditating. Her white hair sprawled on the ground around her as she sat on the surface of one of the planet's two moons— a moon she had claimed entirely for herself.

If one watched closely, they could see the air sparkling and shimmering in her near vicinity. Any impurities had been eviscerated. Even the tiniest speck of dust could not survive within five miles of where she meditated.

Suddenly, her eyes snapped open. "What?" she said. In the next moment, she disappeared, reappearing on the other side of Trial Planet, where a peculiar sight was taking place. Multicolored storm clouds were gathering in space, appearing out of nowhere. Lightning arced and brewed between them.

"A tribulation? For what reason?"

It didn't take long for a few more figures to appear beside her. They were the captains of each starship under her command—all of them C-Grades. One, her personal assistant, floated to stand a step behind her.

"Why would a tribulation appear here, Commander?" he asked respectfully.

"There are not many things worthy of a tribulation," she responded. "Someone using an extremely strong treasure to break through would be one reason. Someone disrespecting the Dao would be another. It could also—Wait. It's firing. Back off!"

All of them flew backward, putting a distance of several dozen miles between them and the tribulation. Eva was intrigued. Where would the tribulation fire? Who was its target?

Lightning cracked and slithered. An explosion came. The clouds were roused. And yet, no lightning bolt flew in any direction.

The C-Grade captains behind Eva started whispering, but she only narrowed her eyes, sensing a spatial turbulation in the midst of the clouds. The lightning bolts were fired, but they were teleported somewhere else. And, if that happened so close to Trial Planet, there could only be one explanation.

"It's aiming at something inside the planet," she said. "But it couldn't be a breakthrough. Such is impossible in Trial Planet. It couldn't be a disrespect of the Dao, either—how could mere mortals attract its attention?"

"Then, what could it be, Commander?" her assistant asked.

"The birth of an incredible beast... or a supreme treasure." She narrowed her eyes. "This has to be connected to the Ancient ruins found inside. Have we discovered anyone suspicious yet?"

"No one, Commander. However, the latest Garden Assault was completed a month ago, and our lady reported two suspicious individuals. A man with extreme divination and unknown power, who was probably affiliated with the Black Hole Church, and a recently Integrated man who developed the power of a lord and managed to steal the Top Treasure under the noses of all three participating lords. The two of them were reported to be friends."

"Has either of them exited the planet?"

"Not yet, Commander. If they have, we haven't found them."

"Hmm." She frowned. "This must be connected to the Black Hole Church representative. Put out a warrant with his details, offering a reward that would tempt even C-Grades. I also want all of you to take shifts and join the squads scanning the planet, to make sure none of them escape. You know the Black Hole Church has its ways—without a C-Grade actively watching, they could easily slip by us, if they haven't already."

"Since this tribulation is happening, they're probably still inside."

"Probably. I will also keep my meditation light so I can intervene at a moment's notice, should anything happens."

"We appreciate that, Commander," the assistant replied, bowing low. Eva returned her gaze to the tribulation, which was still firing away at whatever its target was. Then, she turned, as if she'd suddenly remembered something.

"Did you say that second man hasn't come out either?" she asked.

"Yes, Commander. However, our lady reported that he was trapped in an immortal meditation chamber. According to her, the chances of him escaping are close to nil."

"Hmm. Well, at least he wasn't one of ours. Focus on the Black Hole Church representative. Whatever treasure drew this tribulation, it must be extremely precious. We must not let the Black Hole Church get it. And summon reinforcements from the headquarters—if this really is a supreme treasure, the Church might send B-Grades to retrieve it."

The assistant's eyes shone with fear, but he bowed. "Yes, Commander."

———

Jack still felt the same as before the breakthrough, but that was only because it was not yet completed. Soon, he would be a man anew.

But only if he could survive the tribulation.

He caught the eye of Brock, who nodded with a smile, and Old Man Spirit, who watched impassionately. He then raised his gaze high.

There was a power brewing over him. He couldn't see it, but he could feel it. Like an eye staring at him from far, far away.

It was coming.

The ceiling of the Final Ring cracked. No—it was space itself that cracked, not the ceiling. Clouds slipped in through the opening, expanding until they filled the entire ring. Darkness covered the tiny planet as the sun mushrooms were hidden behind the anger of the universe.

Only flashes of light illuminated Jack's surroundings now. Strands of lightning appeared briefly in the clouds above, arcing between them and gathering more power. They came in all colors of the rainbow. If Jack didn't know they sought his death, they would be beautiful.

As it was, they were nothing short of terrifying.

He still raised his head to stare at them directly. He followed the path of the fist. Even if the sky fell, his head would remain high.

"Good luck, kid," Old Man Spirit muttered.

And then, heaven did fall.

Lightning gathered in the cloud directly above Jack's head and streamed in from all directions, gathering power.

In the instant when it descended, Jack braced himself. The lightning bolt fell straight on his head. He was not prepared for the impact. His mouth screamed without his command; so strong was the shock. His limbs spasmed, his legs threatened to bend, and he could see stars as everything burned.

His regeneration acted up. The power of Life coursed through his body, repairing it and soothing the sharp pain, but the lightning was nowhere near done. One bolt after another crashed down, like an angry giant hammering Jack with his anvil. He screamed. From one moment to the next, the darkness was torn apart by a cascade of lightning, all collapsing from the heavens to Jack's head.

Flashes burned the world. Light spread everywhere. Jack could see nothing, trapped as he was in a hellish cycle of ruin and rebirth. He heard screams—probably his own. His body was constantly burned and regenerated, his nerves were frayed and healed, his heart stopped beating multiple times only to be resuscitated by the same lightning that crippled it in the first place.

When the lightning stopped, Jack stumbled. His entire body was blackened, while smoke rose from his skin. He almost toppled over, then, with a titanic force of will, he forced himself to stay upright, not submitting to the test of the heavens.

Just how was one supposed to survive this without his regeneration?

Yes, he'd cheated to break through. He used a treasure to take a shortcut. That was his choice, and he would take the punishment to prove he was worthy. He refused to fall.

There was no way it was over yet.

"There are three strikes!" Old Man Spirit shouted, as if on cue.

Through the pain, Jack grinned. Of course there were three. "Bring them on!" he shouted to the sky.

The clouds rumbled. More of them appeared, as if angered by his blasphemy, and another round of lightning rained down. It really was like rain. The bolts were blue, this time, and they fell like bullets from the sky. Each was sharp and small, but their piercing power was great. It wasn't just Jack's skin that took the brunt this time. The lightning drops bore into him, sending their shock directly to his nerves.

His entire body went taut. His head was thrown back against his will, and his neck muscles bulged so hard they seemed ready to pop out. The previous round of lightning had charred his skin. This one was burning him inside out.

His limbs went out of control. This time, he did kneel, because he could not control his legs. Shocks and spasms ran over his entire body. He didn't know if he was awake or unconscious—maybe both. A pre-System person's body would have evaporated long ago, but Jack was augmented by the System and his Dao. Even when lightning fell as a storm, he could take it.

When the rain died down, Jack was left on his knees, panting. Smoke escaped from his pores. His regeneration was working overtime to fix him, but that didn't stop the pain. Gritting his teeth was all he could do to avoid screaming even more, and already, he felt exhausted.

The Dao doesn't hold back at all... he thought, vision blurry. This tribulation is so powerful.

And there was one more strike. One more to go. If it was of the same intensity as the previous two, he could take it... but who was he kidding? Of course it would be even stronger.

On cue, the clouds above rumbled a third time. Red was the dominant color now. One by one, more lightning bolts snaked into the cloud above Jack from the surrounding ones, but these strikes were slow, like ribbons made of fire.

Jack braced himself.

And fire rained. This was no lightning. It was a literal torrent, a column of fire that fell from the sky, engulfing him. The grass around him evaporated. Fire poured unendingly, flowing to the limits of where his purple hurricane had been before, forming a small pool that engulfed him.

Jack was covered in the hellish fire, bathed in it. He tried his hardest not to scream, as the fire could enter his mouth and burn his innards. He tried to close his nose and ears, to keep the damage outside his body, where it would hurt him less.

Unfortunately, drowned in searing pain as he was, that was impossible. His eyelids burned. His skin bubbled. His pants evaporated, as did his credit card, leaving him alone in a prison that he could not even scream to avoid.

The pain was indescribable. Jack barely held on to a strand of sanity, realizing that this was equally terrible as when he ingested the Life Drop. But he had succeeded then. He would succeed now.

He would accept this price to become stronger. No matter the pain, no matter the torture, he would persevere. *And win.*

He gritted his teeth and fought hard to retain his sanity.

It was this unending resolve, this indomitable will, that let Jack survive amidst the flames. He didn't know how long it had been. All he knew was that, when the red of the world finally receded, he was blind, deaf, and alone. All his senses had been obliterated by the flames. It was just him, his pain, and his exhaustion.

Touch was the first sense to return. He felt the hot, rough ground under his back. Smell and taste came next—and he really wished they hadn't, for all he could smell was his burnt skin, and all he could taste were ash and iron. When his vision finally recovered, Jack found himself splayed on the ground in a fetal position, protecting himself with the barest instinct he could muster.

The pain was everywhere, even as his regeneration worked hard to repair his body. His burnt-off muscles and tendons were replaced with new ones. His charred skin flaked off to reveal a pristine, pink one. His nerves regrew, returning him control of his limbs, but also the ability to feel the full extent of what he'd endured.

Only then did he stand, pushing through his injuries. He felt like absolute shit.

But he'd survived. He endured the tribulation, proved himself worthy of using the Thousand Essence Flower, and secured a position as an immortal. The barrier that held his Dao back was still there, but it would fall soon, and then...

Then, he would be so strong.

He made himself turn toward Brock and Old Man Spirit. He smiled at them—though he undoubtedly looked horrible. Brock smiled back and gave a thumbs-up. Old Man Spirit nodded in approval.

"You survived," he said. "That's good. You can rest at my—"

His words were cut short and his gaze turned to the sky. Brock made a questioning gesture, to which Old Man Spirit replied, "I'm not sure, but something feels off."

Jack followed the old man's gaze. The ceiling remained covered in clouds, which were dissipating, since the tribulation was over. Everything seemed over... but could the spirit of Trial Planet be wrong?

Suddenly, the purple hurricane around Jack re-emerged. It pulsed with light and rotated faster, almost hiding him from view. The dissipating clouds above froze, then began to re-condense. Jack's eyes widened. So did Old Man Spirit's.

"What is going on!" Old Man Spirit shouted. "This... This shouldn't happen! The tribulation is over! I saw the clouds dissipating. It's three strikes, *always three strikes!*"

CHAPTER ONE HUNDRED EIGHTEEN
A DEADLY INTERVENTION

THE TRUTH WAS IRREFUTABLE. NOT ONLY WERE THE CLOUDS REGATHERING, BUT more and more kept appearing. They formed layers, covering more of the sky until they arrived half a mile above the tiny planet. The arcs of lightning that passed between them were thick like barrels and filled to the brim with power.

Jack's eyes were shaking. Old Man Spirit was gaping in disbelief. Brock tried rushing to Jack, but a lightning bolt fell before his feet and forced him to step back—it was a warning.

"Stay back, Brock!" Jack shouted. "I'll be fine! I'll—"

He didn't have time to finish his words. A thick thunderbolt crashed on his head, frying his entire body. Its power was way beyond the previous ones—and it was just the first bolt.

Old Man Spirit's face hardened, and his eyes narrowed as he shouted in rage, "WHO IS MESSING WITH MY TRIAL PLANET!"

His voice roared louder than the thunder. For a moment, everything went quiet before another lightning bolt fell—directly on Old Man Spirit.

However, this old man was in his element. Even before the lightning crashed, he pointed a finger at it and shouted, "BREAK!"

The bolt broke. The air opened and swallowed it, spitting out to the side. Old Man Spirit floated upward, utterly enraged. "I don't know you are, but if you think you can mess with my Trial Planet, you are deeply mistaken."

He unleashed his complete Dao. Jack was blinded. He had no idea what level of power Old Man Spirit had really reached, but he knew the D-Grade knight he'd faced was nothing but a tiny fraction of what he now witnessed. The Dao itself rocked and seethed as Old Man Spirit waved a hand at the sky. A titanic silver mace appeared, aiming to crash into the clouds and disperse them. The entire world stood at attention.

"Show yourself!" Old Man Spirit demanded.

The moment the mace was about to strike, a second presence blanketed the sky. Jack froze. Old Man Spirit's mace was broken, his Dao was crushed, and his body was flung downward, nailed into the ground as if spiked by a giant.

Old Man Spirit was unfathomably strong, but whoever was here was someone even stronger. A voice rumbled, like the far-off whisper of a God.

"Life is sealed in the dark. To those who wield it, death."

It was a few simple words. Yet, Jack felt his entire world shake and sharpen to a point. He felt equal parts terror and awe. Instinctively, he knew he was really going to die.

His gaze sought solace from Old Man Spirit, but the old man's wide eyes mirrored Jack's emotions. "It can't be..." he whispered. "The Life Drop... The power of Enas... You are... Axelor!"

The voice didn't respond. It disappeared like it'd never been there. The clouds remained, and they were pregnant with deadly lightning of extremely unsafe proportions—all of which was immediately unloaded on Jack's head.

———

On a far-off starship heading away from Trial Planet, a rag-dressed, yellow-toothed man was meditating. His eyes snapped open, and his head whipped toward Trial Planet. "Axelor..." he muttered, a storm brewing in his gaze.

———

The B-Grade Head Enforcer of the Hand of God was still hovering before the tribulation in space, when her eyes narrowed. "Something is wrong," she told her captains. "What is this presence?"

She looked into nothingness, reading the screens before her face. Her eyes widened. "An Old One is interfering! No—two of them!" She turned tail and ran away, while her panicked captains followed suit. "System, intervention detected. Report to headquarters. Contain it immediately!"

An explosion of force. Two divine presences collided next to the tribulation clouds, shattering space for a hundred miles in all directions. Even the clouds, for all their holiness, were dissipated.

When the world stopped shaking, Eva looked back at the clouds from a safe distance—thankfully, the only thing in the radius of impact had been an unaffiliated starship, which was now completely destroyed.

"What is happening?" she wondered aloud. "Why did the will of Old Ones appear here? Who were they? Just what is going on inside Trial Planet!"

———

Jack remained on the ground, standing on burnt grass as an ocean of power thrummed above him. The divine presence had abruptly disappeared, but the clouds remained, and their power was far above the previous tribulation's level.

Only one thing was clear: Someone very powerful wanted him dead.

"Jack!" Old Man Spirit shouted. "I... I can't stop it! I'm sorry!"

"Take Broc—"

Jack didn't have time to finish his sentence. The heavens opened and fire became his whole world, interspersed with lightning of a far greater scale than before. Every bolt shook his soul. The flames threatened to lick his limbs to the bone. The ground was cratered under his feet, melting into a puddle of white-hot liquid.

Jack found himself trapped there, drowning in pain and submerging into temperatures he couldn't possibly endure.

He was going to die.

Then, a second titanic presence flooded his being. This one came from inside him—from the Life Drop, whose depths he was still unable to reach. The presence said one thing: "Two can play this game."

Jack no longer had any idea what was happening. A valve opened from within. The thin barrier containing the Life Drop's powers collapsed, releasing a veritable ocean of life inside him. His entire body was suffused with power. Every single injury he had was healed, and his exhaustion disappeared, reverting him to full power. But a ton of energy still remained, and it escaped his body as a green sphere, pushing back the fire, lightning, and molten dirt. Jack hovered in a sphere of perfect safety in the middle of extreme danger. It was similar to how he had used his Dao to counteract the old man's Dao Domain.

"You have three seconds to prepare," the voice inside him said before disappearing. The Life Drop's barrier reformed, and no more energy escaped. The green sphere protecting him swiftly began to degrade in power, as it was ground down by the incredible heat outside.

Three seconds? Jack wondered. What—

There was no time to think. Three seconds was a considerable amount of time for someone of his level, but not enough to waste on the how and why of the world. All the questions he had could wait. Right now, he had to hurry and prepare, because the barrier would fall soon, and his existence would be snuffed out.

Prepare how? he asked himself, set fully to the task. There is no way I can survive that tribulation. It's just too strong. Unless...

A wild thought crossed his mind, and once it appeared, it refused to go away. He closed his eyes, reaching his soul space, where the multicolored fist hovered powerlessly, still blocked off by the Dao of the universe. After all, officially, his tribulation wasn't over.

Someone up there wasn't playing by the rules. Therefore, neither would Jack.

With a roar, he used the entirety of his mental energy to slam into the thin barrier that contained his Dao. It screeched and cried for help, but the life energy was keeping all other Dao at bay. It was alone.

Jack's soul clenched its fists and tore at the barrier. He smashed it again and again. His punches fell like comets, and before his mind could comprehend exactly what was happening, a crack was formed. It enlarged before the entire barrier broke apart.

For the first time, Jack felt his Dao. It was beautiful. It was him. His entire life and will, crystallized into one shape. It was the sword he'd fight with and the hill he'd die on.

He was discovering a crucial piece of himself that had always been missing. How had he fought without his real Dao? How had he even lived?

He reached out and touched it. It fell into place in his soul. Instantly, his entire world shifted. The Dao currents he'd seen under the effects of the Dao Sprouting Pill were now everywhere—they were part of his normal sight. His body was filled with such power that his mind took some time to comprehend it.

He felt like a god—an immortal.

Jack had broken through. He'd become a D-Grade cultivator. Right here and now, in the unlikeliest of circumstances, with two gods fighting over his head, he somehow succeeded.

And, in a flash of awareness, he realized that breaking that barrier with his own two fists was the most suitable way to break through.

Before he could comprehend the weight of his power increase, blue screens flooded his vision.

Congratulations! Perfect Dao Seed of the Fist (peak+) → Dao Tree of the Fist

Congratulations! E-Grade → D-Grade
Congratulations! You have developed your own, personal Dao, becoming an immortal member of the universe.
All stats +50
Free stat points per Level Up: 5 → 10

Level Up! You have reached Level 125.

Congratulations! The Bare Fist Brotherhood faction has reached the D-Grade. New functions unlocked in the faction screen.

Congratulations! For being the first cultivator on your planet to develop a Dao Tree, you are awarded the Title: Planetary Overlord (1).

Planetary Overlord (1): A Title awarded to the first cultivator to develop a Dao Tree in an Integrated planet. A sign of great potential, marking the owner as a person worthy of the Immortal System's assistance.

Efficacy of all stats +15%.

Jack's body convulsed as it was flooded with power. His stats, which were already extraordinary, had just been pushed through the roof. He felt like he could break a mountain with a single punch.

Although the greatest increase in power wasn't in stats. It was qualitative. His Dao had increased so vastly in potency that he couldn't fathom how he ever beat someone of this level while still an immortal himself. Rather than a piece of a greater Dao that he simply borrowed, he now had a power of his own. The difference was unimaginable.

His soul thrummed with an ocean of power, like he was a god himself, and he felt a resonance with the world around him that went beyond words. By simply willing it, he could exert control over his surroundings, influence them with his Dao.

Of course, at this level, his mind was much faster than a normal human's. Despite all these changes, only two seconds had passed since the voice spoke. One remained. Which meant...

Even amidst the danger, Jack grinned.

STRIKING BACK

Class Upgrade available. Please choose your new Class:

Fist of Tyranny (Elite)
Power is the foundation of everything. Use your strength to step on the weakness of others and develop a fighting style meant to annihilate large groups of weaker opponents.
"Punch until they no longer dare to stand."

THIS FIRST CLASS SEEMED LIKE AN EVOLUTION OF HIS CURRENT ONE, FIEND OF the Iron Fist. However, while the Fiend Class suited Jack's strengths, this one took things way too far. He could see how his path could be interpreted that way, but that wasn't it. He didn't want to lead by fear. The point of his fist wasn't to dominate others, but to liberate himself.

Primal Fist (King)
A Primal Fist channels the spirits and ghosts of the world to enhance themselves. They dominate natural wonders, as well as the hearts of people, becoming forces of nature themselves.
"To live. To prey. That is to be."

That sounded cool. It sounded like Nauja, actually. Since she had a bow, maybe she would one day become a Primal Hunter?

Not to mention it was a King one. Jack had never seen a Class of this tier before, but it was certainly far better than the Elite ones he was used to. Plus, its direction wasn't so far away from his current path.

In any case, this Class intrigued Jack. He went on to read the final one.

Cosmic Fist (King)

Punches like meteors, a body like a celestial object, and a supernova as your war cry. Cosmic Fist is a warrior who uses their body to emulate the wonders of space, harnessing powers that belong to the cosmic scale.
"Punch through the final frontier."

That was... way too suitable. Jack was most certainly intrigued. Not only was this Class a King one, like the Primal Fist, but space had always fascinated him. Even more so after traveling through it for a bit.

All three Classes sounded great. All could lead him to incredible adventures, to the peak of the world. However, the winner was clear in his heart. He knew which path he wanted to follow—one of his skills was already on it, actually.

Congratulations! You are now a Cosmic Fist (King).

Congratulations! Indomitable Body III upgraded into Neutron Star Body II.
Neutron Star Body II: Neutron Stars are made from the densest material in the universe. Your body inherits some of its properties, achieving extraordinary resilience and durability, increased weight and strength, as well as resistance to all elemental attacks.
You also retain the heavy regenerative properties of this skill's previous version.

Congratulations! Ghost Step I upgraded into Space Walk I.
Space Walk I: Space is a constraint you have learned to escape. By
spending a large amount of energy, take a step through the fabric of
space to reappear anywhere within a mile radius.

Both those skills sounded seriously cool. Jack could barely contain his excitement. Even as the sphere of life energy around him was running on its last fumes, he felt so filled with power and potential that no lightning or fire could harm him.

He spent the final fractions of a second to inspect his status screen, feeling his chest swell with pride at how far he'd come. He also invested all free points from his one level up to Physical.

Name: Jack Rust
Species: Human, Earth-387
Faction: Bare Fist Brotherhood (D)
Grade: D
Class: Cosmic Fist (King)
Level: 125

Strength: 650
Dexterity: 605
Constitution: 625
Mental: 120
Will: 190

Dao Skills: Meteor Punch III, Iron Fist Style II, Neutron Star Body II, Brutalizing Aura II, Space Walk I
Daos: Dao Tree of the Fist, Dao Root of Indomitable Will (fused), Dao Root of Life (fused), Dao Root of Power (fused), Dao Root of Weakness (fused)
Titles: Planetary Frontrunner (10), Planetary Torchbearer (1), Ninth Ring Conqueror, Planetary Overlord (1)

There were so many things to take in.

Thanks to the newest title, Planetary Overlord (1), all his stats now had an additional efficacy of ninety percent. Moreover, the fifty points he got in all primary stats—so a hundred and fifty total—were the equivalent of thirty levels in the E-Grade. And he had another ten points from the one level up he gained, from level 124 to 125.

Unfortunately, there was no more time to take in his status screen. He eyed the storm of fire and lightning outside, then clenched his fists.

Someone was trying to kill him. They'd thrown at him a tribulation he couldn't possibly survive. But they hadn't predicted he would break through in the process. Whoever it was, whatever this tribulation meant, Jack would punch it all in the face.

The life barrier dropped. Fire and lightning filled his world. This time, Jack didn't just wait for punishment to fall on him. He had recovered his Dao—he could fight back.

He roared and punched. All colors and sounds were sucked into his fist. Even the tribulation itself lost its vibrancy. His new, reinforced Dao seeped into his fist and, for a moment, made it the most brilliant object in the world.

A purple meteor exploded to life. The air cracked. The fire and lightning were pushed back. Strong winds erupted, striking the ring ceiling a mile above and the ground under Jack's feet. They even parted the molten dirt that surrounded Jack, letting his bare feet touch the torched ground.

The white-hot liquid would close again soon, but that was fine. Jack was no longer going to sit back and watch. He would demand the reins. He would fight back.

He would break the heavens.

His feet pressed hard against the ground, and he shot off. The molten liquid closed under him, but it didn't matter. Not only did he not plan to fall back down, he was also an immortal—he could fly now, as simply as willing it.

Fire and lightning surrounded him in all directions. Jack was trapped in hell, but he used to be a fiend—he knew his way around. Even as the world closed, he punched out again. A meteor shattered the world, like the entire Trial Planet had just rumbled.

The fire and lightning were pushed back yet again, but he was higher up this time, and they were stronger. They recovered, surrounding him and seeking to smother him like constrictor snakes.

Flames rubbed against his skin. Lightning struck his orifices. Jack was swallowed by disaster, but feeling the pain, he only laughed.

"Is that all?" he shouted to the sky, unafraid of opening his mouth. His new Dao gave him control over his surroundings—a control that this tribulation, originally meant for E-Grade mortals, couldn't break. Even if he opened his mouth, the fire couldn't come in. All it could do was strike at his Neutron Star Body, which was now harder than steel. Even this celestial fire could only sizzle his arm hairs, and the lightning ricocheted back to where it came from.

Jack laughed again. "Fuck off!" The Dao erupted from his body, commanding the space like it was his. Every foreign Dao was pushed away or subdued. The fire went out, the lightning coiled around itself, and Jack reigned over his surroundings like a god—like an immortal.

Watching from below, Brock's eyes were filled with stars, while Old Man Spirit was dumbfounded. "A Dao Domain *already*?" he cried out.

Their surprise didn't end there. Jack had had enough. He was so powerful it filled his body and mind, wrestled the world under his control. He shot up, directly toward the clouds, which were preparing for another strike. A column of fire fell on him, hot enough to melt iron.

Jack laughed. He took a step midair, and suddenly, he could see reality fold in on itself, becoming a wrinkled piece of paper on which he could walk. He traversed from one fold to the next and stepped in. When he reappeared, he was now a thousand feet higher than where he used to stand. The column of fire was below him, burning nothing but his afterimage.

Jack's mind reeled with an excitement that not even his exhaustion could overshadow. He'd teleported! He had crossed space from the outside!

Suddenly, he found himself right before the clouds. They stretched over him like a reverse sea, a dark surface that huffed and puffed with power, arcing down in the distance as they followed the curvature of the ring ceiling.

These clouds, and whoever sent them, were trying to kill Jack. He readied a punch, filling it with all his newfound power. Space shuddered. He was practically holding onto a nuclear bomb. The strength in his hand was so rich it nearly burned him—this would be the most powerful strike he'd ever unleashed, and by far.

He couldn't help but grin in exhilaration.

The clouds must have sensed his intentions. They groaned in protest as they gathered all of their power. The clouds in the distance shriveled up and died as the one directly above Jack pulsed and grew, charging up one lightning bolt with the power to level a mountain.

Jack felt his hair rise and his heartbeat quicken. This power was so large that he was instinctively terrified, but he wrestled that feeling down. He was strong now. He could fight this.

"I don't care if you're a God!" he shouted, sending his voice to echo all over the Final Ring. The more he spoke, the more it rose in volume, until the entire ring vibrated to his tune. "I don't care if you're a tribulation! I don't care if you are the Dao, or the System, or the Immortals, or even the Hand of God. You tried to step on my face and kill me. That is unforgivable. So pack your things... and FUCK OFF!"

He punched out. The world darkened. A true meteor appeared around his fist, dominating the world and casting it in shadow. Its purple tail was the only color to be found.

The cloud roared in protest like he'd defiled it with his words. Its lightning bolt streaked to meet him, as thick as a house and as fast as light itself. But Jack's fist was already on the way.

They collided.

The world and the point of impact detonated. Space cracked and ripped. The unleashed power dissolved the clouds, pushing them into the ceiling and the space crack from which they came. The sun mushrooms were destroyed. The entire planet shook as if an earthquake had happened. A shockwave ravaged the floor of the Final Ring.

Brock covered his eyes and hid behind Old Man Spirit, who watched the sky with wide, shocked eyes.

When everything calmed down, Brock hesitantly raised his eyes to the sky. There were no clouds to be seen. No fire, no lightning. Cracks spread across the ceiling, and a single sun mushroom illuminated a man hovering in the air, laughing as he held up a fist.

Brock's eyes were filled with emotion.

"Fuck you, world!" Jack shouted with release. "You can't hold me down! I am Jack Rust, and I. Am. BACK!"

CHAPTER ONE HUNDRED TWENTY
GOODBYE, TRIAL PLANET

EDGAR WAS PREPARING FOR A CELEBRATION, HOISTING LITTLE LIGHTS ON TREES, when the professor came running out of her house. "Edgar!" she shouted, frantic with joy. "Look at the faction screen! Look at the faction screen!"

Perplexed, he obliged.

Faction: Bare Fist Brotherhood (D-Grade)
Leader: Jack Rust
Supervisor: Margaret Rust
Members: 793
Capital: Milky Way galaxy, Milky Way sector, Animal Kingdom constellation, Earth-387 planet, Forest of the Strong dungeon area.

•••

"D-Grade?" he exclaimed. "Professor! Then, Jack—"

"He broke through!" She squealed in a way that didn't at all befit a woman of her age. "Somewhere out there, he became an *immortal*!"

"Hah. Perhaps now he can buy the telepathy function," Edgar replied, laughing.

"This is no joke, Edgar. We must celebrate! We must let the world know! Then, maybe—"

Suddenly, a shiver ran through them, like they were stared at by a beast. The professor looked around, lost, but Edgar directed his gaze upward.

There, three hundred feet above ground, a man was held aloft by a pair of menacing ice wings—and, even from this distance, Edgar could sense the coldness in his eyes.

Sparman appeared next to them instantly. "Oh wow, that guy sure looks angry. But, uh, he's neither in the forest nor threatening it. I can't do anything."

As they scanned him, everyone's eyes widened at the same time. Alexander Petrovic had broken through.

Human (Earth-387), Level 50
Faction: Ice Peak (E-Grade)
Title: Planetary Torchbearer (10)

"Shit," Edgar said.

Alexander roared. His voice covered the entire forest, commanding every ear in a radius of multiple miles. "Edgar Allano! You attacked my faction and killed my people! You crushed my only son to death! I am here to restore my honor. Come out and face me!"

Silence fell over the forest, with only the last of Alexander's words echoing. Before they knew it, everyone turned to Edgar, whose face was impossible to read. He did not reply immediately. Alexander's gaze bore through the trees to land directly on the wizard.

A moment later, Alexander's voice boomed again. "Are you a coward, Edgar Allano? Are you going to hide behind women and robots? Here I am, alone over your headquarters, to take revenge for my son. Come out and fight me if you dare. I challenge you to a duel to the death!"

The entire forest was rife with tension. Of the hundreds of people there, nobody knew how to react. Those in Edgar's vicinity turned to looked at him, lost.

"Don't go," said the professor. "It's meaningless. He's stronger than you."

Edgar chuckled darkly. A thousand thoughts were twisting around in his mind. He thought back to the destruction he'd wrought on the Ice Peak's headquarters. The deaths and pain he had caused.

This wasn't just Alexander Petrovic. It was the consequence of his actions, the just retaliation for what he'd done.

"Can you imagine how the brorillas will look at me if I chicken out, Professor?" he asked.

Her eyes widened. "Edgar, this is stupid! You cannot go! It's not just you; this concerns the future of our entire war! We need you. You cannot risk everything over childish provocations!"

"I know, Professor... and I apologize. Because I still must go."

"This is idiocy! You are better than that, Edgar!"

Edgar only smiled bitterly. He knew exactly how bad of an idea it was to go fight. He wasn't touched by Alexander's provocations, either.

Still, he had to go. Because, in the very core of his being, a breathtaking magic core shone brilliantly. His magic was about wonder, beauty, and awe. And where were those feelings in chickening out of a fair duel? Alexander had every right to request this. His only son had been killed. Edgar had to take responsibility.

What sort of awe-inspiring figure could he aspire to be if he refused this challenge?

He had already betrayed his Dao once by assaulting the Ice Peak headquarters. If he did it again, his Dao Seed would crack, and his path would end forever. He would be stranded.

There was only one path of true magic at this point, and it included accepting this duel. Even if that meant breaking his previous promise of never fighting again.

One more... he thought, sad for having to promise the same thing again. *Just one final time, until the cycle is closed...*

The professor saw through his intentions, and she was livid. Sparman, however, shook his head at her, indicating that there was no point in arguing. Harambe burst from the trees just then, a herculean brorilla, and looked Edgar deep in the eyes. Whatever he saw there, he nodded deeply.

"I'm going, everyone," Edgar said. "If I die, bury me properly... and give my apologies to Jack, for I could not protect what he left behind."

With those final words, he took to the sky.

Edgar and Alexander Petrovic, the only human E-Grades on the planet, faced each other in a duel to the death.

———

One day after his breakthrough, Jack Rust floated over a patch of grass in the Final Ring, which was already fully repaired from his battle against the tribulation. Old Man Spirit had gifted him a set of purple robes, which hung loosely over him like floating silk and left his chest exposed. His hair had regrown when he broke through, and his eyes, though currently closed, sparked in the darkness like hidden stars.

As he meditated, a purple aura spread from him with every breath, and anyone glancing his way would think they saw a clenched fist rather than a man. If a normal human stood beside Jack now, they would instantly fall to their knees and start worshiping.

A young brorilla sat behind Jack, back-to-back with him. He was trying to fuse his new Dao Root of Density—when he succeeded, it would be his second one, raising him to the level of a human Elite.

Jack's eyes opened slowly, gleaming like stars. An old knight appeared before him out of thin air.

"I have gathered the necessary energy," he declared. "You are ready to teleport."

Jack nodded and stood. Since he could now survive long-distance teleportation, Old Man Spirit had agreed to teleport him all the way to the Exploding Sun constellation, from where he could easily reach the faction's headquarters.

Since he liked Jack, the old man had also gifted him a small starship. It was nothing impressive, according to him, but it would let Jack travel between nearby planets.

"Thank you, Old Man Spirit," he said, bowing his head slightly. "Your assistance has saved my life."

"Don't mention it," the old man replied, laughing. "What sort of trial spirit would I be if I didn't favor the competent youth?"

Jack smiled. "Heh. I guess."

"What are you going to do now? Save your planet, as you said?"

"Yes. I will first visit the Exploding Sun faction and see if they are willing to help. With my current strength, I believe they will jump at the opportunity."

"As they should!"

"I will also visit my master there and see if they have anything else to offer me. After that..." His gaze darkened. "There is another faction, the Animal Kingdom, which has been acting as tyrants. They have already tried to bully and kill me on multiple occasions. They are also the ones threatening my planet. Now that I have some real strength, I will not let that stand. In the few months before the grace period is over, what better way to level up than to wage war against a B-Grade faction?"

Old Man Spirit laughed. "That's exactly how young cultivators should think! Good job, Jack. If you don't die, I believe you'll make it far."

"Only thanks to you, Old Man Spirit." Jack bowed again. "I will remember your kindness. In the future, if there is anything I can help you with, don't hesitate to let me know."

"Don't mention it. It's only natural for the old to help the young. Your success would be enough for me. But if I ever need your help with anything, I will be sure to send you a message."

"Returning your kindness would be my honor."

Brock also stood, nodding to Old Man Spirit and stretching out a hand, which the old man shook. "Thanks," he said. "You good guy."

"You are most welcome, Brock. You know, you are quite exceptional in your own right. As long as you keep training, I am sure you will soon blossom into your true potential. One day, you two might even be able to fight side by side."

Jack smiled warmly. "I wouldn't have it any other way."

Brock grinned. "Thanks."

"Now, if you're ready, we can go," Jack said. "Cultivation doesn't wait."

"Of course. Just give me the signal. I'll let your friends outside know to meet you at the Exploding Sun faction, as you said."

"Great. We're ready," Jack said, placing a hand on Brock's shoulder. Since they were spiritual companions, he could bear the full brunt of the teleportation, so Brock could join him. "Goodbye, Old Man Spirit—and thank you for everything."

"Goodbye, Jack and Brock. May your adventures never end."

The old man waved a hand. Suddenly, Jack felt space collapse unstoppably around him. He thought he'd be crushed to death. Then, his Dao Domain sprang to life, shielding them from the turbulations of space as he and Brock shot through the fabric of reality at tremendous speed.

For a moment, he couldn't believe they were finally leaving Trial Planet. It felt like they'd been there forever.

He remembered the ruined surface. The Giant Ring, where he and Brock had dressed up as giant ants to infiltrate an ant hill.

The Barbarian Ring, where he'd met Nauja and her tribe, hunted down a live t-rex, and escaped Bocor.

The Ancient ruins, where he'd inherited the Life Drop and the will of the Ancients.

The Village Ring, where he'd reconvened with Gan Salin and defeated Bocor.

The Space Ring, where Brock had found his Trial, and where they'd surfed on a gigantic horde of space monsters.

The Labyrinth Ring, or Labyring, where he'd journeyed with Longsword and faced an immortal for the first time.

The Garden Ring, where he'd risen in power, faced off against the lords, won the Top Treasure, and developed his final Dao Root after cultivating alone in a dark cave for a month. He'd even released a devil —who knows what happened to that guy.

The Final Ring, where he defeated an immortal head-on, met Old Man Spirit, faced a divine tribulation, and finally became an immortal.

He couldn't believe Trial Planet was over. He had been through so much, met so many people, grown so fast... Despite all the pain and danger, Trial Planet actually left him warm feelings in the end.

Heh. Would you look at that, he thought with a wry smile. How life turns...

But all things came to an end, and if one walked the right path, only better things would follow. Jack had conquered Trial Planet, the galaxy's greatest testing ground, and he was now strong enough to matter, to make a real impact. He was ready to fight the Animal Kingdom and protect his planet.

There would be no rules from now on, no tests or contests. The training gloves were off.

From now on, it would be war.

"Bro, look!" Brock said, snapping Jack out of his thoughts. He was using the Staff of Stone to point in the distance, and Jack followed it.

The feeling of teleportation resembled the one from when they came here with Gan Salin, but so much more vibrant. There was no protective force between him and the space between spaces, just his own Dao. It was the difference between holding your breath underwater and being in a submarine.

Stars shot past. Comets, titanic gas clouds, constellations, planets. An explosion echoed in the distance. A dark void surrounded them, and they were like a purple fist hurtling through infinite space. It was magical.

Jack and Brock were lost in awe. Time had no meaning. Finally, they reached the end. Space shuddered around them, and they were spat back out into reality, in the dark nothingness between celestial bodies. A green planet was visible—their first destination, from where they could use Jack's new strength to access a teleporter and rush for the headquarters of the Exploding Sun.

Brock was no immortal, so he couldn't survive alone here, but it was easy for Jack to engulf him in his Dao Domain and protect him.

Jack reached for his starship, which had the ability to shrink itself to the size of a needle, conveniently stored in his new robes. Unlike his previous pants, these robes had pockets!

However, he paused mid-movement. He turned around to find another starship hovering just behind him, and three figures inspecting him from a hundred feet away. Each were garbed in black, with a cape stretching behind them. Their faces were covered by green, opaque veils that fell from their foreheads.

He recognized them instantly—it was the Hounds who'd been chasing him ever since he left Earth.

"Finally!" one of them cried out. "The diviner was right! You appeared right here, Jack Rust!"

Jack scanned them.

Canine, Level 175

Faction: Animal Kingdom (B-Grade)
Title: Third Ring Conqueror

Canine, Level 178
Canine, Level 171

Since the D-Grade stretched from level 125 to 250, these people were considered middle D-Grades. Normally, any one of them could easily overpower a low D-Grade, like Jack.

Then again, Jack wasn't your average low D-Grade. He'd been able to fight at that level even before breaking through. Now, he was much, much stronger.

But they didn't know that.

"Yup, you got me," he said, raising his hands. "I surrender."

The three Hounds' resolve crumbled a bit. "He became an immortal," said the first.

"That's impossible," added the second.

"And yet, it's true," the third replied. "Capture him first, ask questions later. The bounty will be ours."

Even though they could see he was an immortal, they didn't fear him. After all, he was only level 125, fifty levels below them—that was five hundred stat points.

They approached. One revealed a set of golden handcuffs that somehow felt blurry in Jack's Dao perception. He waited calmly until they were close enough. The leading Hound reached out to cuff him, not thinking for a moment to be on guard.

Jack punched. A meteor was born, and it smashed into the Hound's chest, breaking all his bones and shooting him out like a meteor himself. In the same movement, he used a strand of his Dao to push Brock far back, lest he be touched by the battle's shockwaves.

As the other two Hounds reacted, Jack Space Walked right between them. One used Five Star Grasp on his back. Jack let it land—the fingertips sank two centimeters past his skin, nothing that his regeneration couldn't handle. His left hand shot out faster than sound itself, penetrating the other Hound's chest and emerging from her back. He retrieved his hand even as the Hound floated helplessly in space, breathing her last.

In the blink of an eye, only one Hound was left. His face contorted in mindless fury, and he tried to use Five Star Grasp again. His Dao Domain was finally released, but Jack's met it evenly.

"How!" the Hound shouted, panic coloring his voice. "How can you stop my domain? You're only a low D-Grade!"

"Well, size is not all that matters."

Jack took a step, and space warped around him. When he reappeared, he was behind the Hound, grabbing him by the neck.

"You—" the Hound tried to say, but Jack tightened his grip. Bone bent, and the Hound's words were cut short.

"Answer my questions," Jack ordered calmly. "Who told you I'd be here? And what happened to the *Trampling Ram*, the starship I was previously riding?"

The Hound gurgled blood. His voice still came out, saying, "The Animal Kingdom has its own diviners! As for that starship? Hah! We sent its captain to Hell!"

"Captain Dordok?" Jack's gaze darkened with pain and fury. A purple aura emerged from his body, surrounding the Hound and drowning him. "He was a good man."

"Kill me if you dare!" the Hound screamed. "The Kingdom will know it was you. They will chase you until you die! They will kill your friends and family!"

Jack smiled. "Sure they will. You say they will know it was me who killed you?"

"Of course! The Kingdom knows everything!"

"Perfect," Jack rumbled. He pushed his Dao into his voice, sending it in all directions, echoing in space like the promise of a God. "The Animal Kingdom has bullied me enough. Now, it's my turn. I don't care if they know because I'm coming for them anyway. Let's see how they like being bullied."

The Hound struggled to speak under Jack's tightening grip. "You— What are you saying?" he shouted in incomprehension.

"Is it not clear?" Jack's voice became so loud it shook space itself. "I, Jack Rust, will destroy the Animal Kingdom. I declare *war!*"

The Hound's eyes shot wide open, but he had no time to speak. Jack tightened his grip. The neck in his hand groaned and cracked, then shattered in an explosion of bone. The Hound's head floated above his body, and the veil floated away, revealing an expression permanently frozen in horror and disbelief.

Declaring war on a B-Grade faction... What madman would do that?

Level up! You have reached Level 126.
Level up! You have reached Level 127.
...
Level up! You have reached Level 131.

Jack didn't collect the bodies or their starship. He let them hover there, a grim reminder of his resolve. He withdrew his own starship from his pocket, willed it to enlarge to its normal size, then went in with Brock and closed the door. Soon, they were hurtling through space.

First destination, the Exploding Sun faction. And then, until Earth's grace period was up... Jack would harm the Animal Kingdom as much as he possibly could.

They'd attacked him first. They threatened him, his friends, his family, and his planet. And now, finally, no matter how many C-Grades and B-Grades they had, they would pay.

Because Jack Rust was coming for them.

———

The story will continue in Road to Mastery 3!

THANK YOU FOR READING
ROAD TO MASTERY 2

We hope you enjoyed it as much as we enjoyed bringing it to you. We just wanted to take a moment to encourage you to review the book. Follow this link: Road to Mastery 2 to be directed to the book's Amazon product page to leave your review.

Every review helps further the author's reach and, ultimately, helps them continue writing fantastic books for us all to enjoy.

————

Also in Series:

Road to Mastery
Road to Mastery 2
Road to Mastery 3
Road to Mastery 4

————

Want to discuss our books with other readers and even the authors? Join our Discord server today and be a part of the Aethon community.

Facebook | Instagram | Twitter | Website

You can also join our non-spam mailing list by visiting www.subscribepage.com/AethonReadersGroup and never miss out on future releases. You'll also receive three full books completely Free as our thanks to you.

Looking for more great LitRPG?

Even with an "evil" Class like Necromancer, he can still do good.
With one touch of the Awakening Stone, Tyron receives a forbidden Class and his life changes forever. His bright and promising future as the scion of two famous monster-hunting Slayers is promptly torn apart and he must make a decision. He can allow his Class to be purged from his soul as is required by his society, or can cling to it, abandon all that he knows, and rise to power. Rise from the shadow from his influential parents and prove the world that shunned him wrong. ***Don't miss the start of the next hit LitRPG series from RinoZ, the author of Chrysalis. Book of the Dead takes on all aspects of Necromancy headfirst, from the tactical manuevering of skeletons, to what it's like spending so much time amongst the undead.***

Get Book of the Dead Now!

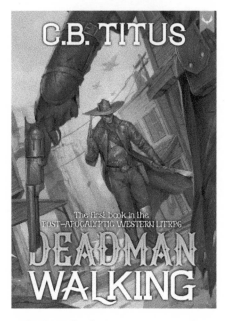

In the wasteland, you do whatever you can to survive... Even after the bombs fell, even after countries unleashed weapons beyond imagination on one another, even after lawlessness became the norm, people still expect their mail. As a deadman, I'm uniquely suited to deliver it. Rads don't bother me, and people who try to hurt me typically wind-up dead. Sure, humans may not like dealing with a face like mine, but hey not like you've got many options here in the wastes. Now in the middle of my route I've come upon a new Job, and maybe the opportunity to start thriving instead of surviving. **Deadman is a Fallout-inspired Apocalyptic LitRPG about a courier braving the irradiated wasteland. Featuring a Weird West vibe, a detailed System, gunfights galore, radiation mutants, saloons, and endless adventure, it's perfect for fans of Fallout, Mad Max, and S.T.A.L.K.E.R. Deadman.**

Get Deadman Walking Now!

———

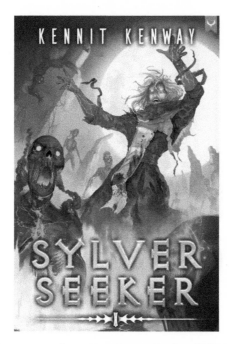